# KINGDOM HEARTS
## CHAIN OF MEMORIES

DISNEP · SQUARE ENIX

KINGDOM HEARTS
CHAIN OF MEMORIES

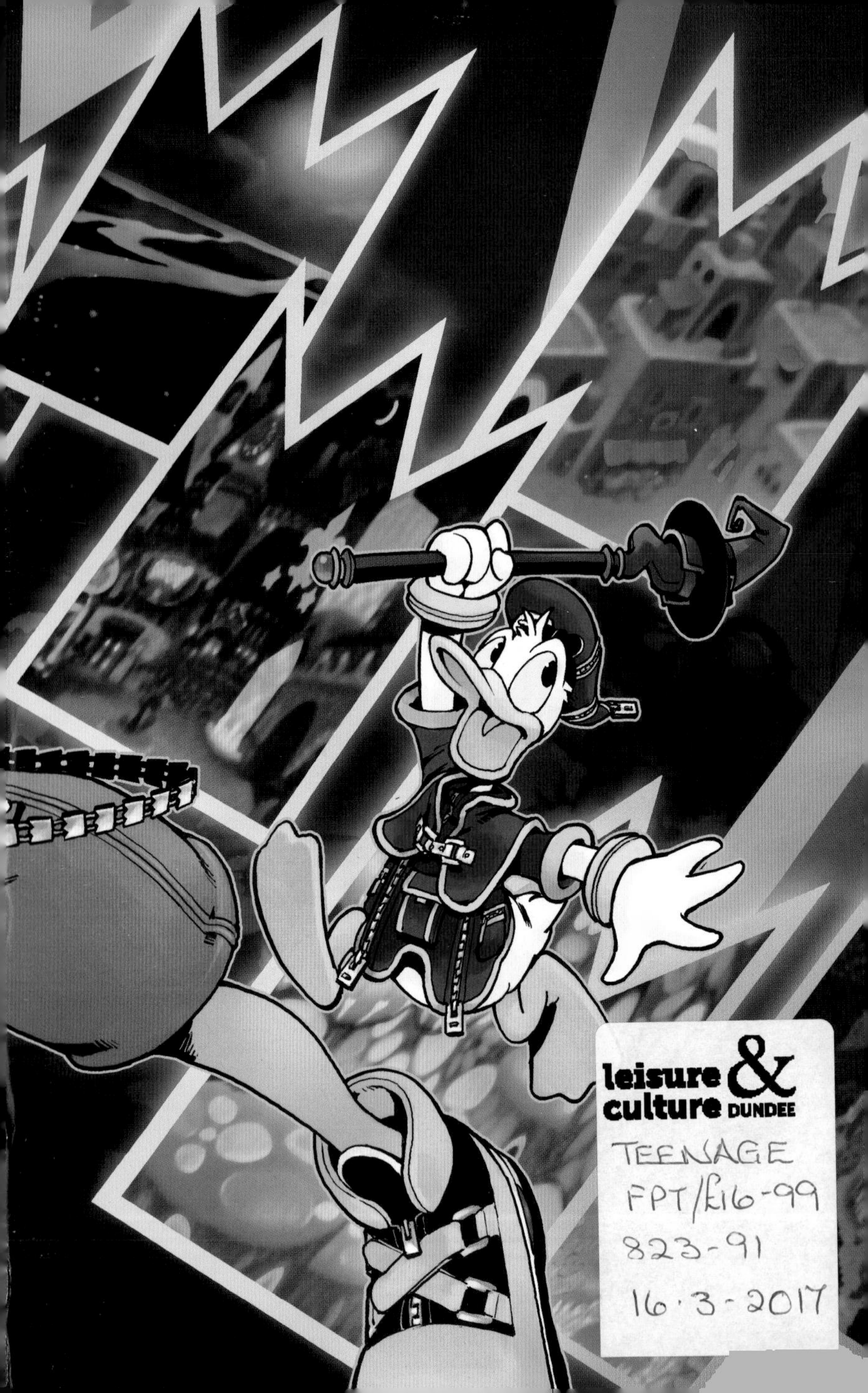

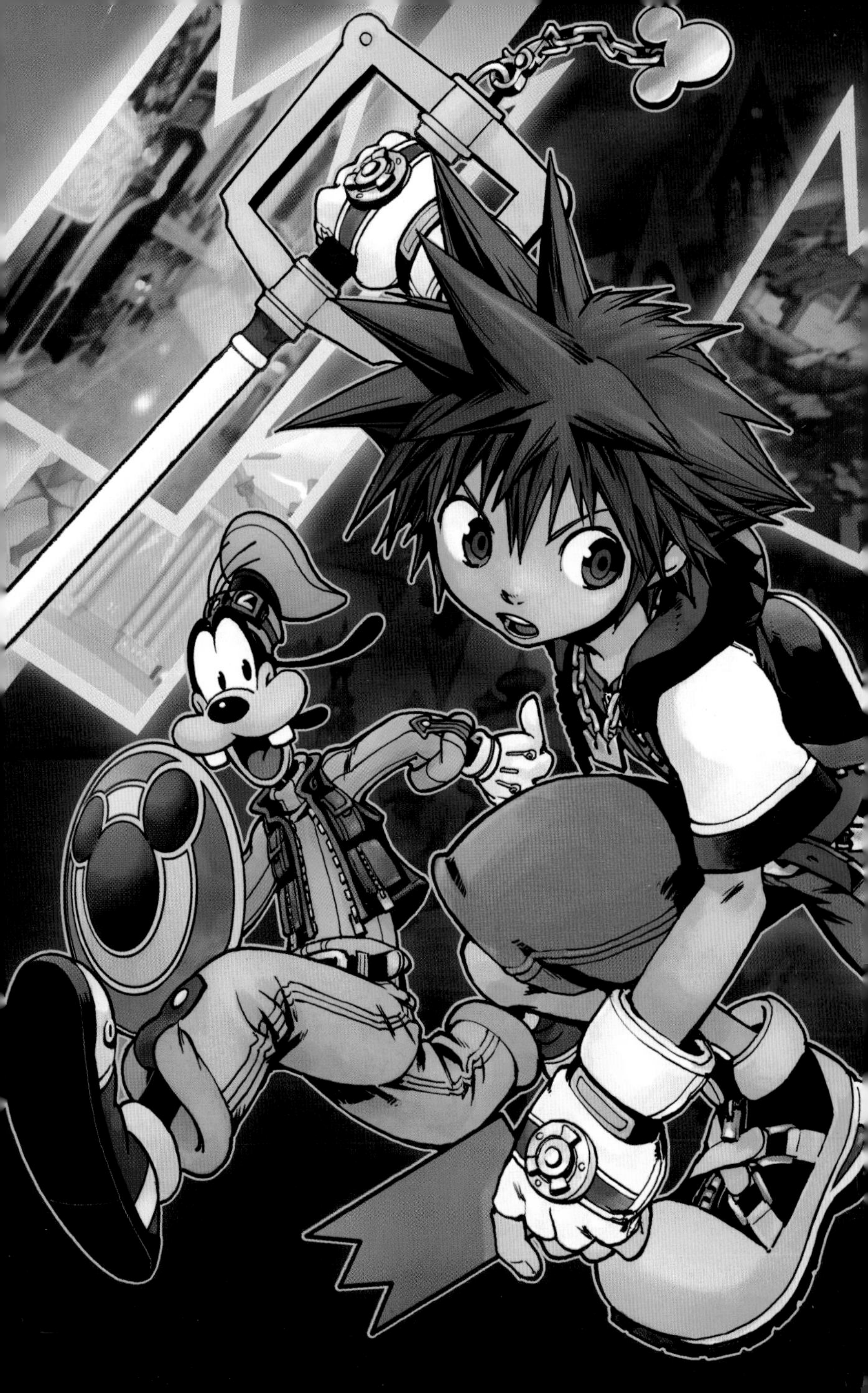

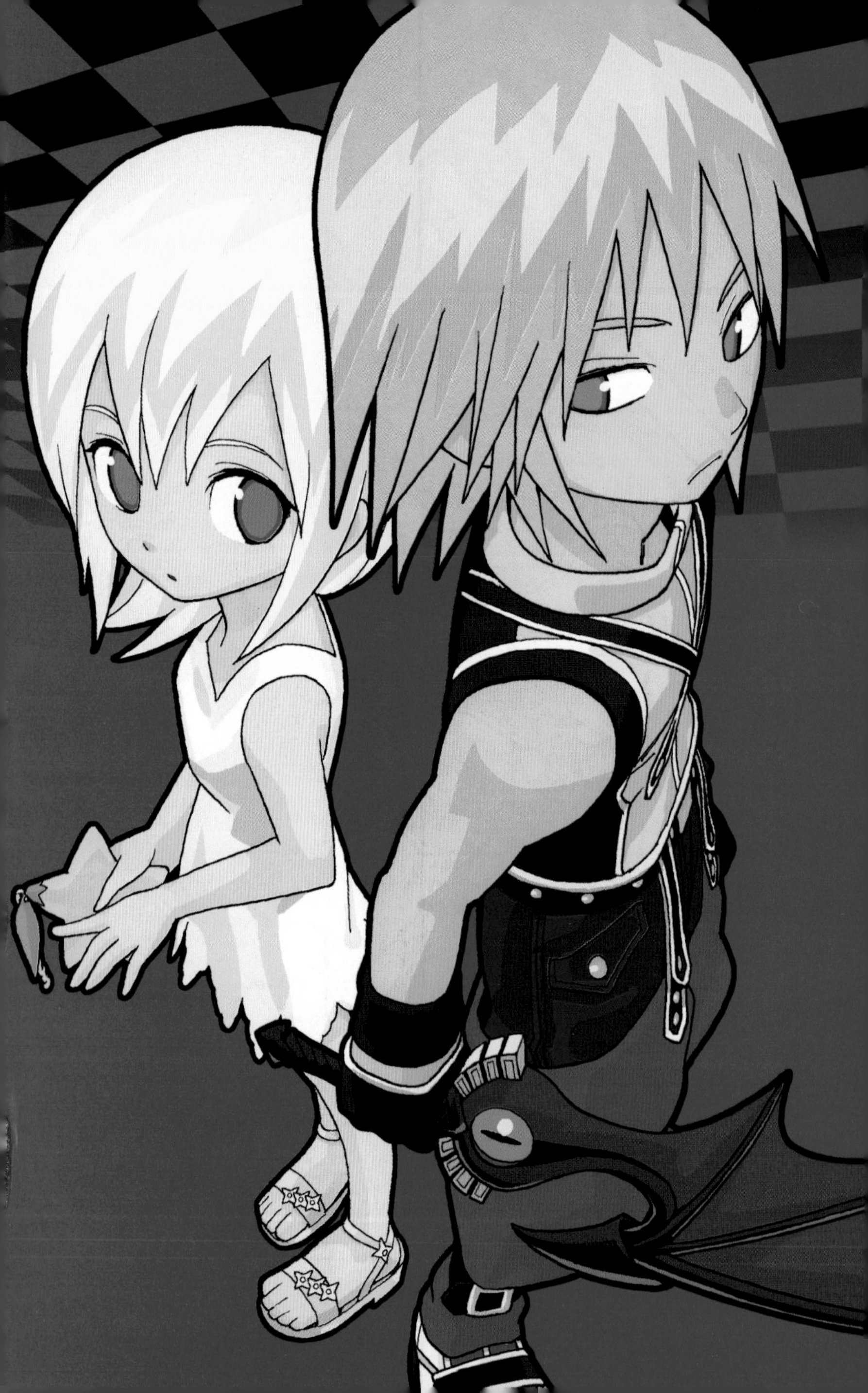

# KINGDOM HEARTS
## CHAIN OF MEMORIES

DISNEY SQUARE ENIX

KINGDOM HEARTS CHAIN OF MEMORIES

SHIRO AMANO
ORIGINAL CONCEPT: TETSUYA NOMURA

## Sora

A boy chosen by the Keyblade—
the key to saving worlds. He continues his
journey to find his missing friend, Riku, and return
with him to their home on Destiny Islands.

## Goofy

He is searching for the
missing King Mickey with
his friends Sora and Donald.
His trademark phrases are
"A-hyuck" and "Gawrsh."

## Donald Duck

Accompanying Sora on his
journey. An expert magician,
he is a helpful duck to
have around, but once he
gets bent out of shape...

# CHARACTERS & STORY

Our hero Sora lived peacefully on Destiny Islands with his best friends, Riku and Kairi, until one night disaster struck his world, and the three were separated, whisked away to faraway worlds. Sora looked for Riku and Kairi in the unfamiliar Traverse Town, but with no clues to finding them, his search was in vain. Then he met Donald and Goofy, who were searching for their missing king, and together, they set off on a quest.

After a long journey across numerous worlds, Sora and his friends found Kairi. They also found Riku and the king on the other side of the door to darkness.

But strange things were happening on the other side of the door. Countless Heartless were crossing its threshold and overflowing into the outside world. To stop them, the door had to be locked, with Riku and the king still on the other side. Seeing Sora's reluctance, the king encouraged him, "There will always be a door to the light." Trusting those words, Sora raised his Keyblade to the sky and locked the door. And in his heart, he vowed to find Riku and the king once more...

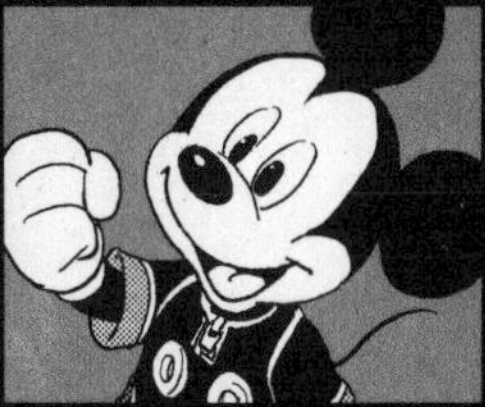

## King Mickey

King of Disney Castle. He is missing along with Riku.

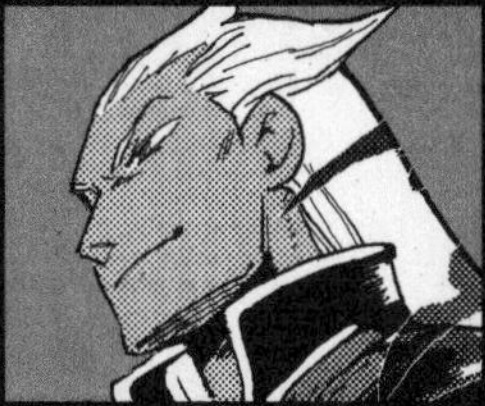

## Ansem

The "Seeker of Darkness" who lurks in Riku's heart, waiting to take control.

## Naminé

A mysterious girl who quietly draws pictures alone in a room of the castle.

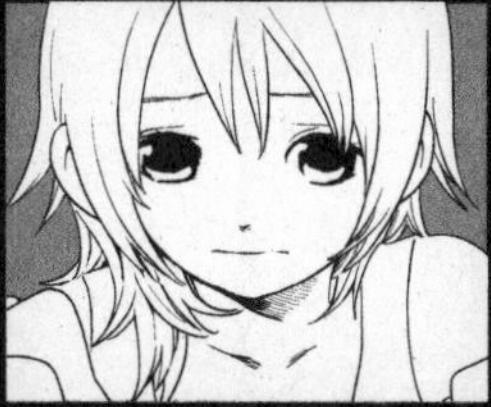

## Kairi

Sora's childhood friend. She waits on Destiny Islands for Sora's return.

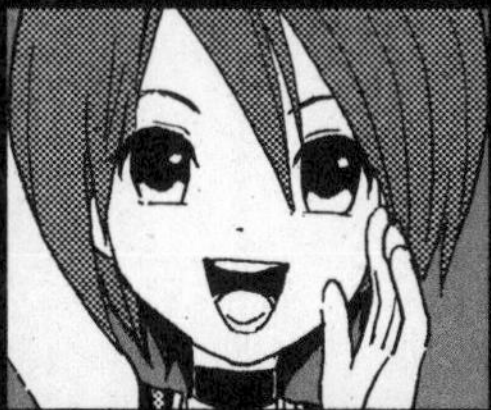

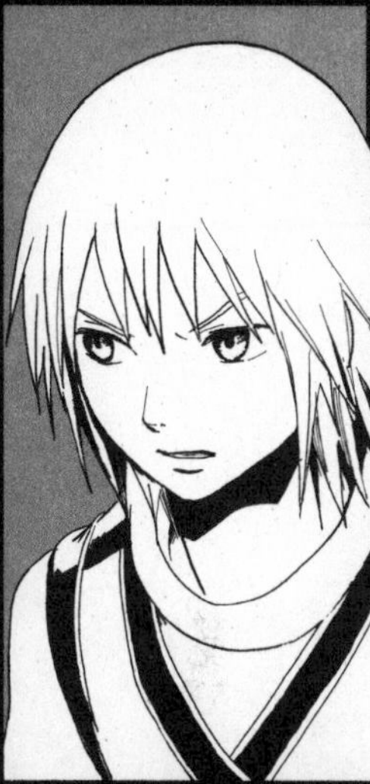

## Riku

Sora's best friend. He closed the door from the inside together with the King and was left behind in the world of darkness.

## MEMBERS OF ORGANIZATION XIII

A mysterious group clad in black cloaks. They seem to be investigating the secrets of the heart...

### BASEMENT TEAM

**ZEXION**

No. 6

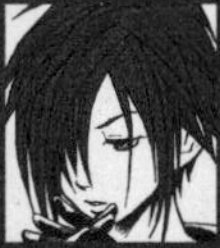

Leader of the Basement Team. Word is he's surprisingly domestic!

**LEXAEUS**

No. 5

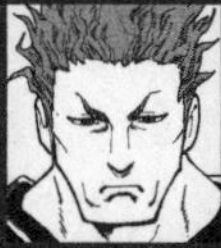

Helps Zexion and Vexen manage things belowground. Avid puzzler.

**VEXEN**

No. 4

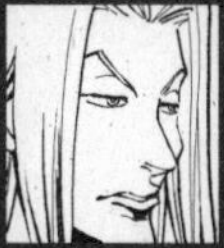

Has the most seniority of all the Organization members at Castle Oblivion. And yet the treatment he receives is...

### ABOVEGROUND TEAM

**LARXENE**

No. 12

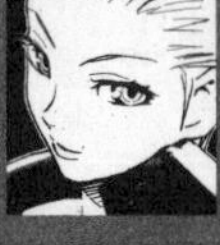

Cold-blooded, temperamental, and really scary. Once she flies off the handle, there's no stopping her.

**MARLUXIA**

No. 11

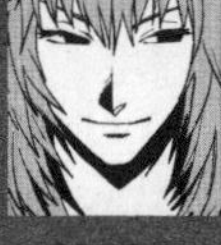

Lover of flowers and leader of operations at Castle Oblivion. It seems he's plotting something...

**AXEL**

No. 8

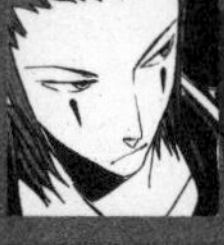

Mysterious individual who appears before Sora from time to time and leaves little bits of advice.

# CONTENTS

ONE HEART THAT IS ALL HEARTS.

ALL HEARTS THAT ARE ONE HEART.

THE HEART OF ALL KINGDOMS—

"KINGDOM HEARTS."

THAT IS THE GREAT HEART.

AND WITHIN, LIES GREAT DARKNESS.

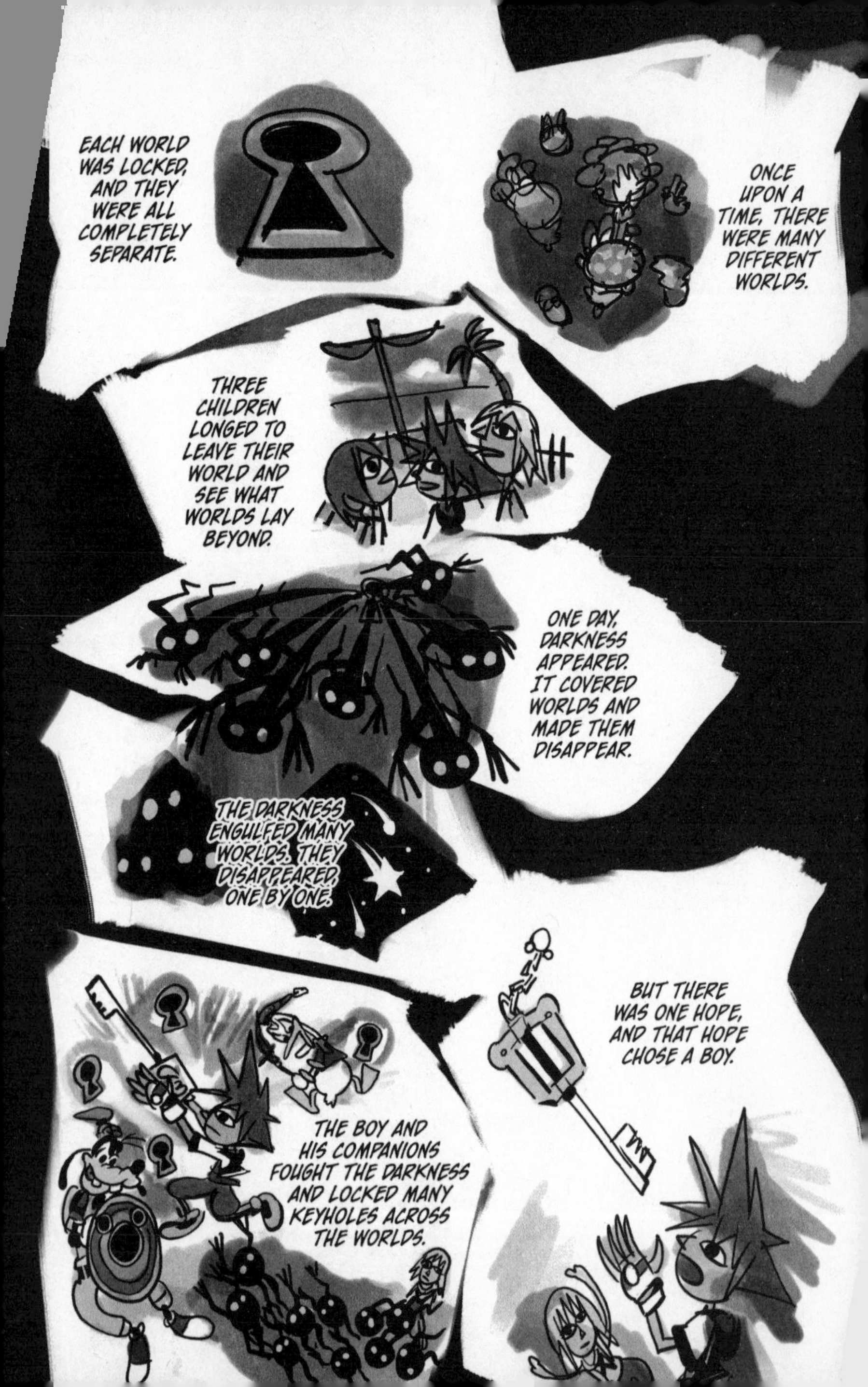
ONCE UPON A TIME, THERE WERE MANY DIFFERENT WORLDS.
EACH WORLD WAS LOCKED, AND THEY WERE ALL COMPLETELY SEPARATE.
THREE CHILDREN LONGED TO LEAVE THEIR WORLD AND SEE WHAT WORLDS LAY BEYOND.
ONE DAY, DARKNESS APPEARED. IT COVERED WORLDS AND MADE THEM DISAPPEAR.
THE DARKNESS ENGULFED MANY WORLDS. THEY DISAPPEARED, ONE BY ONE.
BUT THERE WAS ONE HOPE, AND THAT HOPE CHOSE A BOY.
THE BOY AND HIS COMPANIONS FOUGHT THE DARKNESS AND LOCKED MANY KEYHOLES ACROSS THE WORLDS.

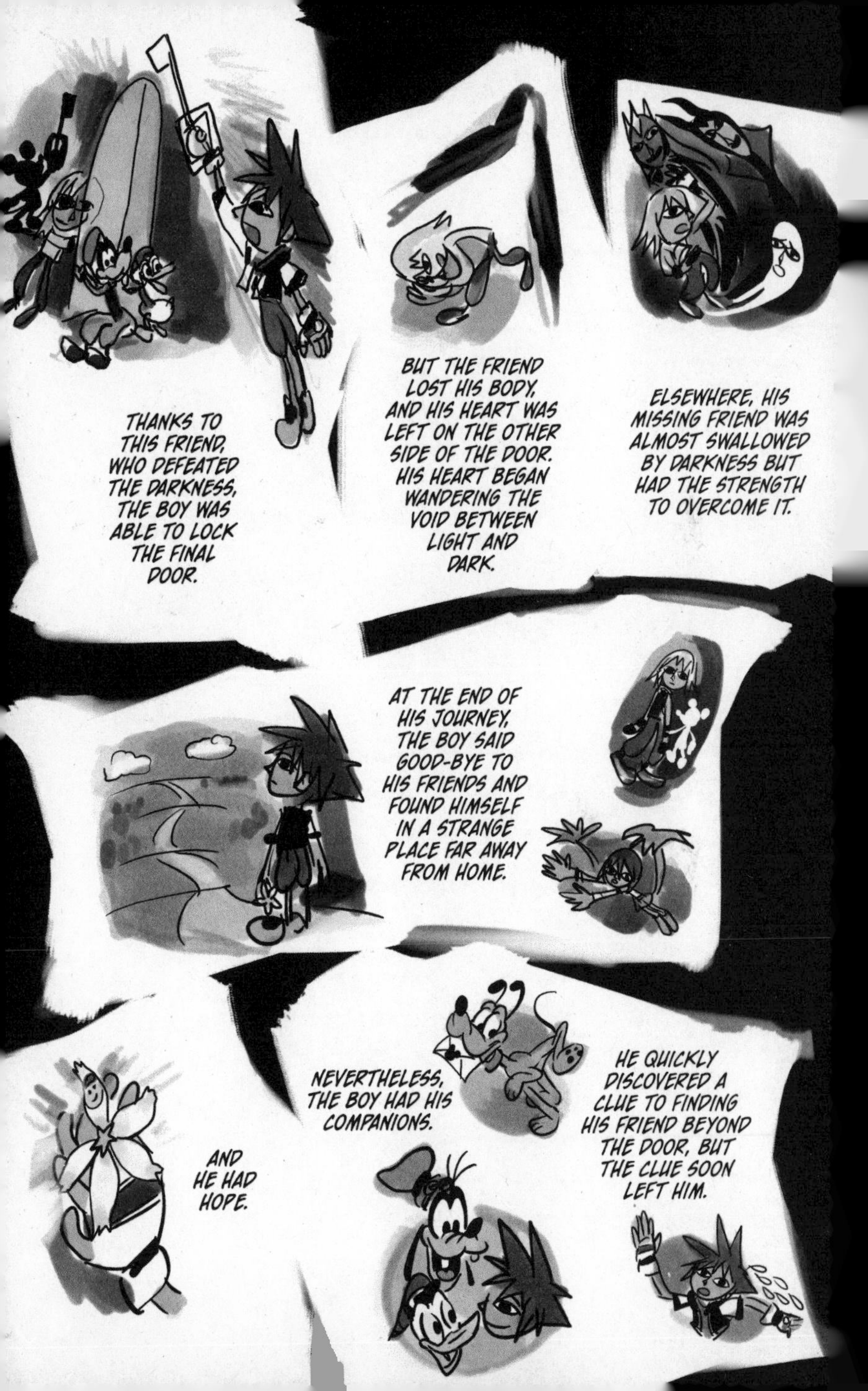
ELSEWHERE, HIS MISSING FRIEND WAS ALMOST SWALLOWED BY DARKNESS BUT HAD THE STRENGTH TO OVERCOME IT.
BUT THE FRIEND LOST HIS BODY, AND HIS HEART WAS LEFT ON THE OTHER SIDE OF THE DOOR. HIS HEART BEGAN WANDERING THE VOID BETWEEN LIGHT AND DARK.
THANKS TO THIS FRIEND, WHO DEFEATED THE DARKNESS, THE BOY WAS ABLE TO LOCK THE FINAL DOOR.
AT THE END OF HIS JOURNEY, THE BOY SAID GOOD-BYE TO HIS FRIENDS AND FOUND HIMSELF IN A STRANGE PLACE FAR AWAY FROM HOME.
HE QUICKLY DISCOVERED A CLUE TO FINDING HIS FRIEND BEYOND THE DOOR, BUT THE CLUE SOON LEFT HIM.
NEVERTHELESS, THE BOY HAD HIS COMPANIONS.
AND HE HAD HOPE.

# Card:01 Castle Oblivion

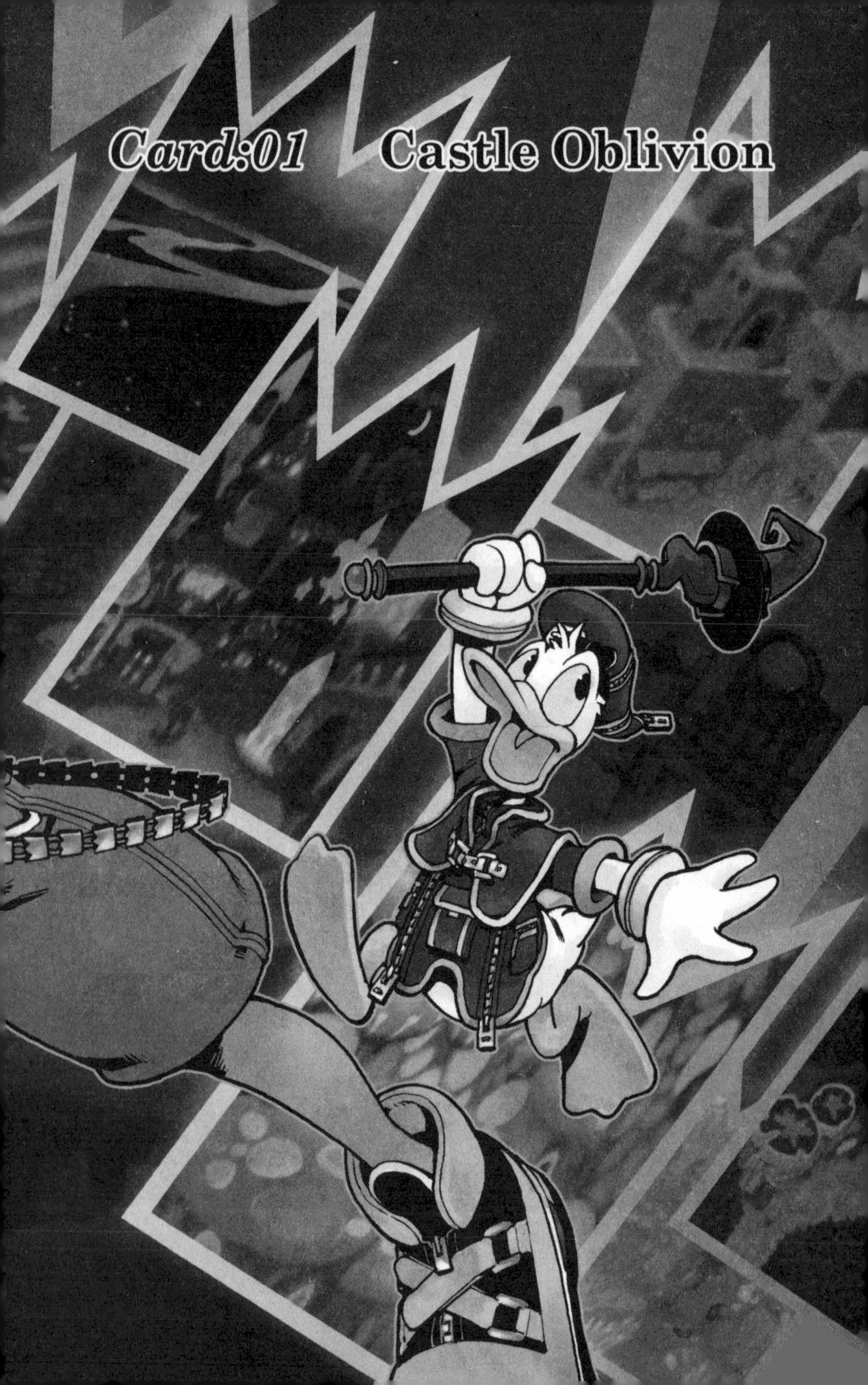

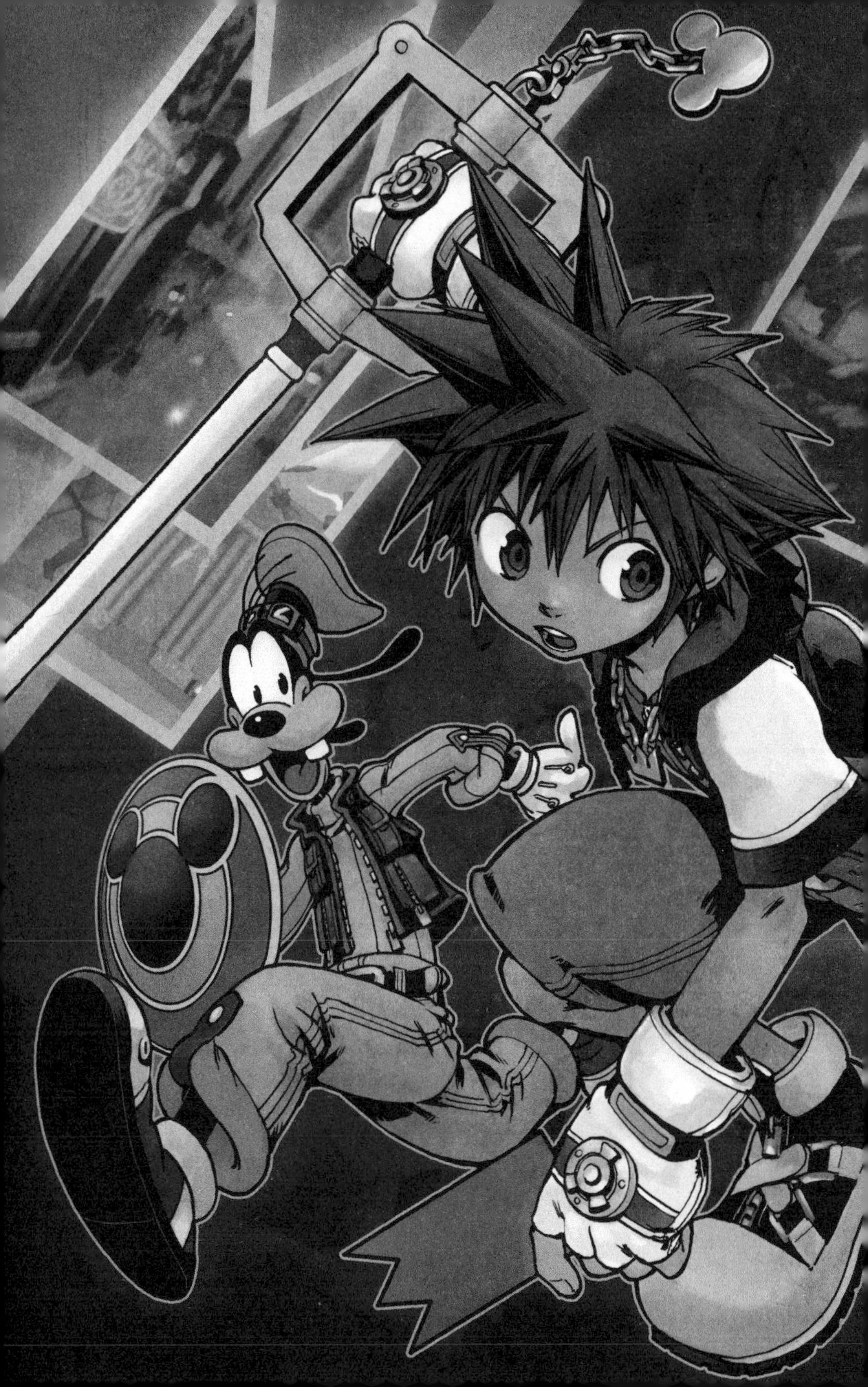

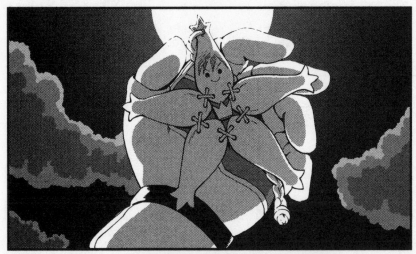

SMOLDER
SMOLDER

SNRRT
ZZZZ

CAN'T
SLEEP?

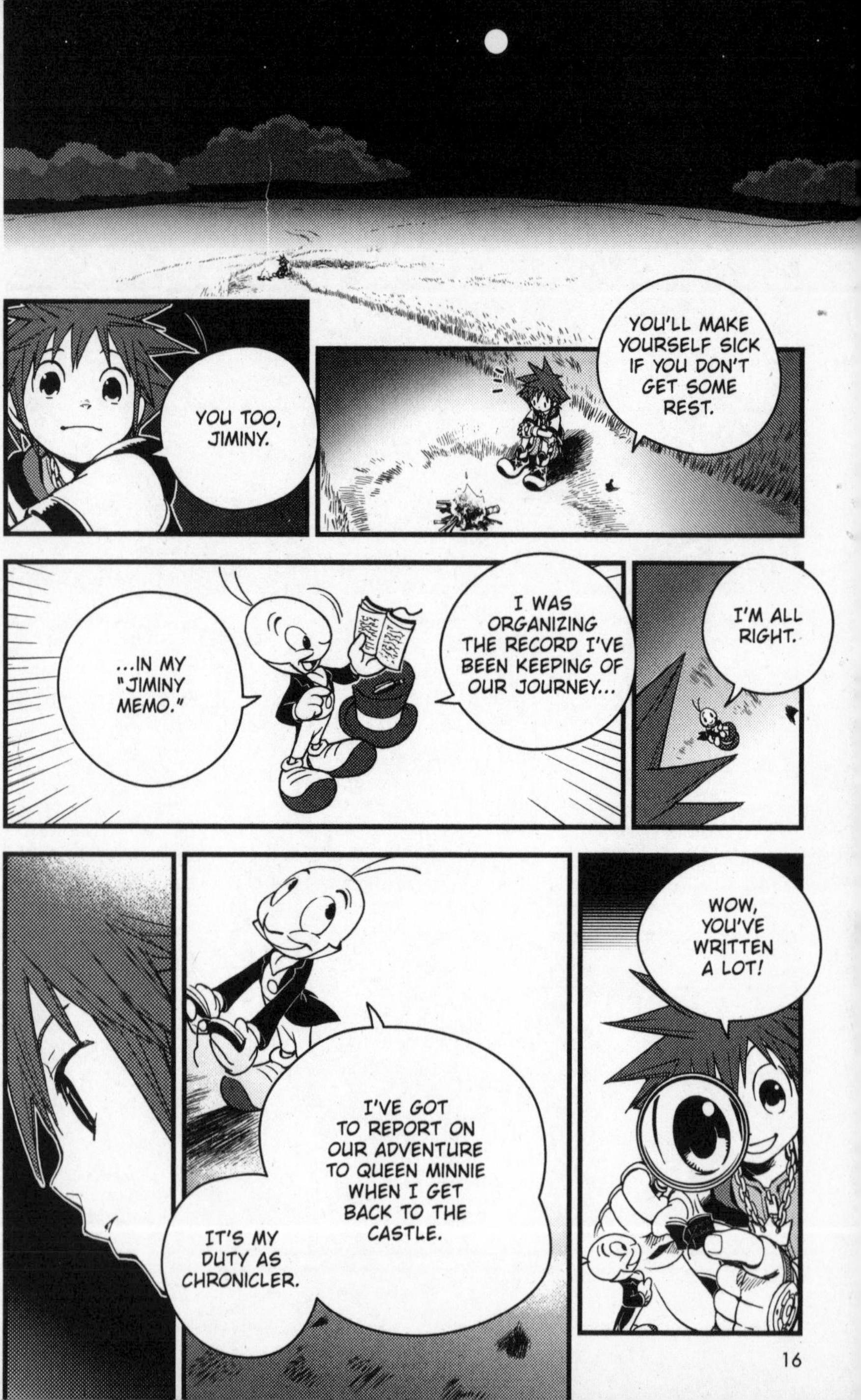
YOU'LL MAKE YOURSELF SICK IF YOU DON'T GET SOME REST.
YOU TOO, JIMINY.
I'M ALL RIGHT.
I WAS ORGANIZING THE RECORD I'VE BEEN KEEPING OF OUR JOURNEY...
...IN MY "JIMINY MEMO."
WOW, YOU'VE WRITTEN A LOT!
I'VE GOT TO REPORT ON OUR ADVENTURE TO QUEEN MINNIE WHEN I GET BACK TO THE CASTLE.
IT'S MY DUTY AS CHRONICLER.

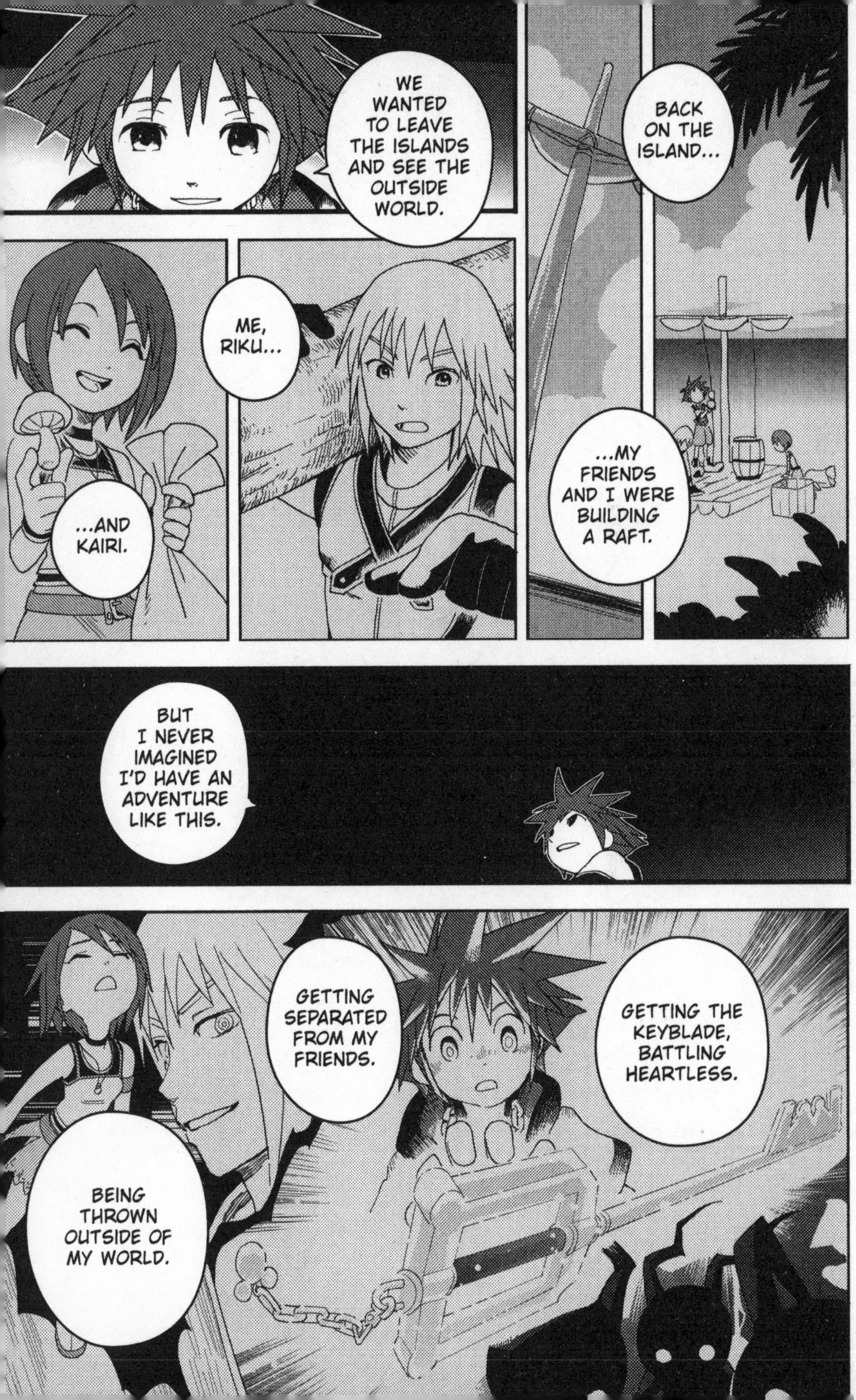
BACK ON THE ISLAND...
...MY FRIENDS AND I WERE BUILDING A RAFT.
WE WANTED TO LEAVE THE ISLANDS AND SEE THE OUTSIDE WORLD.
ME, RIKU...
...AND KAIRI.
BUT I NEVER IMAGINED I'D HAVE AN ADVENTURE LIKE THIS.
GETTING THE KEYBLADE, BATTLING HEARTLESS.
GETTING SEPARATED FROM MY FRIENDS.
BEING THROWN OUTSIDE OF MY WORLD.

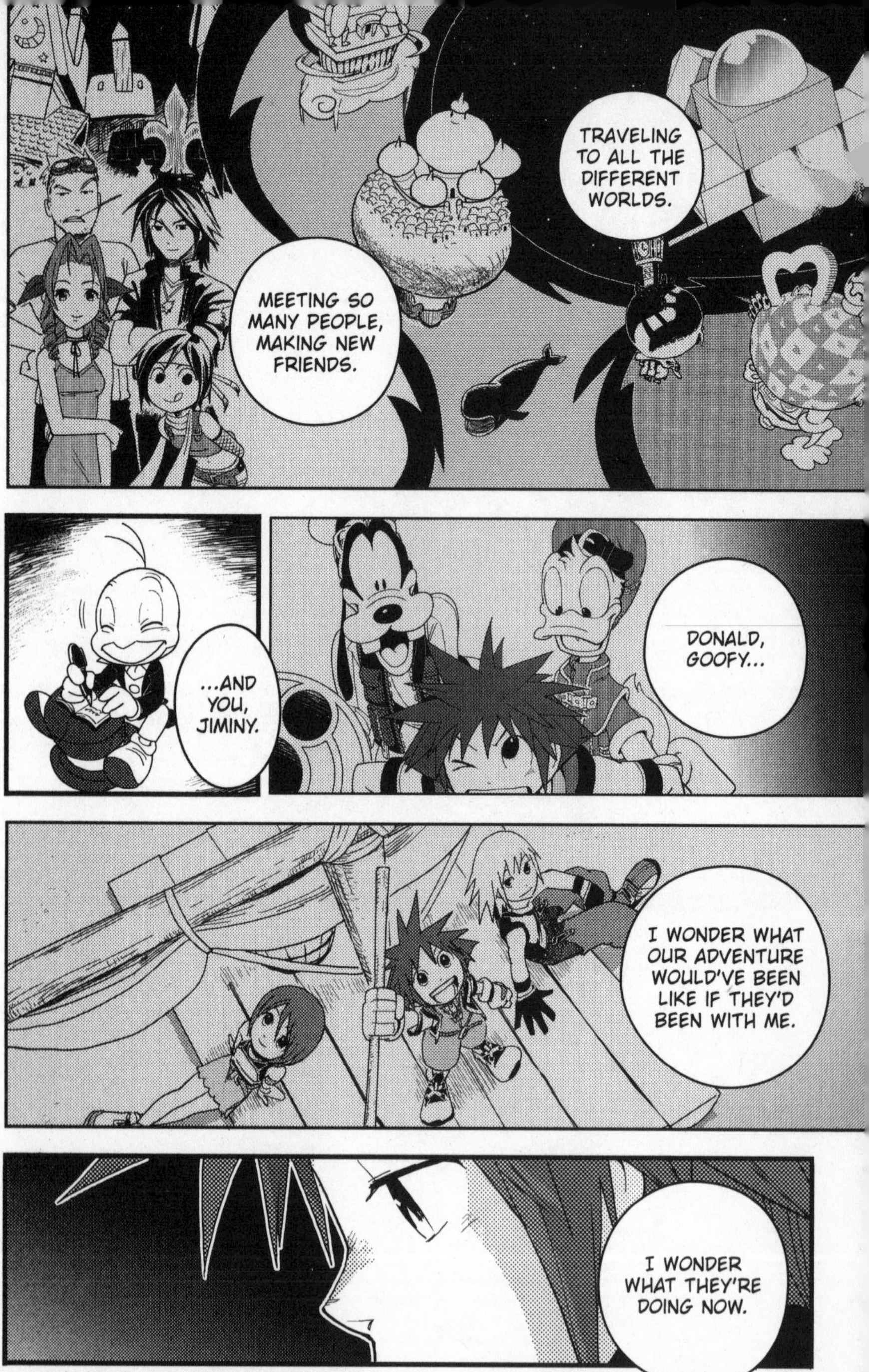
TRAVELING TO ALL THE DIFFERENT WORLDS.
MEETING SO MANY PEOPLE, MAKING NEW FRIENDS.
DONALD, GOOFY...
...AND YOU, JIMINY.
I WONDER WHAT OUR ADVENTURE WOULD'VE BEEN LIKE IF THEY'D BEEN WITH ME.
I WONDER WHAT THEY'RE DOING NOW.

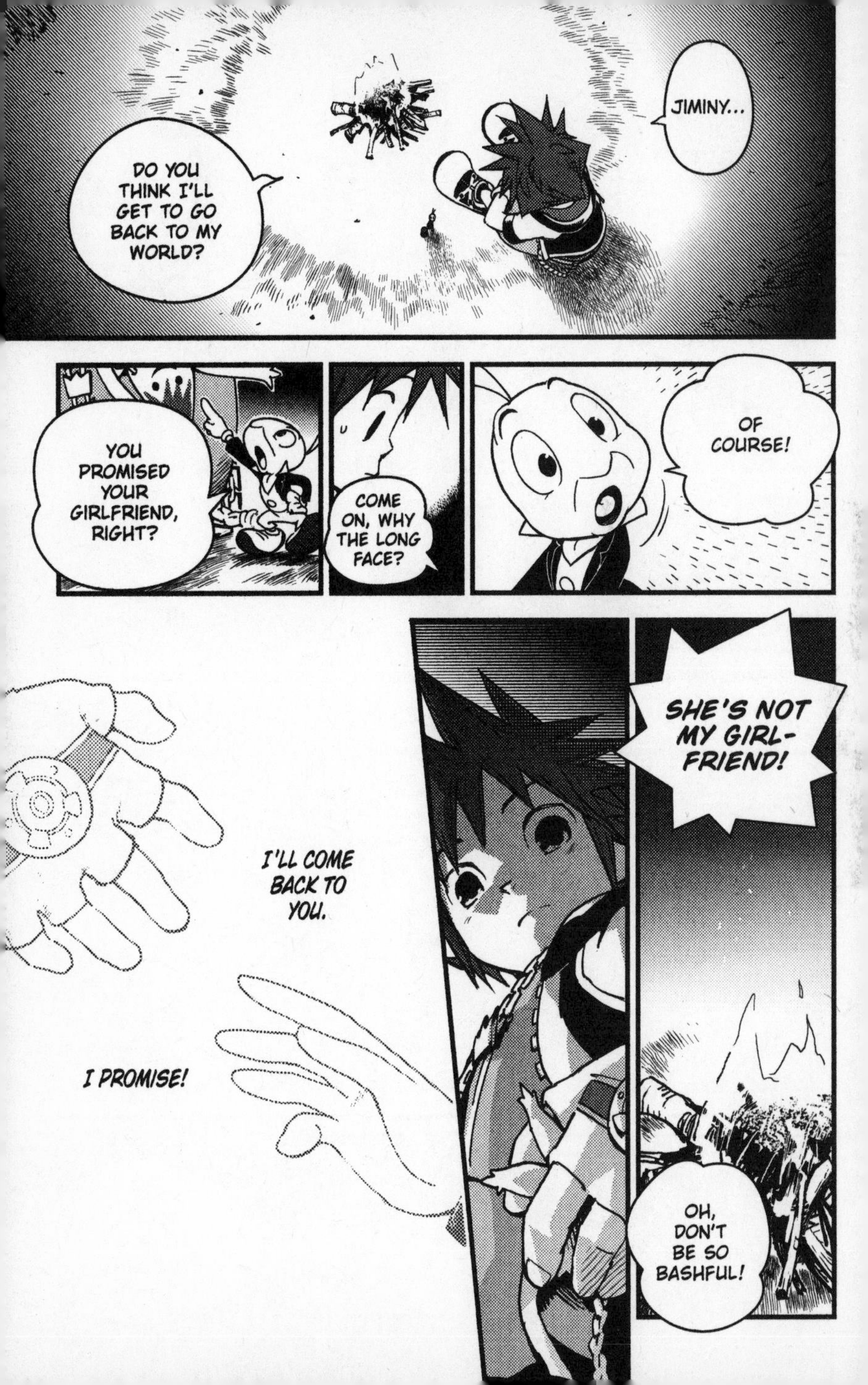
JIMINY...
DO YOU THINK I'LL GET TO GO BACK TO MY WORLD?
OF COURSE!
COME ON, WHY THE LONG FACE?
YOU PROMISED YOUR GIRLFRIEND, RIGHT?
SHE'S NOT MY GIRL-FRIEND!
OH, DON'T BE SO BASHFUL!
I'LL COME BACK TO YOU.
I PROMISE!

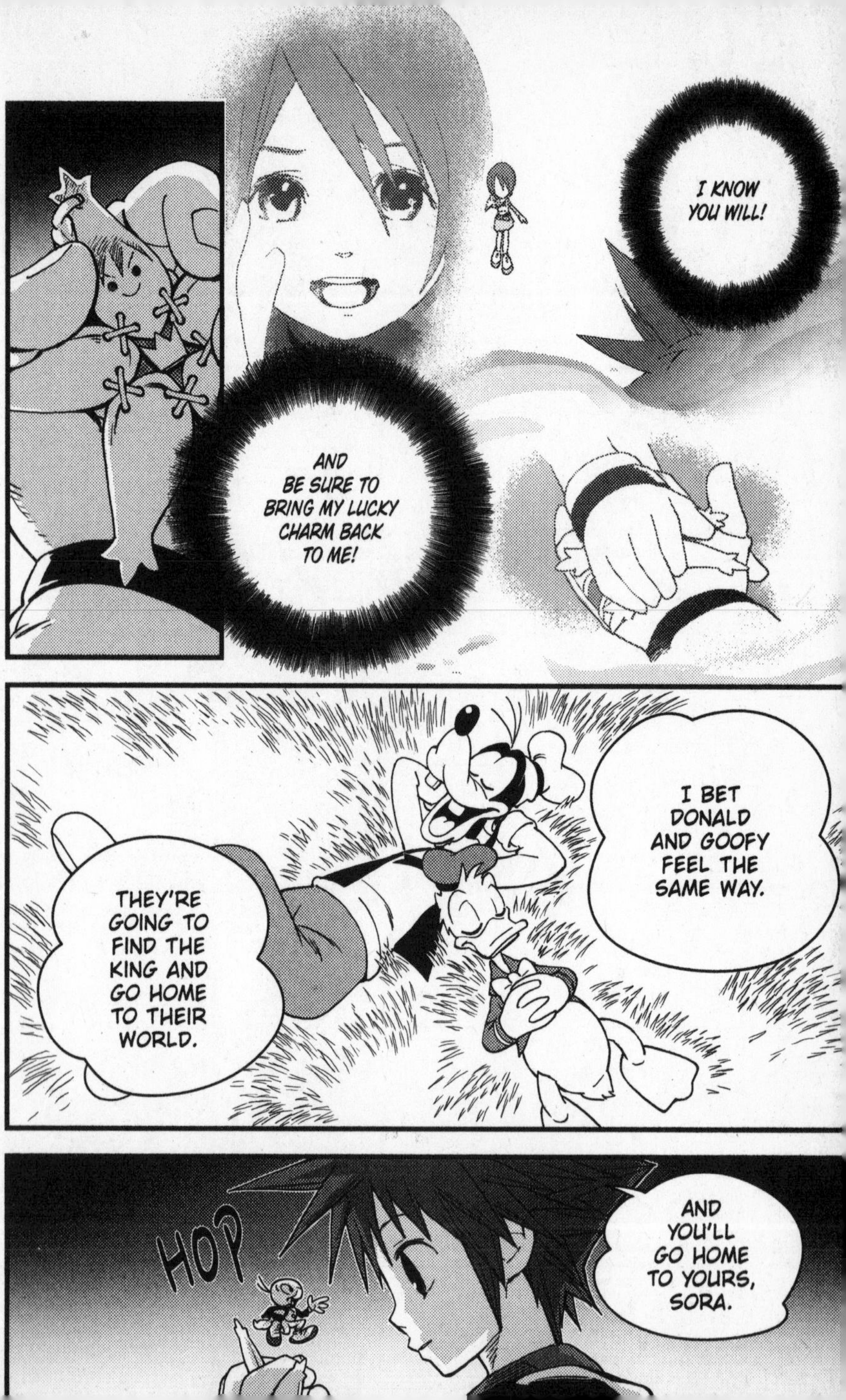
I KNOW YOU WILL!
AND BE SURE TO BRING MY LUCKY CHARM BACK TO ME!
I BET DONALD AND GOOFY FEEL THE SAME WAY.
THEY'RE GOING TO FIND THE KING AND GO HOME TO THEIR WORLD.
AND YOU'LL GO HOME TO YOURS, SORA.
HOP

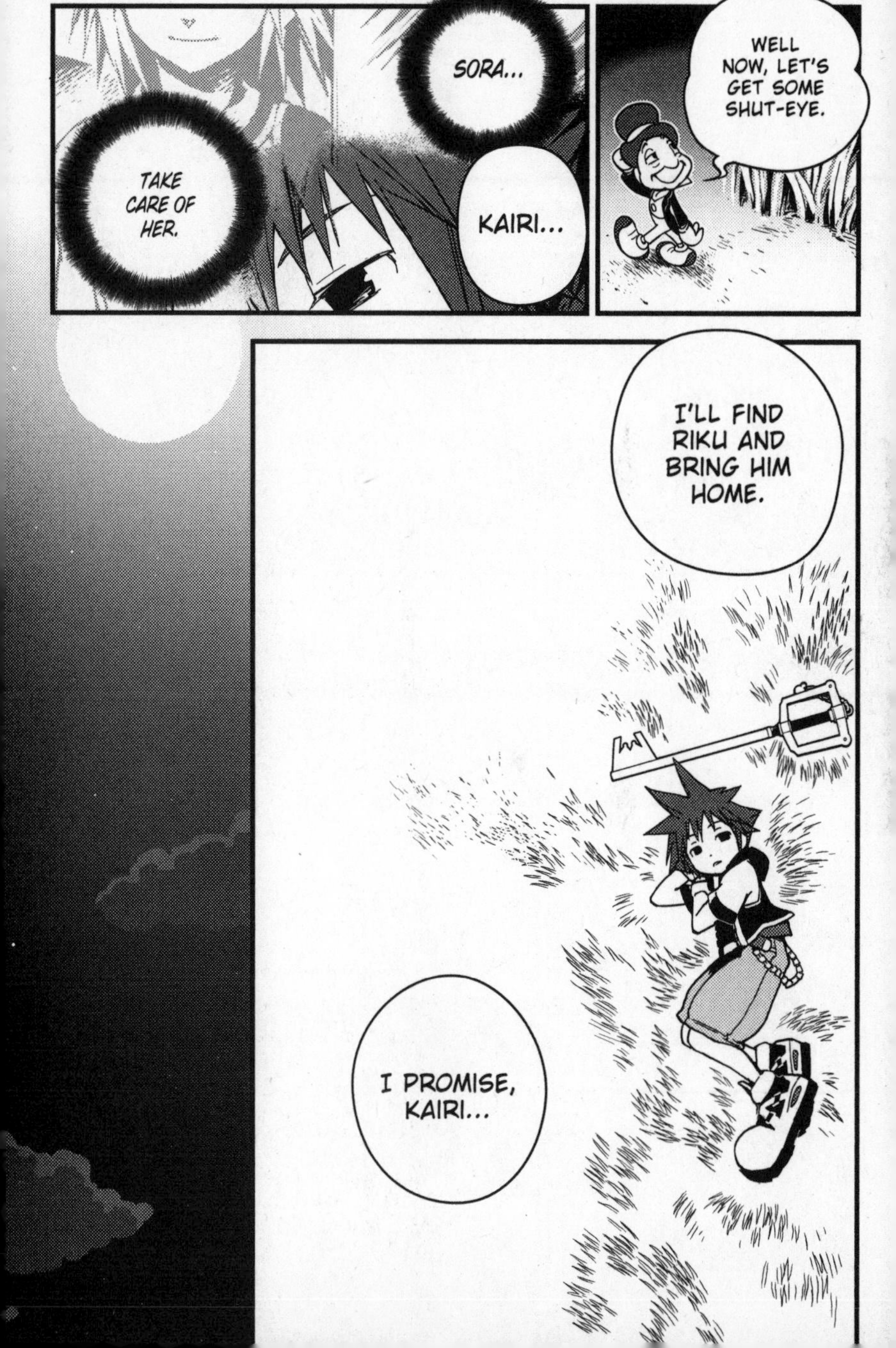
WELL NOW, LET'S GET SOME SHUT-EYE.
SORA...
KAIRI...
TAKE CARE OF HER.
I'LL FIND RIKU AND BRING HIM HOME.
I PROMISE, KAIRI...

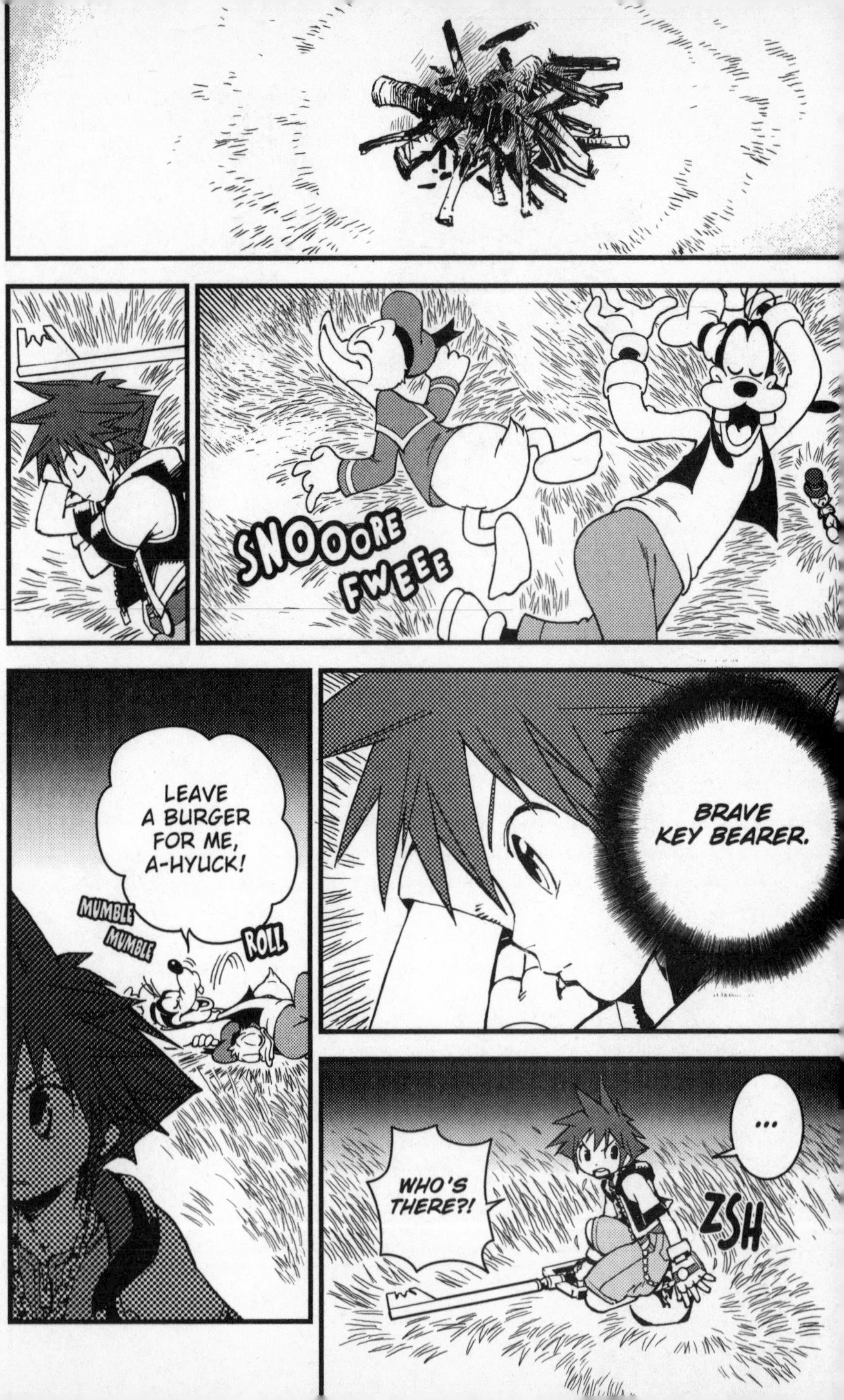
SNOOORE
FWEEE
BRAVE KEY BEARER.
...
WHO'S THERE?!
ZSH
LEAVE A BURGER FOR ME, A-HYUCK!
MUMBLE MUMBLE
ROLL

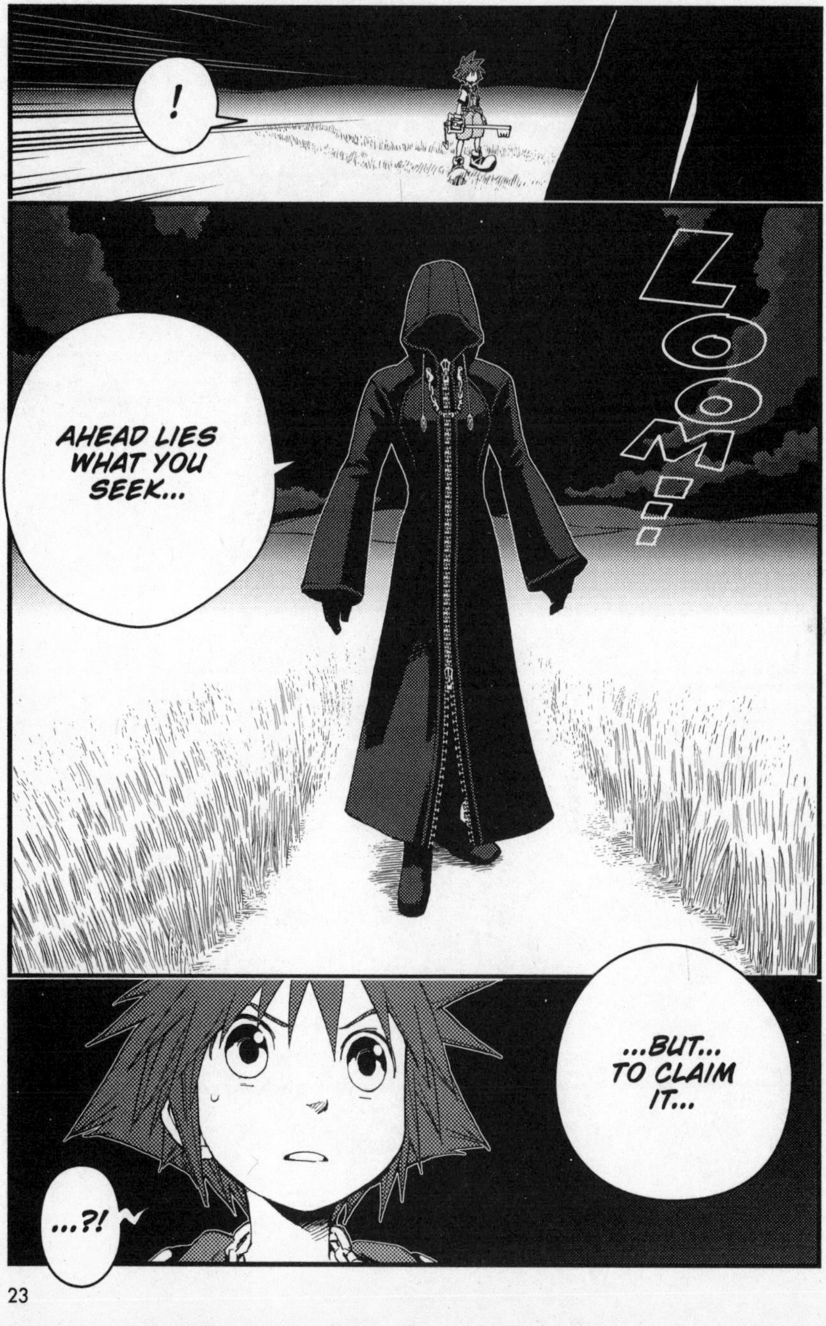
!
LOOM...
AHEAD LIES WHAT YOU SEEK...
...BUT... TO CLAIM IT...
...?!

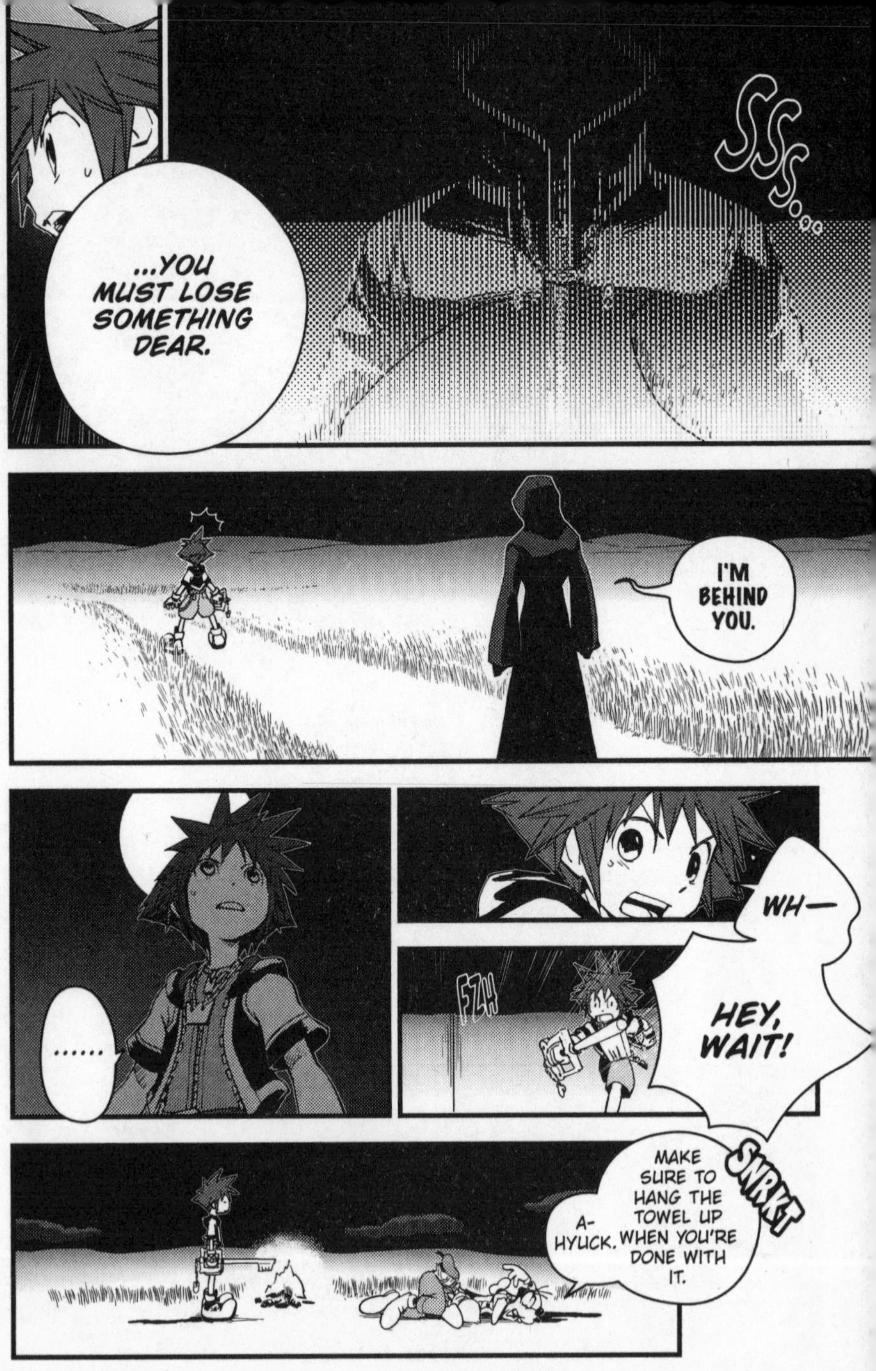
SSS...
...YOU MUST LOSE SOMETHING DEAR.
I'M BEHIND YOU.
WH—
FZH
HEY, WAIT!
......
SNRKT
MAKE SURE TO HANG THE TOWEL UP WHEN YOU'RE DONE WITH IT.
A-HYUCK.

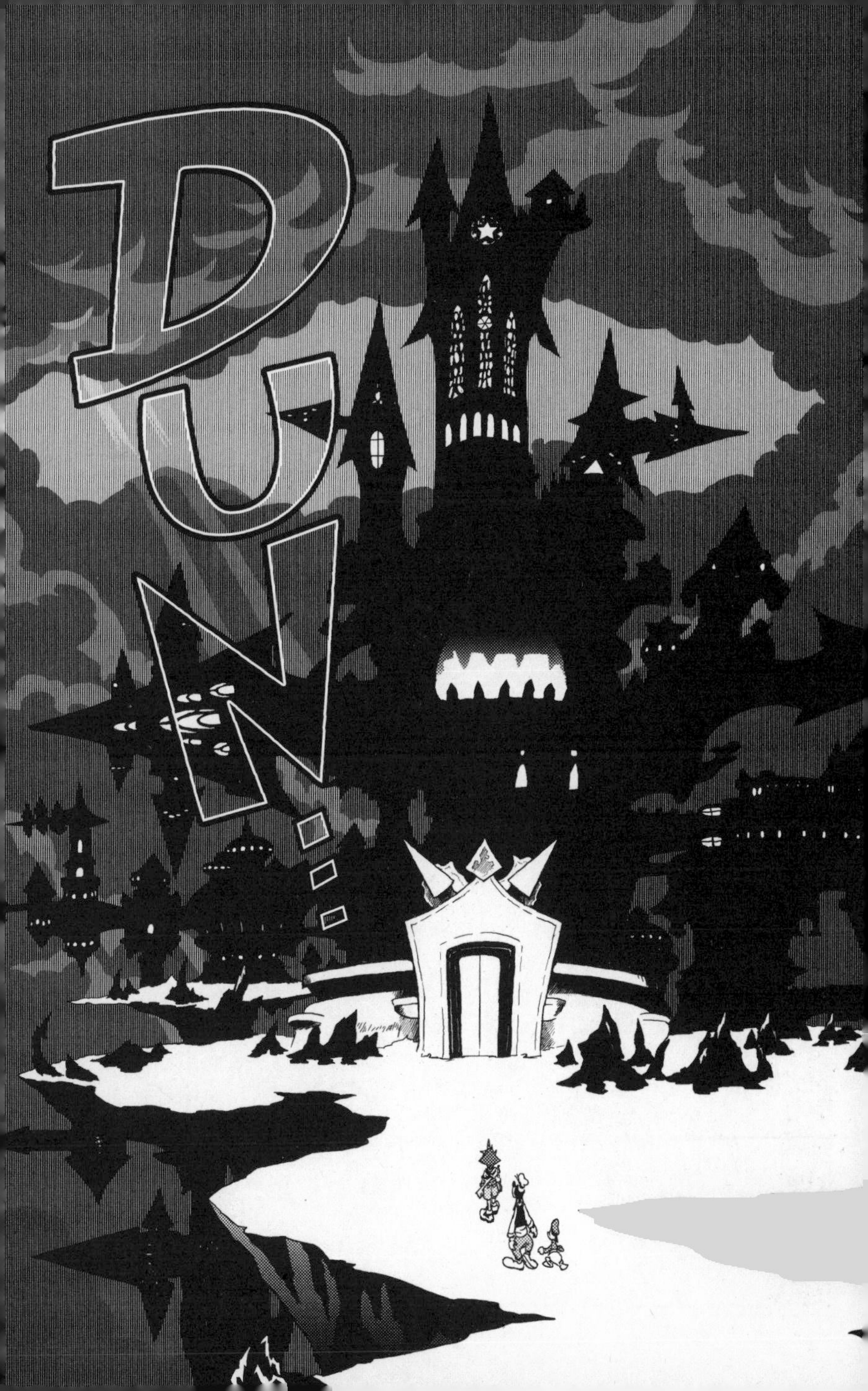
DUN!

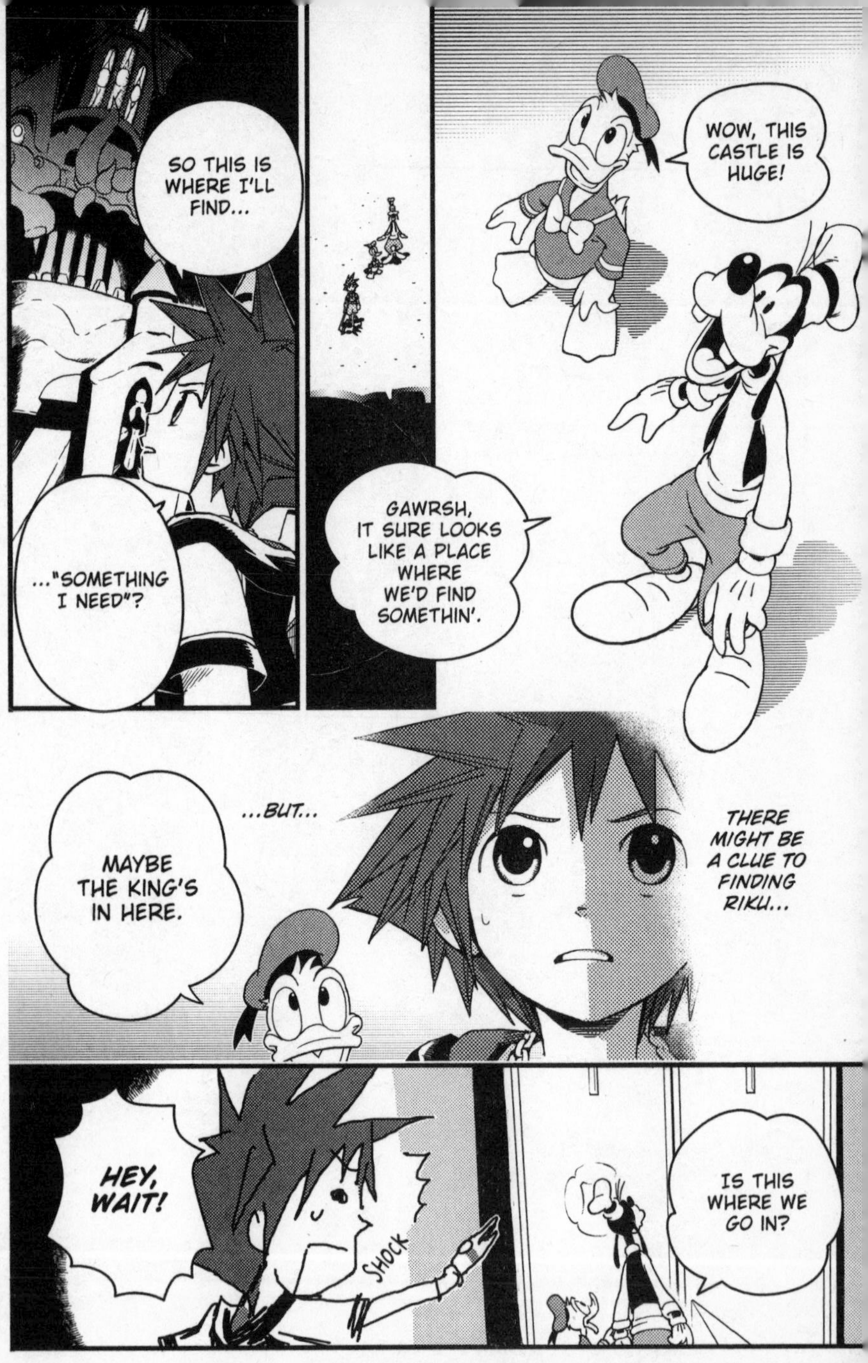
WOW, THIS CASTLE IS HUGE!
GAWRSH, IT SURE LOOKS LIKE A PLACE WHERE WE'D FIND SOMETHIN'.
SO THIS IS WHERE I'LL FIND...
..."SOMETHING I NEED"?
THERE MIGHT BE A CLUE TO FINDING RIKU...
...BUT...
MAYBE THE KING'S IN HERE.
IS THIS WHERE WE GO IN?
HEY, WAIT!
SHOCK

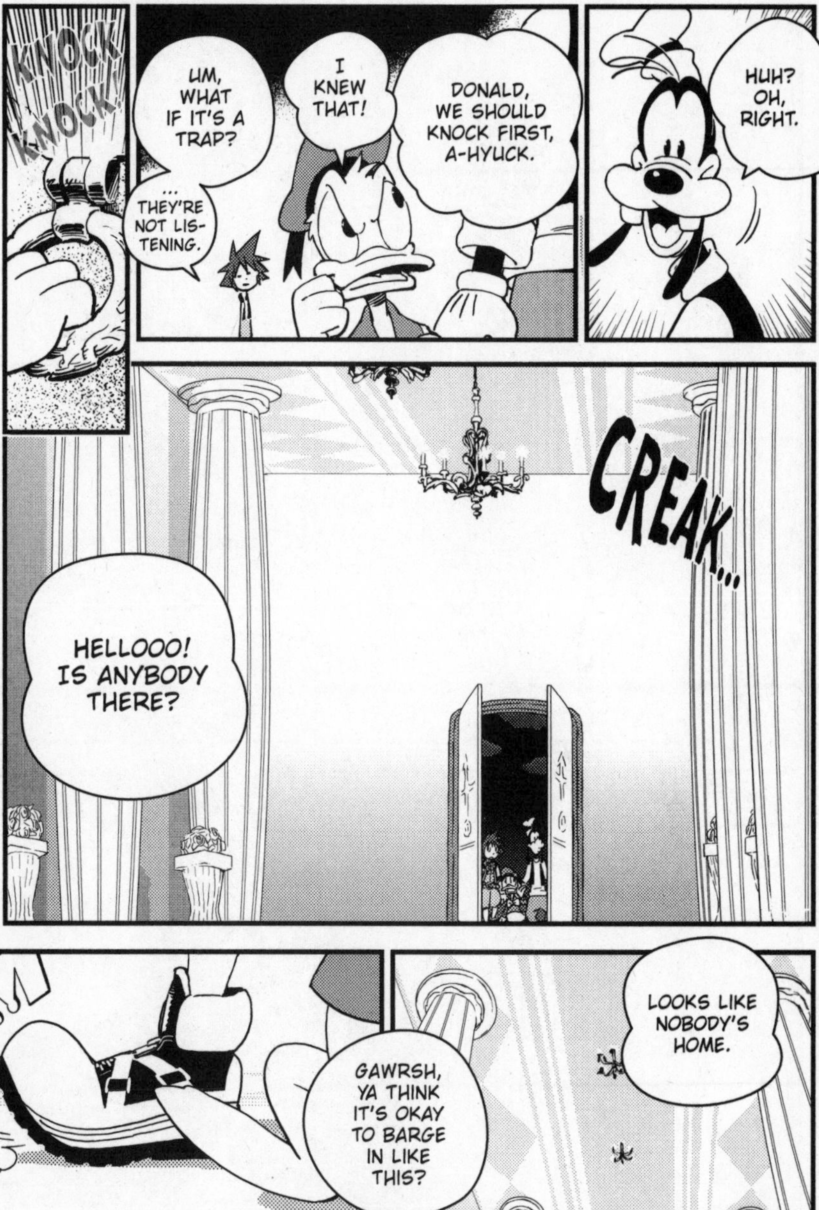
HUH? OH, RIGHT.
DONALD, WE SHOULD KNOCK FIRST, A-HYUCK.
I KNEW THAT!
UM, WHAT IF IT'S A TRAP?
... THEY'RE NOT LIS-TENING.
KNOCK KNOCK
CREAK...
HELLOOO! IS ANYBODY THERE?
LOOKS LIKE NOBODY'S HOME.
GAWRSH, YA THINK IT'S OKAY TO BARGE IN LIKE THIS?

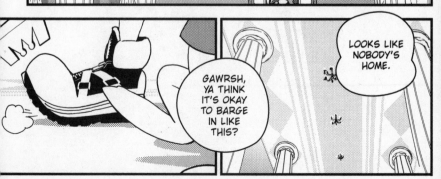

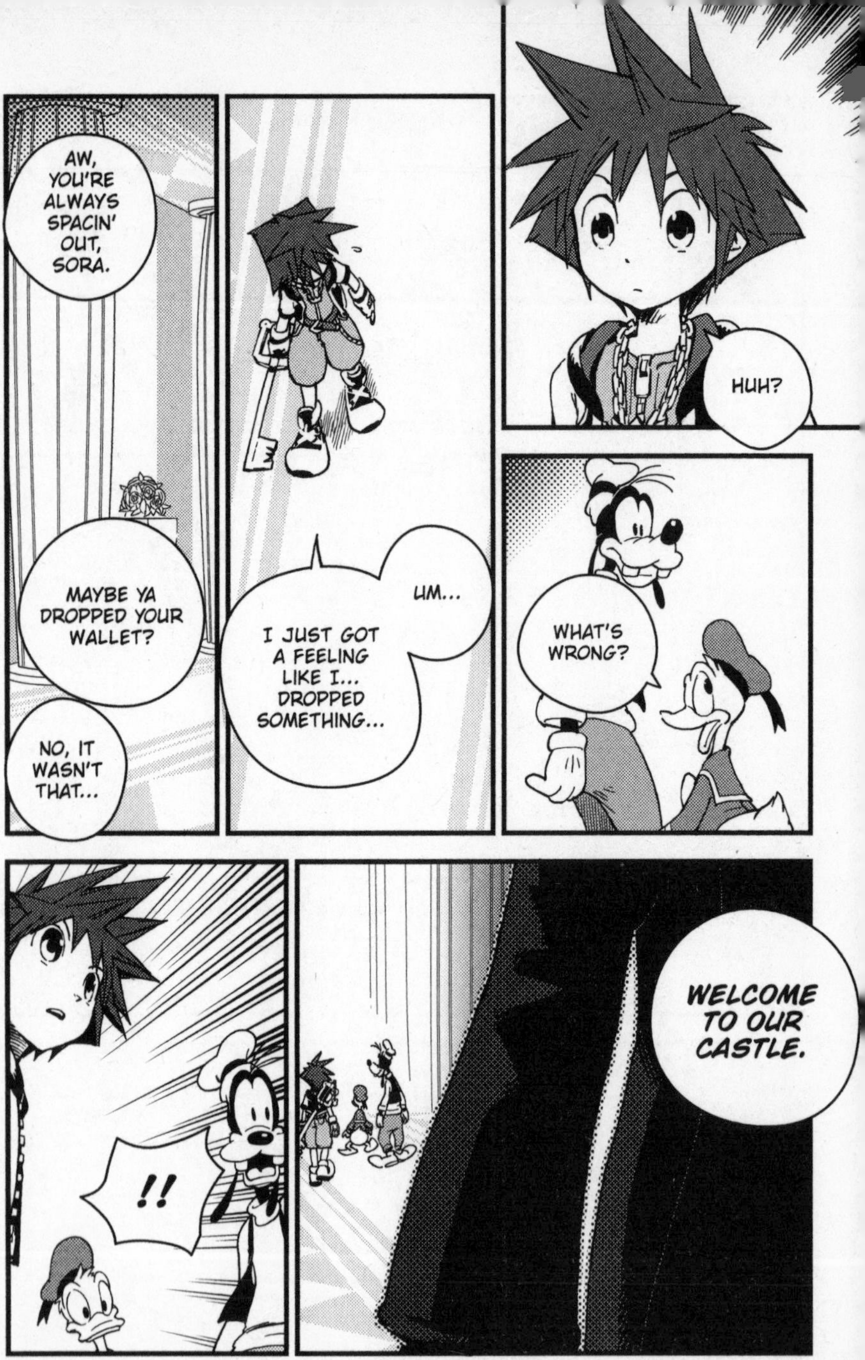
HUH?
WHAT'S WRONG?
UM...
I JUST GOT A FEELING LIKE I... DROPPED SOMETHING...
AW, YOU'RE ALWAYS SPACIN' OUT, SORA.
MAYBE YA DROPPED YOUR WALLET?
NO, IT WASN'T THAT...
WELCOME TO OUR CASTLE.
!!

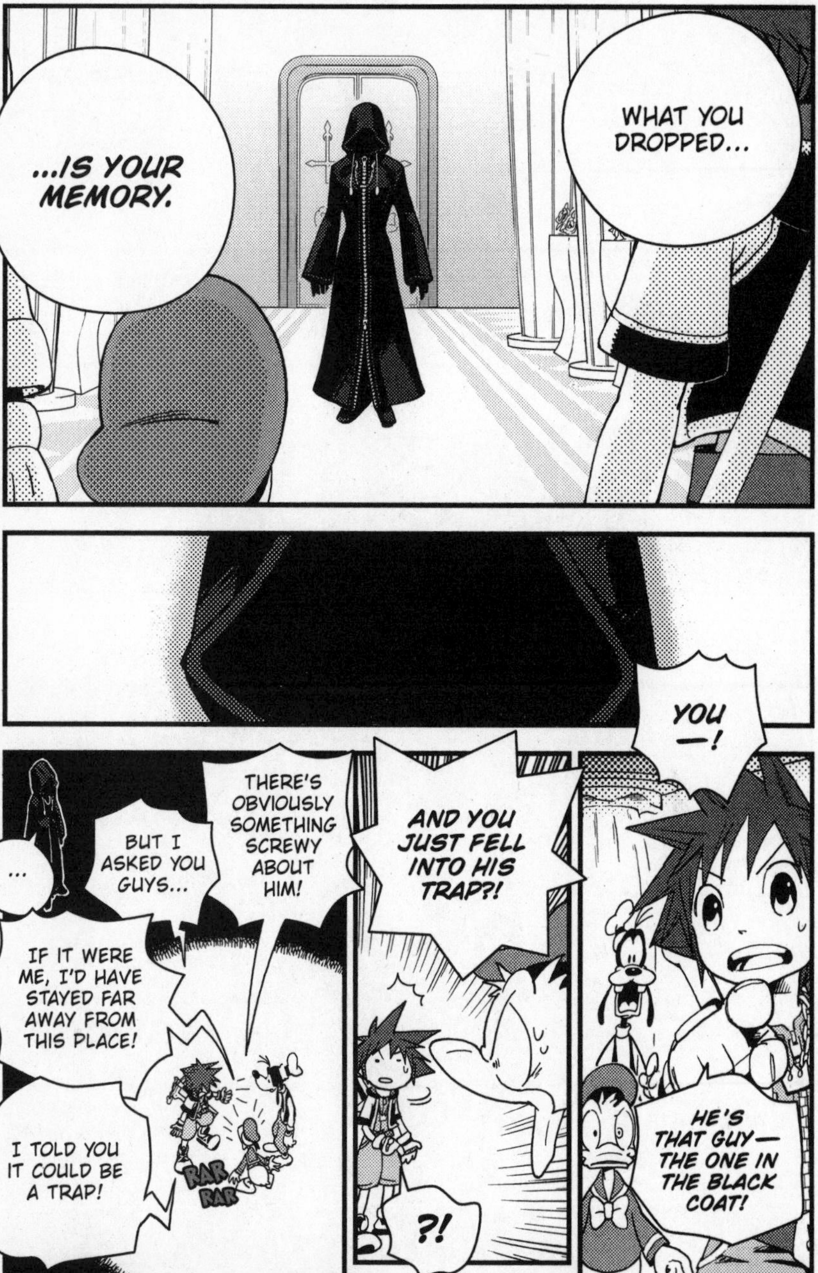
WHAT YOU DROPPED...
...IS YOUR MEMORY.
YOU—!
HE'S THAT GUY—THE ONE IN THE BLACK COAT!
AND YOU JUST FELL INTO HIS TRAP?!
?!
THERE'S OBVIOUSLY SOMETHING SCREWY ABOUT HIM!
BUT I ASKED YOU GUYS...
...
IF IT WERE ME, I'D HAVE STAYED FAR AWAY FROM THIS PLACE!
I TOLD YOU IT COULD BE A TRAP!
RAR RAR

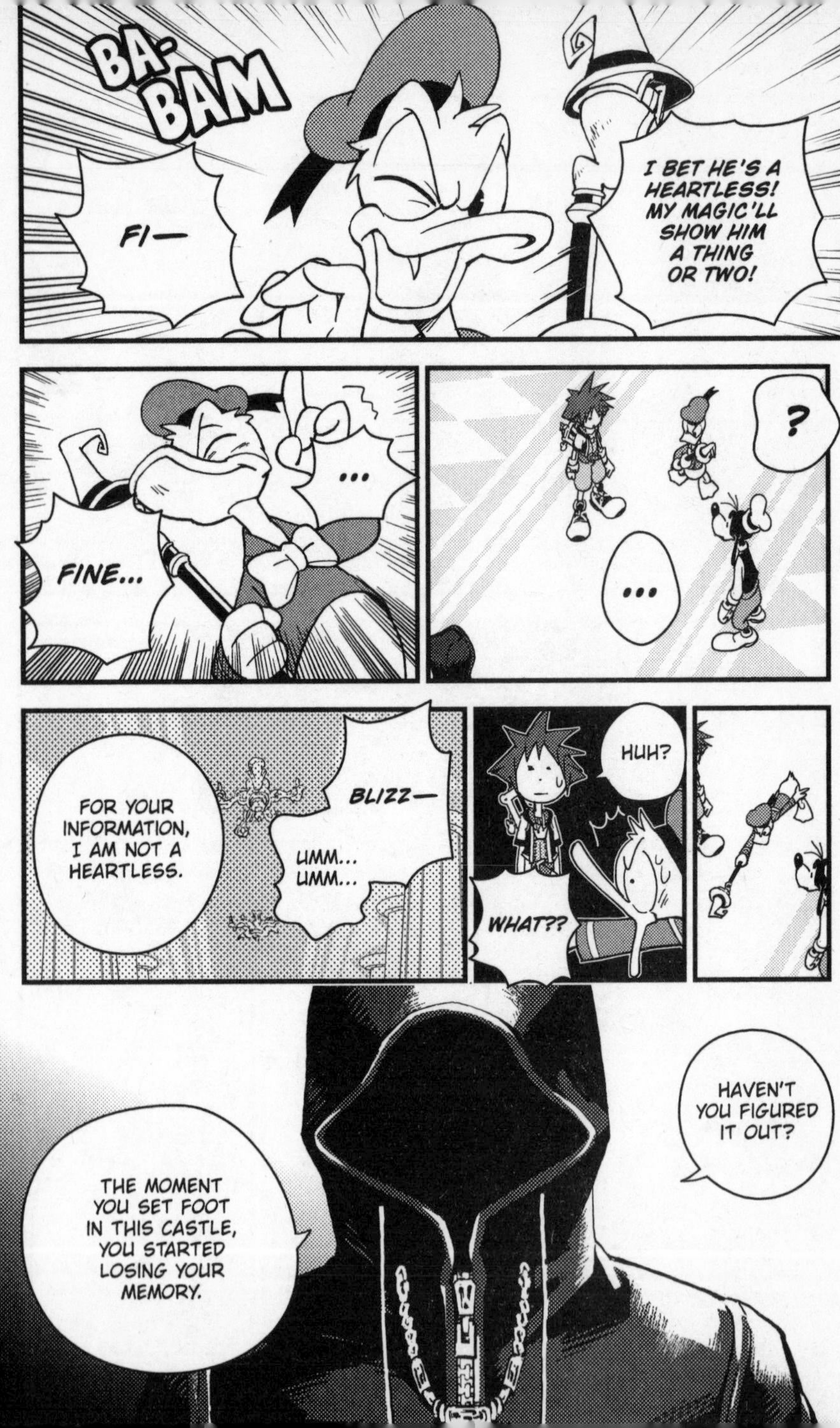
I BET HE'S A HEARTLESS! MY MAGIC'LL SHOW HIM A THING OR TWO!
BA-BAM
FI—
?
...
...
FINE...
HUH?
WHAT??
BLIZZ—
UMM... UMM...
FOR YOUR INFORMATION, I AM NOT A HEARTLESS.
HAVEN'T YOU FIGURED IT OUT?
THE MOMENT YOU SET FOOT IN THIS CASTLE, YOU STARTED LOSING YOUR MEMORY.

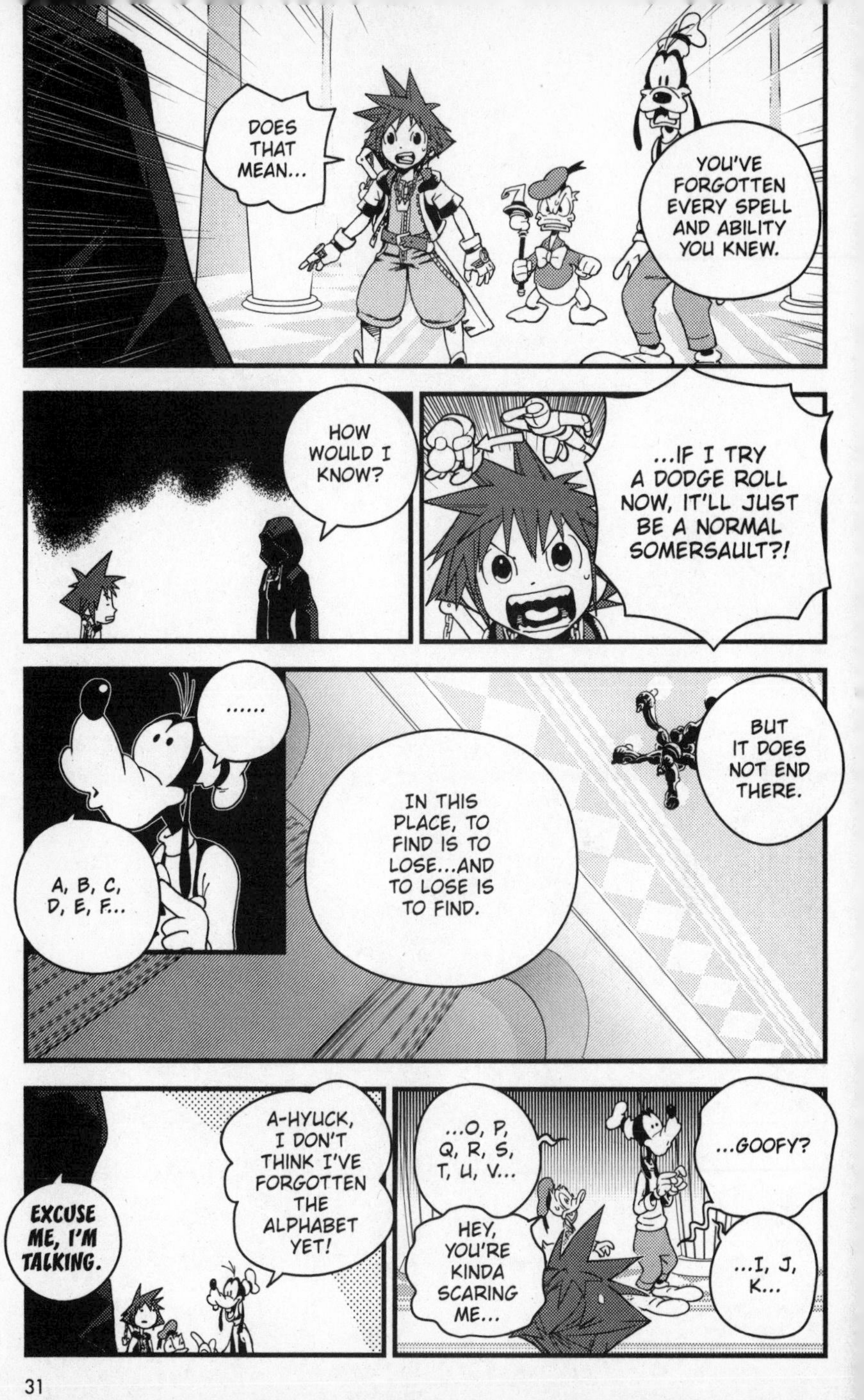
DOES THAT MEAN...
YOU'VE FORGOTTEN EVERY SPELL AND ABILITY YOU KNEW.
...IF I TRY A DODGE ROLL NOW, IT'LL JUST BE A NORMAL SOMERSAULT?!
HOW WOULD I KNOW?
BUT IT DOES NOT END THERE.
IN THIS PLACE, TO FIND IS TO LOSE...AND TO LOSE IS TO FIND.
......
A, B, C, D, E, F...
...GOOFY?
...I, J, K...
...O, P, Q, R, S, T, U, V...
HEY, YOU'RE KINDA SCARING ME...
A-HYUCK, I DON'T THINK I'VE FORGOTTEN THE ALPHABET YET!
EXCUSE ME, I'M TALKING.

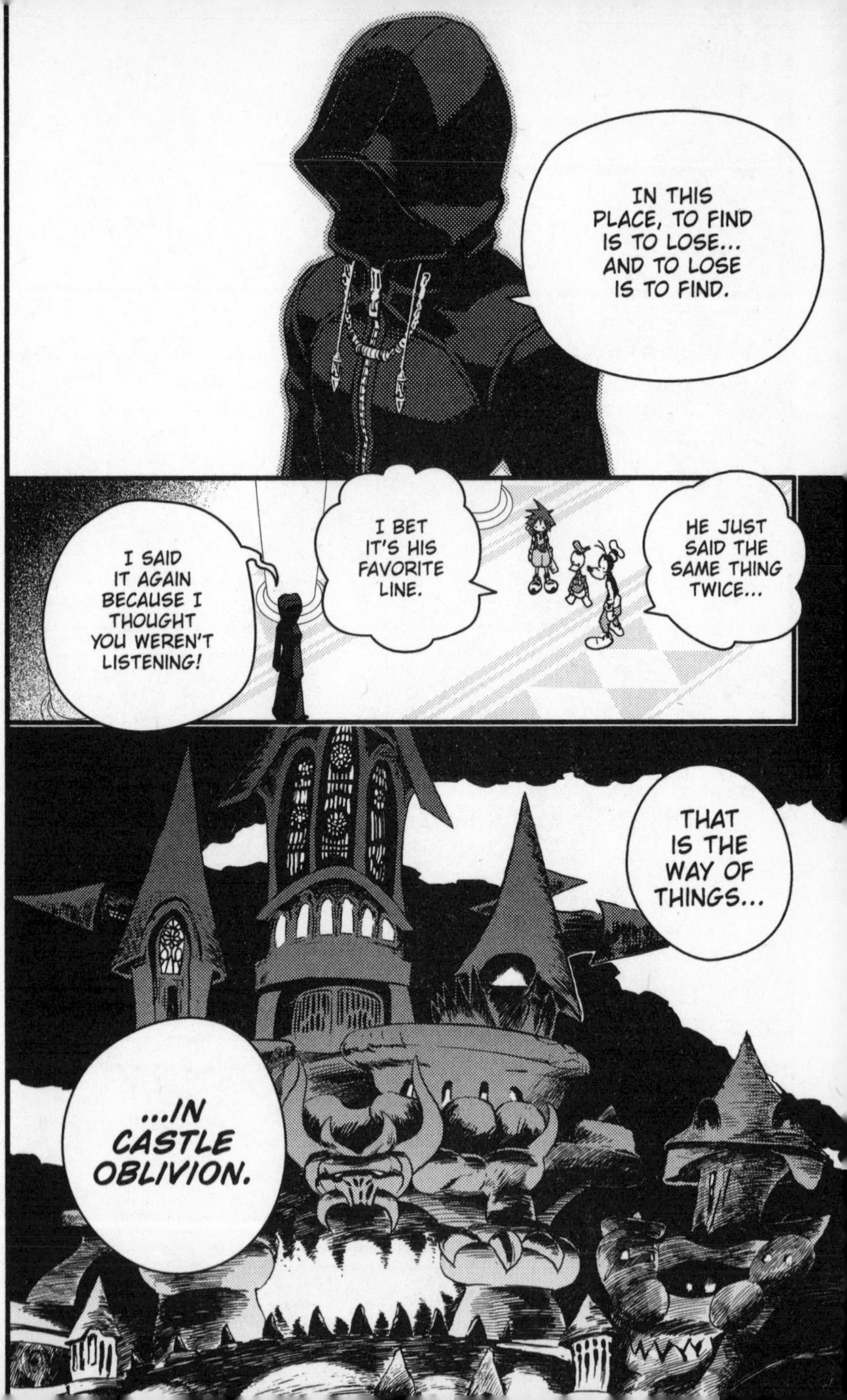
IN THIS PLACE, TO FIND IS TO LOSE... AND TO LOSE IS TO FIND.
HE JUST SAID THE SAME THING TWICE...
I BET IT'S HIS FAVORITE LINE.
I SAID IT AGAIN BECAUSE I THOUGHT YOU WEREN'T LISTENING!
THAT IS THE WAY OF THINGS...
...IN CASTLE OBLIVION.

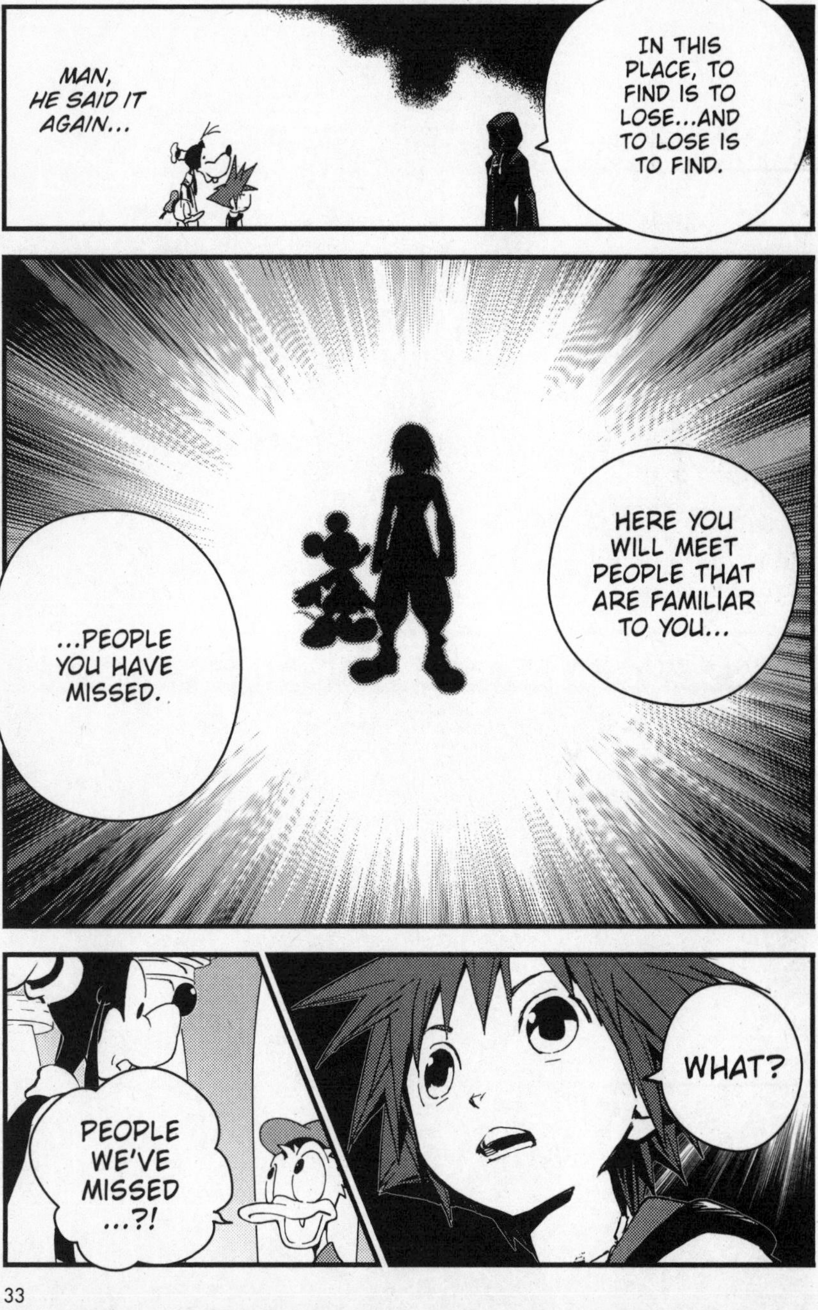
IN THIS PLACE, TO FIND IS TO LOSE...AND TO LOSE IS TO FIND.
MAN, HE SAID IT AGAIN...
HERE YOU WILL MEET PEOPLE THAT ARE FAMILIAR TO YOU...
...PEOPLE YOU HAVE MISSED.
WHAT?
PEOPLE WE'VE MISSED ...?!

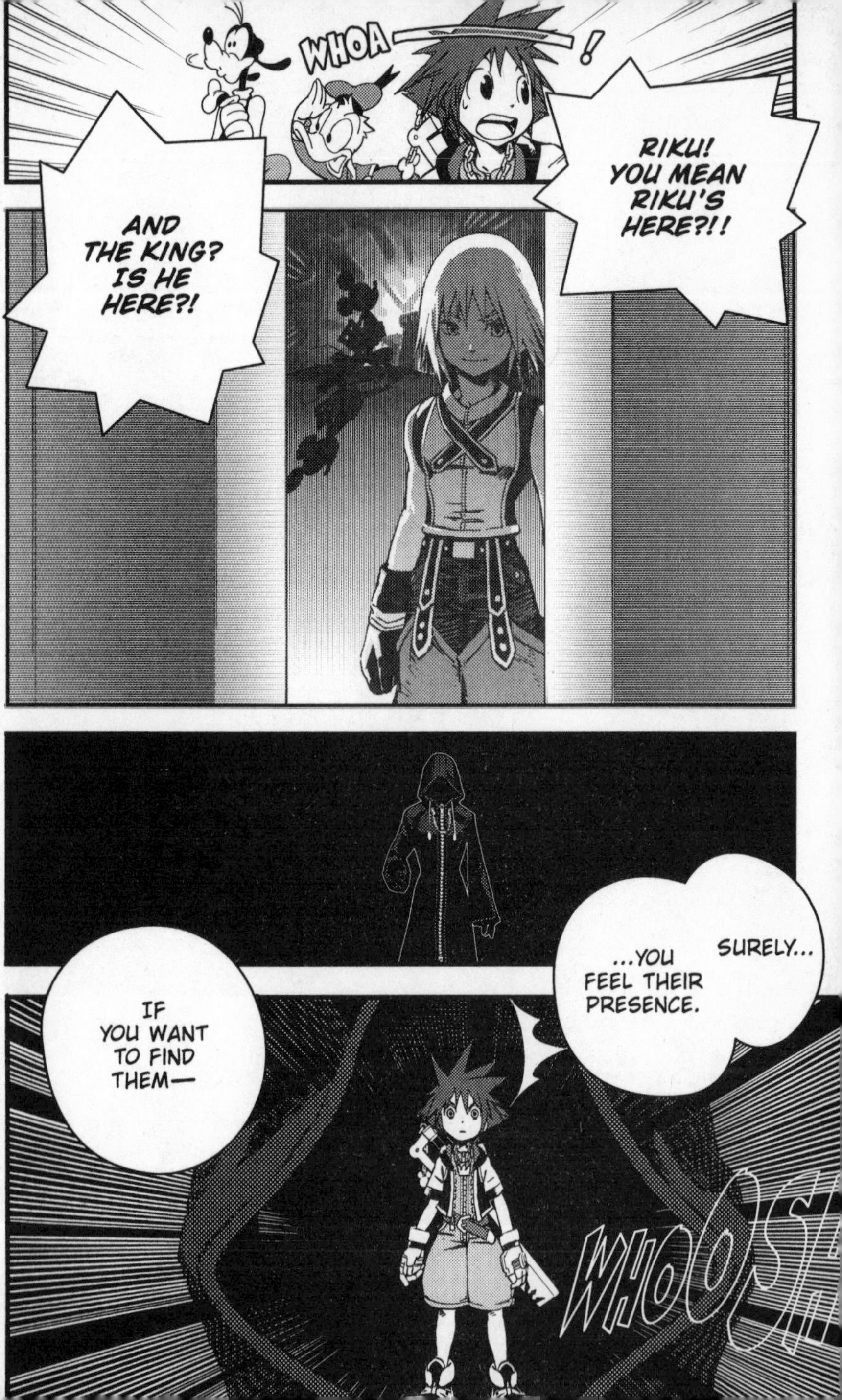
!
WHOA
RIKU! YOU MEAN RIKU'S HERE?!!
AND THE KING? IS HE HERE?!
SURELY...
...YOU FEEL THEIR PRESENCE.
IF YOU WANT TO FIND THEM—
WHOOSH

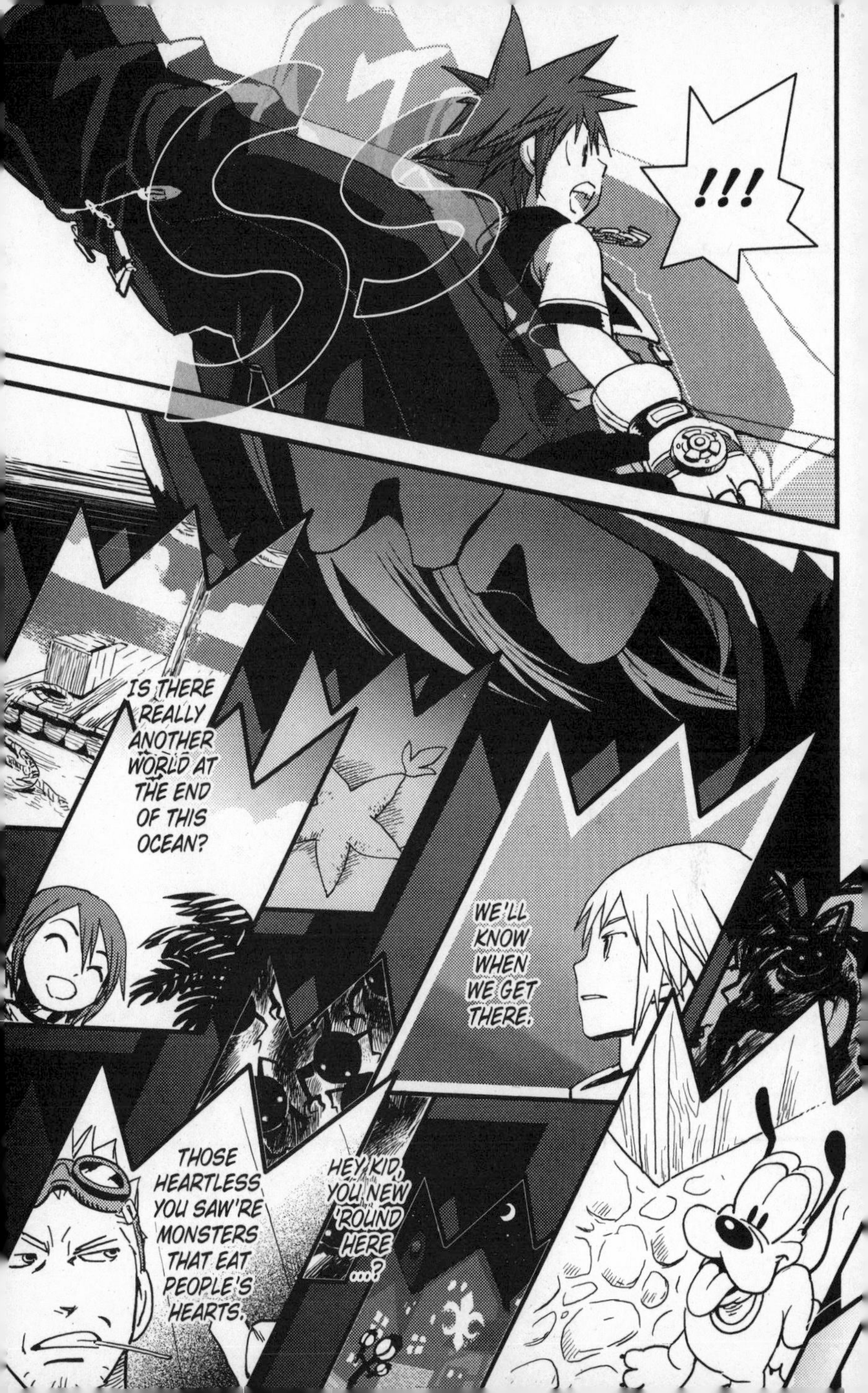
!!!
IS THERE REALLY ANOTHER WORLD AT THE END OF THIS OCEAN?
WE'LL KNOW WHEN WE GET THERE.
HEY KID, YOU NEW 'ROUND HERE ...?
THOSE HEARTLESS YOU SAW'RE MONSTERS THAT EAT PEOPLE'S HEARTS.

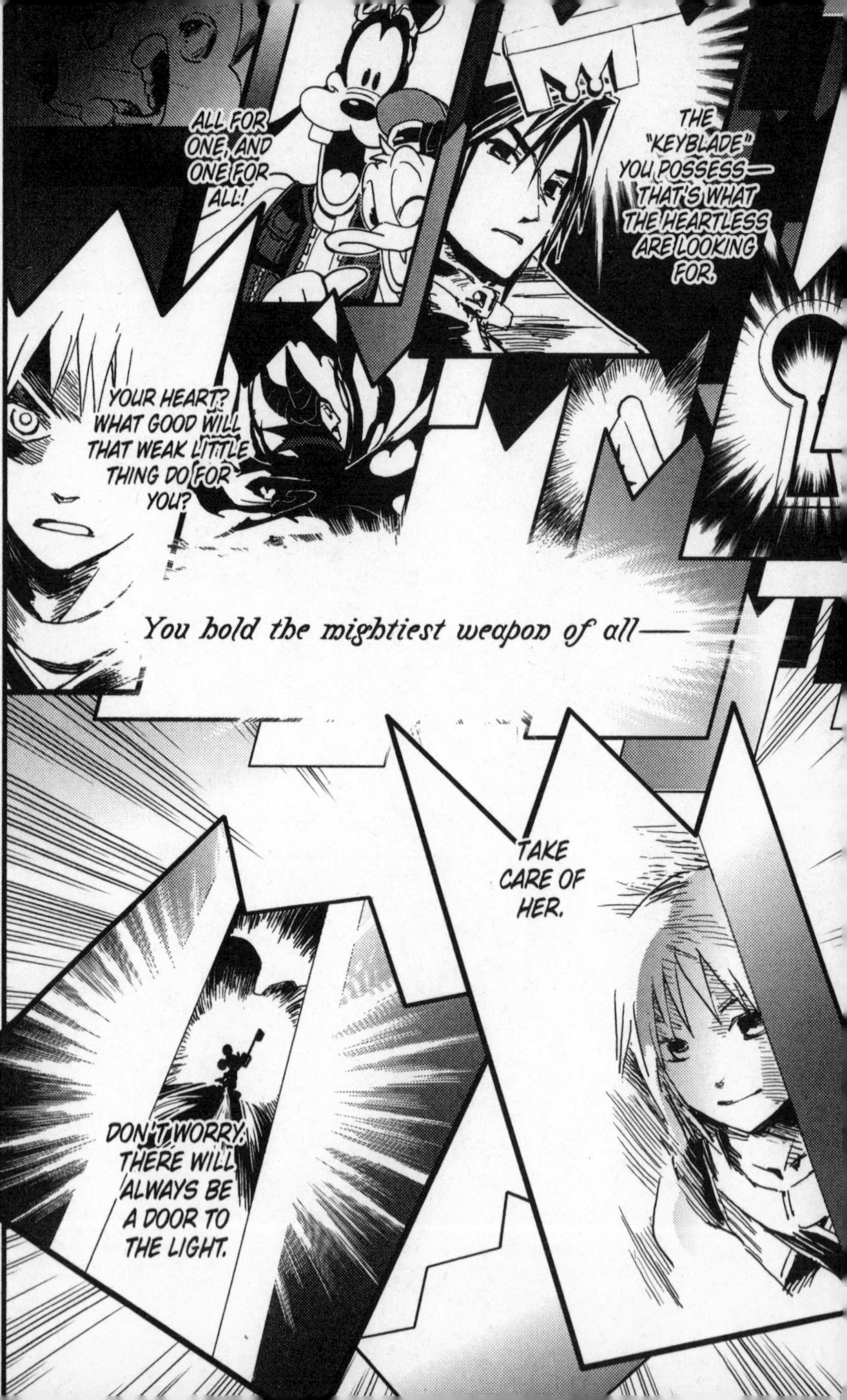
THE "KEYBLADE" YOU POSSESS—THAT'S WHAT THE HEARTLESS ARE LOOKING FOR.
ALL FOR ONE, AND ONE FOR ALL!
YOUR HEART? WHAT GOOD WILL THAT WEAK LITTLE THING DO FOR YOU?
You hold the mightiest weapon of all—
TAKE CARE OF HER.
DON'T WORRY. THERE WILL ALWAYS BE A DOOR TO THE LIGHT.

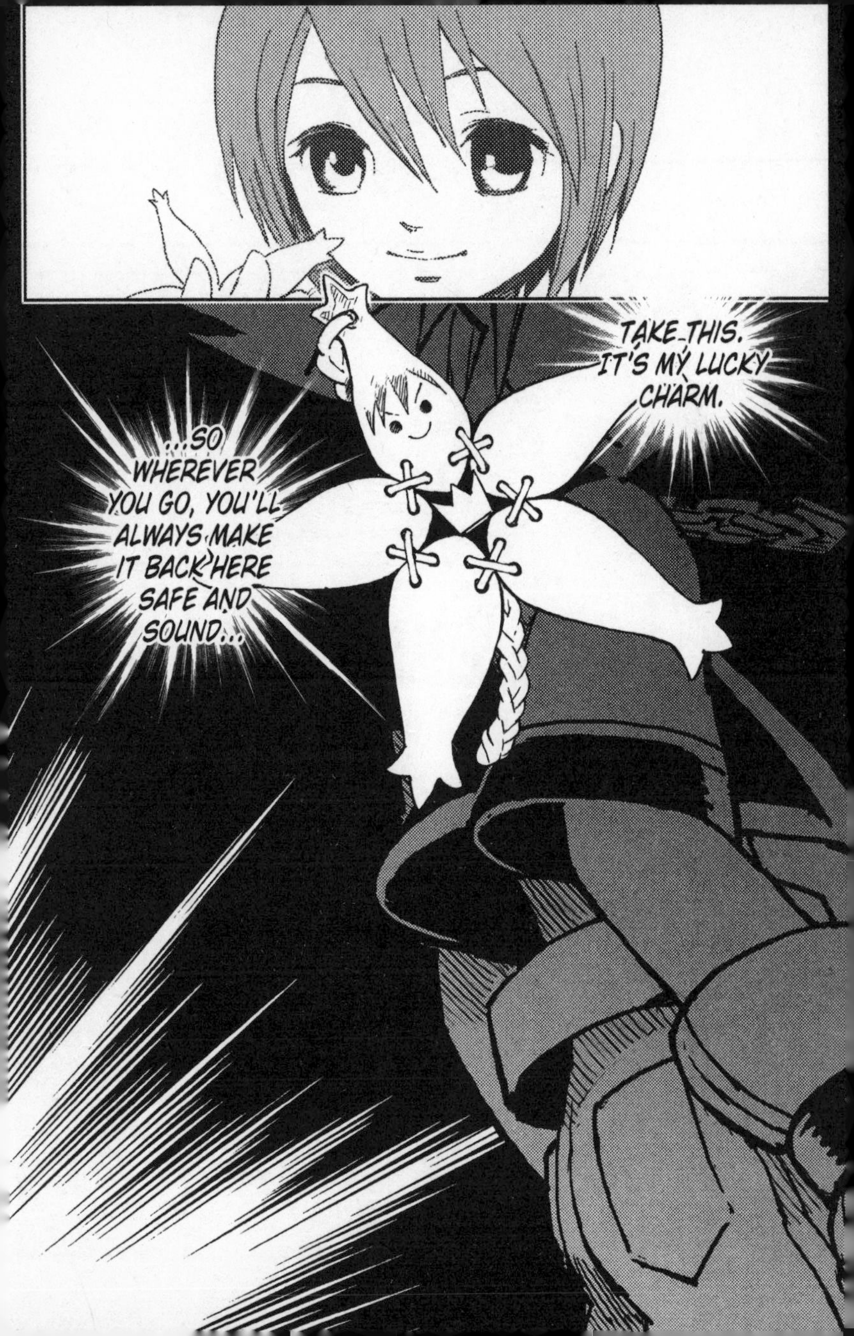
TAKE THIS. IT'S MY LUCKY CHARM.
...SO WHEREVER YOU GO, YOU'LL ALWAYS MAKE IT BACK HERE SAFE AND SOUND...

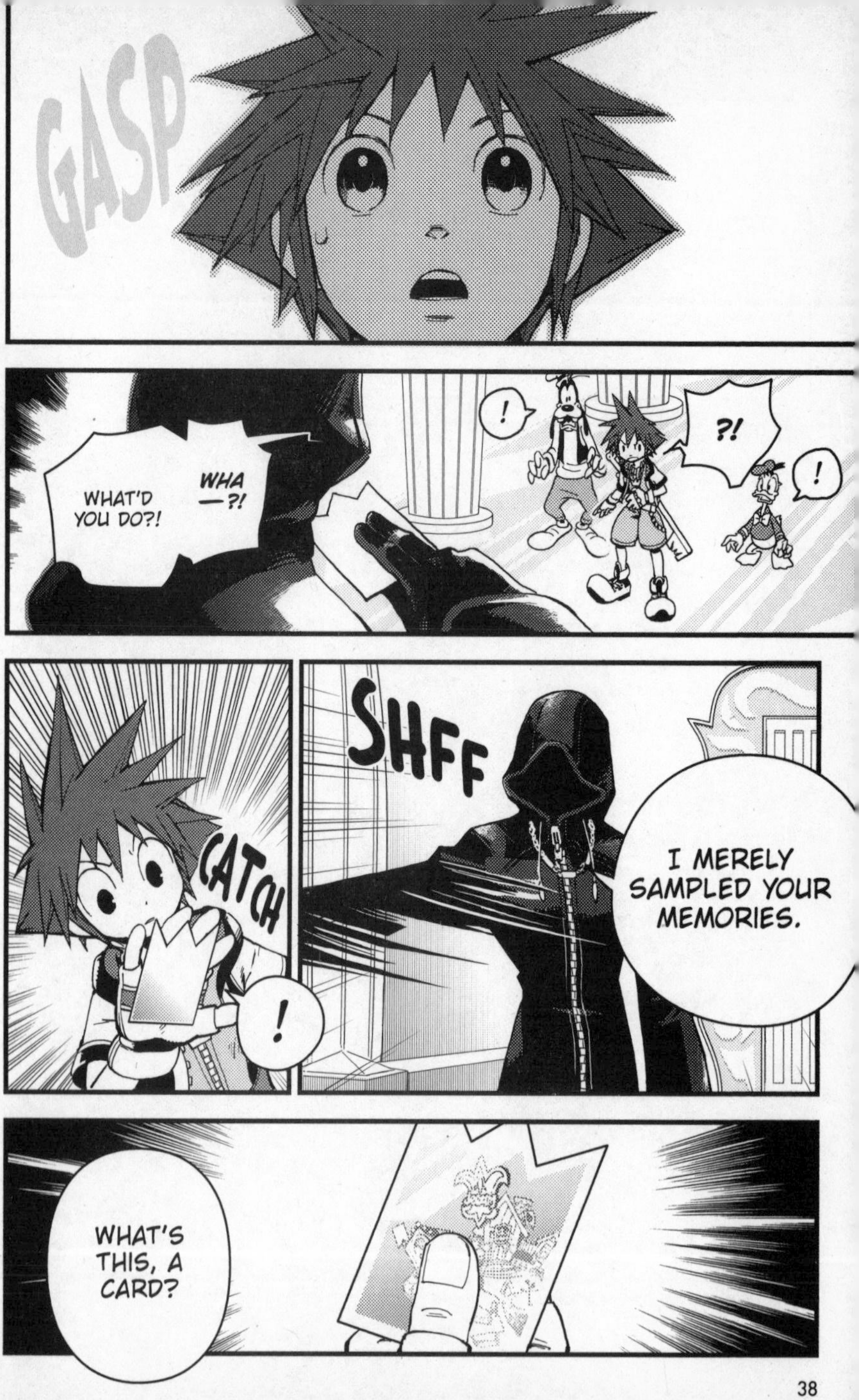
GASP
?!
!
!
WHA—?!
WHAT'D YOU DO?!
SHFF
I MERELY SAMPLED YOUR MEMORIES.
CATCH
!
WHAT'S THIS, A CARD?

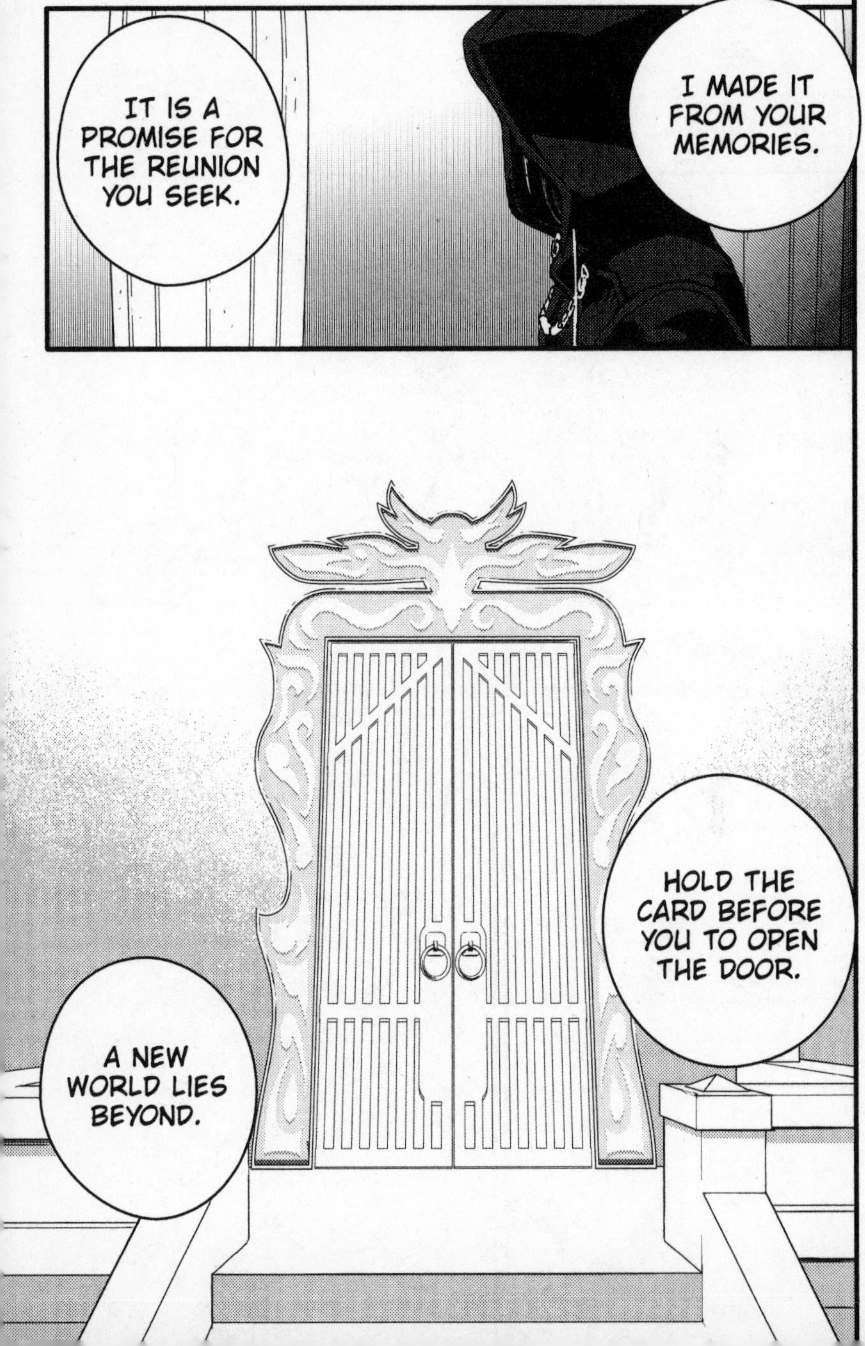
I MADE IT FROM YOUR MEMORIES.
IT IS A PROMISE FOR THE REUNION YOU SEEK.
HOLD THE CARD BEFORE YOU TO OPEN THE DOOR.
A NEW WORLD LIES BEYOND.

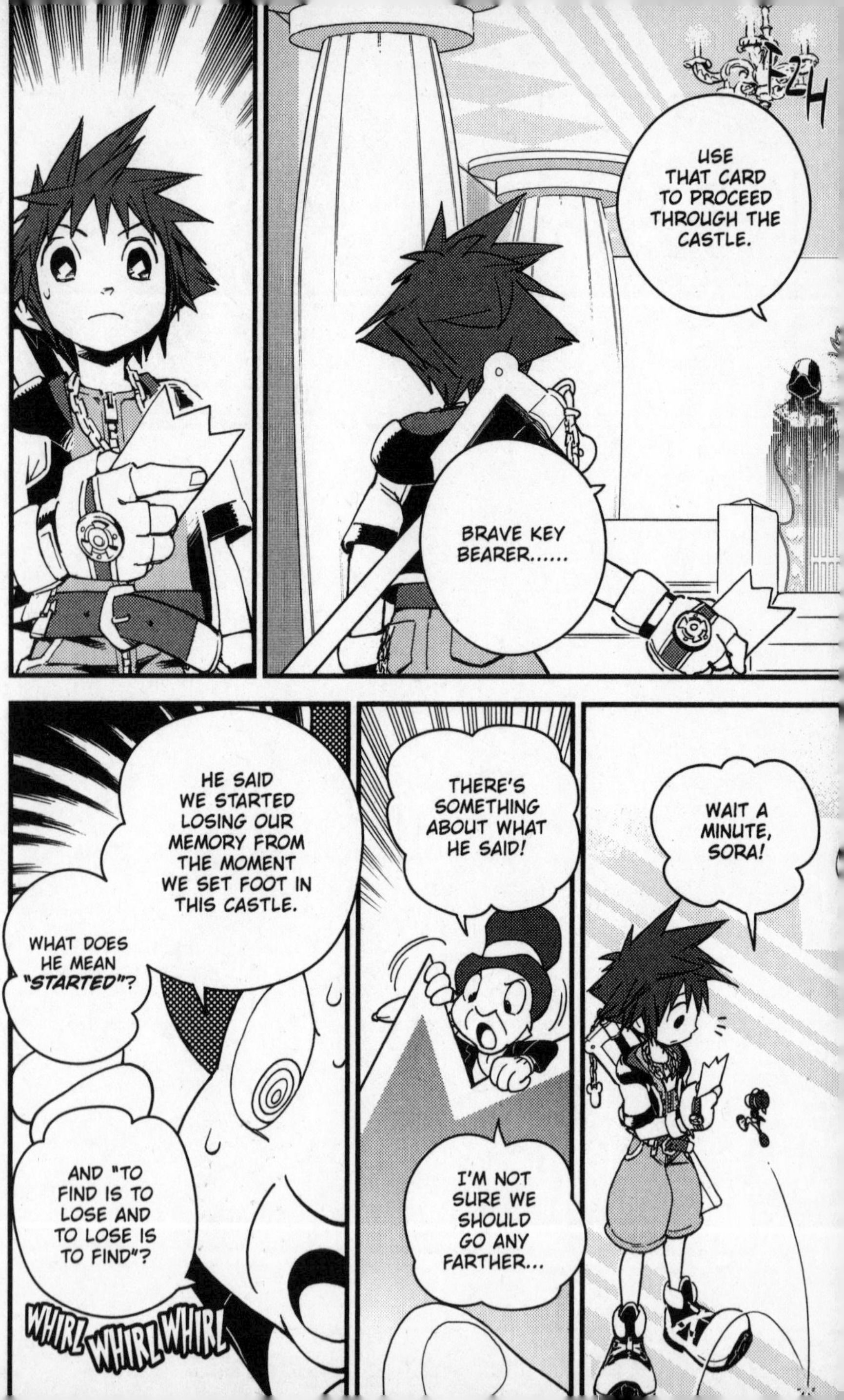
USE THAT CARD TO PROCEED THROUGH THE CASTLE.
BRAVE KEY BEARER......
WAIT A MINUTE, SORA!
THERE'S SOMETHING ABOUT WHAT HE SAID!
I'M NOT SURE WE SHOULD GO ANY FARTHER...
HE SAID WE STARTED LOSING OUR MEMORY FROM THE MOMENT WE SET FOOT IN THIS CASTLE.
WHAT DOES HE MEAN "STARTED"?
AND "TO FIND IS TO LOSE AND TO LOSE IS TO FIND"?
WHIRL WHIRL WHIRL

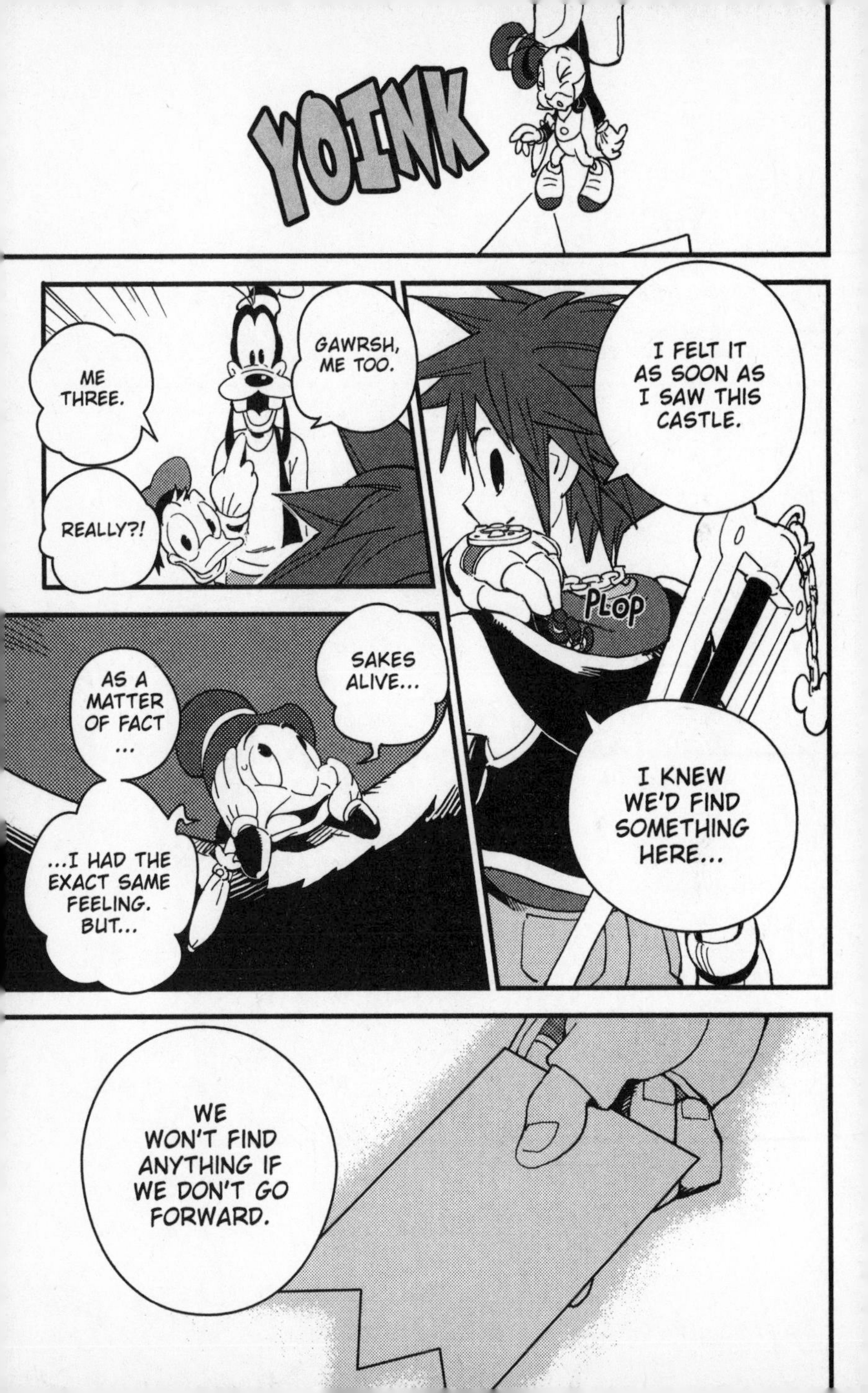
YOINK
I FELT IT AS SOON AS I SAW THIS CASTLE.
PLOP
I KNEW WE'D FIND SOMETHING HERE...
GAWRSH, ME TOO.
ME THREE.
REALLY?!
SAKES ALIVE...
AS A MATTER OF FACT ...
...I HAD THE EXACT SAME FEELING. BUT...
WE WON'T FIND ANYTHING IF WE DON'T GO FORWARD.

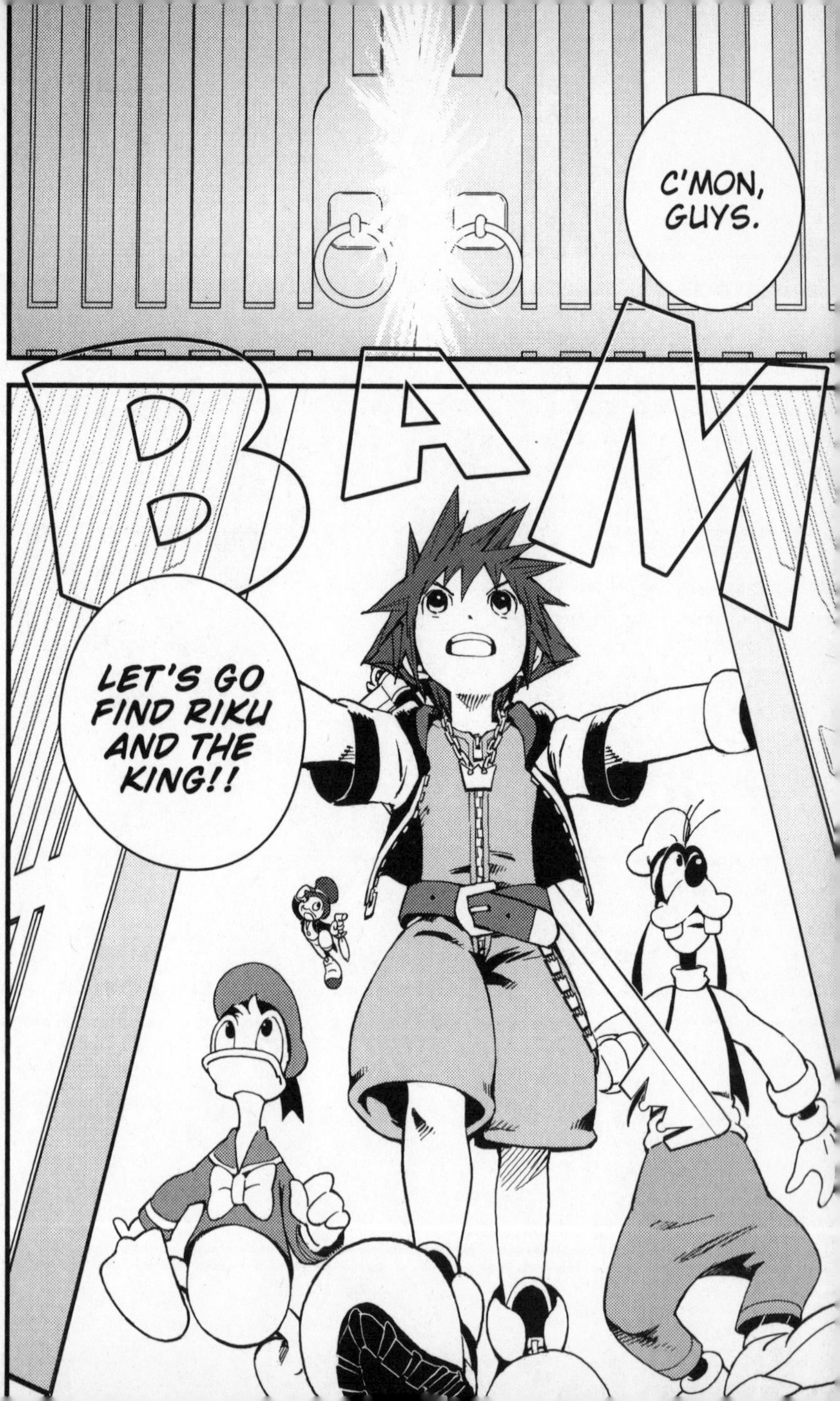
C'MON, GUYS.
BAM
LET'S GO FIND RIKU AND THE KING!!

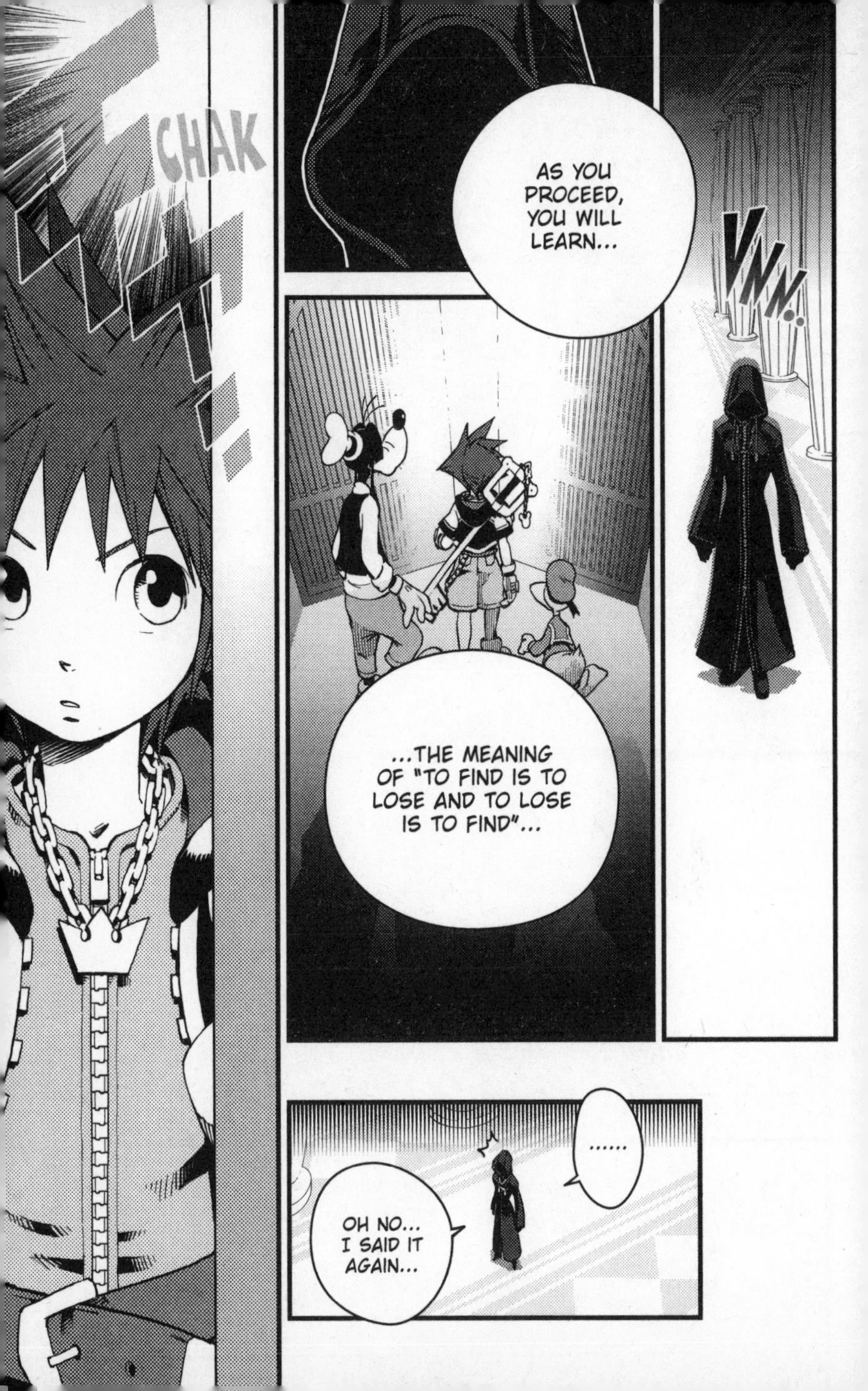
VNN..
AS YOU PROCEED, YOU WILL LEARN...
...THE MEANING OF "TO FIND IS TO LOSE AND TO LOSE IS TO FIND"...
......
OH NO... I SAID IT AGAIN...
CHAK

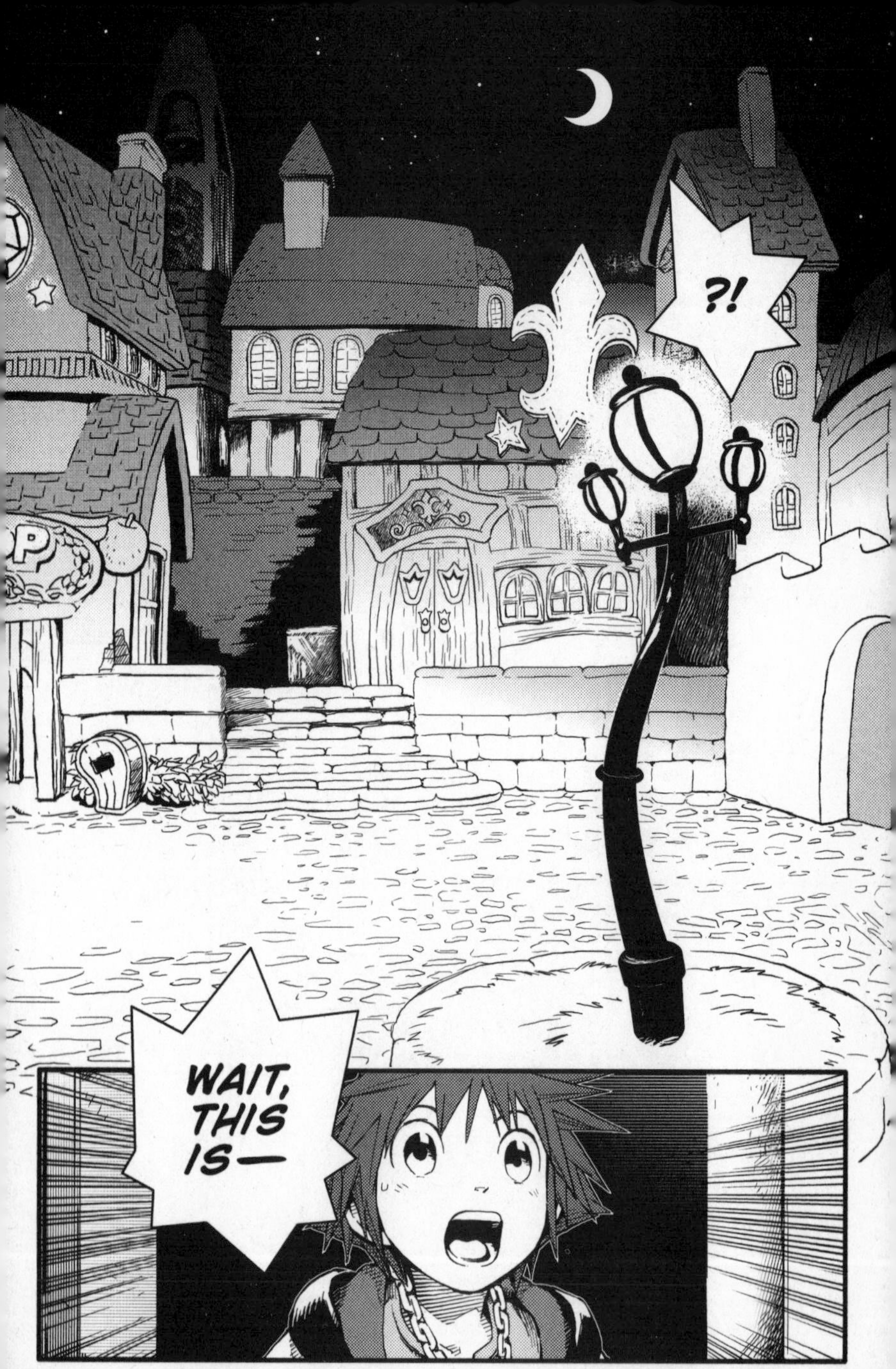
?!
WAIT, THIS IS—

# *Card:02*
# Bellyful Stew

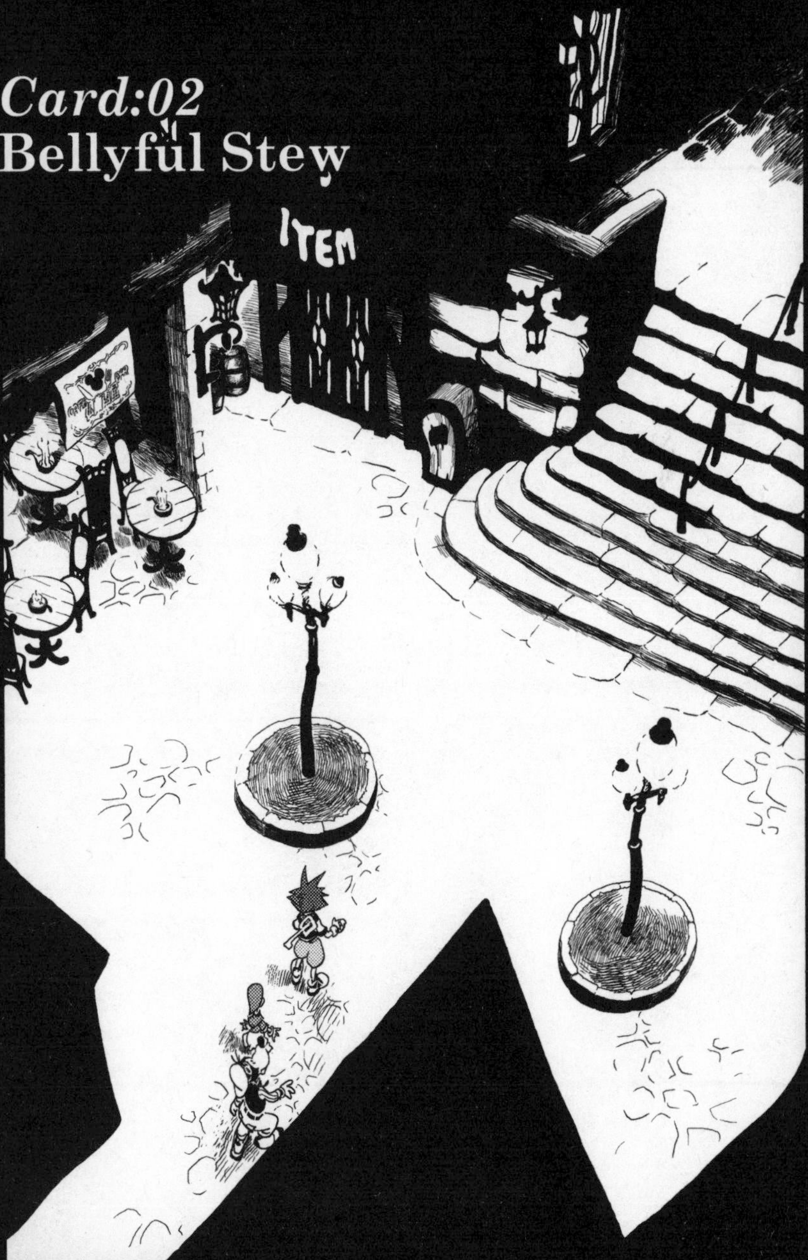
ITEM

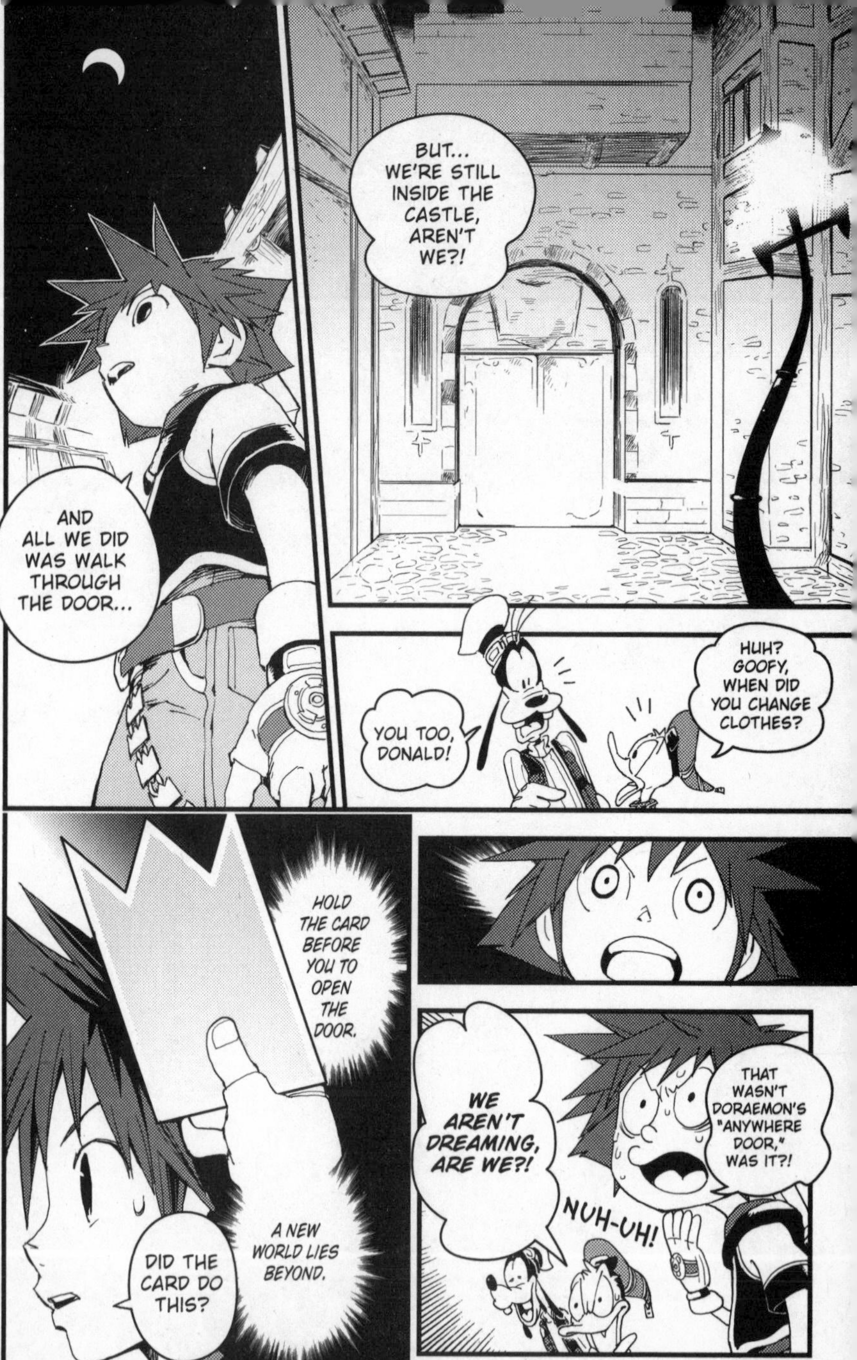

BUT... WE'RE STILL INSIDE THE CASTLE, AREN'T WE?!
HUH? GOOFY, WHEN DID YOU CHANGE CLOTHES?
YOU TOO, DONALD!
AND ALL WE DID WAS WALK THROUGH THE DOOR...
THAT WASN'T DORAEMON'S "ANYWHERE DOOR," WAS IT?!
WE AREN'T DREAMING, ARE WE?!
NUH-UH!
HOLD THE CARD BEFORE YOU TO OPEN THE DOOR.
A NEW WORLD LIES BEYOND.
DID THE CARD DO THIS?

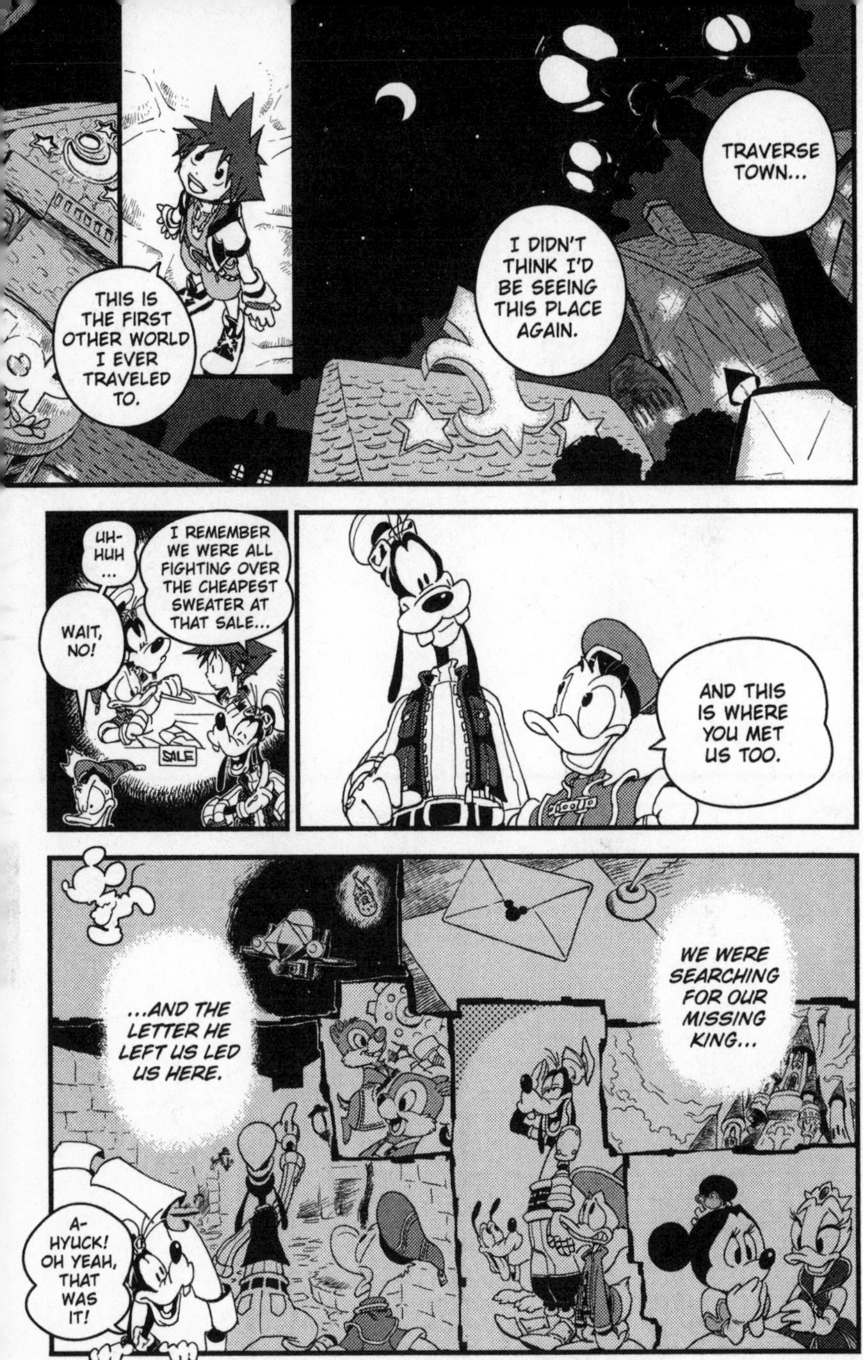
TRAVERSE TOWN...
I DIDN'T THINK I'D BE SEEING THIS PLACE AGAIN.
THIS IS THE FIRST OTHER WORLD I EVER TRAVELED TO.
AND THIS IS WHERE YOU MET US TOO.
I REMEMBER WE WERE ALL FIGHTING OVER THE CHEAPEST SWEATER AT THAT SALE...
UH-HUH...
WAIT, NO!
SALE
WE WERE SEARCHING FOR OUR MISSING KING...
...AND THE LETTER HE LEFT US LED US HERE.
A-HYUCK! OH YEAH, THAT WAS IT!

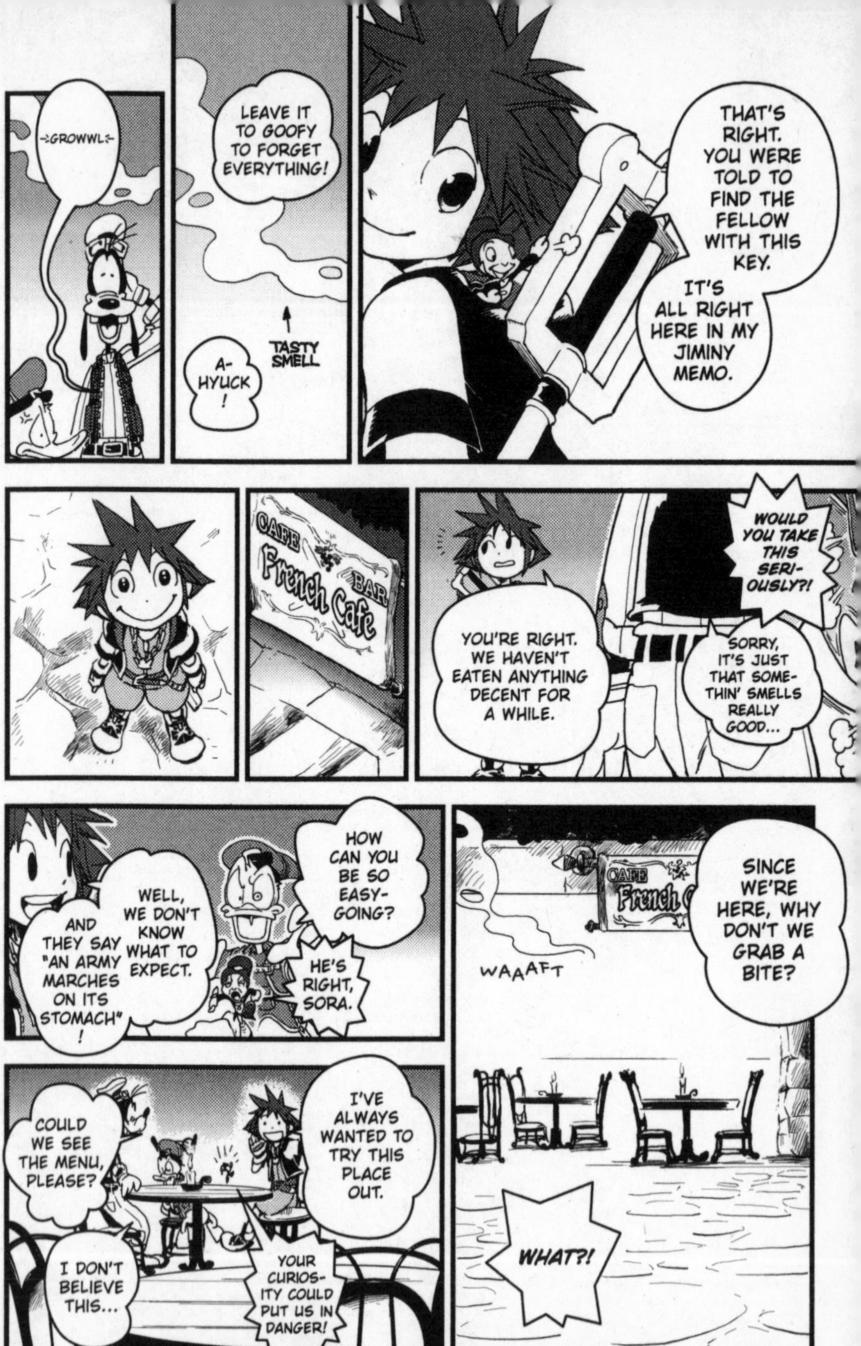
THAT'S RIGHT. YOU WERE TOLD TO FIND THE FELLOW WITH THIS KEY.
IT'S ALL RIGHT HERE IN MY JIMINY MEMO.
LEAVE IT TO GOOFY TO FORGET EVERYTHING!
TASTY SMELL
A-HYUCK!
GROWWL
WOULD YOU TAKE THIS SERI-OUSLY?!
SORRY, IT'S JUST THAT SOME-THIN' SMELLS REALLY GOOD...
YOU'RE RIGHT. WE HAVEN'T EATEN ANYTHING DECENT FOR A WHILE.
CAFE
French Cafe
BAR
SINCE WE'RE HERE, WHY DON'T WE GRAB A BITE?
CAFE
WAAAFT
WHAT?!
HOW CAN YOU BE SO EASY-GOING?
HE'S RIGHT, SORA.
WELL, WE DON'T KNOW WHAT TO EXPECT.
AND THEY SAY "AN ARMY MARCHES ON ITS STOMACH"!
I'VE ALWAYS WANTED TO TRY THIS PLACE OUT.
COULD WE SEE THE MENU, PLEASE?
YOUR CURIOS-ITY COULD PUT US IN DANGER!
I DON'T BELIEVE THIS...

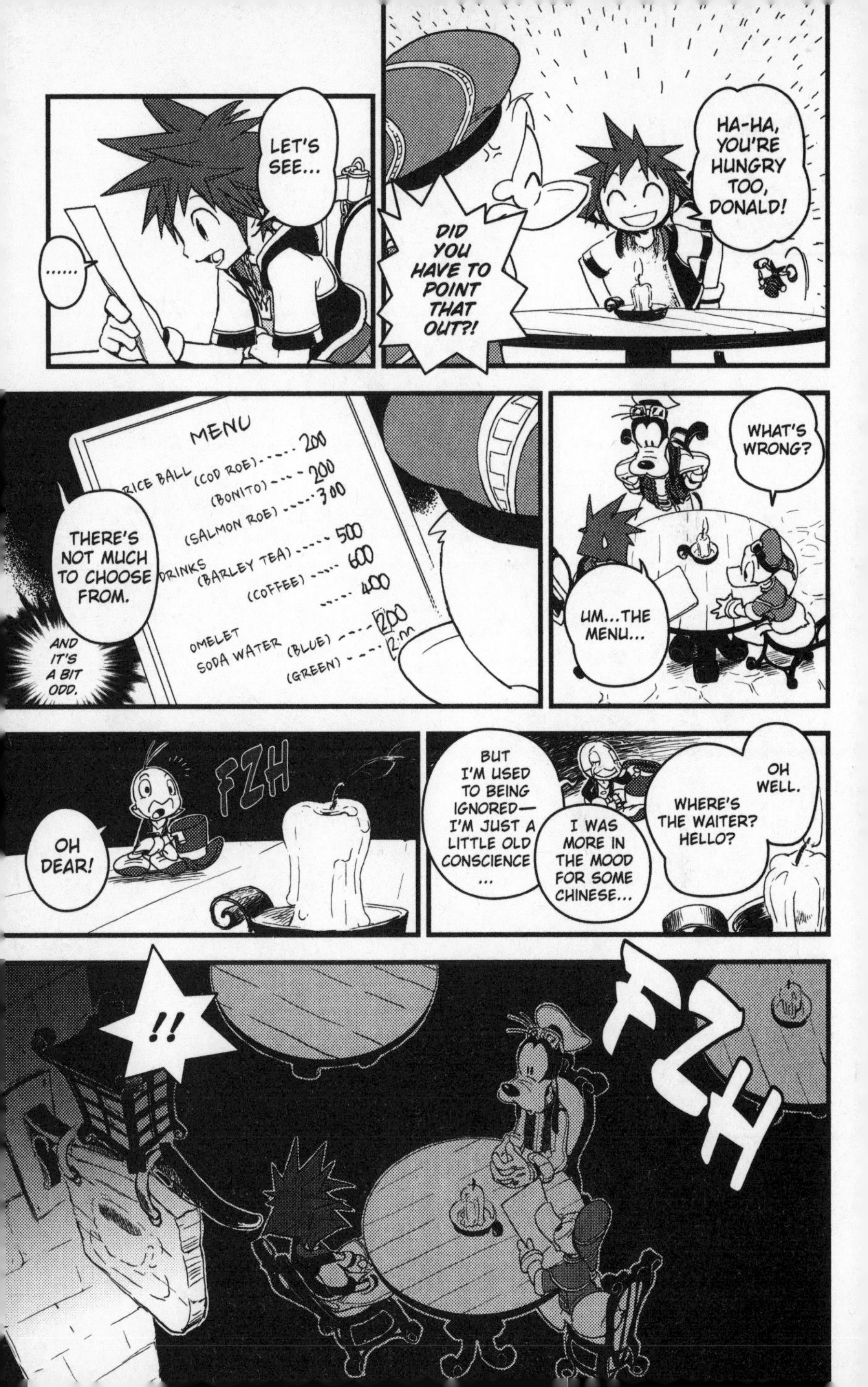
HA-HA, YOU'RE HUNGRY TOO, DONALD!
DID YOU HAVE TO POINT THAT OUT?!
LET'S SEE...
......
WHAT'S WRONG?
UM...THE MENU...
MENU
RICE BALL (COD ROE) 200
(BONITO) 200
(SALMON ROE) 300
DRINKS (BARLEY TEA) 500
(COFFEE) 600
400
OMELET 200
SODA WATER (BLUE)
(GREEN)
THERE'S NOT MUCH TO CHOOSE FROM.
AND IT'S A BIT ODD.
OH WELL.
WHERE'S THE WAITER? HELLO?
I WAS MORE IN THE MOOD FOR SOME CHINESE...
BUT I'M USED TO BEING IGNORED—I'M JUST A LITTLE OLD CONSCIENCE ...
FZH
OH DEAR!
FZH
!!

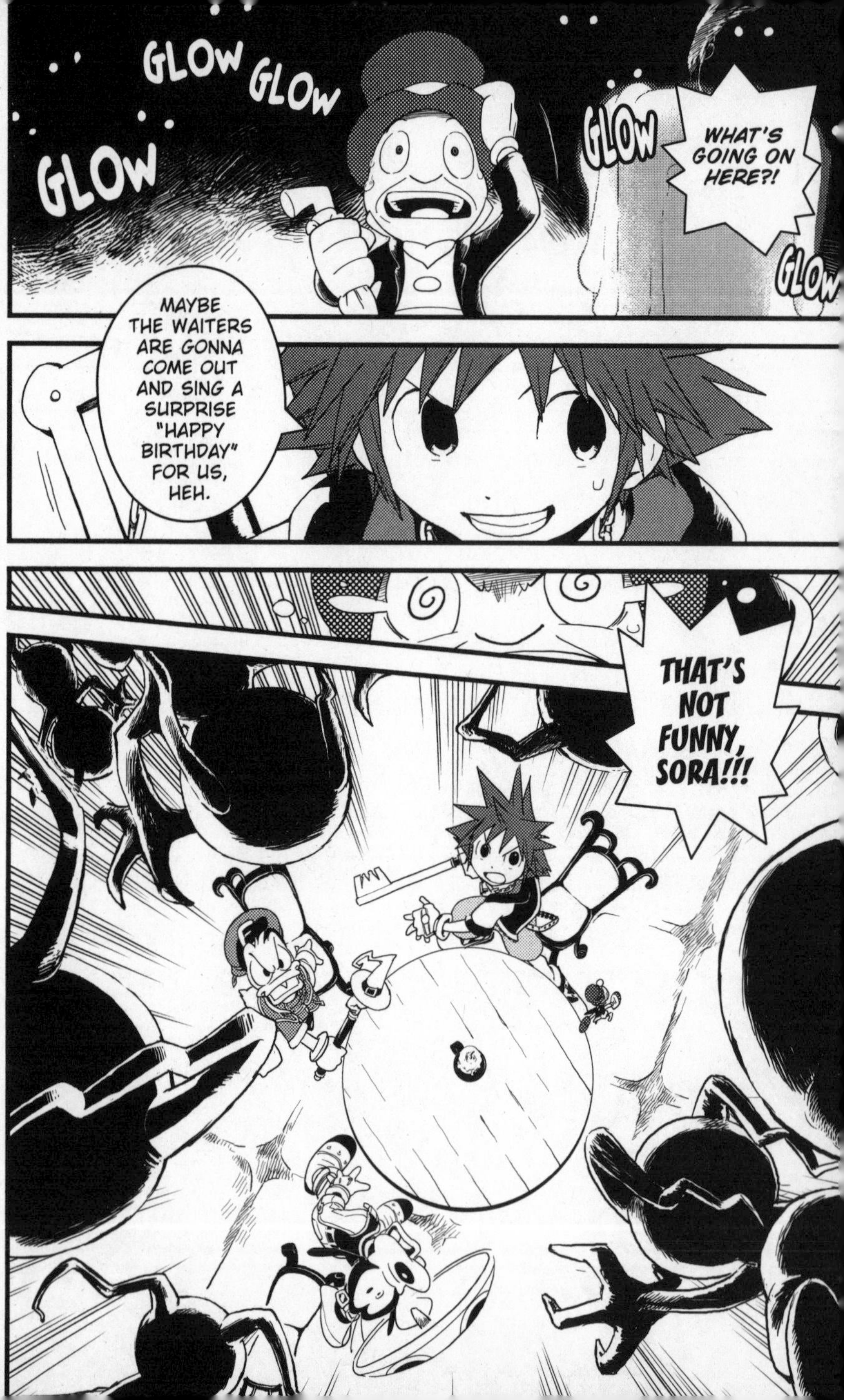
GLOW
GLOW
GLOW
GLOW
GLOW
WHAT'S GOING ON HERE?!
MAYBE THE WAITERS ARE GONNA COME OUT AND SING A SURPRISE "HAPPY BIRTHDAY" FOR US, HEH.
THAT'S NOT FUNNY, SORA!!!

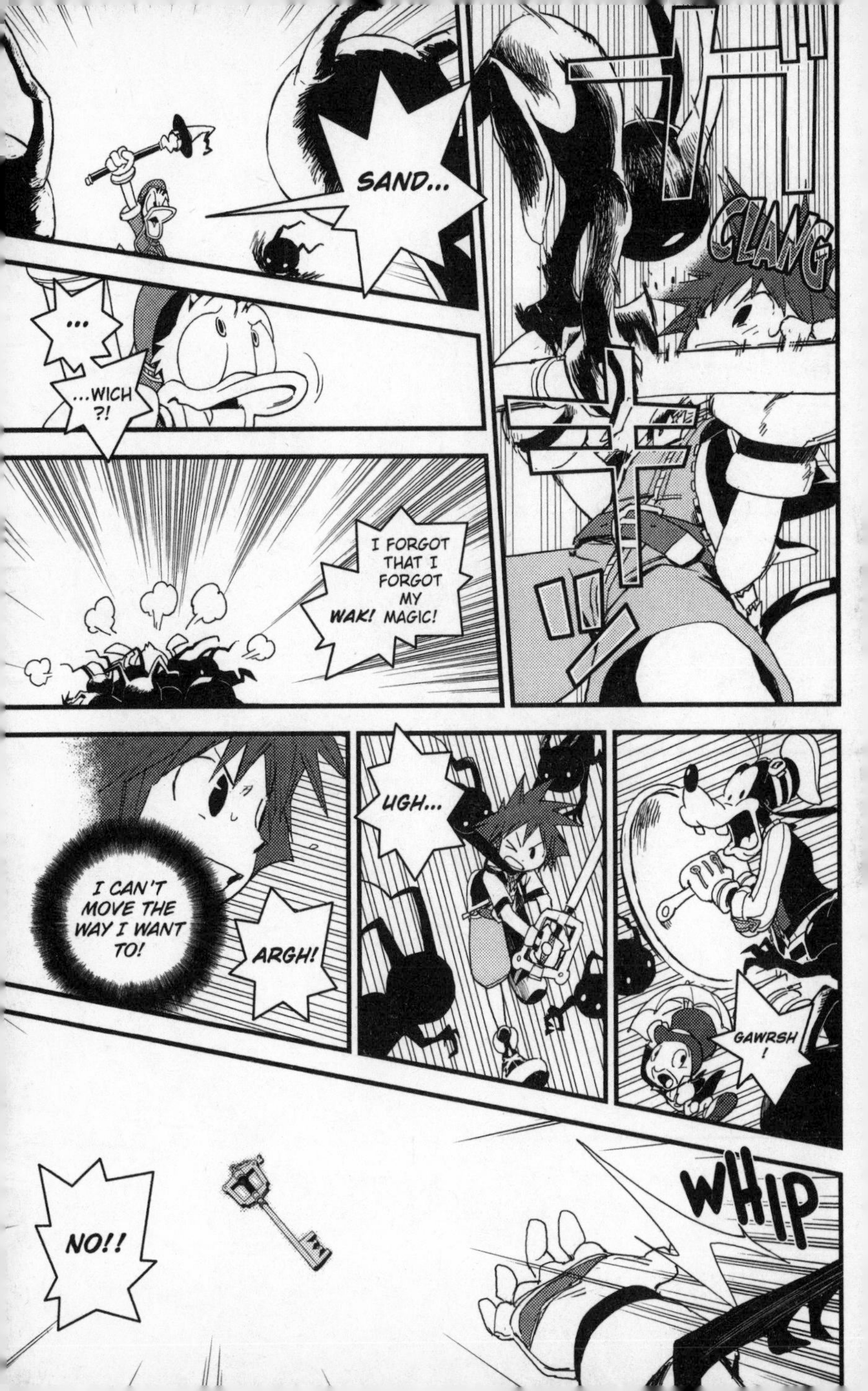
CLANG
SAND...
...
...WICH ?!
I FORGOT THAT I FORGOT MY WAK! MAGIC!
GAWRSH !
UGH...
I CAN'T MOVE THE WAY I WANT TO!
ARGH!
WHIP
NO!!

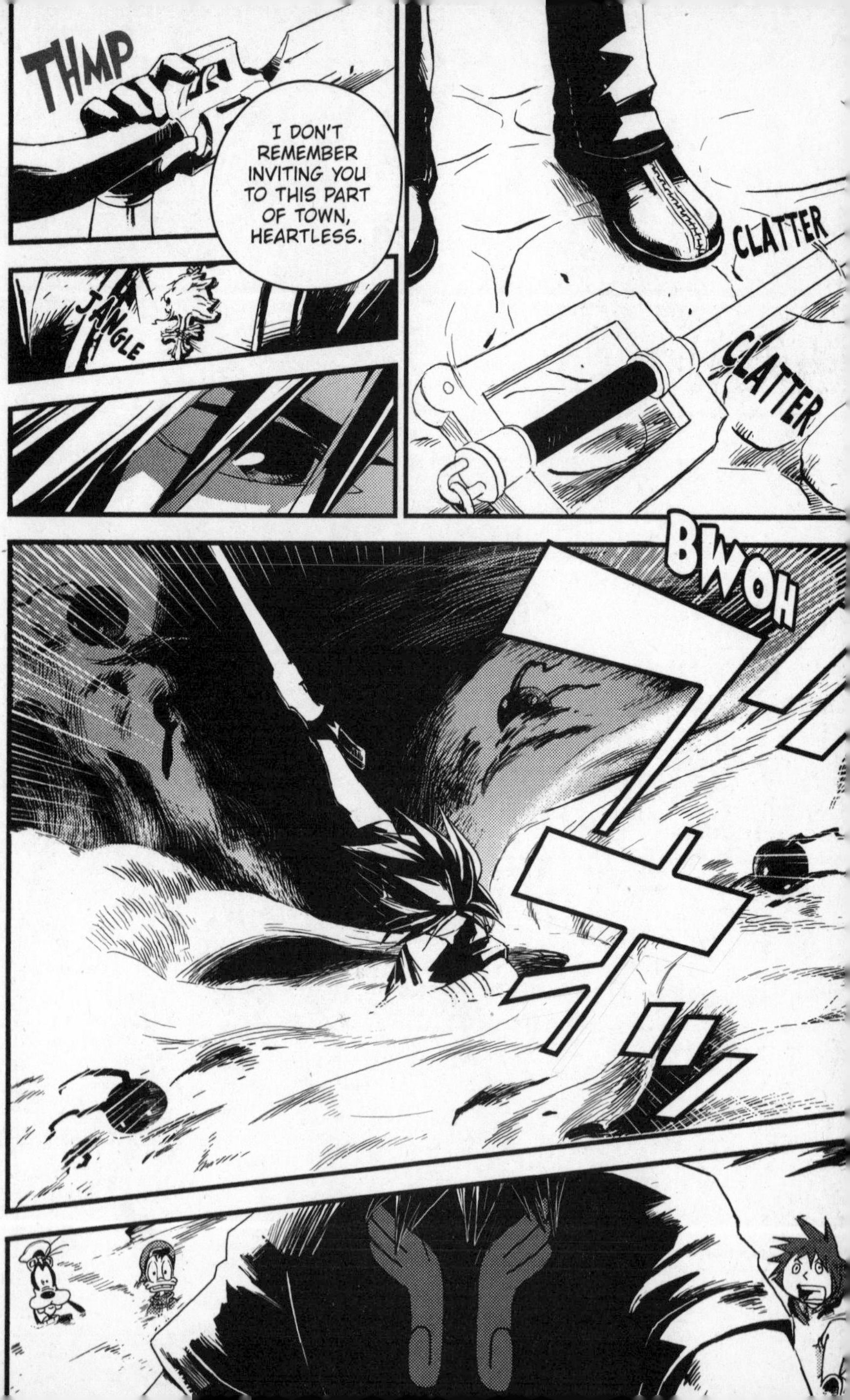
CLATTER
CLATTER
THMP
I DON'T REMEMBER INVITING YOU TO THIS PART OF TOWN, HEARTLESS.
JANGLE
BWOH

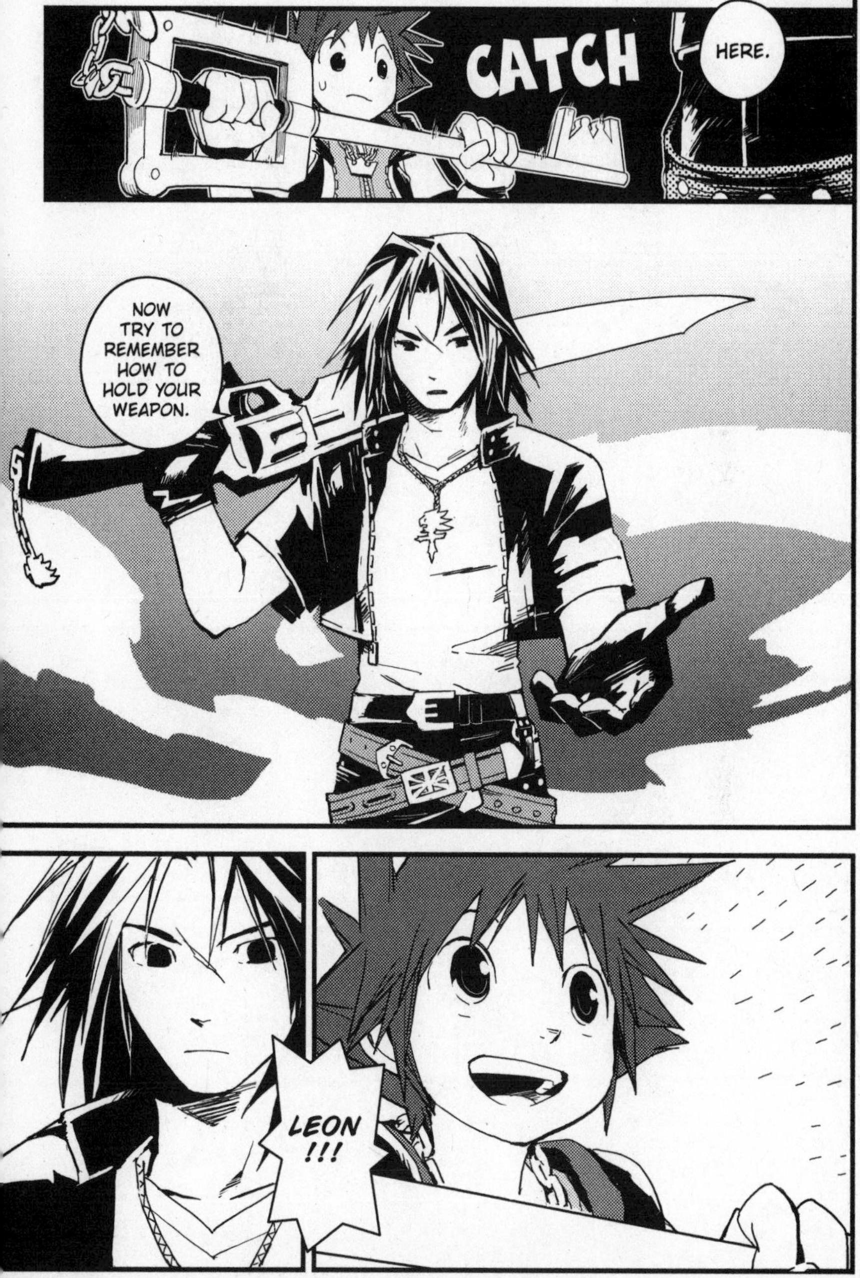
HERE.
CATCH
NOW TRY TO REMEMBER HOW TO HOLD YOUR WEAPON.
LEON !!!

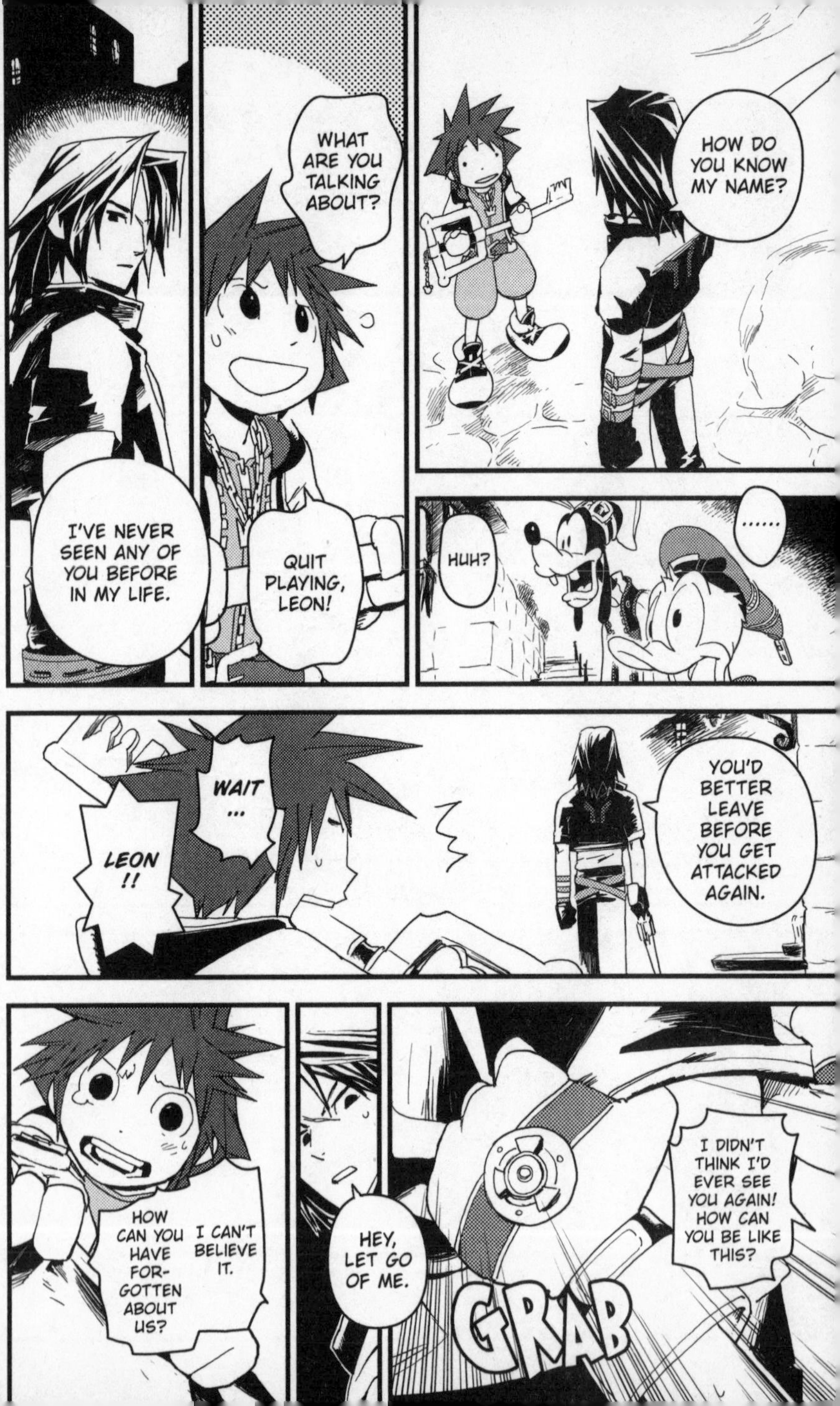

HOW DO YOU KNOW MY NAME?
......
HUH?
WHAT ARE YOU TALKING ABOUT?
QUIT PLAYING, LEON!
I'VE NEVER SEEN ANY OF YOU BEFORE IN MY LIFE.
YOU'D BETTER LEAVE BEFORE YOU GET ATTACKED AGAIN.
WAIT ...
LEON !!
I DIDN'T THINK I'D EVER SEE YOU AGAIN! HOW CAN YOU BE LIKE THIS?
GRAB
HEY, LET GO OF ME.
I CAN'T BELIEVE IT.
HOW CAN YOU HAVE FOR-GOTTEN ABOUT US?

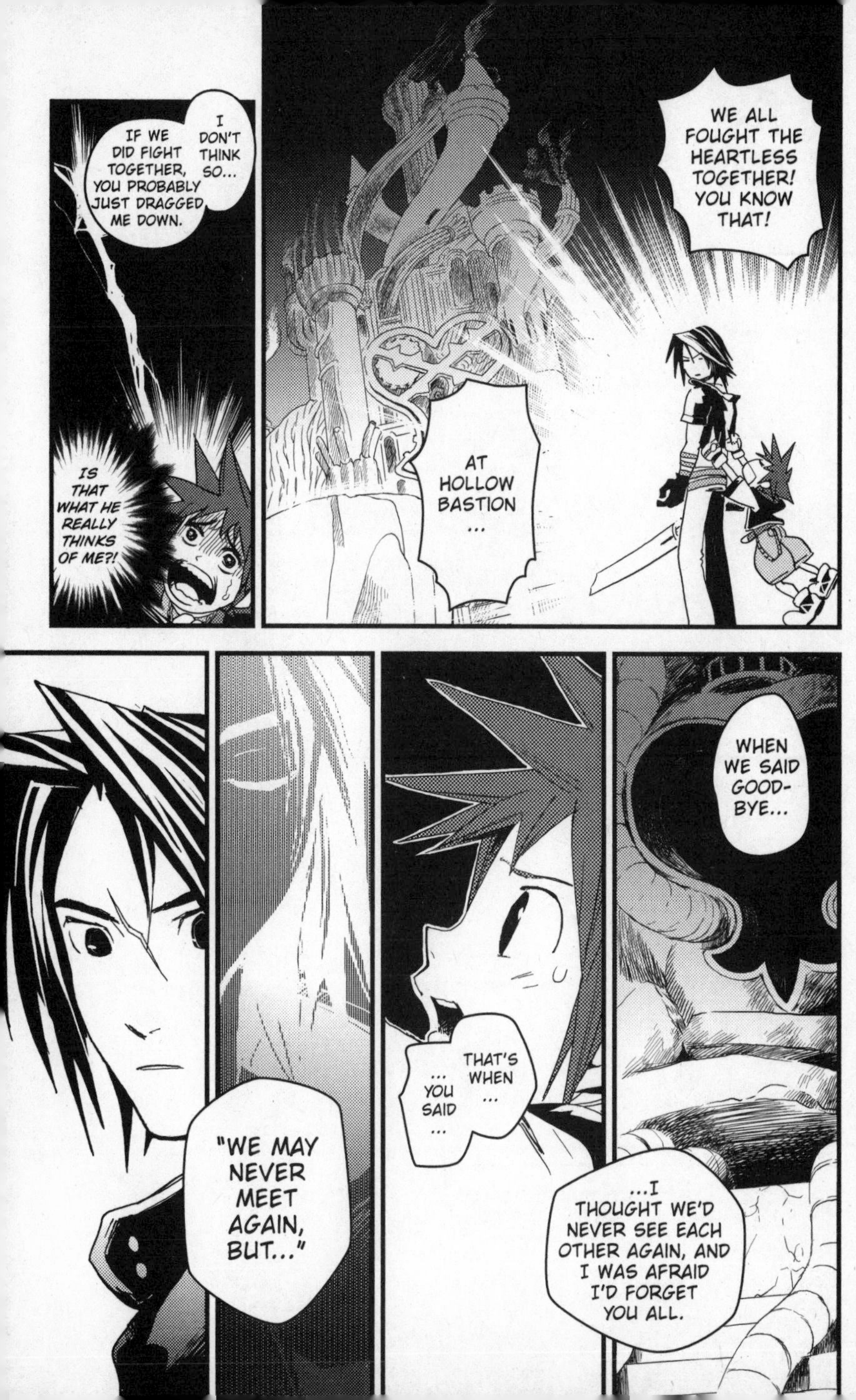
WE ALL FOUGHT THE HEARTLESS TOGETHER! YOU KNOW THAT!
AT HOLLOW BASTION ...
I DON'T THINK SO...
IF WE DID FIGHT TOGETHER, YOU PROBABLY JUST DRAGGED ME DOWN.
IS THAT WHAT HE REALLY THINKS OF ME?!
WHEN WE SAID GOOD-BYE...
...I THOUGHT WE'D NEVER SEE EACH OTHER AGAIN, AND I WAS AFRAID I'D FORGET YOU ALL.
THAT'S WHEN ...
... YOU SAID ...
"WE MAY NEVER MEET AGAIN, BUT..."

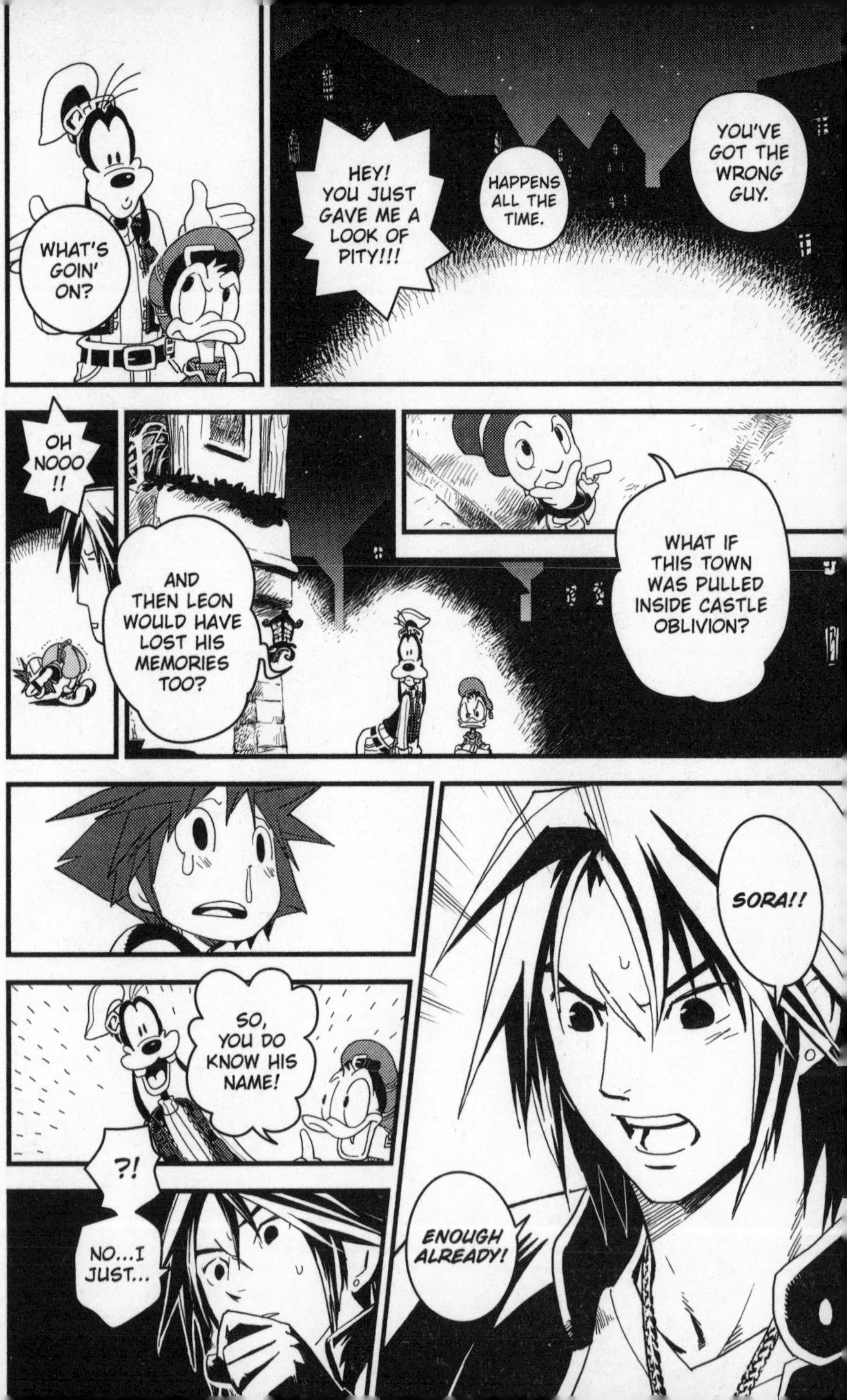
YOU'VE GOT THE WRONG GUY.
HAPPENS ALL THE TIME.
HEY! YOU JUST GAVE ME A LOOK OF PITY!!!
WHAT'S GOIN' ON?
WHAT IF THIS TOWN WAS PULLED INSIDE CASTLE OBLIVION?
AND THEN LEON WOULD HAVE LOST HIS MEMORIES TOO?
OH NOOO !!
SORA!!
ENOUGH ALREADY!
SO, YOU DO KNOW HIS NAME!
?!
NO...I JUST...

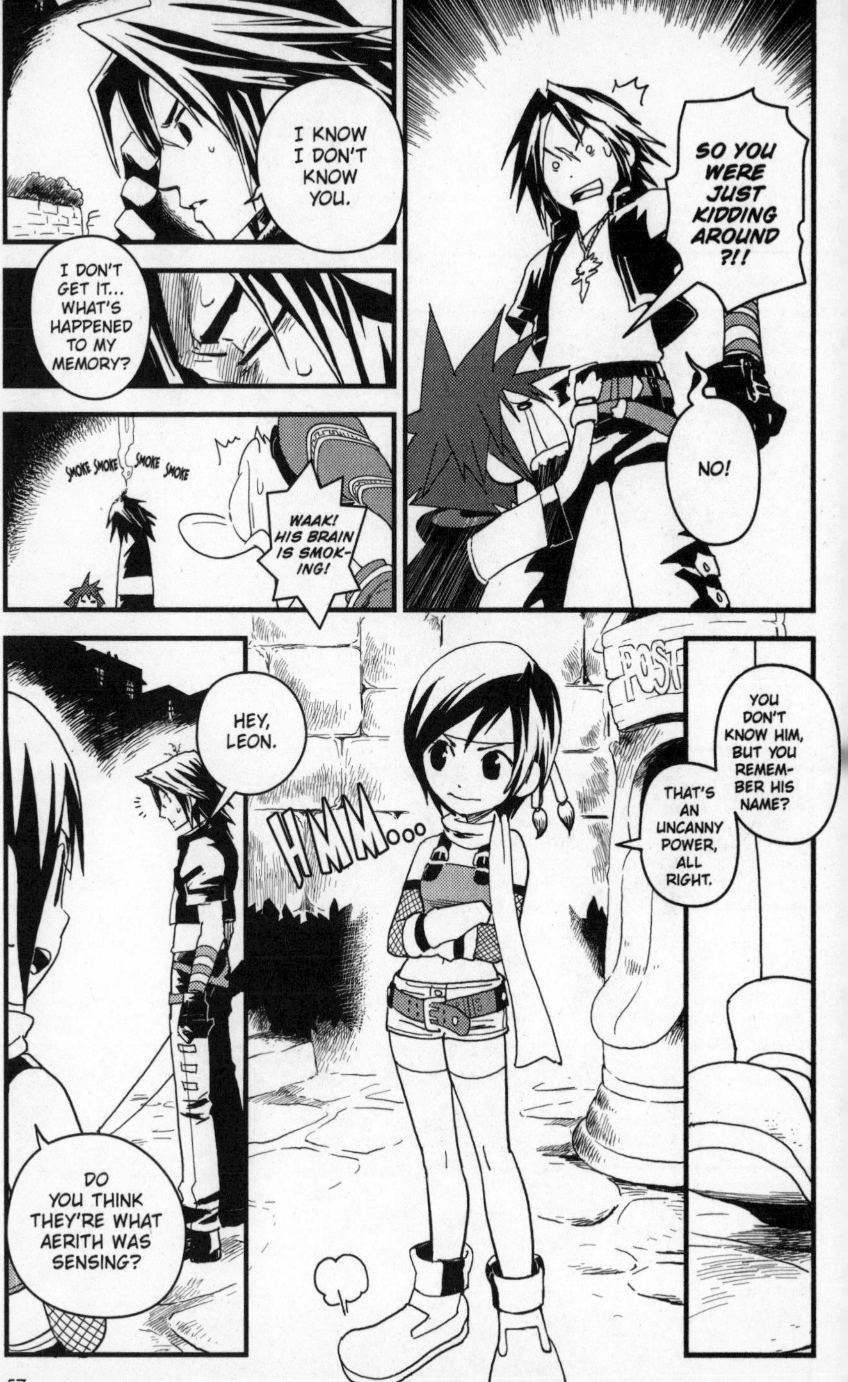
SO YOU WERE JUST KIDDING AROUND ?!!
NO!
I KNOW I DON'T KNOW YOU.
I DON'T GET IT... WHAT'S HAPPENED TO MY MEMORY?
SMOKE SMOKE SMOKE SMOKE
WAAK! HIS BRAIN IS SMOK-ING!
POST
YOU DON'T KNOW HIM, BUT YOU REMEM-BER HIS NAME?
THAT'S AN UNCANNY POWER, ALL RIGHT.
HMM...
HEY, LEON.
DO YOU THINK THEY'RE WHAT AERITH WAS SENSING?

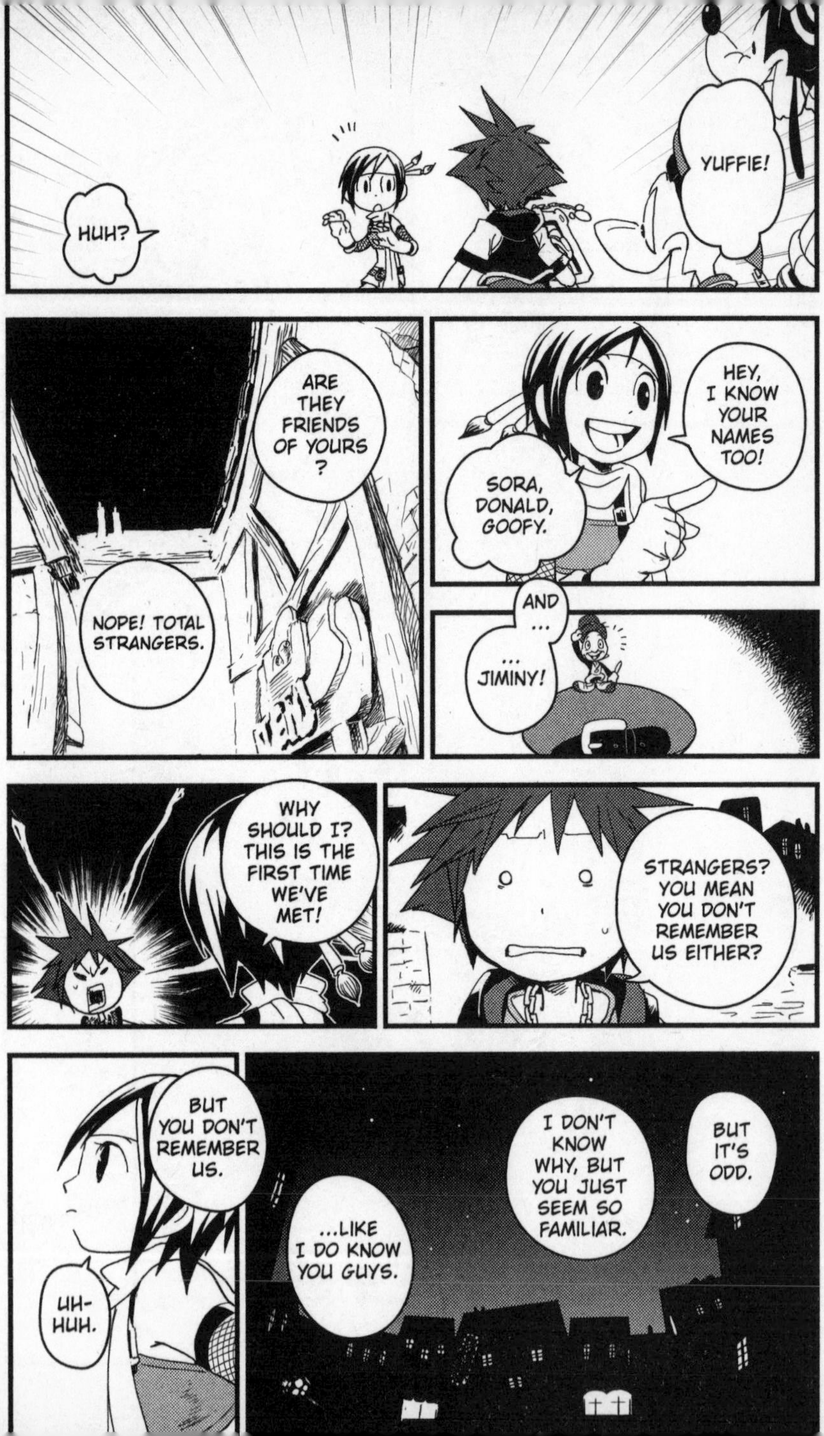
YUFFIE!
HUH?
HEY, I KNOW YOUR NAMES TOO!
SORA, DONALD, GOOFY.
AND ...
... JIMINY!
ARE THEY FRIENDS OF YOURS?
NOPE! TOTAL STRANGERS.
STRANGERS? YOU MEAN YOU DON'T REMEMBER US EITHER?
WHY SHOULD I? THIS IS THE FIRST TIME WE'VE MET!
BUT IT'S ODD.
I DON'T KNOW WHY, BUT YOU JUST SEEM SO FAMILIAR.
...LIKE I DO KNOW YOU GUYS.
BUT YOU DON'T REMEMBER US.
UH-HUH.

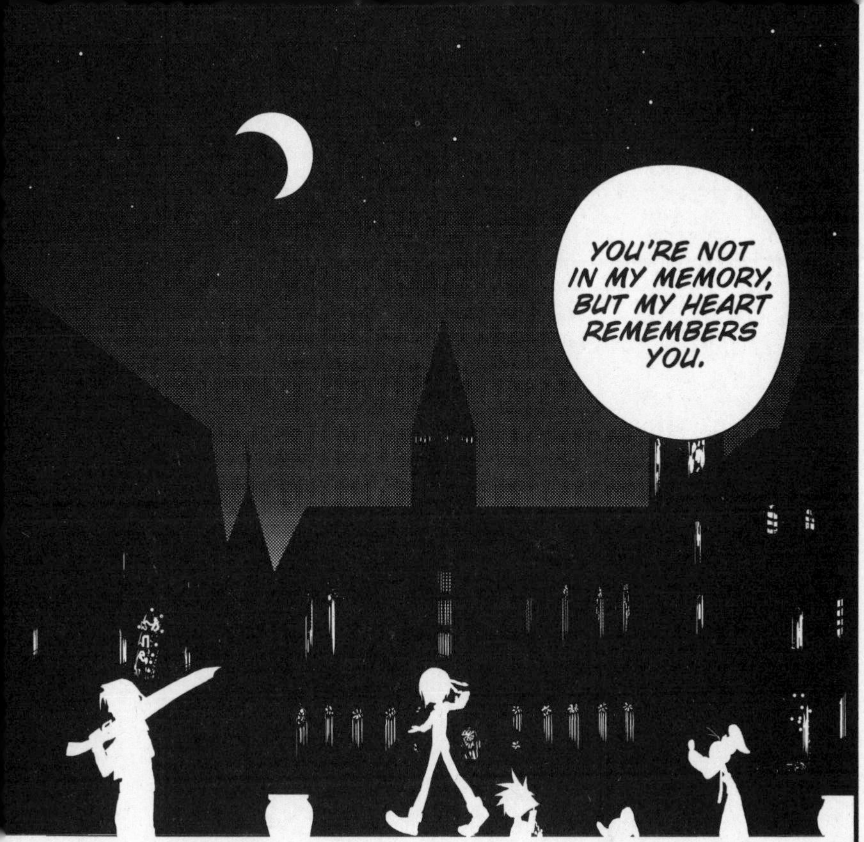
YOU'RE NOT IN MY MEMORY, BUT MY HEART REMEMBERS YOU.
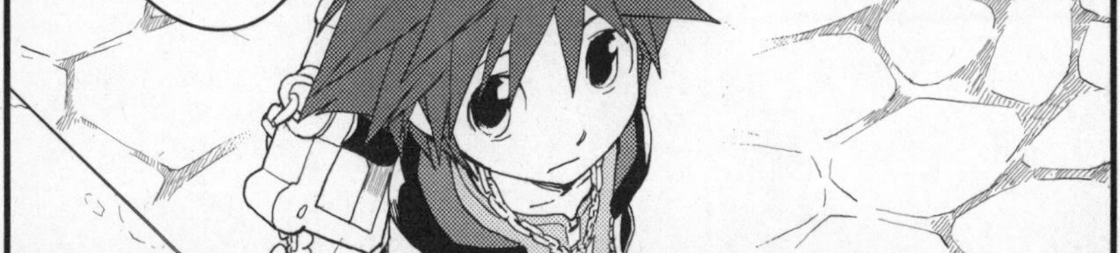
OR... SOMETHING LIKE THAT.

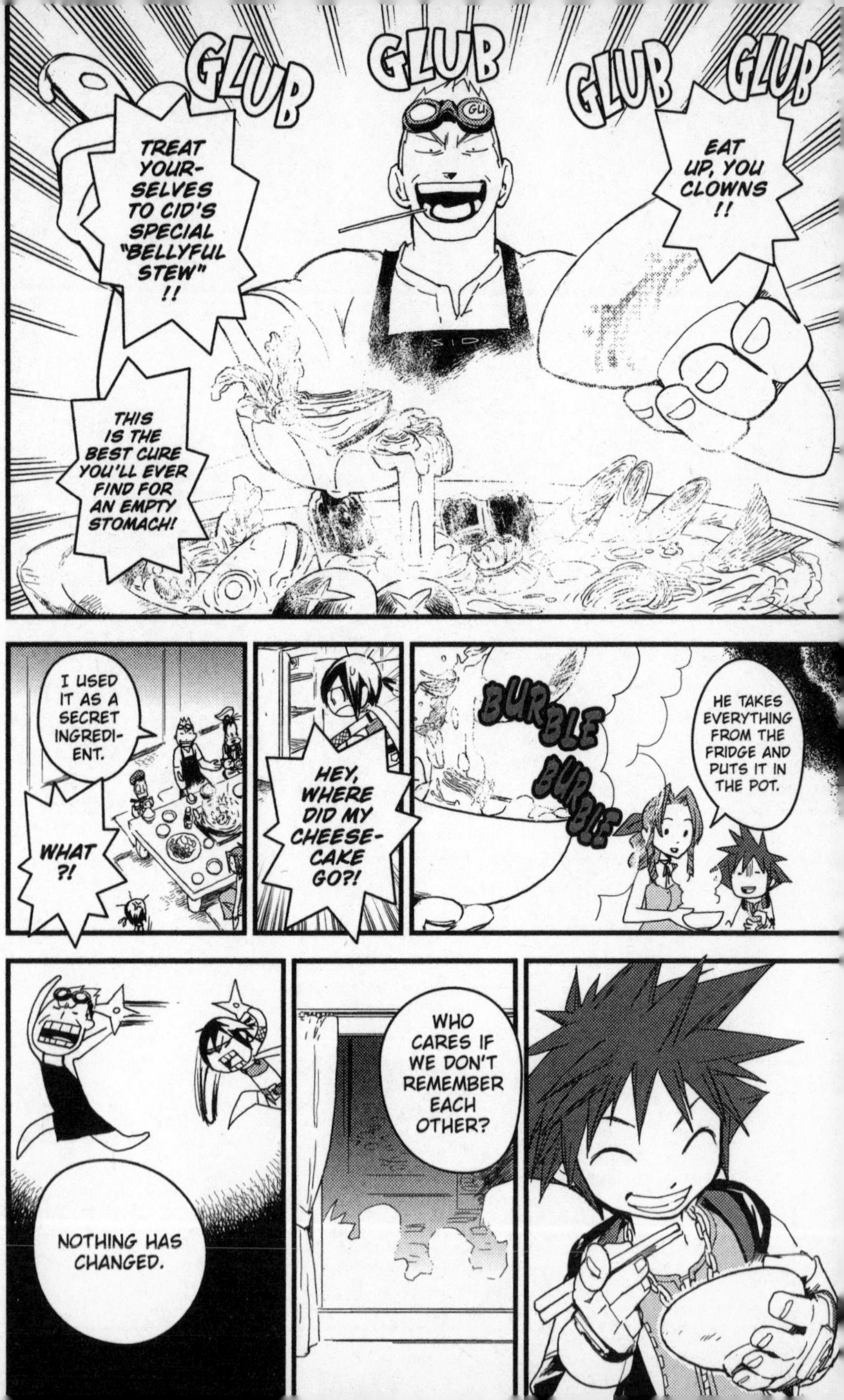
GLUB
GLUB
GLUB
GLUB
EAT UP, YOU CLOWNS!!
TREAT YOURSELVES TO CID'S SPECIAL "BELLYFUL STEW"!!
THIS IS THE BEST CURE YOU'LL EVER FIND FOR AN EMPTY STOMACH!
HE TAKES EVERYTHING FROM THE FRIDGE AND PUTS IT IN THE POT.
BURBLE
BURBLE
HEY, WHERE DID MY CHEESECAKE GO?!
I USED IT AS A SECRET INGREDIENT.
WHAT?!
WHO CARES IF WE DON'T REMEMBER EACH OTHER?
NOTHING HAS CHANGED.

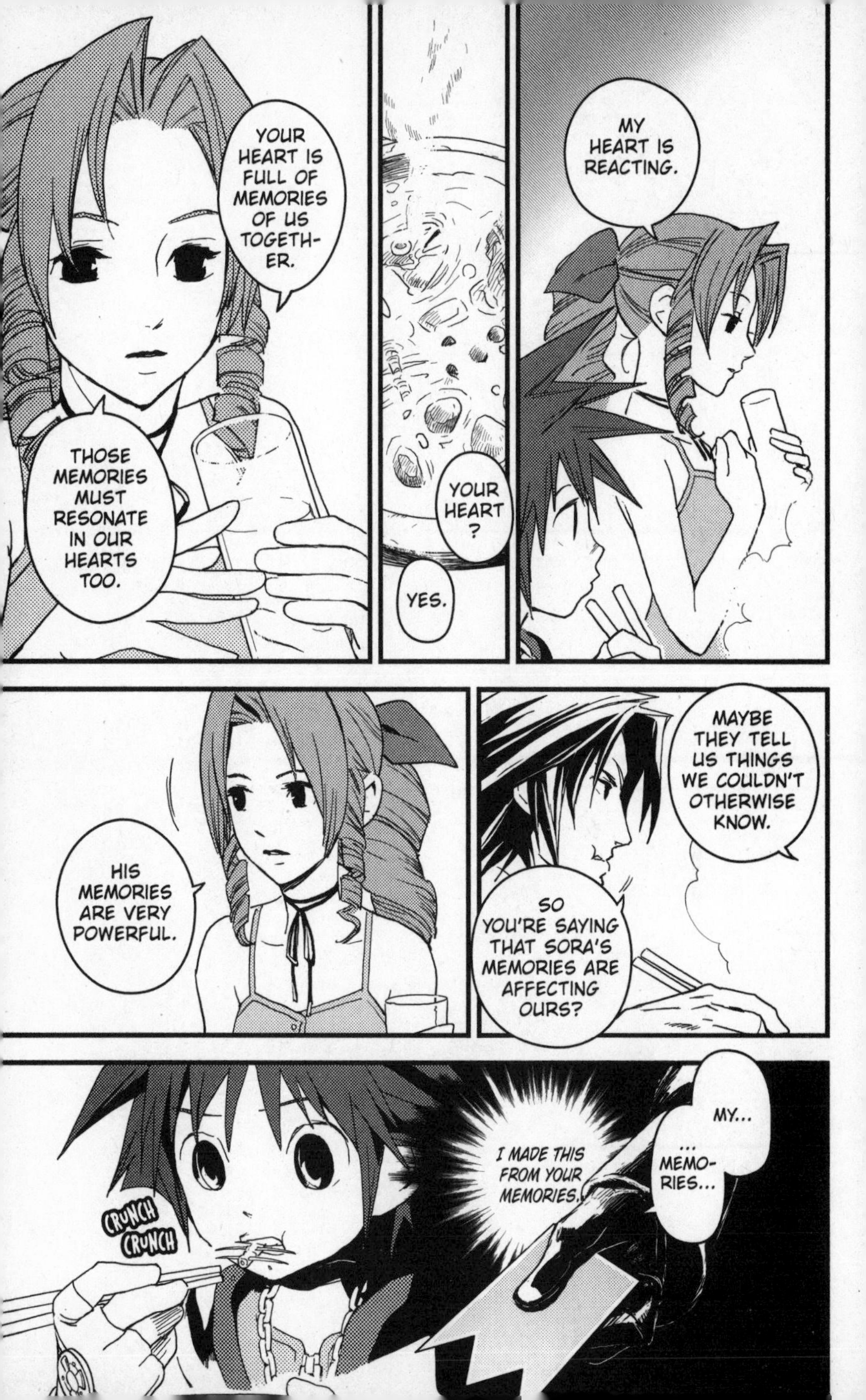
MY HEART IS REACTING.
YOUR HEART?
YES.
YOUR HEART IS FULL OF MEMORIES OF US TOGETH-ER.
THOSE MEMORIES MUST RESONATE IN OUR HEARTS TOO.
MAYBE THEY TELL US THINGS WE COULDN'T OTHERWISE KNOW.
SO YOU'RE SAYING THAT SORA'S MEMORIES ARE AFFECTING OURS?
HIS MEMORIES ARE VERY POWERFUL.
MY...
... MEMO-RIES...
I MADE THIS FROM YOUR MEMORIES.
CRUNCH CRUNCH

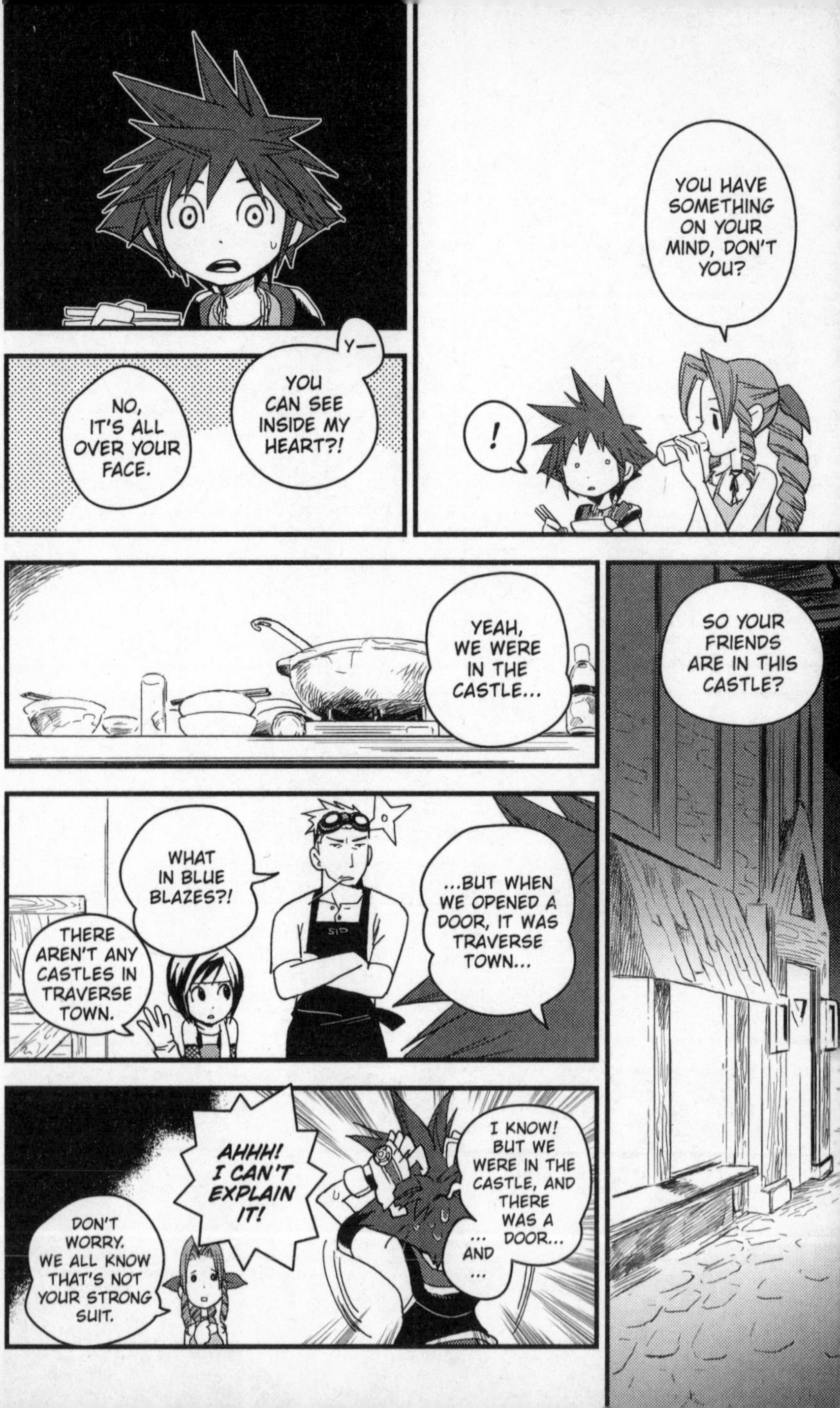
YOU HAVE SOMETHING ON YOUR MIND, DON'T YOU?
!
Y—
YOU CAN SEE INSIDE MY HEART?!
NO, IT'S ALL OVER YOUR FACE.
SO YOUR FRIENDS ARE IN THIS CASTLE?
YEAH, WE WERE IN THE CASTLE...
...BUT WHEN WE OPENED A DOOR, IT WAS TRAVERSE TOWN...
WHAT IN BLUE BLAZES?!
THERE AREN'T ANY CASTLES IN TRAVERSE TOWN.
I KNOW! BUT WE WERE IN THE CASTLE, AND THERE WAS A DOOR...
... AND ...
AHHH! I CAN'T EXPLAIN IT!
DON'T WORRY. WE ALL KNOW THAT'S NOT YOUR STRONG SUIT.

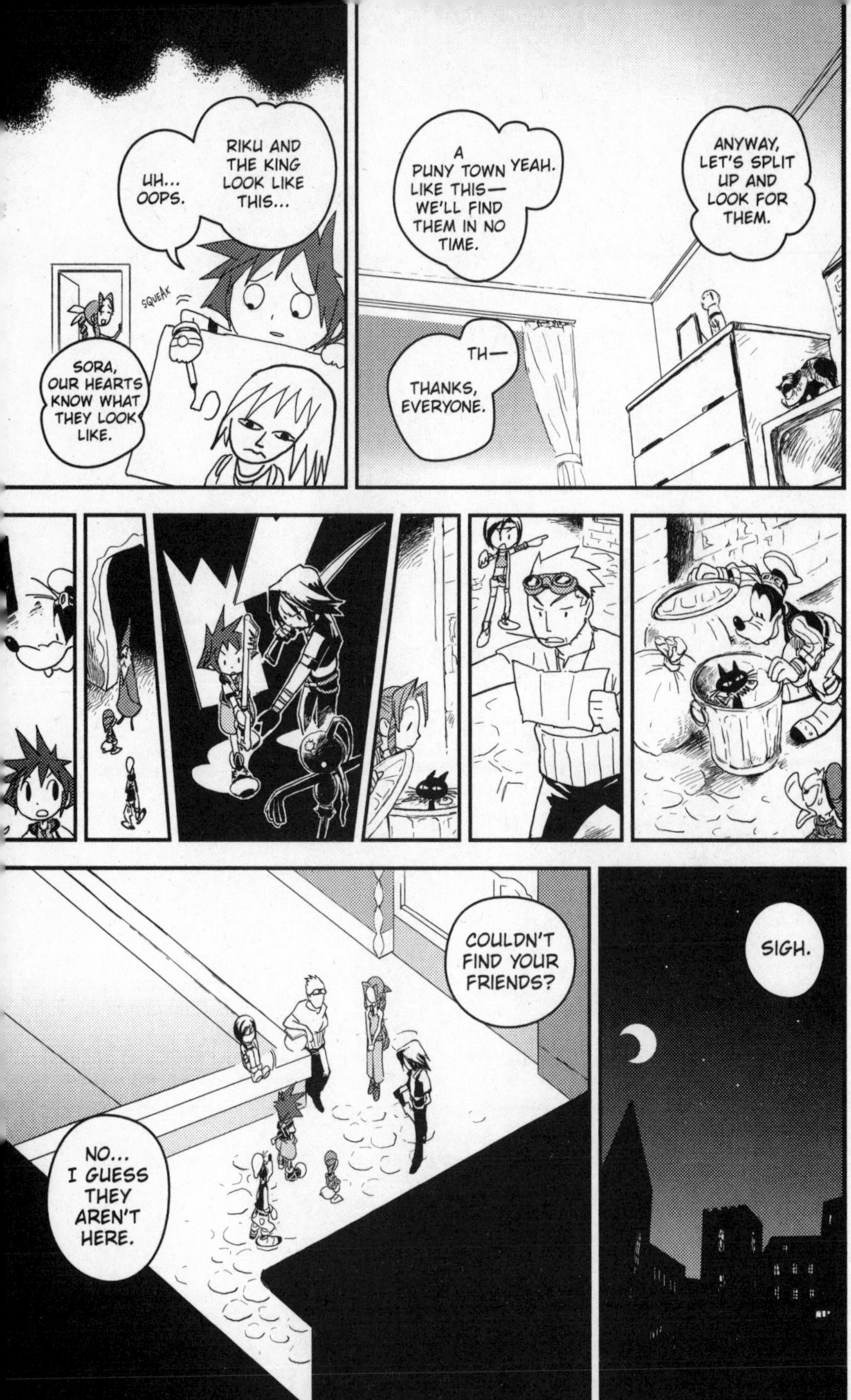
ANYWAY, LET'S SPLIT UP AND LOOK FOR THEM.
YEAH.
A PUNY TOWN LIKE THIS— WE'LL FIND THEM IN NO TIME.
TH—
THANKS, EVERYONE.
RIKU AND THE KING LOOK LIKE THIS...
UH... OOPS.
SQUEAK
SORA, OUR HEARTS KNOW WHAT THEY LOOK LIKE.
SIGH.
COULDN'T FIND YOUR FRIENDS?
NO... I GUESS THEY AREN'T HERE.

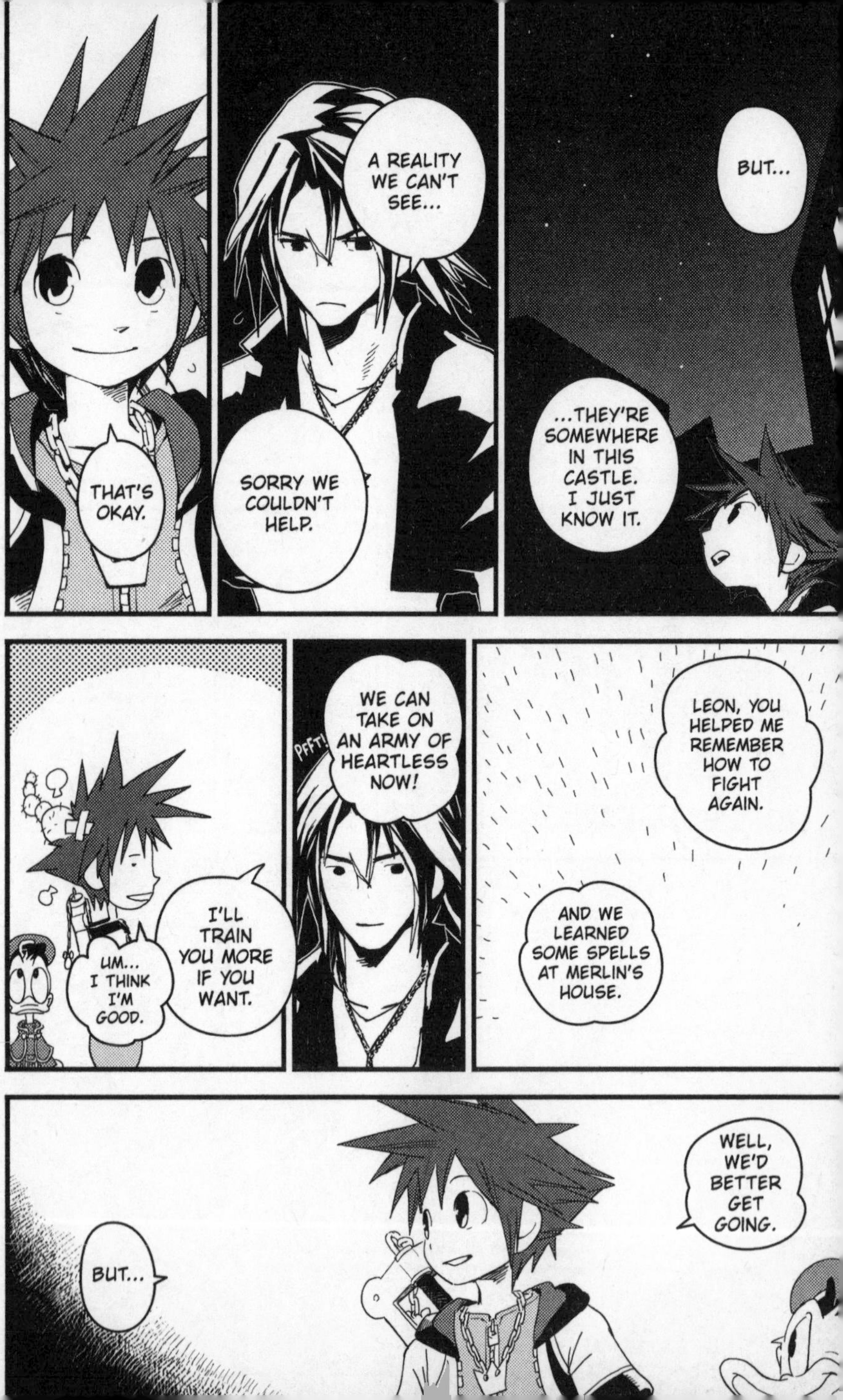
BUT...
...THEY'RE SOMEWHERE IN THIS CASTLE. I JUST KNOW IT.
A REALITY WE CAN'T SEE...
SORRY WE COULDN'T HELP.
THAT'S OKAY.
LEON, YOU HELPED ME REMEMBER HOW TO FIGHT AGAIN.
AND WE LEARNED SOME SPELLS AT MERLIN'S HOUSE.
WE CAN TAKE ON AN ARMY OF HEARTLESS NOW!
PFFT!
I'LL TRAIN YOU MORE IF YOU WANT.
UM... I THINK I'M GOOD.
WELL, WE'D BETTER GET GOING.
BUT...

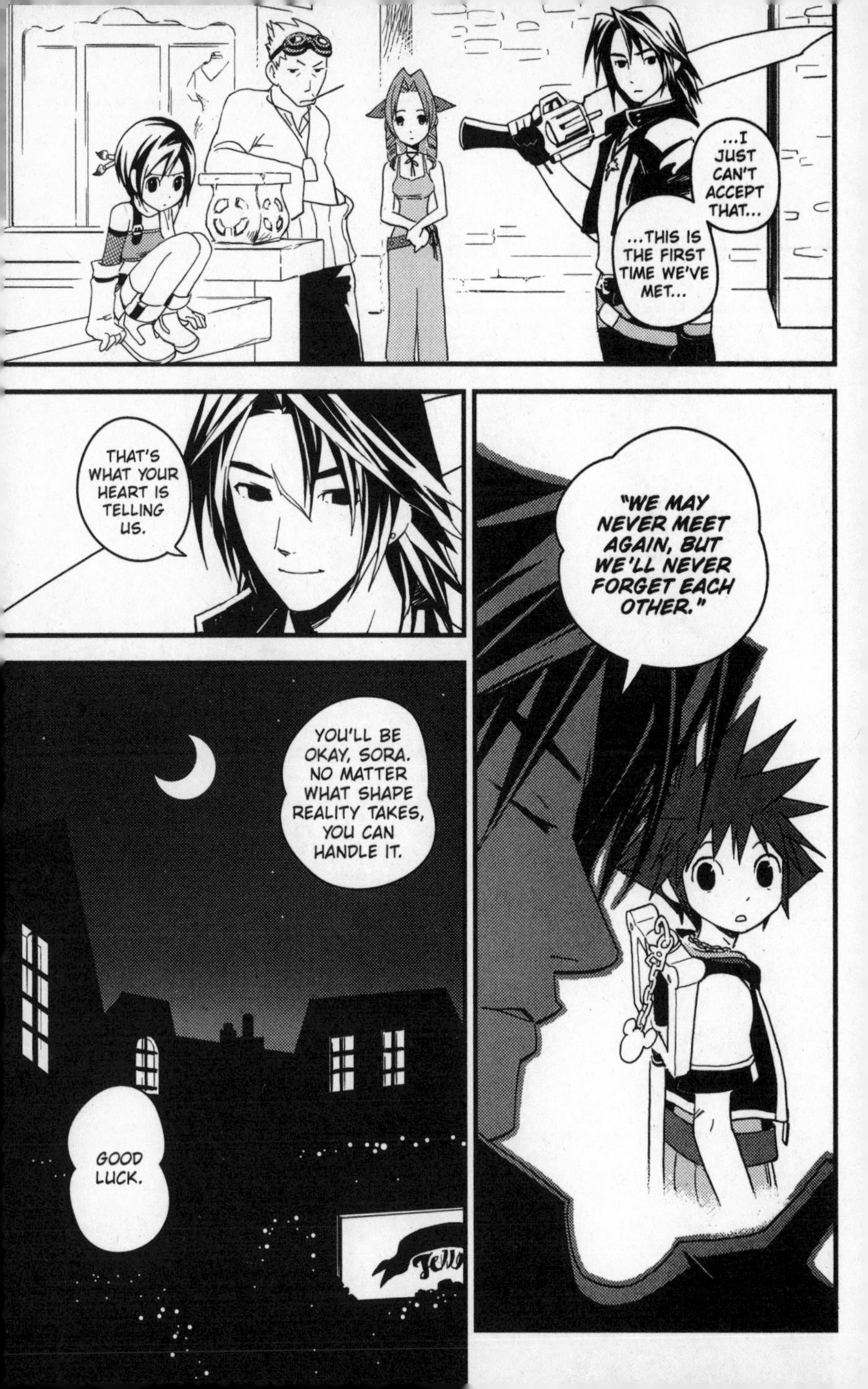
...I JUST CAN'T ACCEPT THAT...
...THIS IS THE FIRST TIME WE'VE MET...
"WE MAY NEVER MEET AGAIN, BUT WE'LL NEVER FORGET EACH OTHER."
THAT'S WHAT YOUR HEART IS TELLING US.
YOU'LL BE OKAY, SORA. NO MATTER WHAT SHAPE REALITY TAKES, YOU CAN HANDLE IT.
GOOD LUCK.

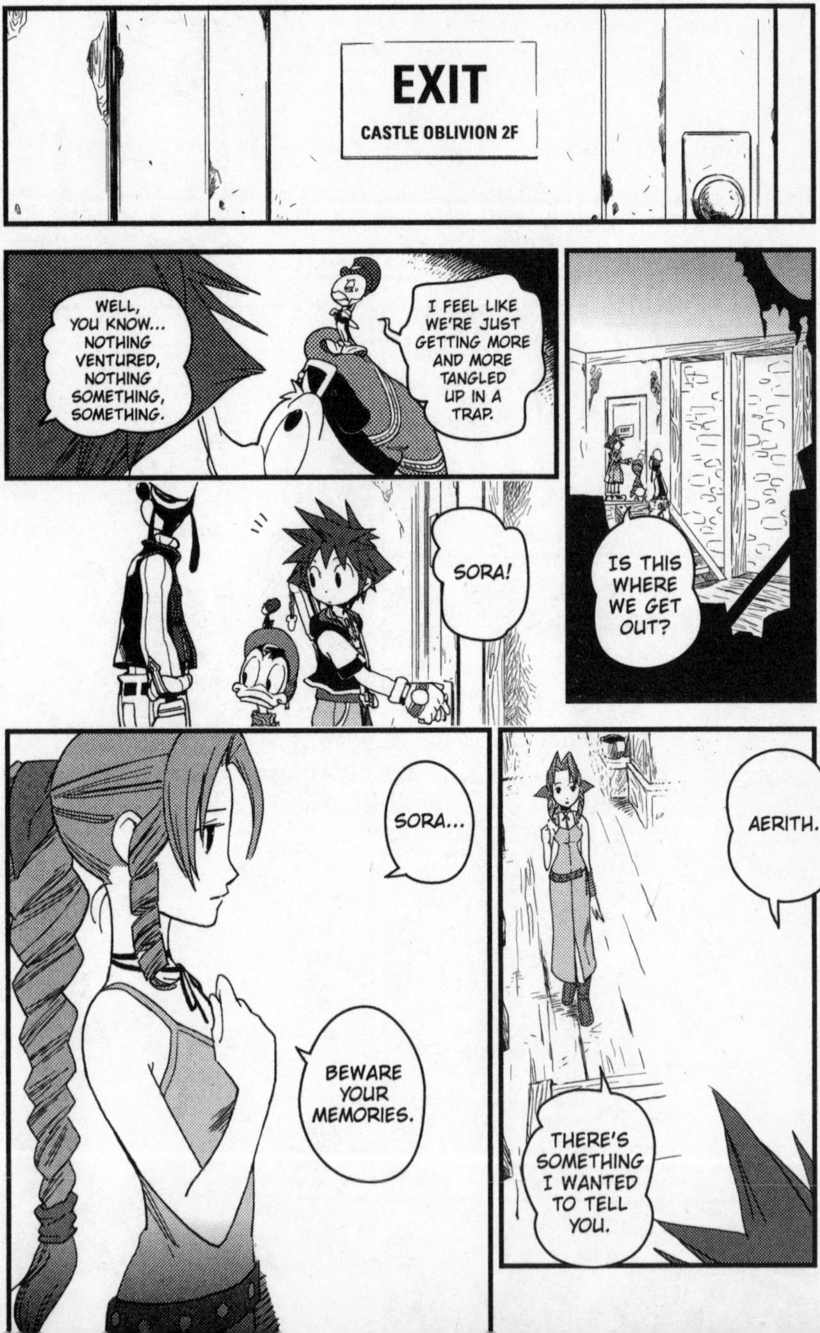
EXIT
CASTLE OBLIVION 2F
IS THIS WHERE WE GET OUT?
I FEEL LIKE WE'RE JUST GETTING MORE AND MORE TANGLED UP IN A TRAP.
WELL, YOU KNOW... NOTHING VENTURED, NOTHING SOMETHING, SOMETHING.
SORA!
AERITH.
THERE'S SOMETHING I WANTED TO TELL YOU.
SORA...
BEWARE YOUR MEMORIES.

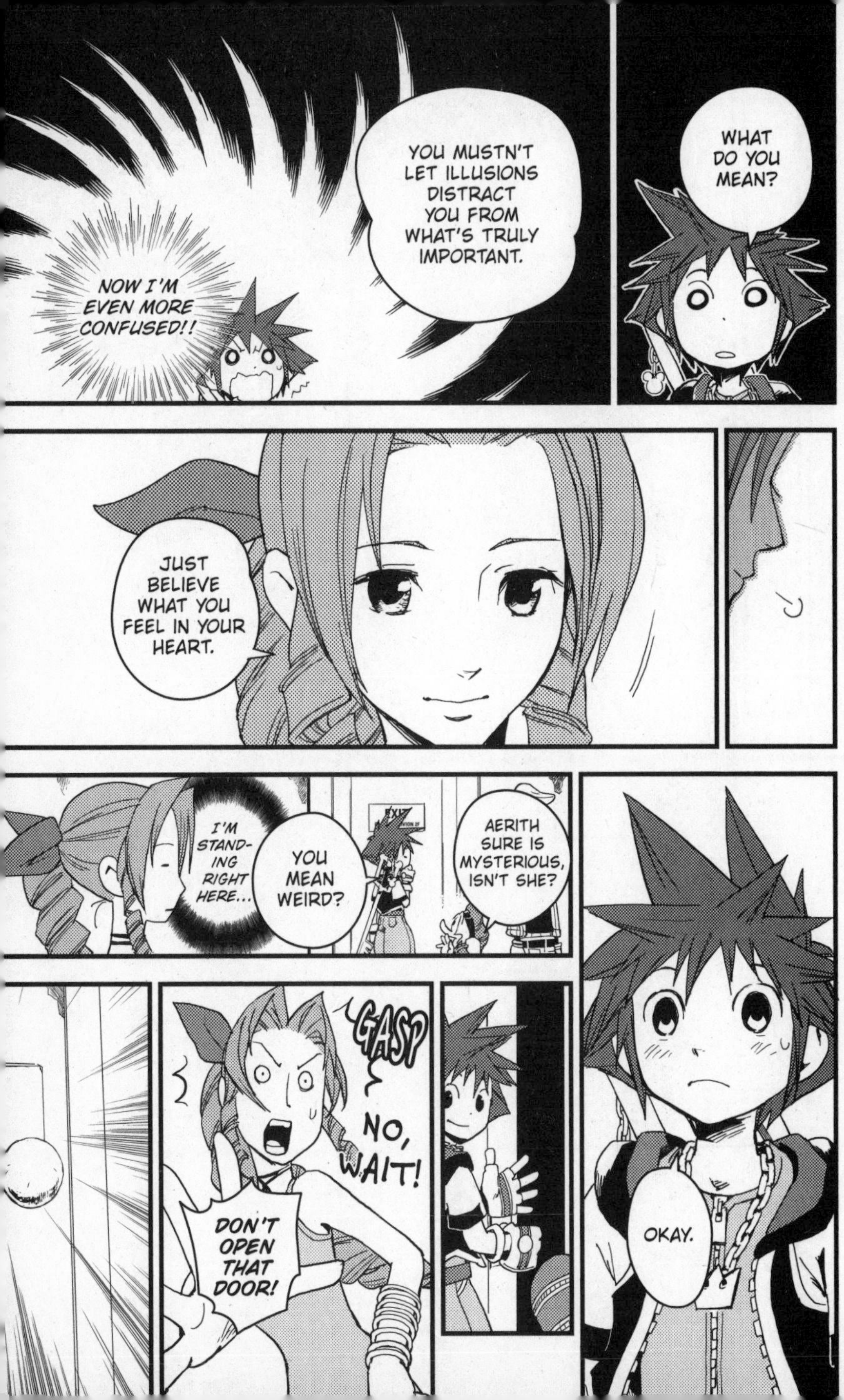
WHAT DO YOU MEAN?
YOU MUSTN'T LET ILLUSIONS DISTRACT YOU FROM WHAT'S TRULY IMPORTANT.
NOW I'M EVEN MORE CONFUSED!!
JUST BELIEVE WHAT YOU FEEL IN YOUR HEART.
OKAY.
AERITH SURE IS MYSTERIOUS, ISN'T SHE?
YOU MEAN WEIRD?
I'M STAND-ING RIGHT HERE...
GASP
NO, WAIT!
DON'T OPEN THAT DOOR!

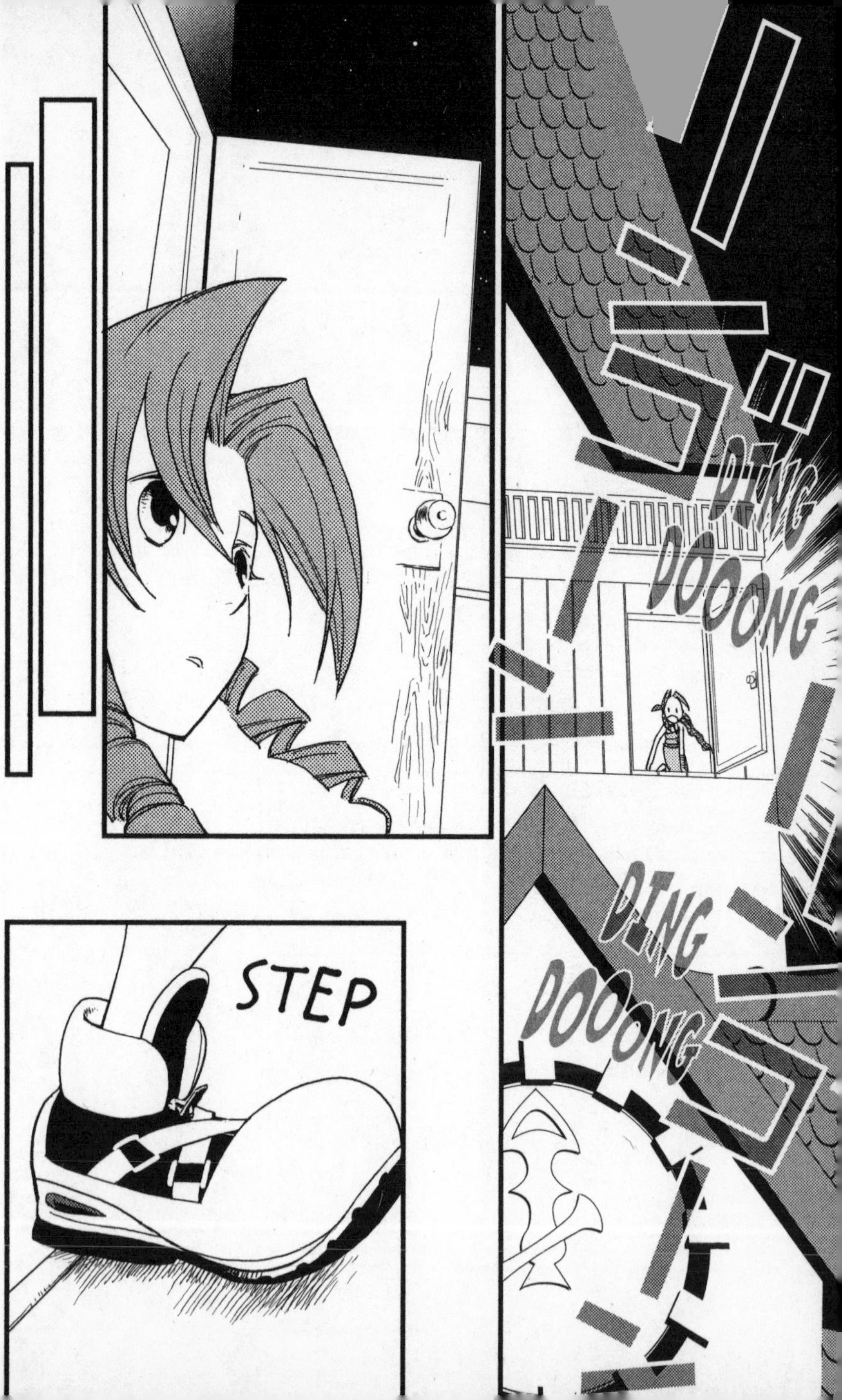
DING DOOONG
DING DOOONG
STEP

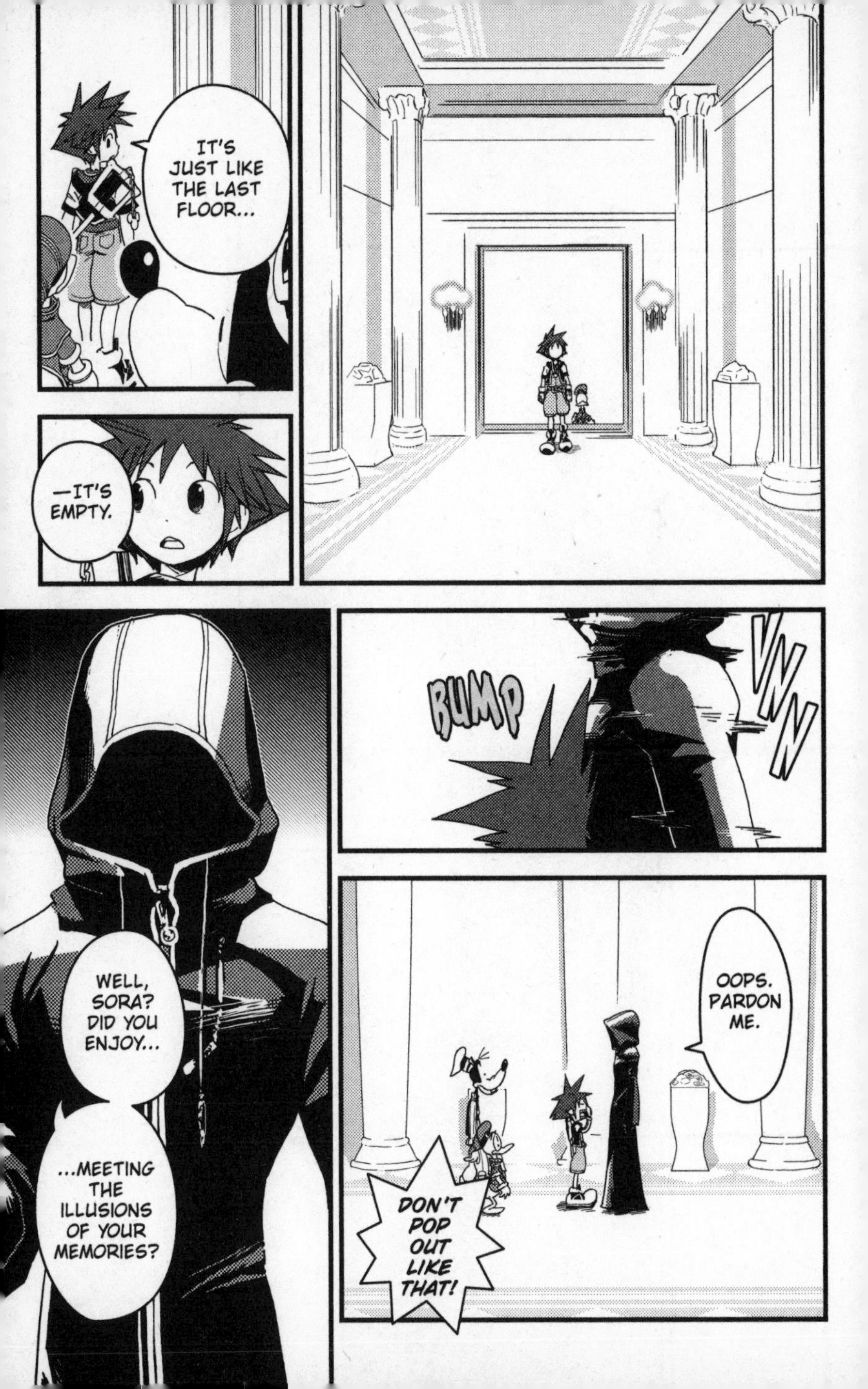
IT'S JUST LIKE THE LAST FLOOR...
—IT'S EMPTY.
VNNN
BUMP
OOPS. PARDON ME.
DON'T POP OUT LIKE THAT!
WELL, SORA? DID YOU ENJOY...
...MEETING THE ILLUSIONS OF YOUR MEMORIES?

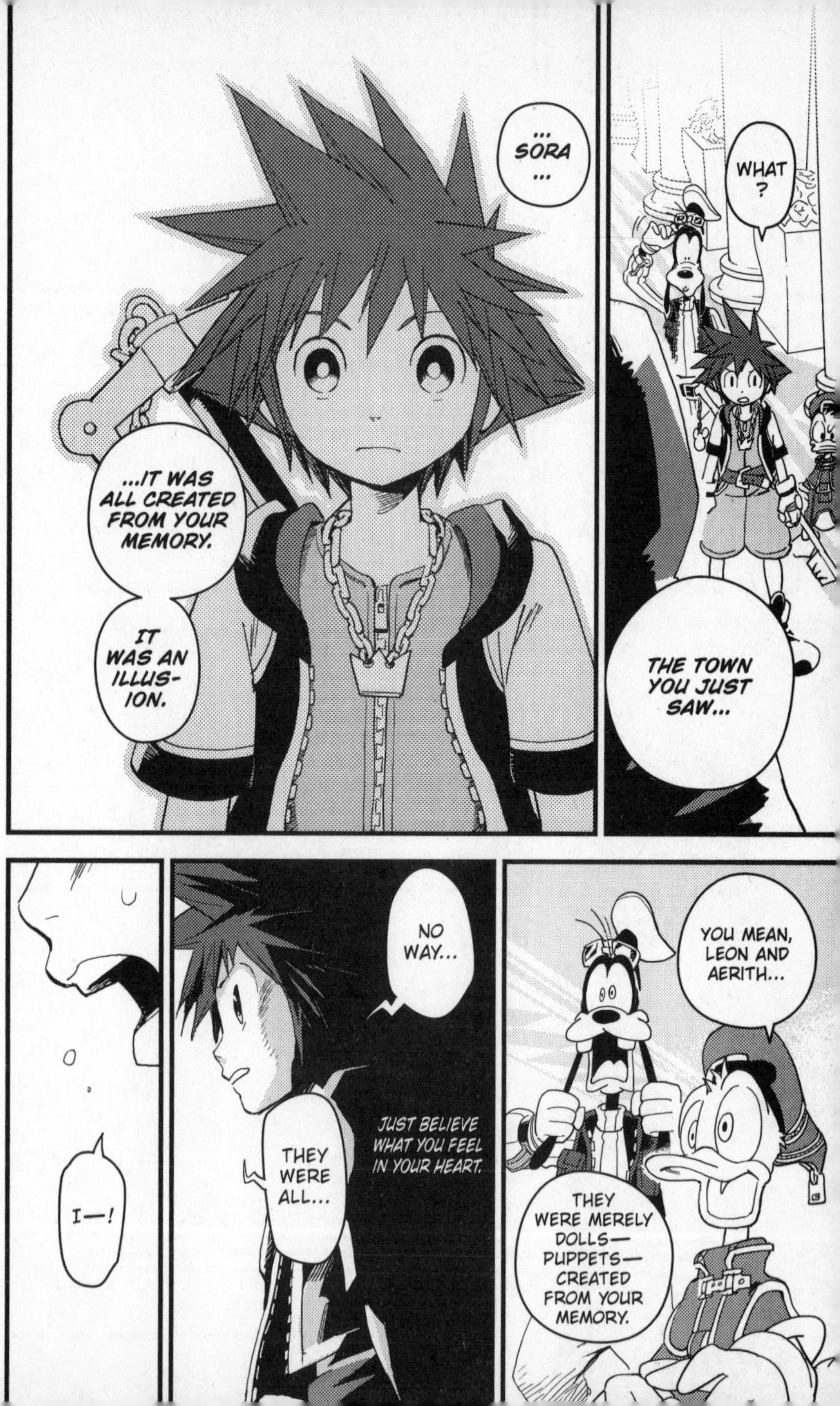
WHAT?
THE TOWN YOU JUST SAW...
... SORA ...
...IT WAS ALL CREATED FROM YOUR MEMORY.
IT WAS AN ILLUSION.
YOU MEAN, LEON AND AERITH...
THEY WERE MERELY DOLLS—PUPPETS—CREATED FROM YOUR MEMORY.
NO WAY...
JUST BELIEVE WHAT YOU FEEL IN YOUR HEART.
THEY WERE ALL...
I—!

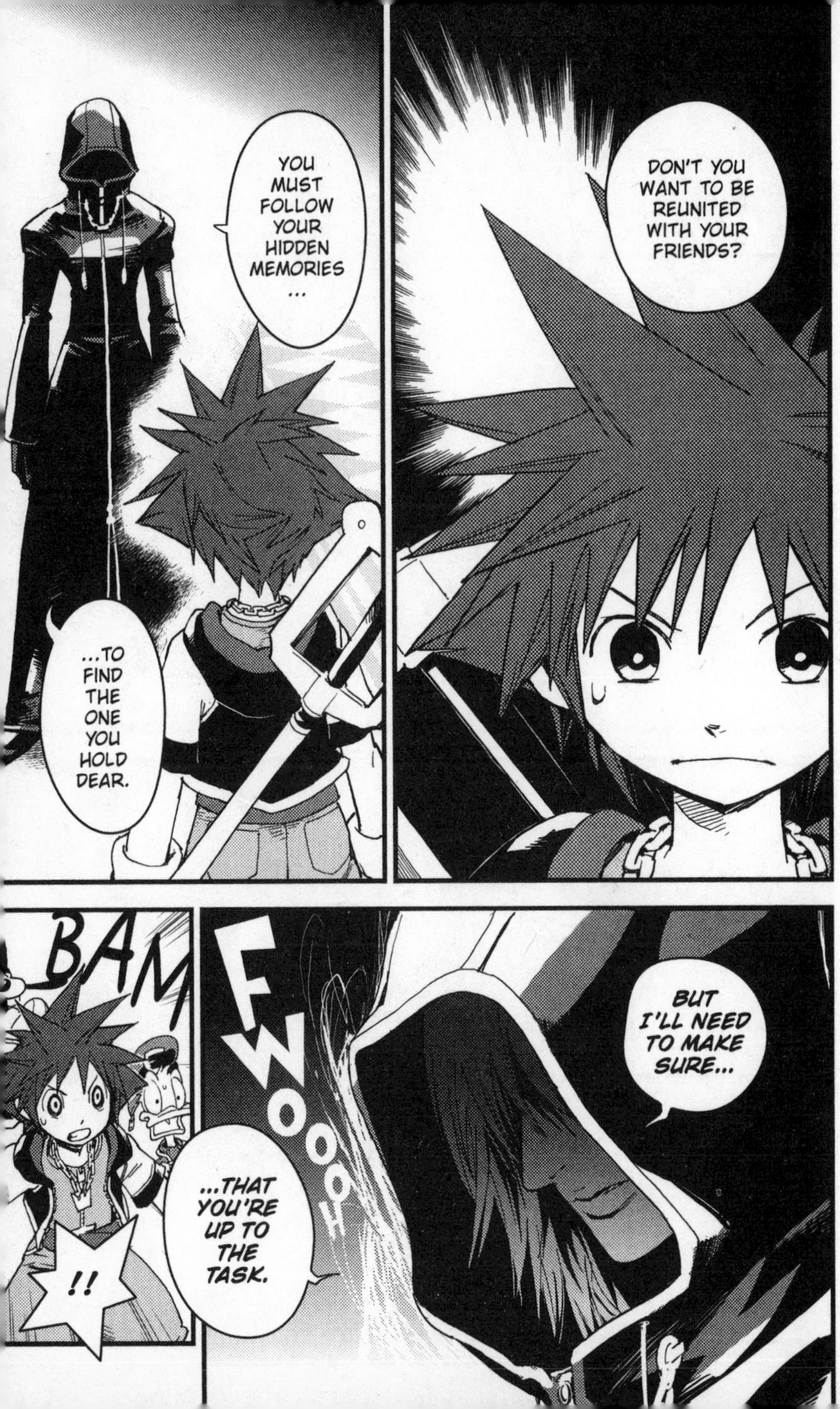
DON'T YOU WANT TO BE REUNITED WITH YOUR FRIENDS?
YOU MUST FOLLOW YOUR HIDDEN MEMORIES ...
...TO FIND THE ONE YOU HOLD DEAR.
BUT I'LL NEED TO MAKE SURE...
...THAT YOU'RE UP TO THE TASK.
FWOOOOH
BAM
!!

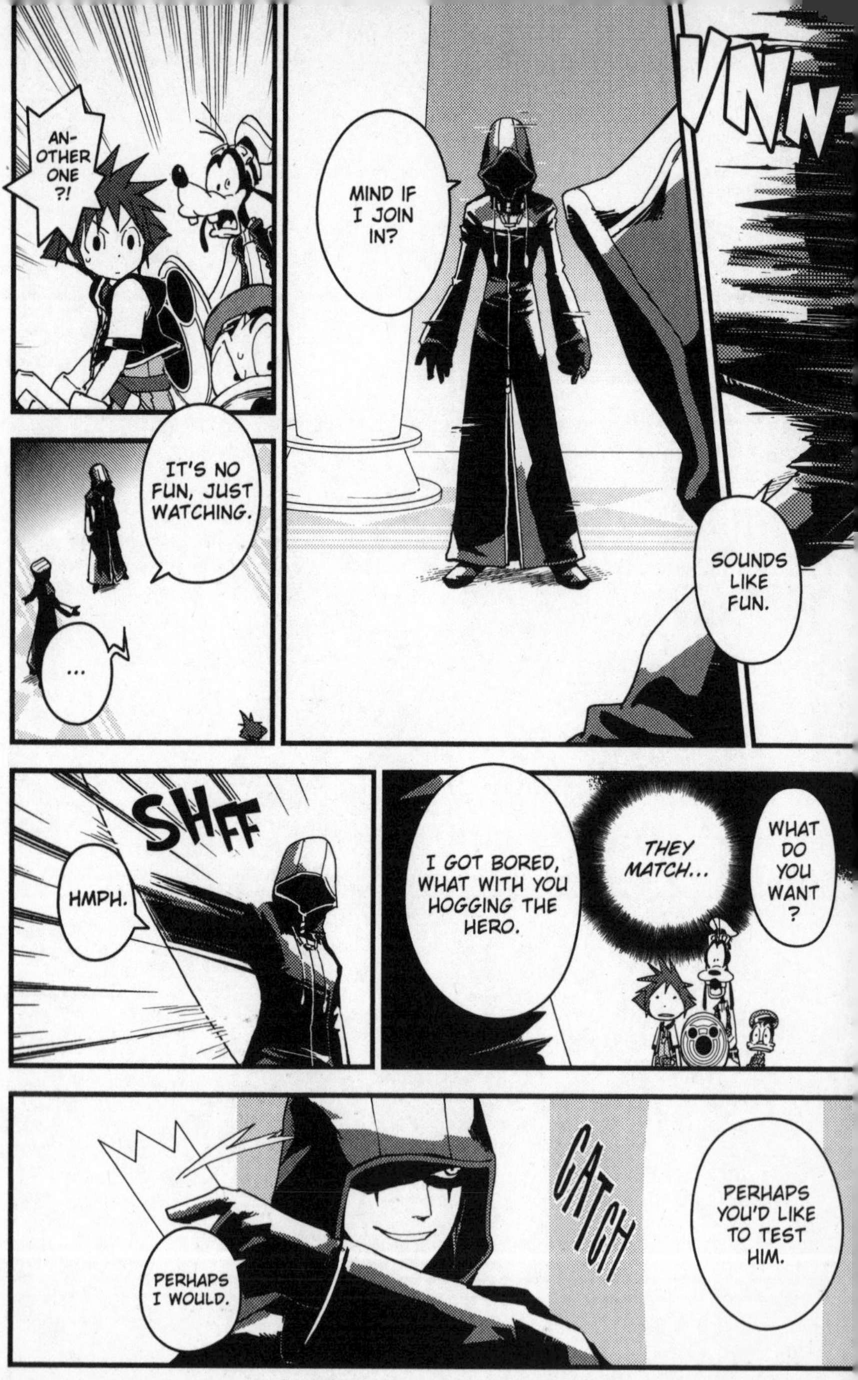
VNN
SOUNDS LIKE FUN.
MIND IF I JOIN IN?
AN-OTHER ONE?!
IT'S NO FUN, JUST WATCHING.
...
WHAT DO YOU WANT?
THEY MATCH...
I GOT BORED, WHAT WITH YOU HOGGING THE HERO.
SHFF
HMPH.
PERHAPS YOU'D LIKE TO TEST HIM.
CATCH
PERHAPS I WOULD.

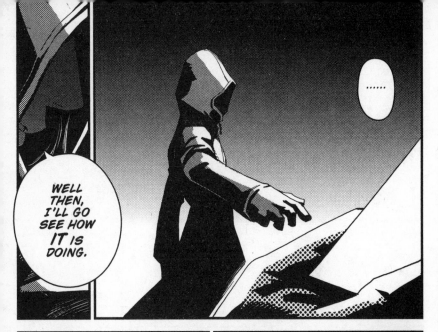

......

WELL THEN, I'LL GO SEE HOW IT IS DOING.

LOOKS LIKE IT'S MY SHOW NOW...

...KEY-BLADE MASTER.

SEE YA...

MY NAME IS AXEL.

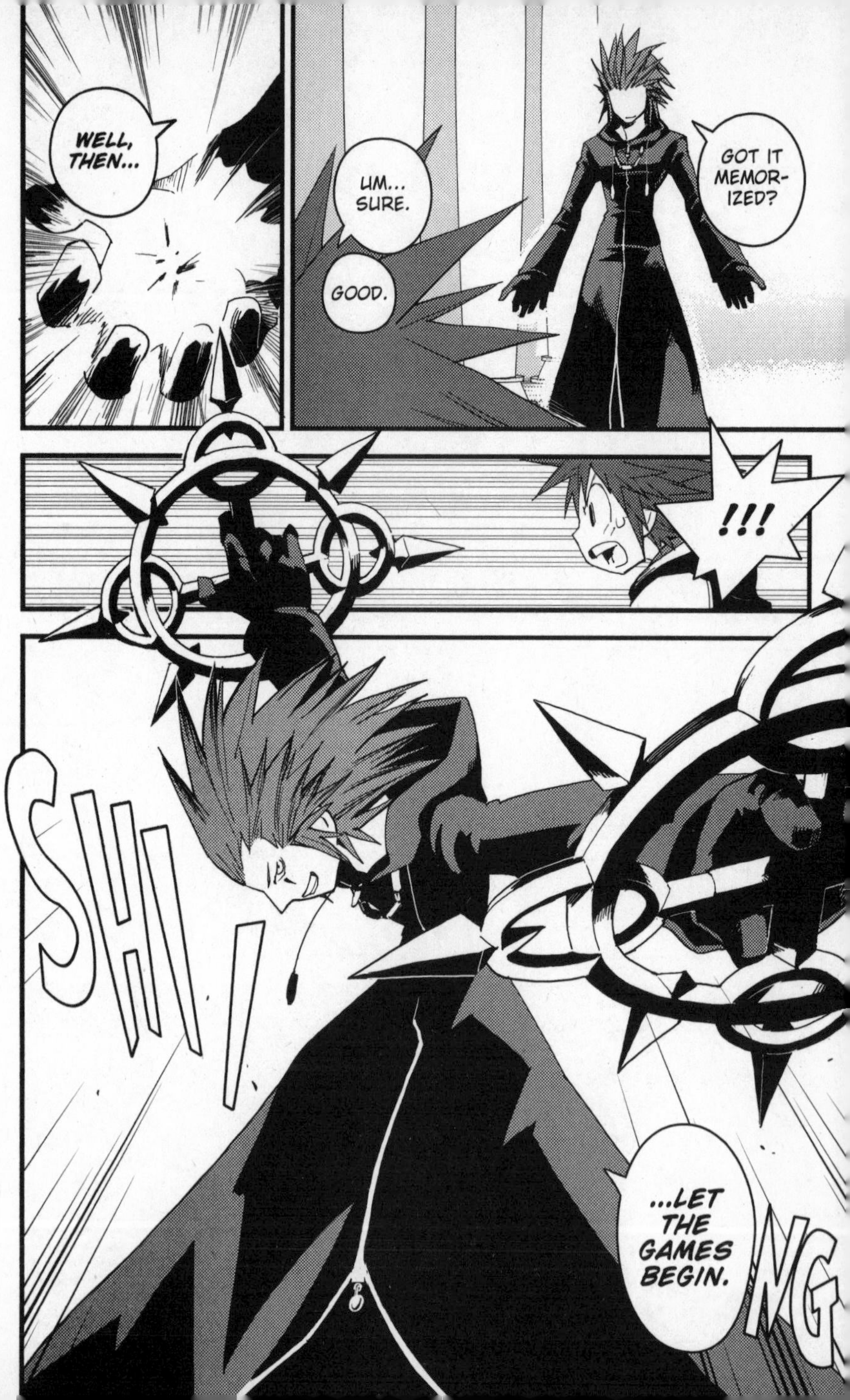

GOT IT MEMOR-IZED?
UM... SURE.
GOOD.
WELL, THEN...
!!!
...LET THE GAMES BEGIN.
SHII
NG

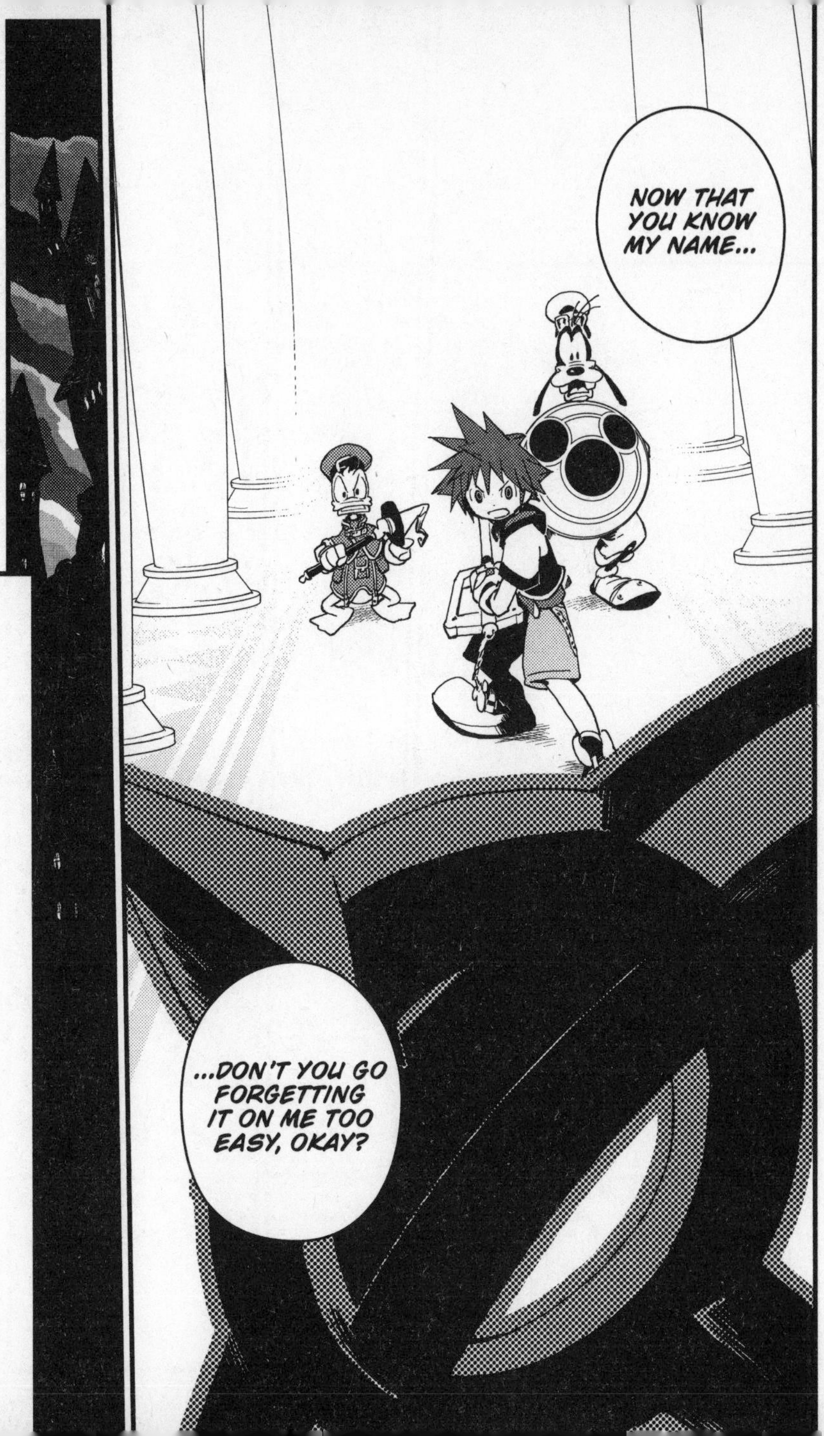
NOW THAT YOU KNOW MY NAME...
...DON'T YOU GO FORGETTING IT ON ME TOO EASY, OKAY?

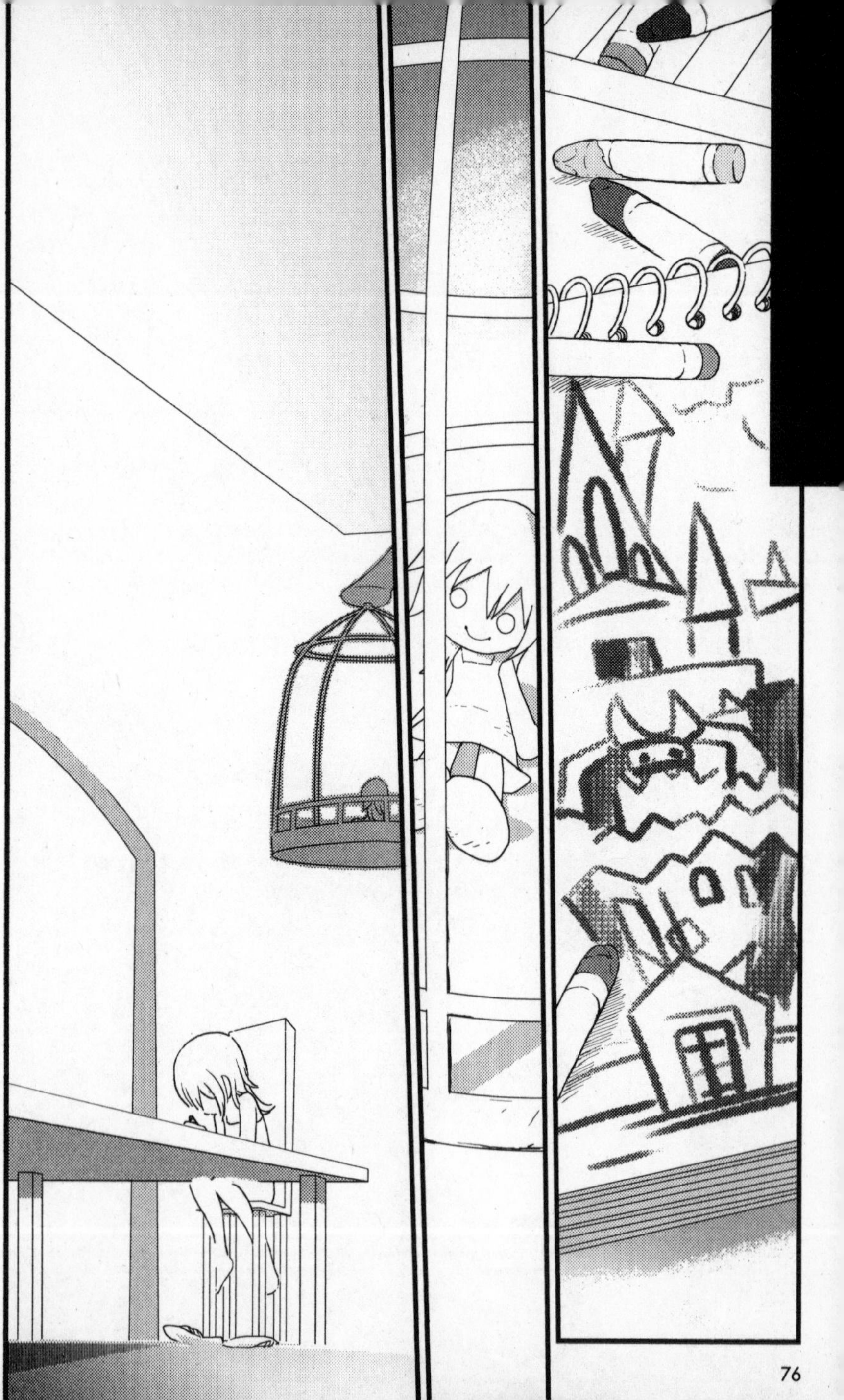

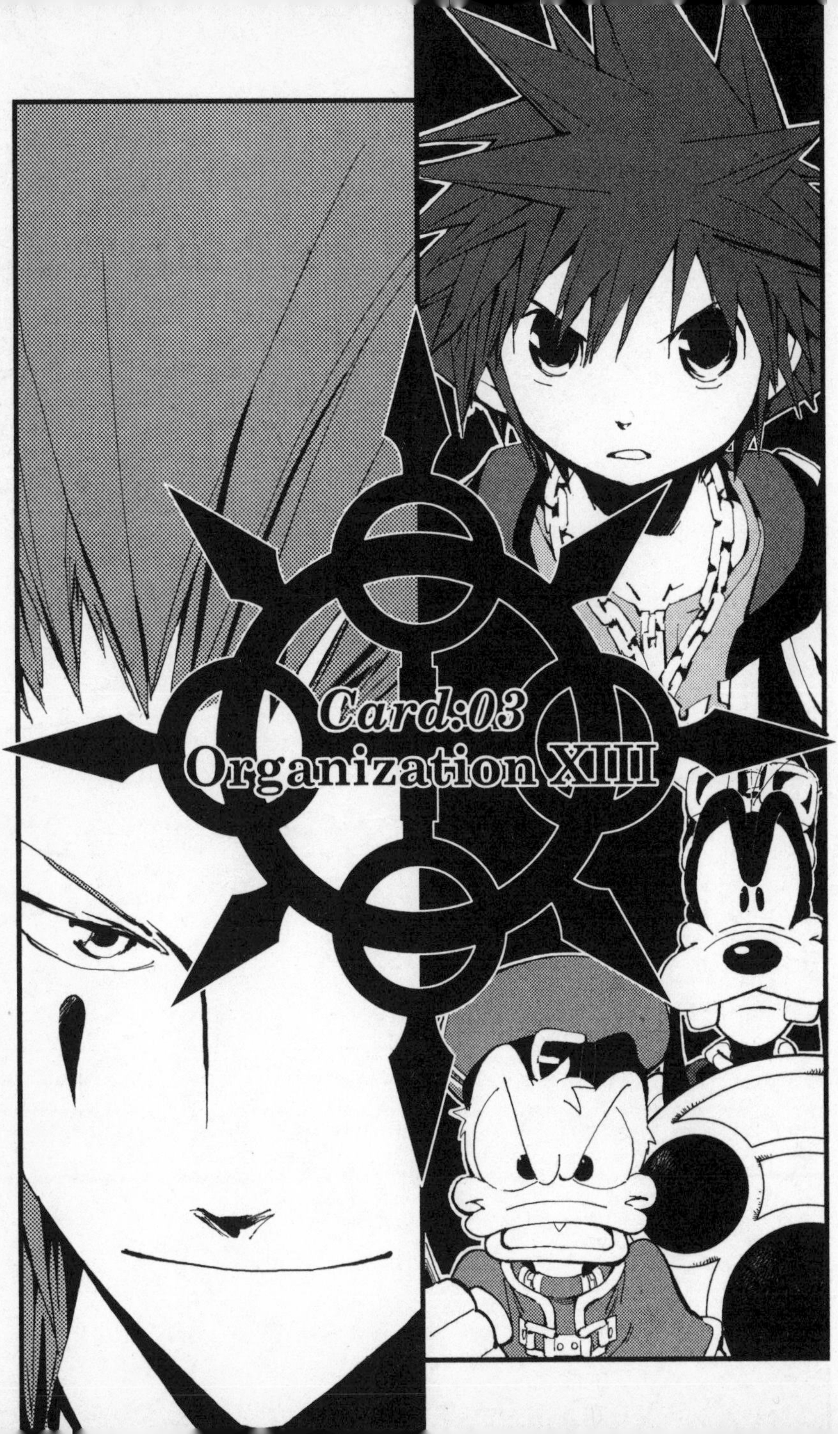
Card:03
Organization XIII

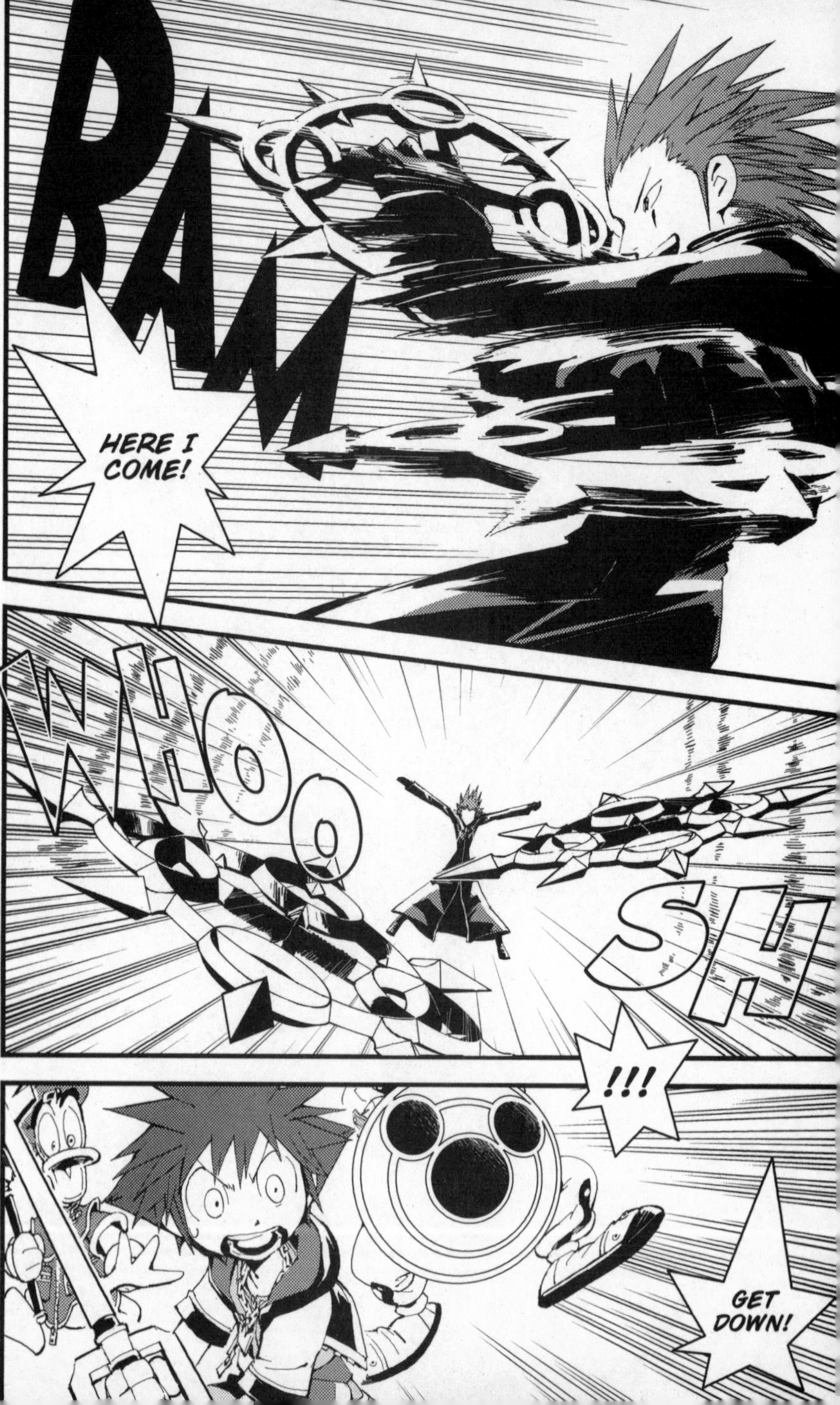
BAM
HERE I COME!
WHOOOSH
!!!
GET DOWN!

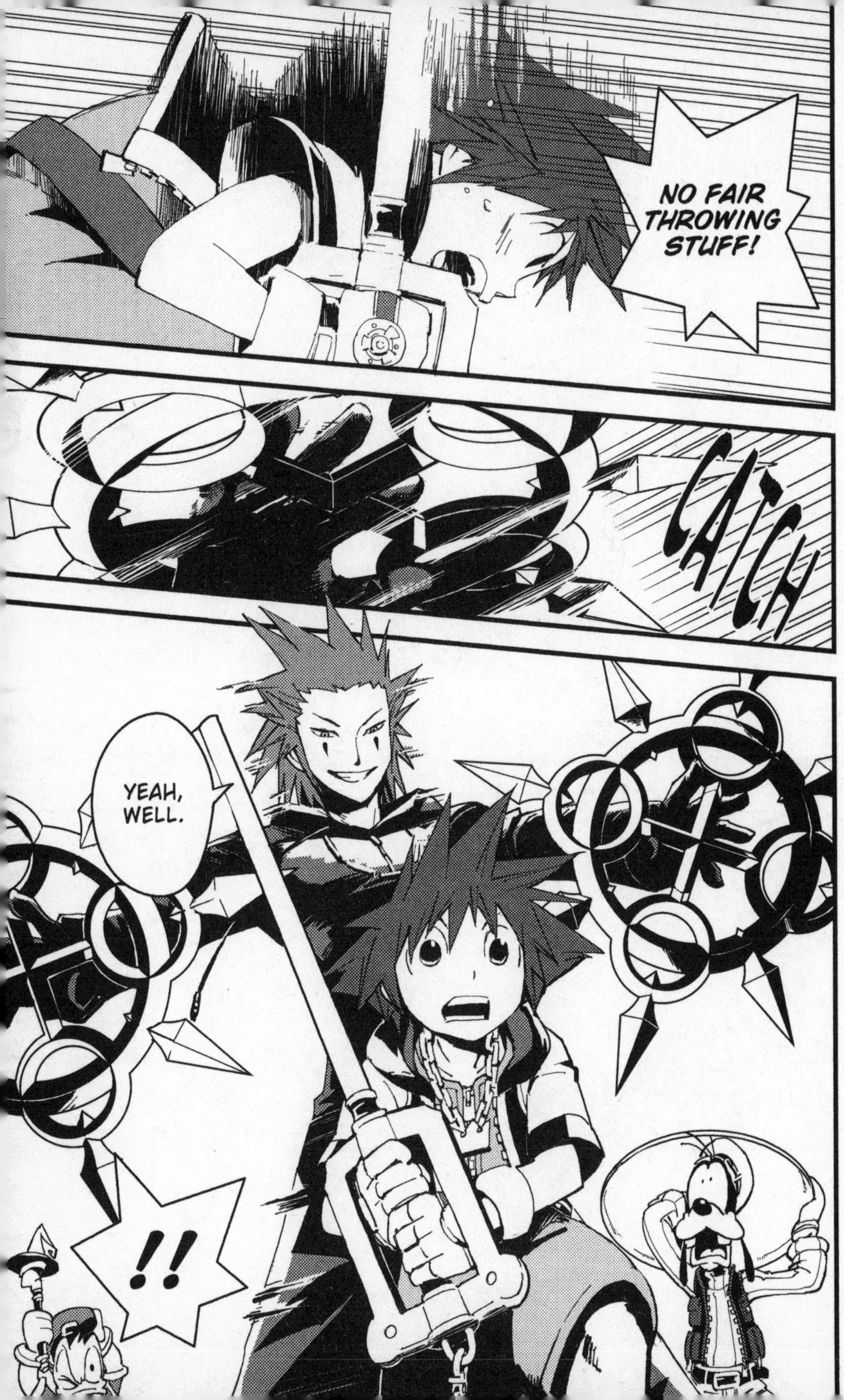
NO FAIR THROWING STUFF!
CATCH
YEAH, WELL.
!!

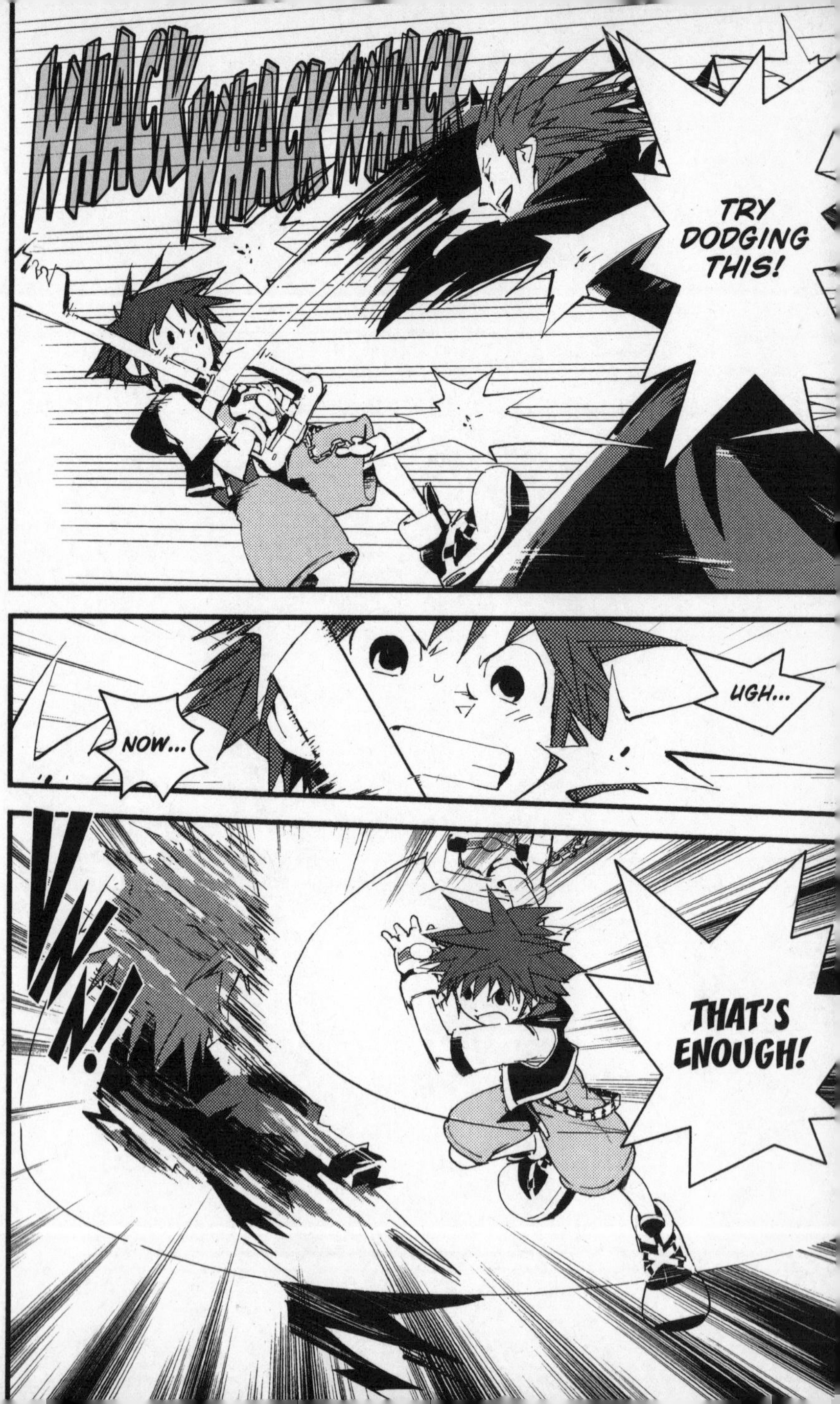
TRY DODGING THIS!
WHACK WHACK WHACK
UGH...
NOW...
THAT'S ENOUGH!
WN!

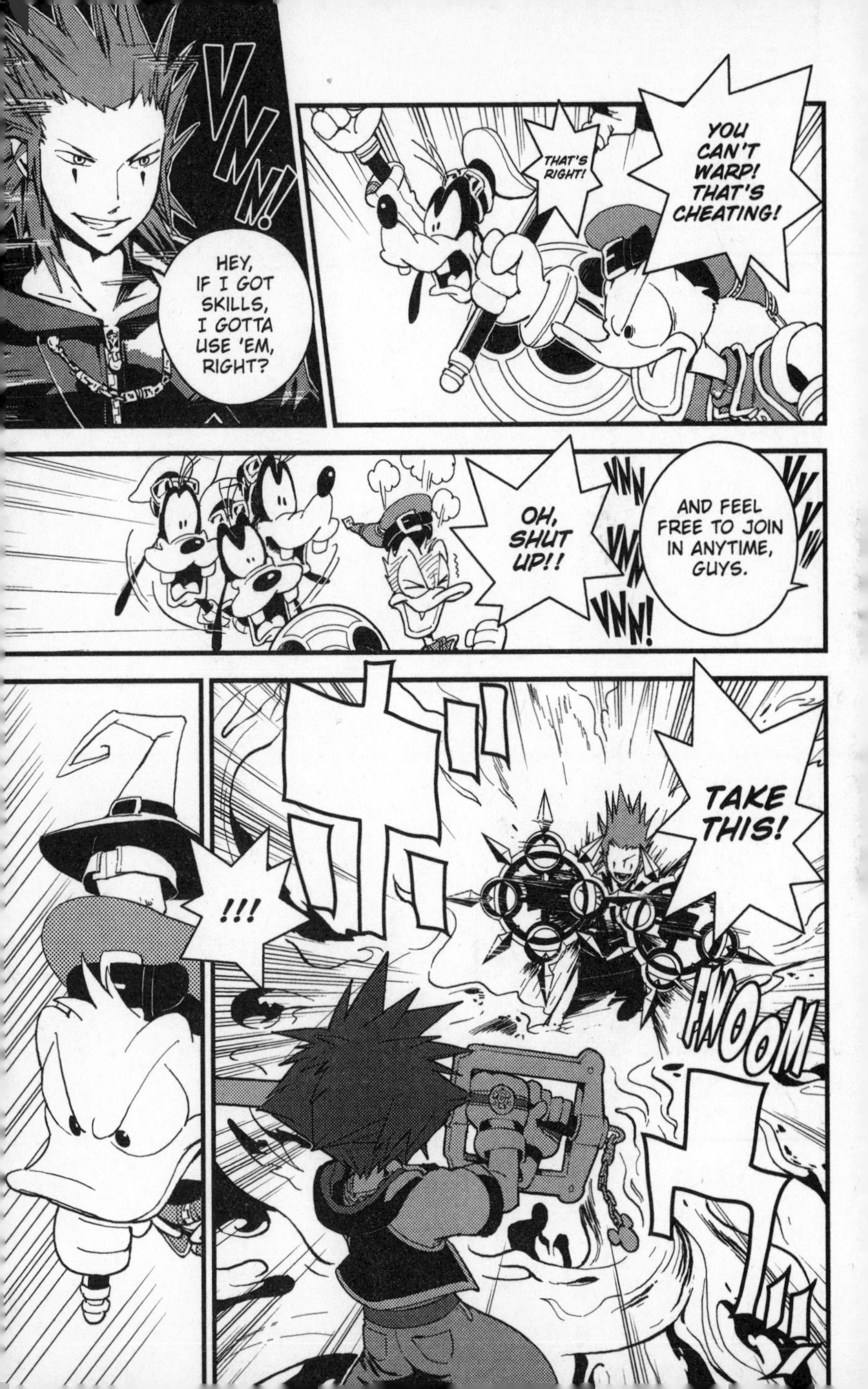
YOU CAN'T WARP! THAT'S CHEATING!
THAT'S RIGHT!
VNNN!
HEY, IF I GOT SKILLS, I GOTTA USE 'EM, RIGHT?
AND FEEL FREE TO JOIN IN ANYTIME, GUYS.
VNN VNN VNN!
OH, SHUT UP!!
TAKE THIS!
FWOOM
!!!

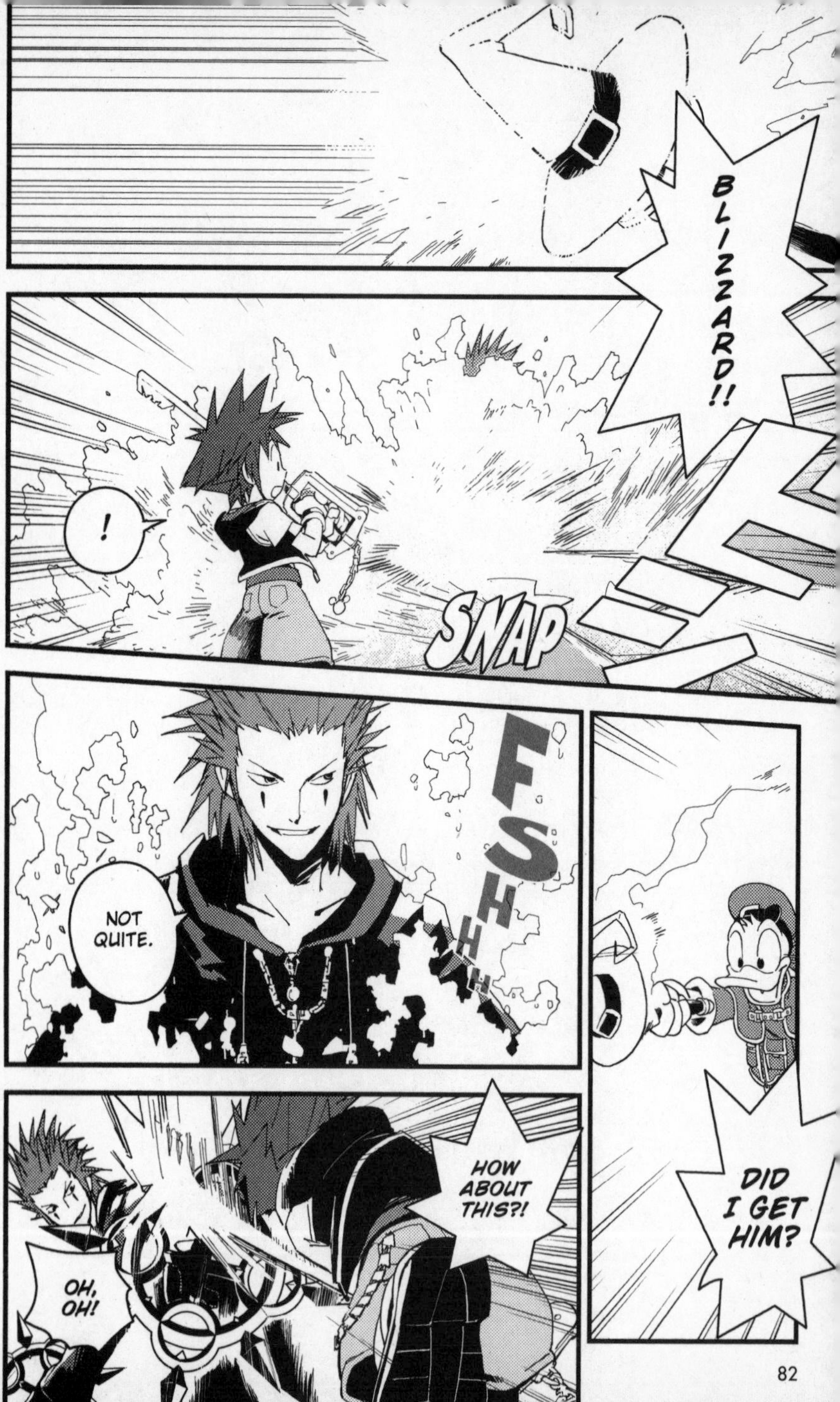
BLIZZARD!!
!
SNAP
DID I GET HIM?
FSHHH
NOT QUITE.
HOW ABOUT THIS?!
OH, OH!

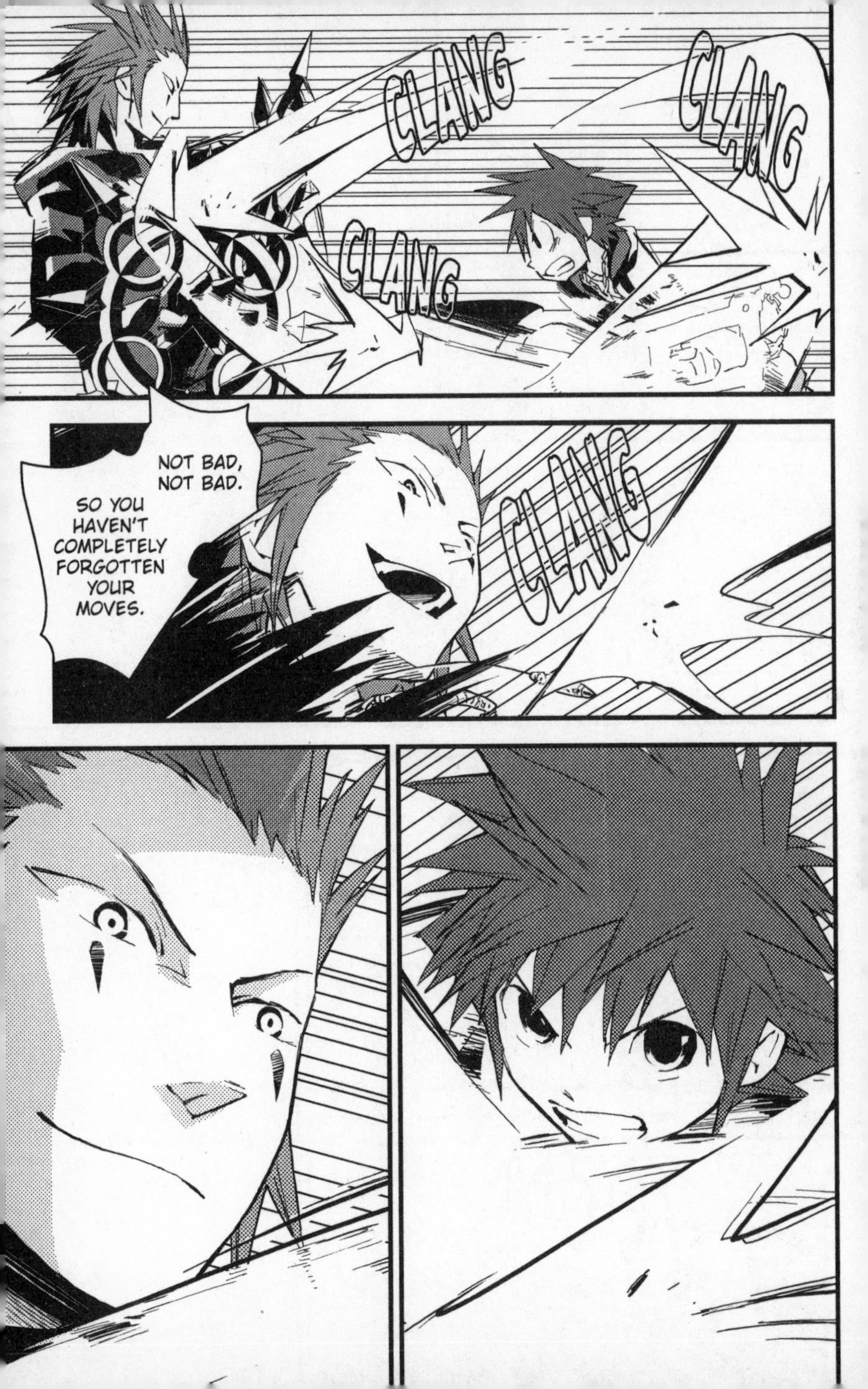
CLANG
CLANG
CLANG
CLANG
NOT BAD, NOT BAD.
SO YOU HAVEN'T COMPLETELY FORGOTTEN YOUR MOVES.

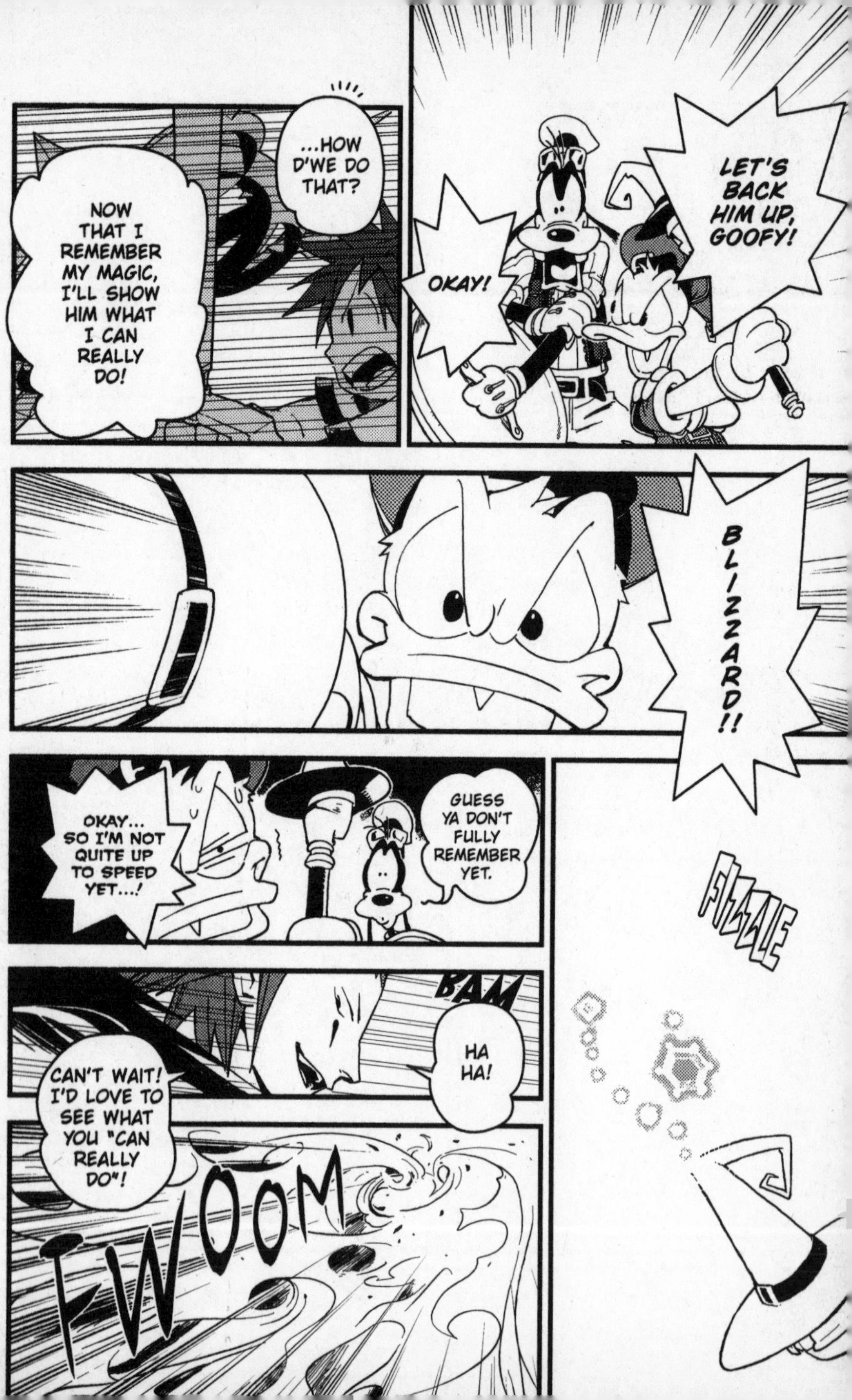
LET'S BACK HIM UP, GOOFY!
OKAY!
...HOW D'WE DO THAT?
NOW THAT I REMEMBER MY MAGIC, I'LL SHOW HIM WHAT I CAN REALLY DO!
BLIZZARD!!
FIZZLE
GUESS YA DON'T FULLY REMEMBER YET.
OKAY... SO I'M NOT QUITE UP TO SPEED YET...!
BAM
HA HA!
CAN'T WAIT! I'D LOVE TO SEE WHAT YOU "CAN REALLY DO"!
FWOOM

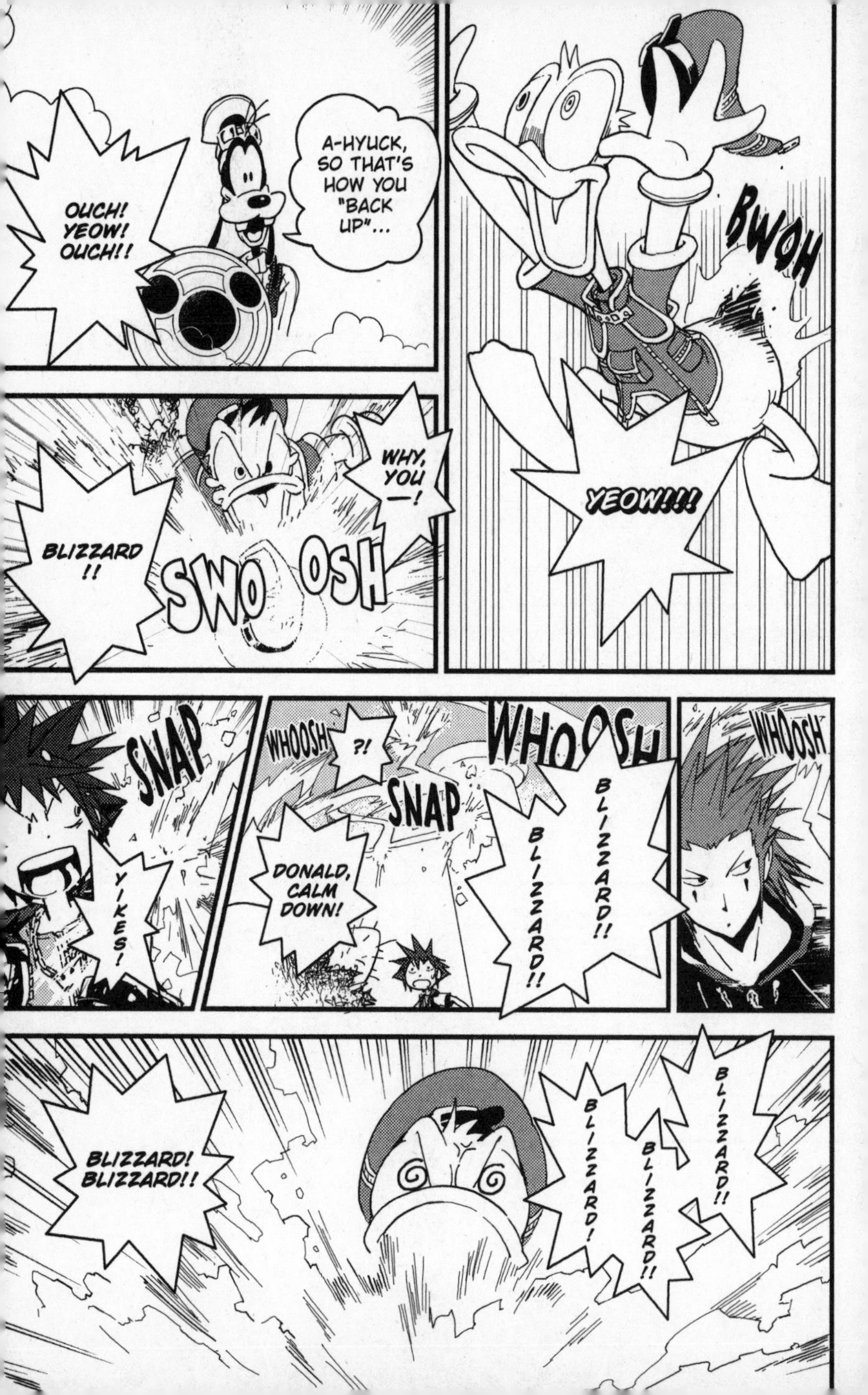
BWOH
YEOW!!!
A-HYUCK, SO THAT'S HOW YOU "BACK UP"...
OUCH! YEOW! OUCH!!
WHY, YOU—!
SWOOSH
BLIZZARD!!
WHOOSH
WHOOSH
BLIZZARD!!
BLIZZARD!!
SNAP
?!
WHOOSH
DONALD, CALM DOWN!
SNAP
YIKES!
BLIZZARD!!
BLIZZARD!!
BLIZZARD!
BLIZZARD! BLIZZARD!!

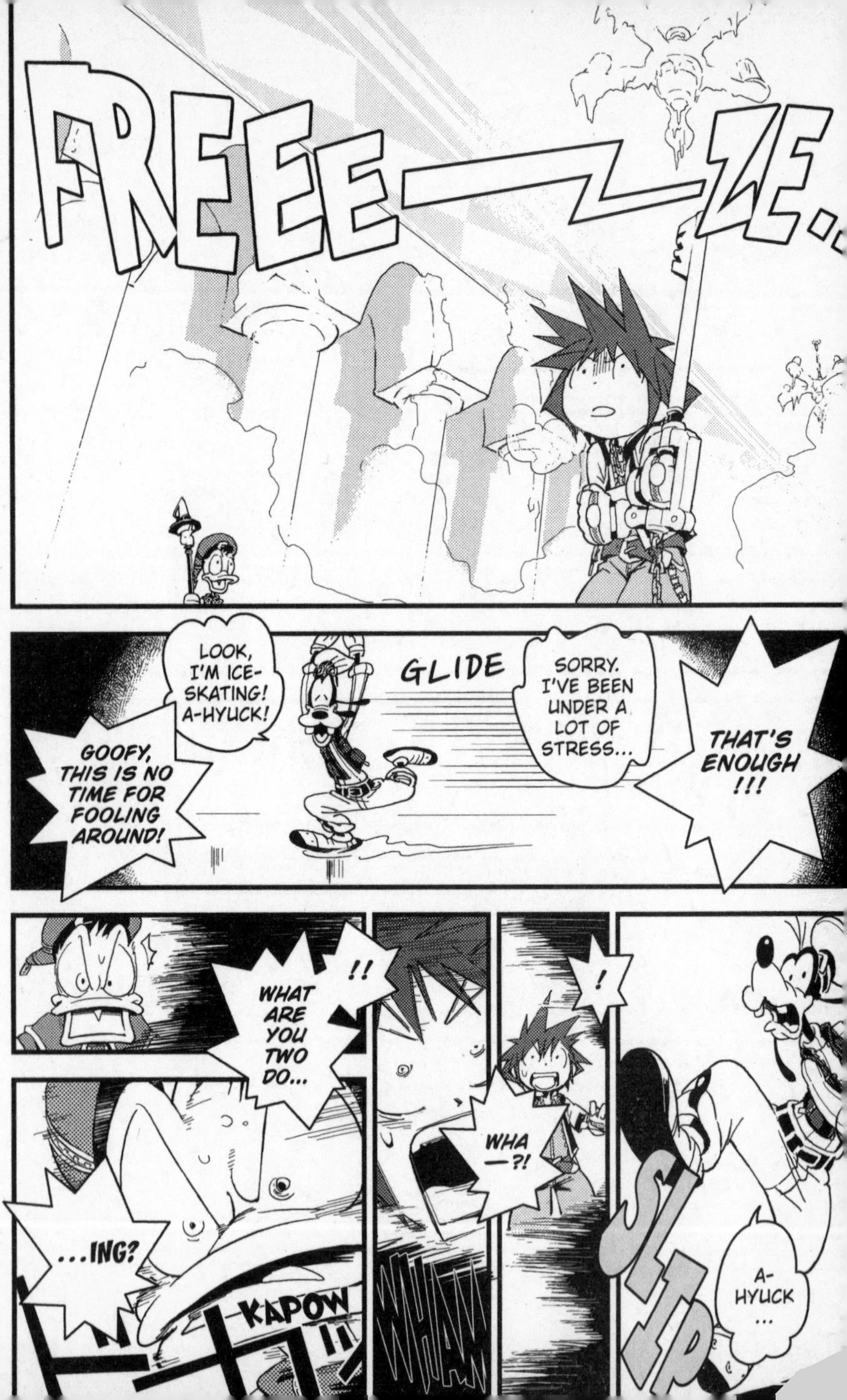
FREEE—ZE...
THAT'S ENOUGH !!!
SORRY. I'VE BEEN UNDER A LOT OF STRESS...
GLIDE
LOOK, I'M ICE-SKATING! A-HYUCK!
GOOFY, THIS IS NO TIME FOR FOOLING AROUND!
SLIP
A-HYUCK ...
!
WHA—?!
WHAM
!!
WHAT ARE YOU TWO DO...
...ING?
KAPOW

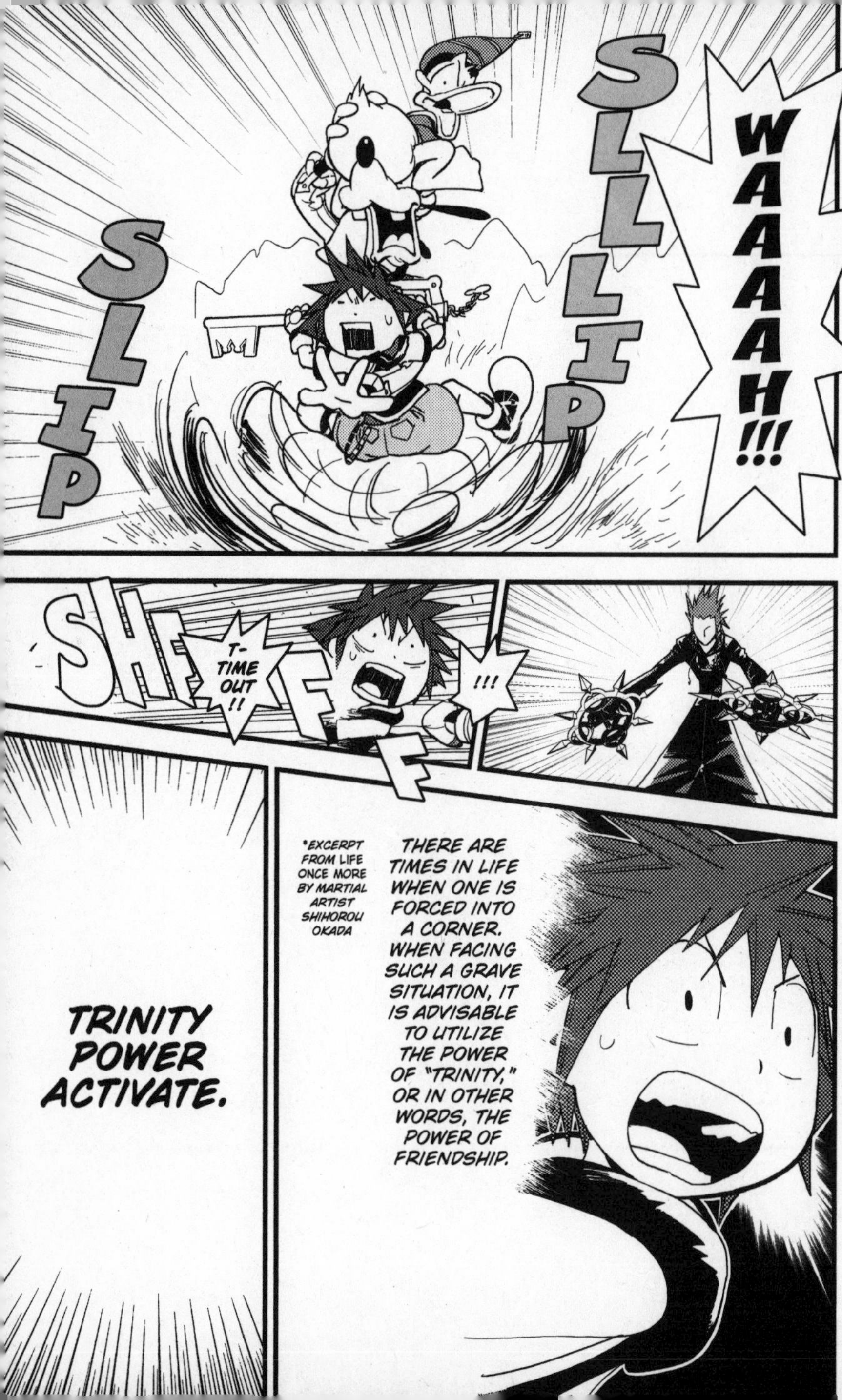
WAAAAH!!!
SLLIP
SLIP
!!!
T-TIME OUT!!
SHFF
THERE ARE TIMES IN LIFE WHEN ONE IS FORCED INTO A CORNER. WHEN FACING SUCH A GRAVE SITUATION, IT IS ADVISABLE TO UTILIZE THE POWER OF "TRINITY," OR IN OTHER WORDS, THE POWER OF FRIENDSHIP.
*EXCERPT FROM LIFE ONCE MORE BY MARTIAL ARTIST SHIHOROU OKADA
TRINITY POWER ACTIVATE.

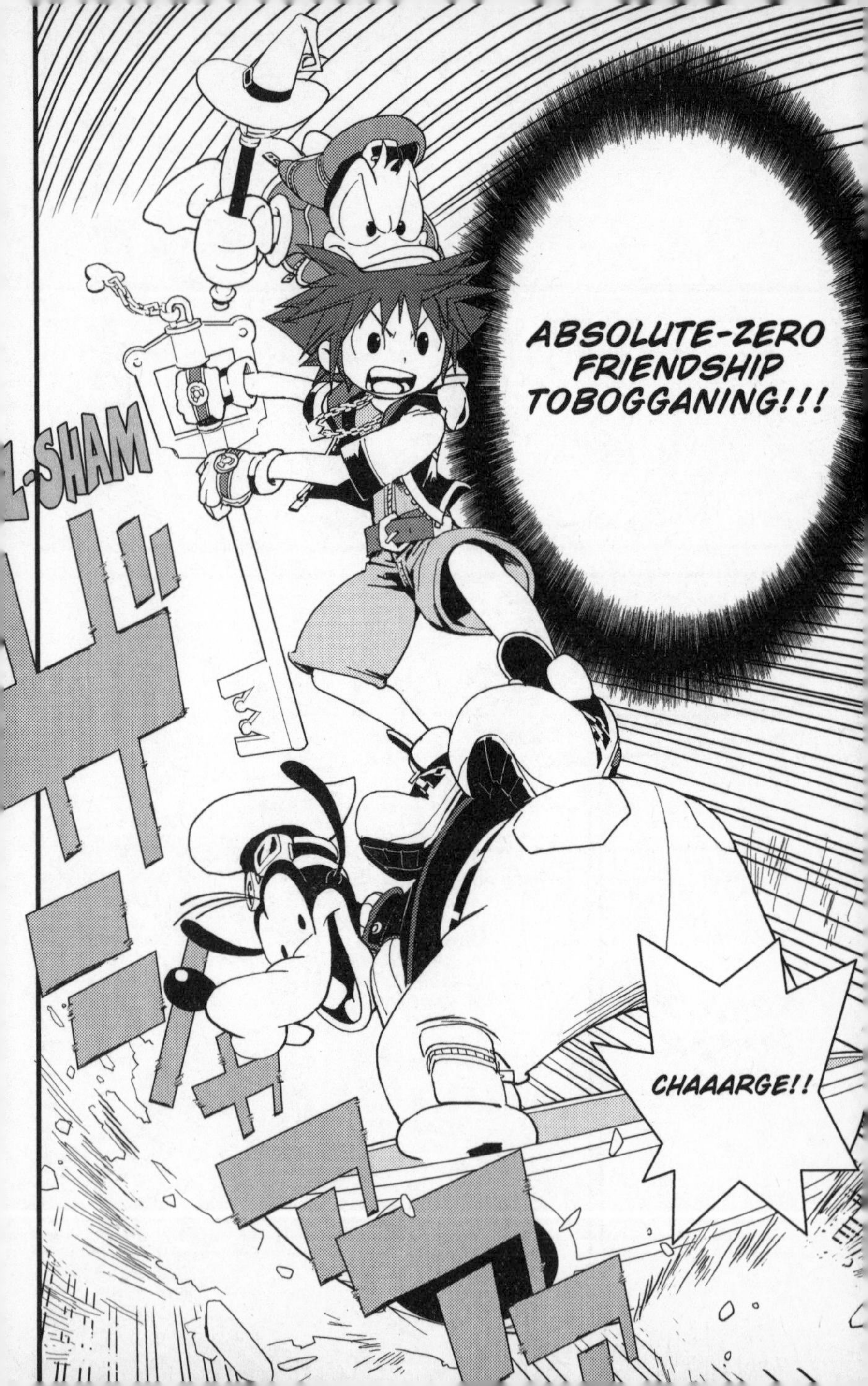
ABSOLUTE-ZERO FRIENDSHIP TOBOGGANING!!!
-SHAM
CHAAARGE!!

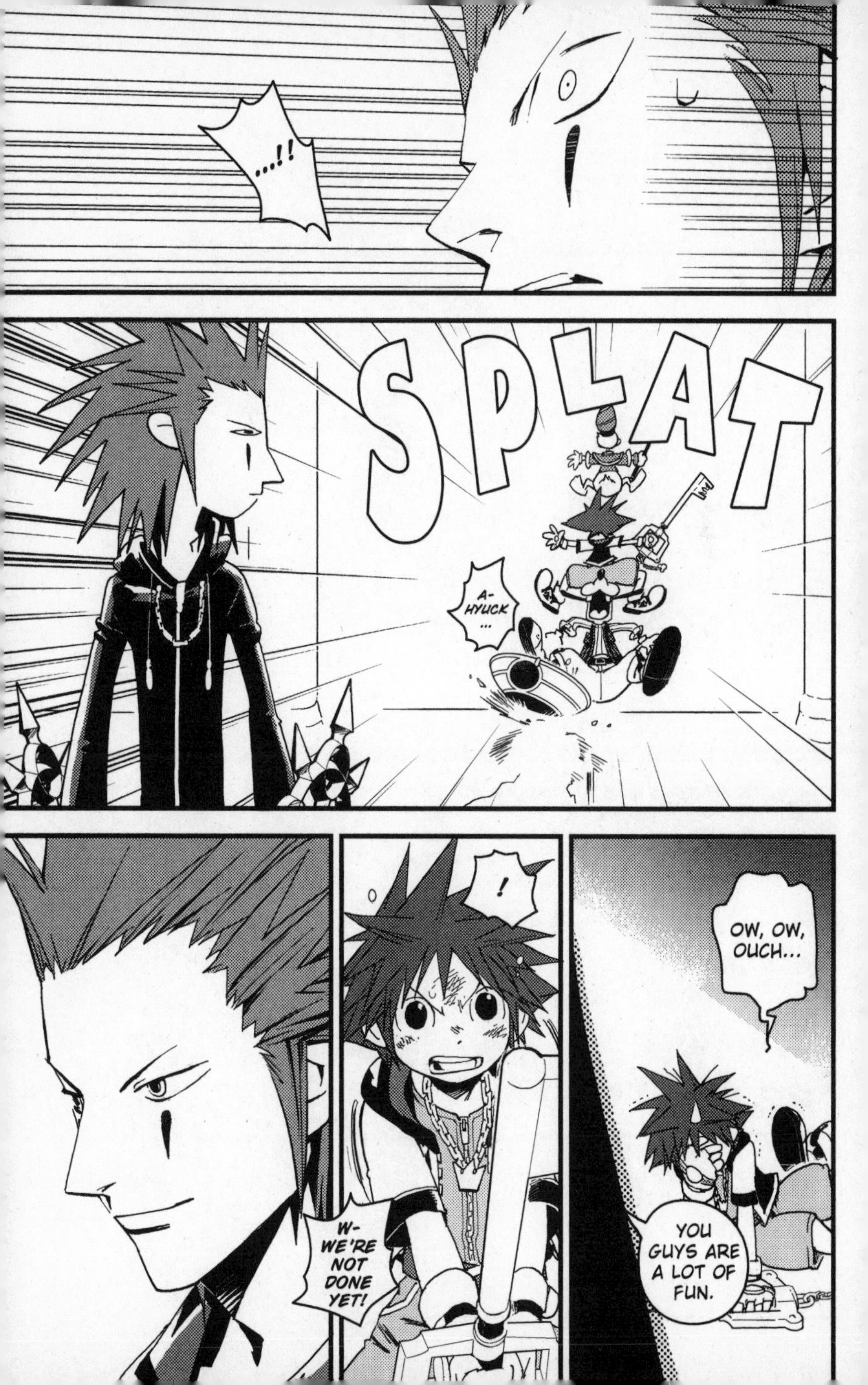
...!!
SPLAT
A-HYUCK ...
OW, OW, OUCH...
YOU GUYS ARE A LOT OF FUN.
!
W-WE'RE NOT DONE YET!

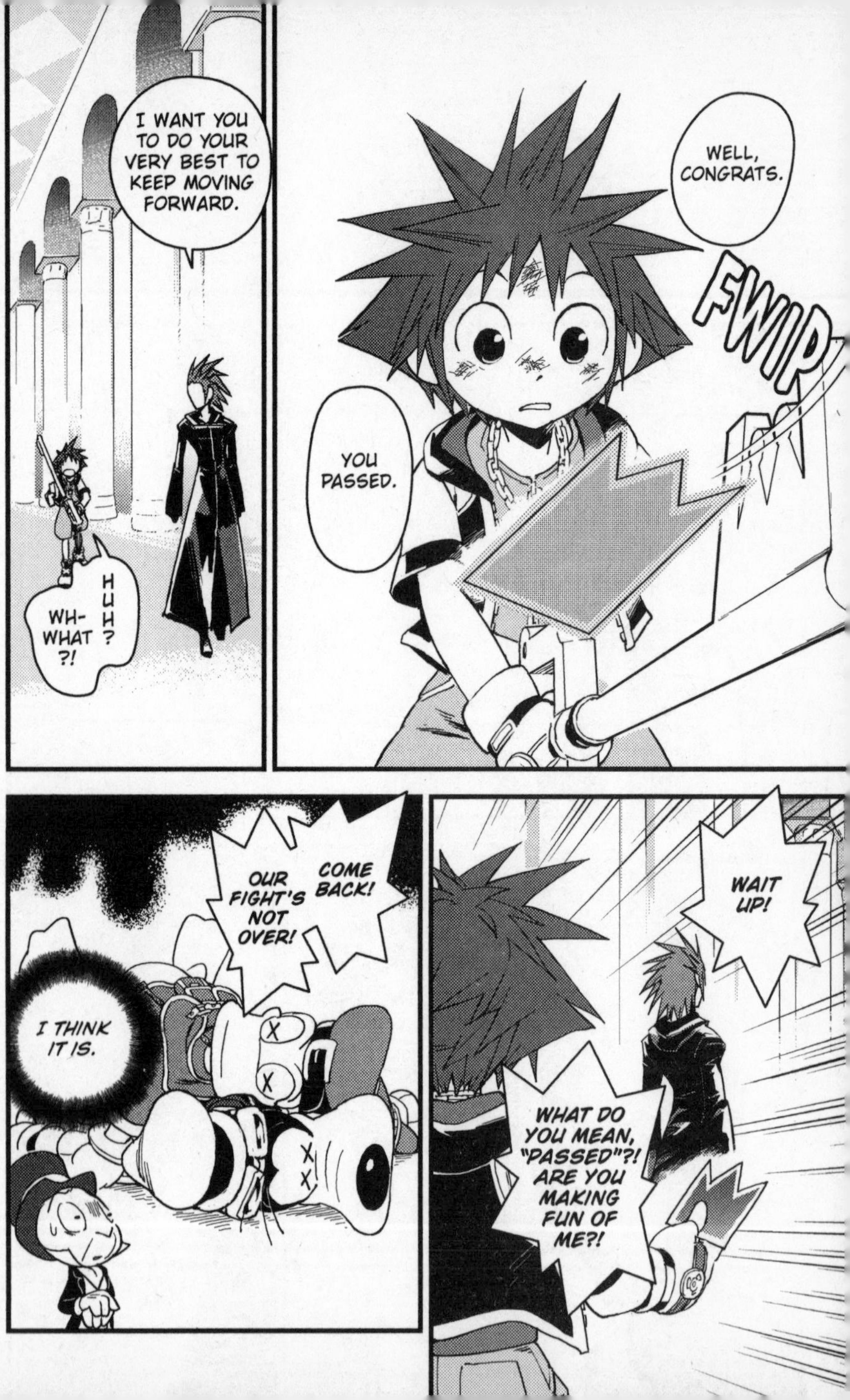
WELL, CONGRATS.
FWIP
YOU PASSED.
I WANT YOU TO DO YOUR VERY BEST TO KEEP MOVING FORWARD.
HUH?
WH-WHAT?!
WAIT UP!
WHAT DO YOU MEAN, "PASSED"?! ARE YOU MAKING FUN OF ME?!
COME BACK!
OUR FIGHT'S NOT OVER!
I THINK IT IS.

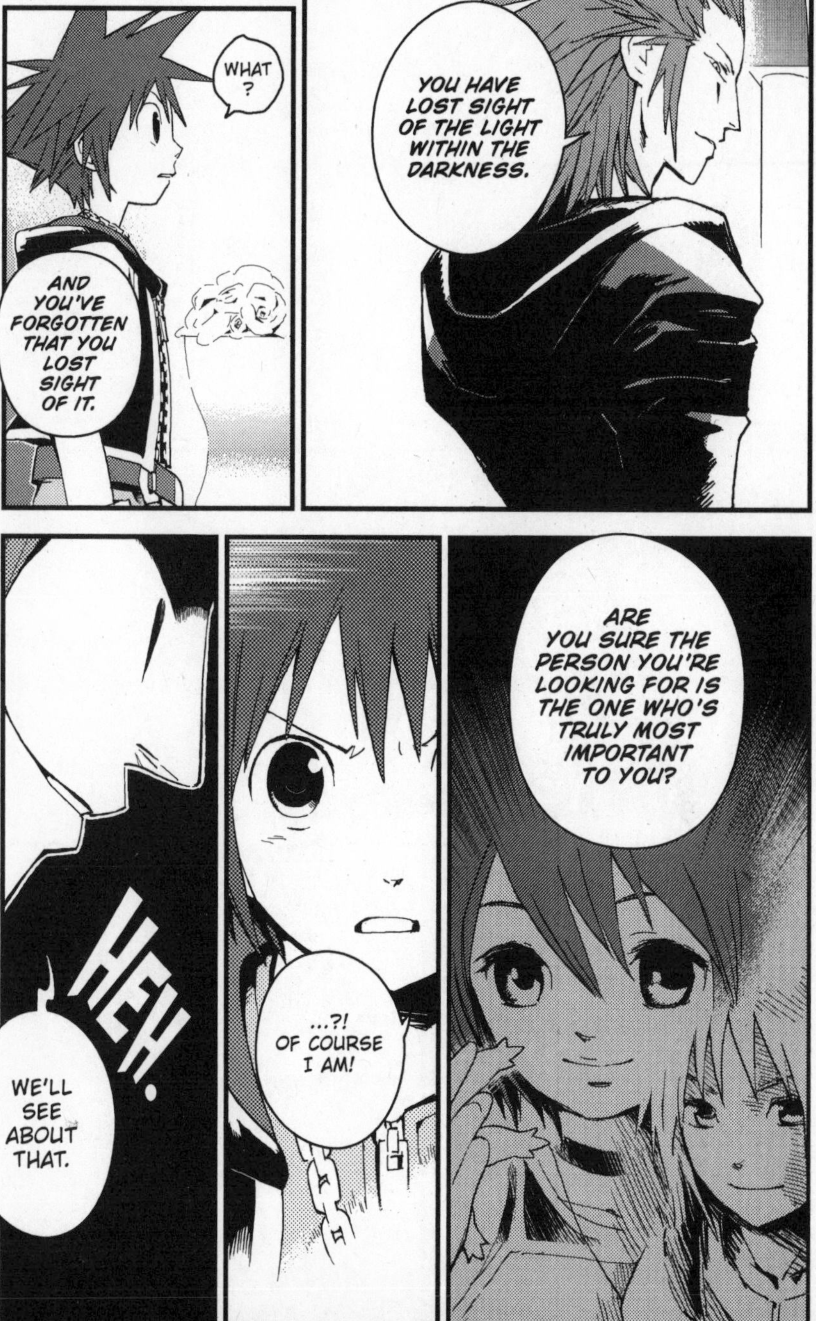
YOU HAVE LOST SIGHT OF THE LIGHT WITHIN THE DARKNESS.
WHAT?
AND YOU'VE FORGOTTEN THAT YOU LOST SIGHT OF IT.
ARE YOU SURE THE PERSON YOU'RE LOOKING FOR IS THE ONE WHO'S TRULY MOST IMPORTANT TO YOU?
...?! OF COURSE I AM!
HEH.
WE'LL SEE ABOUT THAT.

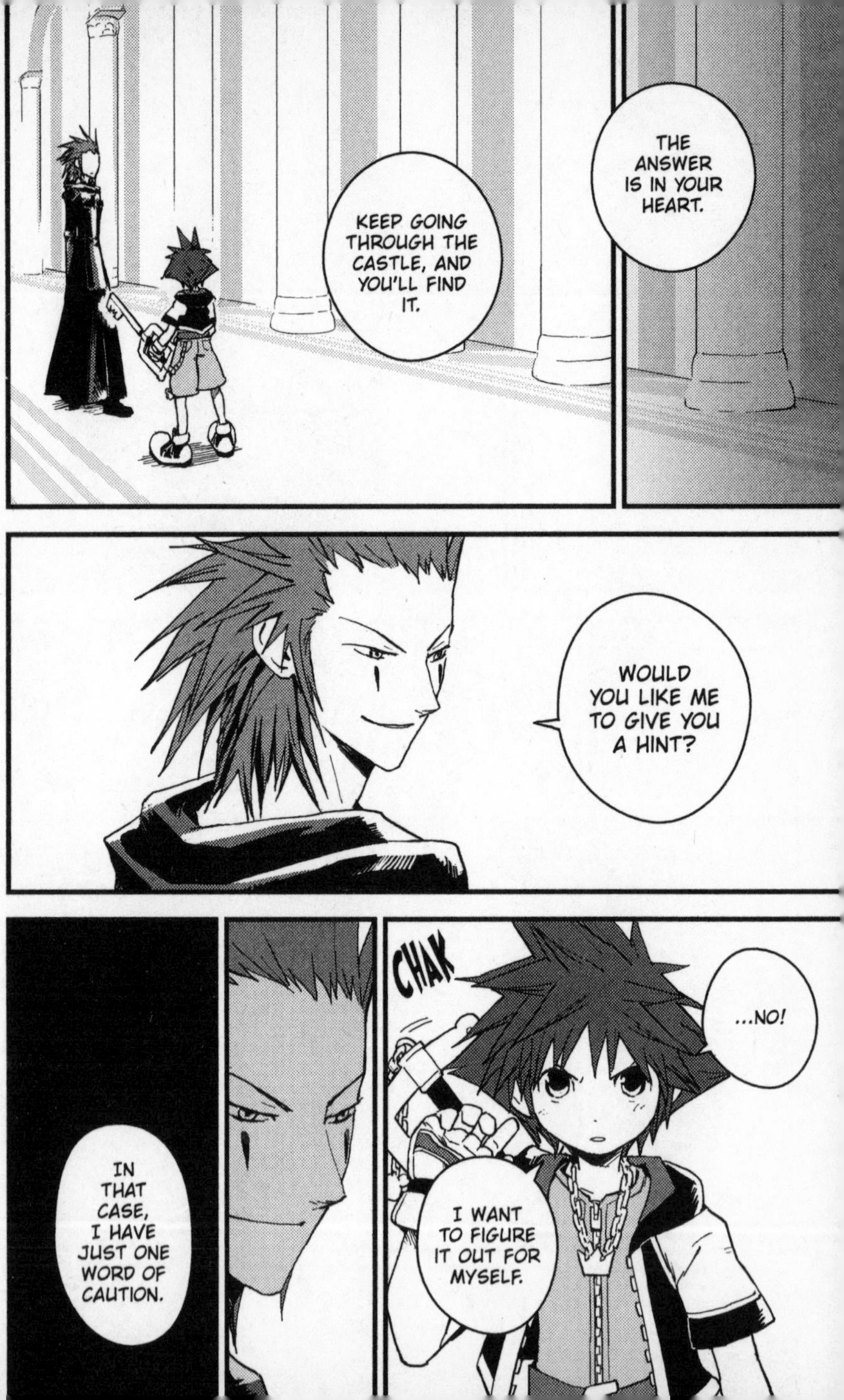
THE ANSWER IS IN YOUR HEART.
KEEP GOING THROUGH THE CASTLE, AND YOU'LL FIND IT.
WOULD YOU LIKE ME TO GIVE YOU A HINT?
CHAK
...NO!
I WANT TO FIGURE IT OUT FOR MYSELF.
IN THAT CASE, I HAVE JUST ONE WORD OF CAUTION.

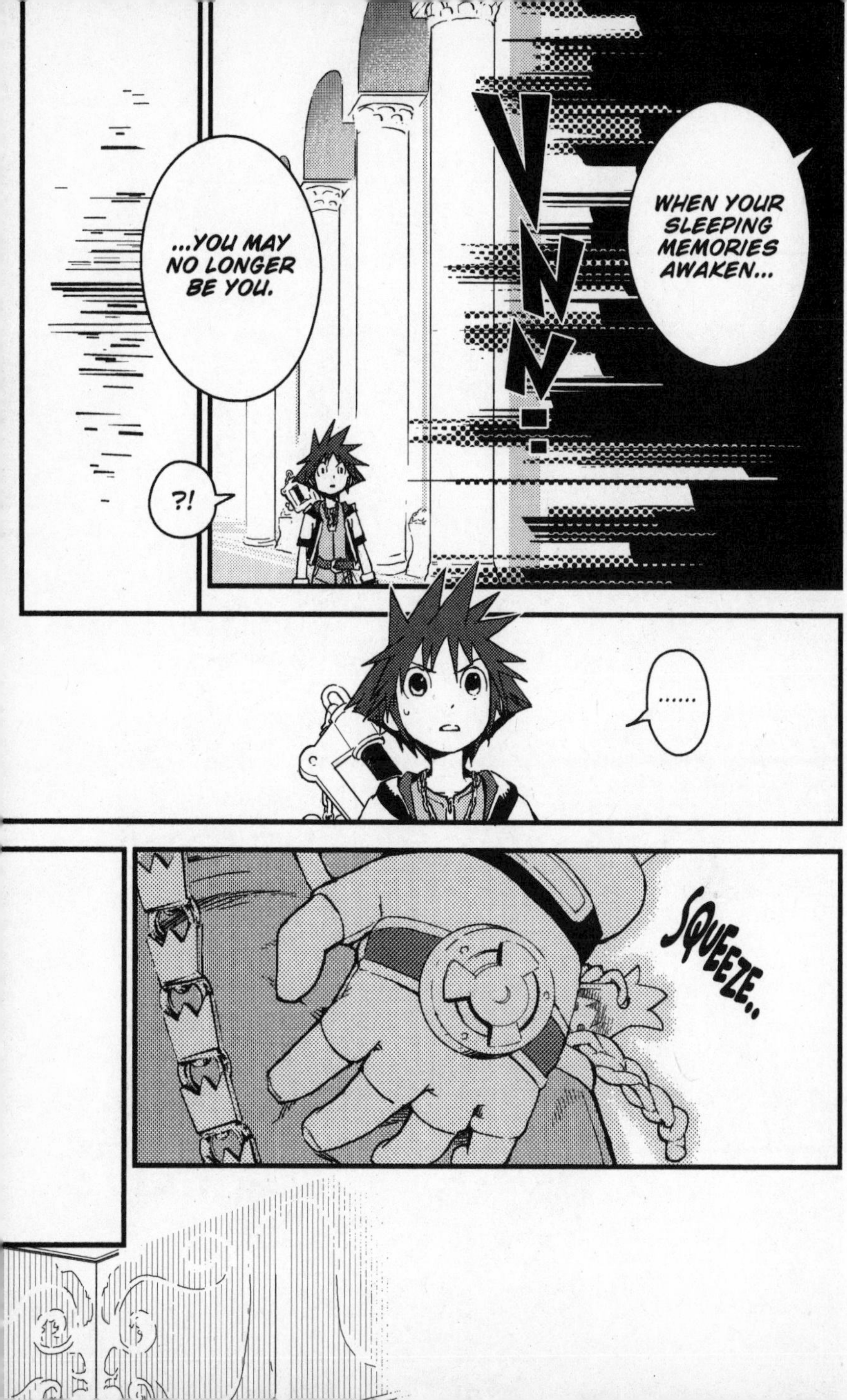
WHEN YOUR SLEEPING MEMORIES AWAKEN...
VNNN!
...YOU MAY NO LONGER BE YOU.
?!
......
SQUEEZE..

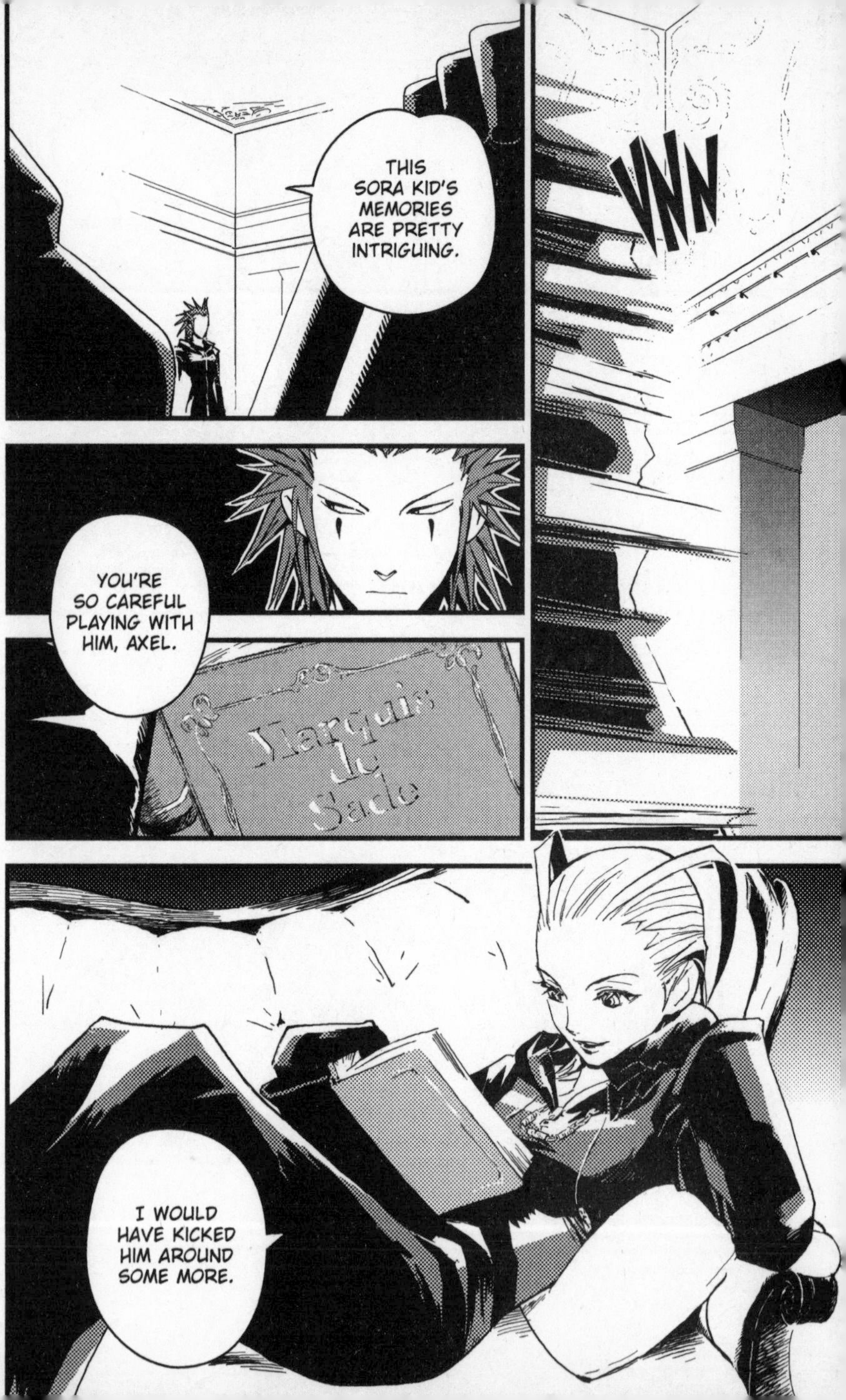
VNN
THIS SORA KID'S MEMORIES ARE PRETTY INTRIGUING.
YOU'RE SO CAREFUL PLAYING WITH HIM, AXEL.
Marquis de Sade
I WOULD HAVE KICKED HIM AROUND SOME MORE.

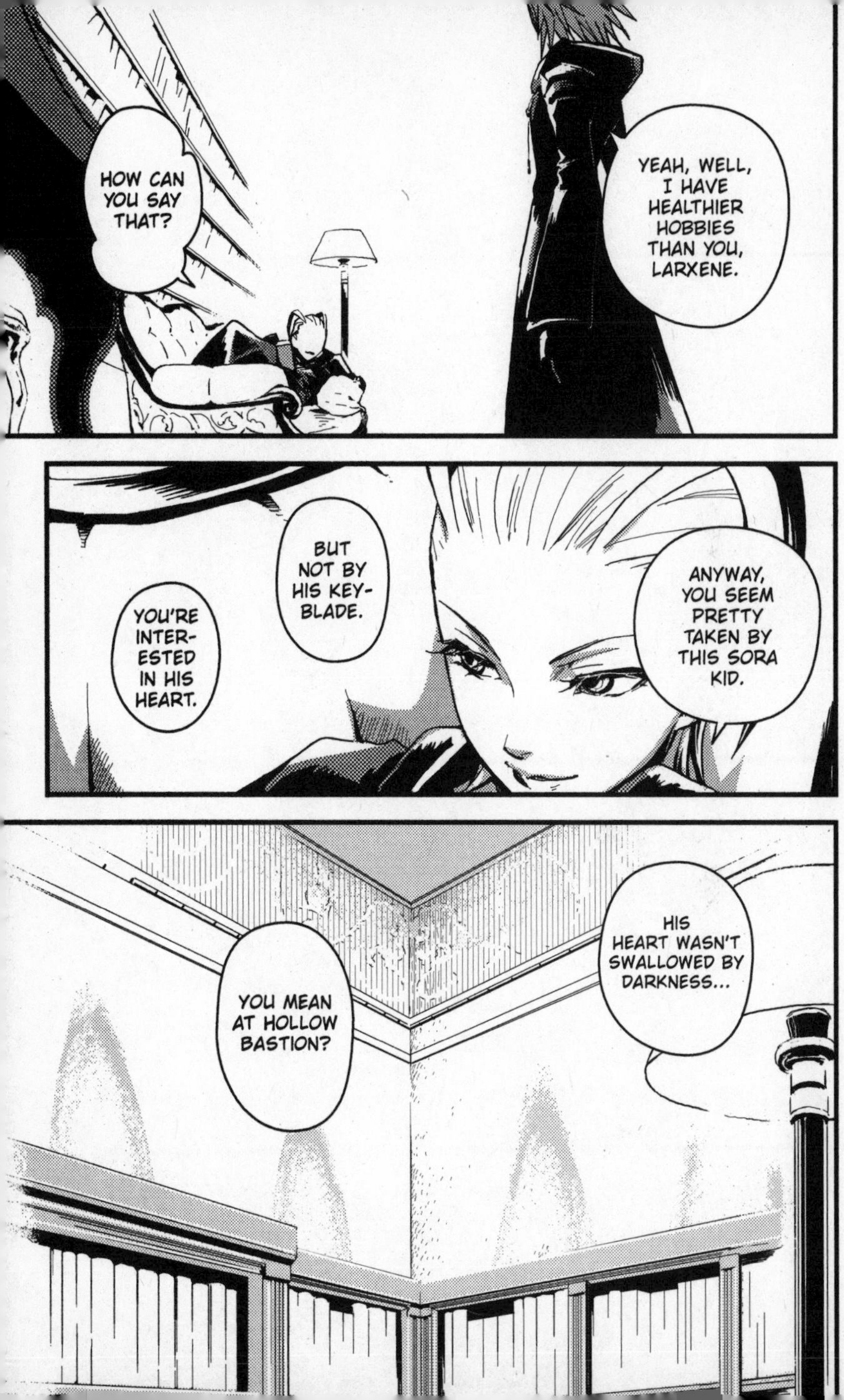
YEAH, WELL, I HAVE HEALTHIER HOBBIES THAN YOU, LARXENE.
HOW CAN YOU SAY THAT?
ANYWAY, YOU SEEM PRETTY TAKEN BY THIS SORA KID.
BUT NOT BY HIS KEY-BLADE.
YOU'RE INTER-ESTED IN HIS HEART.
HIS HEART WASN'T SWALLOWED BY DARKNESS...
YOU MEAN AT HOLLOW BASTION?

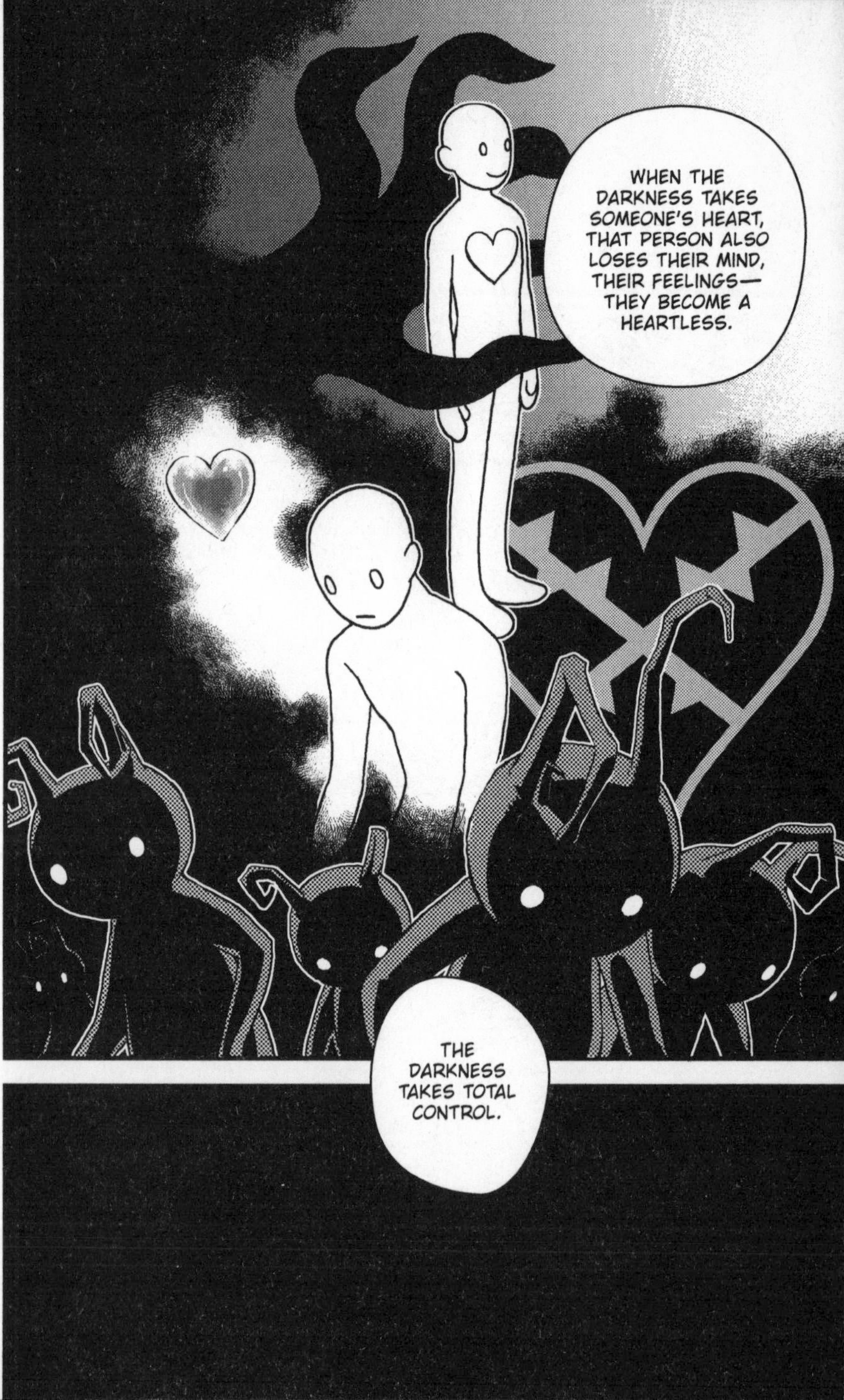
WHEN THE DARKNESS TAKES SOMEONE'S HEART, THAT PERSON ALSO LOSES THEIR MIND, THEIR FEELINGS—THEY BECOME A HEARTLESS.
THE DARKNESS TAKES TOTAL CONTROL.

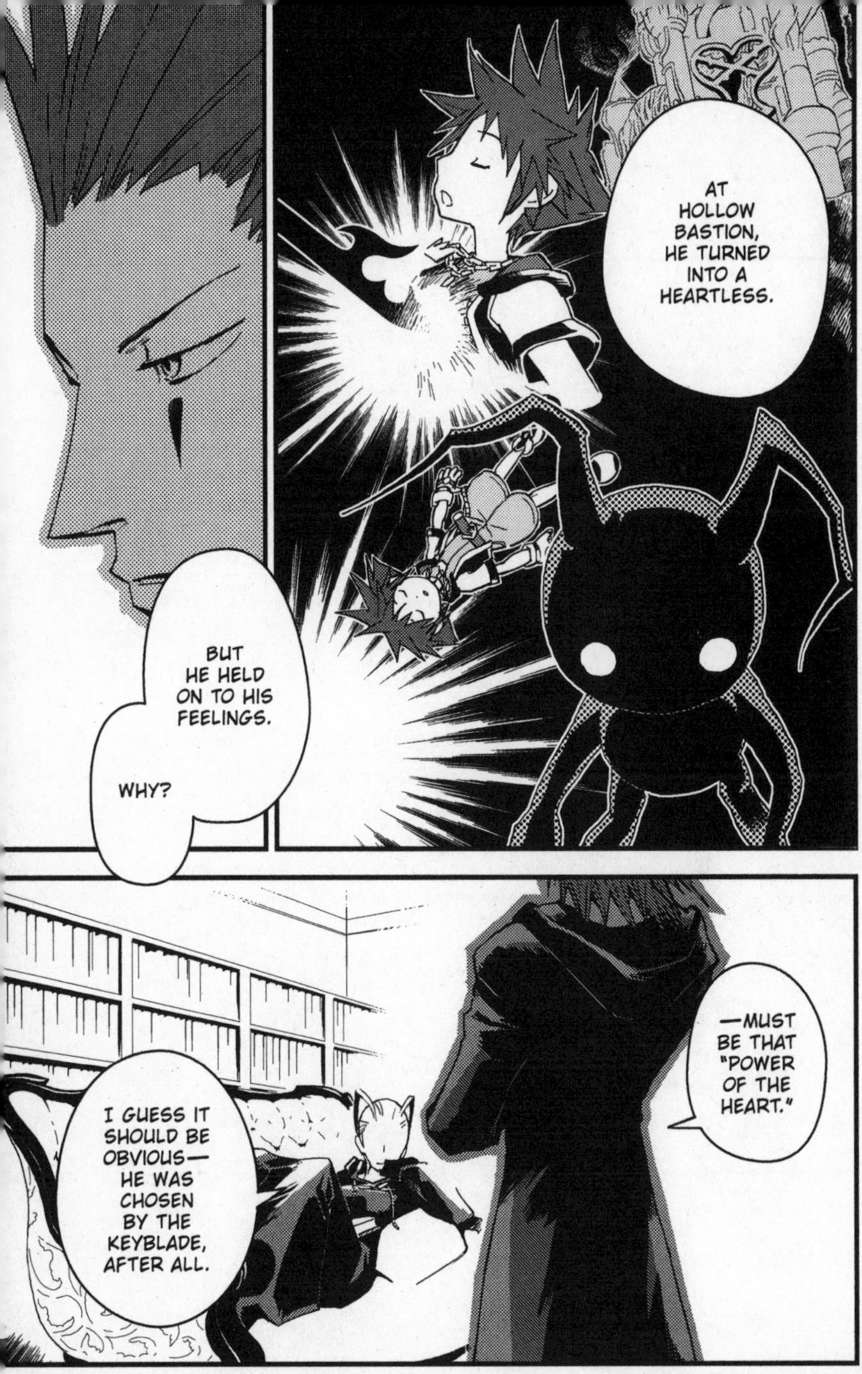
AT HOLLOW BASTION, HE TURNED INTO A HEARTLESS.
BUT HE HELD ON TO HIS FEELINGS.
WHY?
—MUST BE THAT "POWER OF THE HEART."
I GUESS IT SHOULD BE OBVIOUS— HE WAS CHOSEN BY THE KEYBLADE, AFTER ALL.

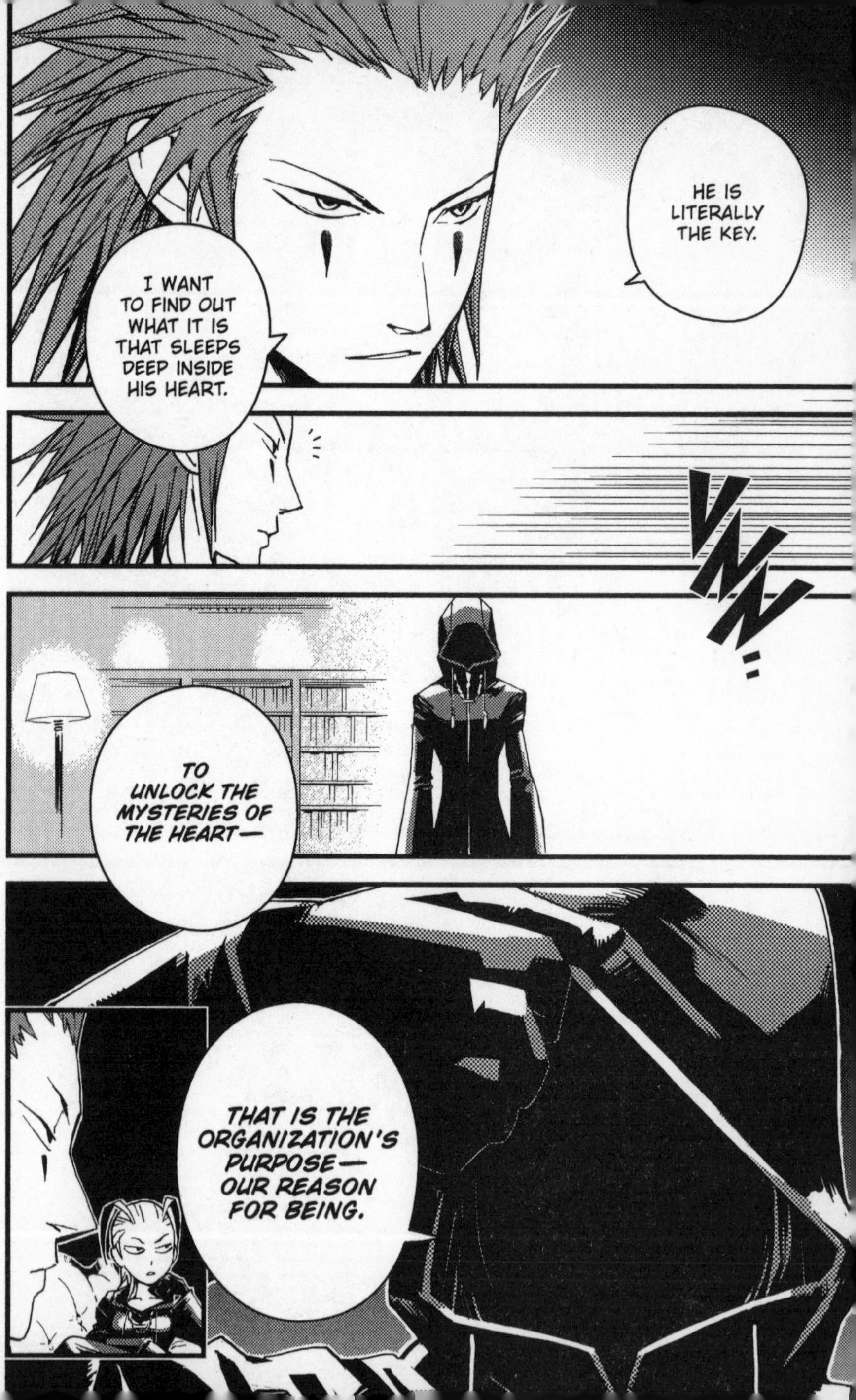
HE IS LITERALLY THE KEY.
I WANT TO FIND OUT WHAT IT IS THAT SLEEPS DEEP INSIDE HIS HEART.
VNN
TO UNLOCK THE MYSTERIES OF THE HEART—
THAT IS THE ORGANIZATION'S PURPOSE— OUR REASON FOR BEING.

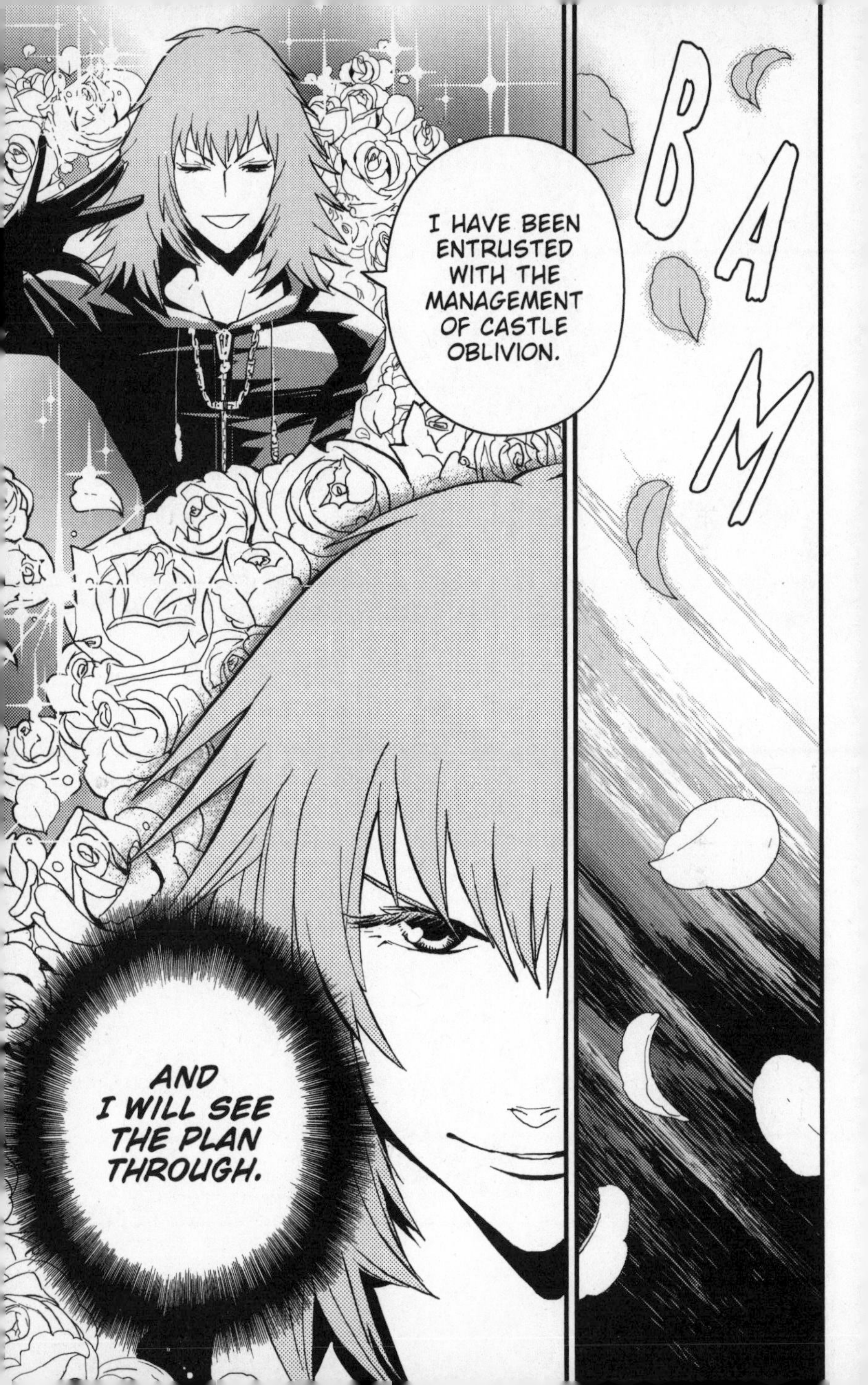
BAM
I HAVE BEEN ENTRUSTED WITH THE MANAGEMENT OF CASTLE OBLIVION.
AND I WILL SEE THE PLAN THROUGH.

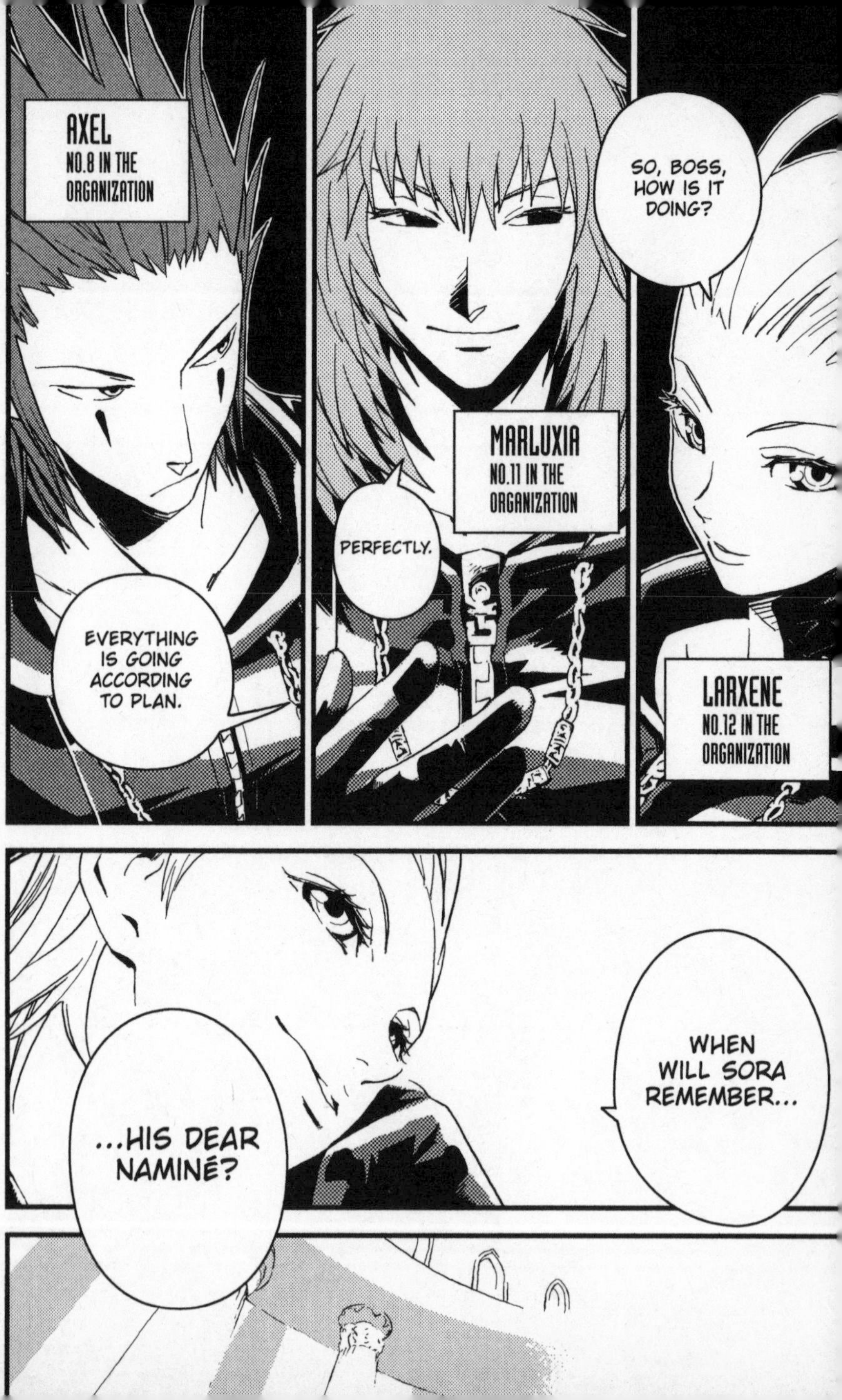
SO, BOSS, HOW IS IT DOING?
LARXENE
NO.12 IN THE ORGANIZATION
MARLUXIA
NO.11 IN THE ORGANIZATION
PERFECTLY.
AXEL
NO.8 IN THE ORGANIZATION
EVERYTHING IS GOING ACCORDING TO PLAN.
WHEN WILL SORA REMEMBER...
...HIS DEAR NAMINÉ?

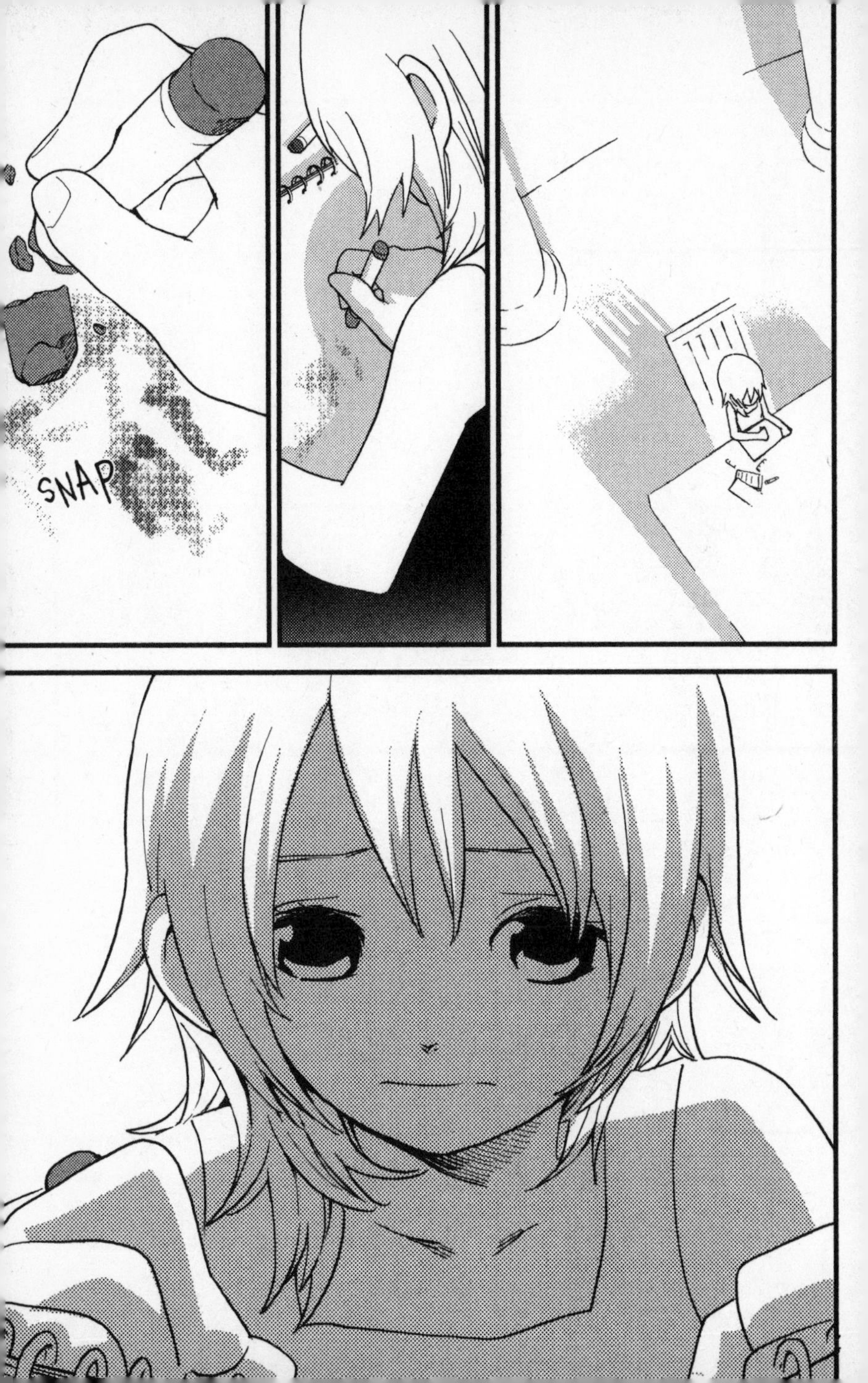
SNAP

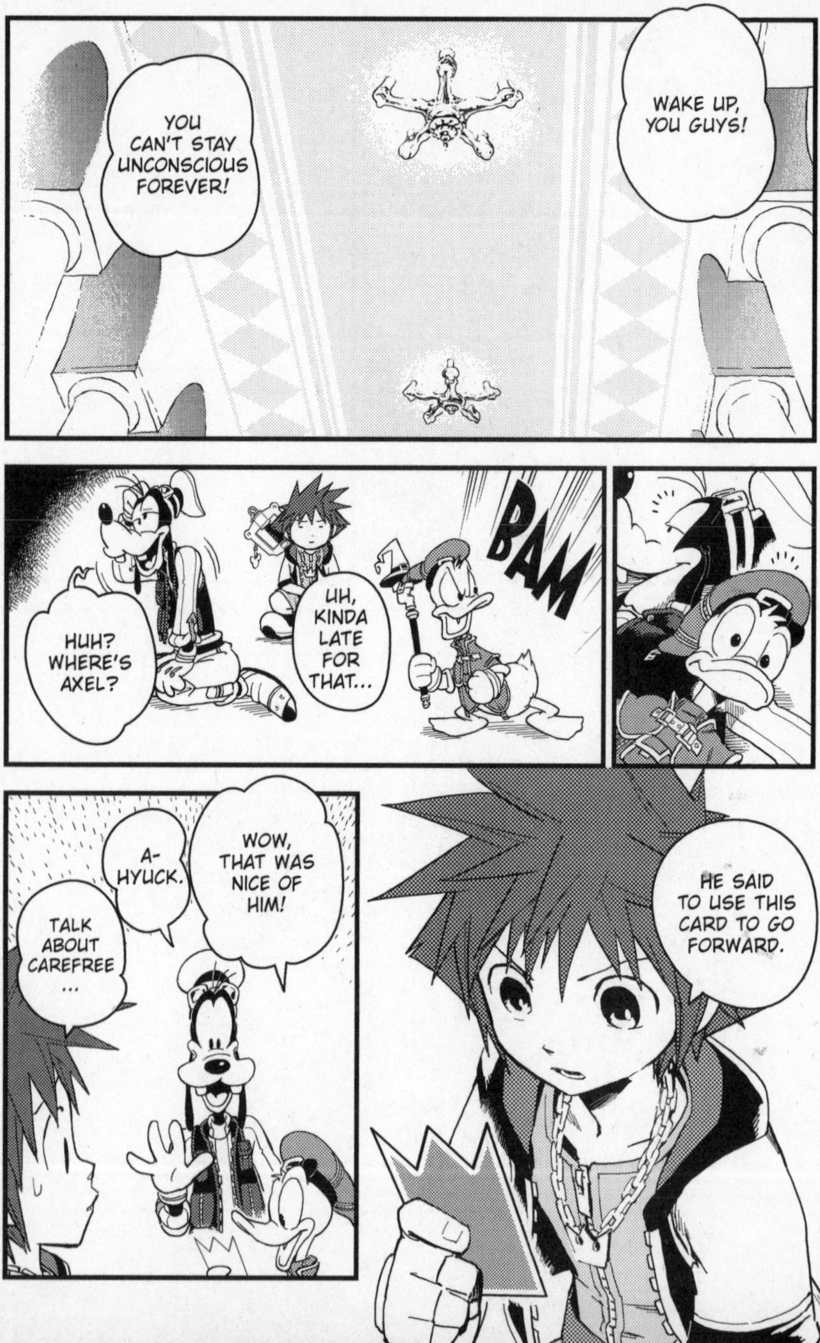
WAKE UP, YOU GUYS!
YOU CAN'T STAY UNCONSCIOUS FOREVER!
BAM
UH, KINDA LATE FOR THAT...
HUH? WHERE'S AXEL?
HE SAID TO USE THIS CARD TO GO FORWARD.
WOW, THAT WAS NICE OF HIM!
A-HYUCK.
TALK ABOUT CAREFREE ...

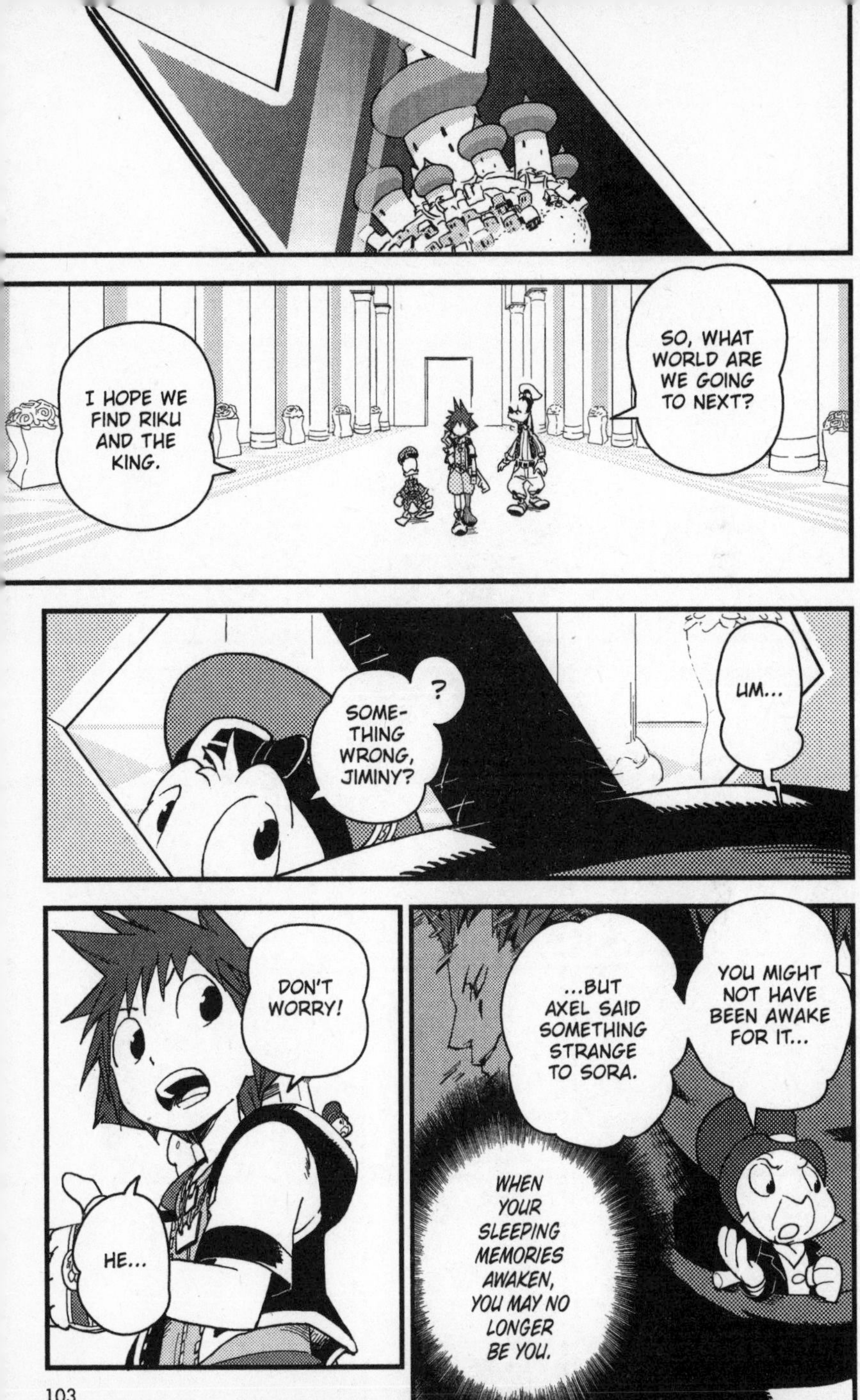
SO, WHAT WORLD ARE WE GOING TO NEXT?
I HOPE WE FIND RIKU AND THE KING.
UM...
?
SOME-THING WRONG, JIMINY?
YOU MIGHT NOT HAVE BEEN AWAKE FOR IT...
...BUT AXEL SAID SOMETHING STRANGE TO SORA.
WHEN YOUR SLEEPING MEMORIES AWAKEN, YOU MAY NO LONGER BE YOU.
DON'T WORRY!
HE...

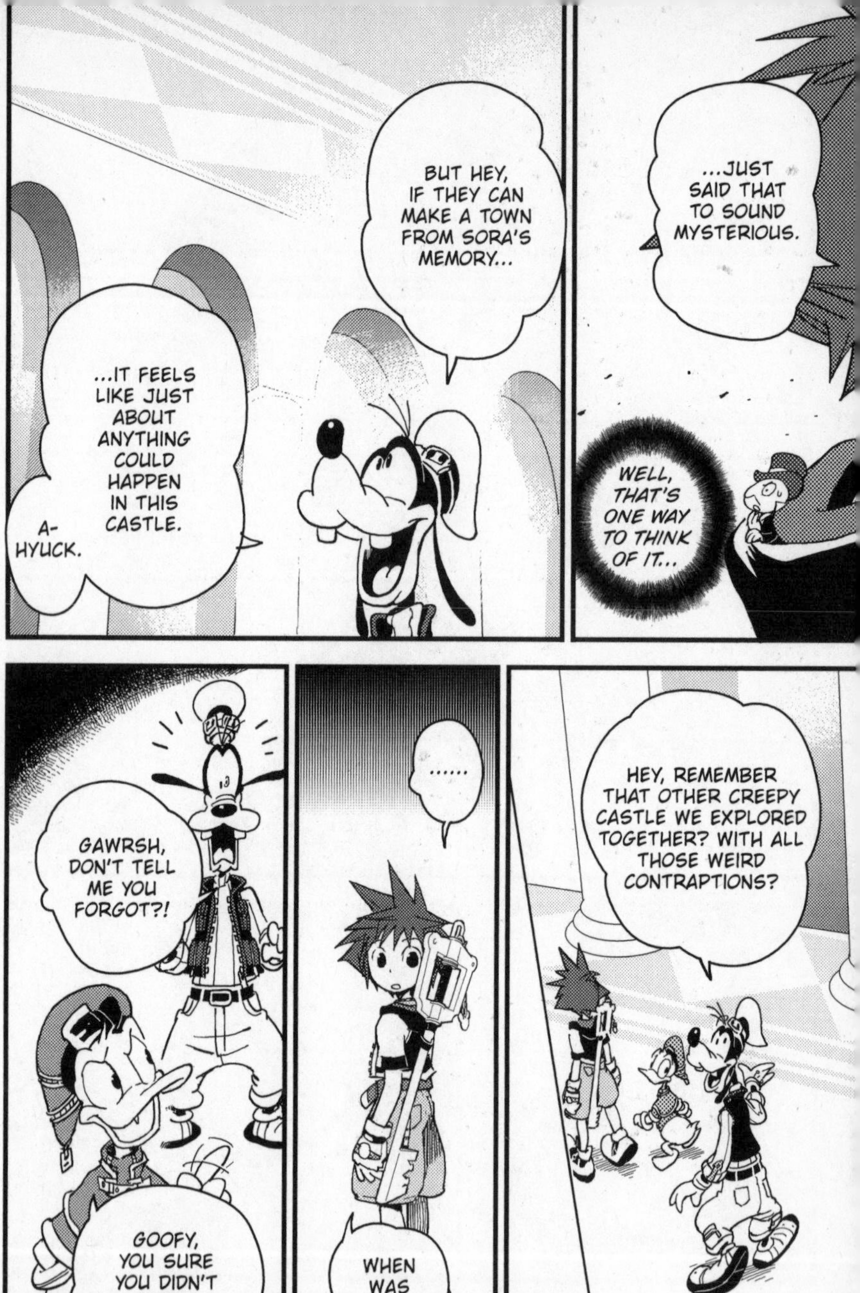
...JUST SAID THAT TO SOUND MYSTERIOUS.
WELL, THAT'S ONE WAY TO THINK OF IT...
BUT HEY, IF THEY CAN MAKE A TOWN FROM SORA'S MEMORY...
...IT FEELS LIKE JUST ABOUT ANYTHING COULD HAPPEN IN THIS CASTLE.
A-HYUCK.
HEY, REMEMBER THAT OTHER CREEPY CASTLE WE EXPLORED TOGETHER? WITH ALL THOSE WEIRD CONTRAPTIONS?
......
WHEN WAS THAT?
GAWRSH, DON'T TELL ME YOU FORGOT?!
GOOFY, YOU SURE YOU DIDN'T MAKE IT UP?

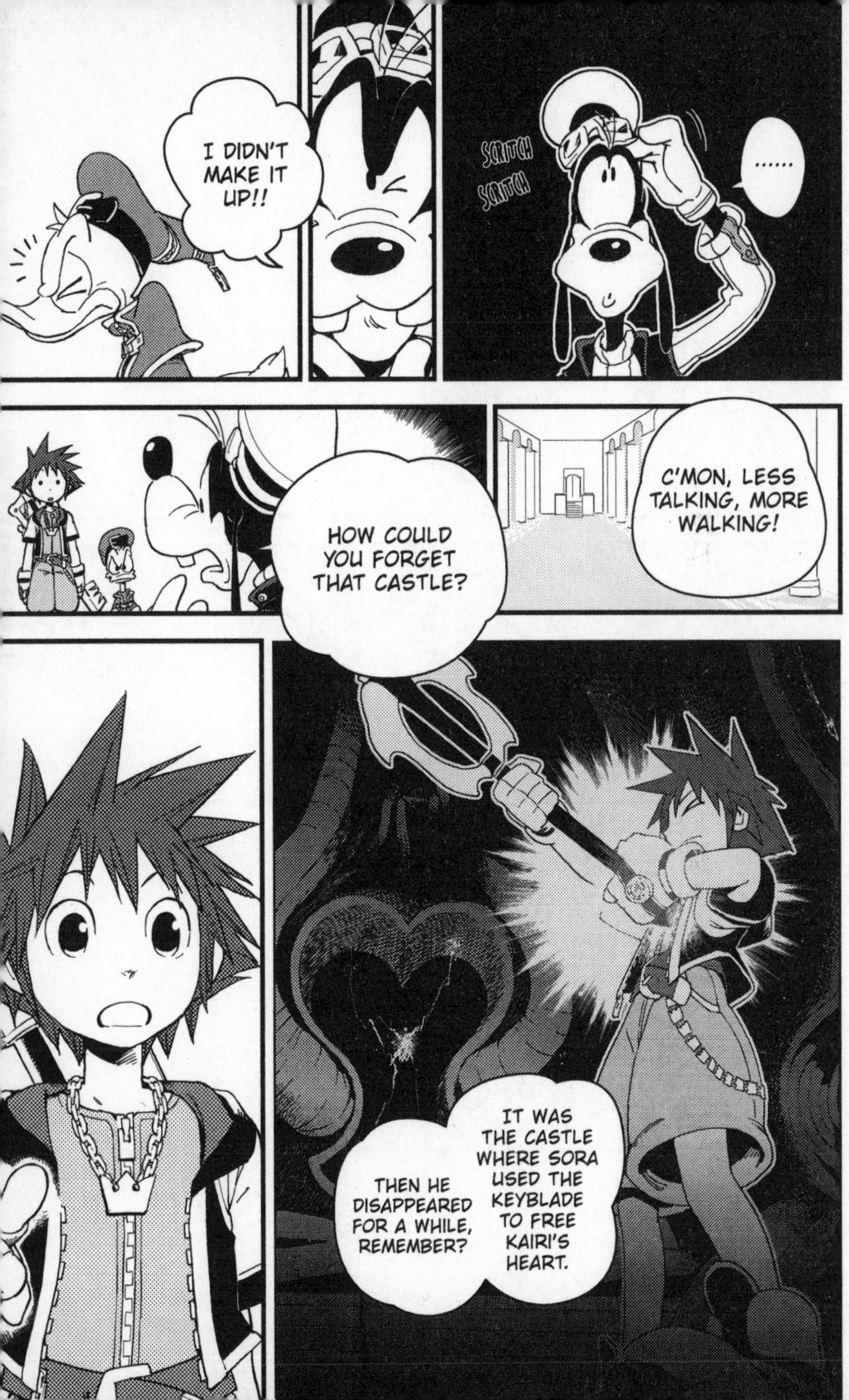
......
SCRITCH
SCRITCH
I DIDN'T MAKE IT UP!!
C'MON, LESS TALKING, MORE WALKING!
HOW COULD YOU FORGET THAT CASTLE?
IT WAS THE CASTLE WHERE SORA USED THE KEYBLADE TO FREE KAIRI'S HEART.
THEN HE DISAPPEARED FOR A WHILE, REMEMBER?

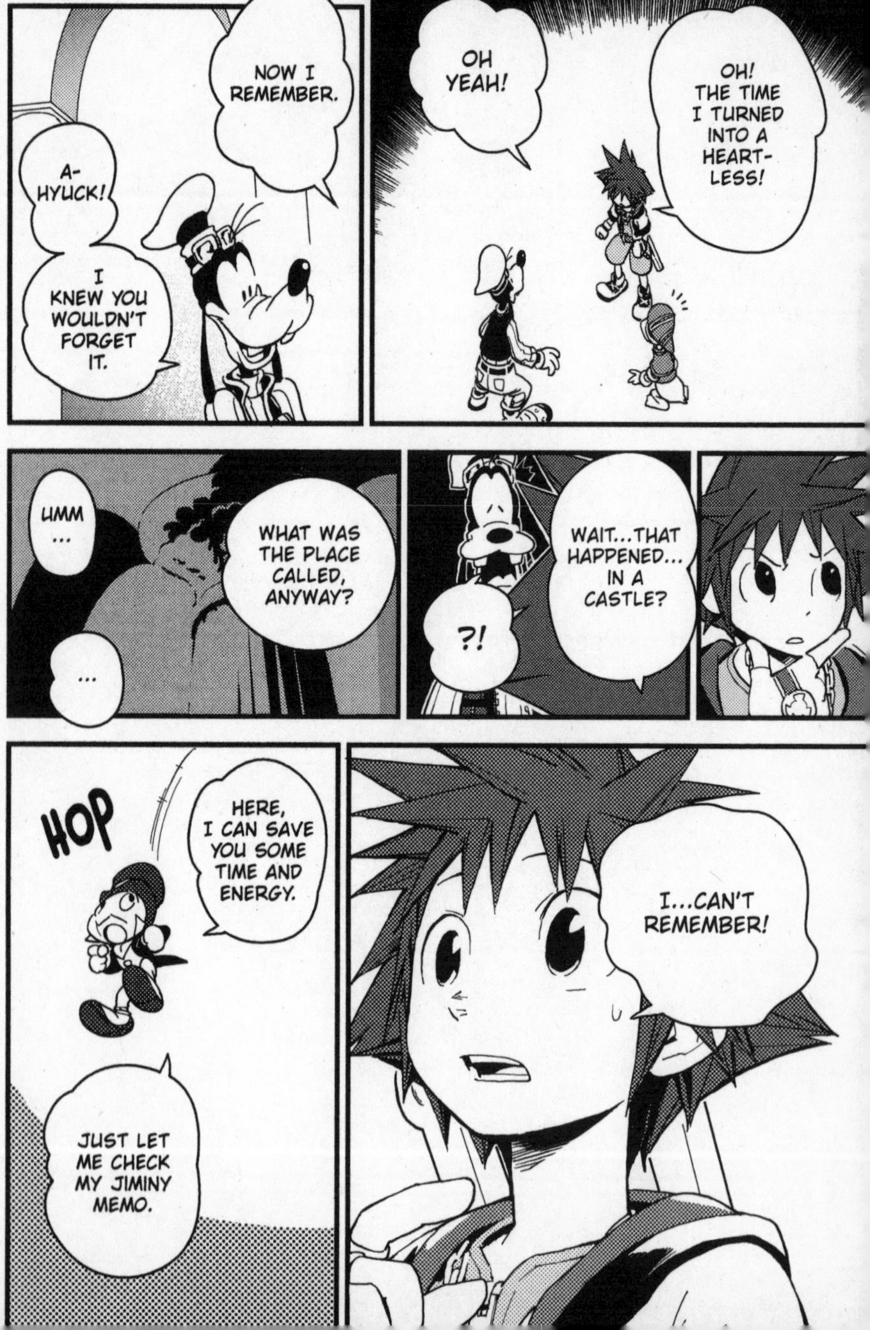
OH! THE TIME I TURNED INTO A HEART-LESS!
OH YEAH!
NOW I REMEMBER.
A-HYUCK!
I KNEW YOU WOULDN'T FORGET IT.
WAIT...THAT HAPPENED... IN A CASTLE?
?!
WHAT WAS THE PLACE CALLED, ANYWAY?
UMM ...
...
I...CAN'T REMEMBER!
HOP
HERE, I CAN SAVE YOU SOME TIME AND ENERGY.
JUST LET ME CHECK MY JIMINY MEMO.

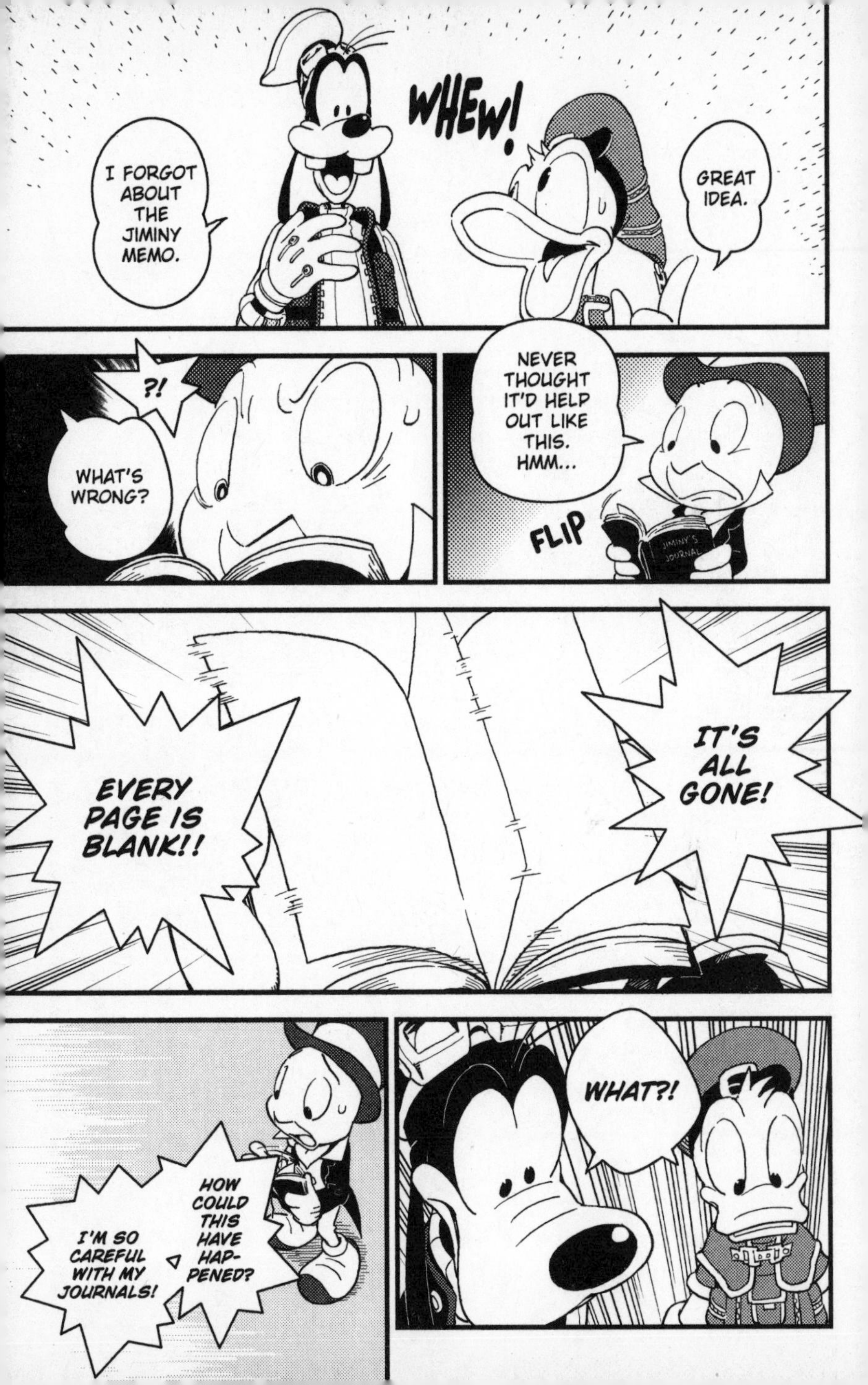
WHEW!
I FORGOT ABOUT THE JIMINY MEMO.
GREAT IDEA.
NEVER THOUGHT IT'D HELP OUT LIKE THIS. HMM...
FLIP
JIMINY'S JOURNAL
?!
WHAT'S WRONG?
IT'S ALL GONE!
EVERY PAGE IS BLANK!!
WHAT?!
HOW COULD THIS HAVE HAP-PENED?
I'M SO CAREFUL WITH MY JOURNALS!

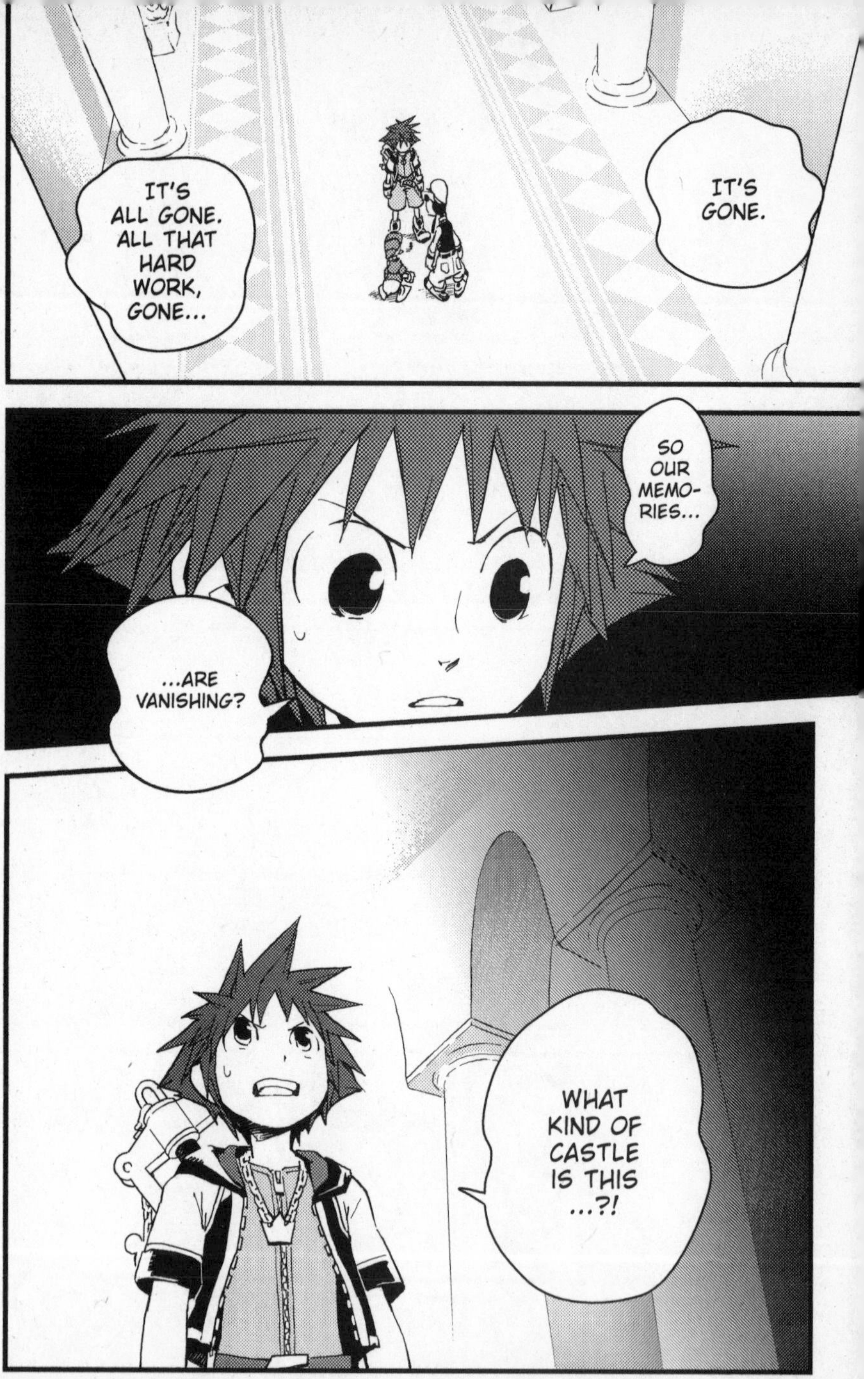
IT'S GONE.
IT'S ALL GONE. ALL THAT HARD WORK, GONE...
SO OUR MEMO-RIES...
...ARE VANISHING?
WHAT KIND OF CASTLE IS THIS ...?!

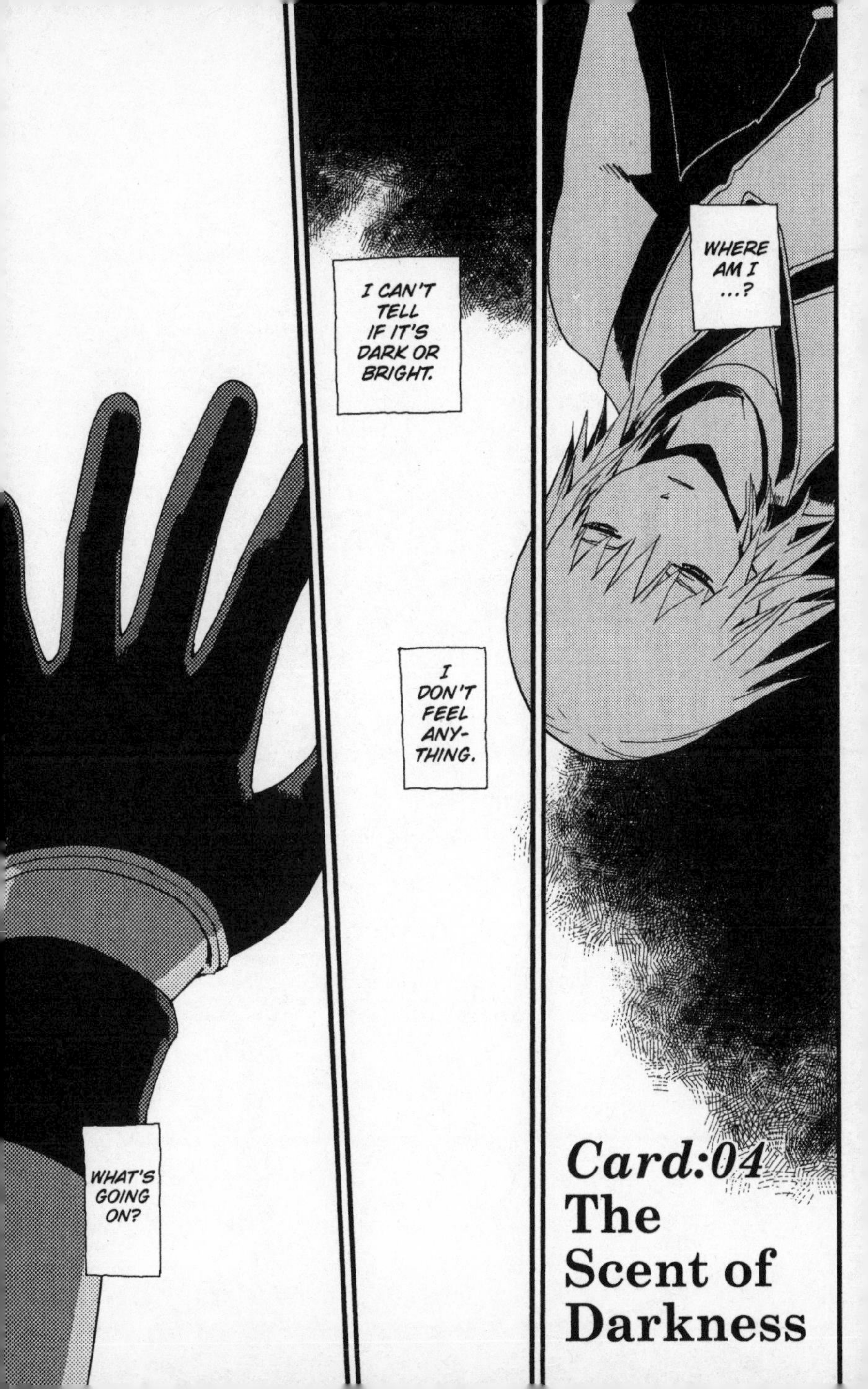
WHERE AM I ...?
Card:04 The Scent of Darkness
I CAN'T TELL IF IT'S DARK OR BRIGHT.
I DON'T FEEL ANYTHING.
WHAT'S GOING ON?

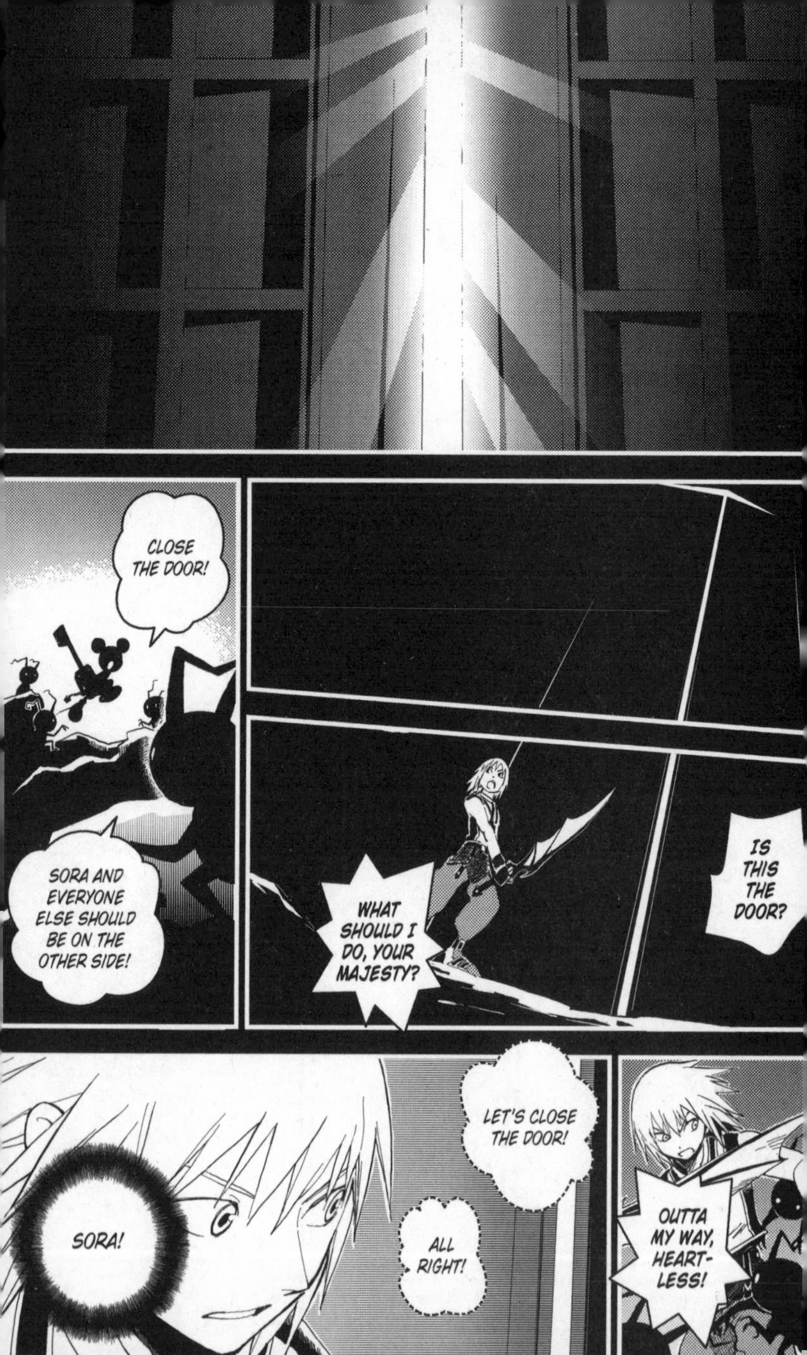
IS THIS THE DOOR?
WHAT SHOULD I DO, YOUR MAJESTY?
CLOSE THE DOOR!
SORA AND EVERYONE ELSE SHOULD BE ON THE OTHER SIDE!
OUTTA MY WAY, HEARTLESS!
LET'S CLOSE THE DOOR!
ALL RIGHT!
SORA!

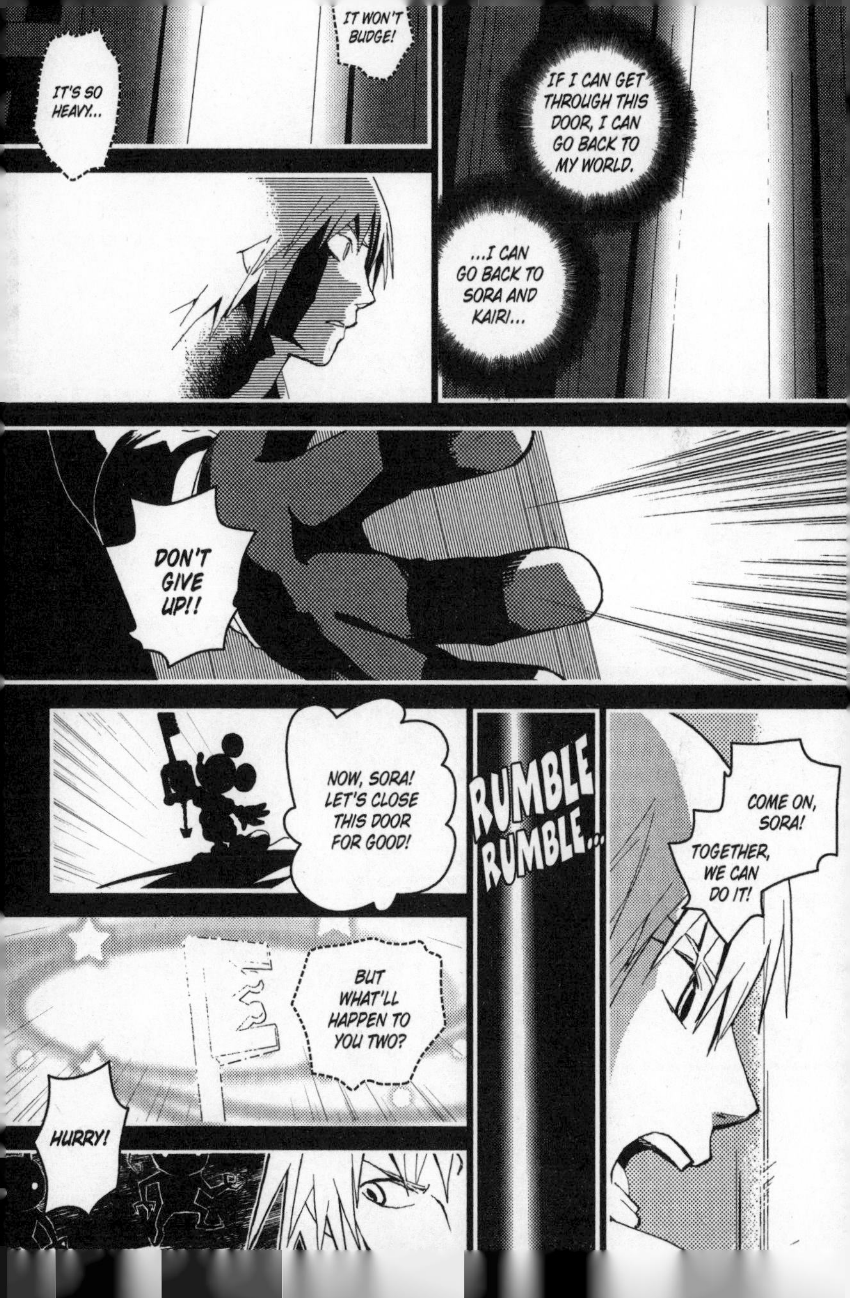
IF I CAN GET THROUGH THIS DOOR, I CAN GO BACK TO MY WORLD.
...I CAN GO BACK TO SORA AND KAIRI...
IT WON'T BUDGE!
IT'S SO HEAVY...
DON'T GIVE UP!!
COME ON, SORA!
TOGETHER, WE CAN DO IT!
RUMBLE RUMBLE...
NOW, SORA! LET'S CLOSE THIS DOOR FOR GOOD!
BUT WHAT'LL HAPPEN TO YOU TWO?
HURRY!

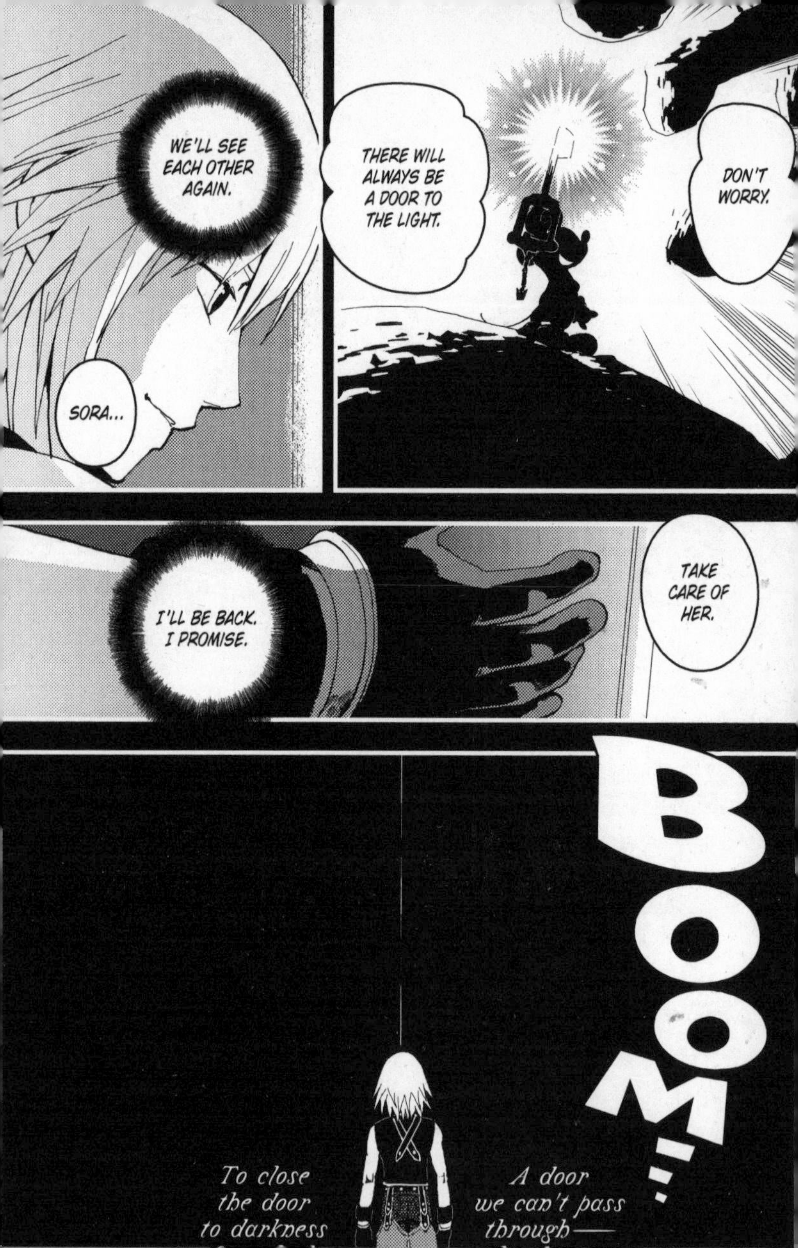
DON'T WORRY.
THERE WILL ALWAYS BE A DOOR TO THE LIGHT.
WE'LL SEE EACH OTHER AGAIN.
SORA...
TAKE CARE OF HER.
I'LL BE BACK. I PROMISE.
BOOM!!
A door we can't pass through—
To close the door to darkness

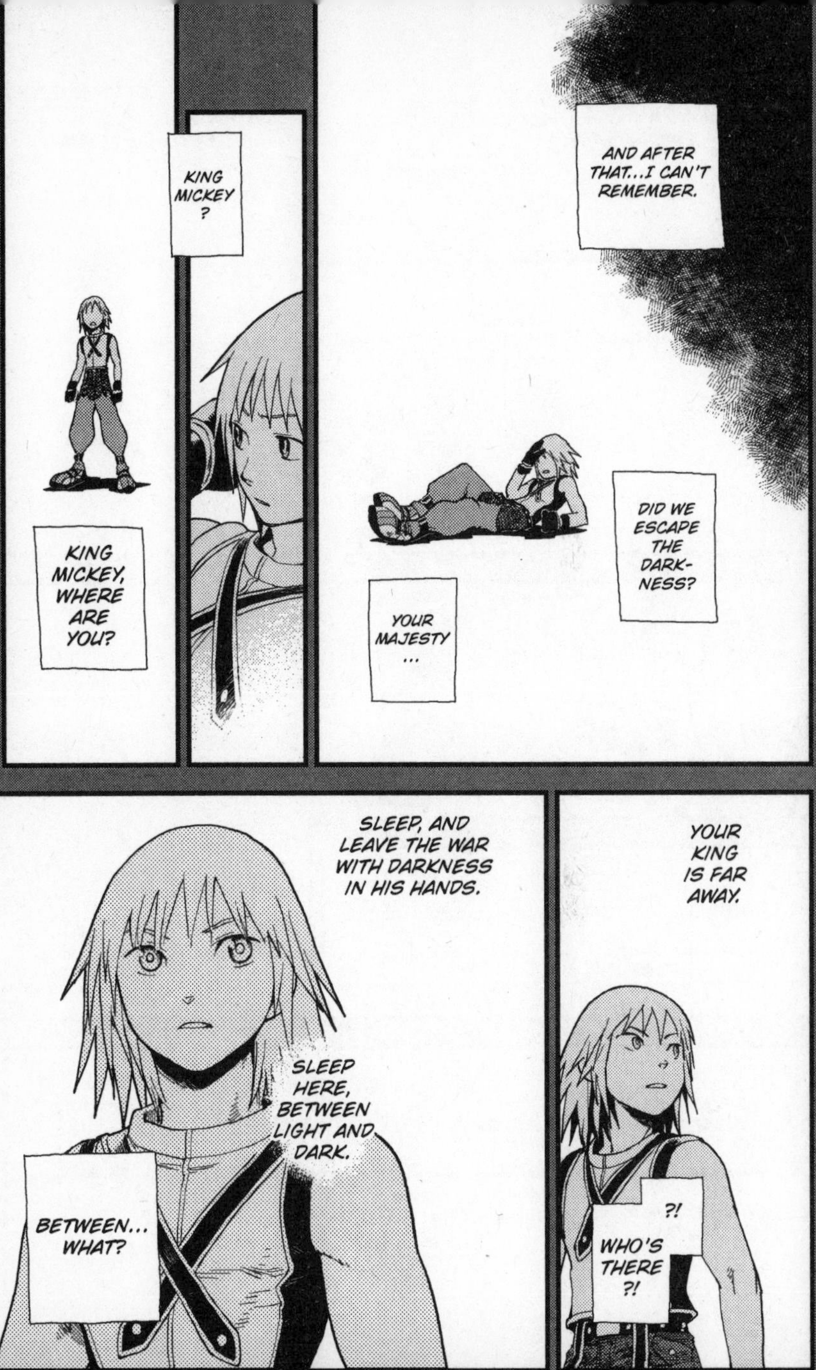
AND AFTER THAT...I CAN'T REMEMBER.
DID WE ESCAPE THE DARK-NESS?
YOUR MAJESTY...
KING MICKEY?
KING MICKEY, WHERE ARE YOU?
YOUR KING IS FAR AWAY.
?!
WHO'S THERE?!
SLEEP, AND LEAVE THE WAR WITH DARKNESS IN HIS HANDS.
SLEEP HERE, BETWEEN LIGHT AND DARK.
BETWEEN... WHAT?

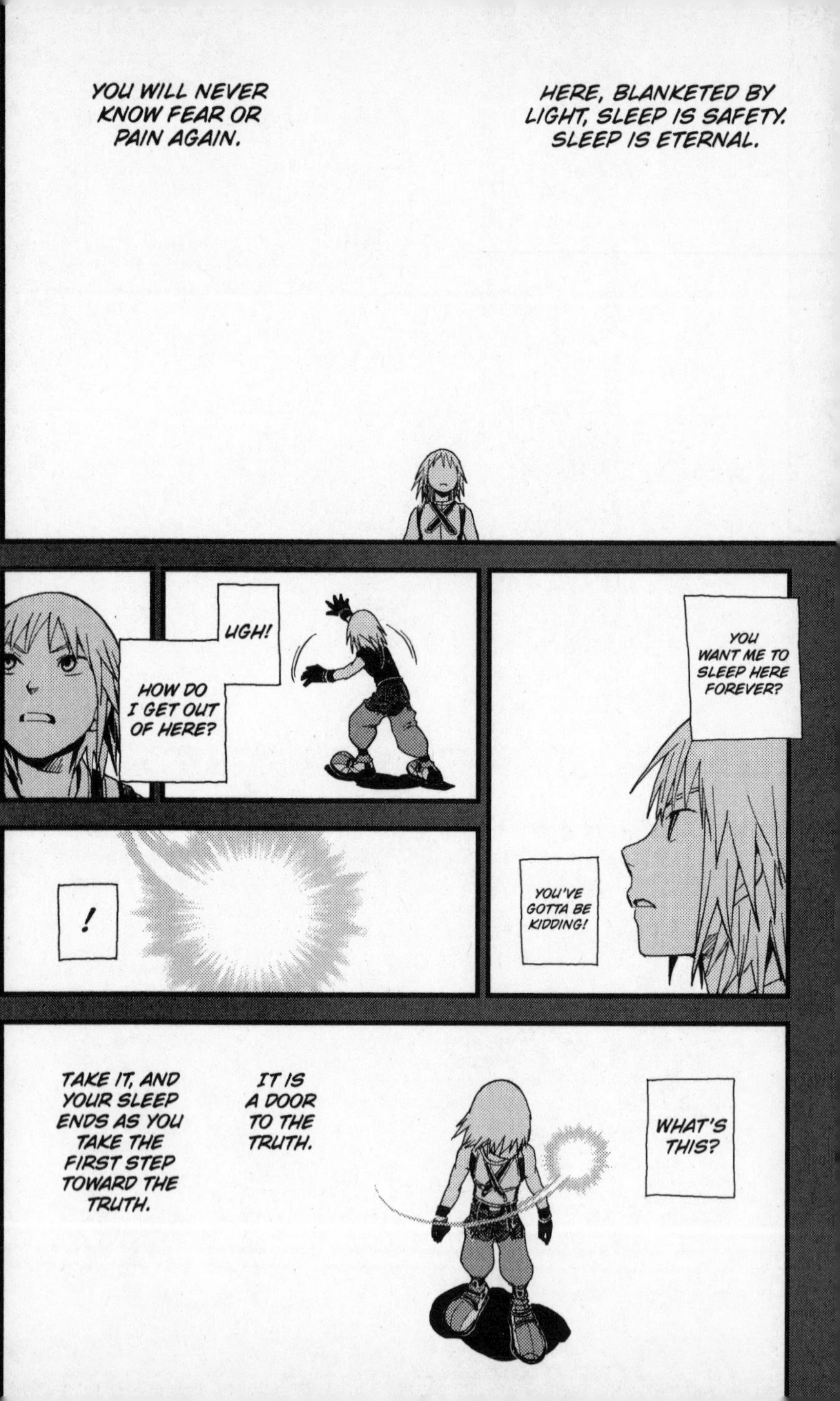
HERE, BLANKETED BY LIGHT, SLEEP IS SAFETY. SLEEP IS ETERNAL.
YOU WILL NEVER KNOW FEAR OR PAIN AGAIN.
YOU WANT ME TO SLEEP HERE FOREVER?
YOU'VE GOTTA BE KIDDING!
UGH!
HOW DO I GET OUT OF HERE?
!
WHAT'S THIS?
IT IS A DOOR TO THE TRUTH.
TAKE IT, AND YOUR SLEEP ENDS AS YOU TAKE THE FIRST STEP TOWARD THE TRUTH.

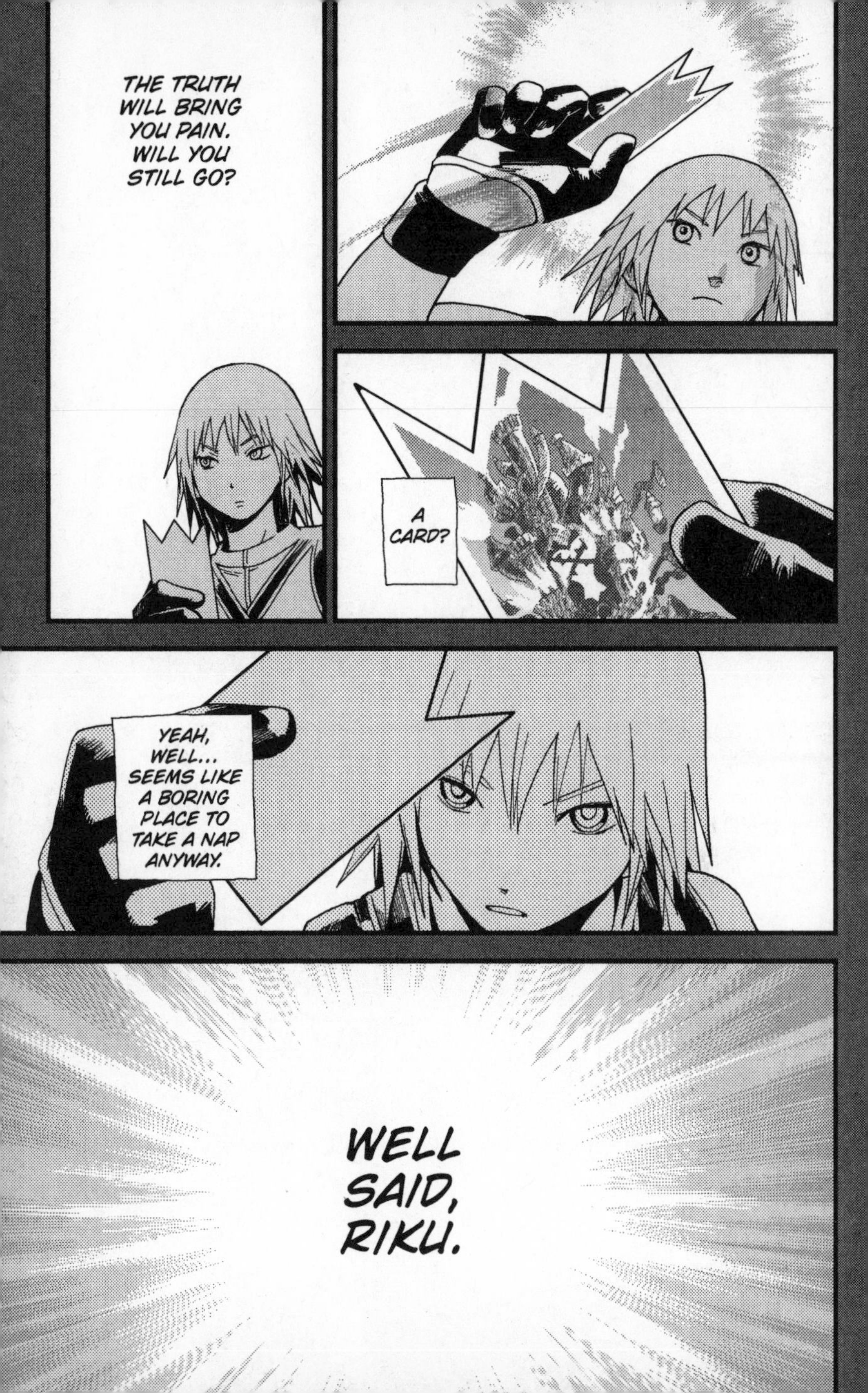
A CARD?
THE TRUTH WILL BRING YOU PAIN. WILL YOU STILL GO?
YEAH, WELL... SEEMS LIKE A BORING PLACE TO TAKE A NAP ANYWAY.
WELL SAID, RIKU.

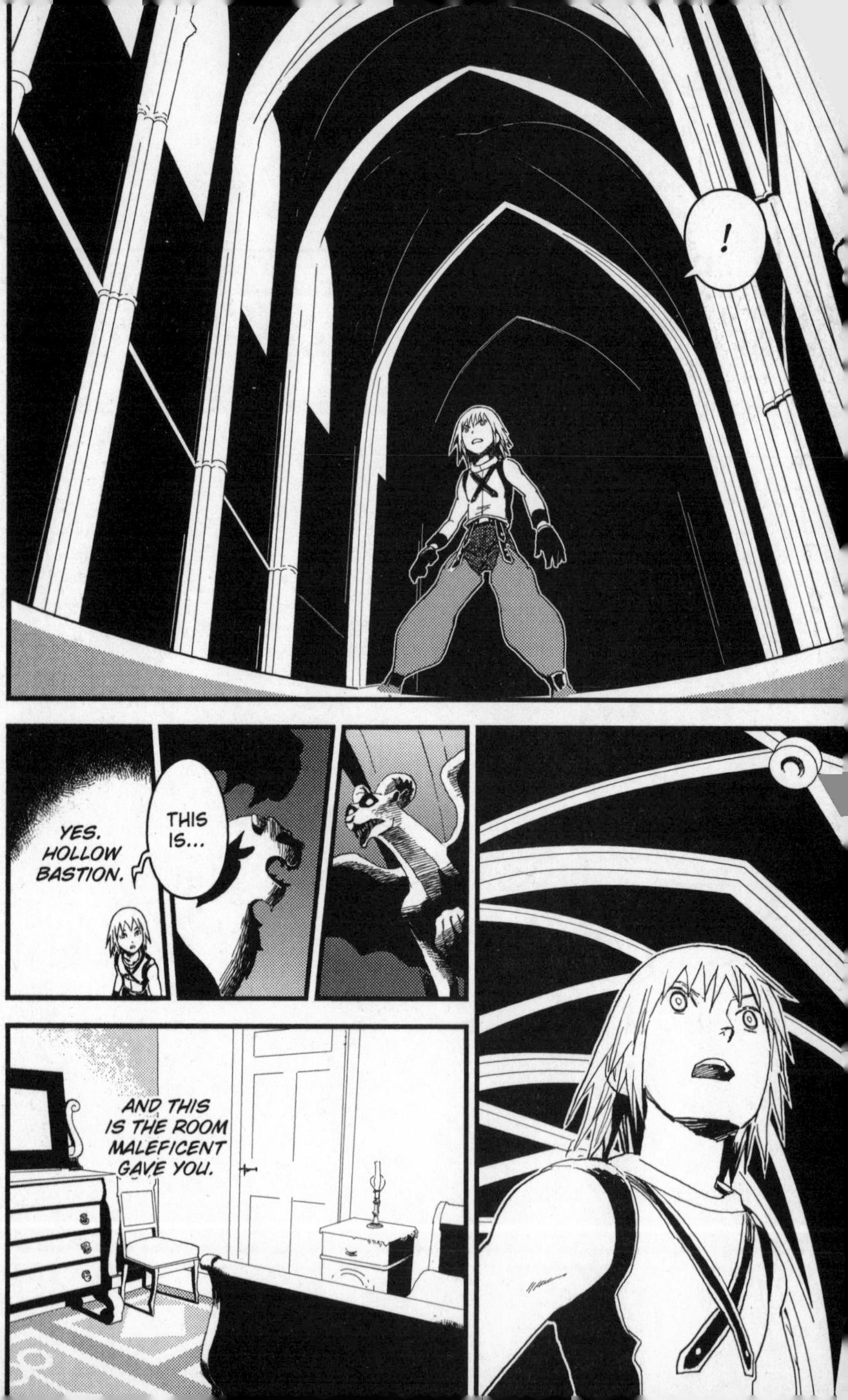
!
THIS IS...
YES. HOLLOW BASTION.
AND THIS IS THE ROOM MALEFICENT GAVE YOU.

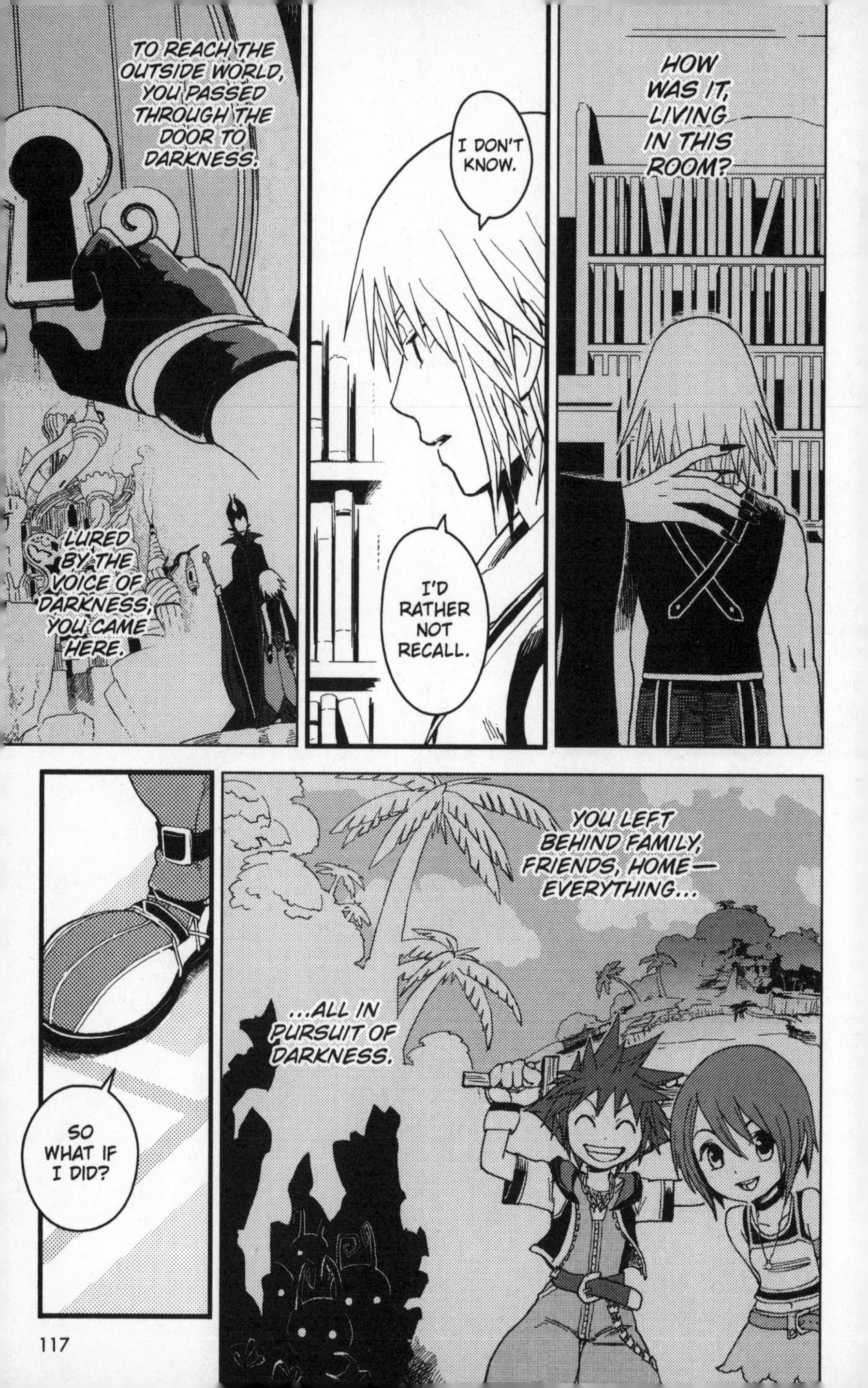
HOW WAS IT, LIVING IN THIS ROOM?
I DON'T KNOW.
I'D RATHER NOT RECALL.
TO REACH THE OUTSIDE WORLD, YOU PASSED THROUGH THE DOOR TO DARKNESS.
LURED BY THE VOICE OF DARKNESS, YOU CAME HERE.
YOU LEFT BEHIND FAMILY, FRIENDS, HOME— EVERYTHING...
...ALL IN PURSUIT OF DARKNESS.
SO WHAT IF I DID?

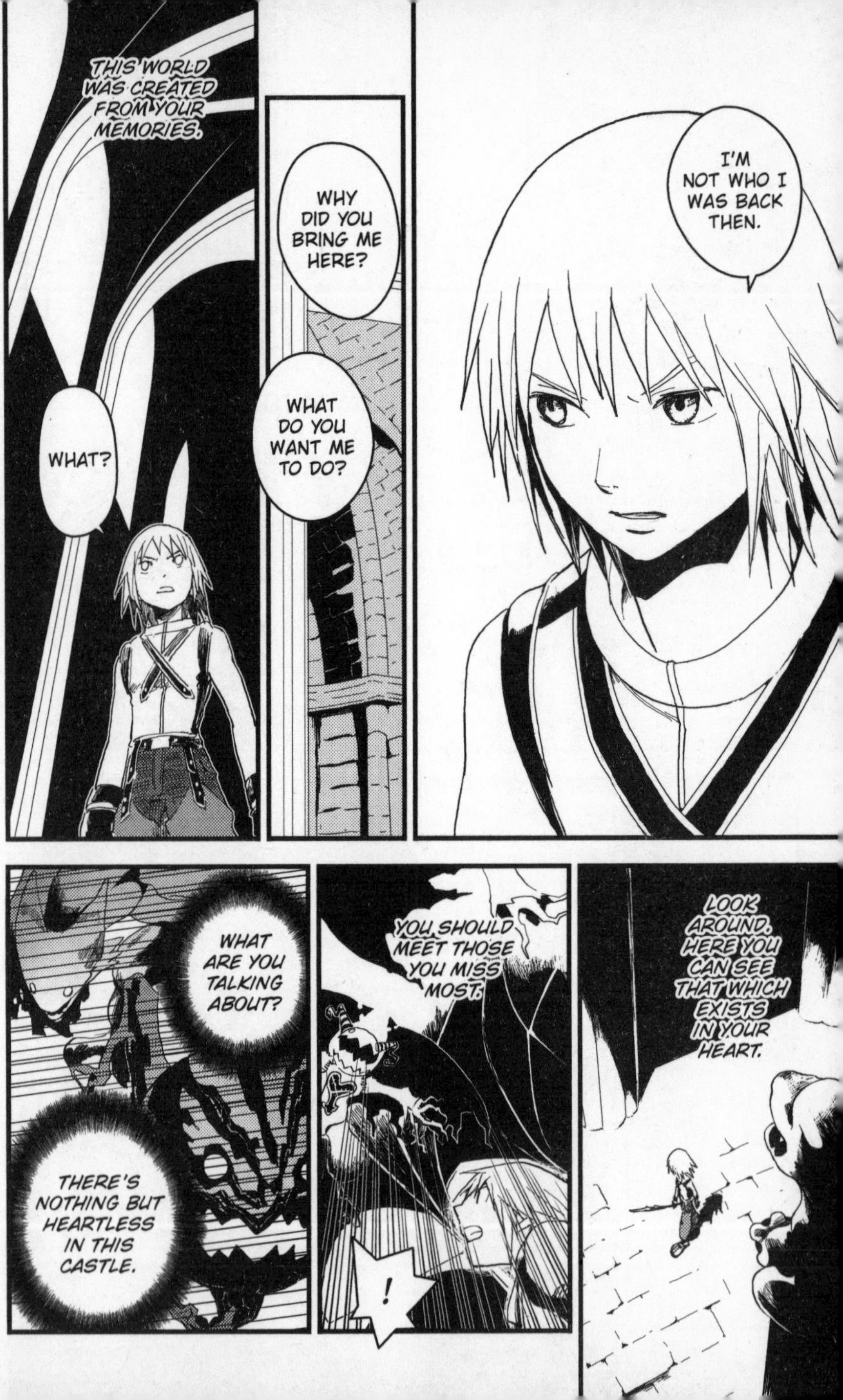
I'M NOT WHO I WAS BACK THEN.
WHY DID YOU BRING ME HERE?
WHAT DO YOU WANT ME TO DO?
THIS WORLD WAS CREATED FROM YOUR MEMORIES.
WHAT?
LOOK AROUND. HERE YOU CAN SEE THAT WHICH EXISTS IN YOUR HEART.
YOU SHOULD MEET THOSE YOU MISS MOST.
!
WHAT ARE YOU TALKING ABOUT?
THERE'S NOTHING BUT HEARTLESS IN THIS CASTLE.

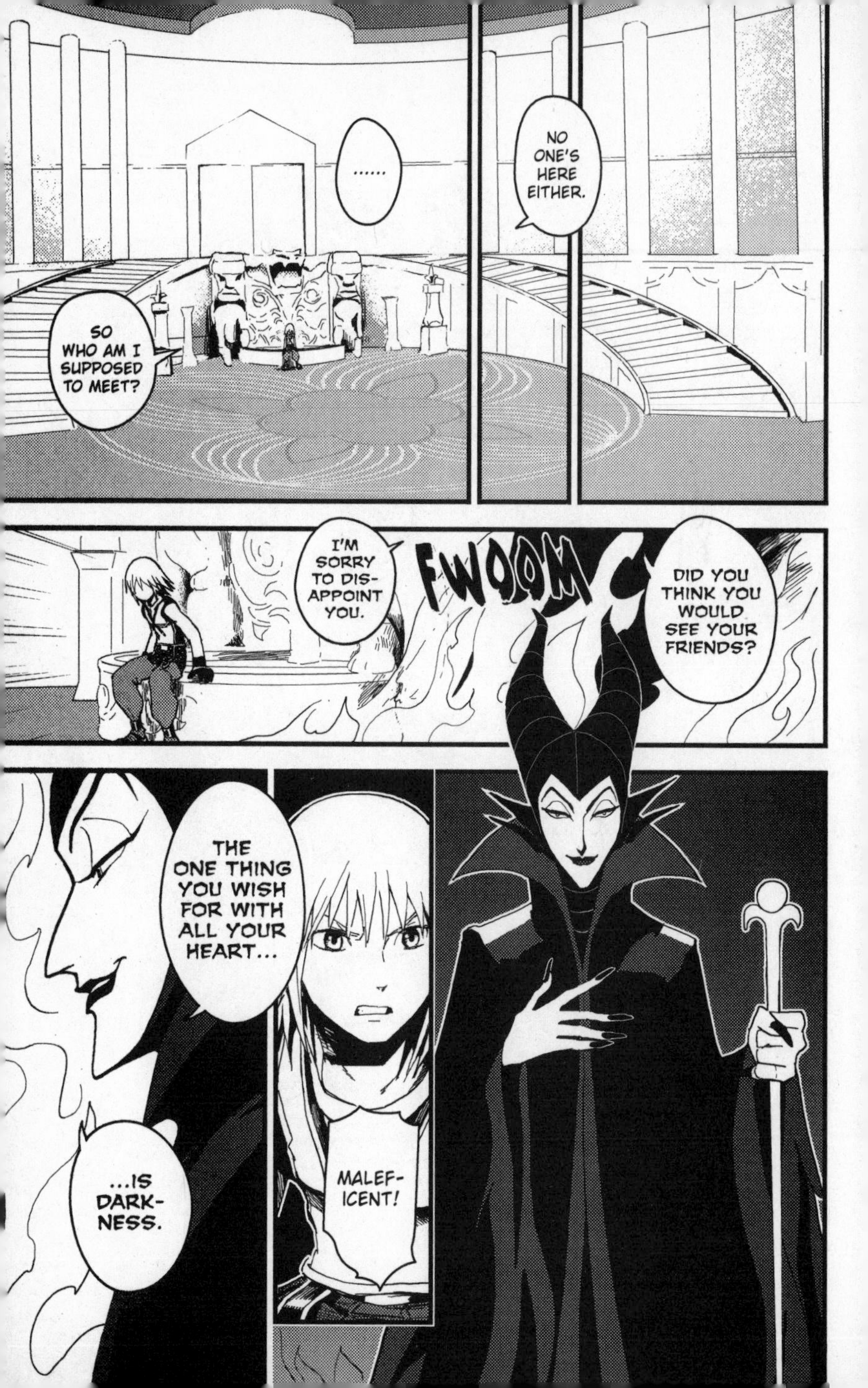
NO ONE'S HERE EITHER.
......
SO WHO AM I SUPPOSED TO MEET?
DID YOU THINK YOU WOULD SEE YOUR FRIENDS?
FWOOM
I'M SORRY TO DIS-APPOINT YOU.
MALEF-ICENT!
THE ONE THING YOU WISH FOR WITH ALL YOUR HEART...
...IS DARK-NESS.

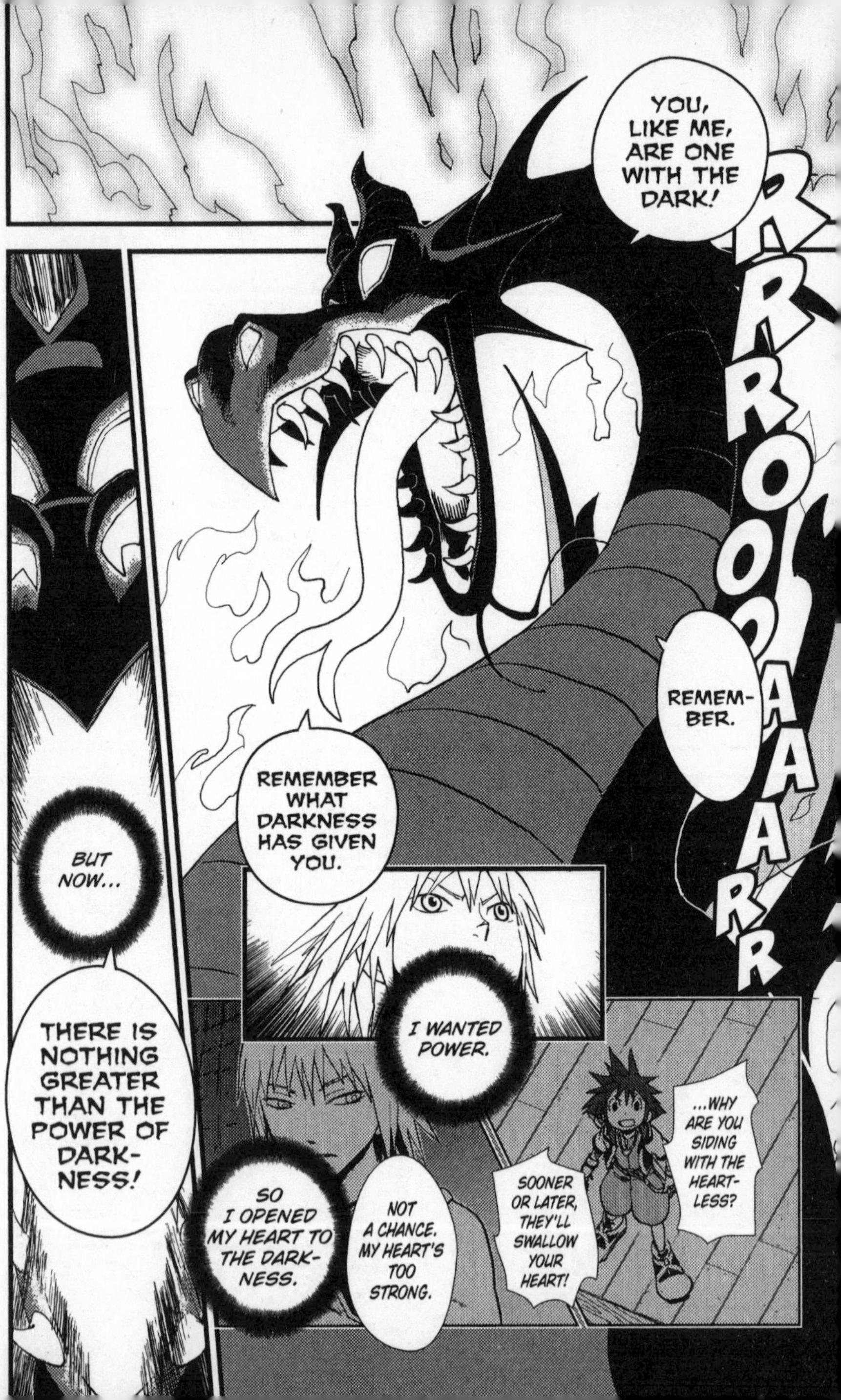
YOU, LIKE ME, ARE ONE WITH THE DARK!
RRROOOAAARR
REMEM-BER.
REMEMBER WHAT DARKNESS HAS GIVEN YOU.
...WHY ARE YOU SIDING WITH THE HEART-LESS?
SOONER OR LATER, THEY'LL SWALLOW YOUR HEART!
NOT A CHANCE. MY HEART'S TOO STRONG.
I WANTED POWER.
SO I OPENED MY HEART TO THE DARK-NESS.
BUT NOW...
THERE IS NOTHING GREATER THAN THE POWER OF DARK-NESS!

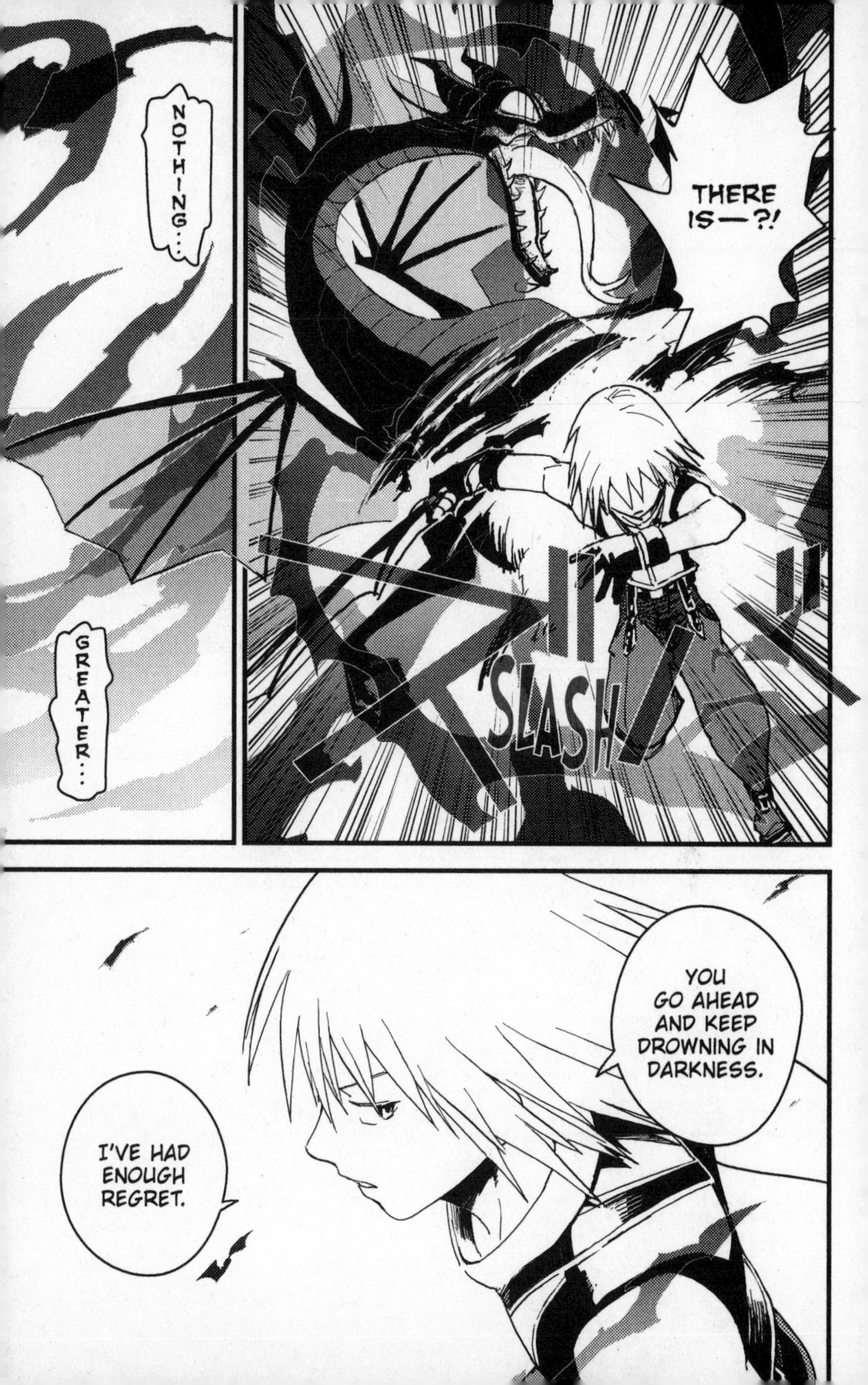
THERE IS—?!
SLASH
NOTHING...
GREATER...
YOU GO AHEAD AND KEEP DROWNING IN DARKNESS.
I'VE HAD ENOUGH REGRET.

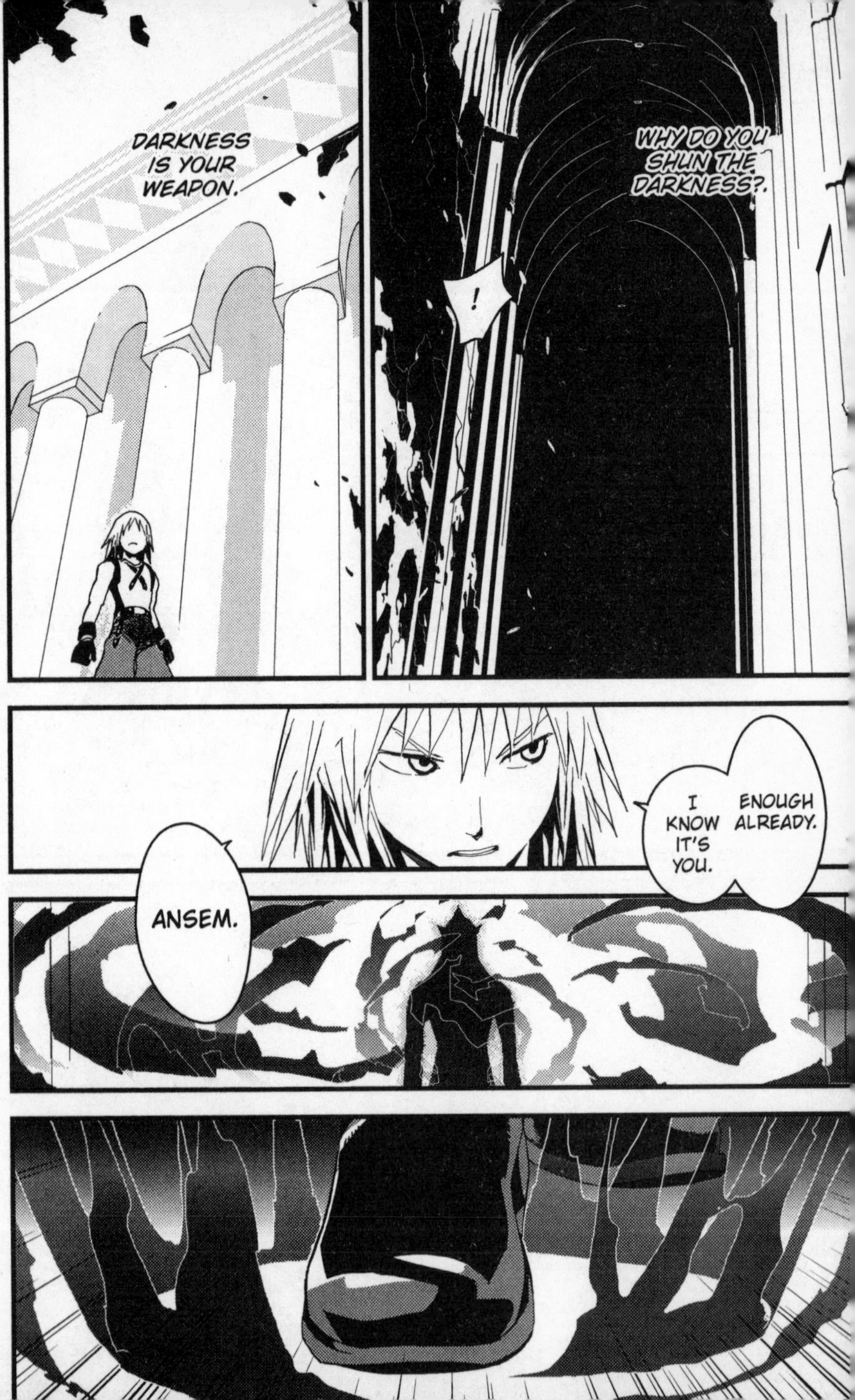
WHY DO YOU SHUN THE DARKNESS?.
!
DARKNESS IS YOUR WEAPON.
ENOUGH ALREADY.
I KNOW IT'S YOU.
ANSEM.

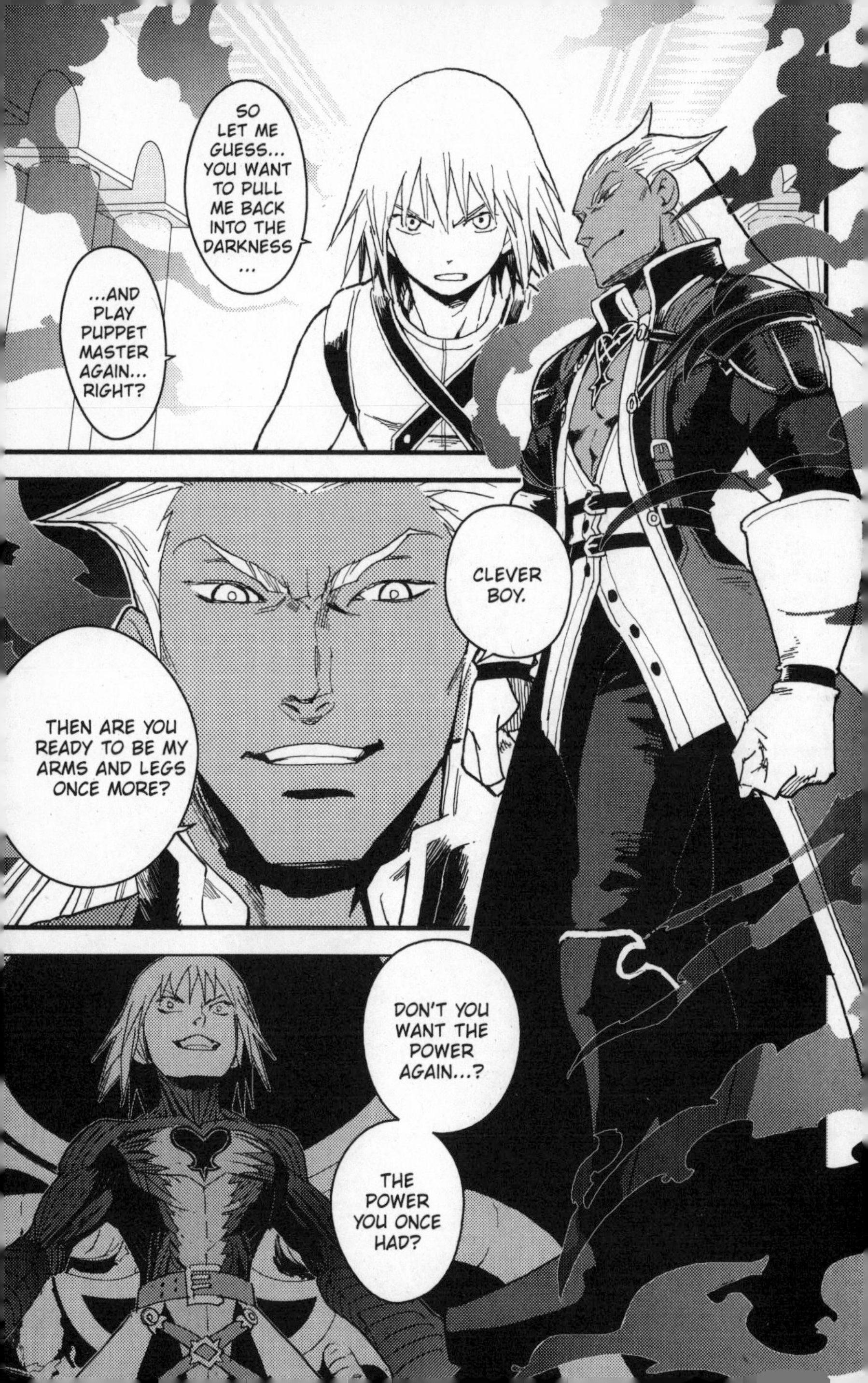
SO LET ME GUESS... YOU WANT TO PULL ME BACK INTO THE DARKNESS...
...AND PLAY PUPPET MASTER AGAIN... RIGHT?
CLEVER BOY.
THEN ARE YOU READY TO BE MY ARMS AND LEGS ONCE MORE?
DON'T YOU WANT THE POWER AGAIN...?
THE POWER YOU ONCE HAD?

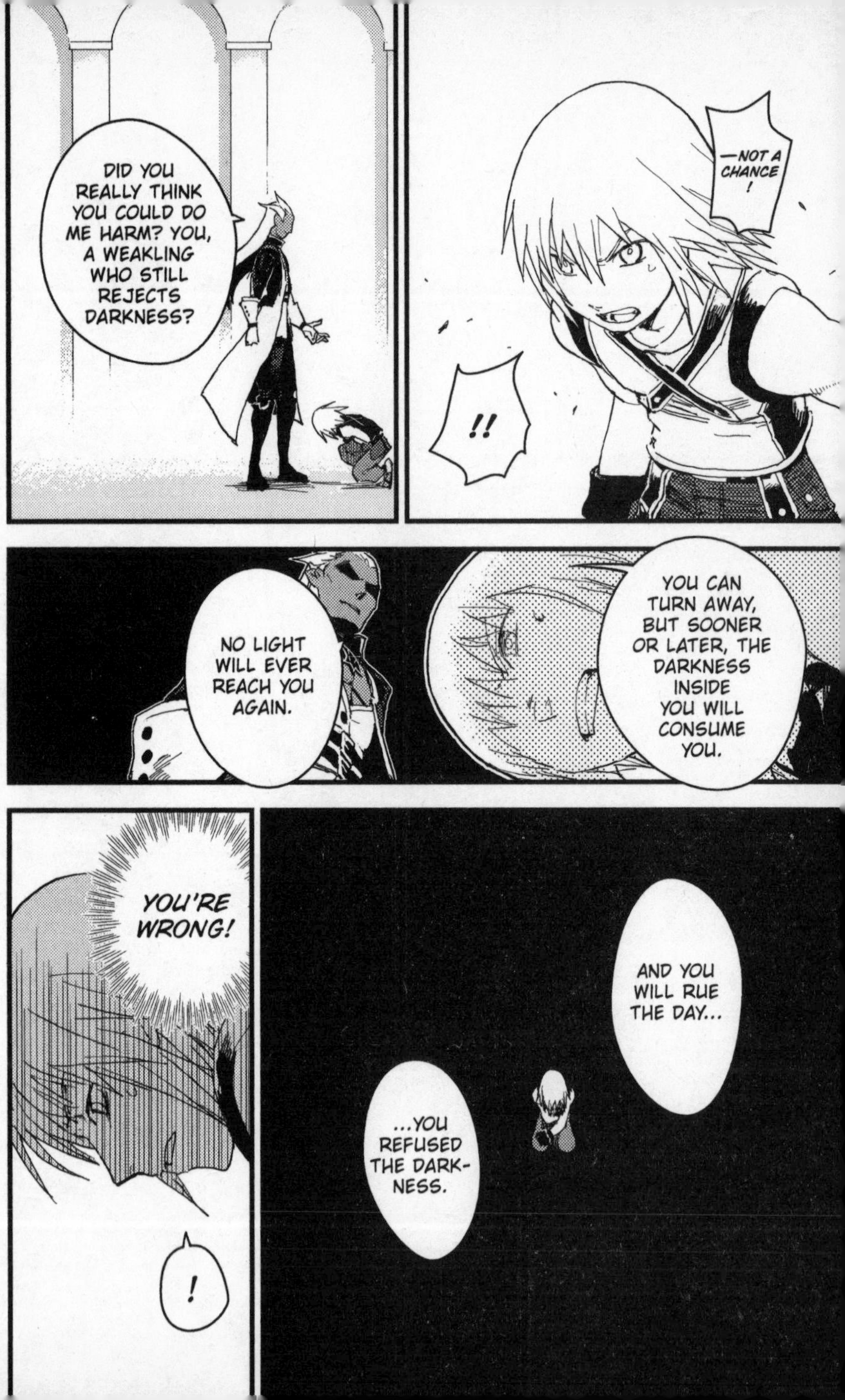
—NOT A CHANCE !
!!
DID YOU REALLY THINK YOU COULD DO ME HARM? YOU, A WEAKLING WHO STILL REJECTS DARKNESS?
YOU CAN TURN AWAY, BUT SOONER OR LATER, THE DARKNESS INSIDE YOU WILL CONSUME YOU.
NO LIGHT WILL EVER REACH YOU AGAIN.
AND YOU WILL RUE THE DAY...
...YOU REFUSED THE DARK-NESS.
YOU'RE WRONG!
!

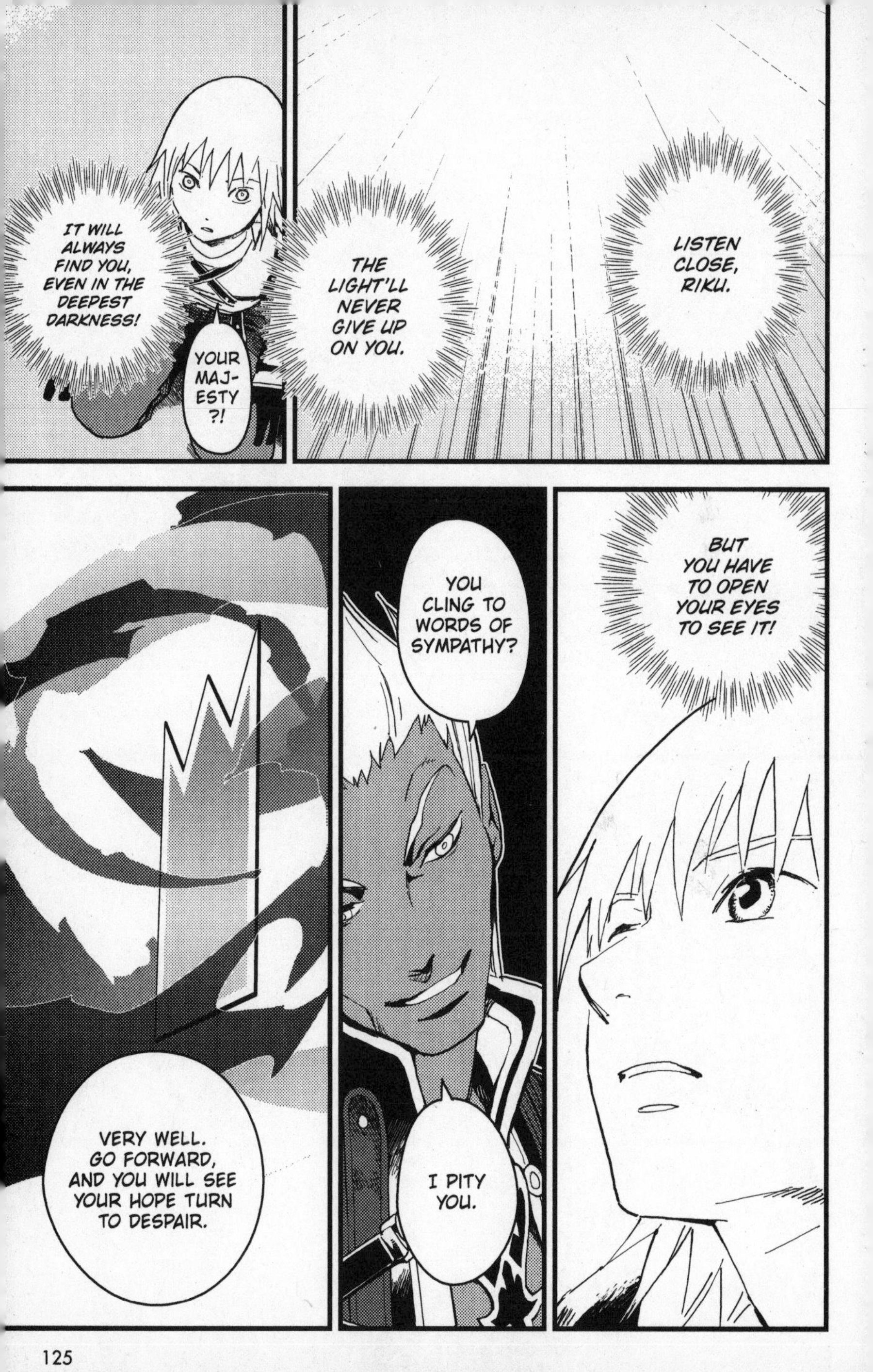
LISTEN CLOSE, RIKU.
THE LIGHT'LL NEVER GIVE UP ON YOU.
IT WILL ALWAYS FIND YOU, EVEN IN THE DEEPEST DARKNESS!
YOUR MAJ-ESTY ?!
BUT YOU HAVE TO OPEN YOUR EYES TO SEE IT!
YOU CLING TO WORDS OF SYMPATHY?
I PITY YOU.
VERY WELL. GO FORWARD, AND YOU WILL SEE YOUR HOPE TURN TO DESPAIR.

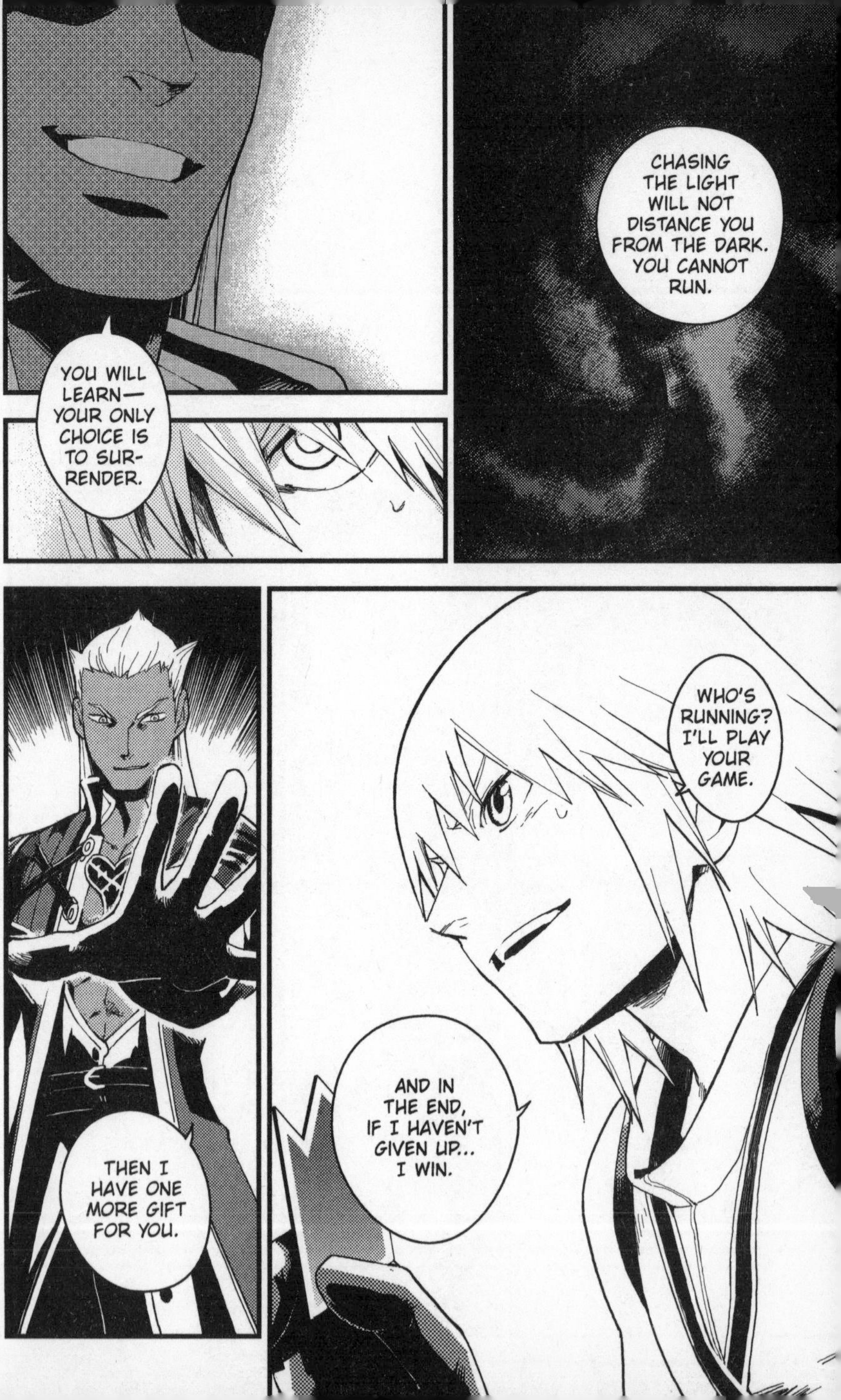
CHASING THE LIGHT WILL NOT DISTANCE YOU FROM THE DARK. YOU CANNOT RUN.
YOU WILL LEARN— YOUR ONLY CHOICE IS TO SUR- RENDER.
WHO'S RUNNING? I'LL PLAY YOUR GAME.
AND IN THE END, IF I HAVEN'T GIVEN UP... I WIN.
THEN I HAVE ONE MORE GIFT FOR YOU.

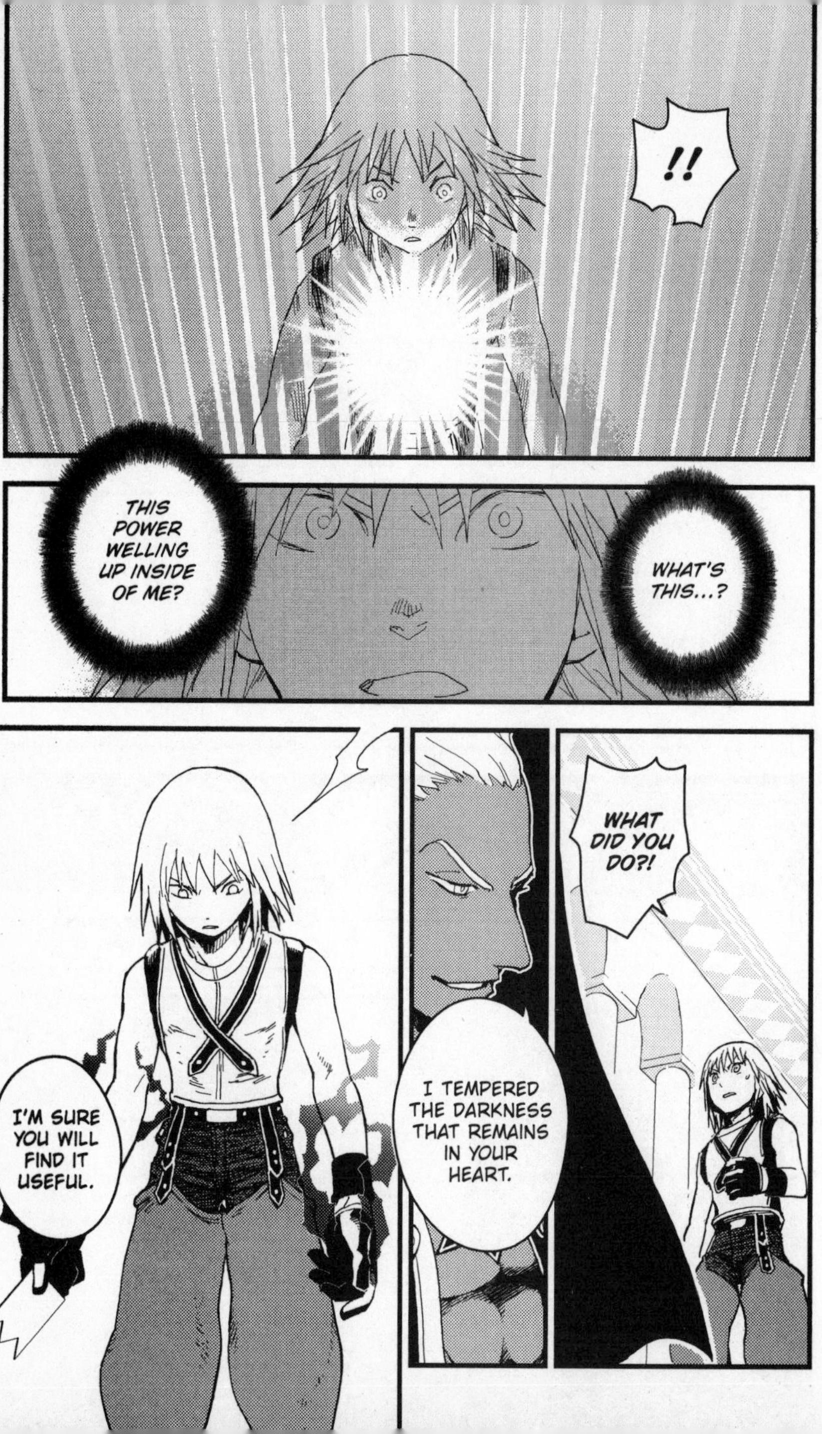
!!
WHAT'S THIS...?
THIS POWER WELLING UP INSIDE OF ME?
WHAT DID YOU DO?!
I TEMPERED THE DARKNESS THAT REMAINS IN YOUR HEART.
I'M SURE YOU WILL FIND IT USEFUL.

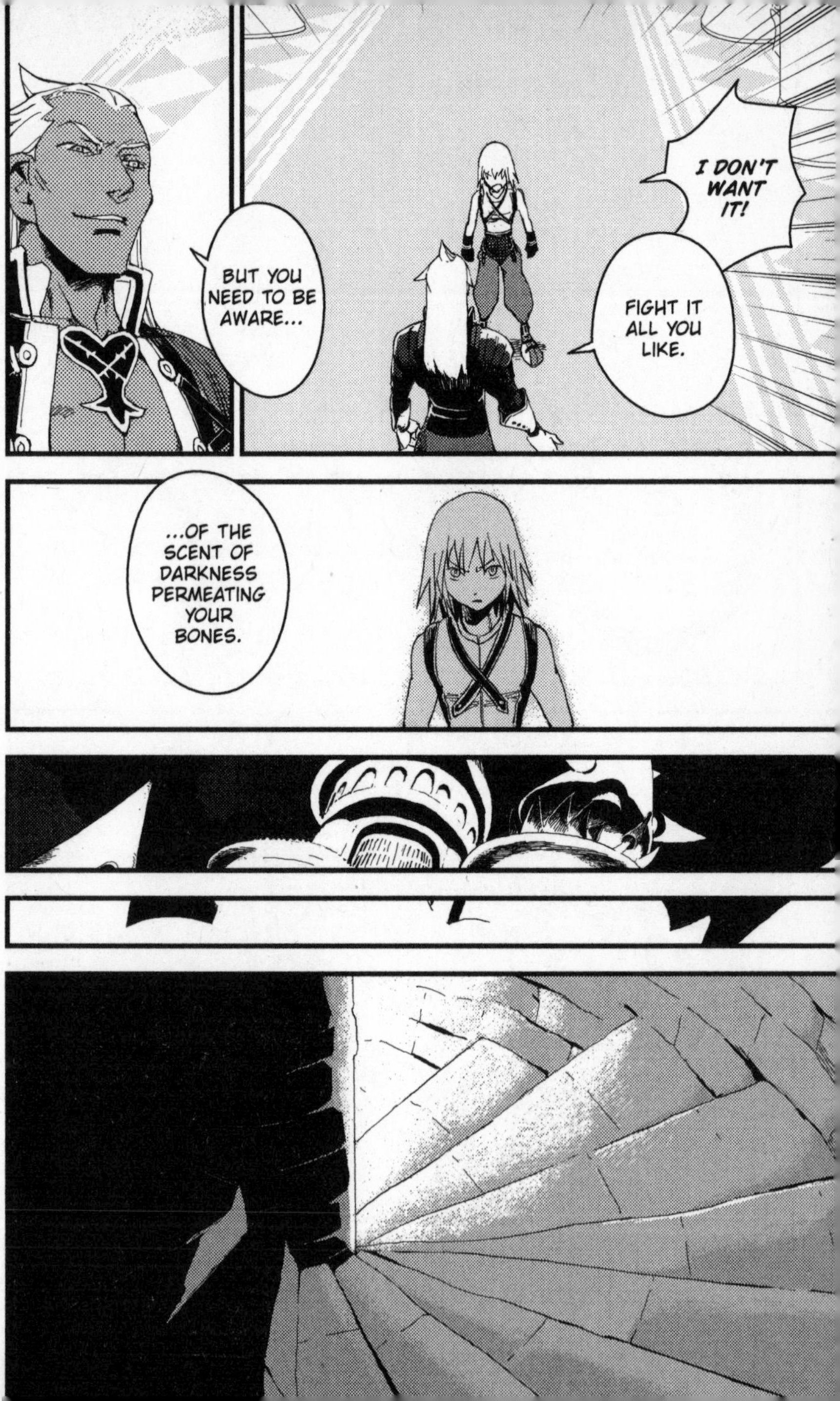
I DON'T WANT IT!
FIGHT IT ALL YOU LIKE.
BUT YOU NEED TO BE AWARE...
...OF THE SCENT OF DARKNESS PERMEATING YOUR BONES.

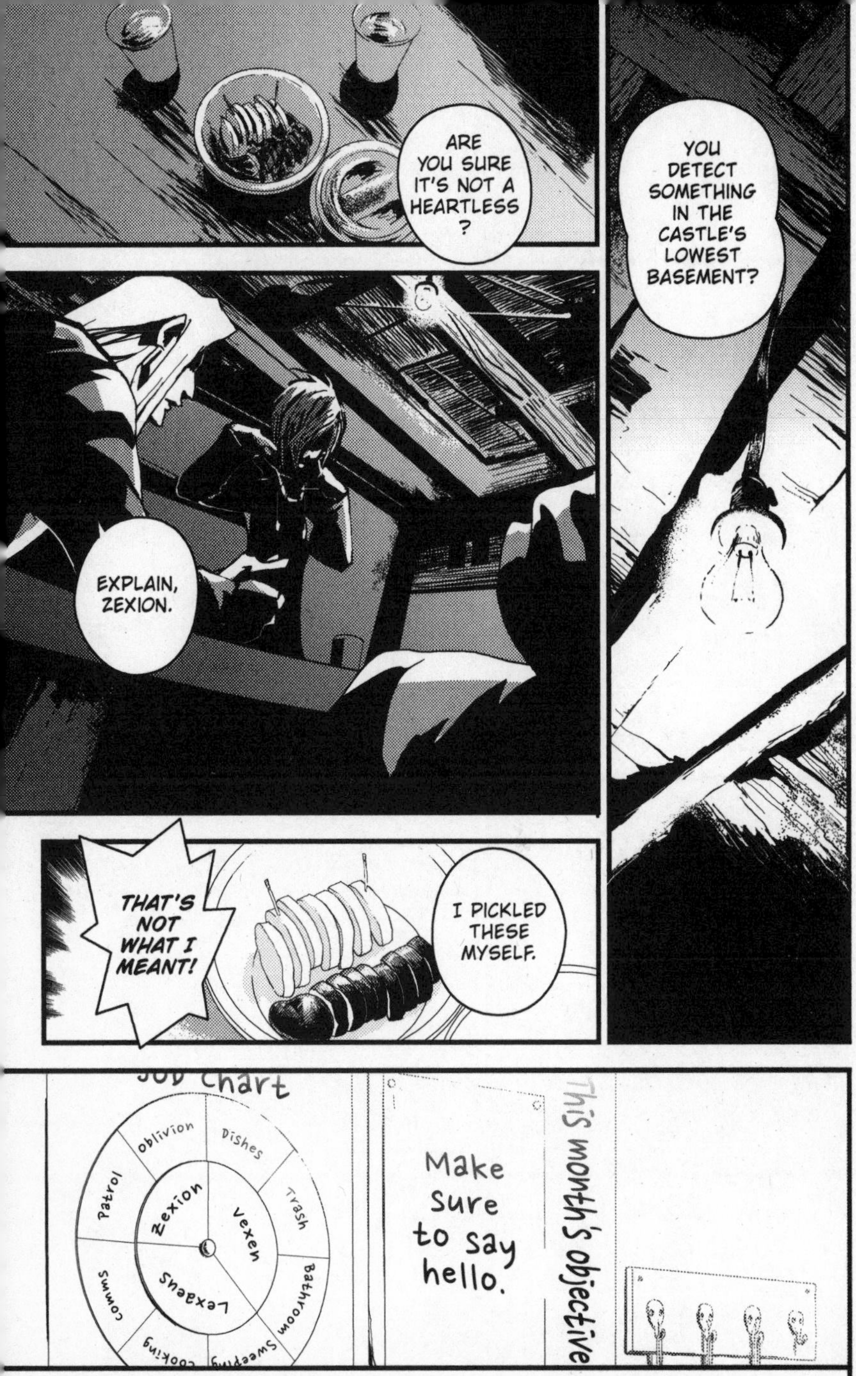
YOU DETECT SOMETHING IN THE CASTLE'S LOWEST BASEMENT?
ARE YOU SURE IT'S NOT A HEARTLESS ?
EXPLAIN, ZEXION.
I PICKLED THESE MYSELF.
THAT'S NOT WHAT I MEANT!
This month's objective
Make sure to say hello.
Chart
Oblivion
Dishes
Trash
Bathroom
Sweeping
Cooking
Comms
Patrol
Zexion
Vexen
Lexaeus

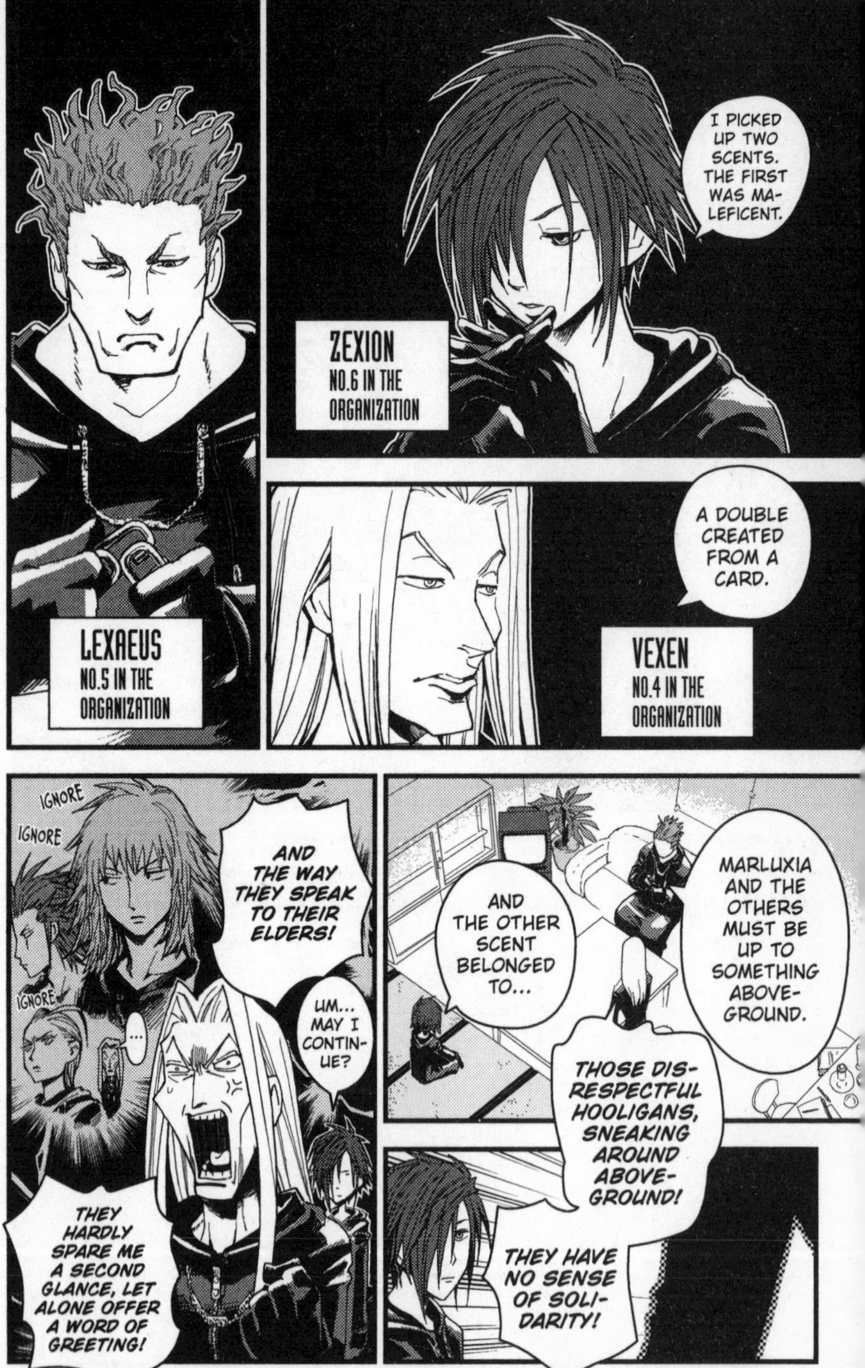
I PICKED UP TWO SCENTS. THE FIRST WAS MALEFICENT.
ZEXION
NO.6 IN THE ORGANIZATION
A DOUBLE CREATED FROM A CARD.
VEXEN
NO.4 IN THE ORGANIZATION
LEXAEUS
NO.5 IN THE ORGANIZATION
MARLUXIA AND THE OTHERS MUST BE UP TO SOMETHING ABOVE-GROUND.
AND THE OTHER SCENT BELONGED TO...
THOSE DIS-RESPECTFUL HOOLIGANS, SNEAKING AROUND ABOVE-GROUND!
THEY HAVE NO SENSE OF SOLI-DARITY!
AND THE WAY THEY SPEAK TO THEIR ELDERS!
IGNORE
IGNORE
IGNORE
UM... MAY I CONTIN-UE?
...
THEY HARDLY SPARE ME A SECOND GLANCE, LET ALONE OFFER A WORD OF GREETING!

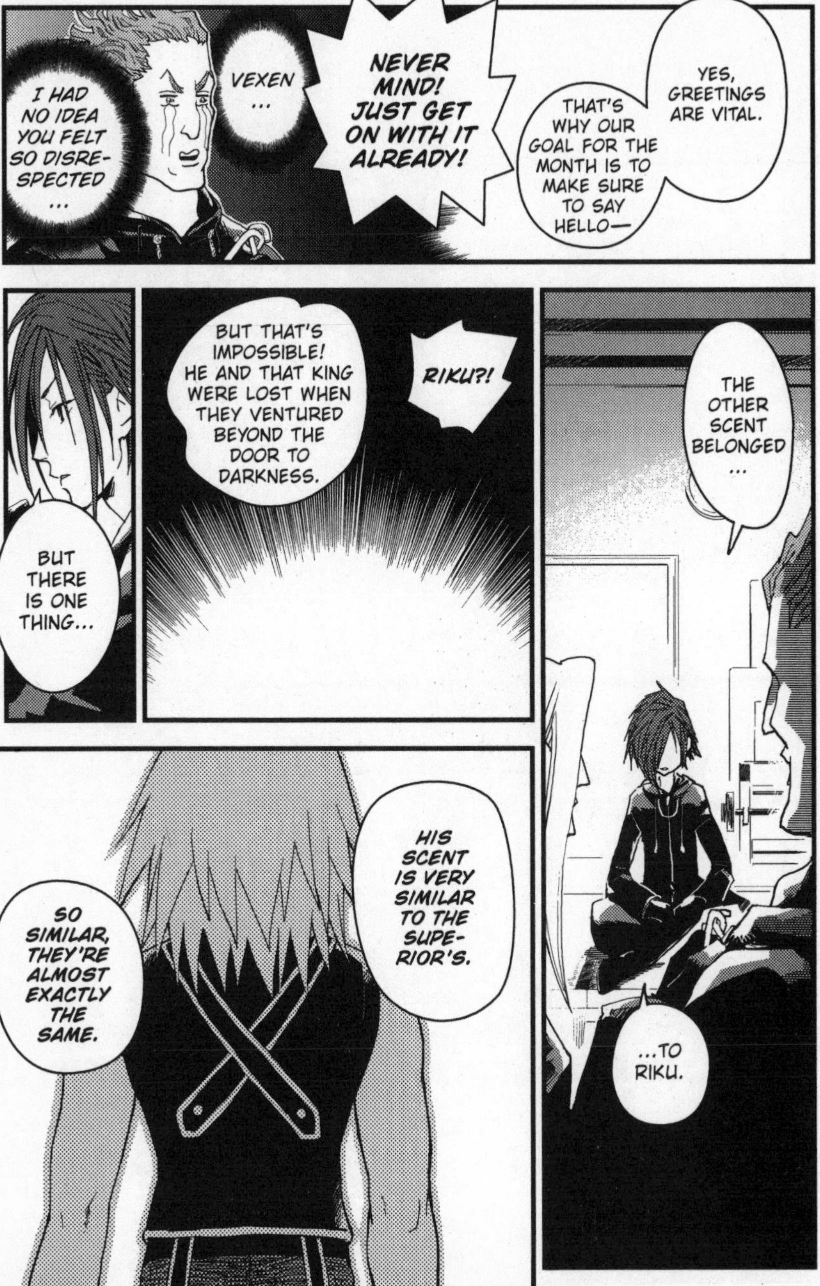
YES, GREETINGS ARE VITAL.
THAT'S WHY OUR GOAL FOR THE MONTH IS TO MAKE SURE TO SAY HELLO—
NEVER MIND! JUST GET ON WITH IT ALREADY!
VEXEN...
I HAD NO IDEA YOU FELT SO DISRESPECTED...
THE OTHER SCENT BELONGED...
...TO RIKU.
RIKU?!
BUT THAT'S IMPOSSIBLE! HE AND THAT KING WERE LOST WHEN THEY VENTURED BEYOND THE DOOR TO DARKNESS.
BUT THERE IS ONE THING...
HIS SCENT IS VERY SIMILAR TO THE SUPERIOR'S.
SO SIMILAR, THEY'RE ALMOST EXACTLY THE SAME.

MAYBE THEY'RE USING THE SAME COLOGNE?

SLUMP

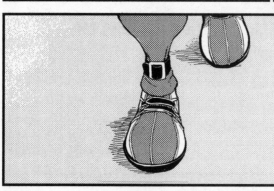

BUT YOU NEED TO BE AWARE...

...OF THE SCENT OF DARKNESS PERMEATING YOUR BONES.

HEH.

HA HA...

SNIFF...

......

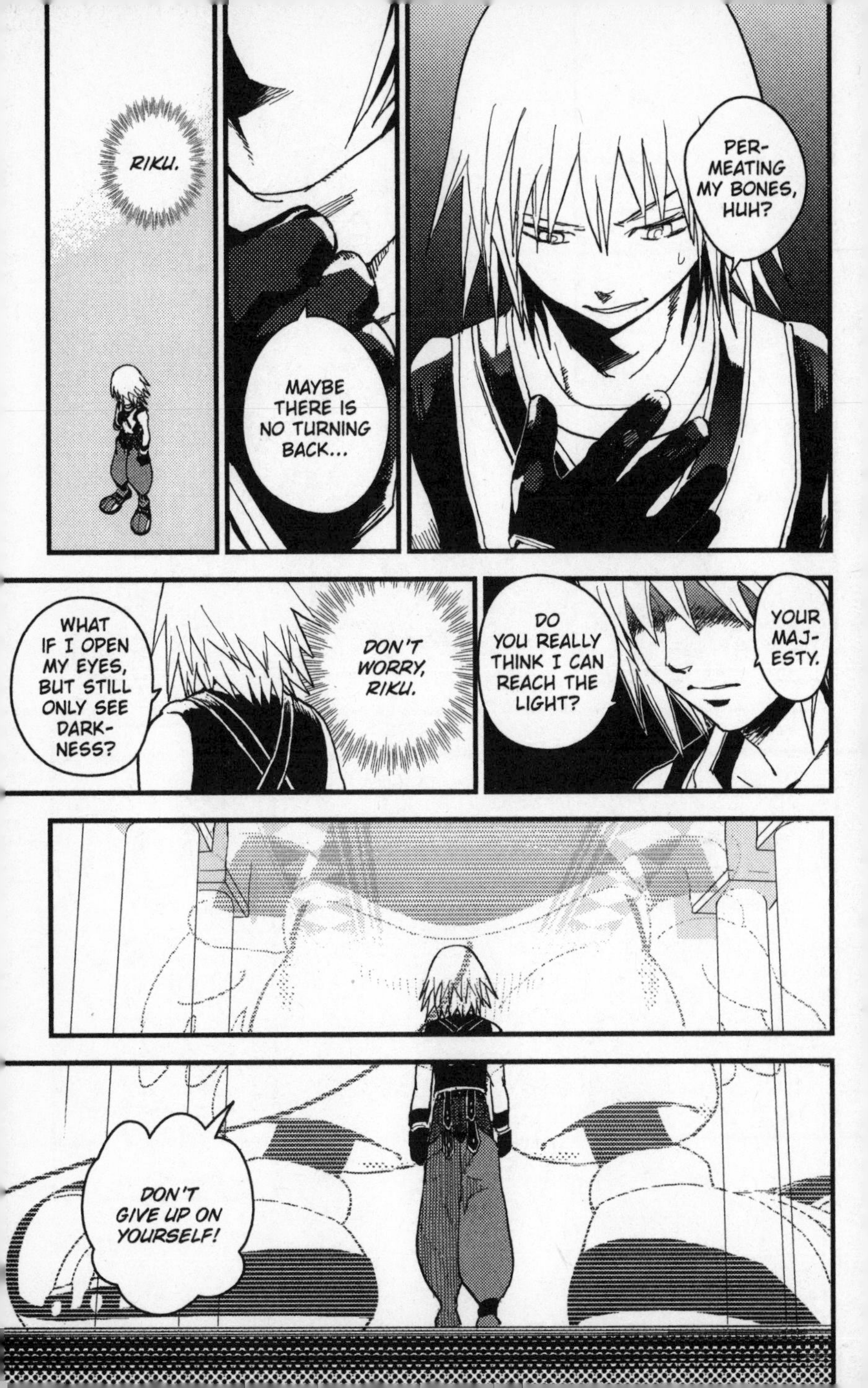
PER-MEATING MY BONES, HUH?
MAYBE THERE IS NO TURNING BACK...
RIKU.
YOUR MAJ-ESTY.
DO YOU REALLY THINK I CAN REACH THE LIGHT?
WHAT IF I OPEN MY EYES, BUT STILL ONLY SEE DARK-NESS?
DON'T WORRY, RIKU.
DON'T GIVE UP ON YOURSELF!

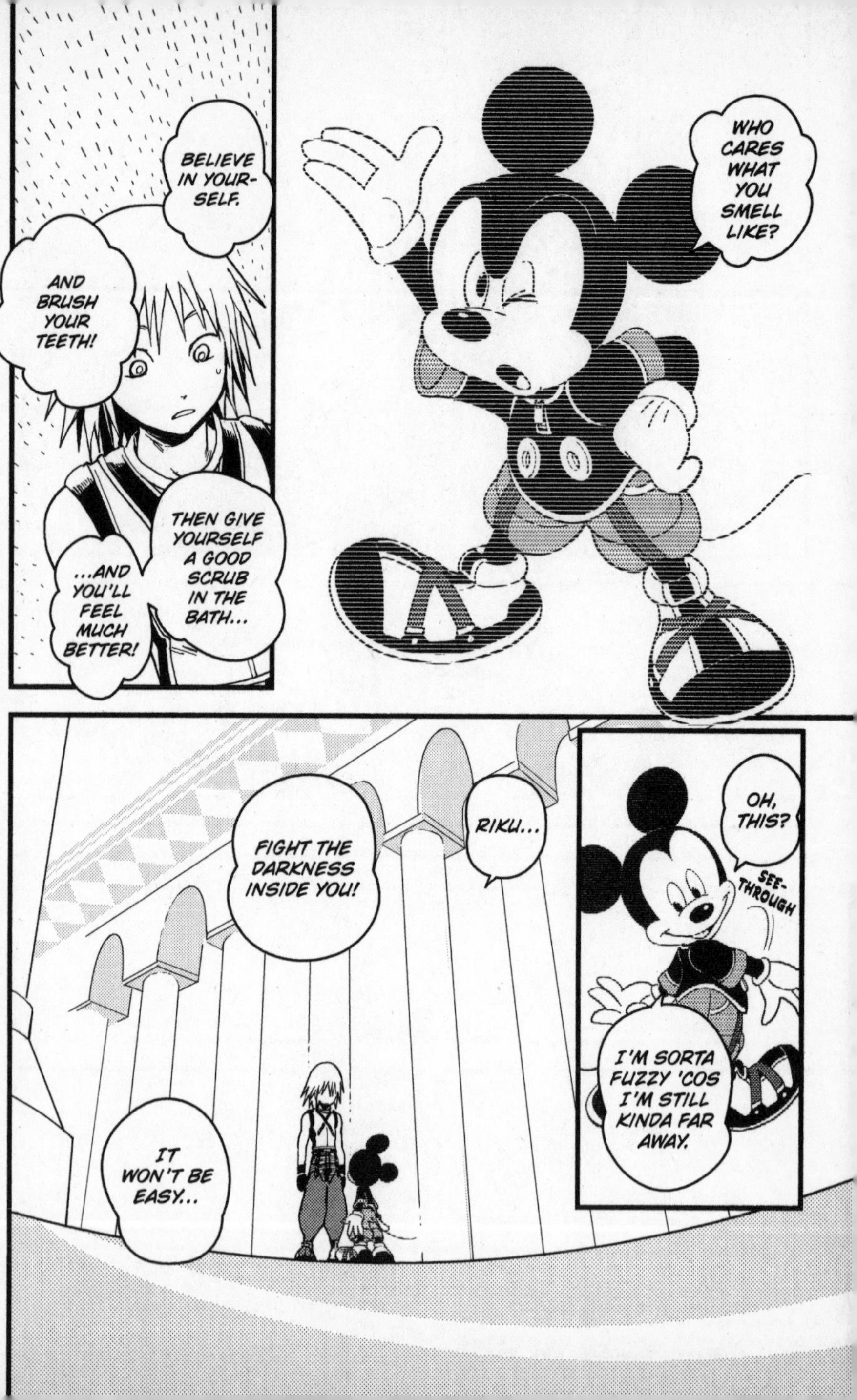
WHO CARES WHAT YOU SMELL LIKE?
BELIEVE IN YOURSELF.
AND BRUSH YOUR TEETH!
THEN GIVE YOURSELF A GOOD SCRUB IN THE BATH...
...AND YOU'LL FEEL MUCH BETTER!
OH, THIS?
SEE-THROUGH
I'M SORTA FUZZY 'COS I'M STILL KINDA FAR AWAY.
RIKU...
FIGHT THE DARKNESS INSIDE YOU!
IT WON'T BE EASY...

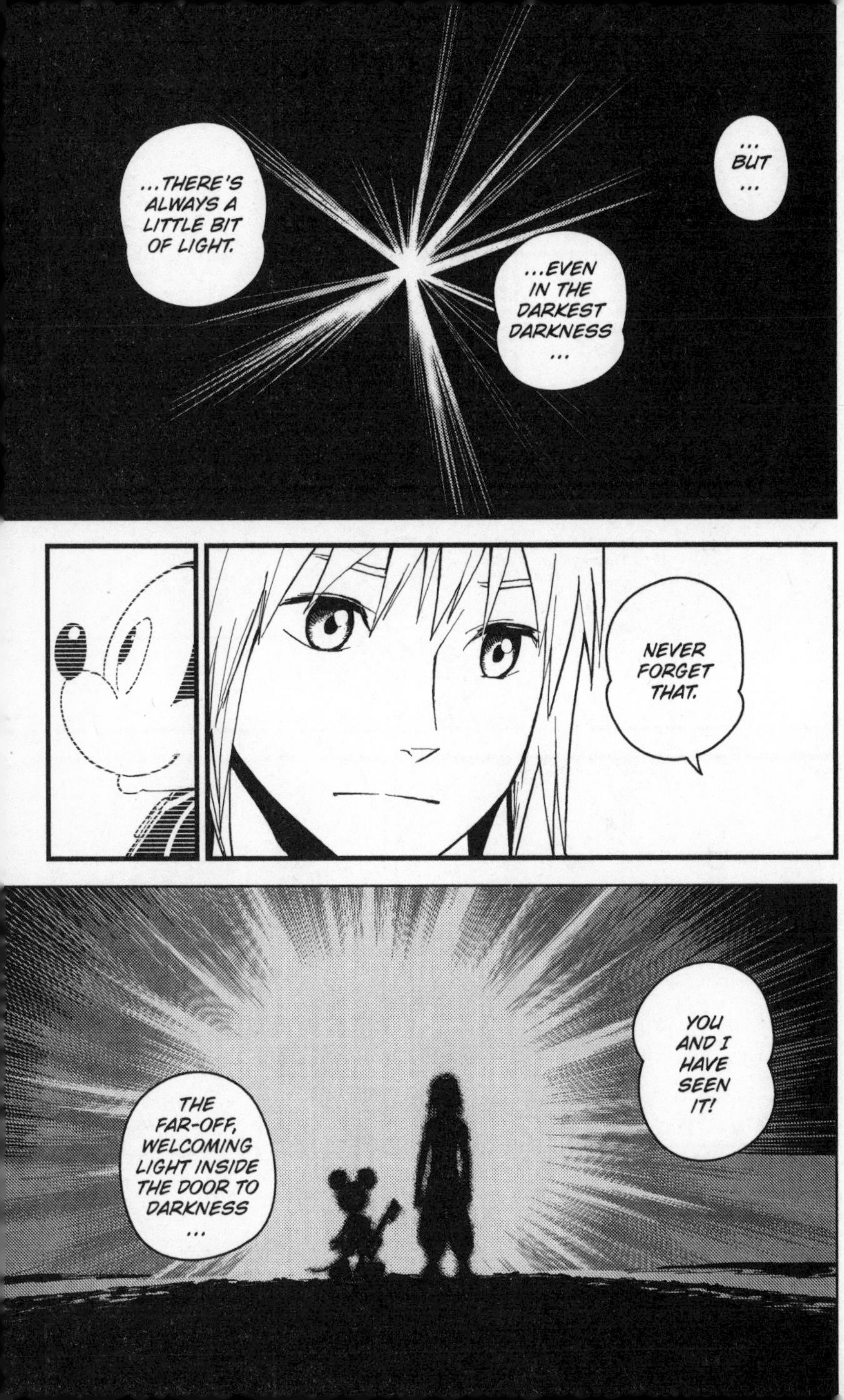

...BUT...
...EVEN IN THE DARKEST DARKNESS...
...THERE'S ALWAYS A LITTLE BIT OF LIGHT.
NEVER FORGET THAT.
YOU AND I HAVE SEEN IT!
THE FAR-OFF, WELCOMING LIGHT INSIDE THE DOOR TO DARKNESS...

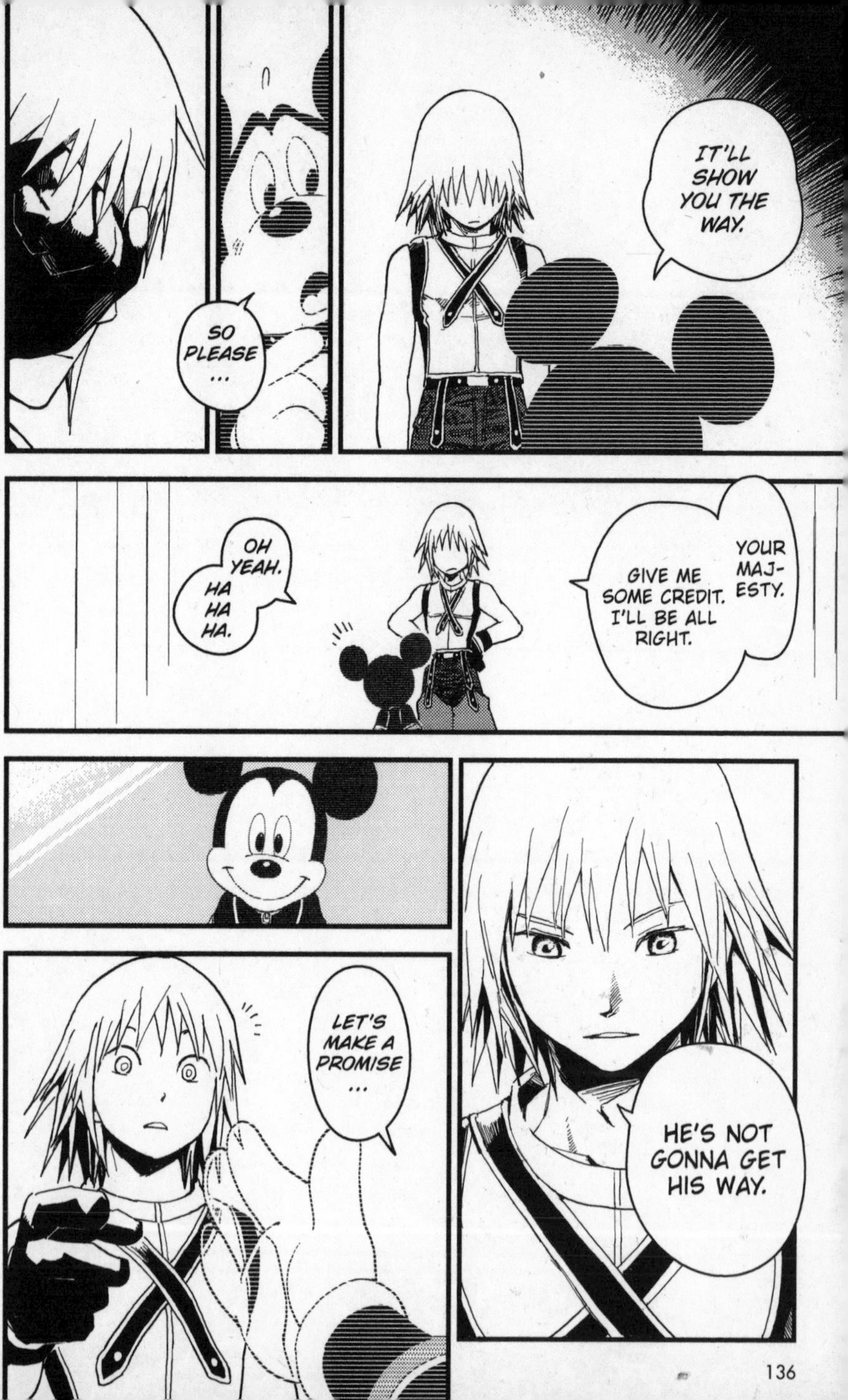
IT'LL SHOW YOU THE WAY.
SO PLEASE ...
YOUR MAJ-ESTY.
GIVE ME SOME CREDIT. I'LL BE ALL RIGHT.
OH YEAH. HA HA HA.
HE'S NOT GONNA GET HIS WAY.
LET'S MAKE A PROMISE ...

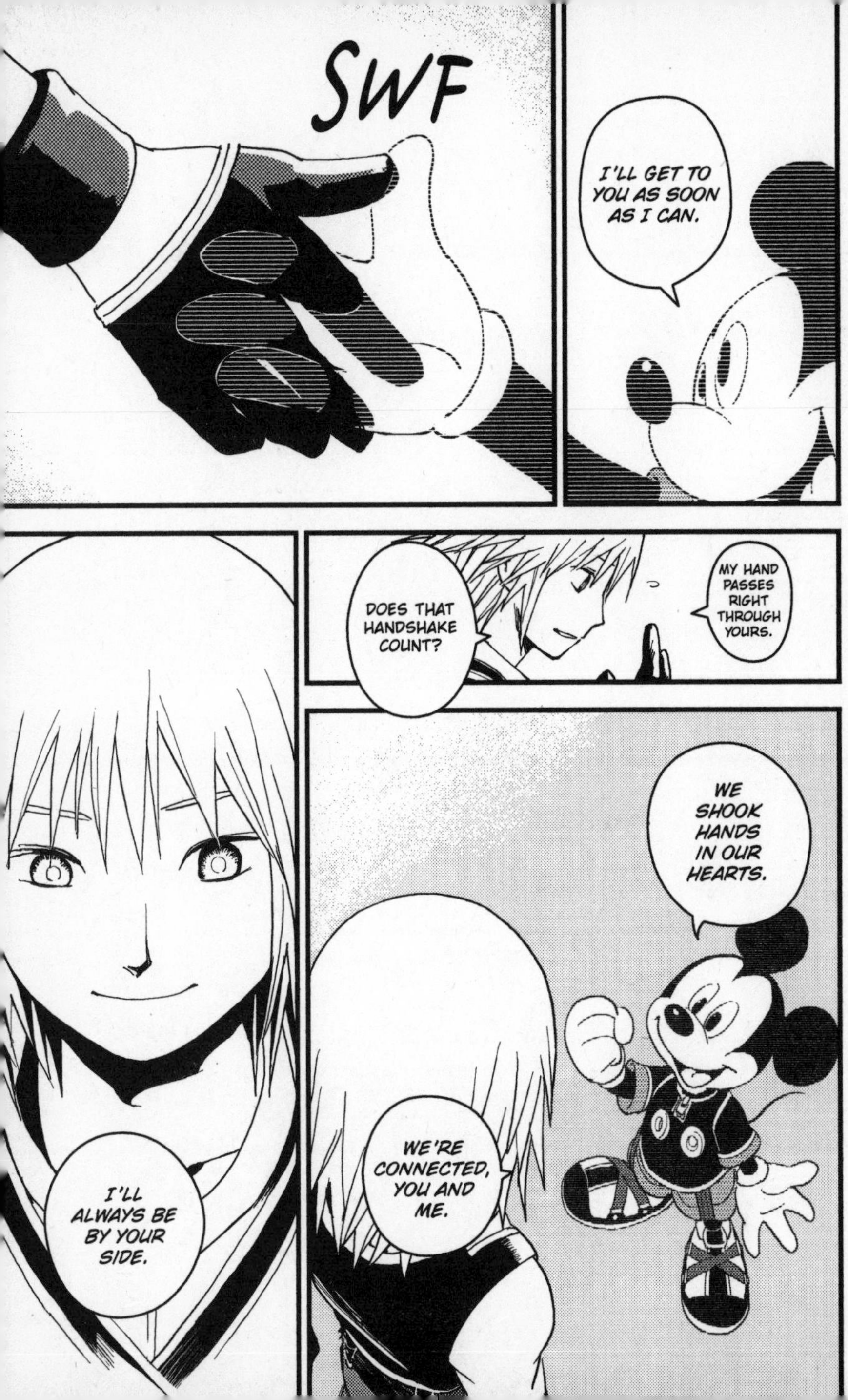
I'LL GET TO YOU AS SOON AS I CAN.
SWF
MY HAND PASSES RIGHT THROUGH YOURS.
DOES THAT HANDSHAKE COUNT?
WE SHOOK HANDS IN OUR HEARTS.
WE'RE CONNECTED, YOU AND ME.
I'LL ALWAYS BE BY YOUR SIDE.

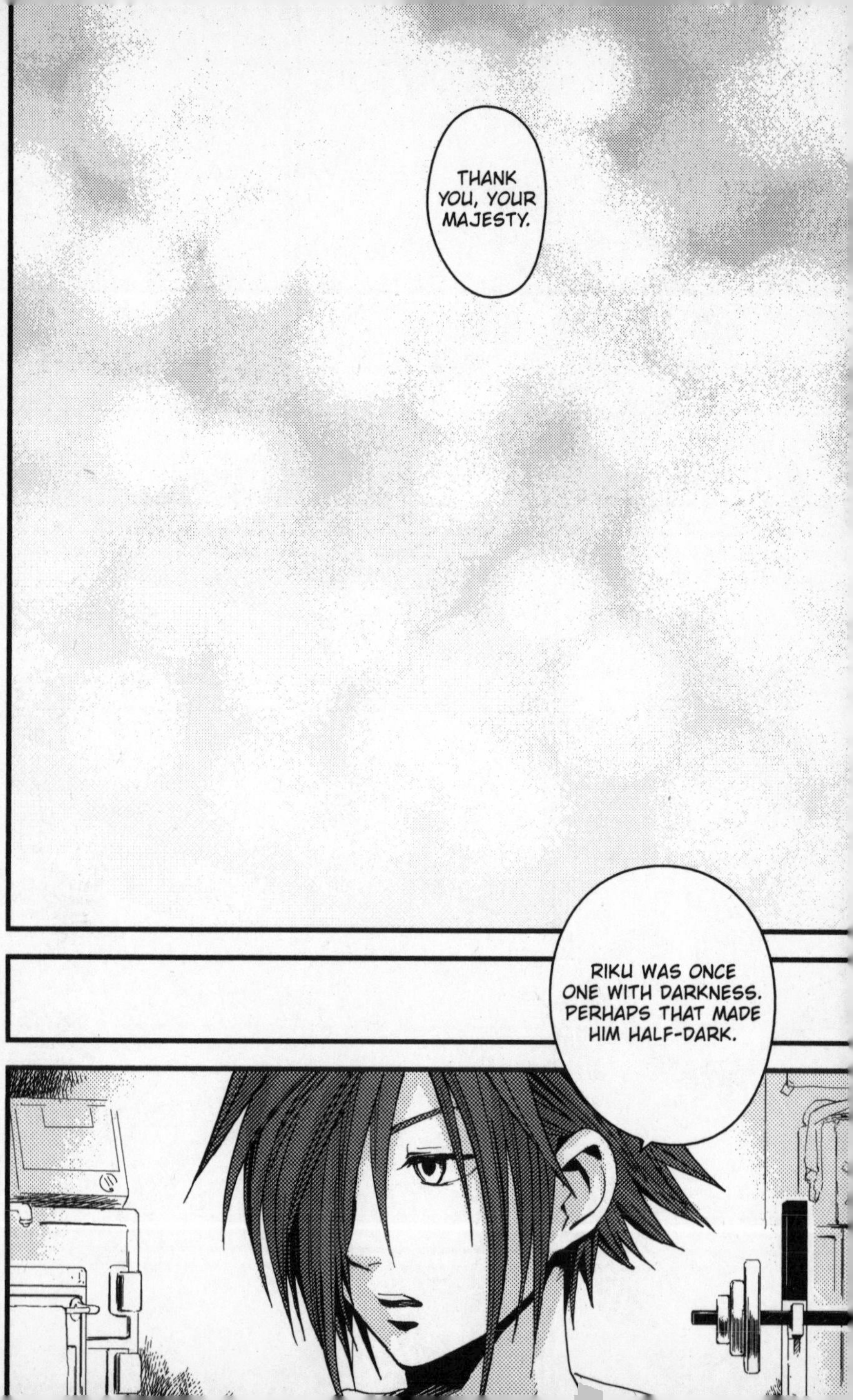
THANK YOU, YOUR MAJESTY.
RIKU WAS ONCE ONE WITH DARKNESS. PERHAPS THAT MADE HIM HALF-DARK.

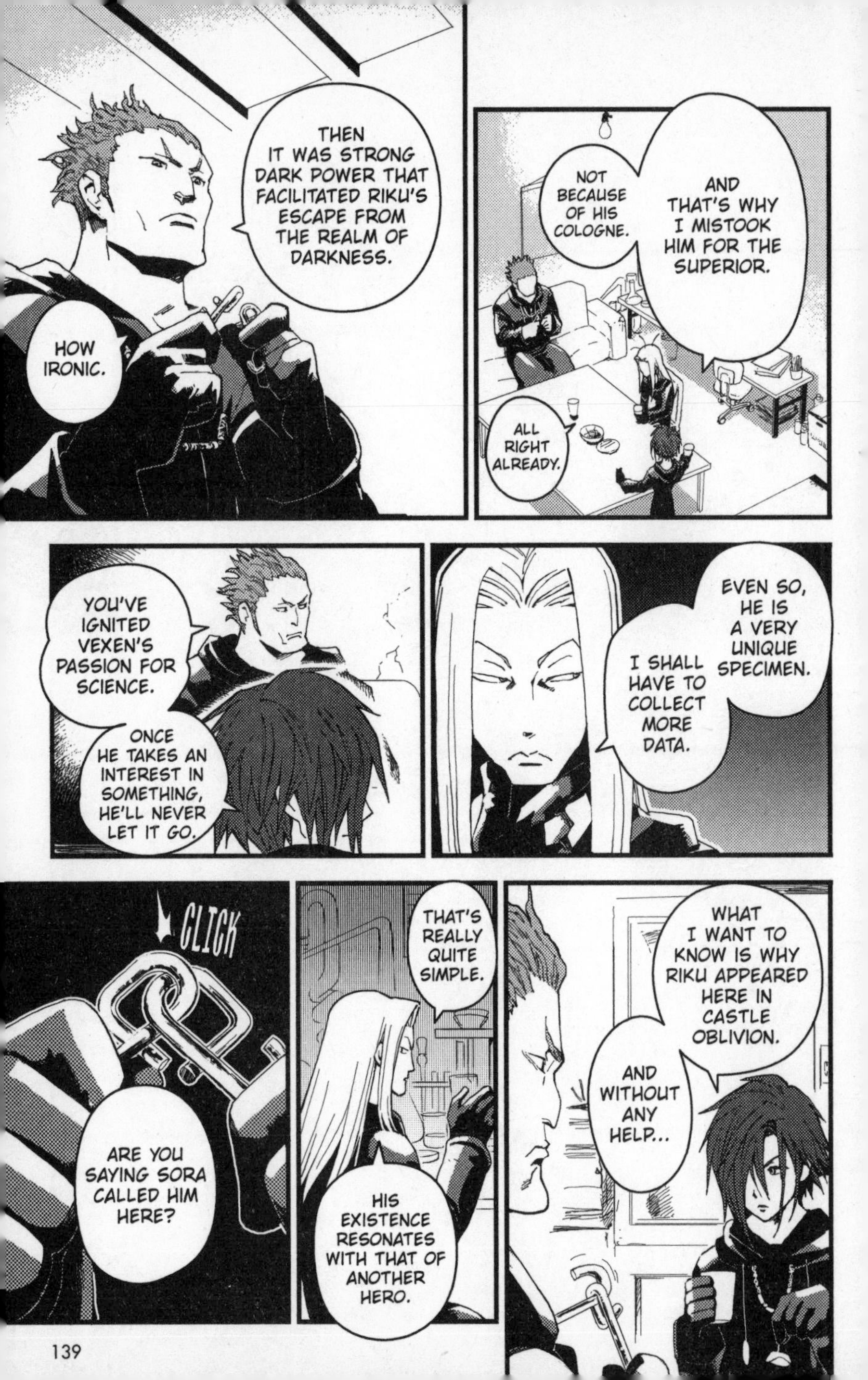
AND THAT'S WHY I MISTOOK HIM FOR THE SUPERIOR.
NOT BECAUSE OF HIS COLOGNE.
ALL RIGHT ALREADY.
THEN IT WAS STRONG DARK POWER THAT FACILITATED RIKU'S ESCAPE FROM THE REALM OF DARKNESS.
HOW IRONIC.
EVEN SO, HE IS A VERY UNIQUE SPECIMEN.
I SHALL HAVE TO COLLECT MORE DATA.
YOU'VE IGNITED VEXEN'S PASSION FOR SCIENCE.
ONCE HE TAKES AN INTEREST IN SOMETHING, HE'LL NEVER LET IT GO.
WHAT I WANT TO KNOW IS WHY RIKU APPEARED HERE IN CASTLE OBLIVION.
AND WITHOUT ANY HELP...
THAT'S REALLY QUITE SIMPLE.
HIS EXISTENCE RESONATES WITH THAT OF ANOTHER HERO.
CLICK
ARE YOU SAYING SORA CALLED HIM HERE?

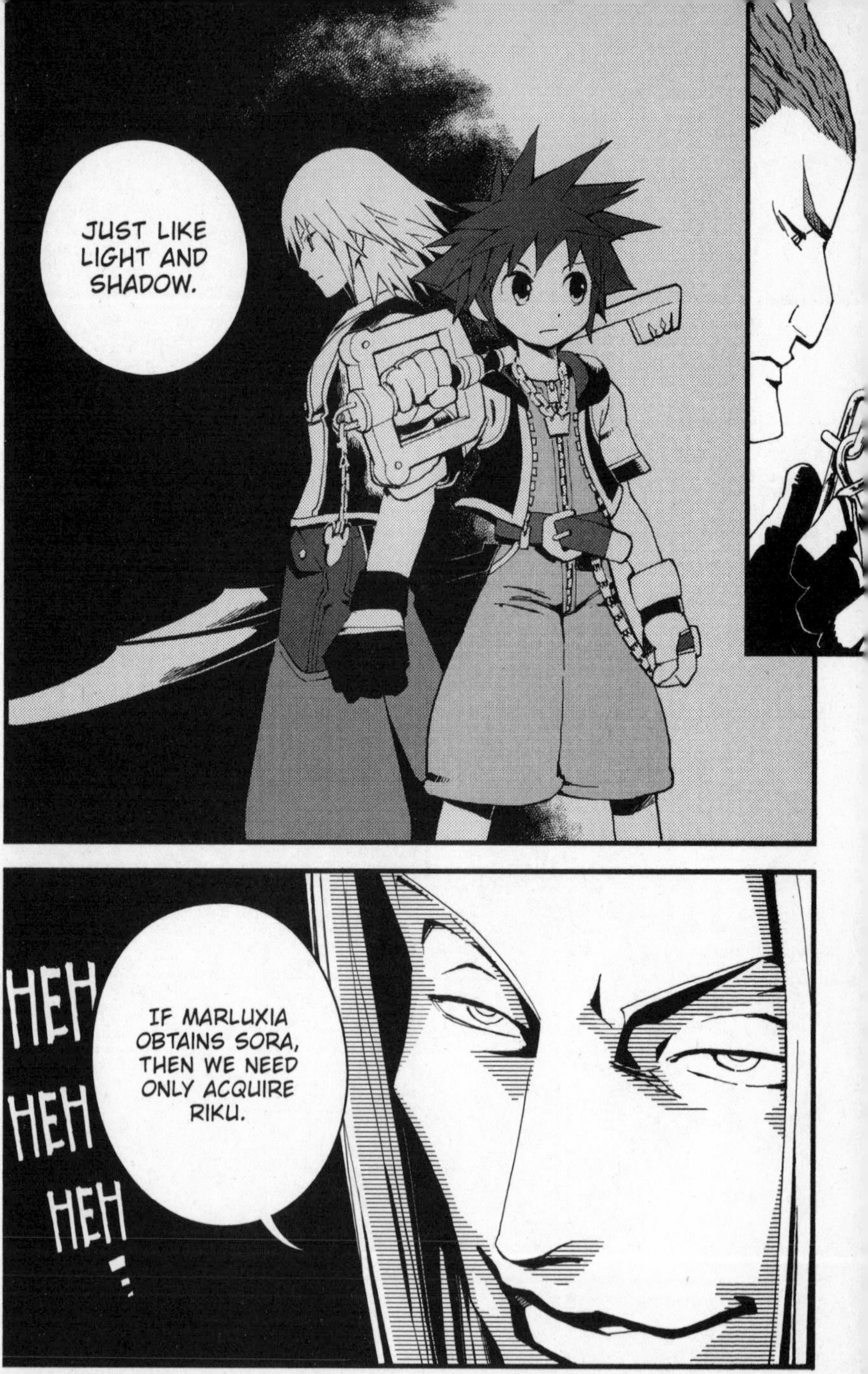
JUST LIKE LIGHT AND SHADOW.
IF MARLUXIA OBTAINS SORA, THEN WE NEED ONLY ACQUIRE RIKU.
HEH HEH HEH

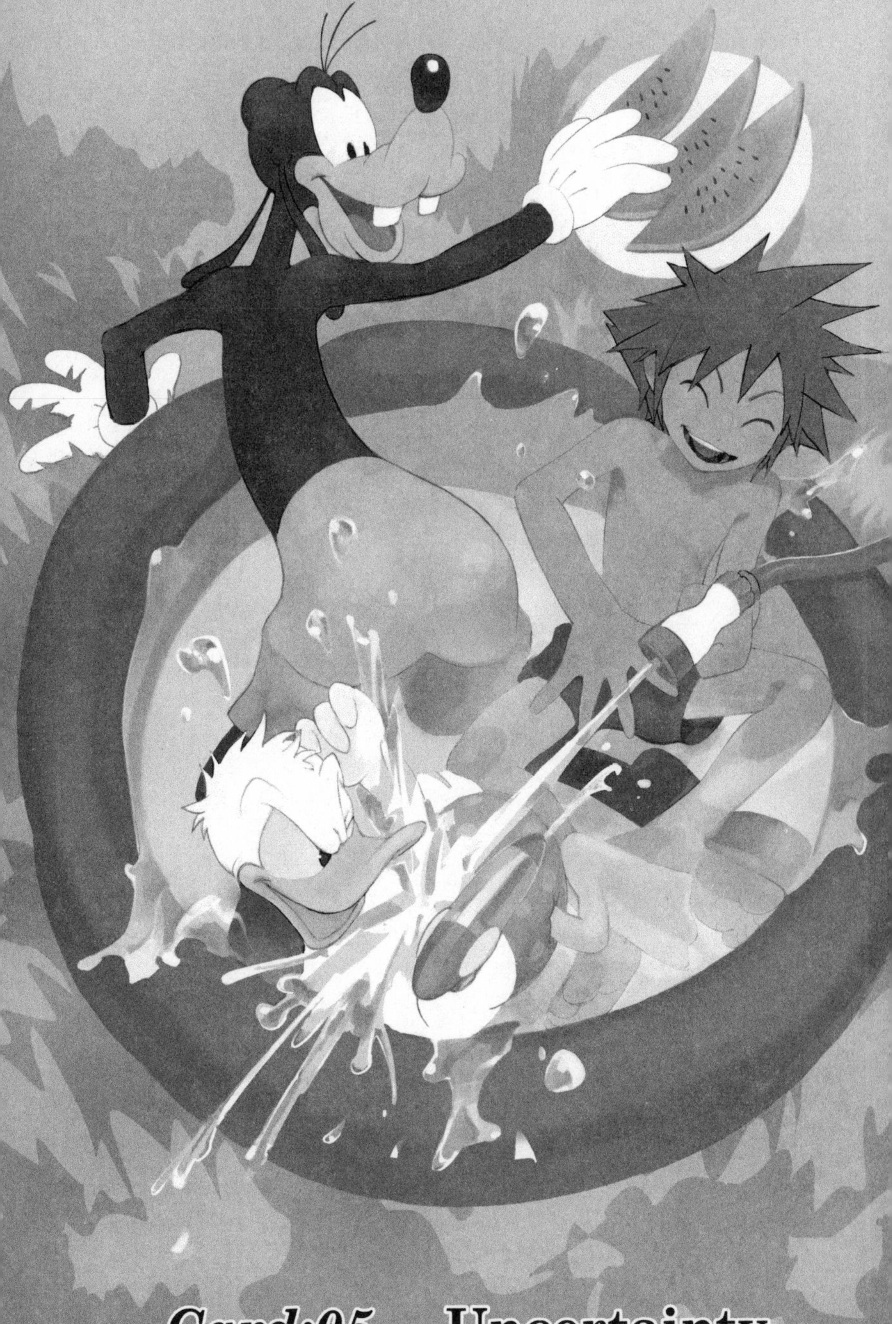

## Card:05 Uncertainty

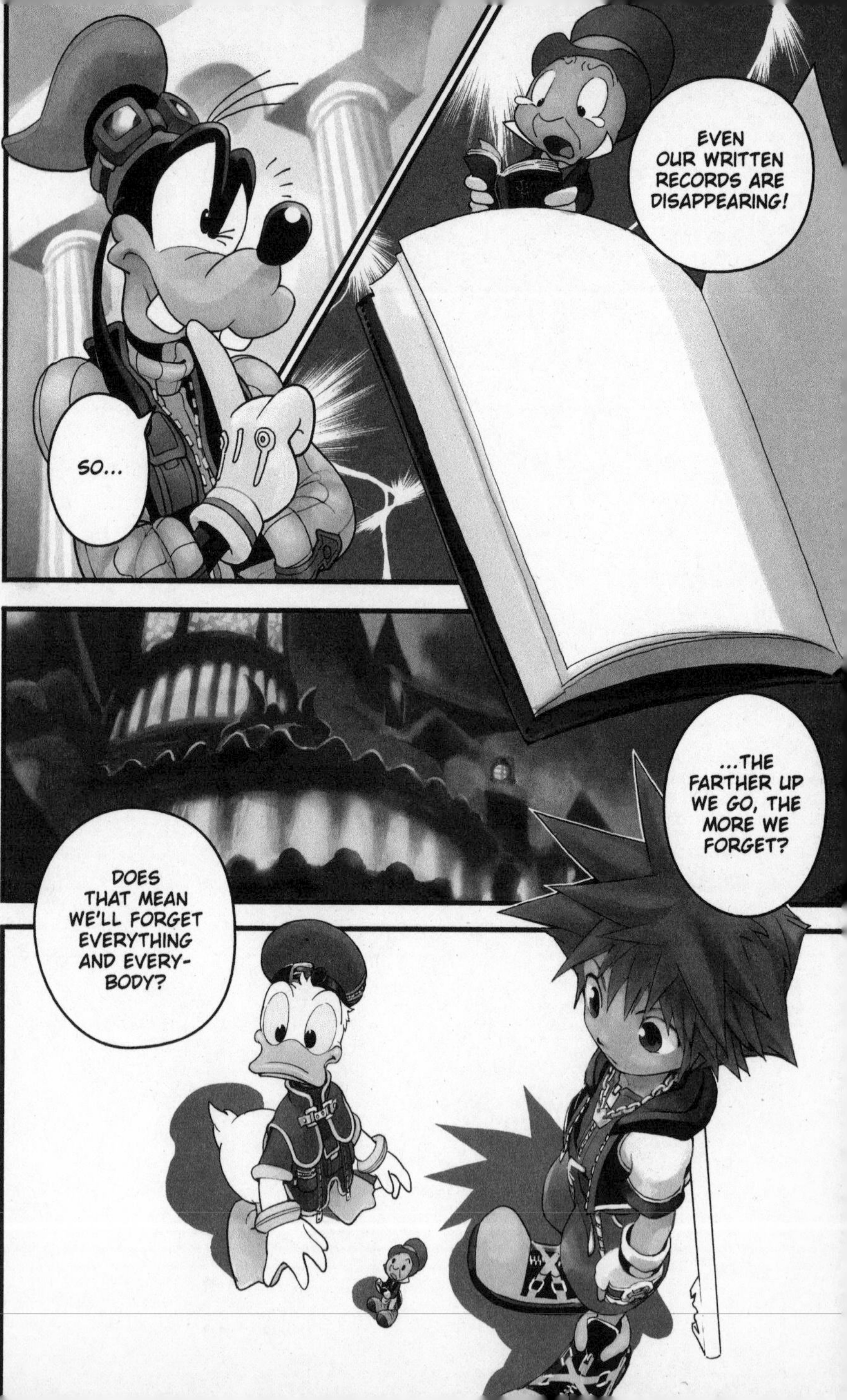
EVEN OUR WRITTEN RECORDS ARE DISAPPEARING!
SO...
...THE FARTHER UP WE GO, THE MORE WE FORGET?
DOES THAT MEAN WE'LL FORGET EVERYTHING AND EVERY-BODY?

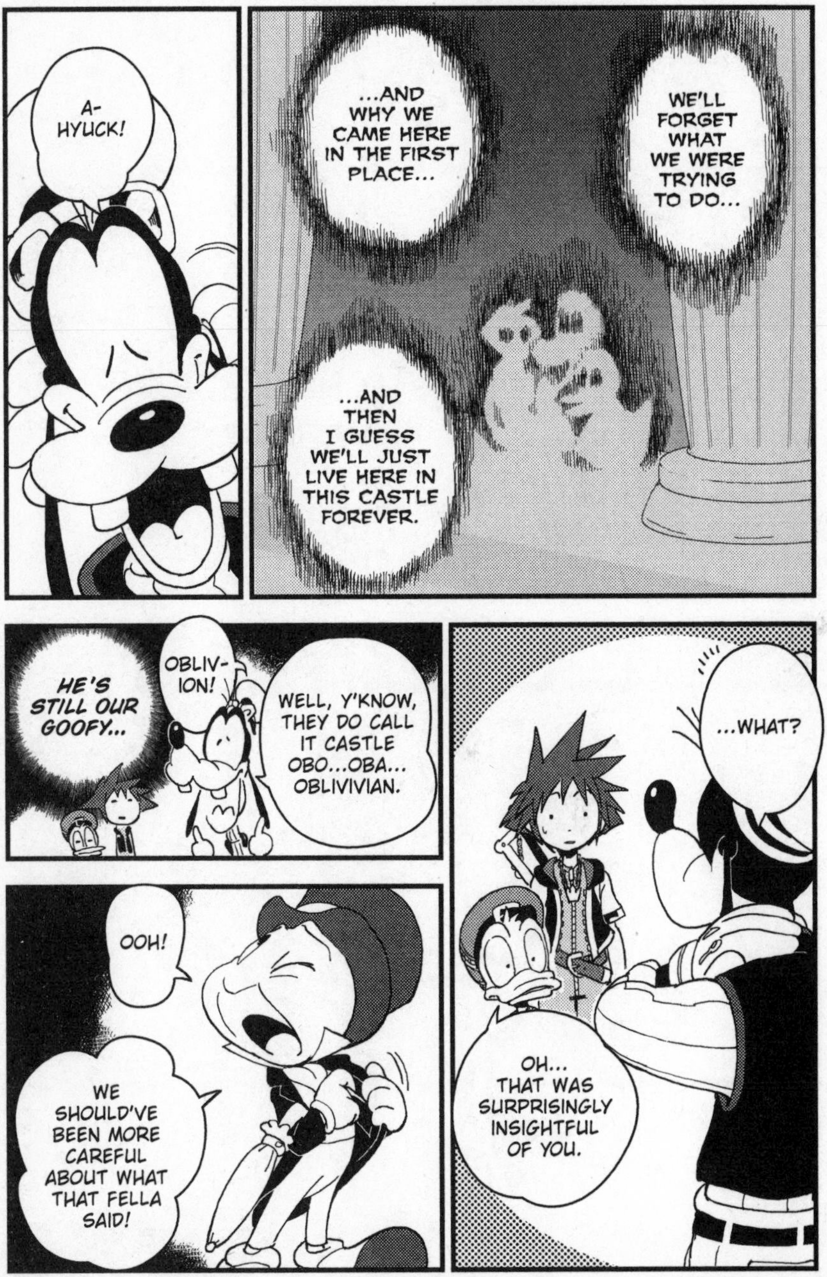
WE'LL FORGET WHAT WE WERE TRYING TO DO...
...AND WHY WE CAME HERE IN THE FIRST PLACE...
...AND THEN I GUESS WE'LL JUST LIVE HERE IN THIS CASTLE FOREVER.
A-HYUCK!
...WHAT?
OH... THAT WAS SURPRISINGLY INSIGHTFUL OF YOU.
WELL, Y'KNOW, THEY DO CALL IT CASTLE OBO...OBA... OBLIVIVIAN.
OBLIV-ION!
HE'S STILL OUR GOOFY...
OOH!
WE SHOULD'VE BEEN MORE CAREFUL ABOUT WHAT THAT FELLA SAID!

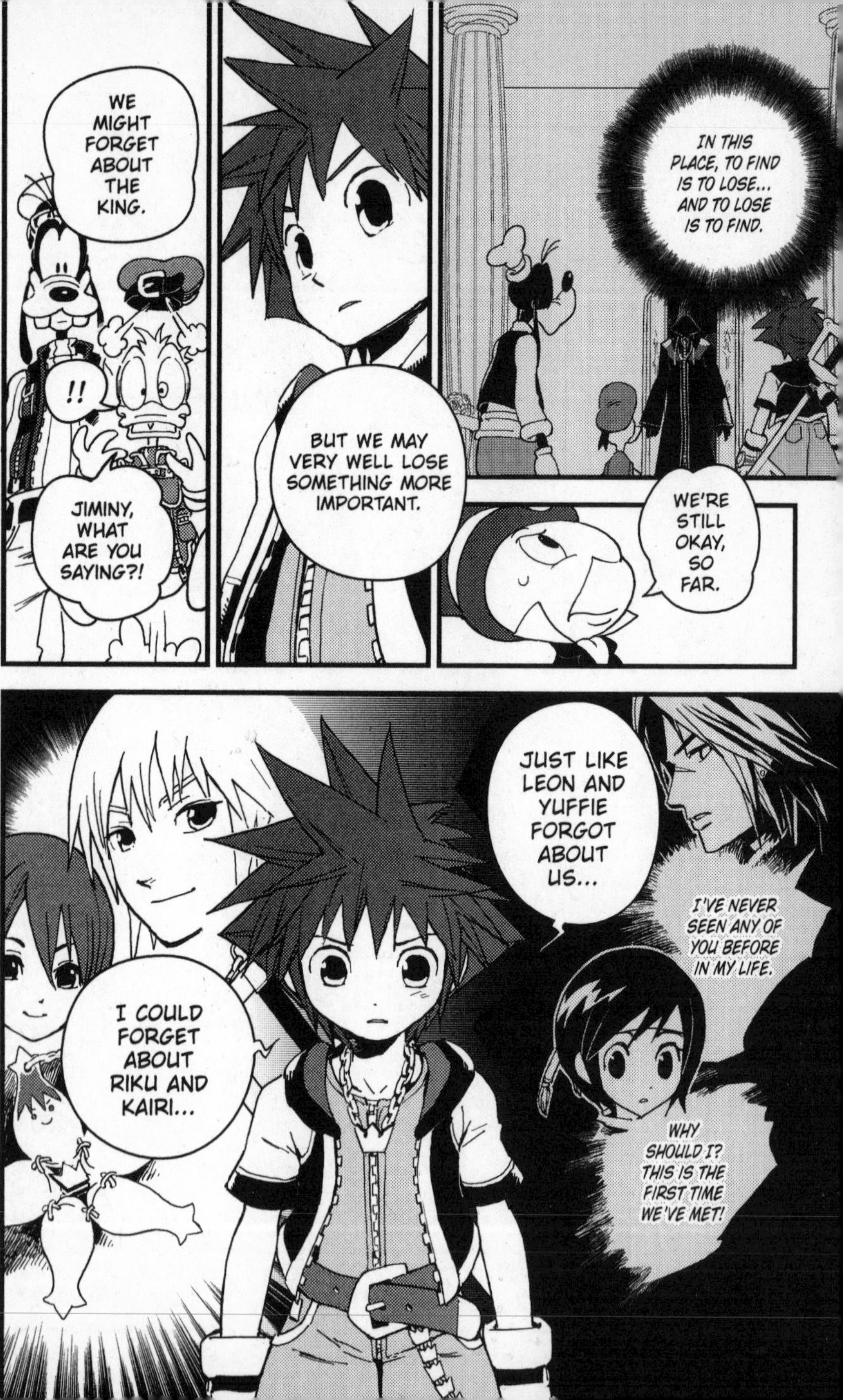
IN THIS PLACE, TO FIND IS TO LOSE... AND TO LOSE IS TO FIND.
WE'RE STILL OKAY, SO FAR.
BUT WE MAY VERY WELL LOSE SOMETHING MORE IMPORTANT.
WE MIGHT FORGET ABOUT THE KING.
!!
JIMINY, WHAT ARE YOU SAYING?!
JUST LIKE LEON AND YUFFIE FORGOT ABOUT US...
I'VE NEVER SEEN ANY OF YOU BEFORE IN MY LIFE.
WHY SHOULD I? THIS IS THE FIRST TIME WE'VE MET!
I COULD FORGET ABOUT RIKU AND KAIRI...

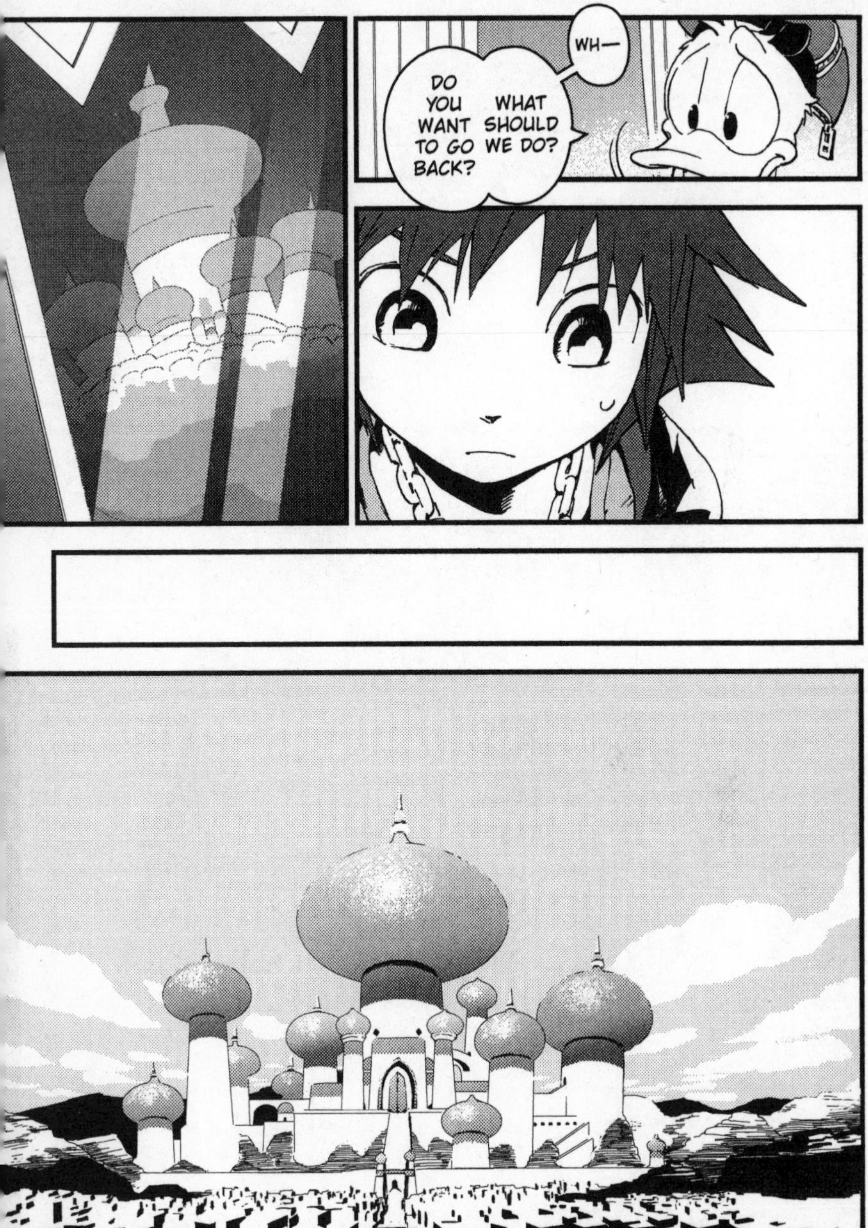
WH—
WHAT SHOULD WE DO?
DO YOU WANT TO GO BACK?

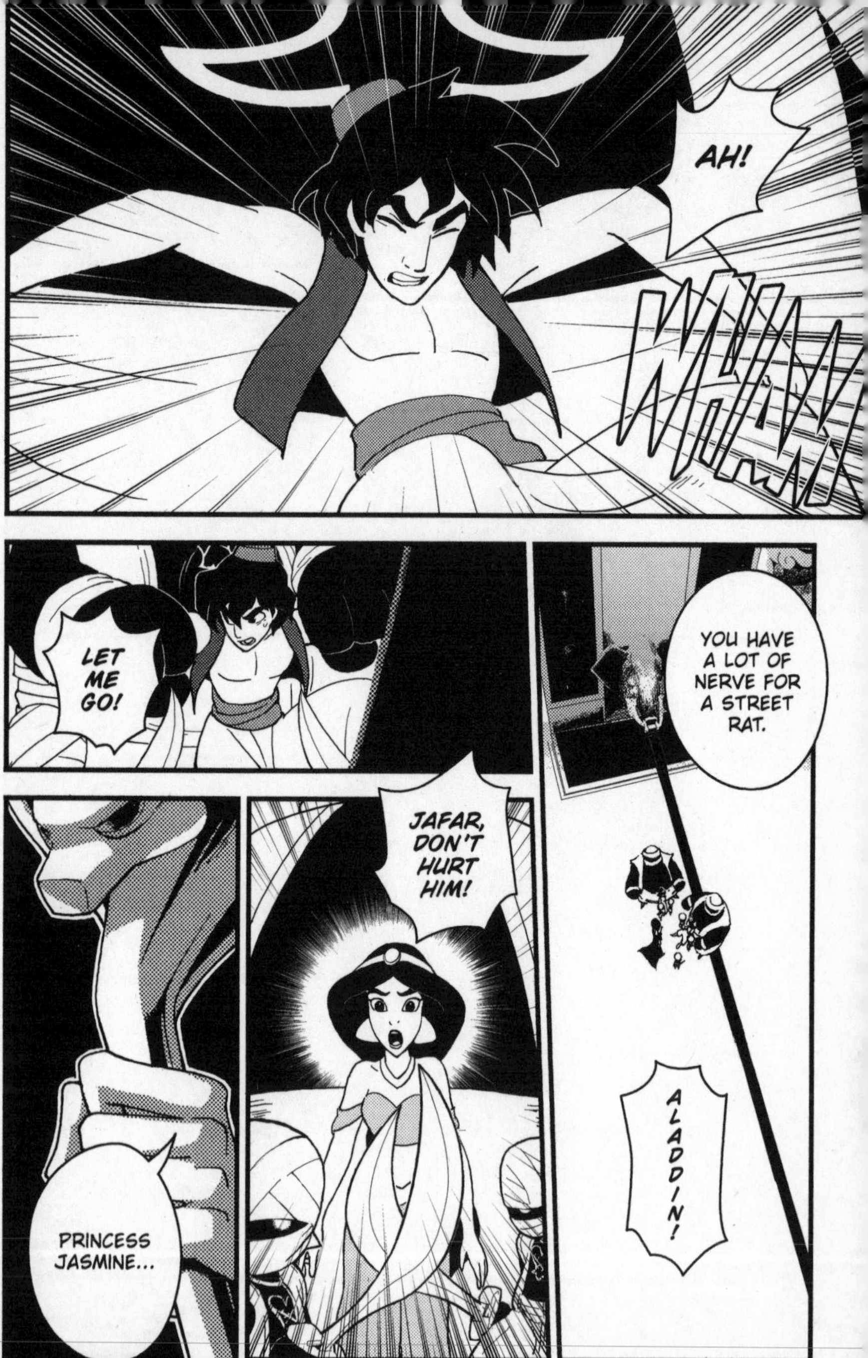
AH!
YOU HAVE A LOT OF NERVE FOR A STREET RAT.
ALADDIN!
LET ME GO!
JAFAR, DON'T HURT HIM!
PRINCESS JASMINE...

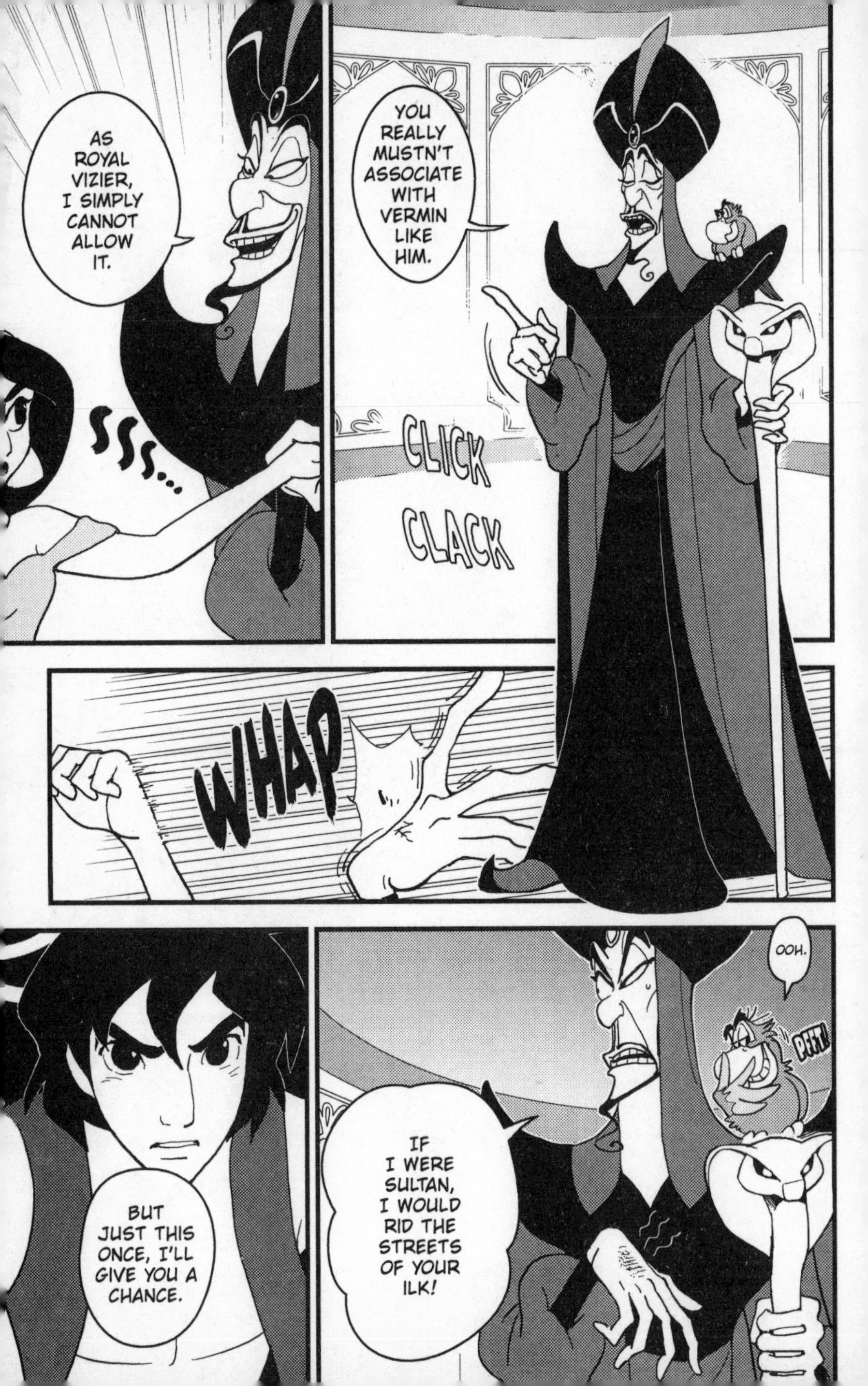
YOU REALLY MUSTN'T ASSOCIATE WITH VERMIN LIKE HIM.
CLICK
CLACK
AS ROYAL VIZIER, I SIMPLY CANNOT ALLOW IT.
SSS...
WHAP
OOH.
PFFT!
IF I WERE SULTAN, I WOULD RID THE STREETS OF YOUR ILK!
BUT JUST THIS ONCE, I'LL GIVE YOU A CHANCE.

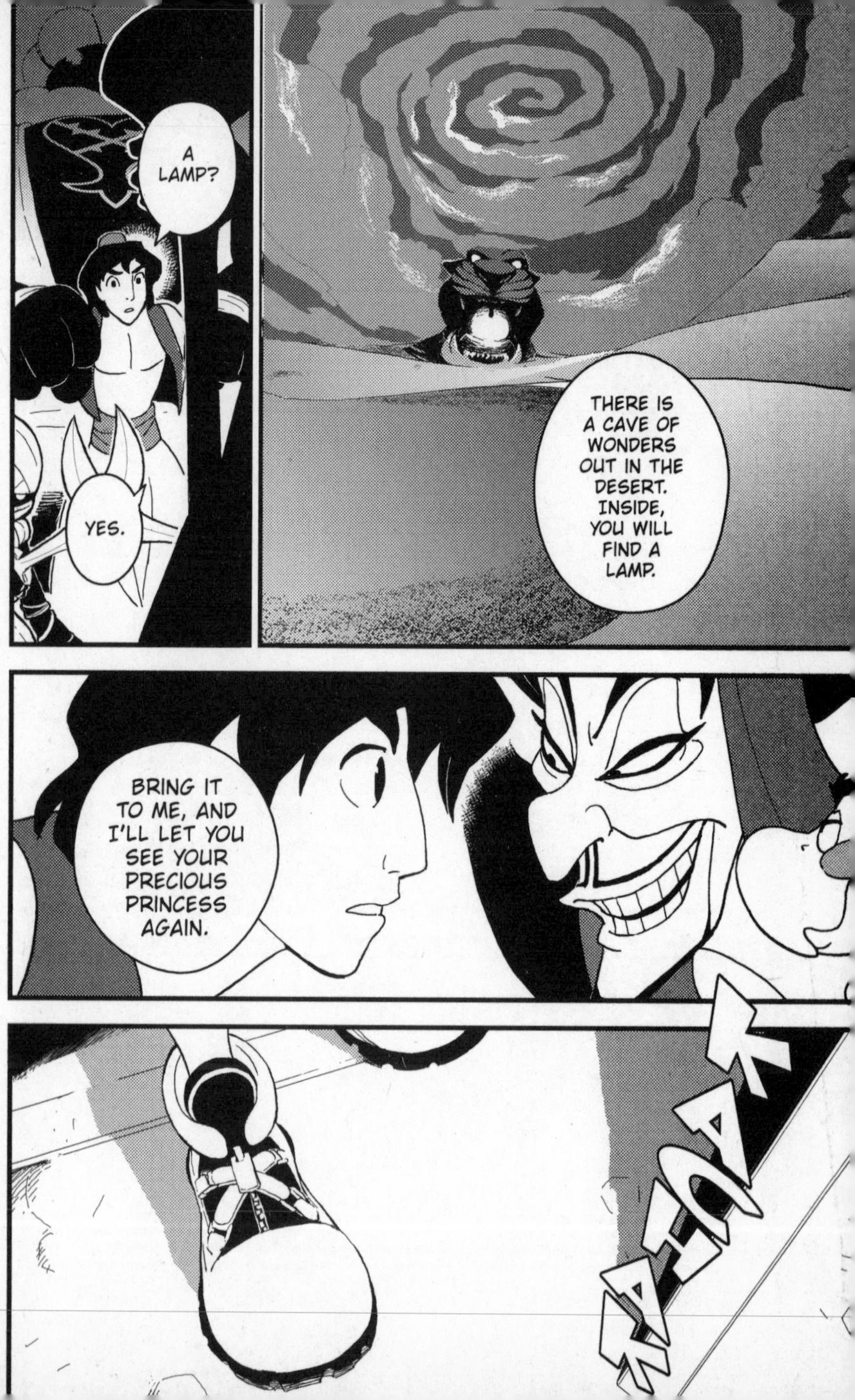
THERE IS A CAVE OF WONDERS OUT IN THE DESERT. INSIDE, YOU WILL FIND A LAMP.
A LAMP?
YES.
BRING IT TO ME, AND I'LL LET YOU SEE YOUR PRECIOUS PRINCESS AGAIN.
KACHAK

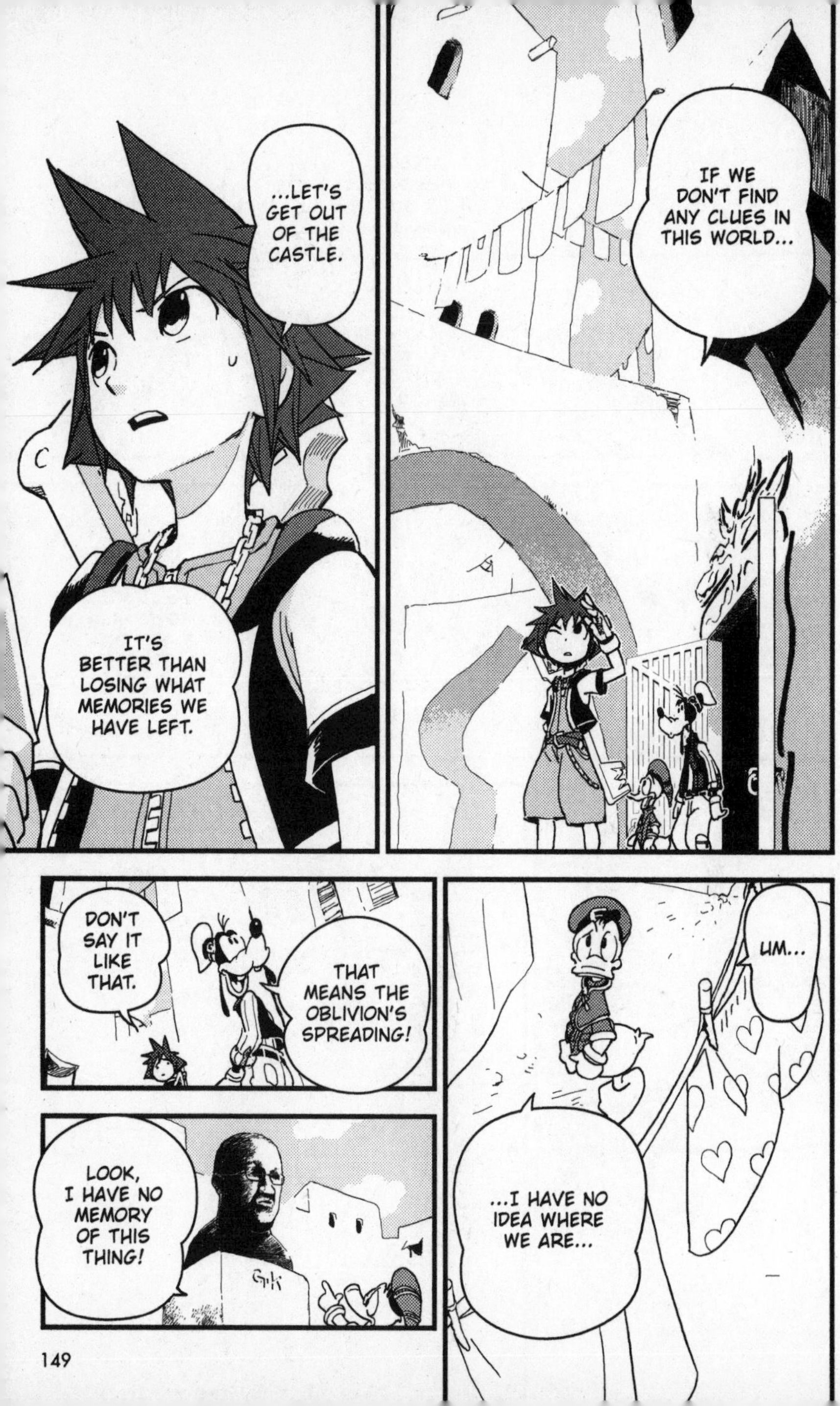
IF WE DON'T FIND ANY CLUES IN THIS WORLD...
...LET'S GET OUT OF THE CASTLE.
IT'S BETTER THAN LOSING WHAT MEMORIES WE HAVE LEFT.
UM...
...I HAVE NO IDEA WHERE WE ARE...
THAT MEANS THE OBLIVION'S SPREADING!
DON'T SAY IT LIKE THAT.
LOOK, I HAVE NO MEMORY OF THIS THING!

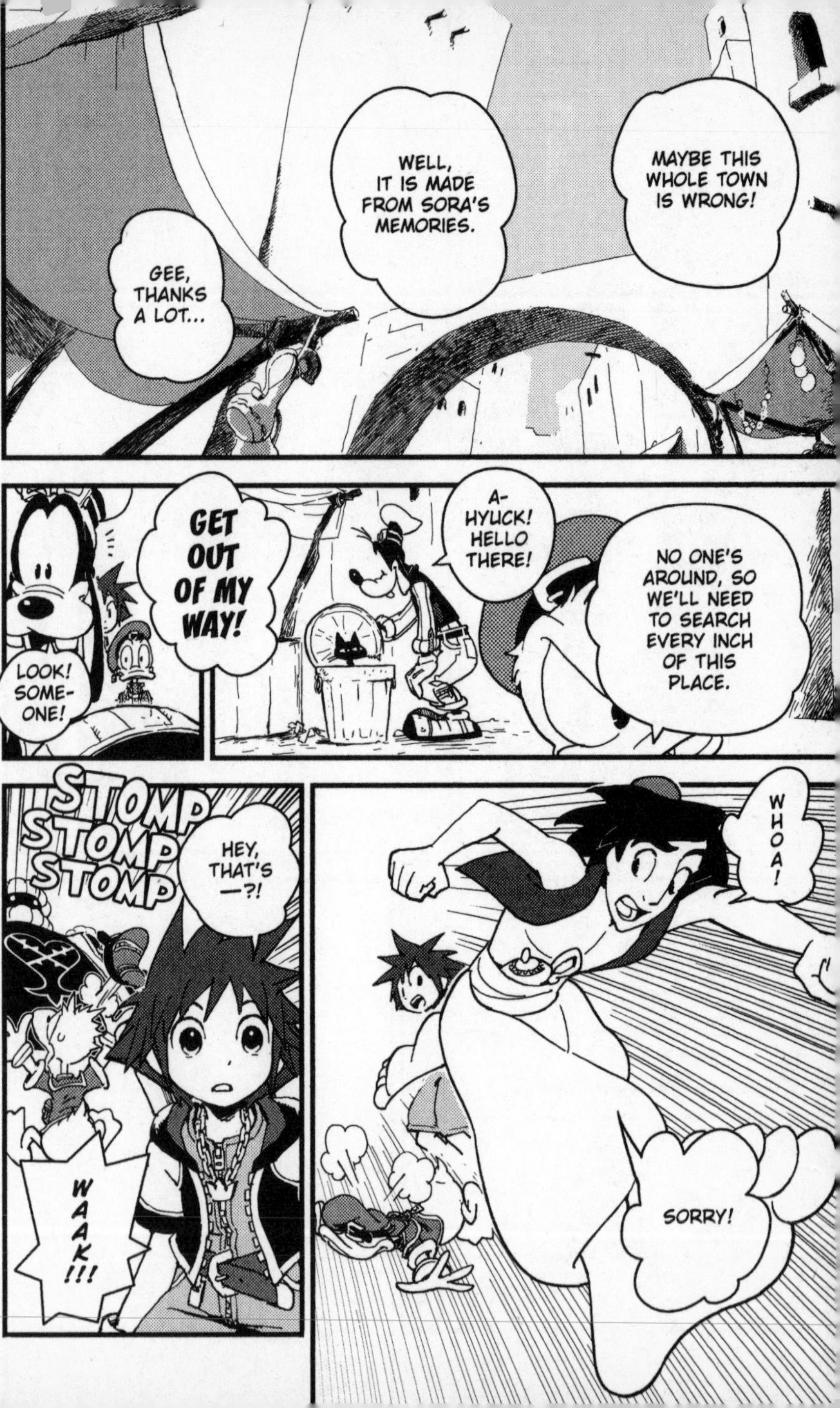
MAYBE THIS WHOLE TOWN IS WRONG!
WELL, IT IS MADE FROM SORA'S MEMORIES.
GEE, THANKS A LOT...
NO ONE'S AROUND, SO WE'LL NEED TO SEARCH EVERY INCH OF THIS PLACE.
A-HYUCK! HELLO THERE!
GET OUT OF MY WAY!
LOOK! SOMEONE!
WHOA!
SORRY!
STOMP STOMP STOMP
HEY, THAT'S—?!
WAAAK!!!

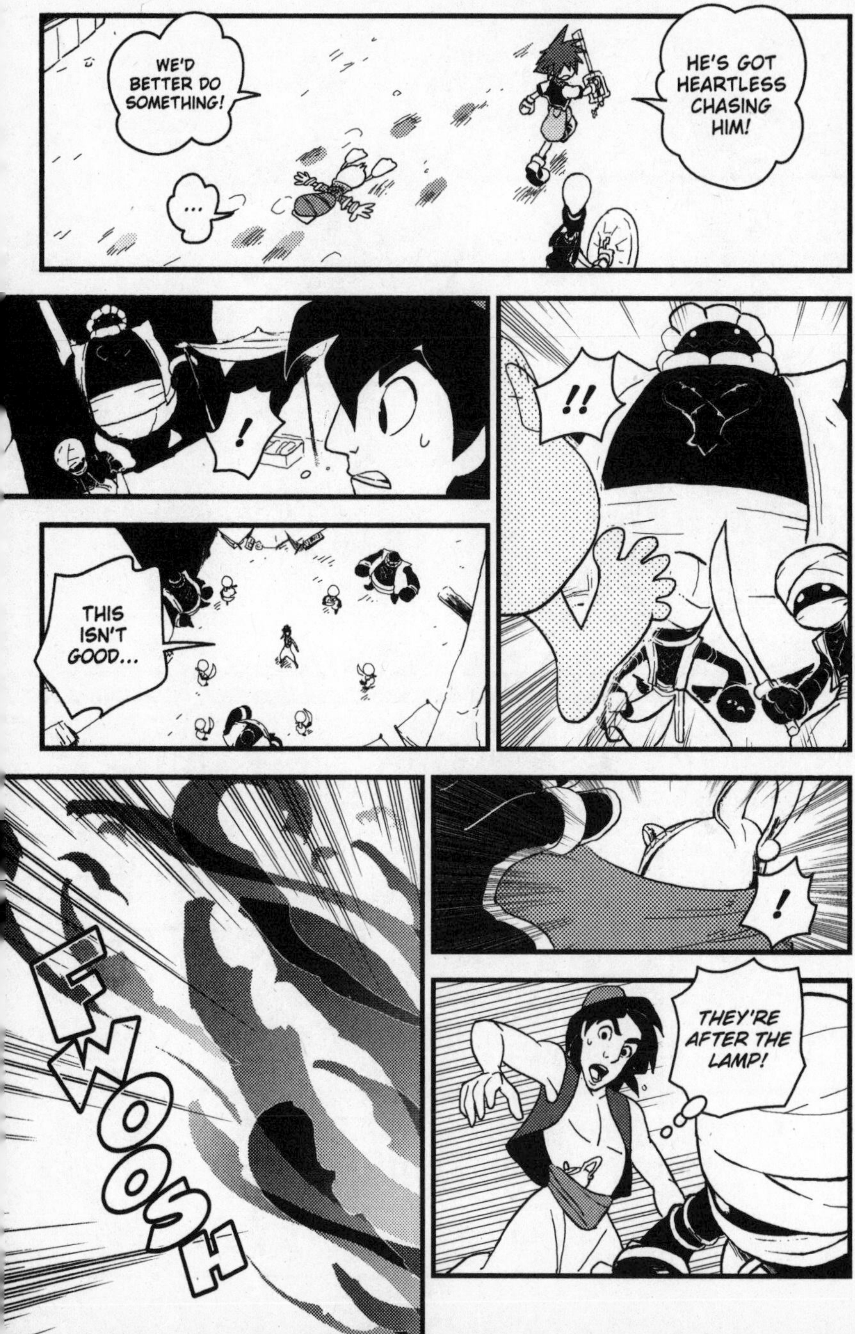
HE'S GOT HEARTLESS CHASING HIM!
WE'D BETTER DO SOMETHING!
...
!!
!
THIS ISN'T GOOD...
!
THEY'RE AFTER THE LAMP!
FWOOSH

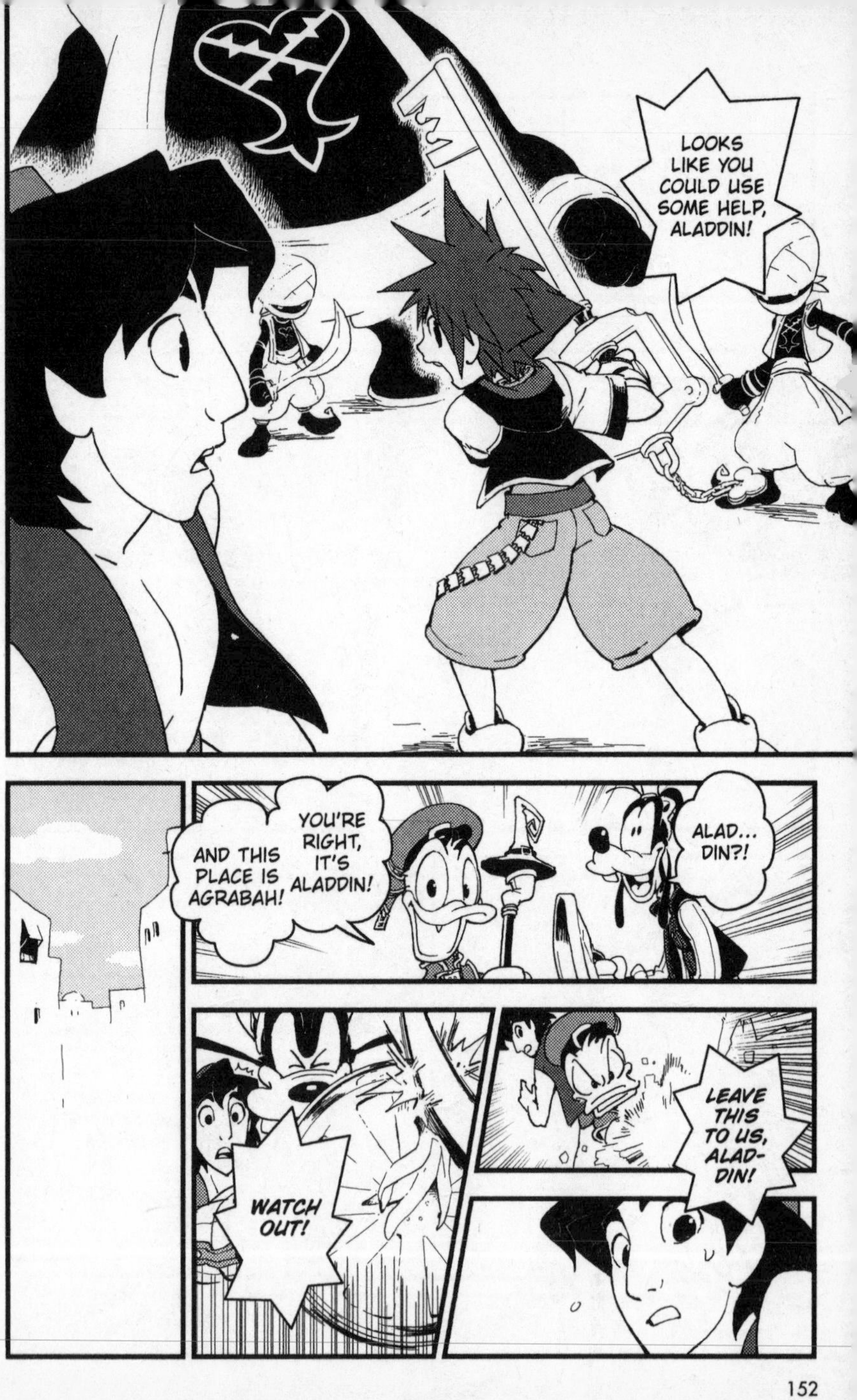
LOOKS LIKE YOU COULD USE SOME HELP, ALADDIN!
ALAD... DIN?!
YOU'RE RIGHT, IT'S ALADDIN!
AND THIS PLACE IS AGRABAH!
LEAVE THIS TO US, ALAD-DIN!
WATCH OUT!

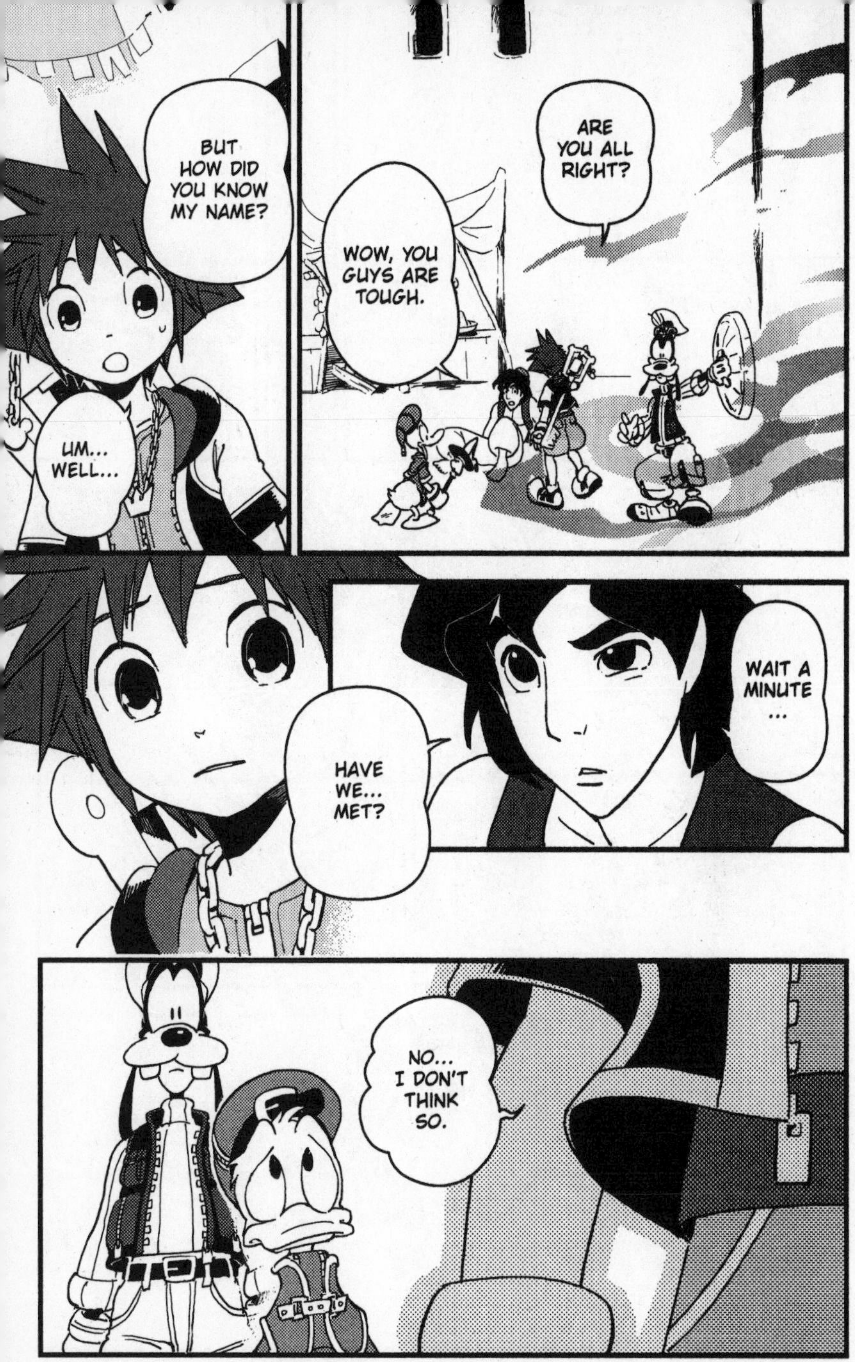
ARE YOU ALL RIGHT?
WOW, YOU GUYS ARE TOUGH.
BUT HOW DID YOU KNOW MY NAME?
UM... WELL...
WAIT A MINUTE ...
HAVE WE... MET?
NO... I DON'T THINK SO.

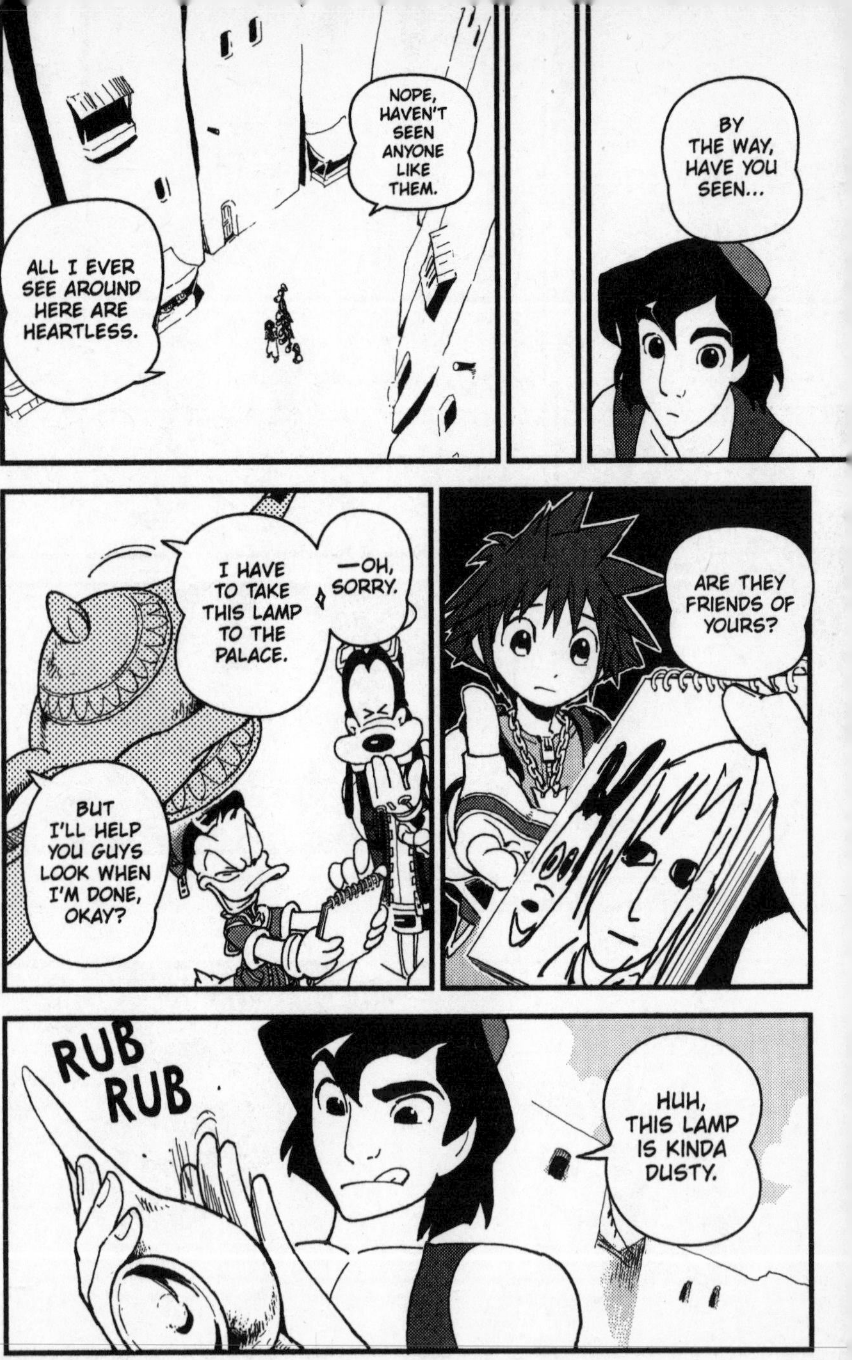
BY THE WAY, HAVE YOU SEEN...
NOPE, HAVEN'T SEEN ANYONE LIKE THEM.
ALL I EVER SEE AROUND HERE ARE HEARTLESS.
ARE THEY FRIENDS OF YOURS?
—OH, SORRY.
I HAVE TO TAKE THIS LAMP TO THE PALACE.
BUT I'LL HELP YOU GUYS LOOK WHEN I'M DONE, OKAY?
HUH, THIS LAMP IS KINDA DUSTY.
RUB RUB

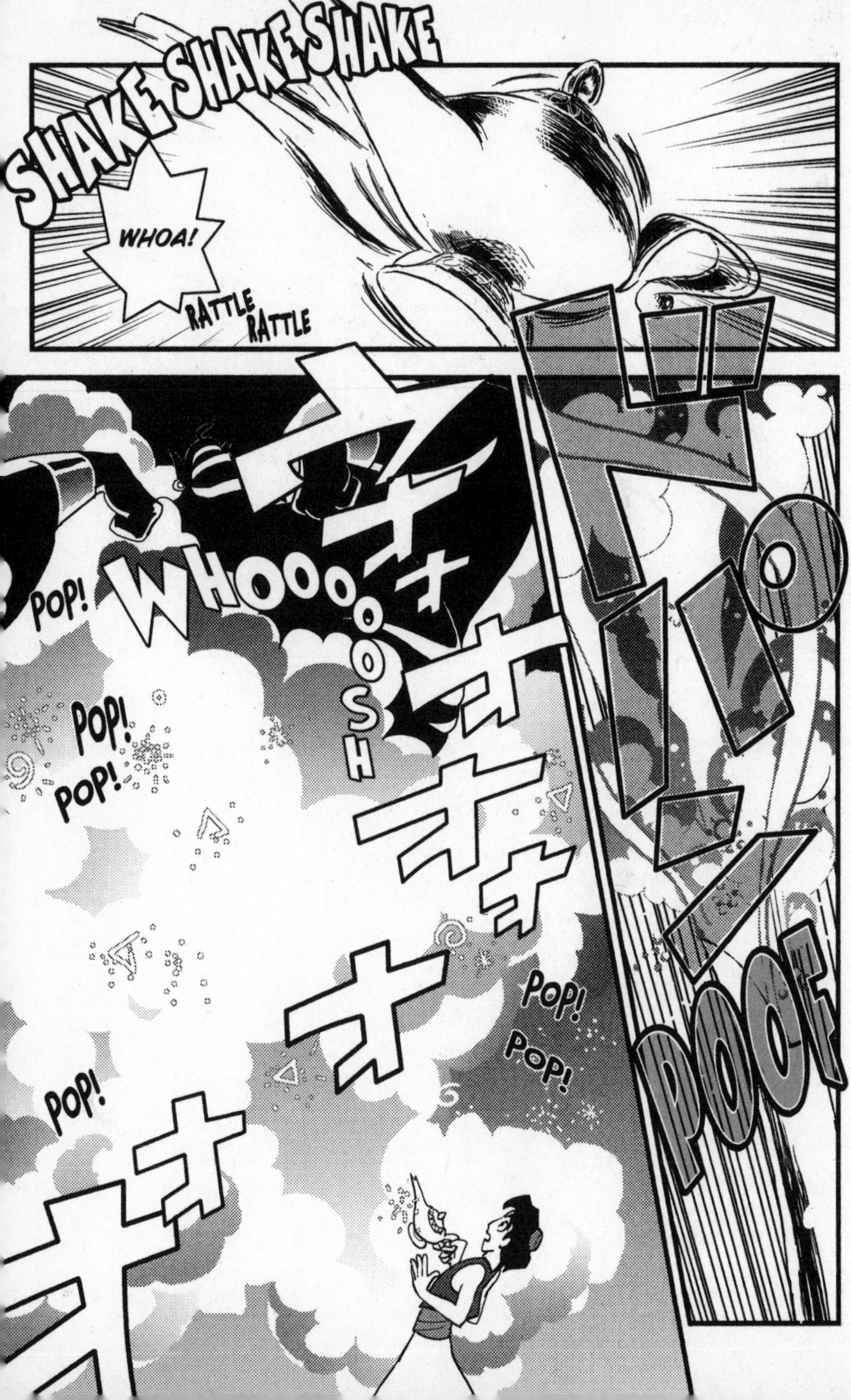
SHAKE SHAKE SHAKE
WHOA!
RATTLE RATTLE
POOF
WHOOOOOOSH
POP!
POP!
POP!
POP!
POP!
POP!

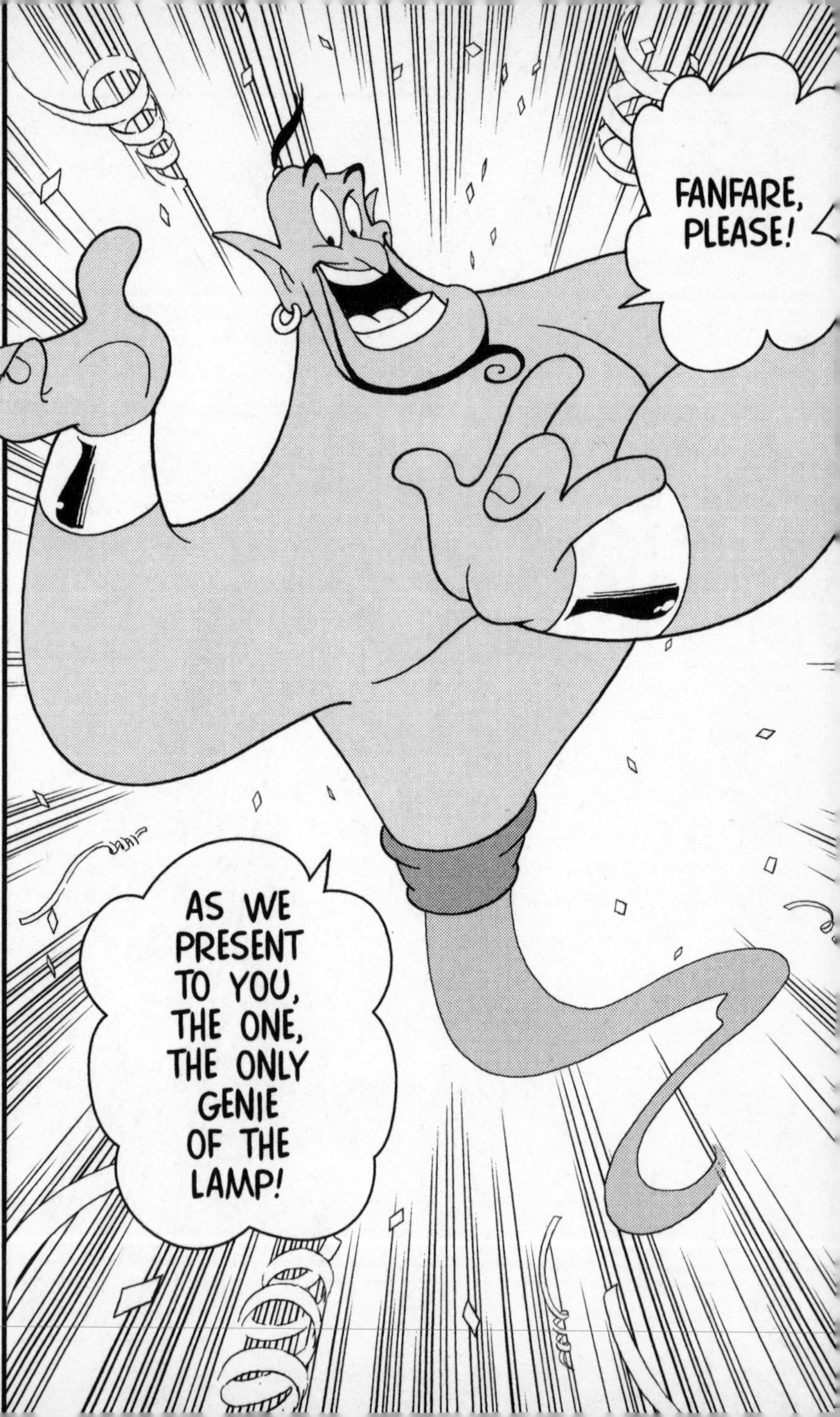
FANFARE, PLEASE!
AS WE PRESENT TO YOU, THE ONE, THE ONLY GENIE OF THE LAMP!

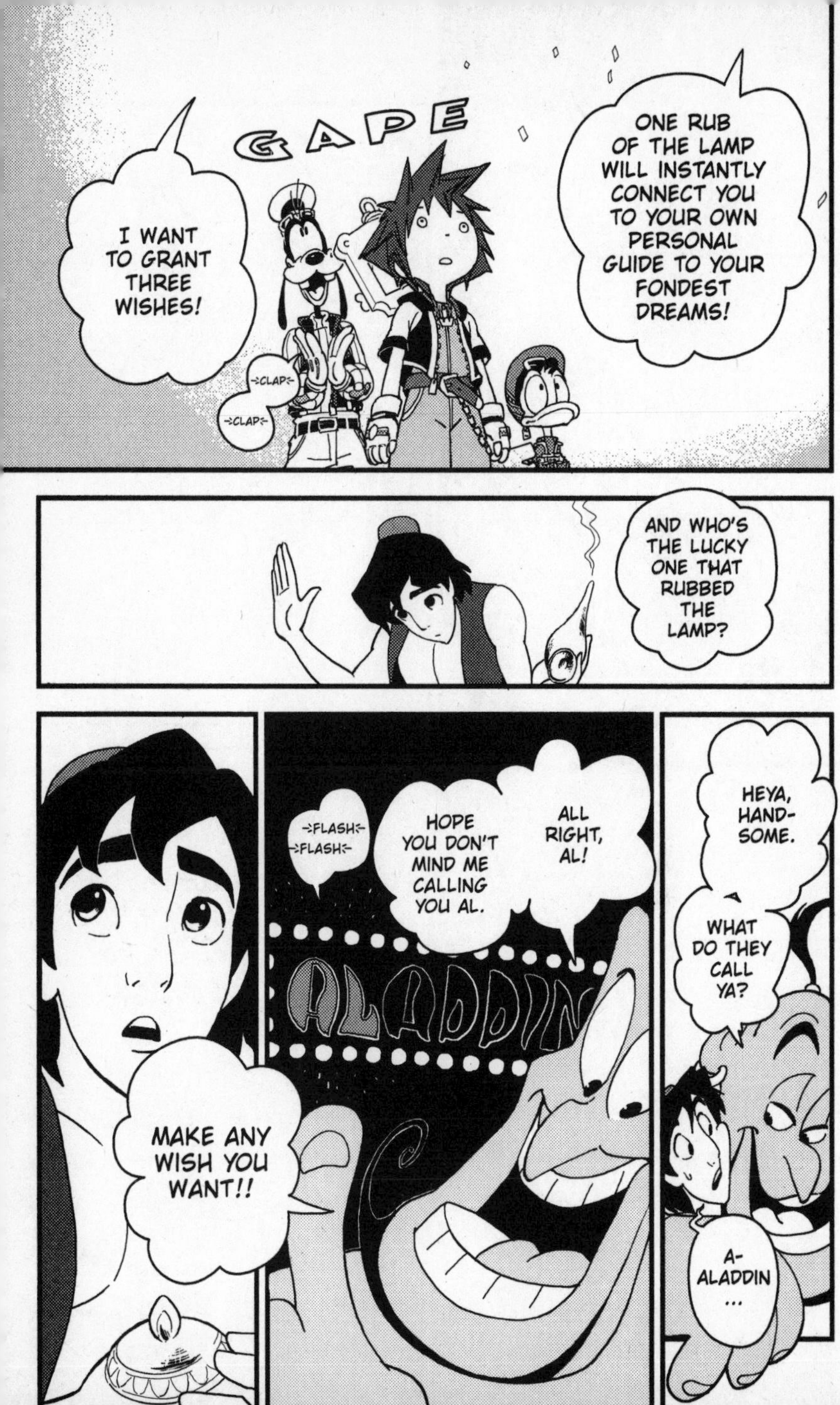
ONE RUB OF THE LAMP WILL INSTANTLY CONNECT YOU TO YOUR OWN PERSONAL GUIDE TO YOUR FONDEST DREAMS!
GAPE
I WANT TO GRANT THREE WISHES!
CLAP
CLAP
AND WHO'S THE LUCKY ONE THAT RUBBED THE LAMP?
HEYA, HANDSOME.
WHAT DO THEY CALL YA?
A-ALADDIN...
ALL RIGHT, AL!
HOPE YOU DON'T MIND ME CALLING YOU AL.
FLASH
FLASH
ALADDIN
MAKE ANY WISH YOU WANT!!

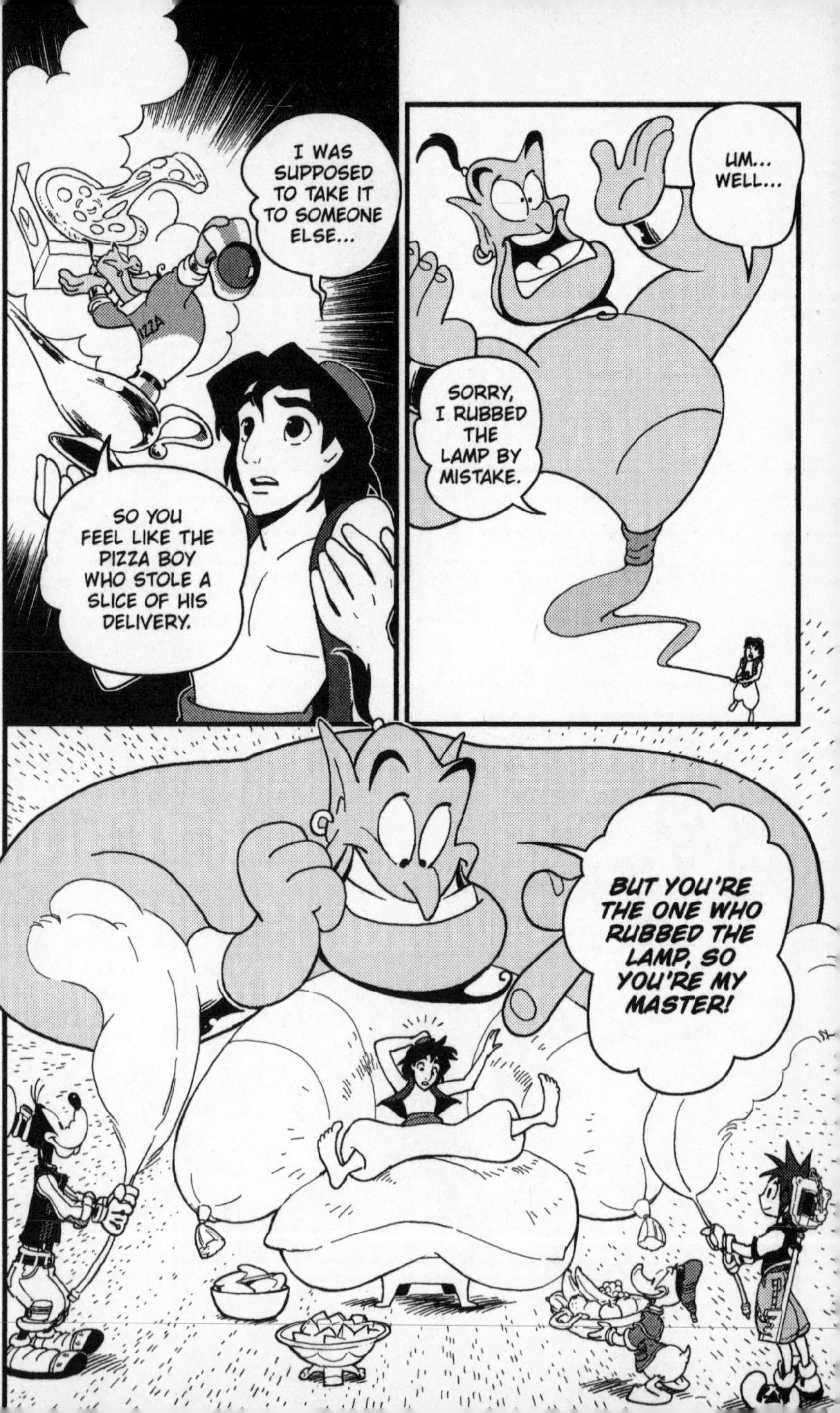
UM... WELL...
SORRY, I RUBBED THE LAMP BY MISTAKE.
I WAS SUPPOSED TO TAKE IT TO SOMEONE ELSE...
SO YOU FEEL LIKE THE PIZZA BOY WHO STOLE A SLICE OF HIS DELIVERY.
PIZZA
BUT YOU'RE THE ONE WHO RUBBED THE LAMP, SO YOU'RE MY MASTER!

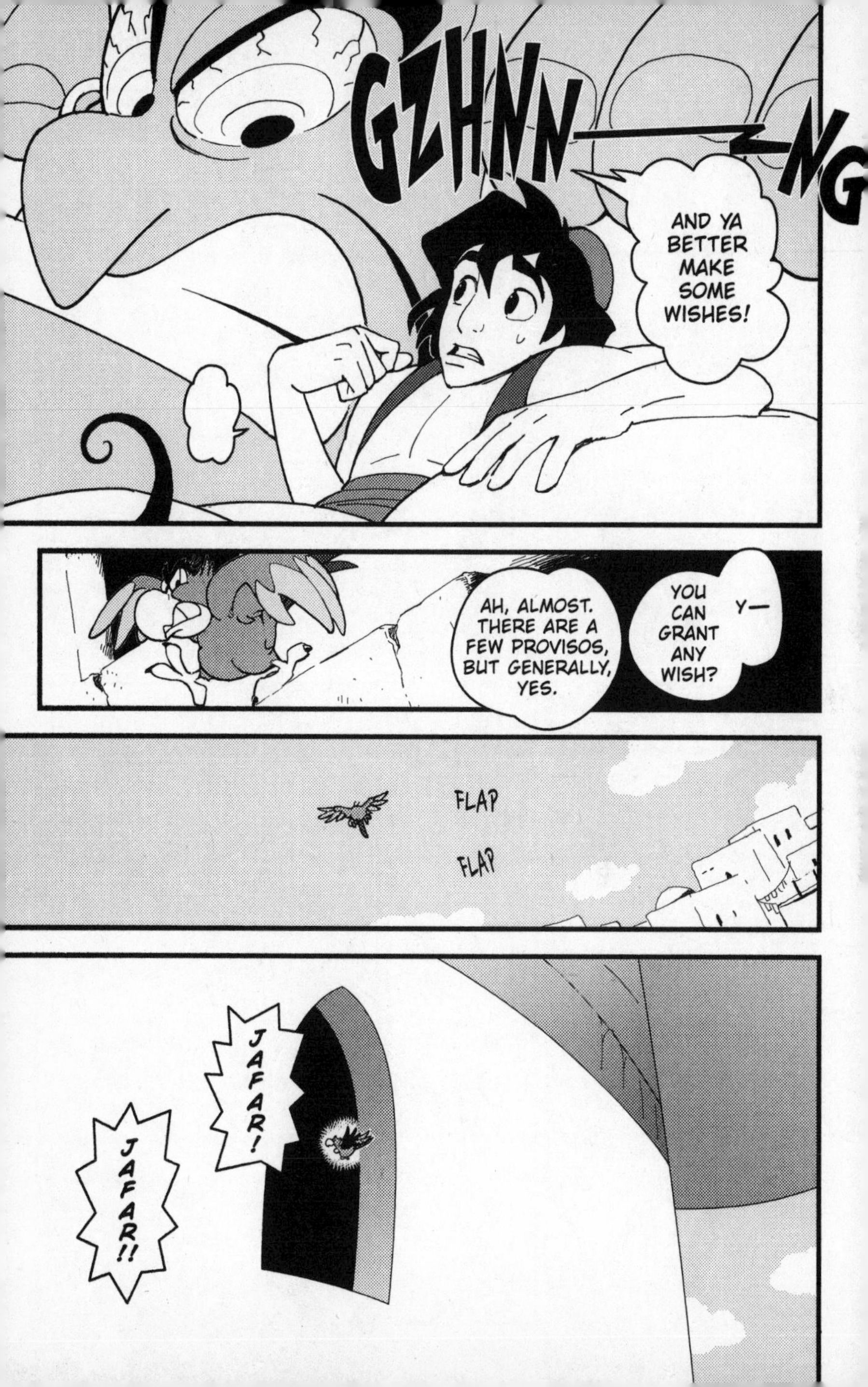
GZHNN—NG
AND YA BETTER MAKE SOME WISHES!
Y— YOU CAN GRANT ANY WISH?
AH, ALMOST. THERE ARE A FEW PROVISOS, BUT GENERALLY, YES.
FLAP
FLAP
JAFAR!
JAFAR!!

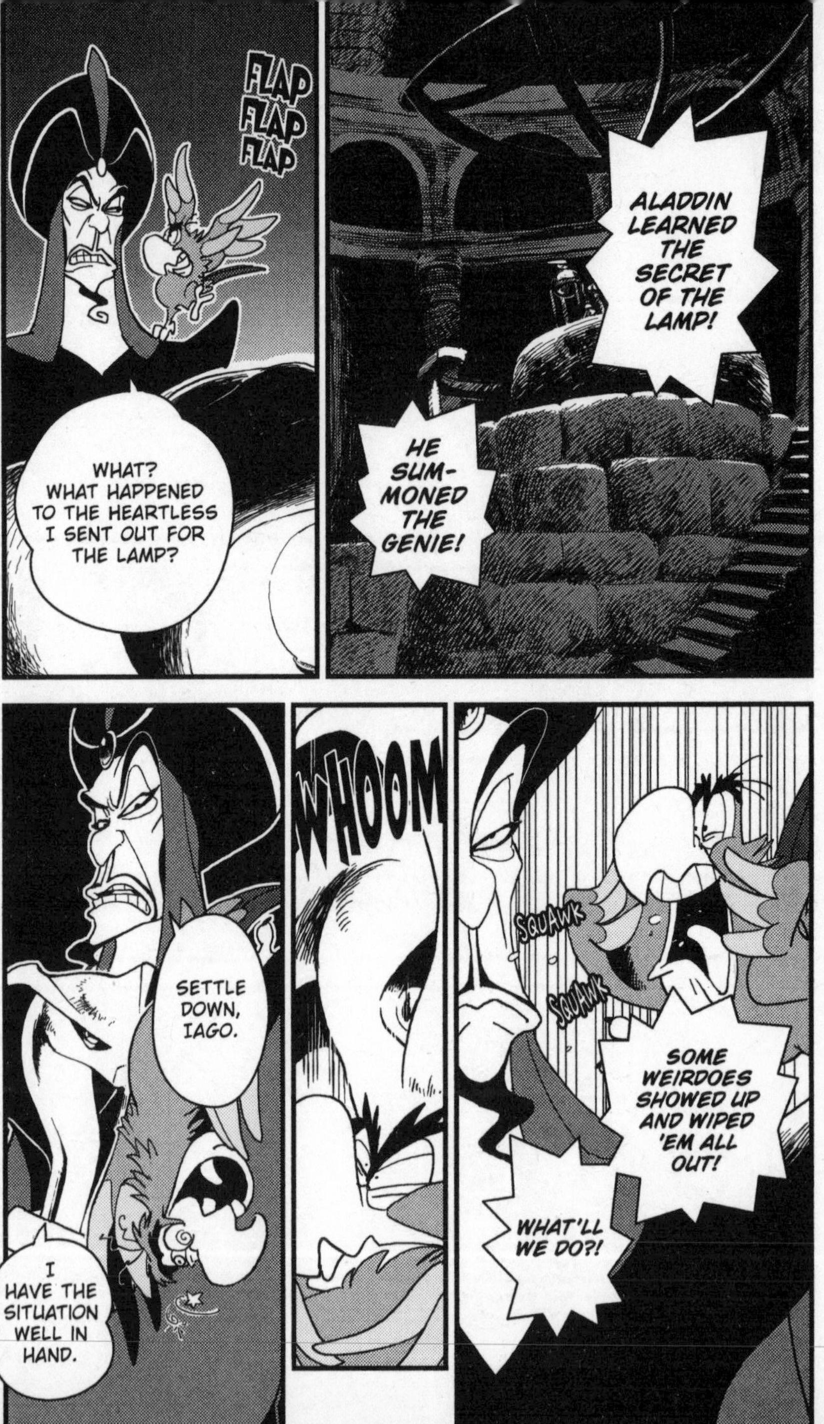
ALADDIN LEARNED THE SECRET OF THE LAMP!
HE SUMMONED THE GENIE!
FLAP FLAP FLAP
WHAT? WHAT HAPPENED TO THE HEARTLESS I SENT OUT FOR THE LAMP?
SQUAWK
SQUAWK
SOME WEIRDOES SHOWED UP AND WIPED 'EM ALL OUT!
WHAT'LL WE DO?!
WHOOM
SETTLE DOWN, IAGO.
I HAVE THE SITUATION WELL IN HAND.

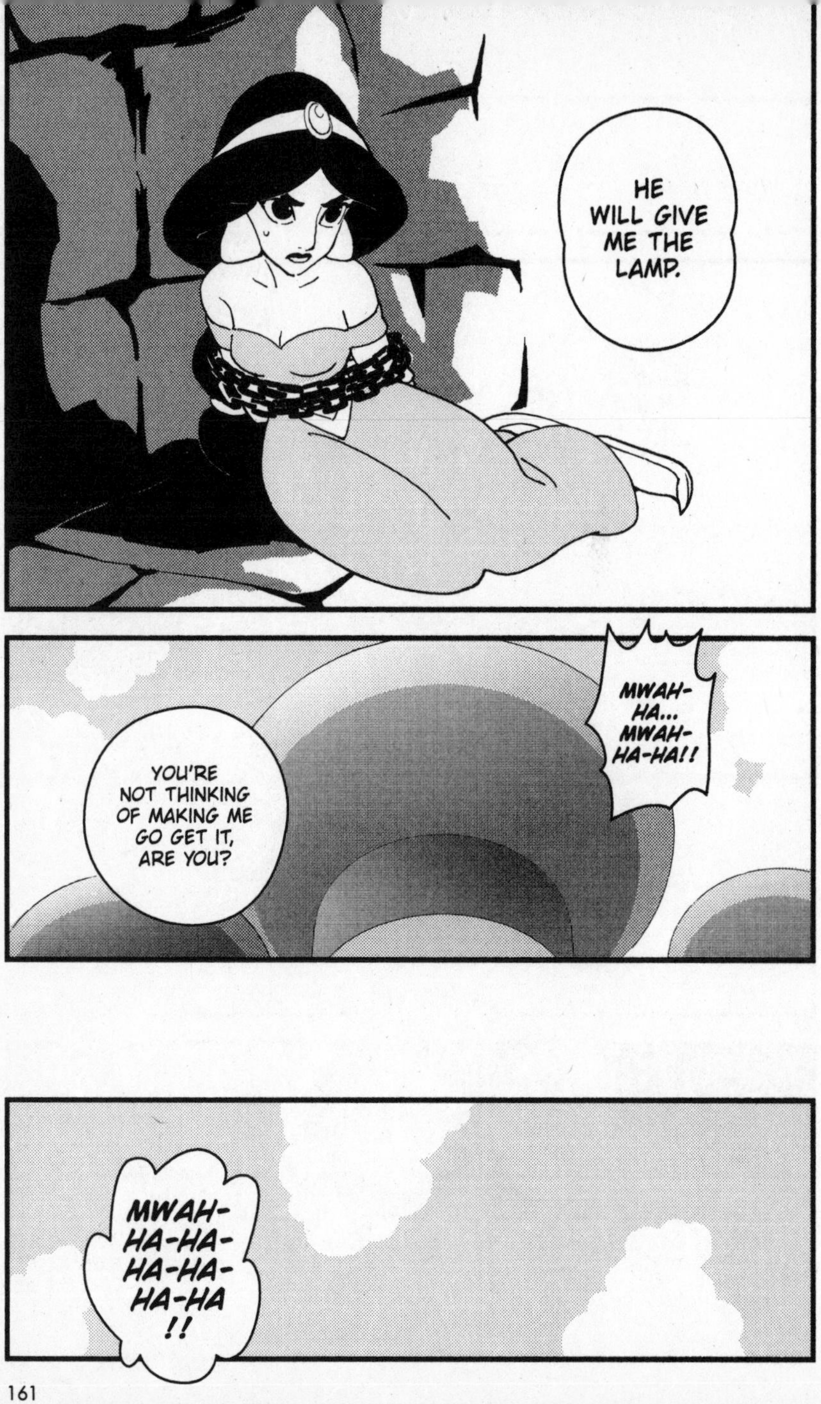
HE WILL GIVE ME THE LAMP.
MWAH-HA... MWAH-HA-HA!!
YOU'RE NOT THINKING OF MAKING ME GO GET IT, ARE YOU?
MWAH-HA-HA-HA-HA-HA-HA !!

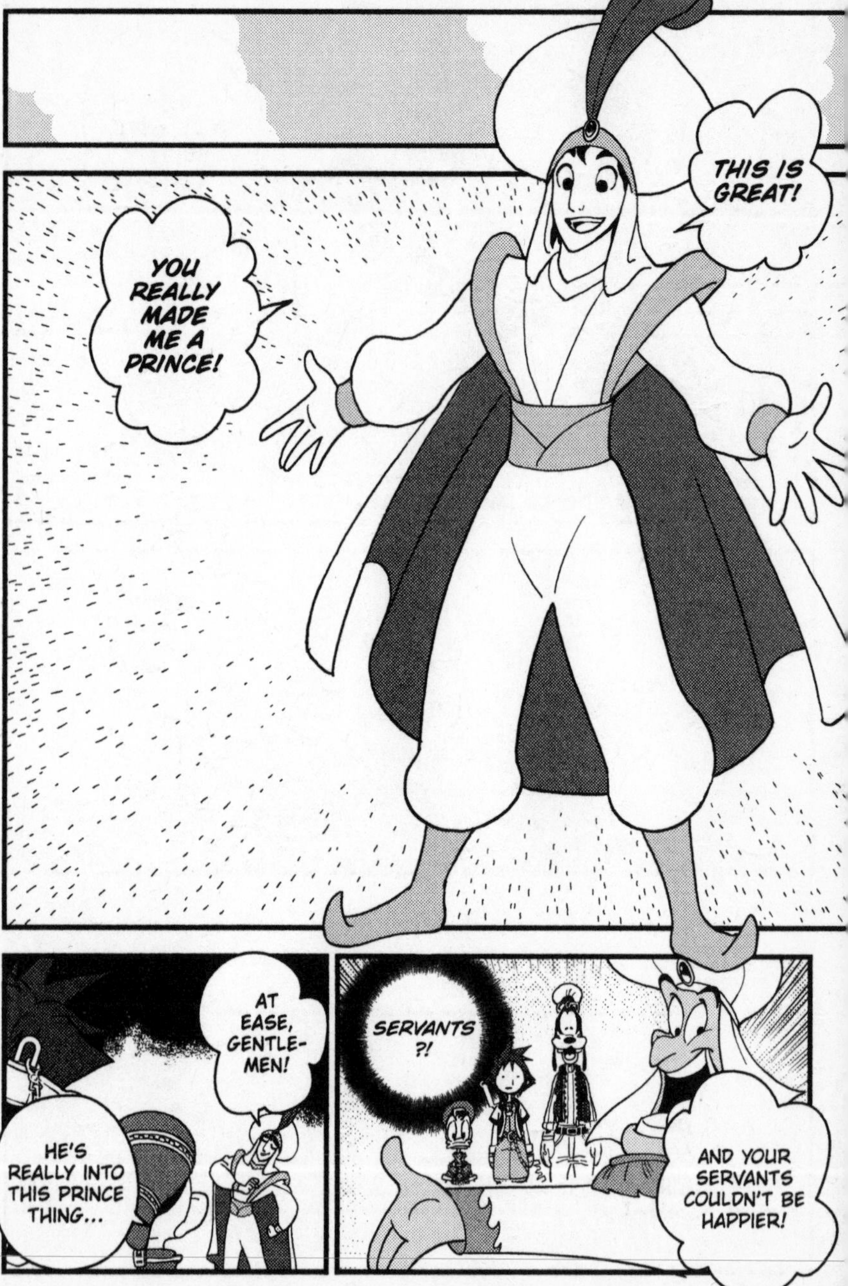
THIS IS GREAT!
YOU REALLY MADE ME A PRINCE!
AND YOUR SERVANTS COULDN'T BE HAPPIER!
SERVANTS?!
AT EASE, GENTLE-MEN!
HE'S REALLY INTO THIS PRINCE THING...

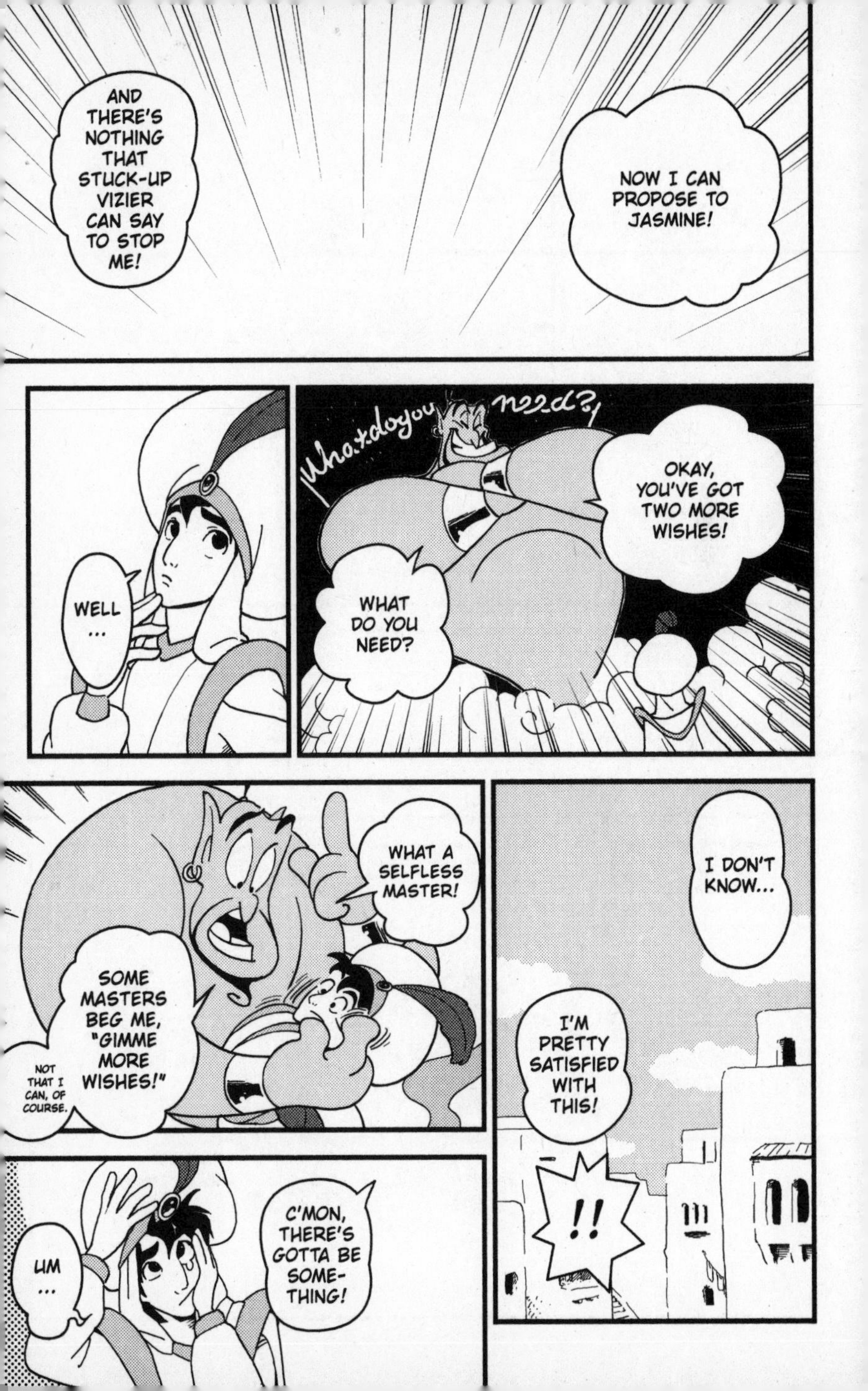
NOW I CAN PROPOSE TO JASMINE!
AND THERE'S NOTHING THAT STUCK-UP VIZIER CAN SAY TO STOP ME!
What do you need?!
OKAY, YOU'VE GOT TWO MORE WISHES!
WHAT DO YOU NEED?
WELL ...
I DON'T KNOW...
I'M PRETTY SATISFIED WITH THIS!
!!
WHAT A SELFLESS MASTER!
SOME MASTERS BEG ME, "GIMME MORE WISHES!"
NOT THAT I CAN, OF COURSE.
C'MON, THERE'S GOTTA BE SOME-THING!
UM ...

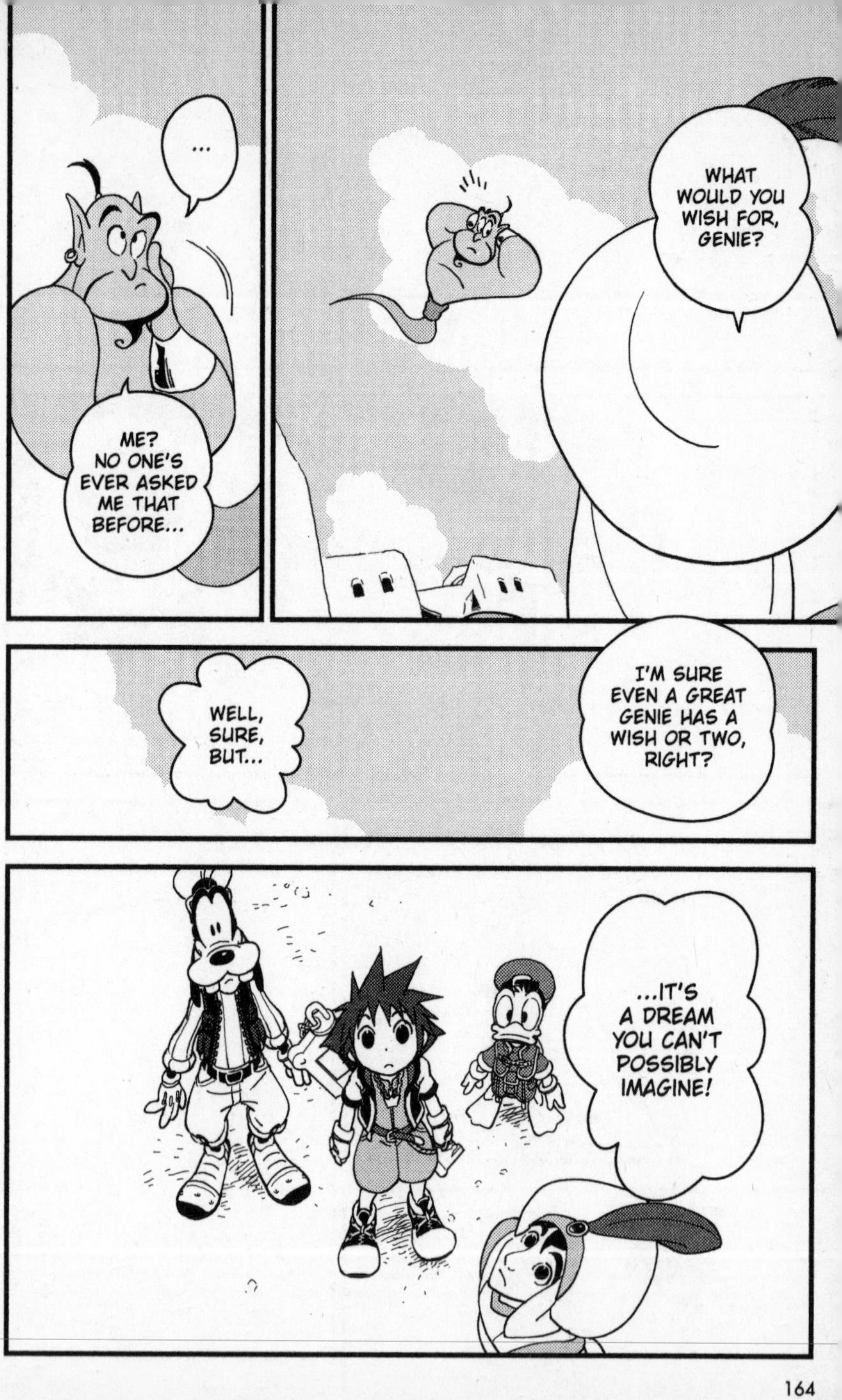
WHAT WOULD YOU WISH FOR, GENIE?
...
ME? NO ONE'S EVER ASKED ME THAT BEFORE...
I'M SURE EVEN A GREAT GENIE HAS A WISH OR TWO, RIGHT?
WELL, SURE, BUT...
...IT'S A DREAM YOU CAN'T POSSIBLY IMAGINE!

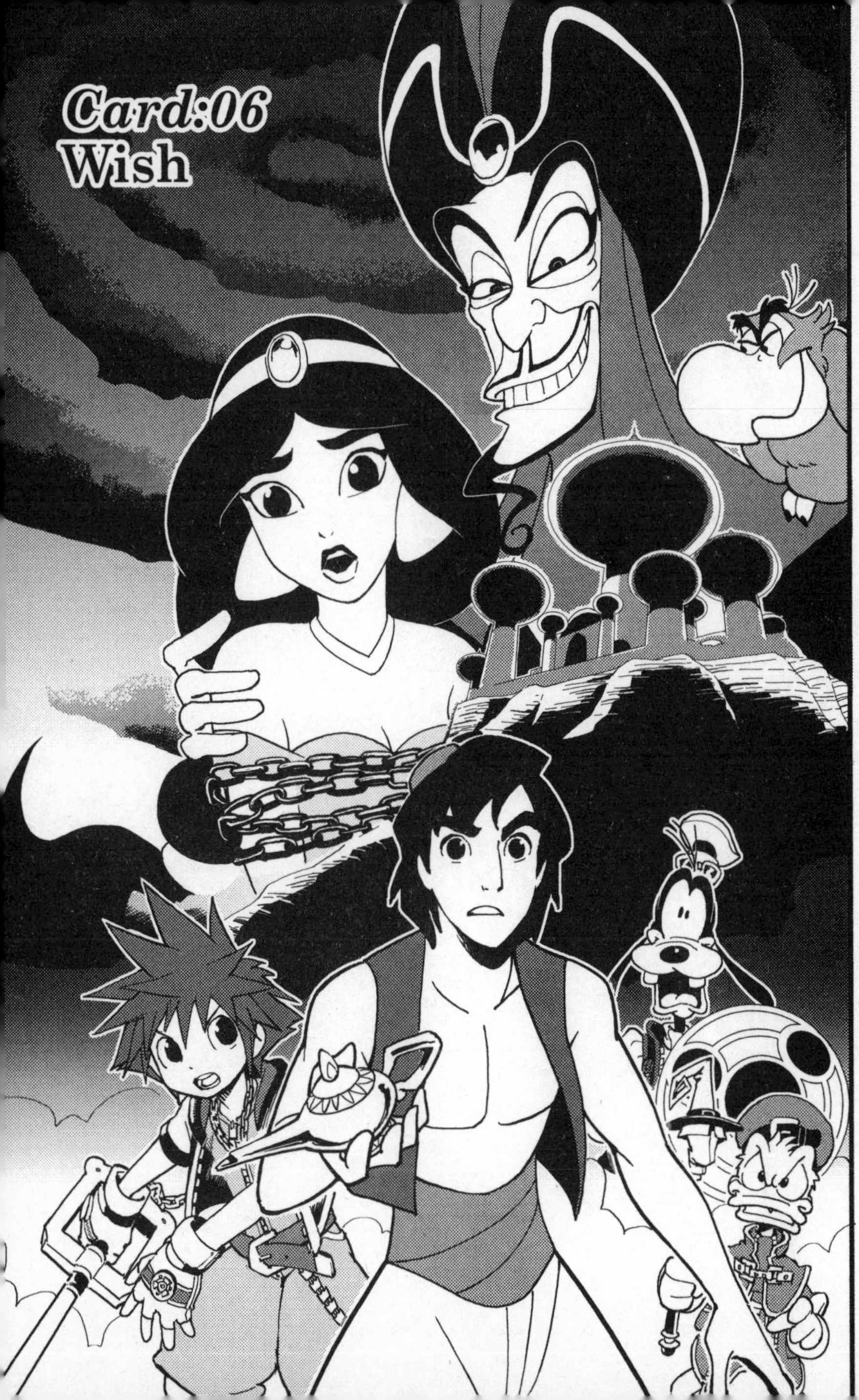
Card:06
Wish

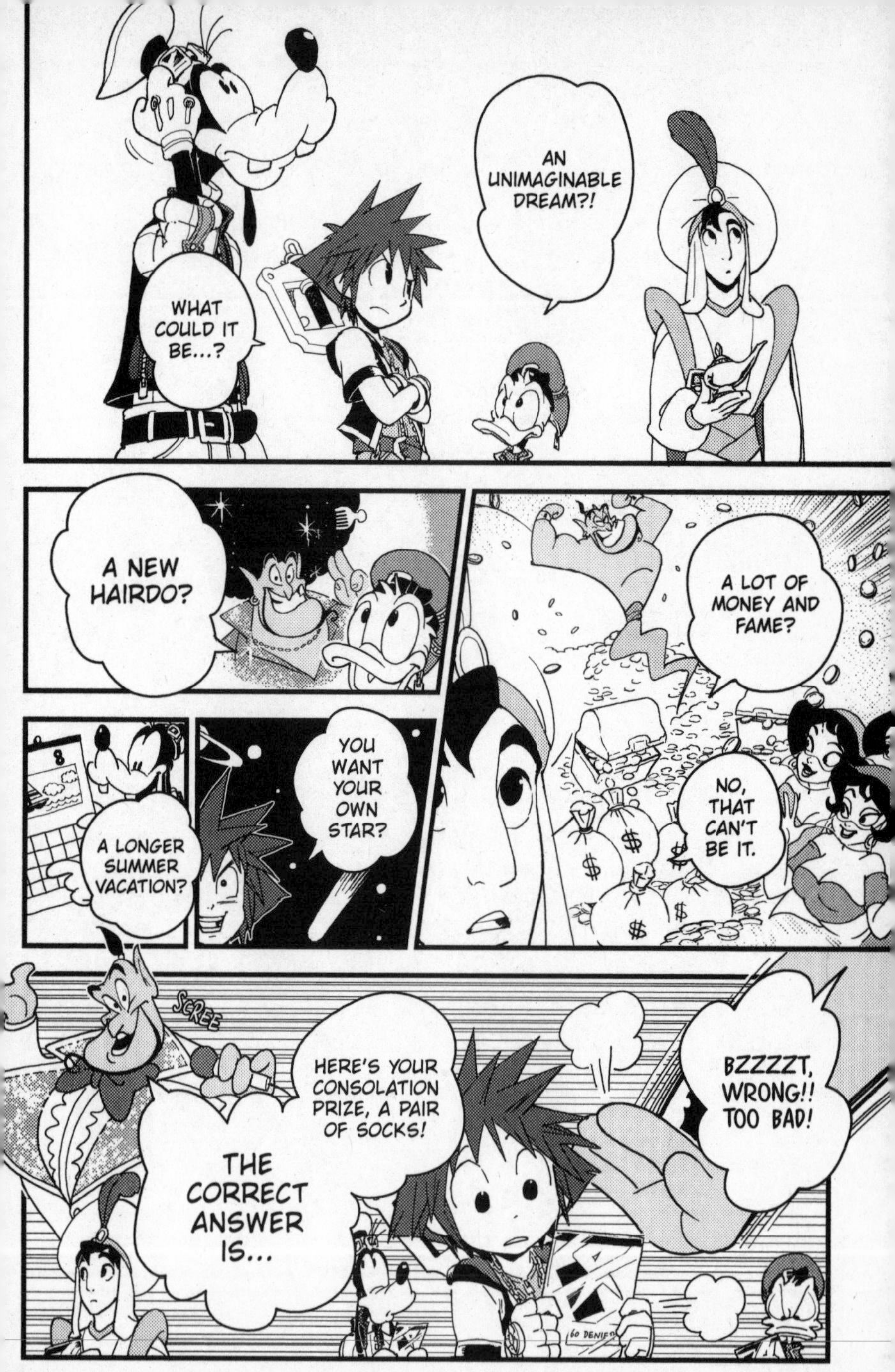
AN UNIMAGINABLE DREAM?!
WHAT COULD IT BE...?
A LOT OF MONEY AND FAME?
NO, THAT CAN'T BE IT.
A NEW HAIRDO?
YOU WANT YOUR OWN STAR?
A LONGER SUMMER VACATION?
BZZZZT, WRONG!! TOO BAD!
HERE'S YOUR CONSOLATION PRIZE, A PAIR OF SOCKS!
SCREE
THE CORRECT ANSWER IS...

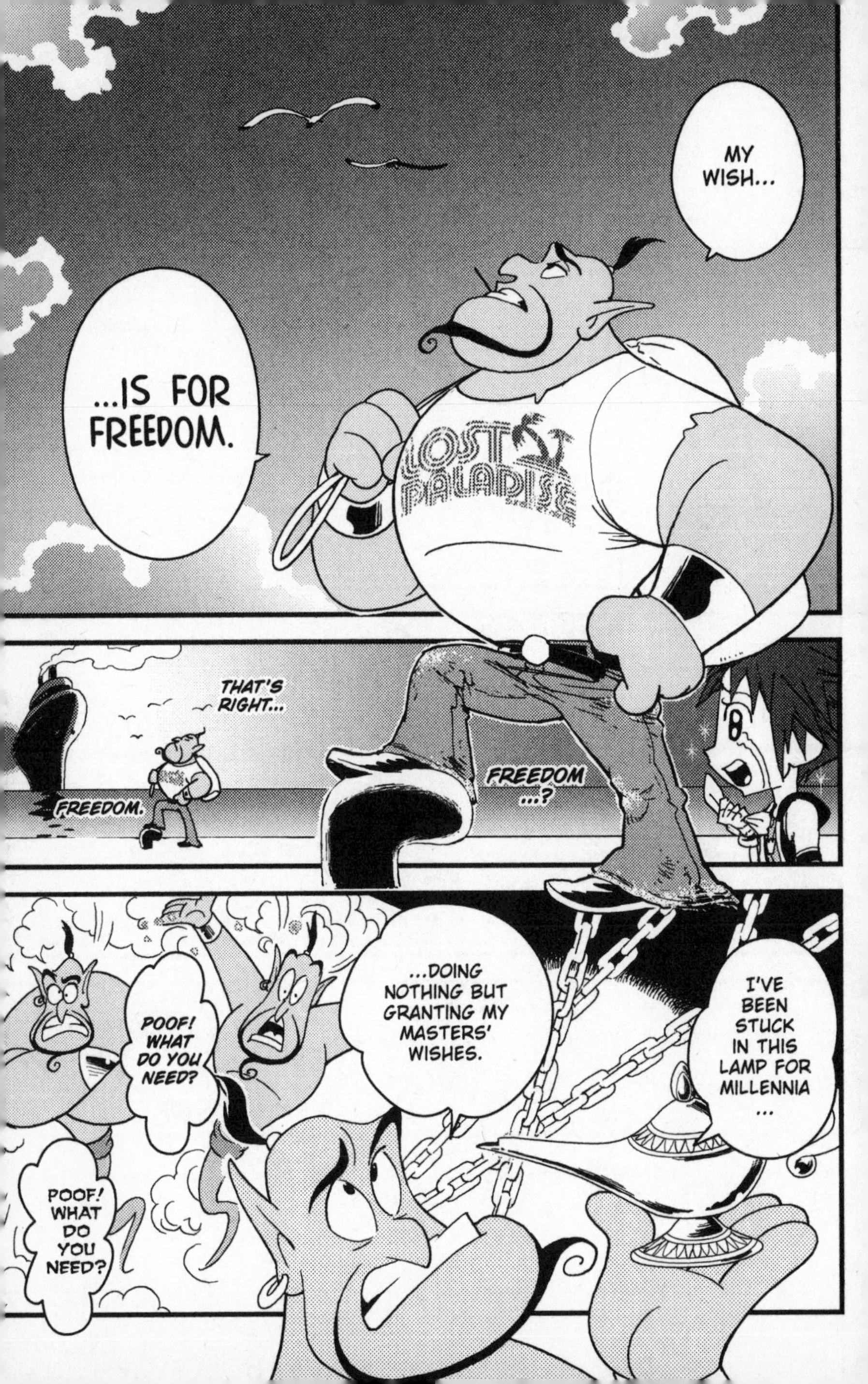
MY WISH...
...IS FOR FREEDOM.
FREEDOM ...?
THAT'S RIGHT...
FREEDOM.
I'VE BEEN STUCK IN THIS LAMP FOR MILLENNIA ...
...DOING NOTHING BUT GRANTING MY MASTERS' WISHES.
POOF! WHAT DO YOU NEED?
POOF! WHAT DO YOU NEED?

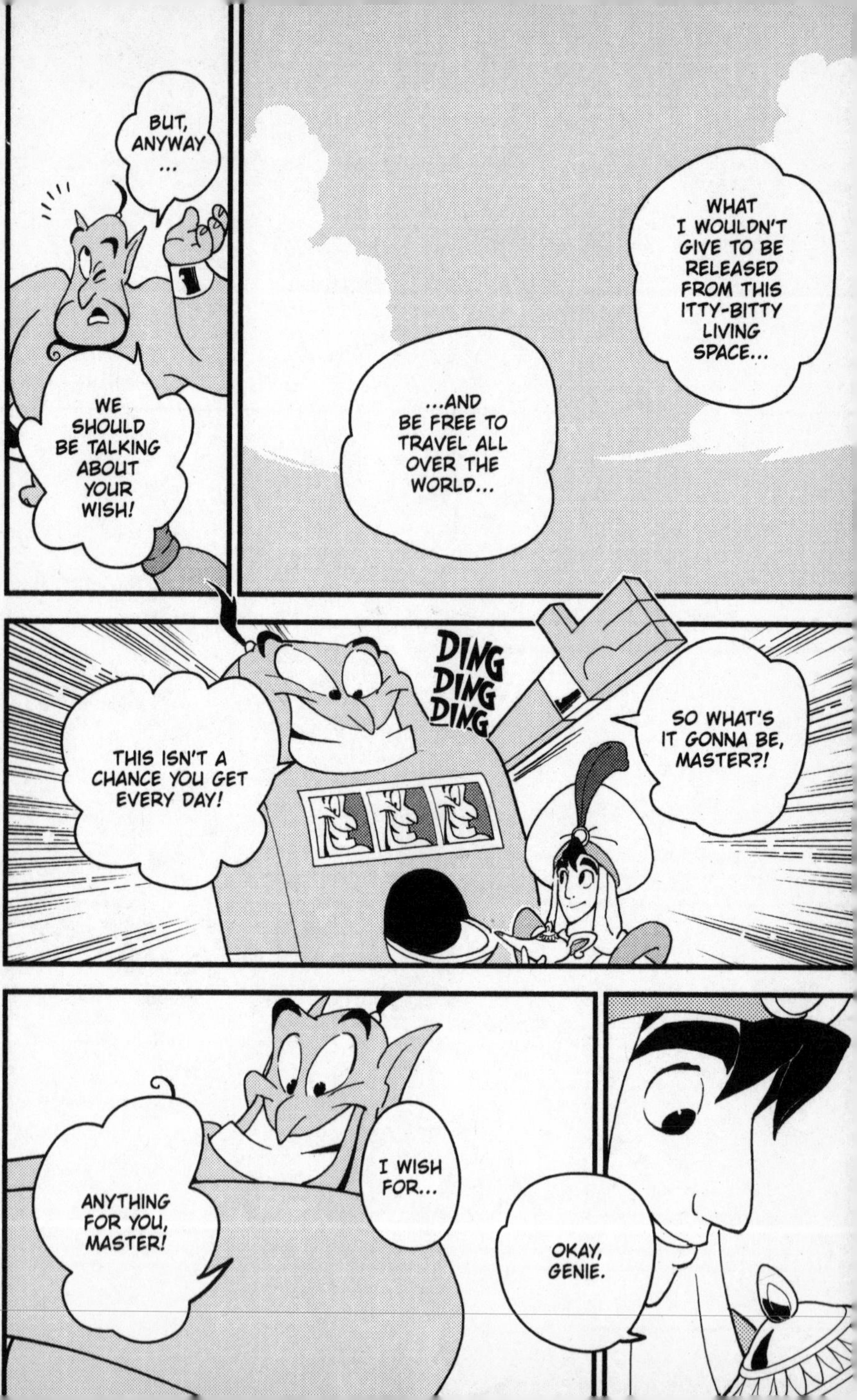
WHAT I WOULDN'T GIVE TO BE RELEASED FROM THIS ITTY-BITTY LIVING SPACE...
...AND BE FREE TO TRAVEL ALL OVER THE WORLD...
BUT, ANYWAY...
WE SHOULD BE TALKING ABOUT YOUR WISH!
DING DING DING
SO WHAT'S IT GONNA BE, MASTER?!
THIS ISN'T A CHANCE YOU GET EVERY DAY!
OKAY, GENIE.
I WISH FOR...
ANYTHING FOR YOU, MASTER!

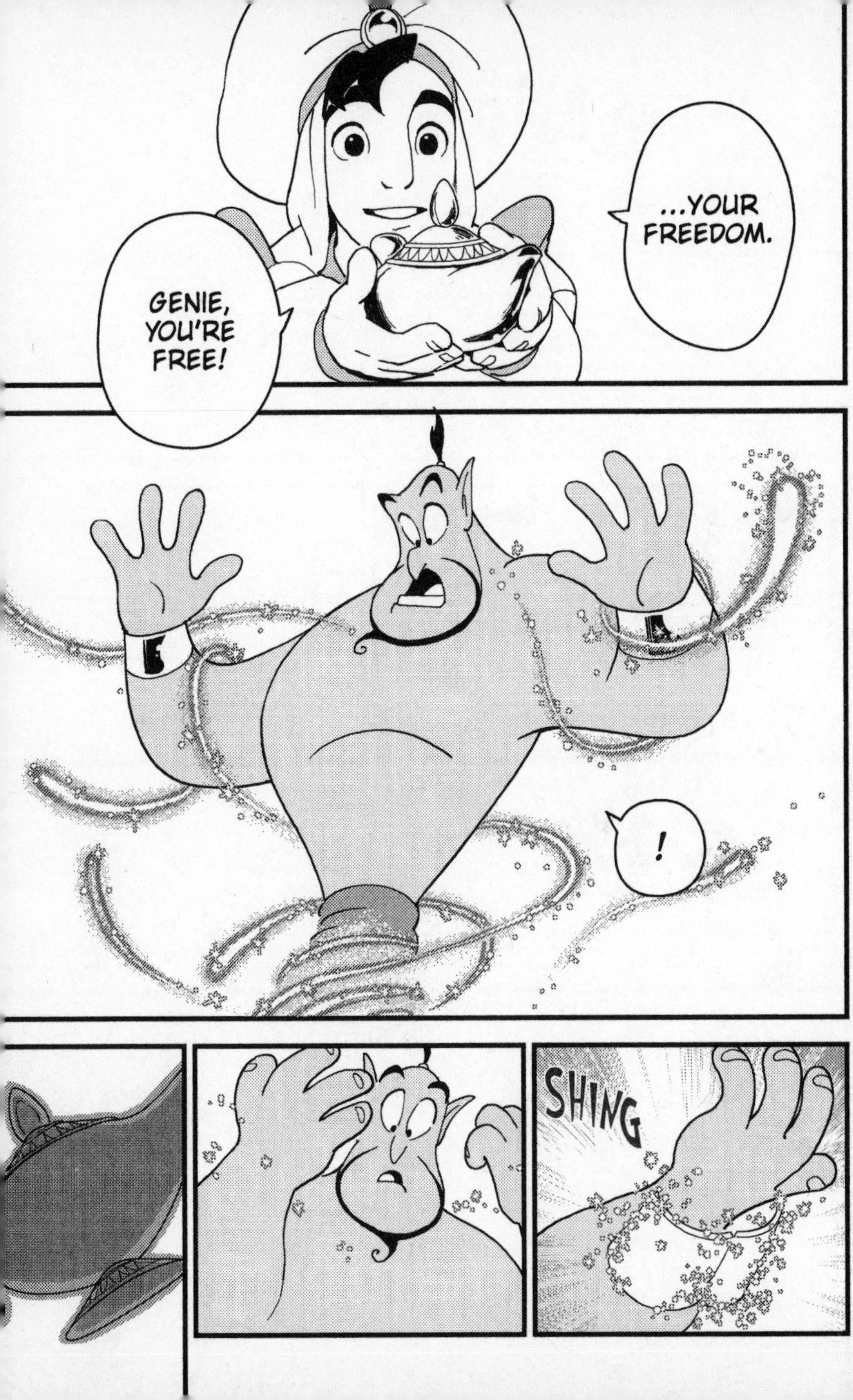
...YOUR FREEDOM.
GENIE, YOU'RE FREE!
!
SHING

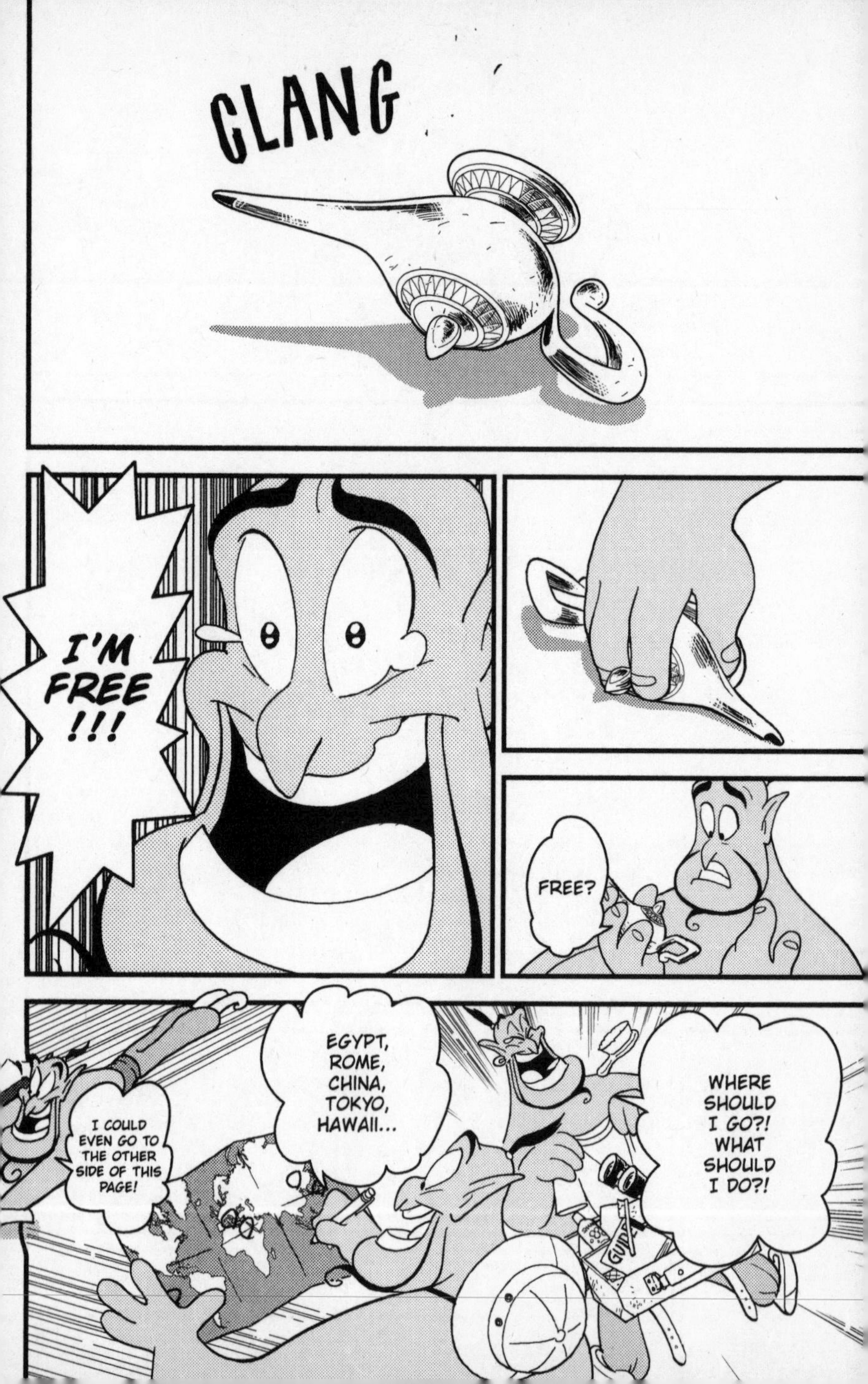
CLANG
FREE?
I'M FREE!!!
WHERE SHOULD I GO?! WHAT SHOULD I DO?!
EGYPT, ROME, CHINA, TOKYO, HAWAII...
I COULD EVEN GO TO THE OTHER SIDE OF THIS PAGE!

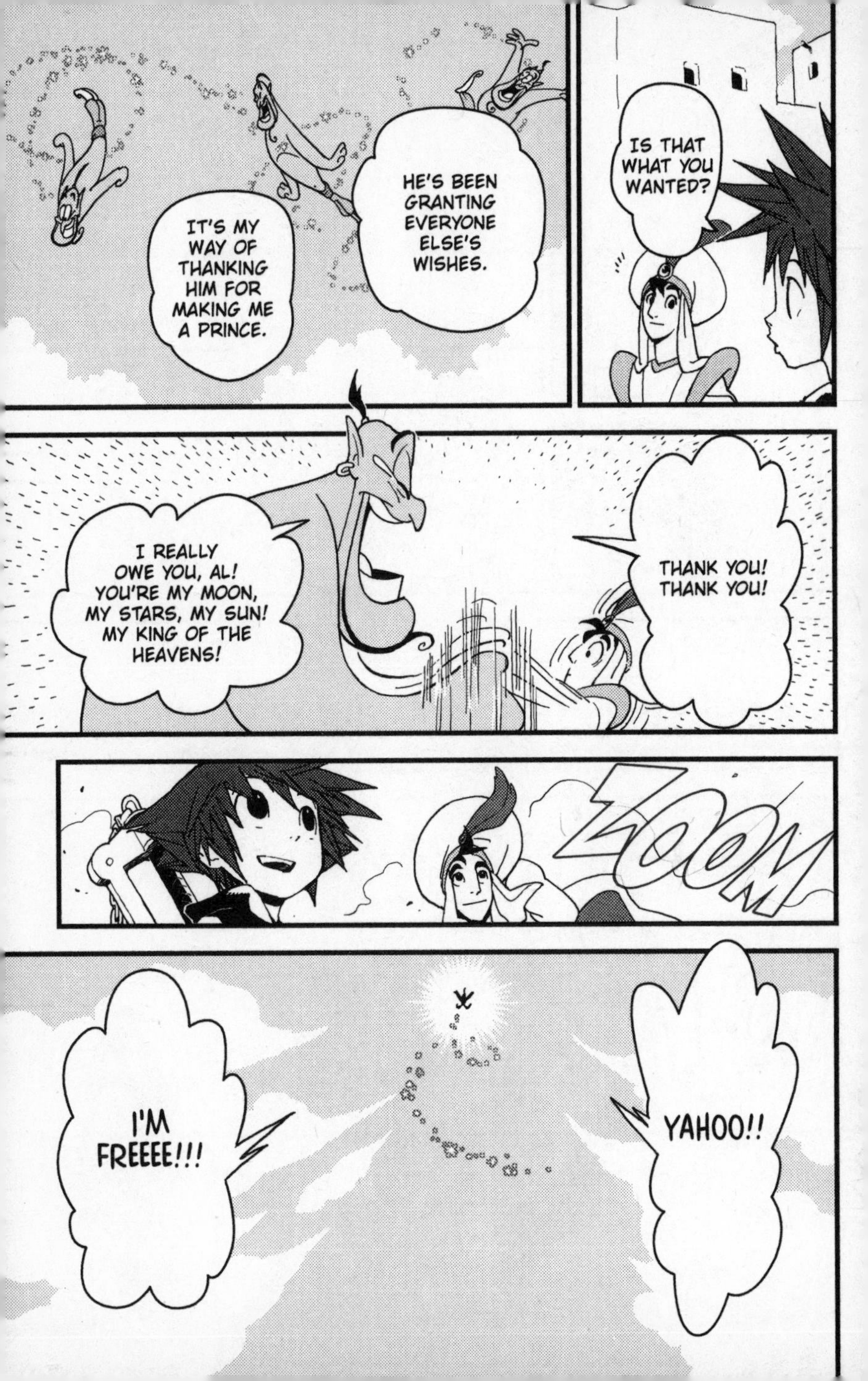
IS THAT WHAT YOU WANTED?
HE'S BEEN GRANTING EVERYONE ELSE'S WISHES.
IT'S MY WAY OF THANKING HIM FOR MAKING ME A PRINCE.
THANK YOU! THANK YOU!
I REALLY OWE YOU, AL! YOU'RE MY MOON, MY STARS, MY SUN! MY KING OF THE HEAVENS!
ZOOM
YAHOO!!
I'M FREEEE!!!

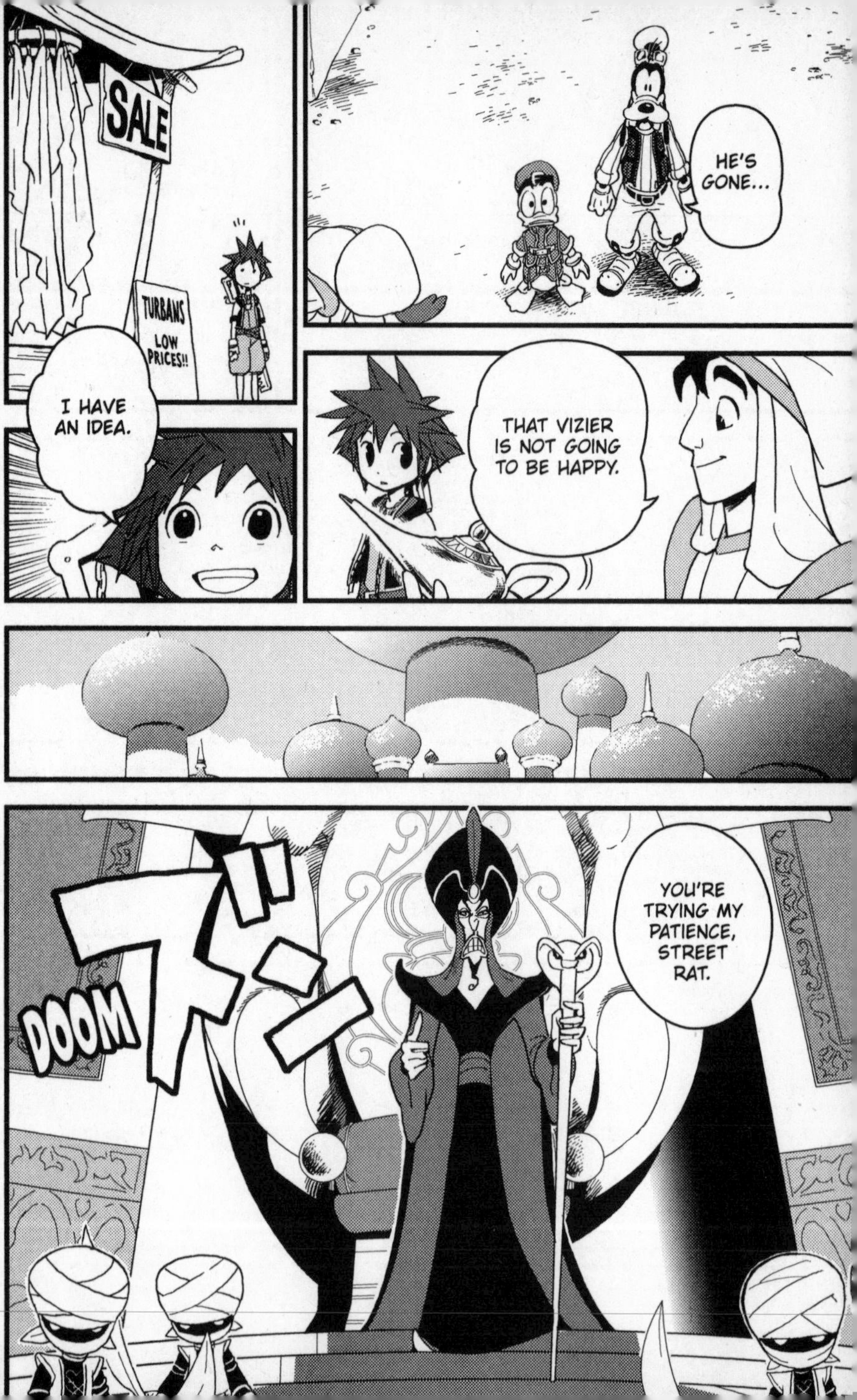
HE'S GONE...
SALE
TURBANS LOW PRICES!!
THAT VIZIER IS NOT GOING TO BE HAPPY.
I HAVE AN IDEA.
YOU'RE TRYING MY PATIENCE, STREET RAT.
DOOM

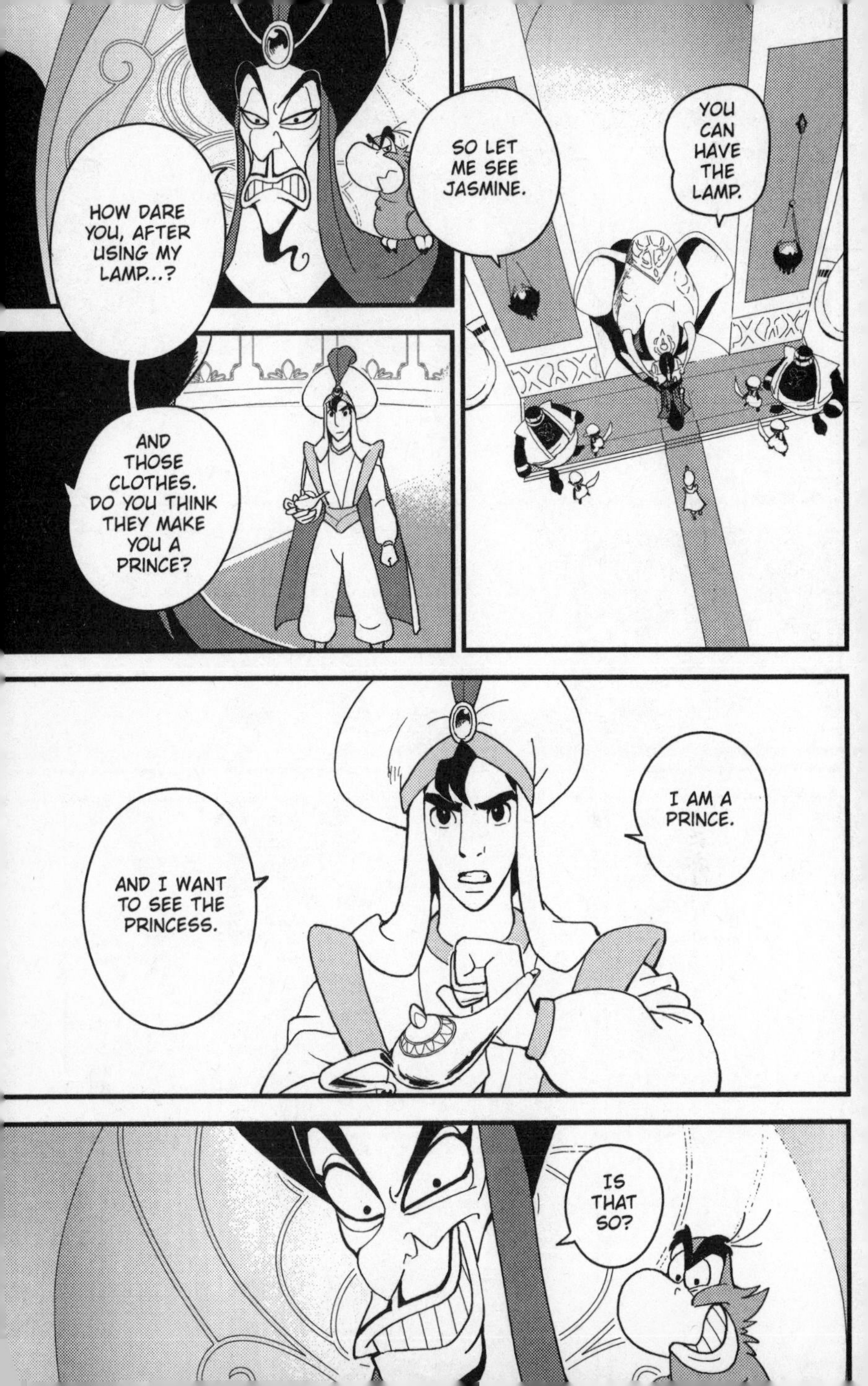
YOU CAN HAVE THE LAMP.
SO LET ME SEE JASMINE.
HOW DARE YOU, AFTER USING MY LAMP...?
AND THOSE CLOTHES. DO YOU THINK THEY MAKE YOU A PRINCE?
I AM A PRINCE.
AND I WANT TO SEE THE PRINCESS.
IS THAT SO?

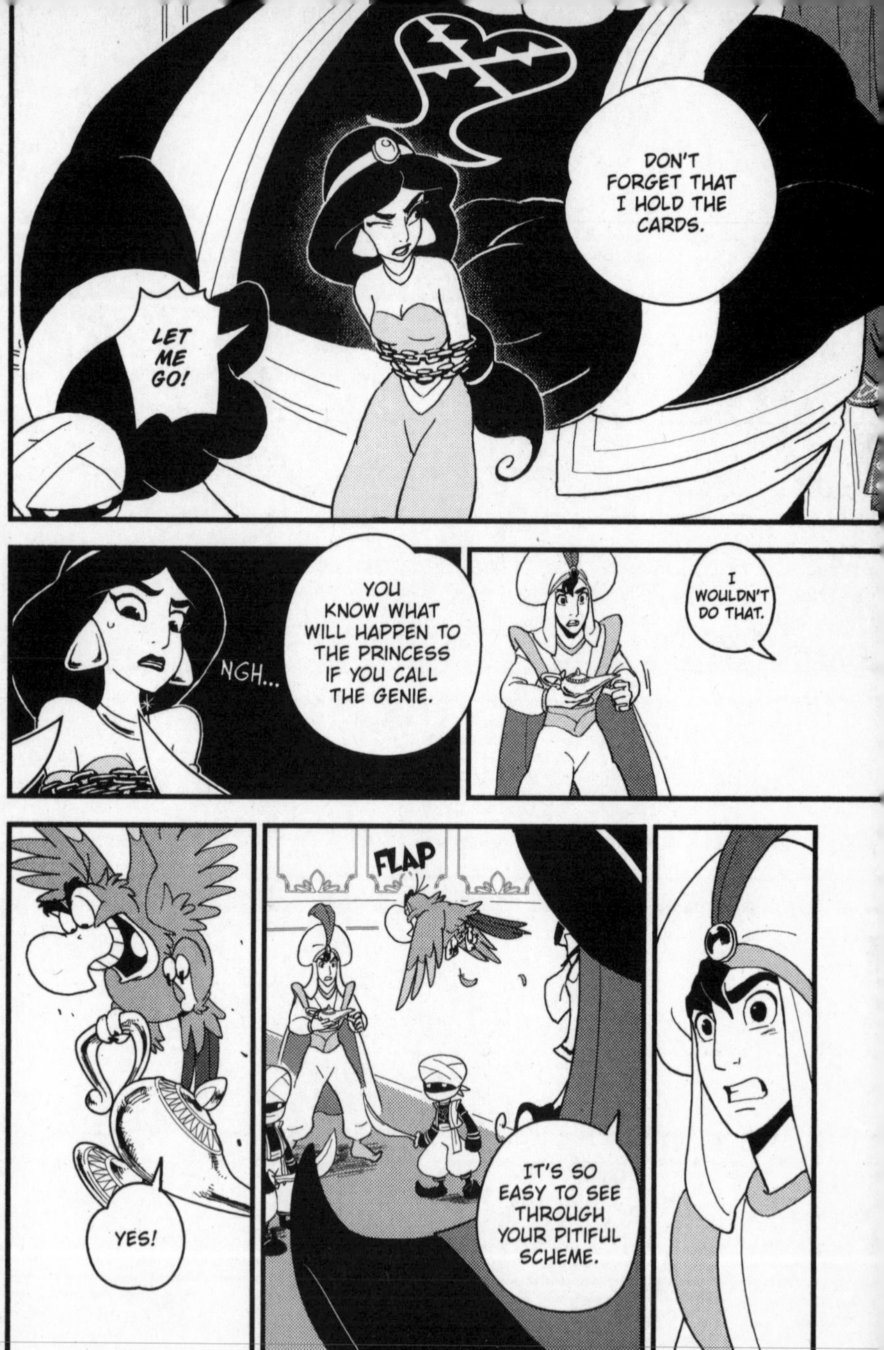

DON'T FORGET THAT I HOLD THE CARDS.
LET ME GO!
I WOULDN'T DO THAT.
YOU KNOW WHAT WILL HAPPEN TO THE PRINCESS IF YOU CALL THE GENIE.
NGH...
FLAP
IT'S SO EASY TO SEE THROUGH YOUR PITIFUL SCHEME.
YES!

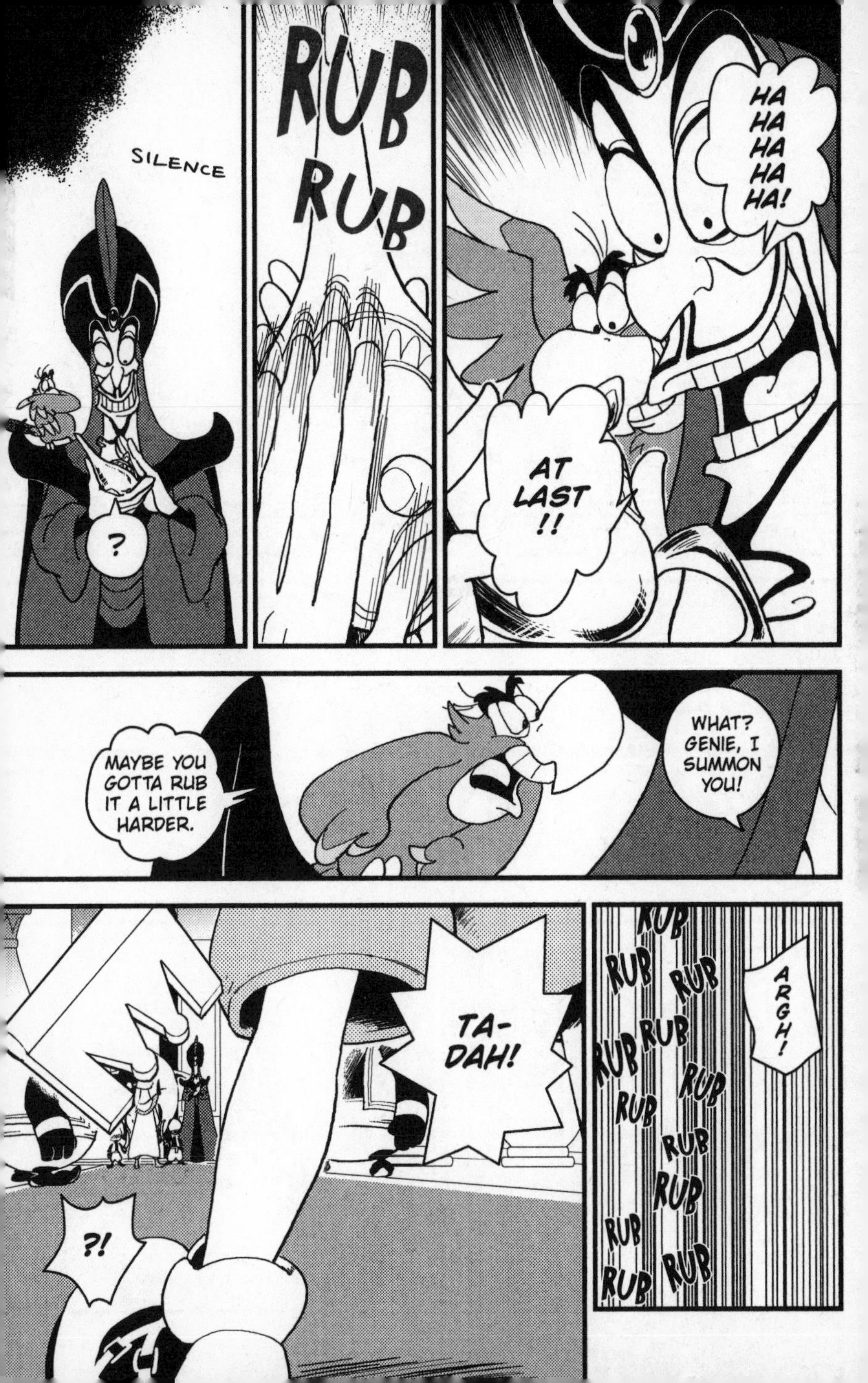
HA HA HA HA HA!
AT LAST!!
RUB RUB
SILENCE
?
WHAT? GENIE, I SUMMON YOU!
MAYBE YOU GOTTA RUB IT A LITTLE HARDER.
ARGH!
RUB
RUB
RUB
RUB
RUB
RUB
RUB
RUB
RUB
RUB
RUB
RUB
RUB
TA-DAH!
?!

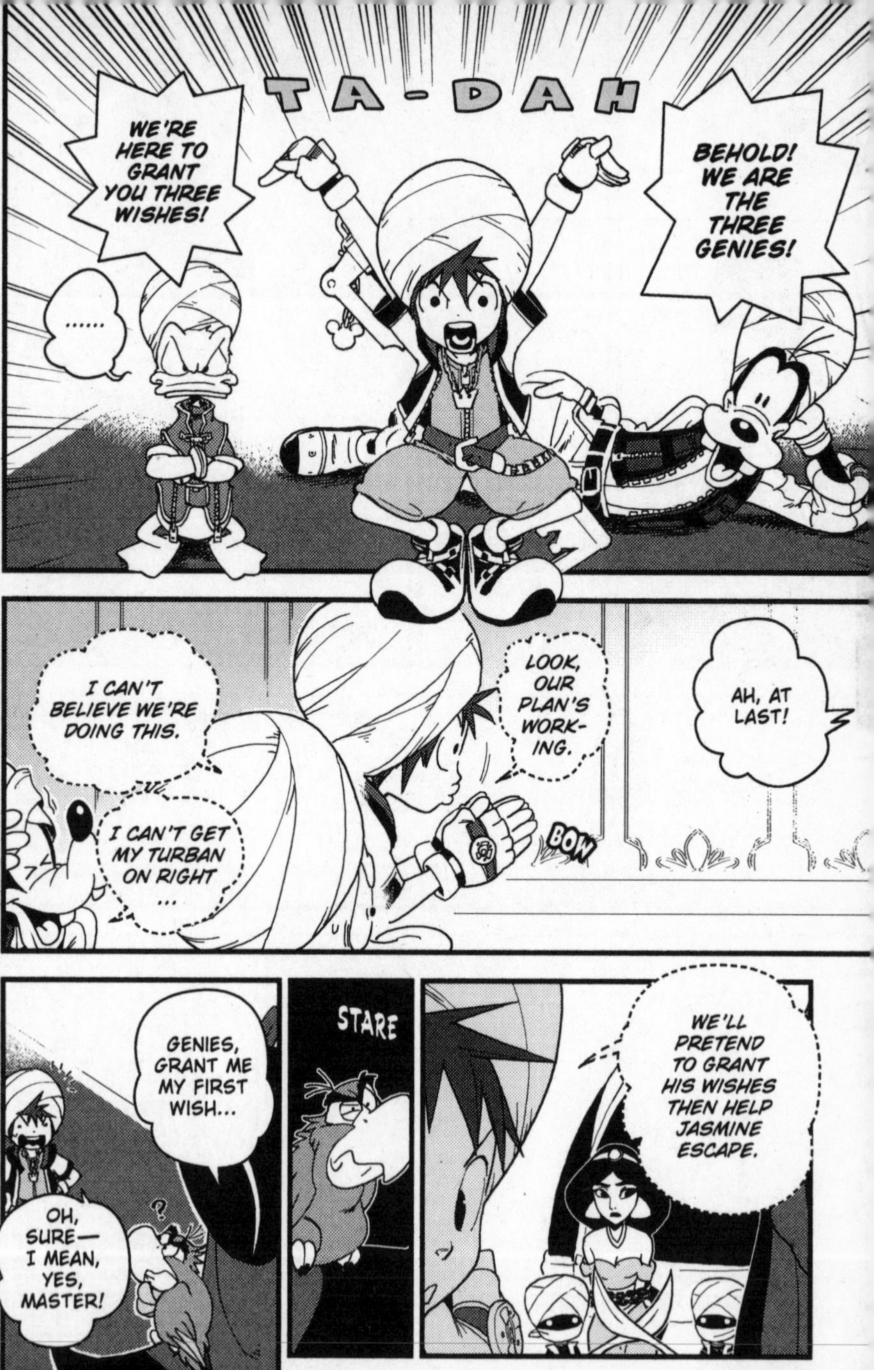
TA-DAH
BEHOLD! WE ARE THE THREE GENIES!
WE'RE HERE TO GRANT YOU THREE WISHES!
......
AH, AT LAST!
LOOK, OUR PLAN'S WORKING.
I CAN'T BELIEVE WE'RE DOING THIS.
BOW
I CAN'T GET MY TURBAN ON RIGHT ...
WE'LL PRETEND TO GRANT HIS WISHES THEN HELP JASMINE ESCAPE.
STARE
GENIES, GRANT ME MY FIRST WISH...
OH, SURE— I MEAN, YES, MASTER!

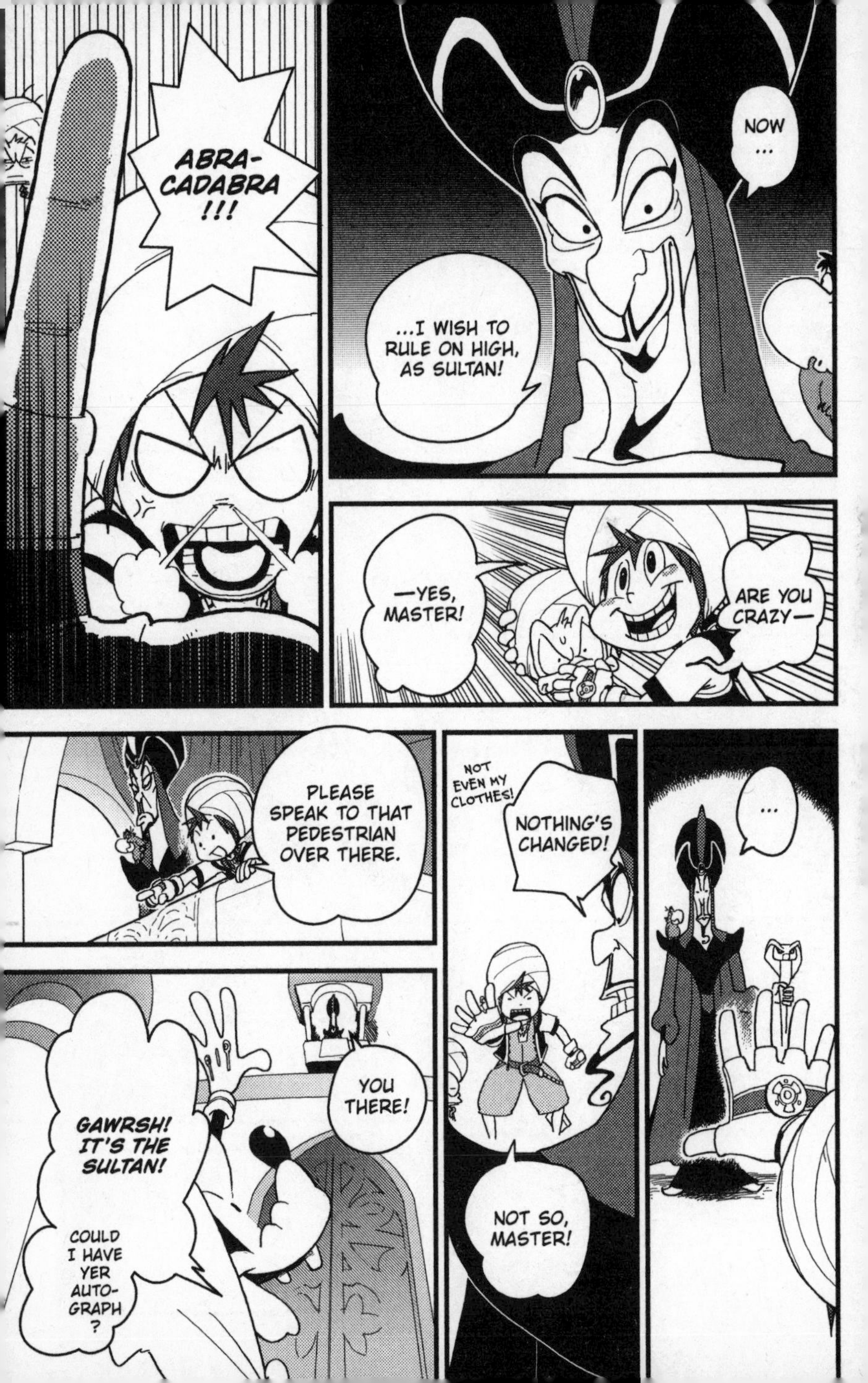
NOW...
...I WISH TO RULE ON HIGH, AS SULTAN!
ARE YOU CRAZY—
—YES, MASTER!
ABRA-CADABRA!!!
...
NOTHING'S CHANGED!
NOT EVEN MY CLOTHES!
NOT SO, MASTER!
PLEASE SPEAK TO THAT PEDESTRIAN OVER THERE.
YOU THERE!
GAWRSH! IT'S THE SULTAN!
COULD I HAVE YER AUTOGRAPH?

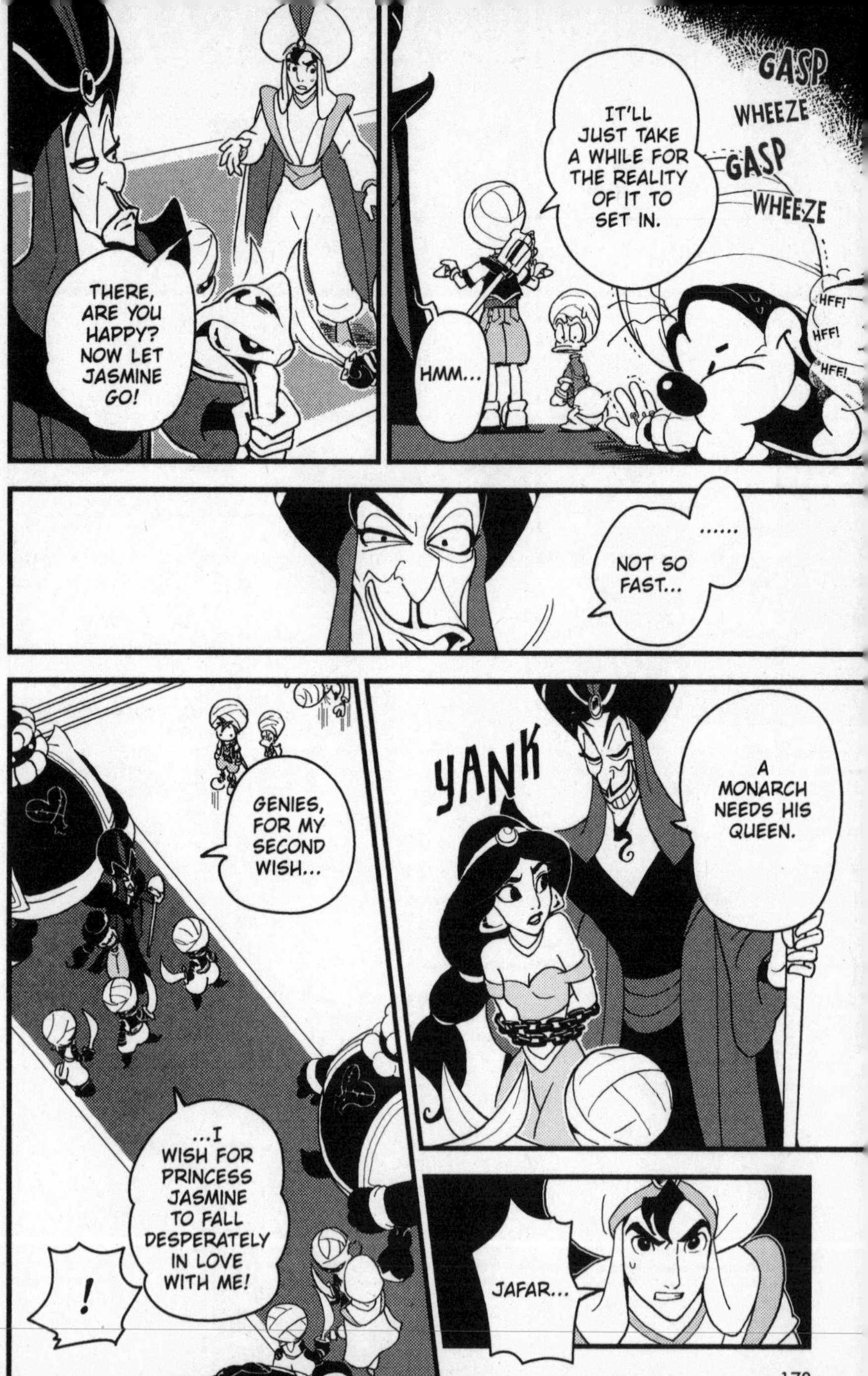
GASP
WHEEZE
GASP
WHEEZE
IT'LL JUST TAKE A WHILE FOR THE REALITY OF IT TO SET IN.
HFF!
HFF!
HFF!
HMM...
THERE, ARE YOU HAPPY? NOW LET JASMINE GO!
......
NOT SO FAST...
A MONARCH NEEDS HIS QUEEN.
YANK
JAFAR...
GENIES, FOR MY SECOND WISH...
...I WISH FOR PRINCESS JASMINE TO FALL DESPERATELY IN LOVE WITH ME!
!

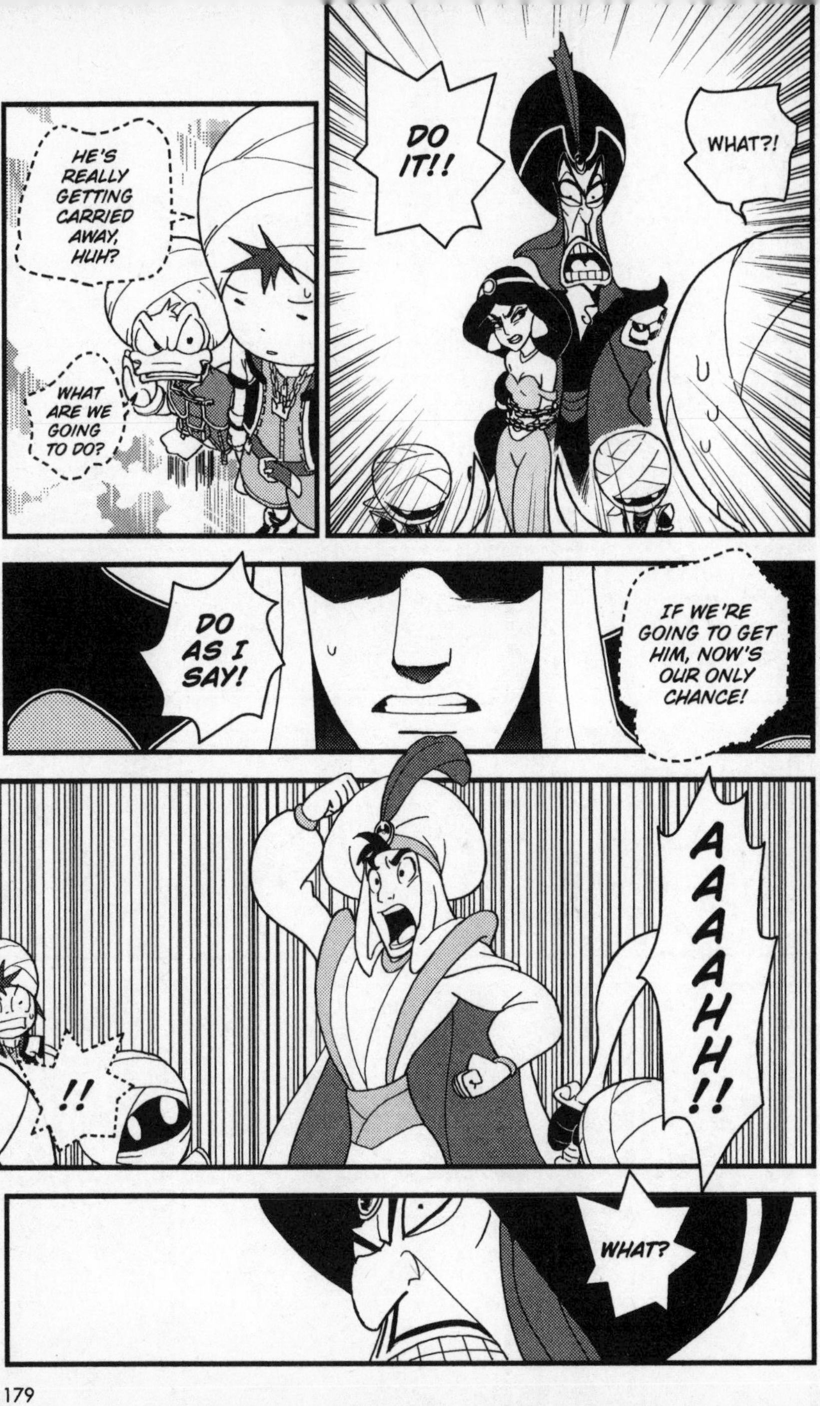
WHAT?!
DO IT!!
HE'S REALLY GETTING CARRIED AWAY, HUH?
WHAT ARE WE GOING TO DO?
IF WE'RE GOING TO GET HIM, NOW'S OUR ONLY CHANCE!
DO AS I SAY!
AAAAAHH!!
!!
WHAT?

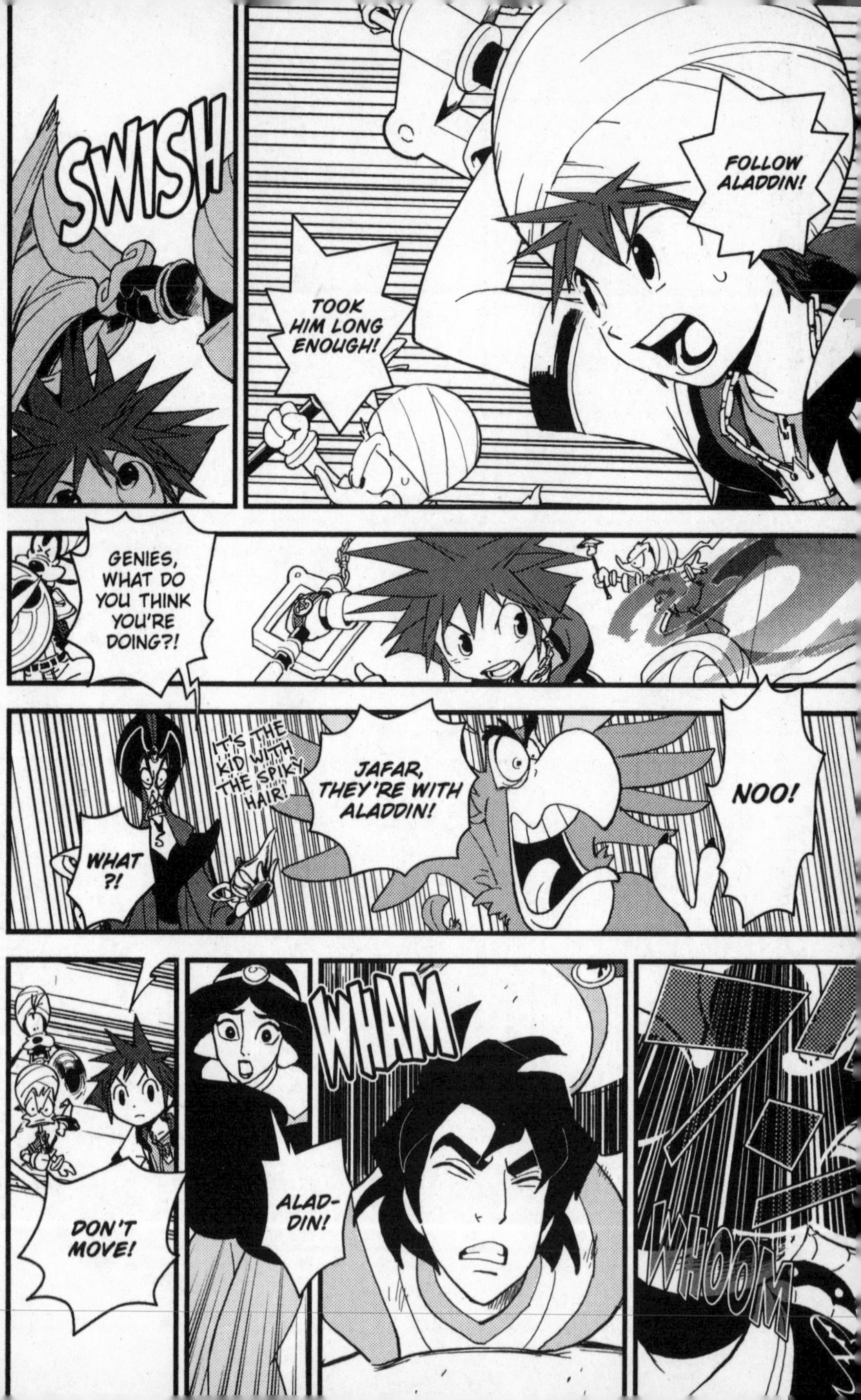
FOLLOW ALADDIN!
TOOK HIM LONG ENOUGH!
SWISH
GENIES, WHAT DO YOU THINK YOU'RE DOING?!
NOO!
JAFAR, THEY'RE WITH ALADDIN!
IT'S THE KID WITH THE SPIKY HAIR!
WHAT?!
WHOOM
WHAM
ALAD-DIN!
DON'T MOVE!

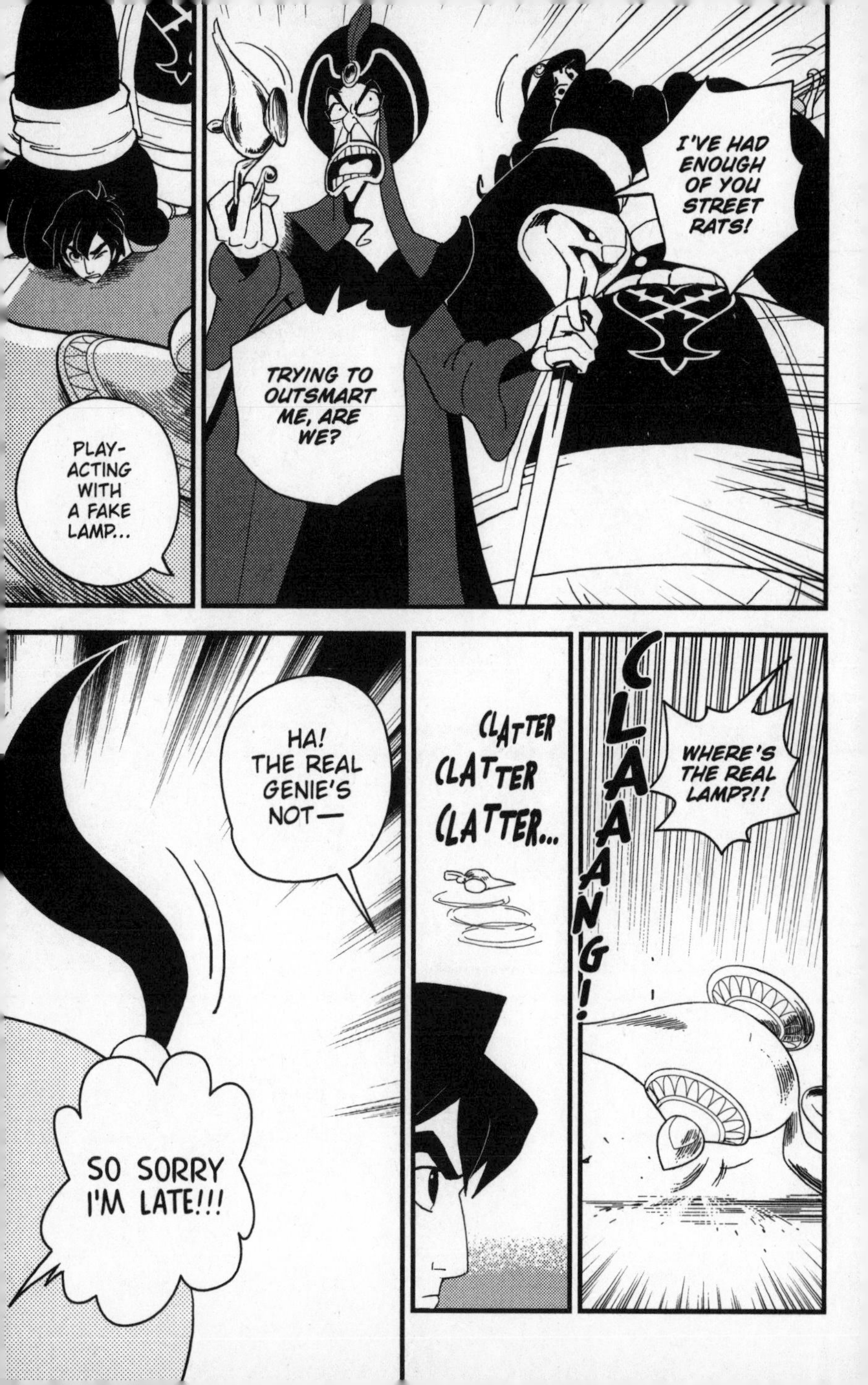
I'VE HAD ENOUGH OF YOU STREET RATS!
TRYING TO OUTSMART ME, ARE WE?
PLAY-ACTING WITH A FAKE LAMP...
CLAAAANG!!
WHERE'S THE REAL LAMP?!!
CLATTER CLATTER CLATTER...
HA! THE REAL GENIE'S NOT—
SO SORRY I'M LATE!!!

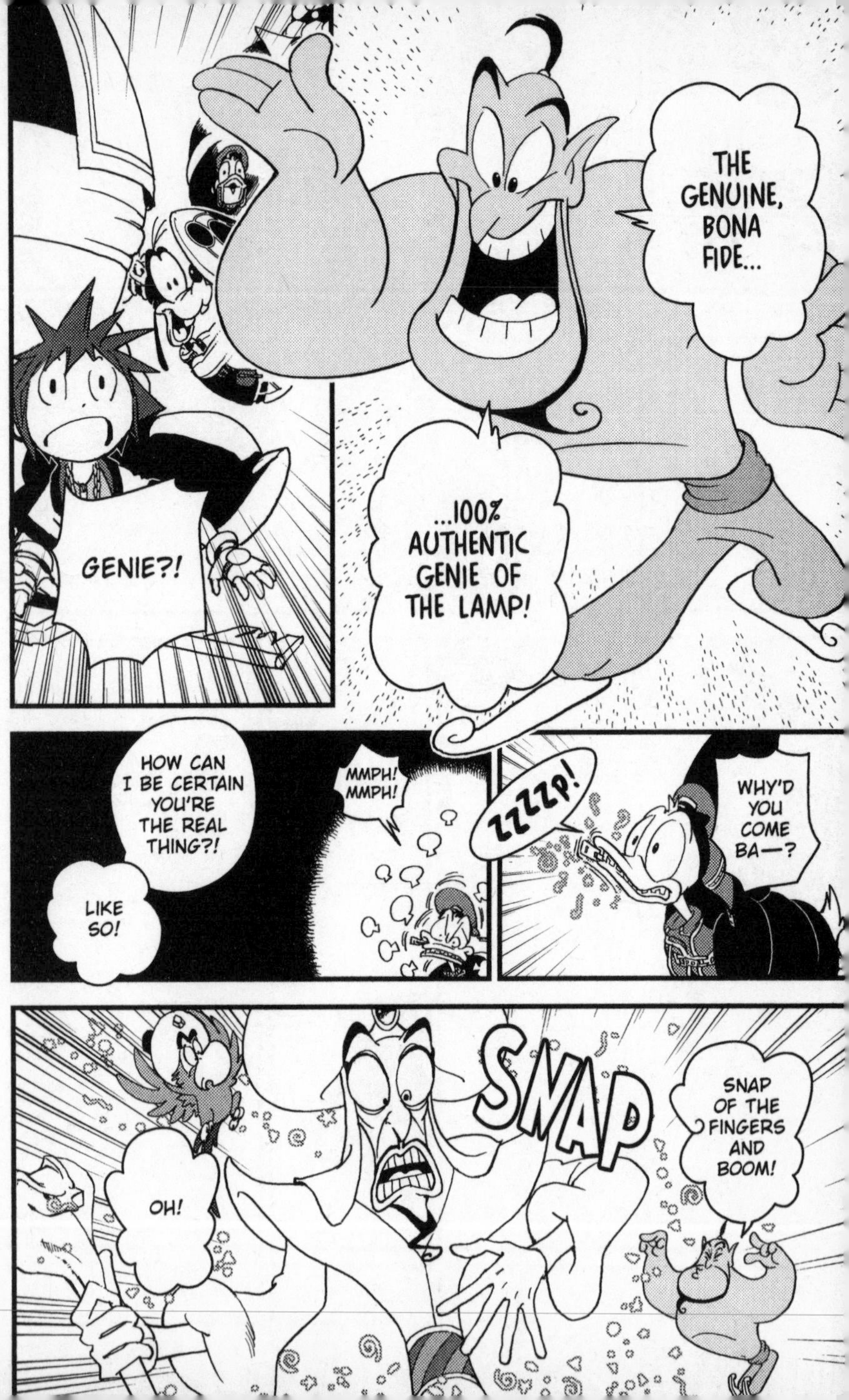
THE GENUINE, BONA FIDE...
...100% AUTHENTIC GENIE OF THE LAMP!
GENIE?!
ZZZZP!
WHY'D YOU COME BA—?
MMPH! MMPH!
HOW CAN I BE CERTAIN YOU'RE THE REAL THING?!
LIKE SO!
SNAP OF THE FINGERS AND BOOM!
SNAP
OH!

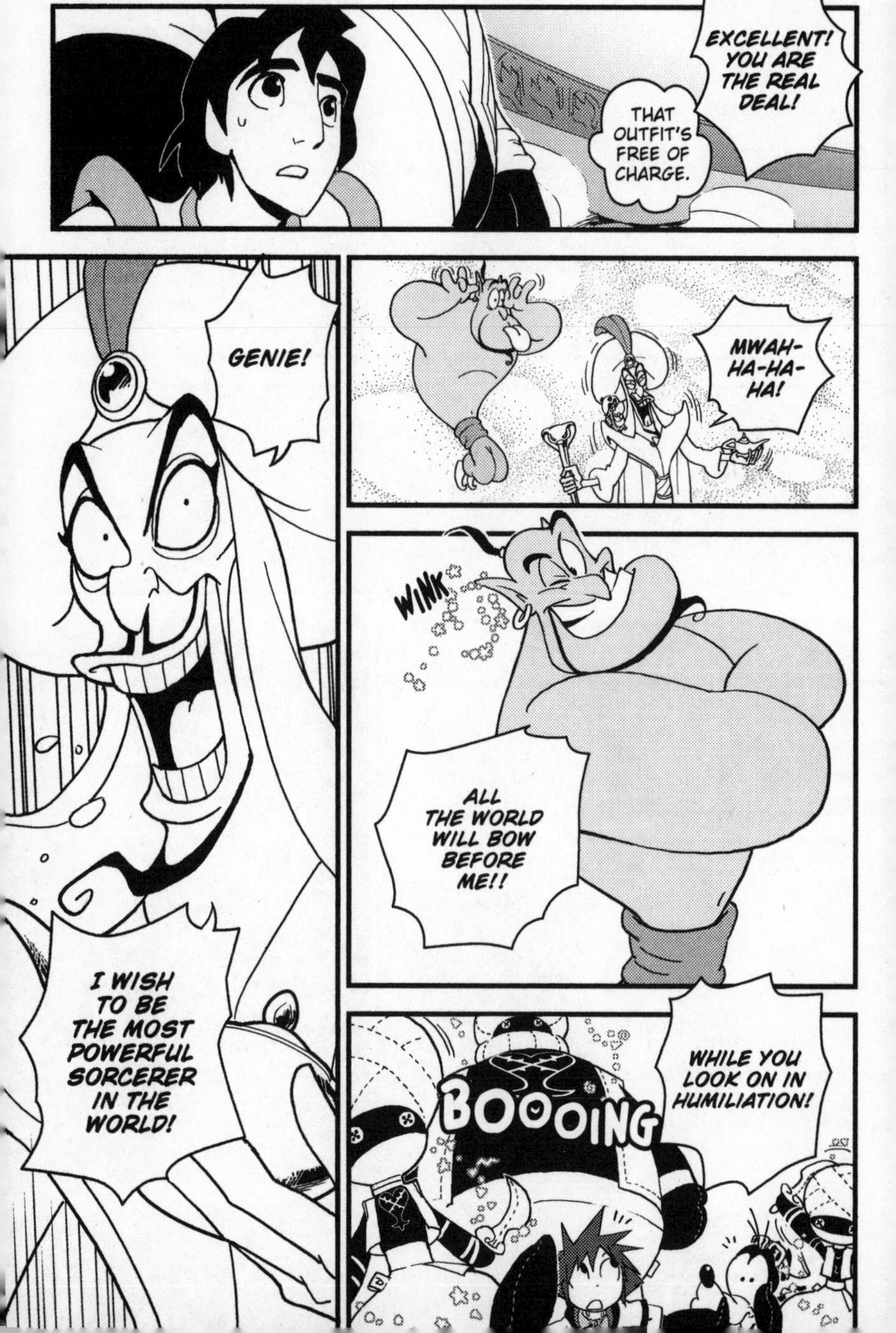
EXCELLENT! YOU ARE THE REAL DEAL!
THAT OUTFIT'S FREE OF CHARGE.
MWAH-HA-HA-HA!
WINK
ALL THE WORLD WILL BOW BEFORE ME!!
WHILE YOU LOOK ON IN HUMILIATION!
BOOOING
GENIE!
I WISH TO BE THE MOST POWERFUL SORCERER IN THE WORLD!

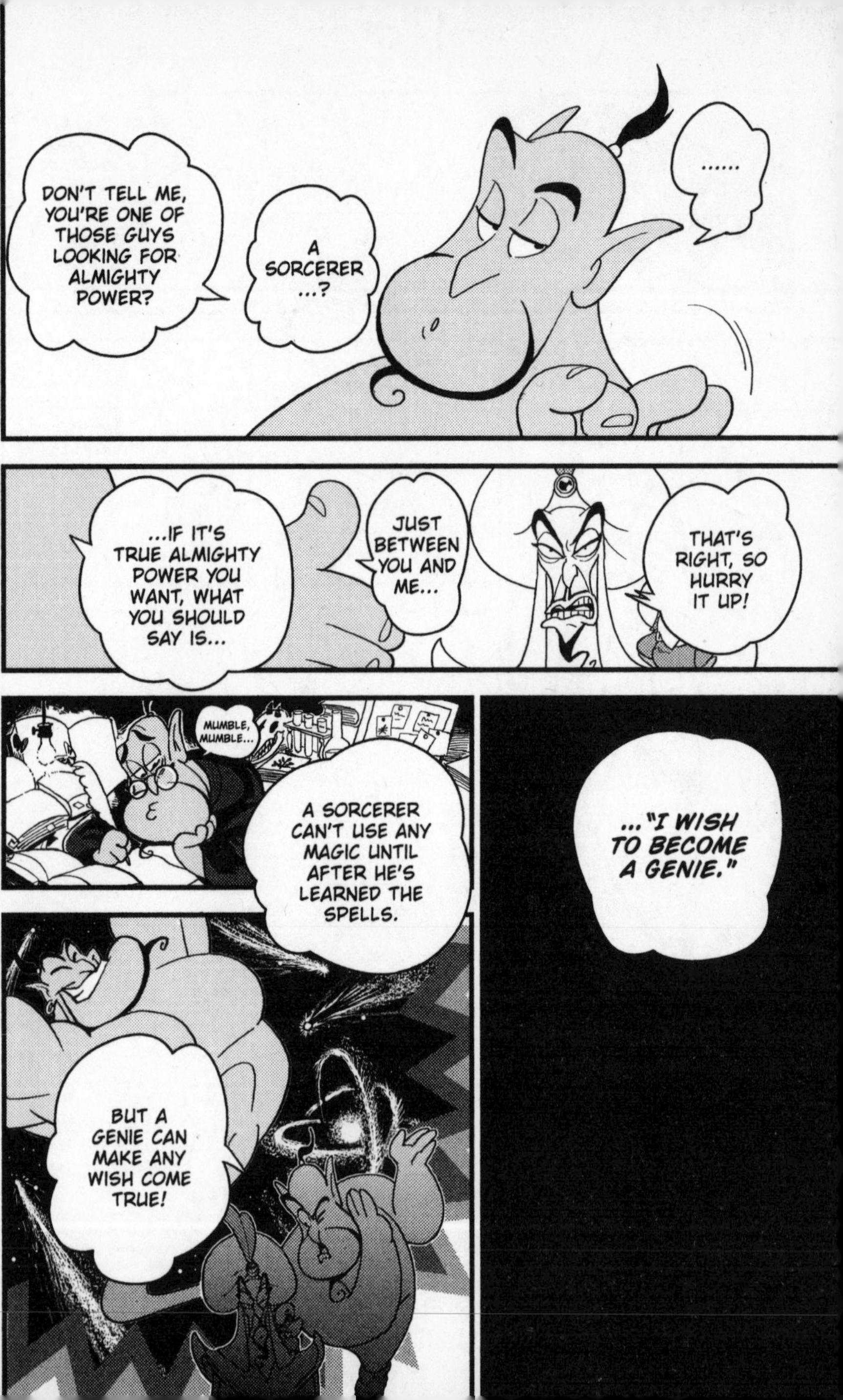
......
A SORCERER ...?
DON'T TELL ME, YOU'RE ONE OF THOSE GUYS LOOKING FOR ALMIGHTY POWER?
THAT'S RIGHT, SO HURRY IT UP!
JUST BETWEEN YOU AND ME...
...IF IT'S TRUE ALMIGHTY POWER YOU WANT, WHAT YOU SHOULD SAY IS...
..."I WISH TO BECOME A GENIE."
MUMBLE, MUMBLE...
A SORCERER CAN'T USE ANY MAGIC UNTIL AFTER HE'S LEARNED THE SPELLS.
BUT A GENIE CAN MAKE ANY WISH COME TRUE!

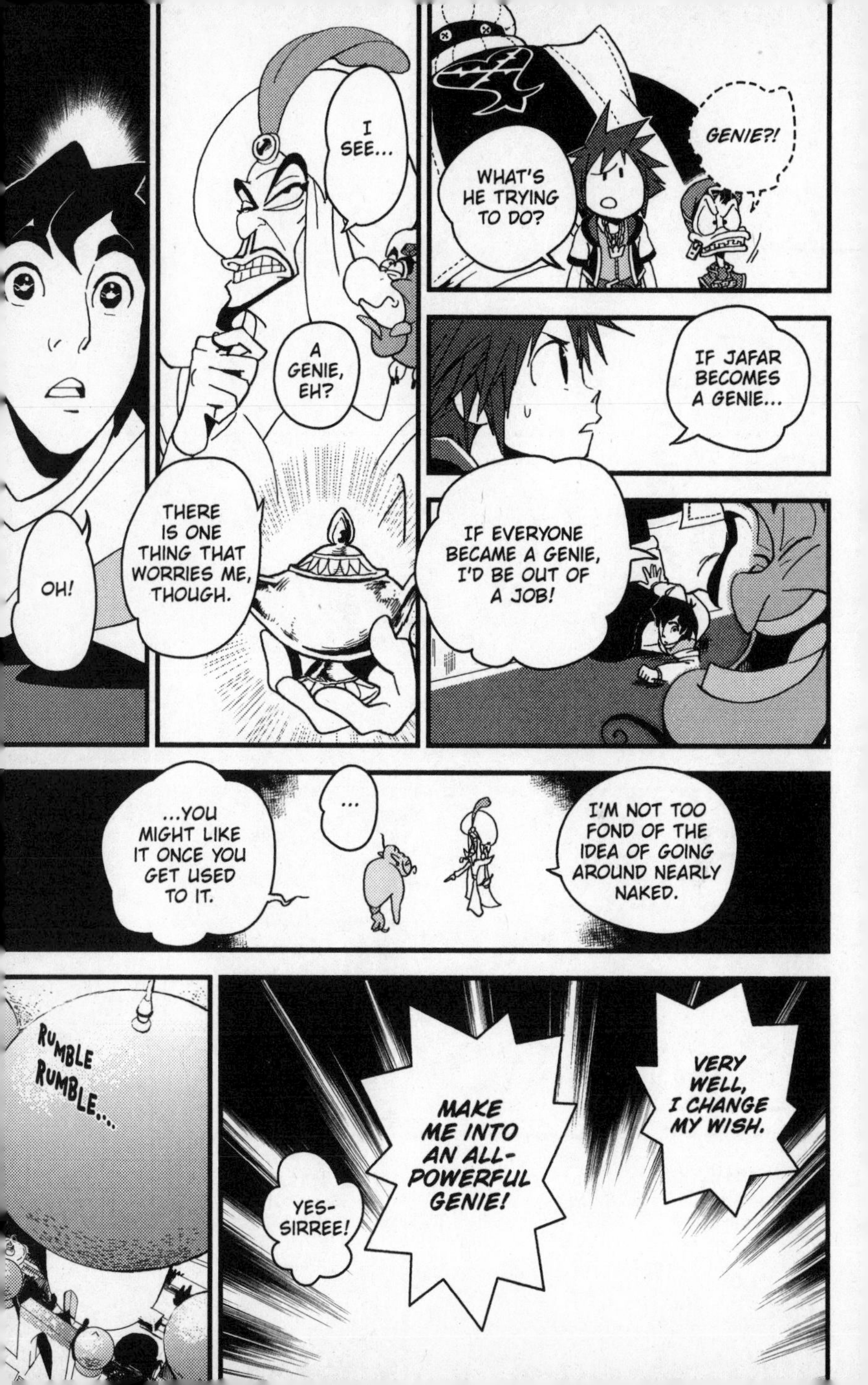
GENIE?!
WHAT'S HE TRYING TO DO?
IF JAFAR BECOMES A GENIE...
IF EVERYONE BECAME A GENIE, I'D BE OUT OF A JOB!
I SEE...
A GENIE, EH?
THERE IS ONE THING THAT WORRIES ME, THOUGH.
OH!
I'M NOT TOO FOND OF THE IDEA OF GOING AROUND NEARLY NAKED.
...
...YOU MIGHT LIKE IT ONCE YOU GET USED TO IT.
VERY WELL, I CHANGE MY WISH.
MAKE ME INTO AN ALL-POWERFUL GENIE!
YES-SIRREE!
RUMBLE RUMBLE...

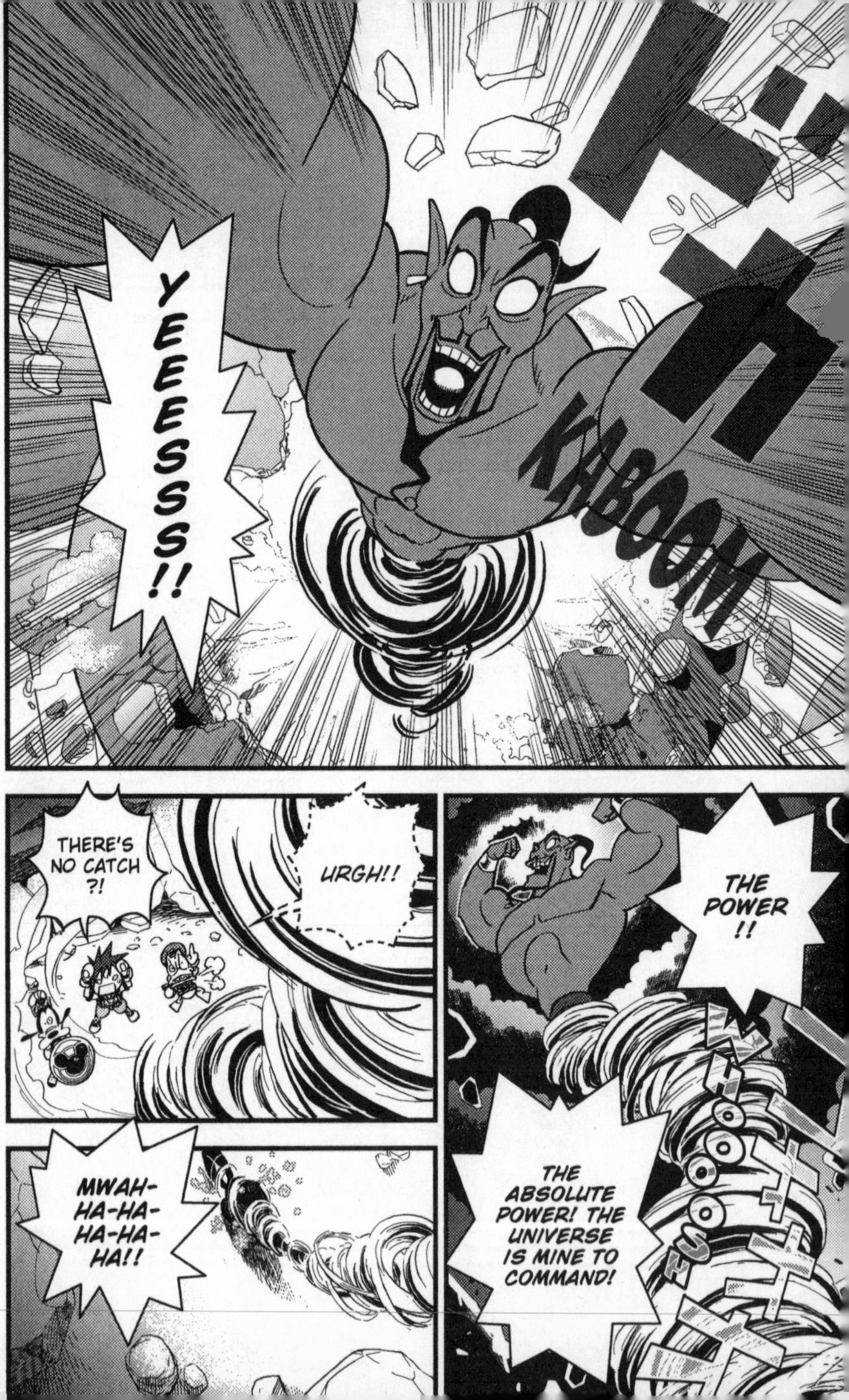
ドカ
KABOOM
YEEEESSSS!!
THE POWER !!
WHOOOOSH
THE ABSOLUTE POWER! THE UNIVERSE IS MINE TO COMMAND!
URGH!!
THERE'S NO CATCH ?!
MWAH-HA-HA-HA-HA-HA!!

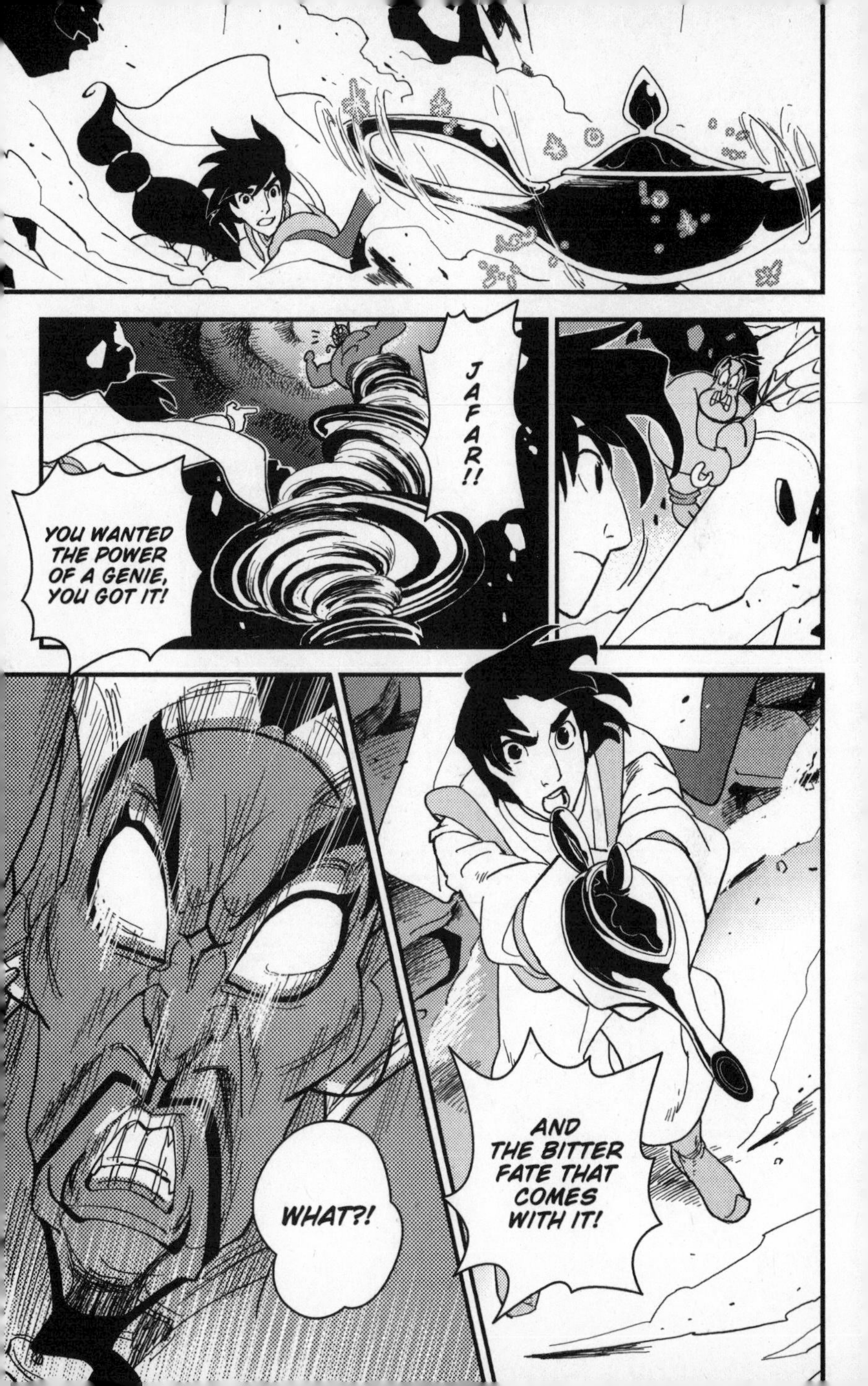
JAFAR!!
YOU WANTED THE POWER OF A GENIE, YOU GOT IT!
AND THE BITTER FATE THAT COMES WITH IT!
WHAT?!

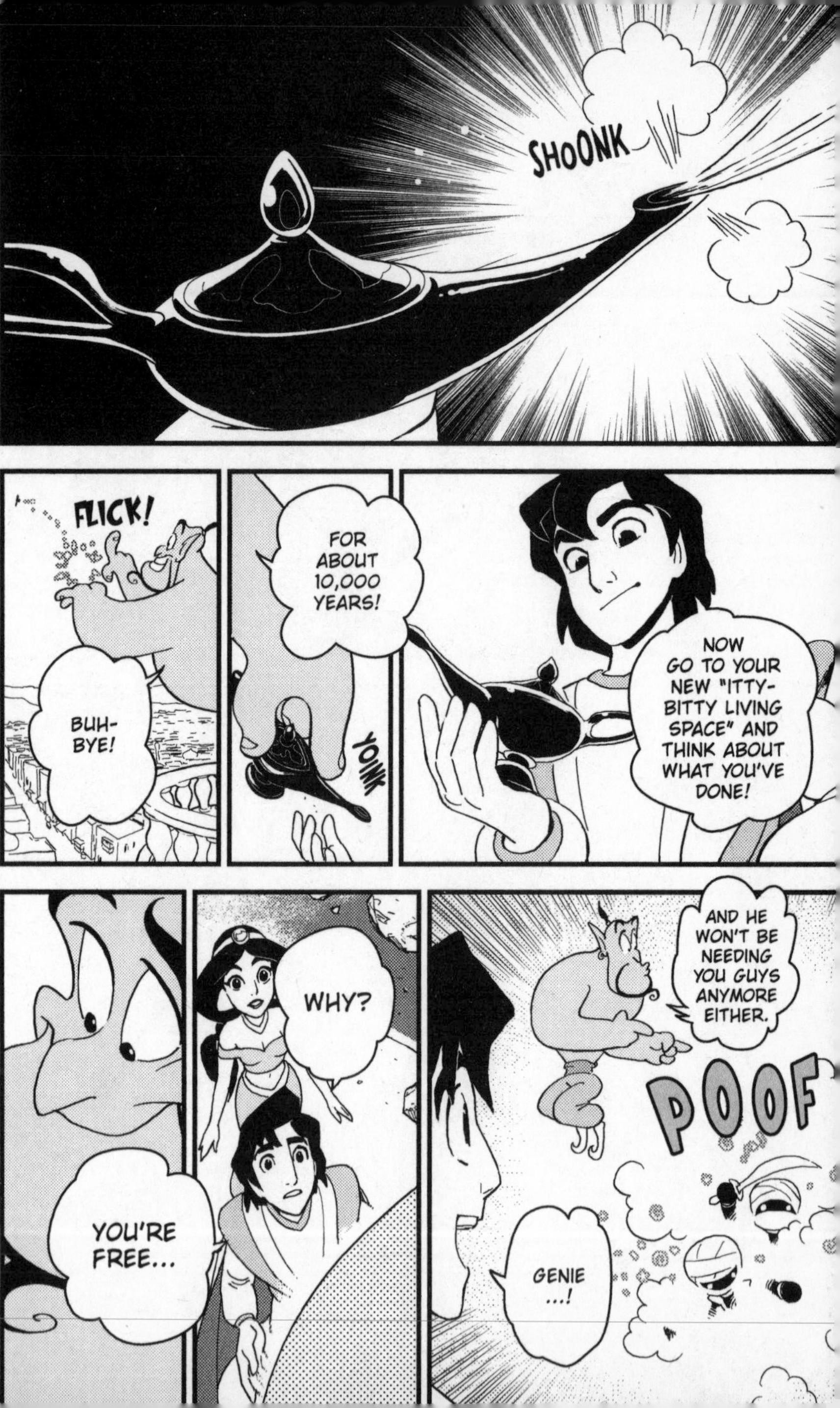
SHOONK
NOW GO TO YOUR NEW "ITTY-BITTY LIVING SPACE" AND THINK ABOUT WHAT YOU'VE DONE!
FOR ABOUT 10,000 YEARS!
YOINK
FLICK!
BUH-BYE!
AND HE WON'T BE NEEDING YOU GUYS ANYMORE EITHER.
POOF
GENIE ...!
WHY?
YOU'RE FREE...

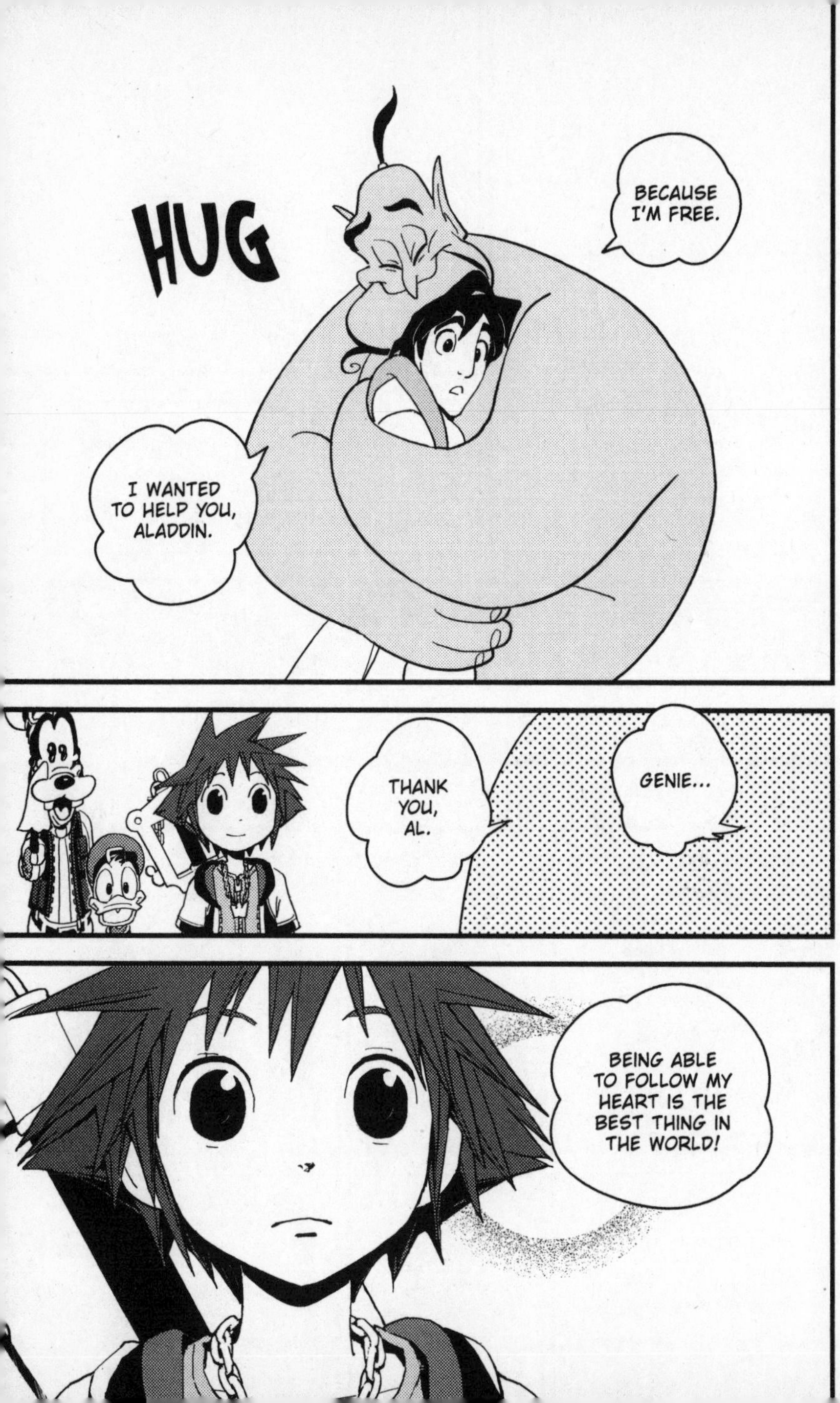
BECAUSE I'M FREE.
HUG
I WANTED TO HELP YOU, ALADDIN.
GENIE...
THANK YOU, AL.
BEING ABLE TO FOLLOW MY HEART IS THE BEST THING IN THE WORLD!

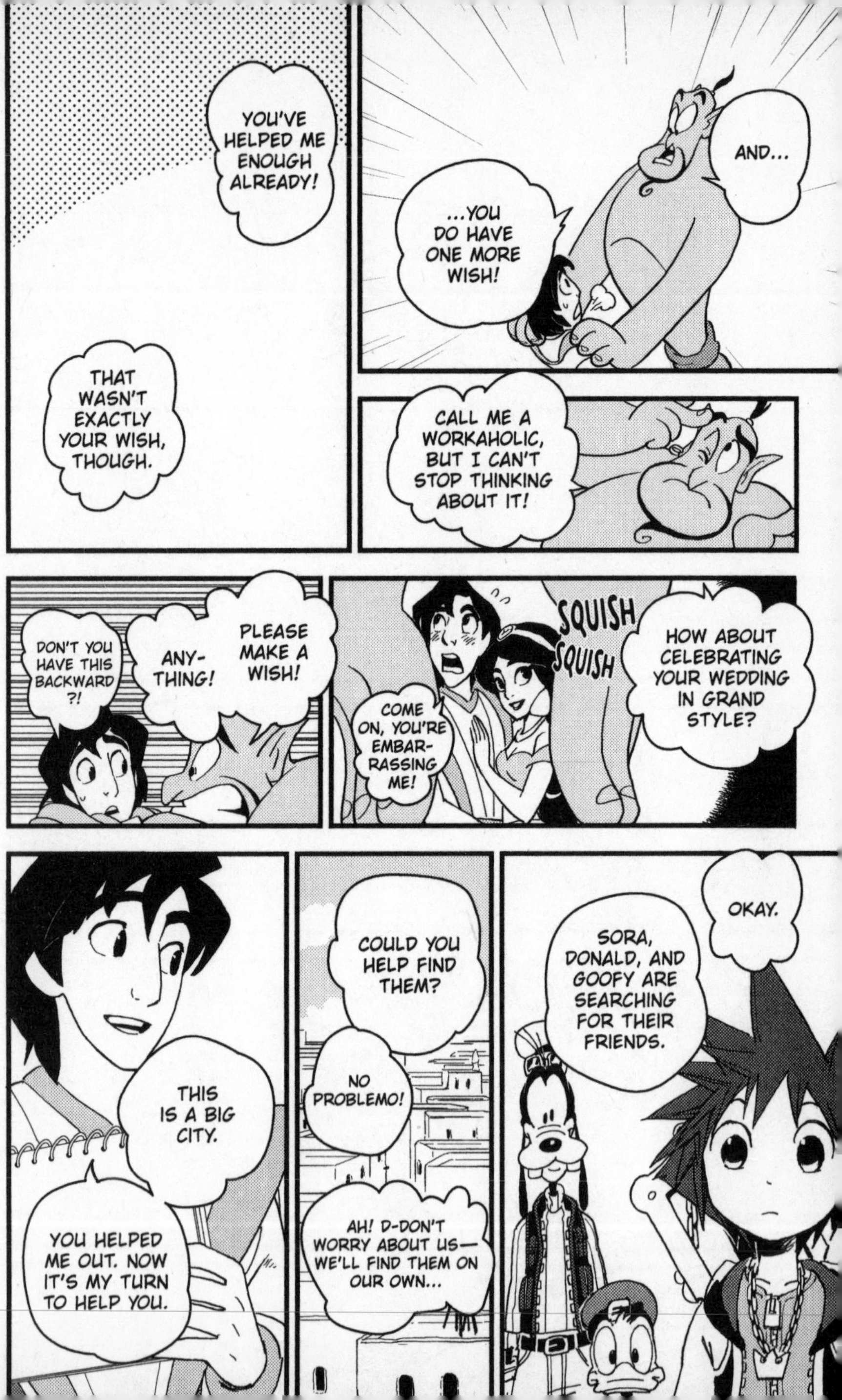
AND...
...YOU DO HAVE ONE MORE WISH!
CALL ME A WORKAHOLIC, BUT I CAN'T STOP THINKING ABOUT IT!
YOU'VE HELPED ME ENOUGH ALREADY!
THAT WASN'T EXACTLY YOUR WISH, THOUGH.
HOW ABOUT CELEBRATING YOUR WEDDING IN GRAND STYLE?
SQUISH
SQUISH
COME ON, YOU'RE EMBAR-RASSING ME!
PLEASE MAKE A WISH!
ANY-THING!
DON'T YOU HAVE THIS BACKWARD?!
OKAY.
SORA, DONALD, AND GOOFY ARE SEARCHING FOR THEIR FRIENDS.
COULD YOU HELP FIND THEM?
NO PROBLEMO!
AH! D-DON'T WORRY ABOUT US— WE'LL FIND THEM ON OUR OWN...
THIS IS A BIG CITY.
YOU HELPED ME OUT. NOW IT'S MY TURN TO HELP YOU.

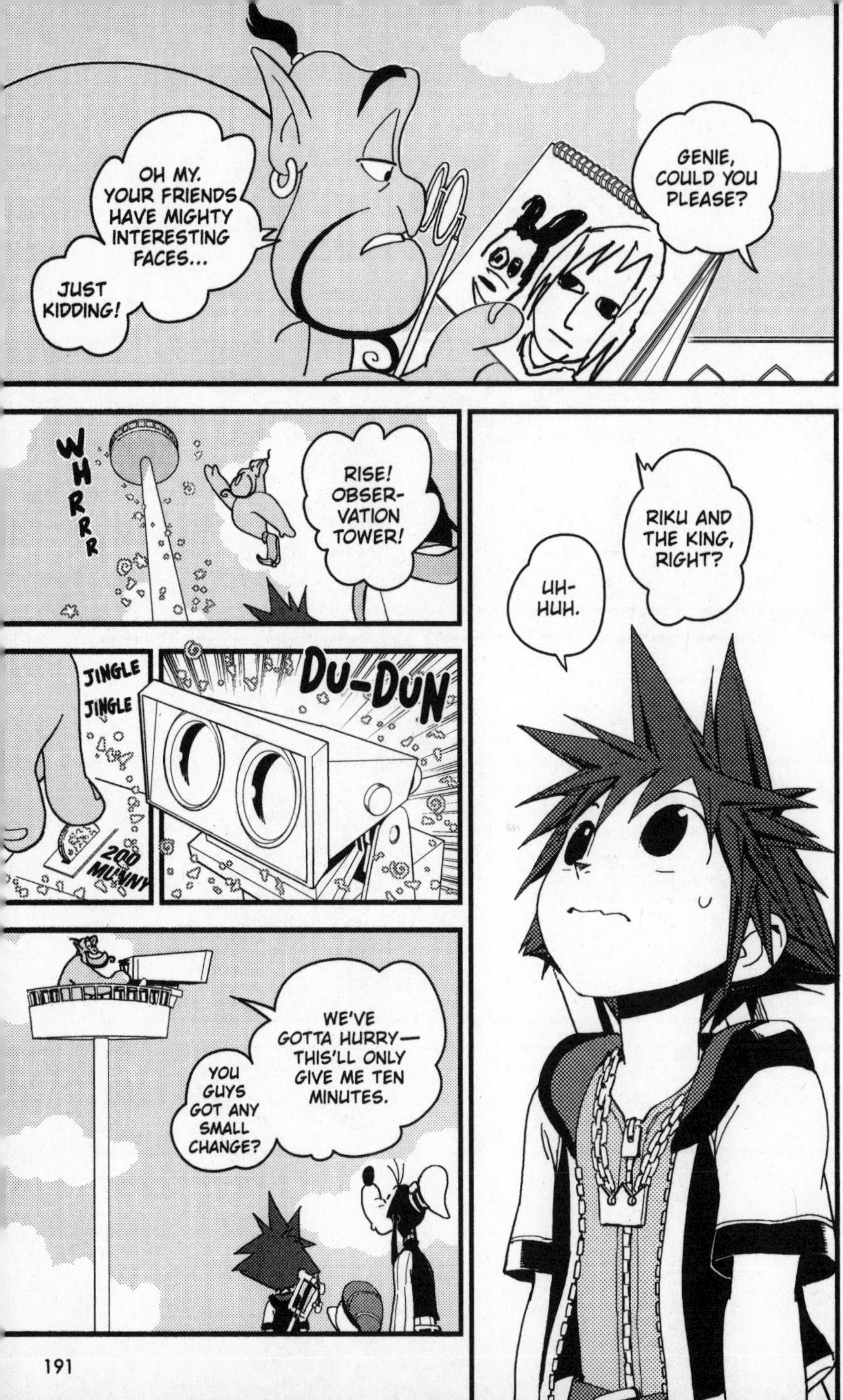
GENIE, COULD YOU PLEASE?
OH MY. YOUR FRIENDS HAVE MIGHTY INTERESTING FACES...
JUST KIDDING!
RIKU AND THE KING, RIGHT?
UH-HUH.
RISE! OBSER-VATION TOWER!
WHRRR
DU-DUN
JINGLE JINGLE
200 MUNNY
WE'VE GOTTA HURRY— THIS'LL ONLY GIVE ME TEN MINUTES.
YOU GUYS GOT ANY SMALL CHANGE?

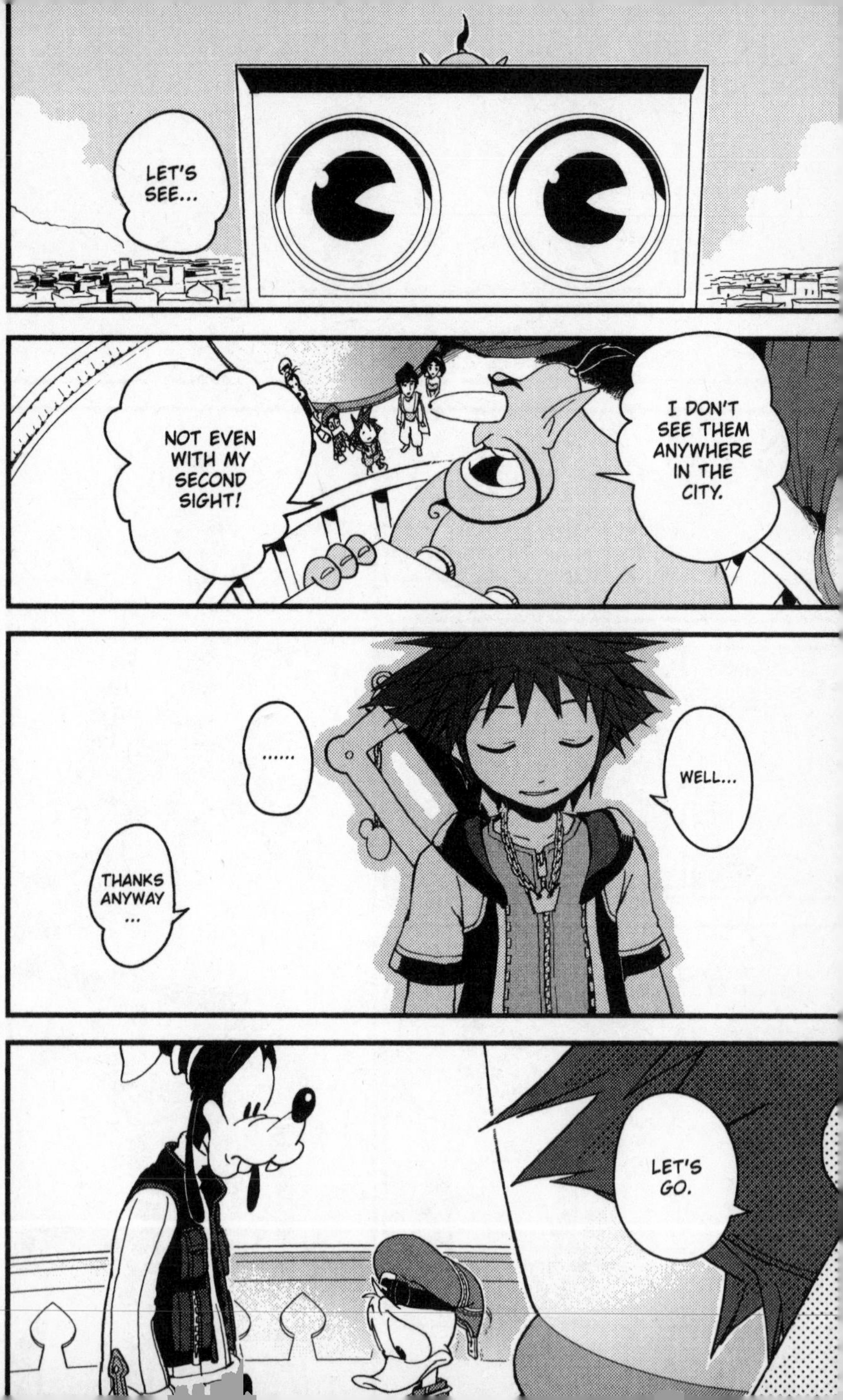
LET'S SEE...
I DON'T SEE THEM ANYWHERE IN THE CITY.
NOT EVEN WITH MY SECOND SIGHT!
WELL...
......
THANKS ANYWAY ...
LET'S GO.

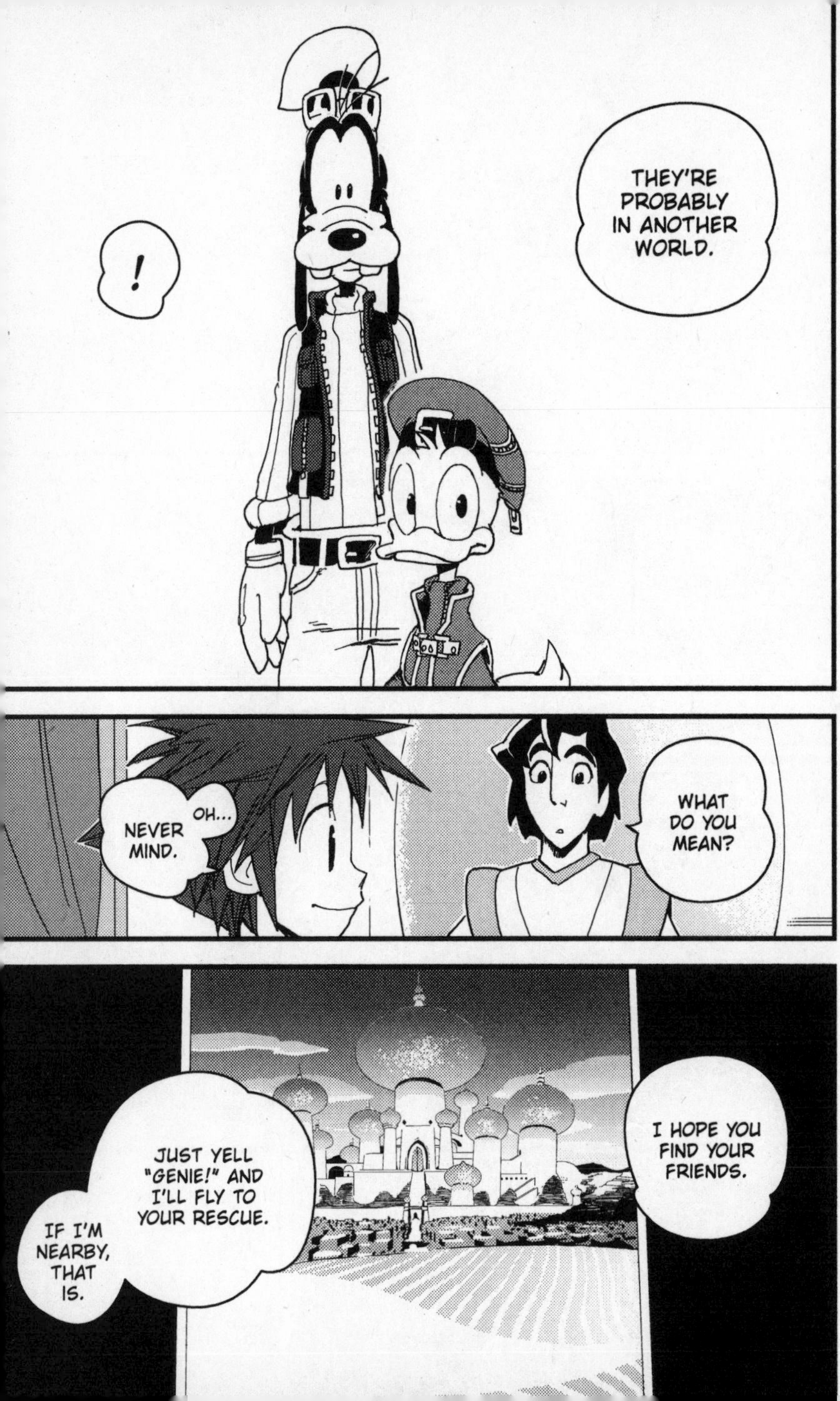
THEY'RE PROBABLY IN ANOTHER WORLD.
!
WHAT DO YOU MEAN?
OH... NEVER MIND.
I HOPE YOU FIND YOUR FRIENDS.
JUST YELL "GENIE!" AND I'LL FLY TO YOUR RESCUE.
IF I'M NEARBY, THAT IS.

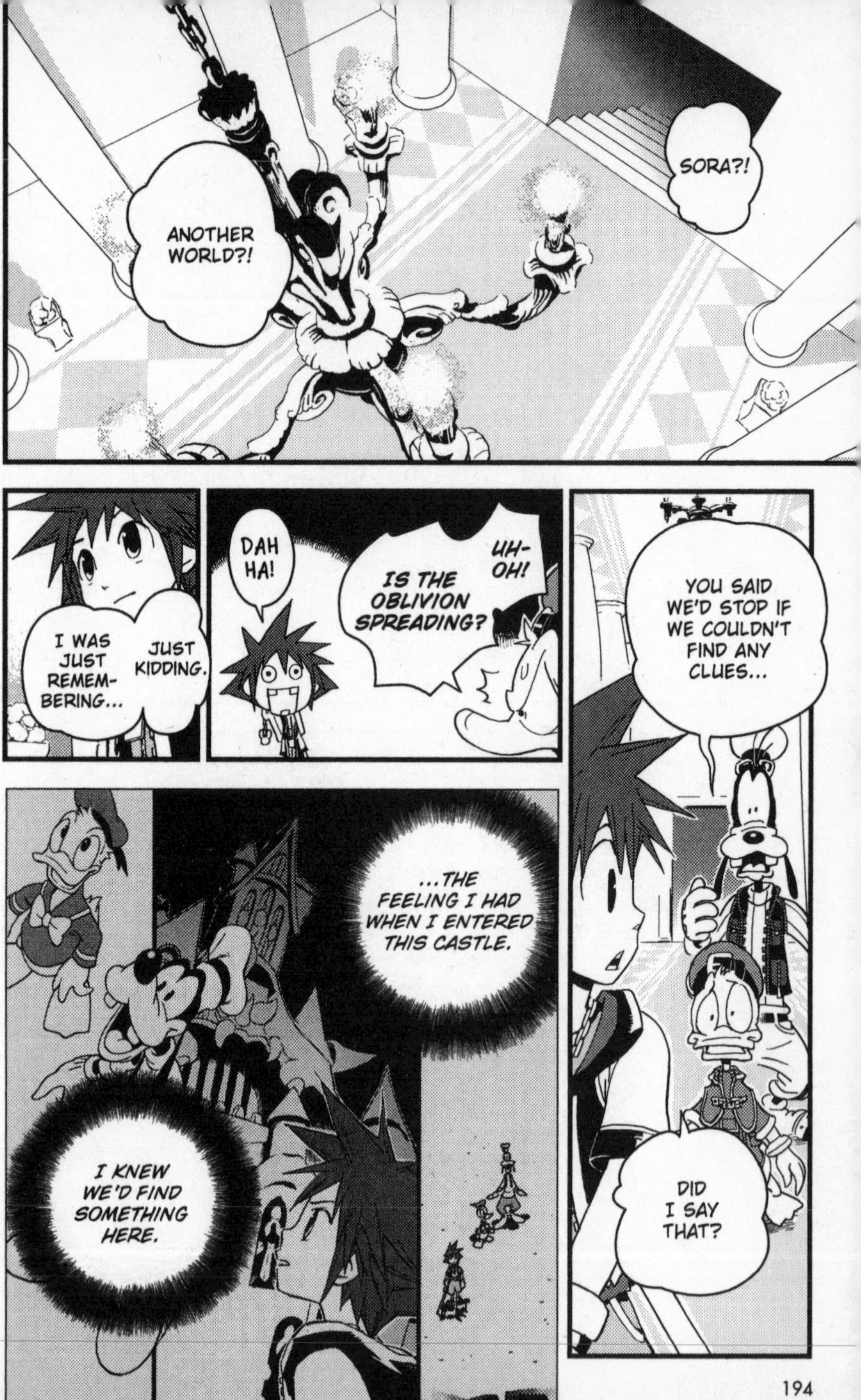
SORA?!
ANOTHER WORLD?!
YOU SAID WE'D STOP IF WE COULDN'T FIND ANY CLUES...
DID I SAY THAT?
UH-OH!
IS THE OBLIVION SPREADING?
DAH HA!
JUST KIDDING.
I WAS JUST REMEMBERING...
...THE FEELING I HAD WHEN I ENTERED THIS CASTLE.
I KNEW WE'D FIND SOMETHING HERE.

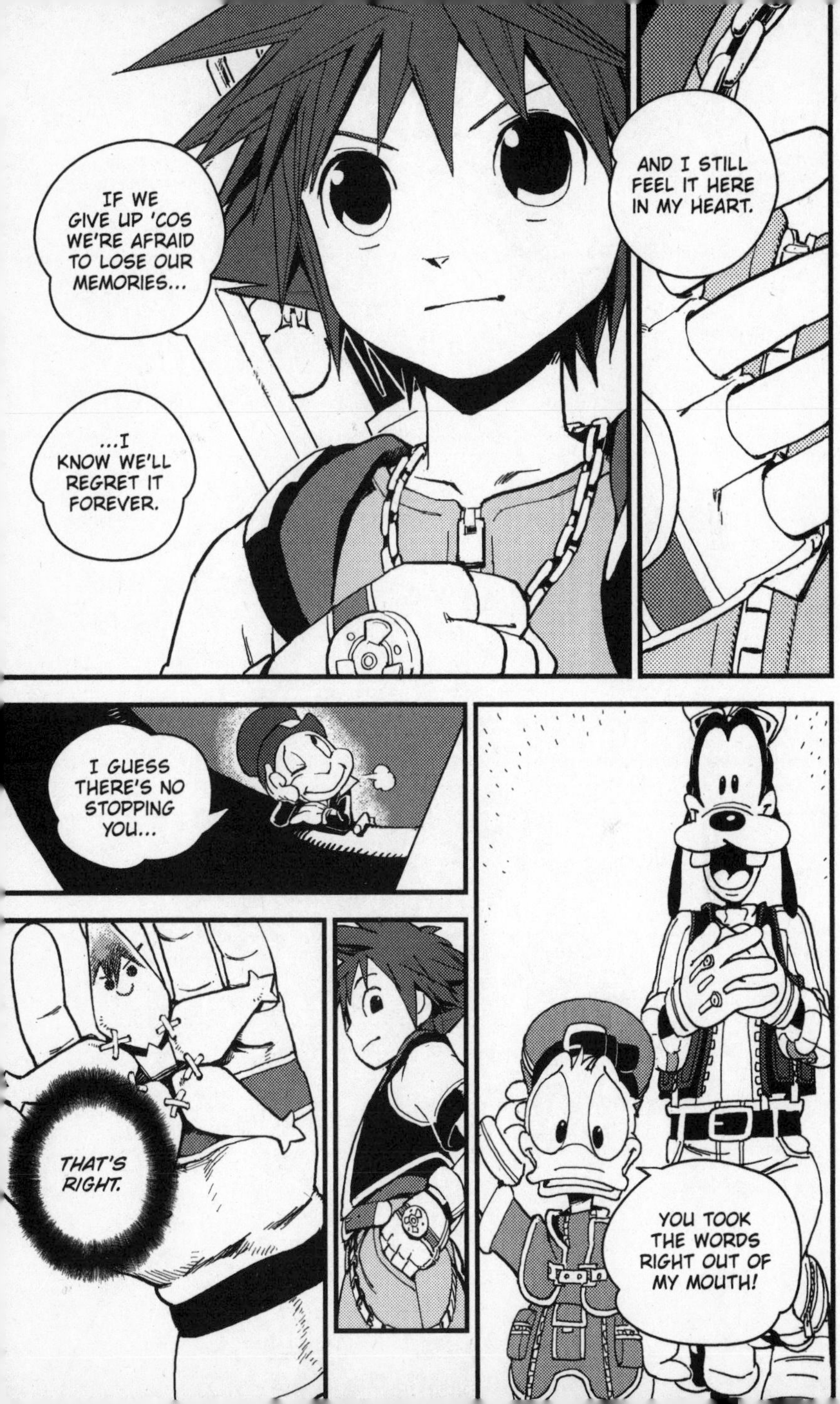
AND I STILL FEEL IT HERE IN MY HEART.
IF WE GIVE UP 'COS WE'RE AFRAID TO LOSE OUR MEMORIES...
...I KNOW WE'LL REGRET IT FOREVER.
YOU TOOK THE WORDS RIGHT OUT OF MY MOUTH!
I GUESS THERE'S NO STOPPING YOU...
THAT'S RIGHT.

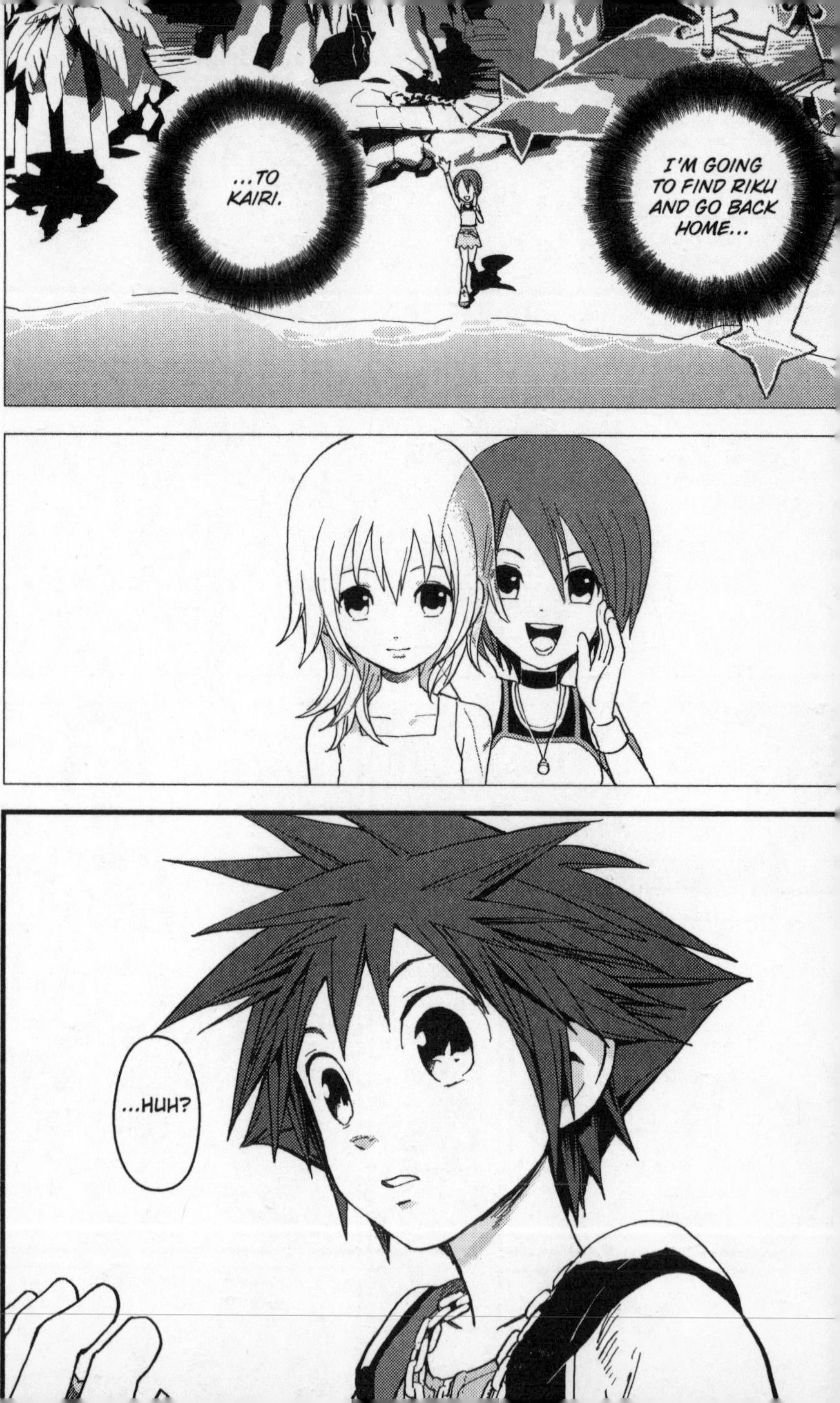
I'M GOING TO FIND RIKU AND GO BACK HOME...
...TO KAIRI.
...HUH?

NEXT ISSUE PREVIEW ILLUSTRATION
[JULY 2005 ISSUE]

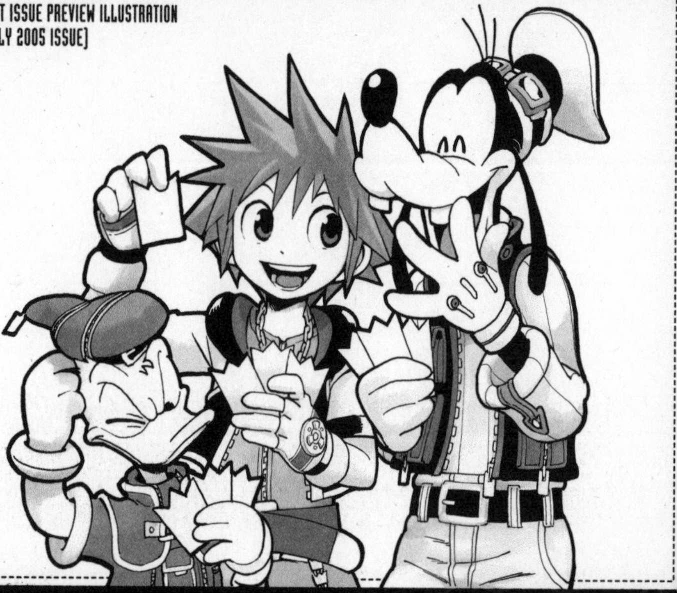

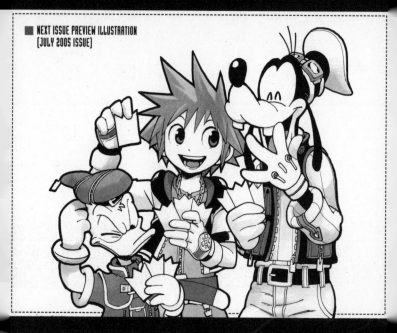

# ILLUST COLLECTION

Take a peek at the cover and preview illustrations published in MONTHLY SHONEN GANGAN!

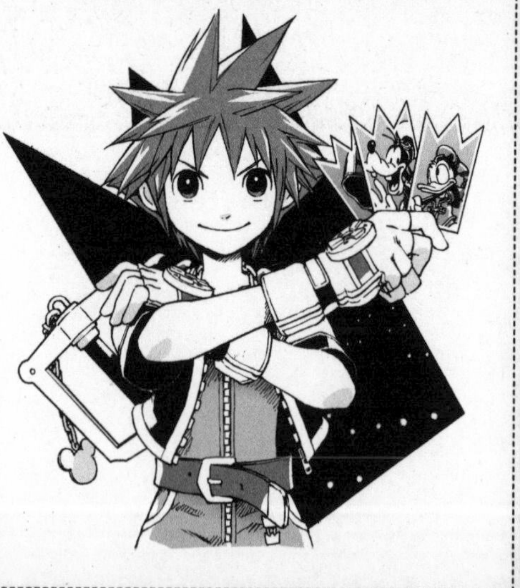

SERIES PREVIEW ILLUSTRATION
[MARCH 2005 ISSUE]

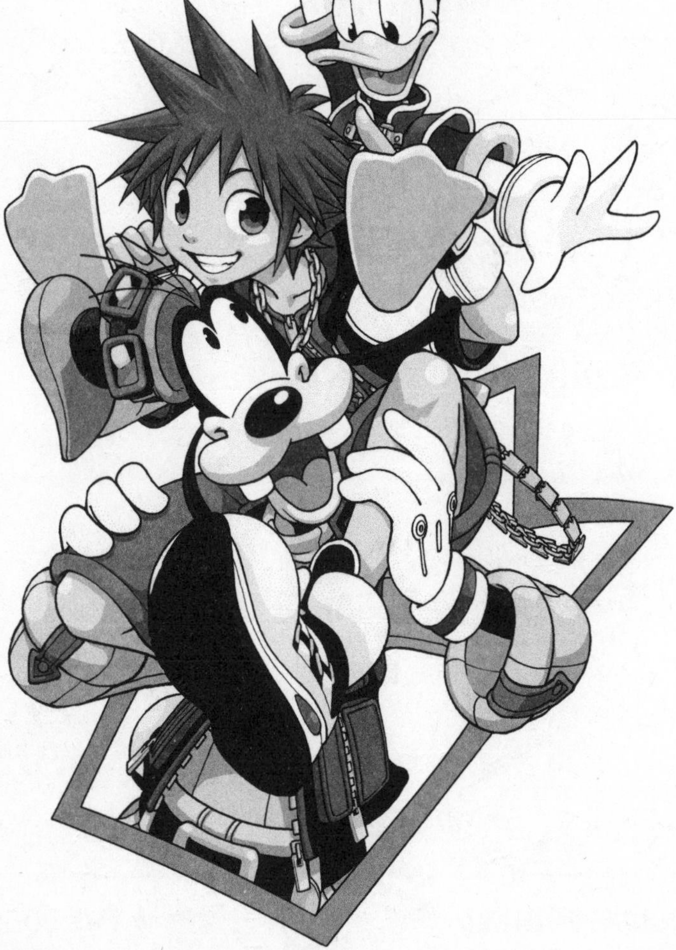

MAGAZINE COVER ILLUSTRATION [APRIL 2005 ISSUE]

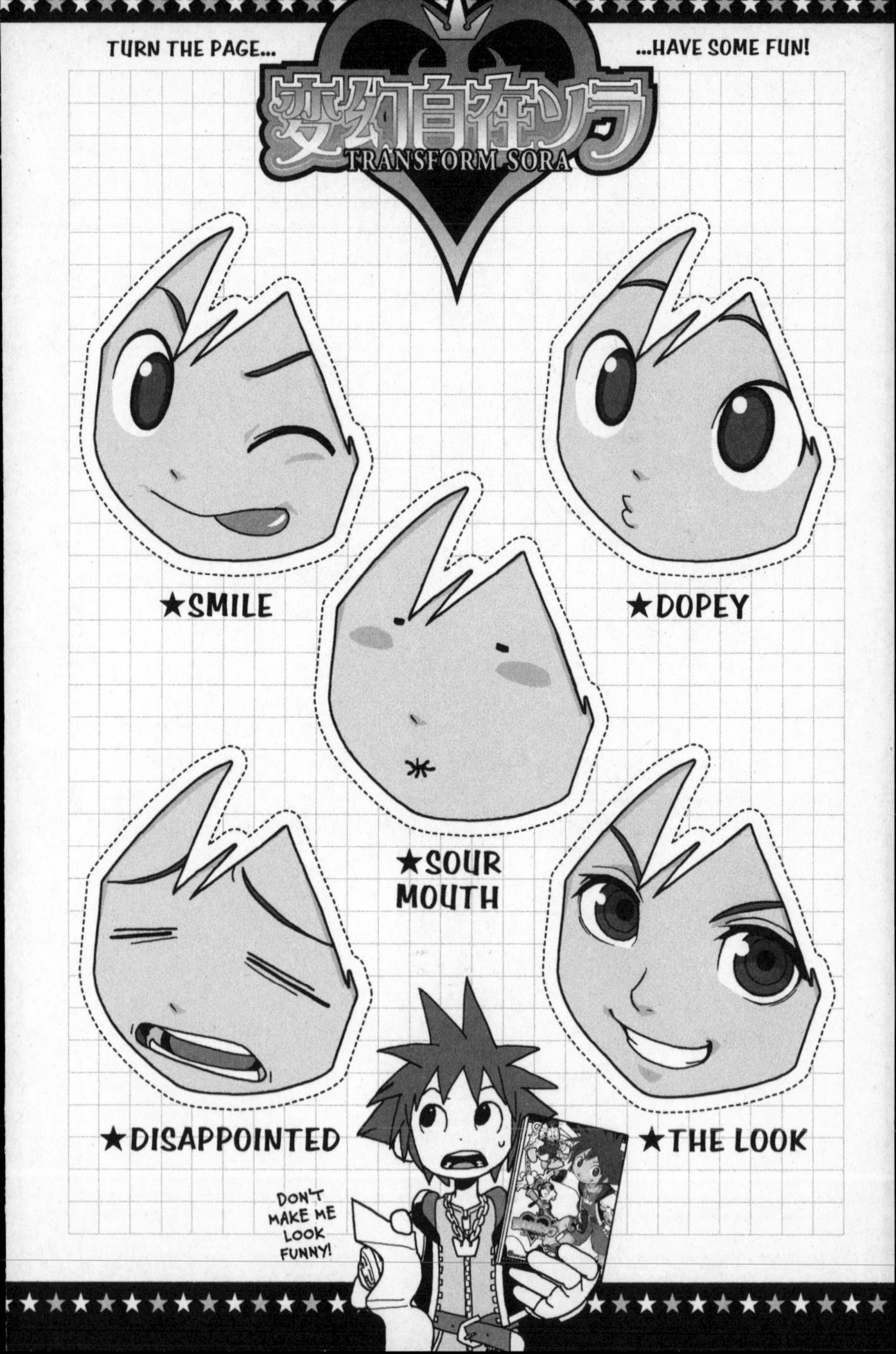
TURN THE PAGE...
...HAVE SOME FUN!
変幻自在ソラ
TRANSFORM SORA
★SMILE
★DOPEY
★SOUR MOUTH
★DISAPPOINTED
★THE LOOK
DON'T MAKE ME LOOK FUNNY!

DISNEY SQUARE ENIX

KINGDOM HEARTS
CHAIN OF MEMORIES

# KINGDOM HEARTS
## CHAIN OF MEMORIES

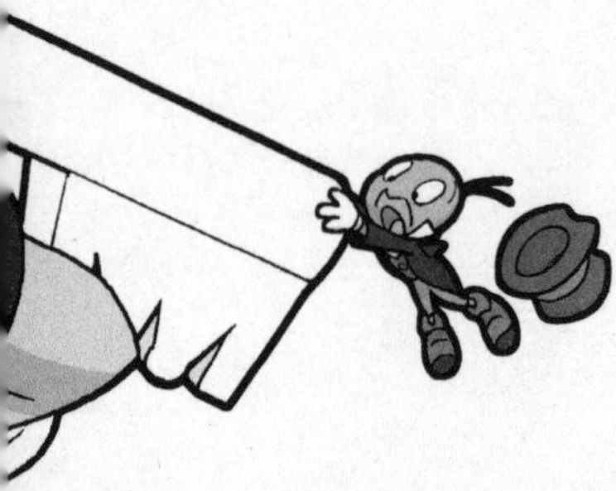

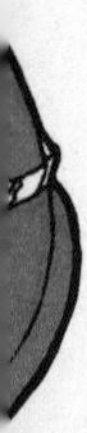

EXAMPLE:

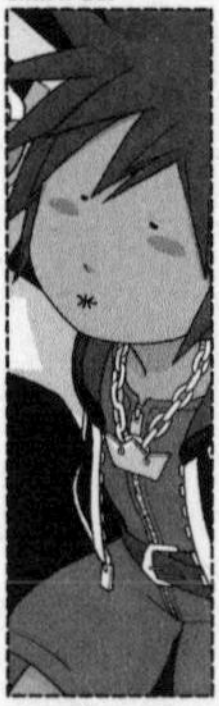

VOILA!
SOURPUSS SORA!

YOU CAN COLOR HIM IN TOO!

**HOW TO TRANSFORM SORA**

1. COPY PAGE 200 AND CUT OUT THE FACES.
2. PUT A FACE IN PLACE, LINING IT UP WITH THE OUTLINE OF SORA'S FACE.
3. ALL DONE!

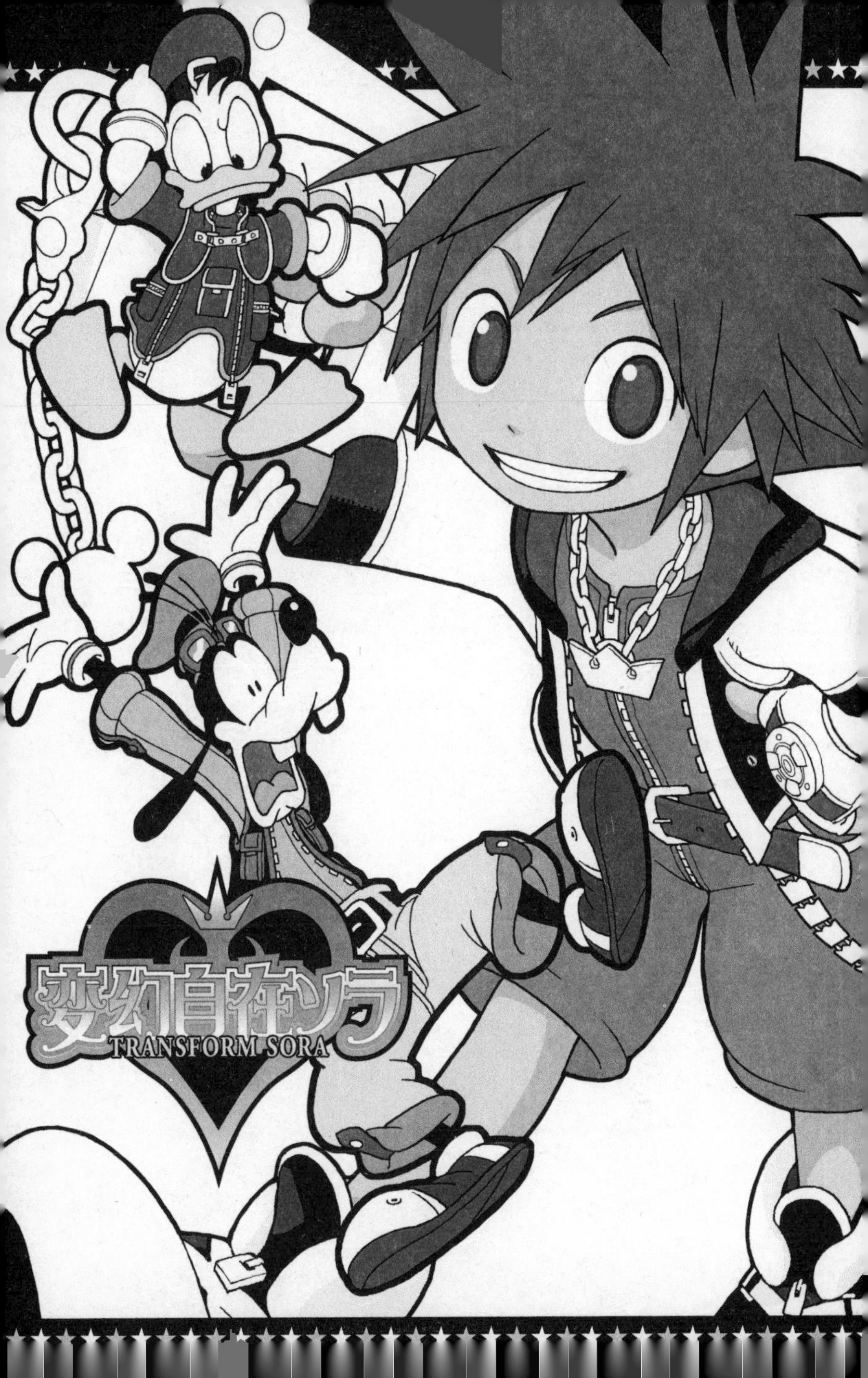
変幻自在ソラ
TRANSFORM SORA

Disney SQUARE ENIX

KINGDOM HEARTS
CHAIN OF MEMORIES

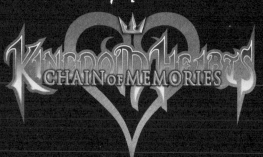

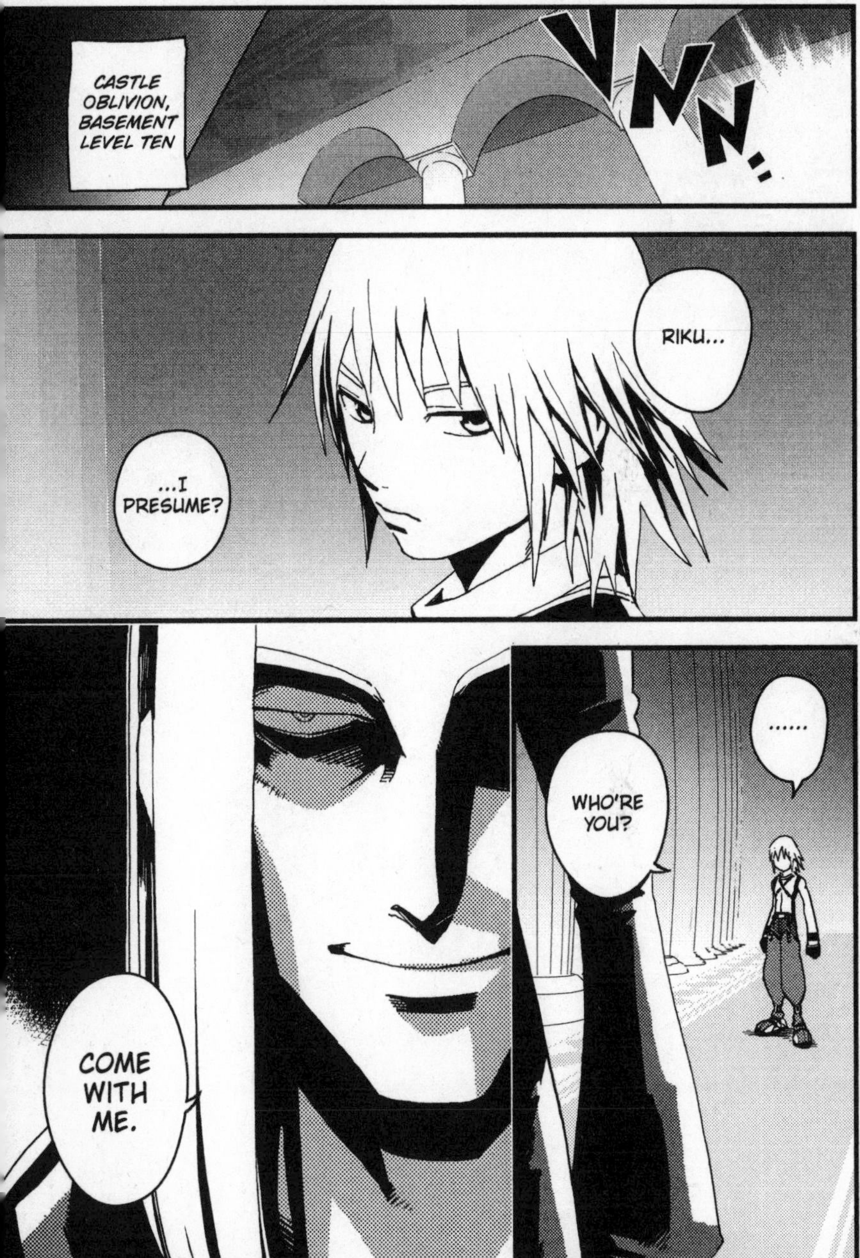
VNN..
CASTLE OBLIVION, BASEMENT LEVEL TEN
RIKU...
...I PRESUME?
......
WHO'RE YOU?
COME WITH ME.

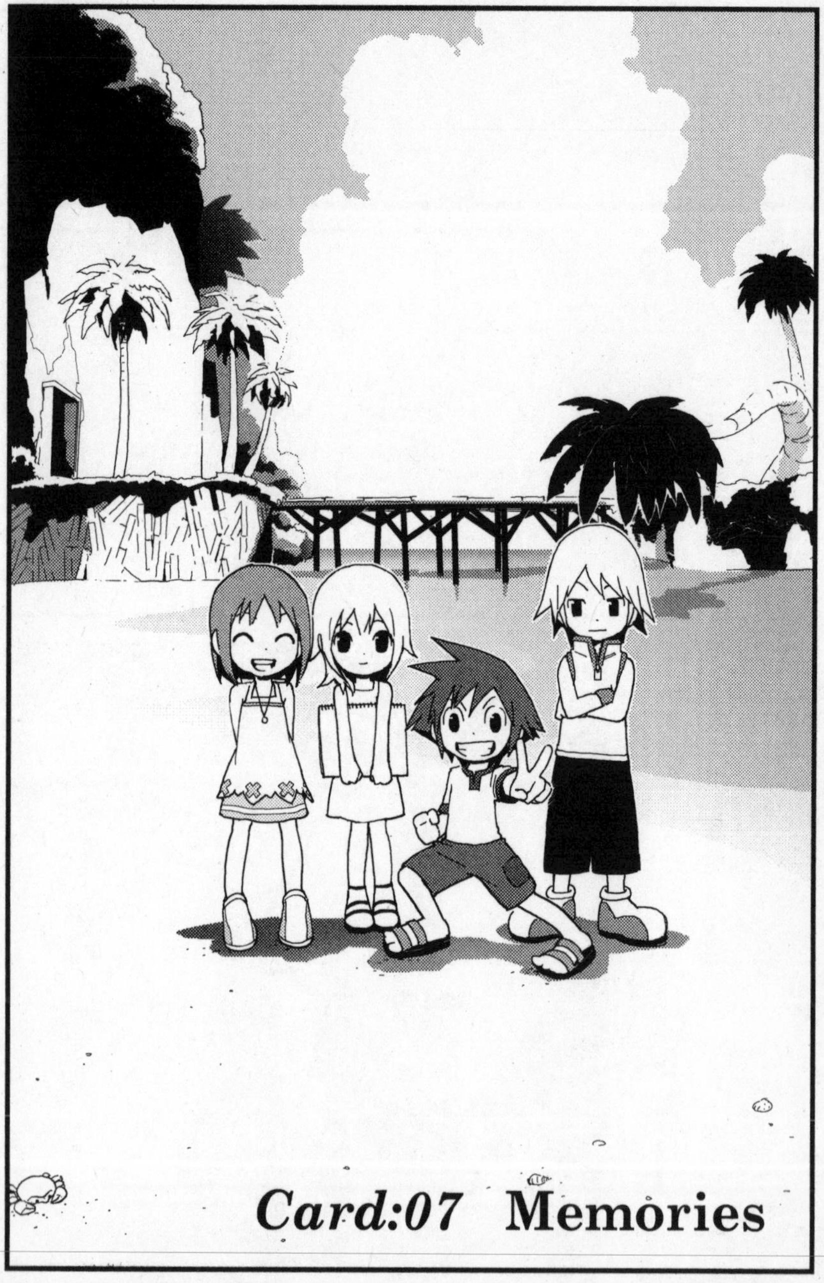

# Card:07 Memories

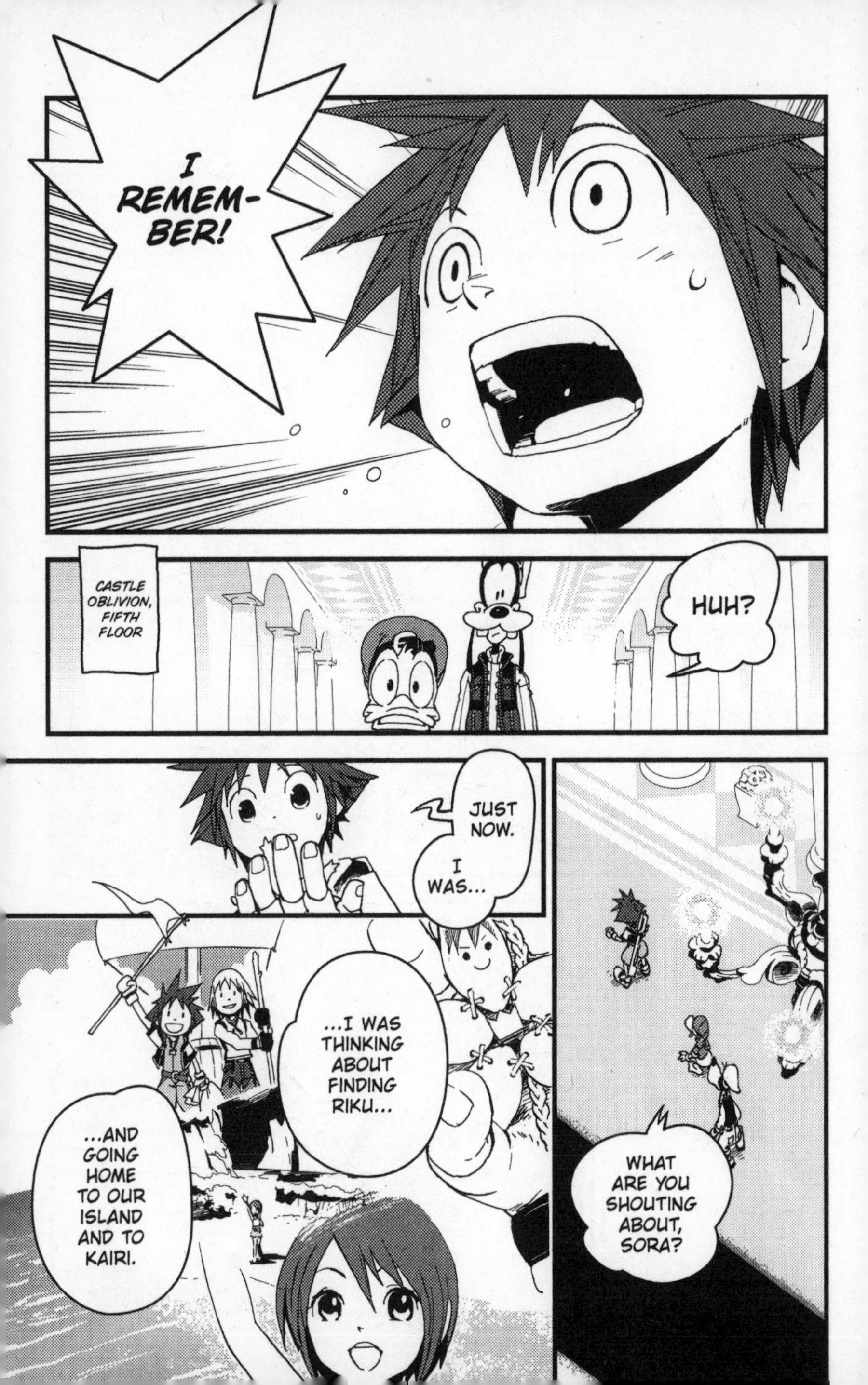
I REMEMBER!
HUH?
CASTLE OBLIVION, FIFTH FLOOR
WHAT ARE YOU SHOUTING ABOUT, SORA?
JUST NOW.
I WAS...
...I WAS THINKING ABOUT FINDING RIKU...
...AND GOING HOME TO OUR ISLAND AND TO KAIRI.

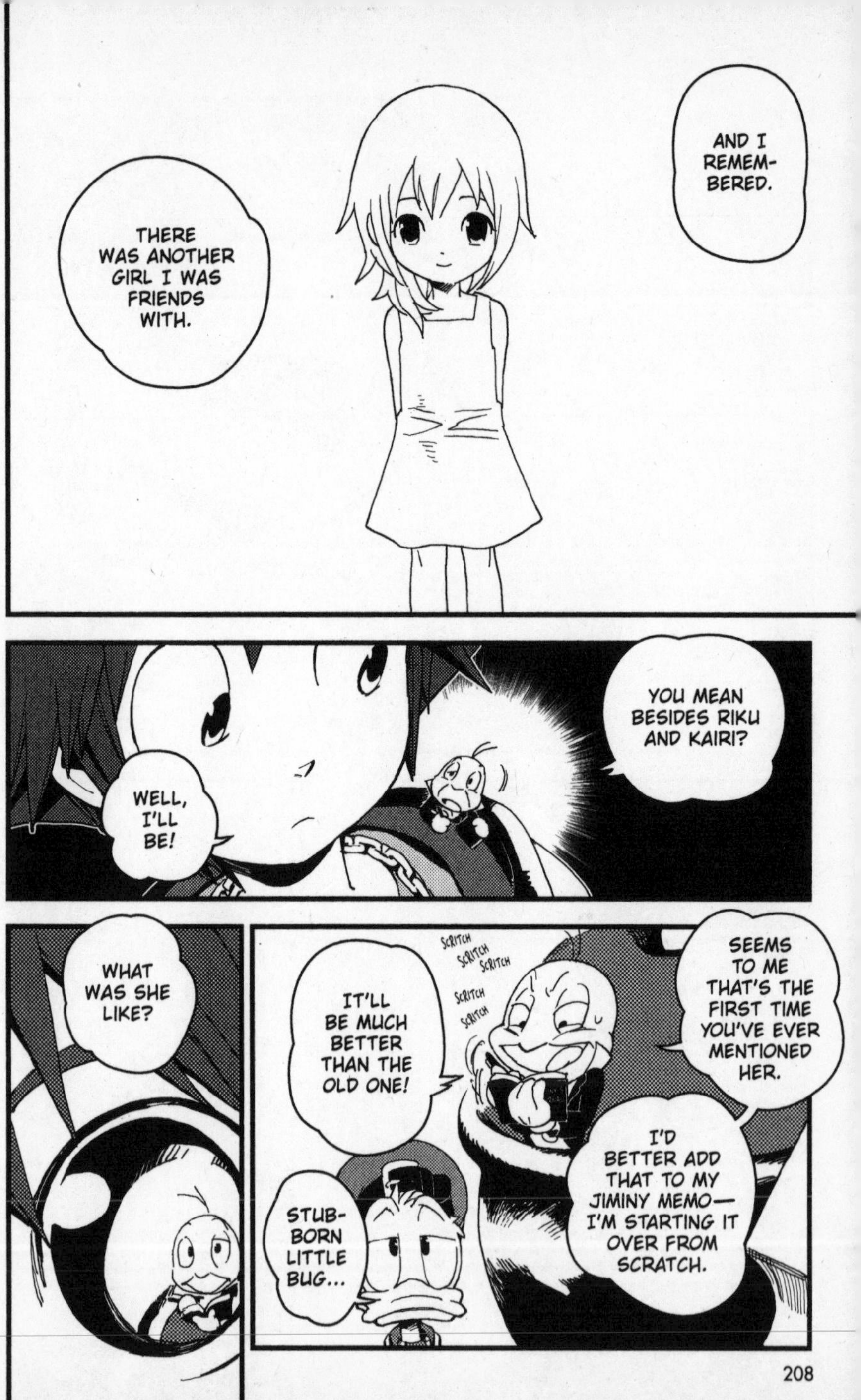
AND I REMEMBERED.
THERE WAS ANOTHER GIRL I WAS FRIENDS WITH.
YOU MEAN BESIDES RIKU AND KAIRI?
WELL, I'LL BE!
SEEMS TO ME THAT'S THE FIRST TIME YOU'VE EVER MENTIONED HER.
SCRITCH SCRITCH SCRITCH SCRITCH SCRITCH
I'D BETTER ADD THAT TO MY JIMINY MEMO—I'M STARTING IT OVER FROM SCRATCH.
IT'LL BE MUCH BETTER THAN THE OLD ONE!
STUBBORN LITTLE BUG...
WHAT WAS SHE LIKE?

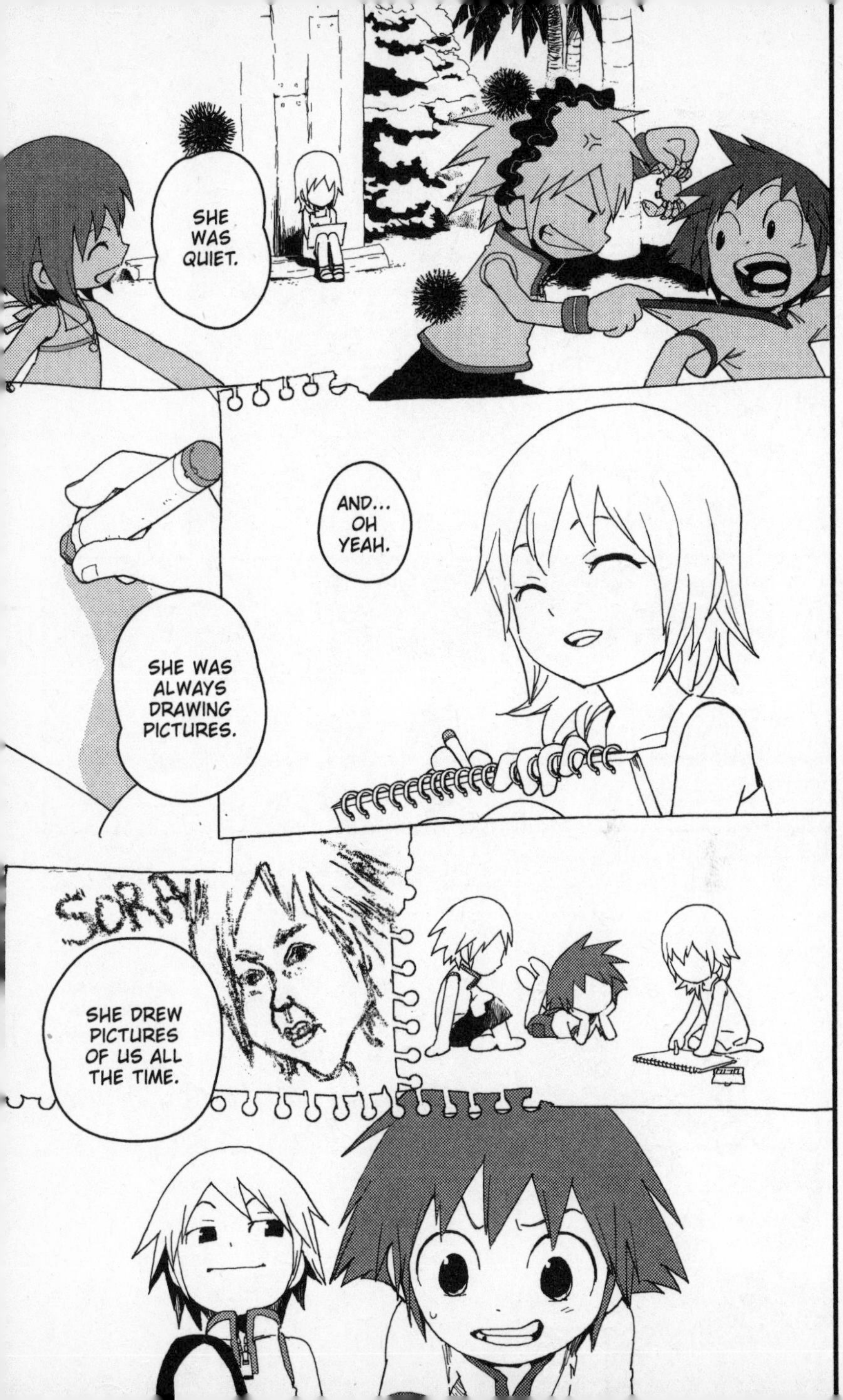
SHE WAS QUIET.
AND... OH YEAH.
SHE WAS ALWAYS DRAWING PICTURES.
SORA!!
SHE DREW PICTURES OF US ALL THE TIME.

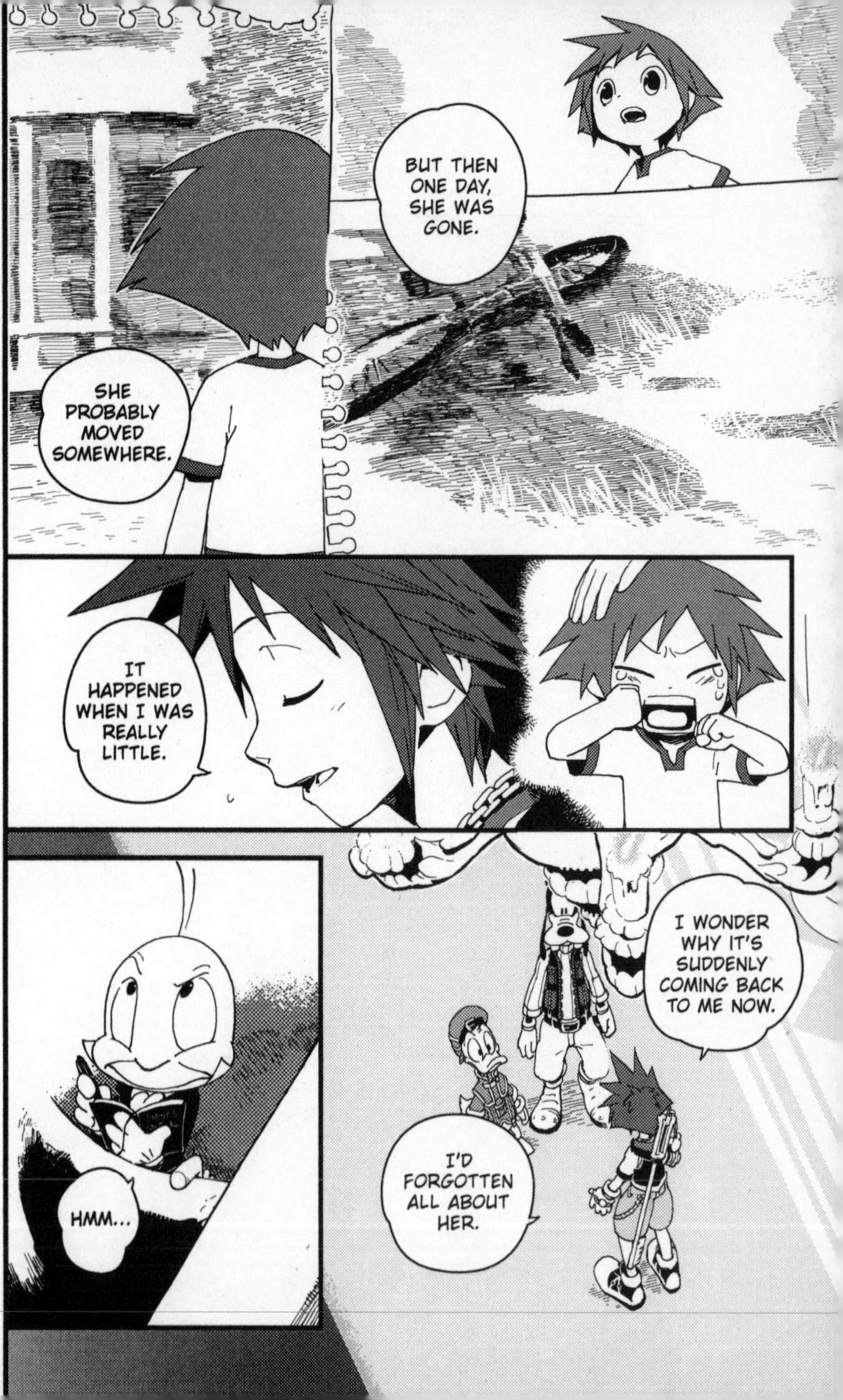
BUT THEN ONE DAY, SHE WAS GONE.
SHE PROBABLY MOVED SOMEWHERE.
IT HAPPENED WHEN I WAS REALLY LITTLE.
I WONDER WHY IT'S SUDDENLY COMING BACK TO ME NOW.
I'D FORGOTTEN ALL ABOUT HER.
HMM...

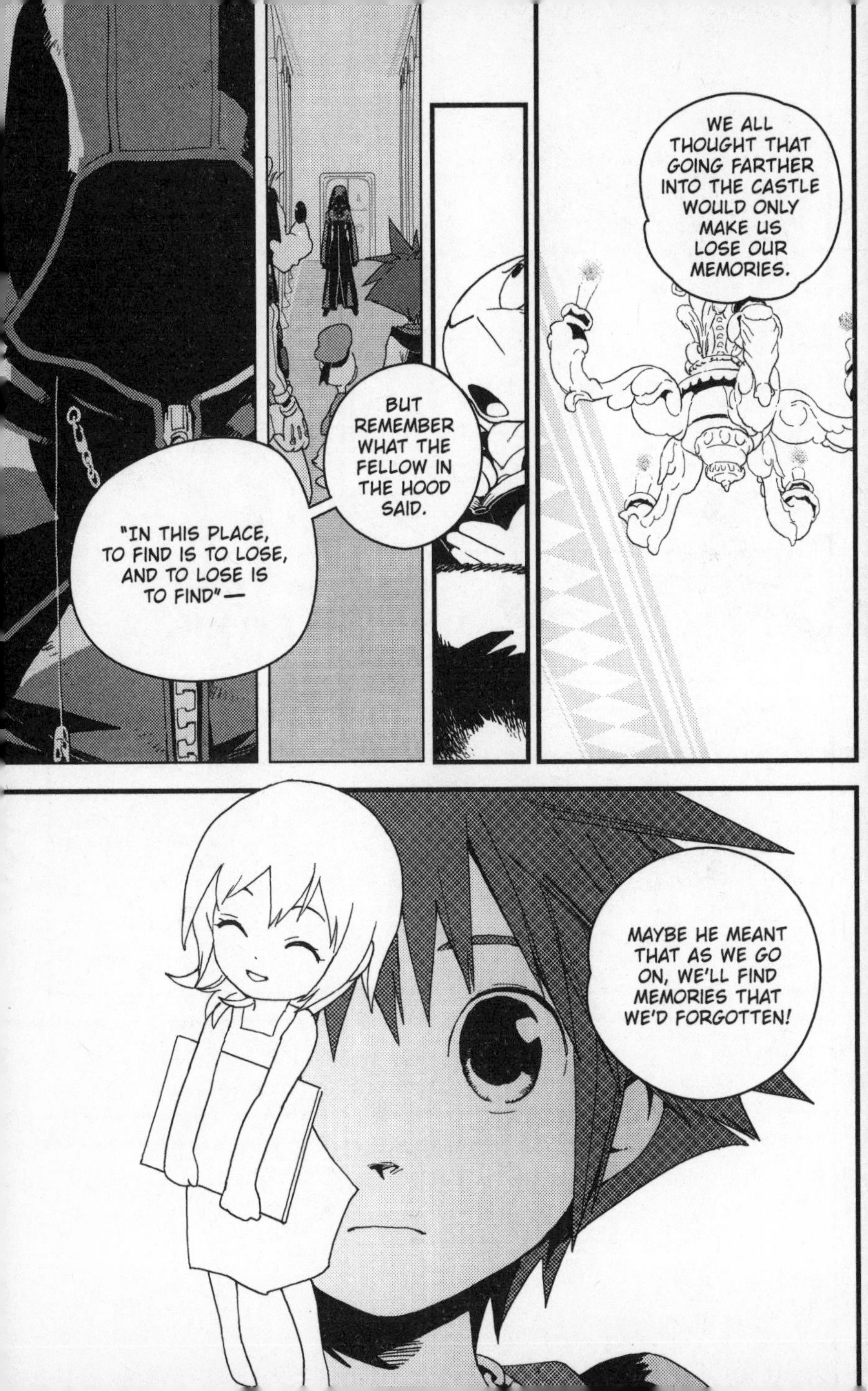
WE ALL THOUGHT THAT GOING FARTHER INTO THE CASTLE WOULD ONLY MAKE US LOSE OUR MEMORIES.
BUT REMEMBER WHAT THE FELLOW IN THE HOOD SAID.
"IN THIS PLACE, TO FIND IS TO LOSE, AND TO LOSE IS TO FIND"—
MAYBE HE MEANT THAT AS WE GO ON, WE'LL FIND MEMORIES THAT WE'D FORGOTTEN!

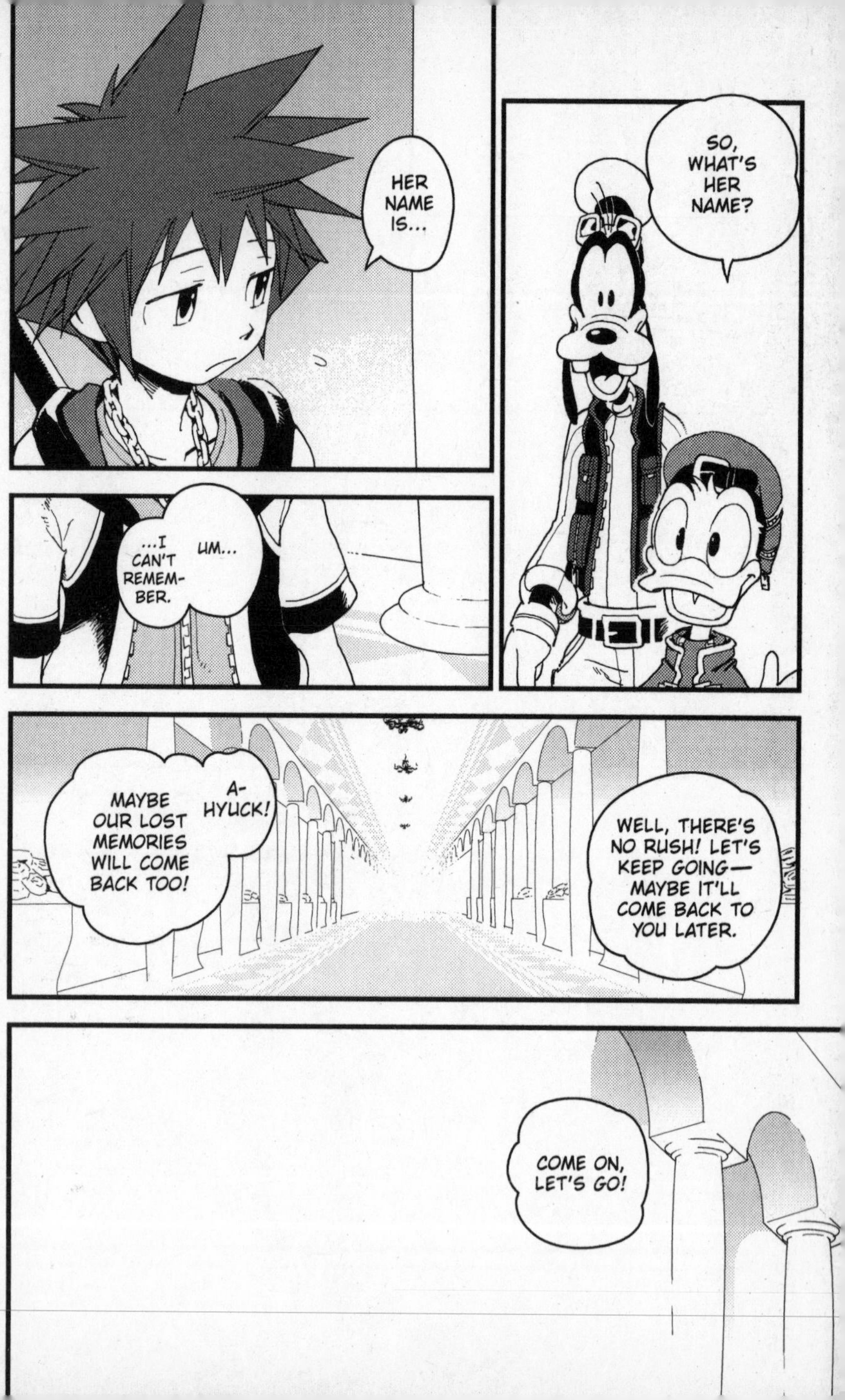
SO, WHAT'S HER NAME?
HER NAME IS...
UM...
...I CAN'T REMEMBER.
WELL, THERE'S NO RUSH! LET'S KEEP GOING—MAYBE IT'LL COME BACK TO YOU LATER.
A-HYUCK!
MAYBE OUR LOST MEMORIES WILL COME BACK TOO!
COME ON, LET'S GO!

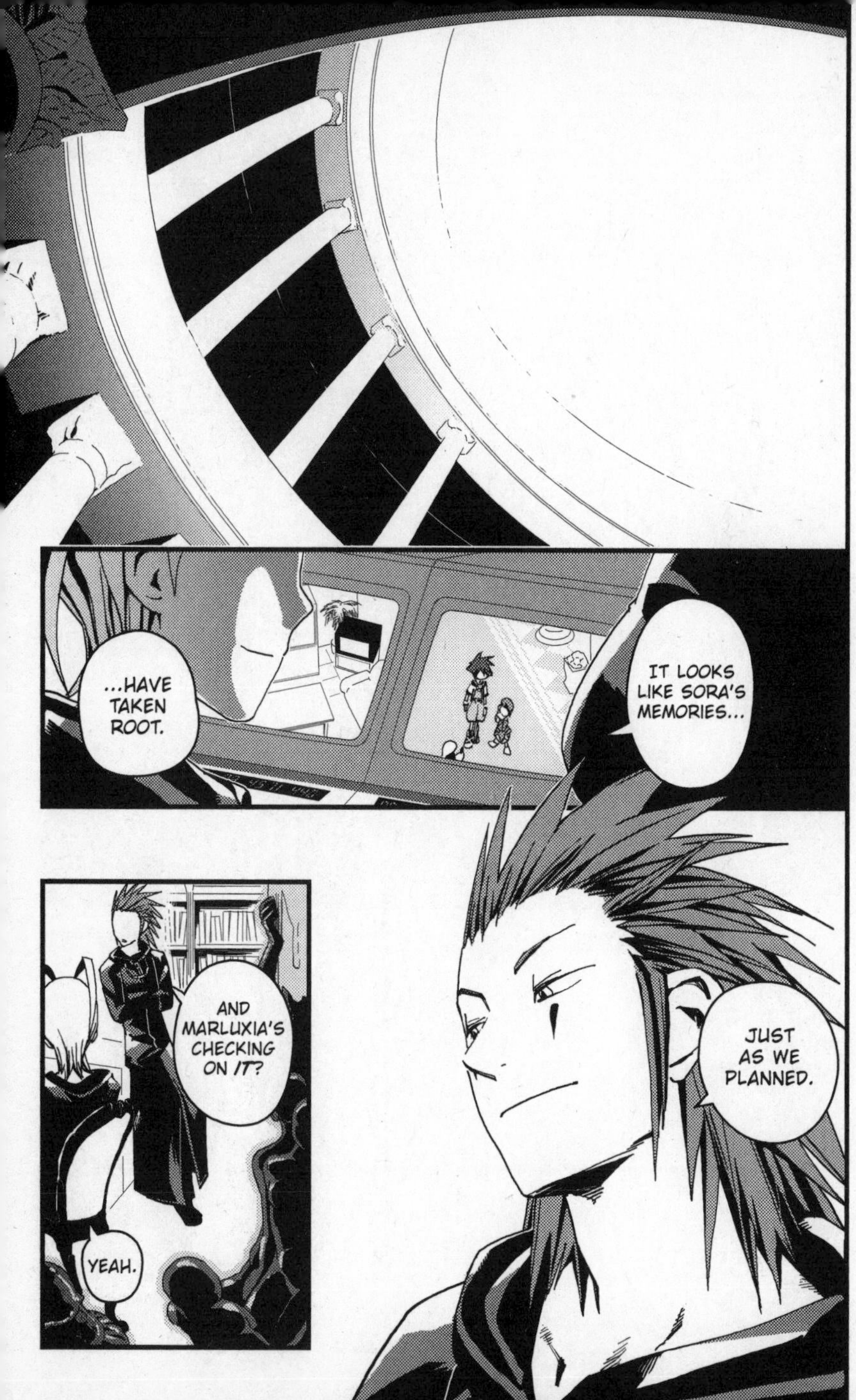
IT LOOKS LIKE SORA'S MEMORIES...
...HAVE TAKEN ROOT.
JUST AS WE PLANNED.
AND MARLUXIA'S CHECKING ON *IT*?
YEAH.

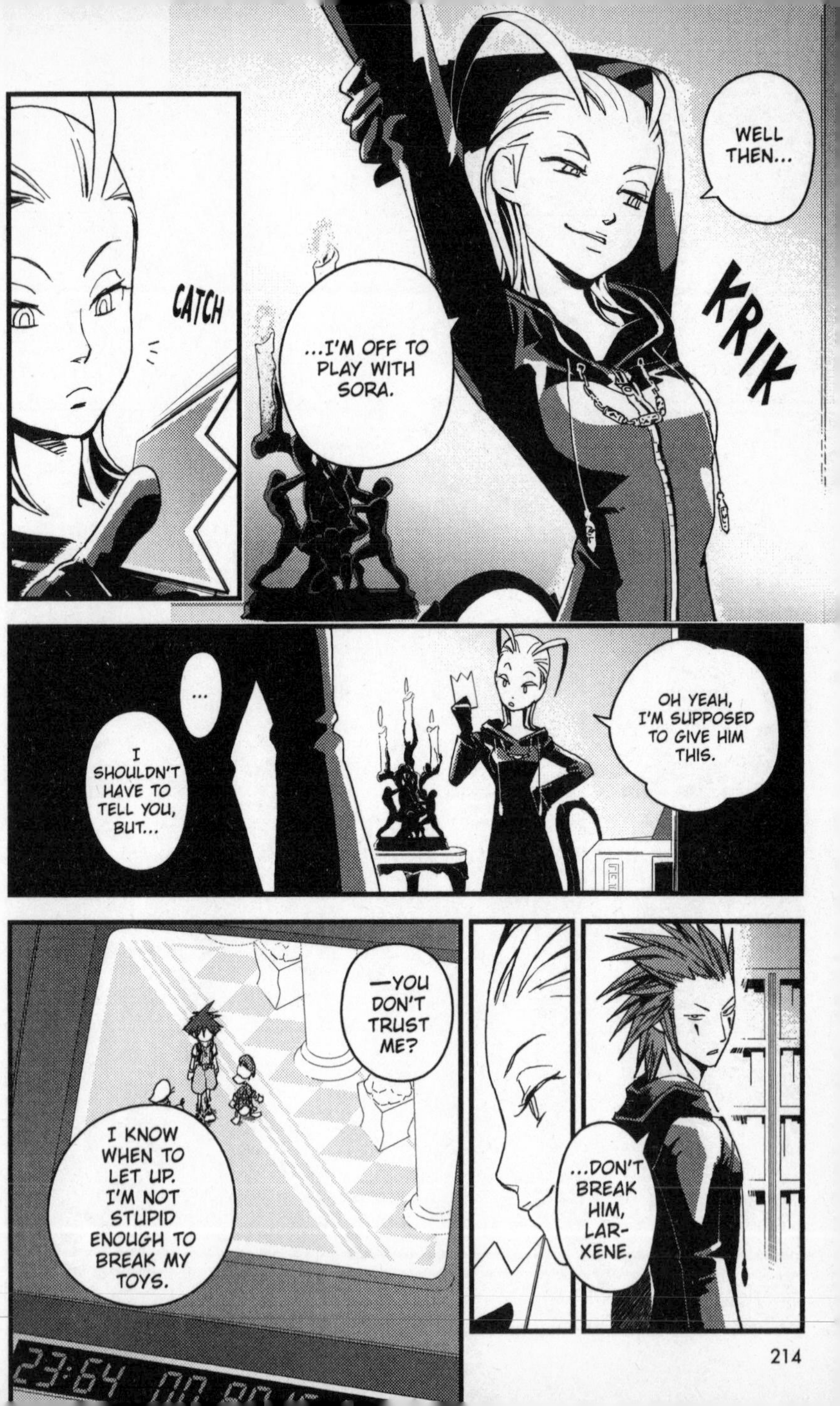
WELL THEN...
KRIK
...I'M OFF TO PLAY WITH SORA.
CATCH
OH YEAH, I'M SUPPOSED TO GIVE HIM THIS.
...
I SHOULDN'T HAVE TO TELL YOU, BUT...
...DON'T BREAK HIM, LAR-XENE.
—YOU DON'T TRUST ME?
I KNOW WHEN TO LET UP. I'M NOT STUPID ENOUGH TO BREAK MY TOYS.

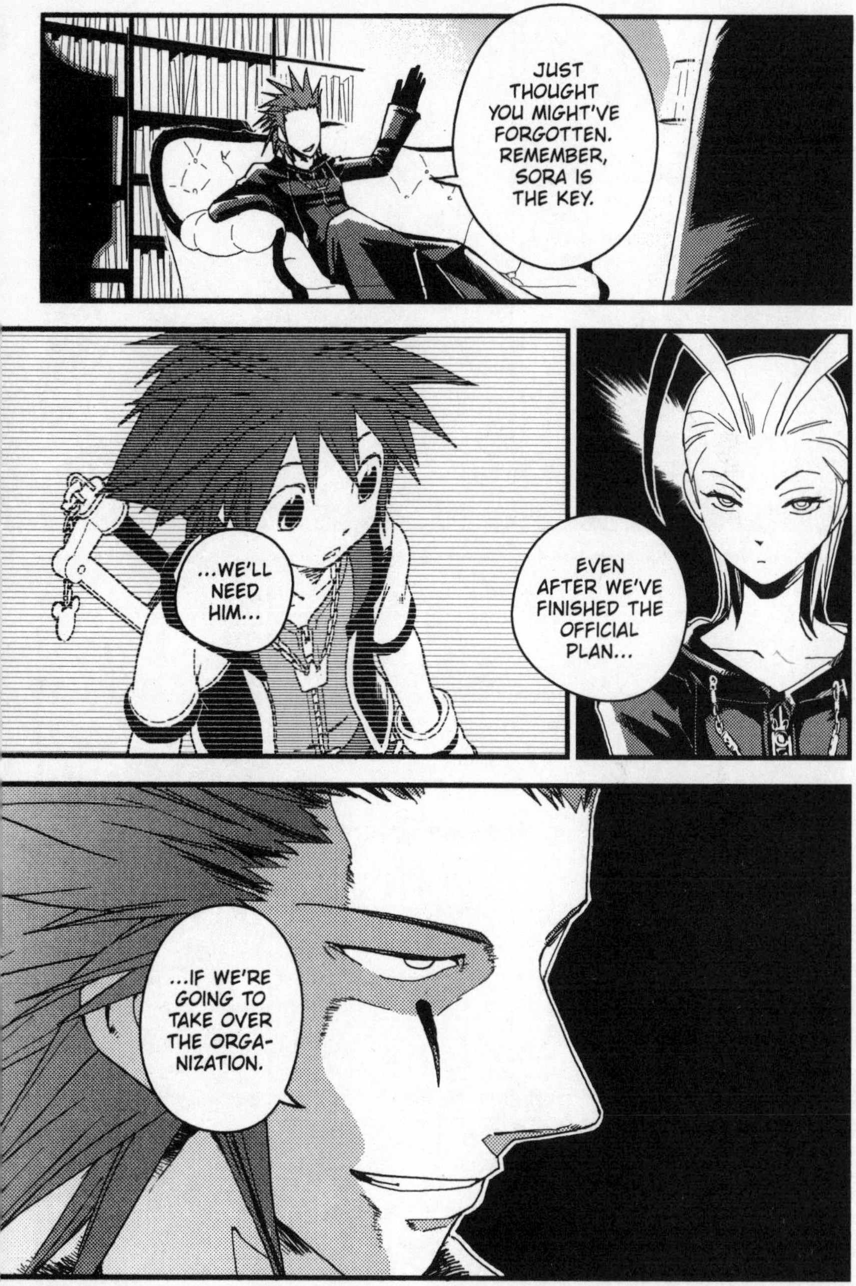
JUST THOUGHT YOU MIGHT'VE FORGOTTEN. REMEMBER, SORA IS THE KEY.
EVEN AFTER WE'VE FINISHED THE OFFICIAL PLAN...
...WE'LL NEED HIM...
...IF WE'RE GOING TO TAKE OVER THE ORGA-NIZATION.

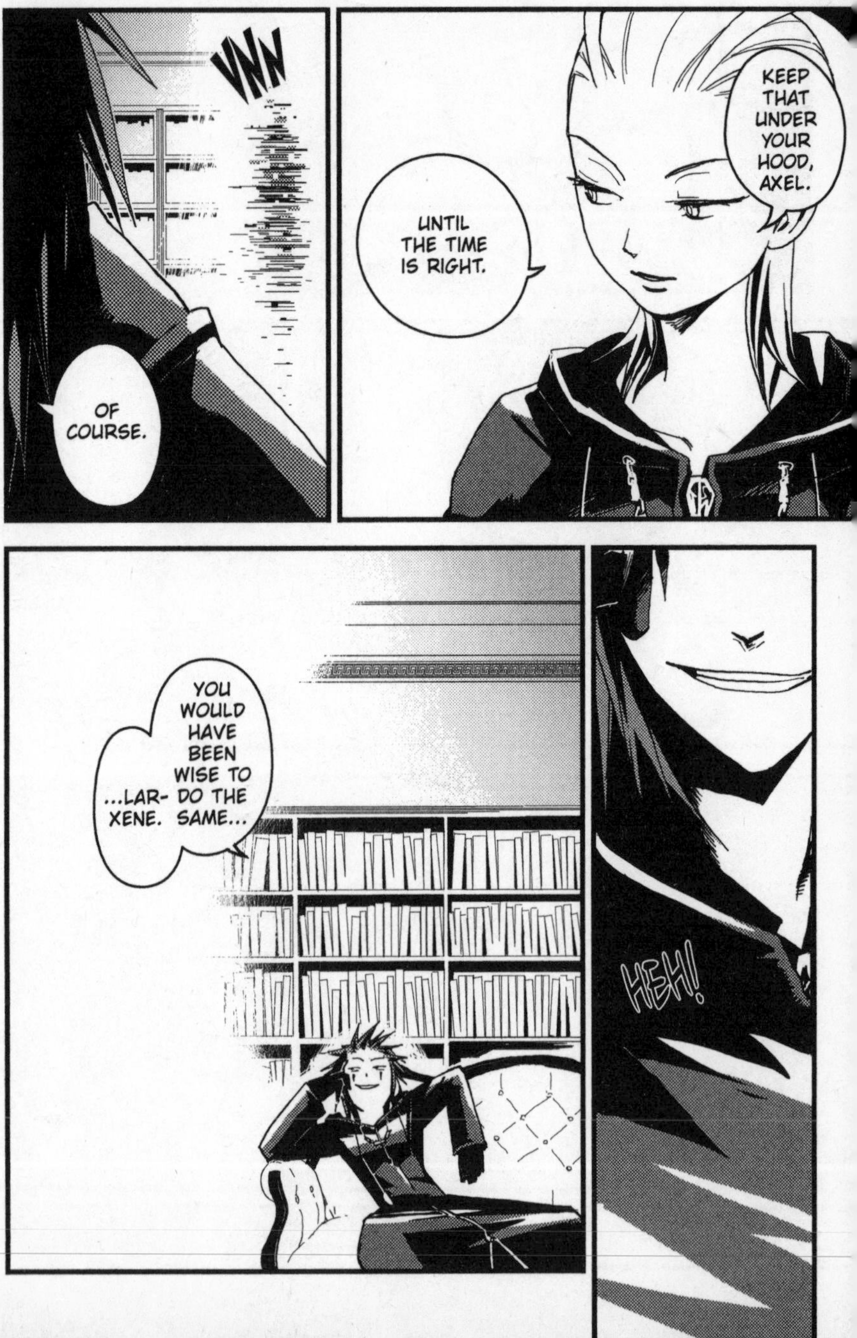
KEEP THAT UNDER YOUR HOOD, AXEL.
UNTIL THE TIME IS RIGHT.
VNN
OF COURSE.
HEH!
YOU WOULD HAVE BEEN WISE TO DO THE SAME...
...LAR- XENE.

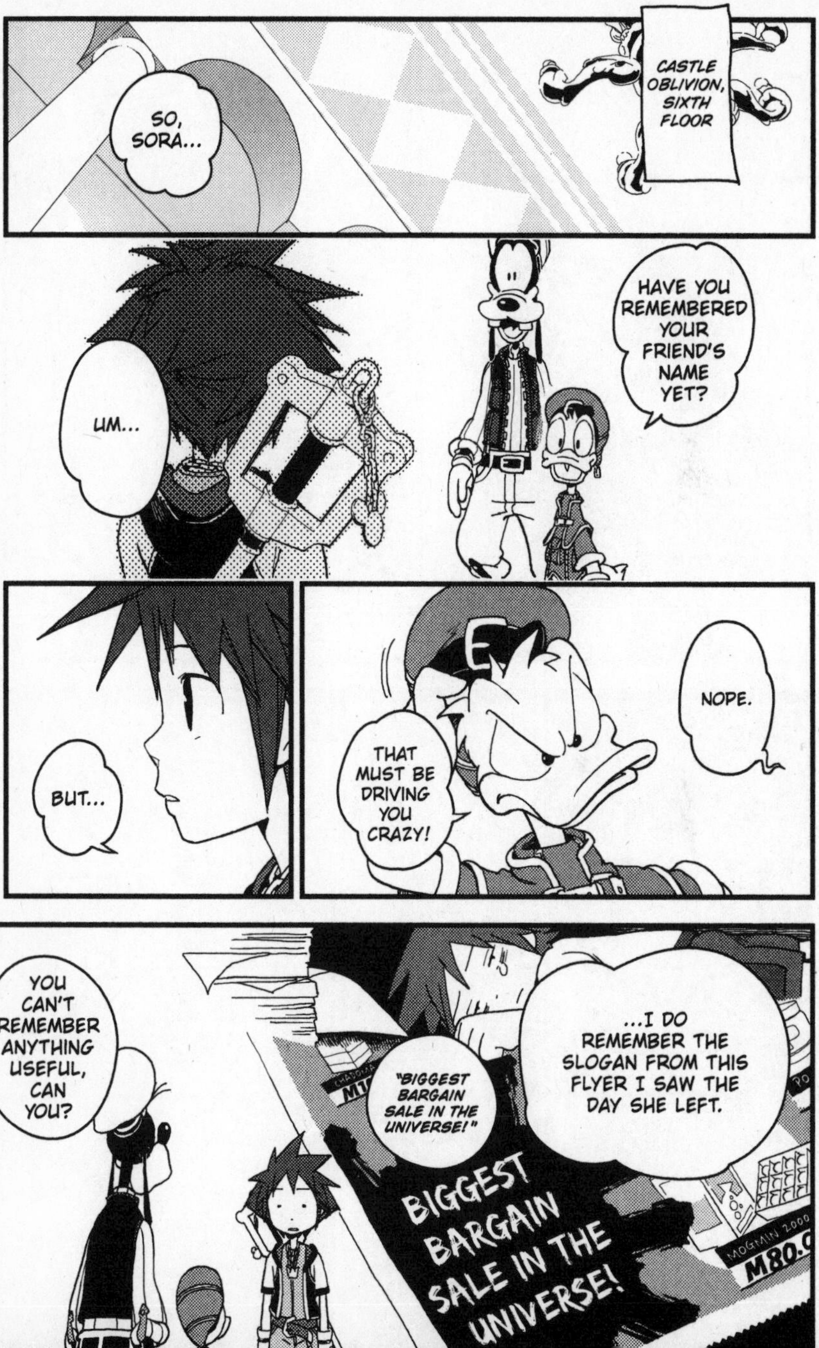
CASTLE OBLIVION, SIXTH FLOOR
SO, SORA...
HAVE YOU REMEMBERED YOUR FRIEND'S NAME YET?
UM...
NOPE.
THAT MUST BE DRIVING YOU CRAZY!
BUT...
...I DO REMEMBER THE SLOGAN FROM THIS FLYER I SAW THE DAY SHE LEFT.
"BIGGEST BARGAIN SALE IN THE UNIVERSE!"
YOU CAN'T REMEMBER ANYTHING USEFUL, CAN YOU?
BIGGEST BARGAIN SALE IN THE UNIVERSE!
MOGMIN 2000

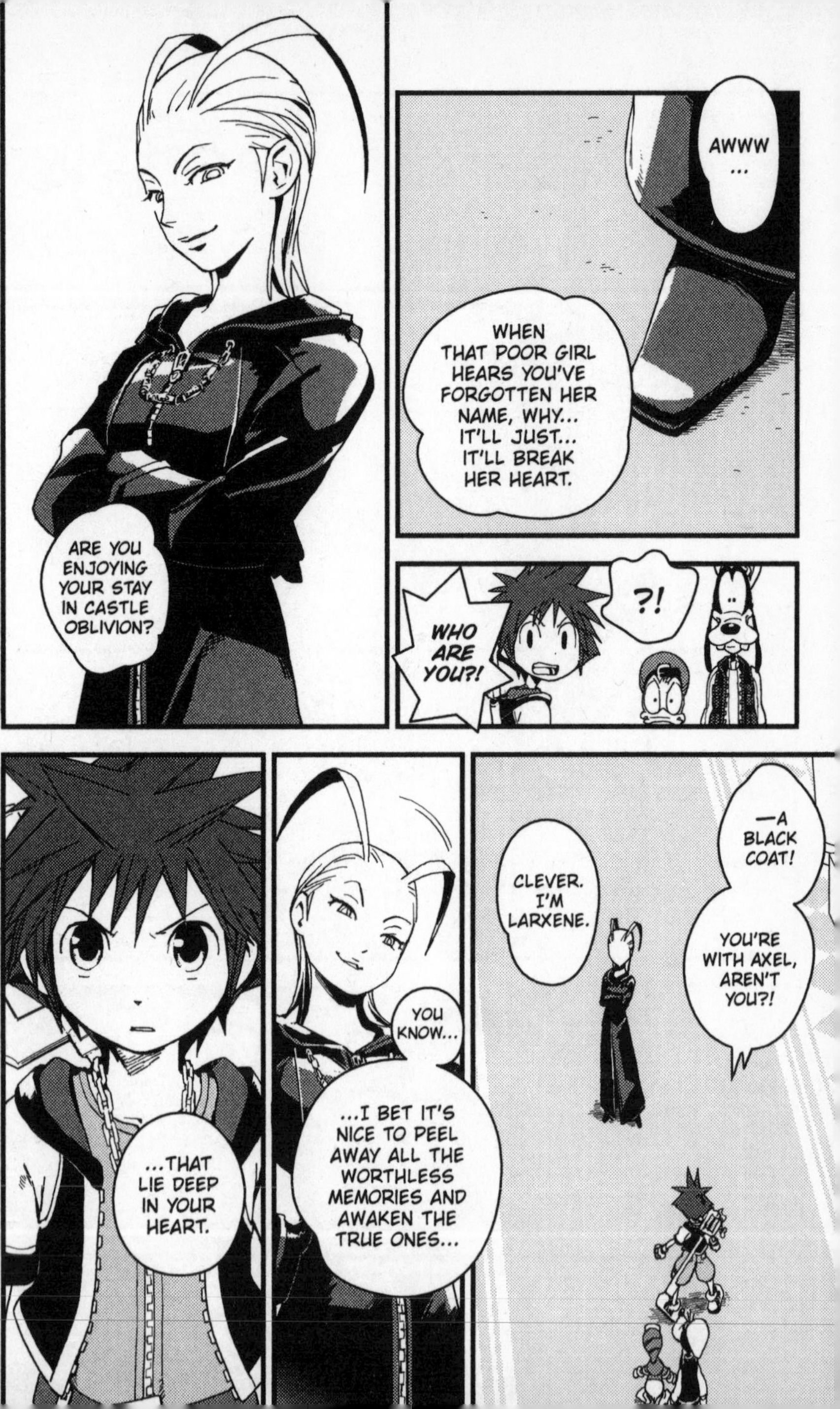
AWWW...
WHEN THAT POOR GIRL HEARS YOU'VE FORGOTTEN HER NAME, WHY... IT'LL JUST... IT'LL BREAK HER HEART.
?!
WHO ARE YOU?!
ARE YOU ENJOYING YOUR STAY IN CASTLE OBLIVION?
—A BLACK COAT!
YOU'RE WITH AXEL, AREN'T YOU?!
CLEVER. I'M LARXENE.
YOU KNOW...
...I BET IT'S NICE TO PEEL AWAY ALL THE WORTHLESS MEMORIES AND AWAKEN THE TRUE ONES...
...THAT LIE DEEP IN YOUR HEART.

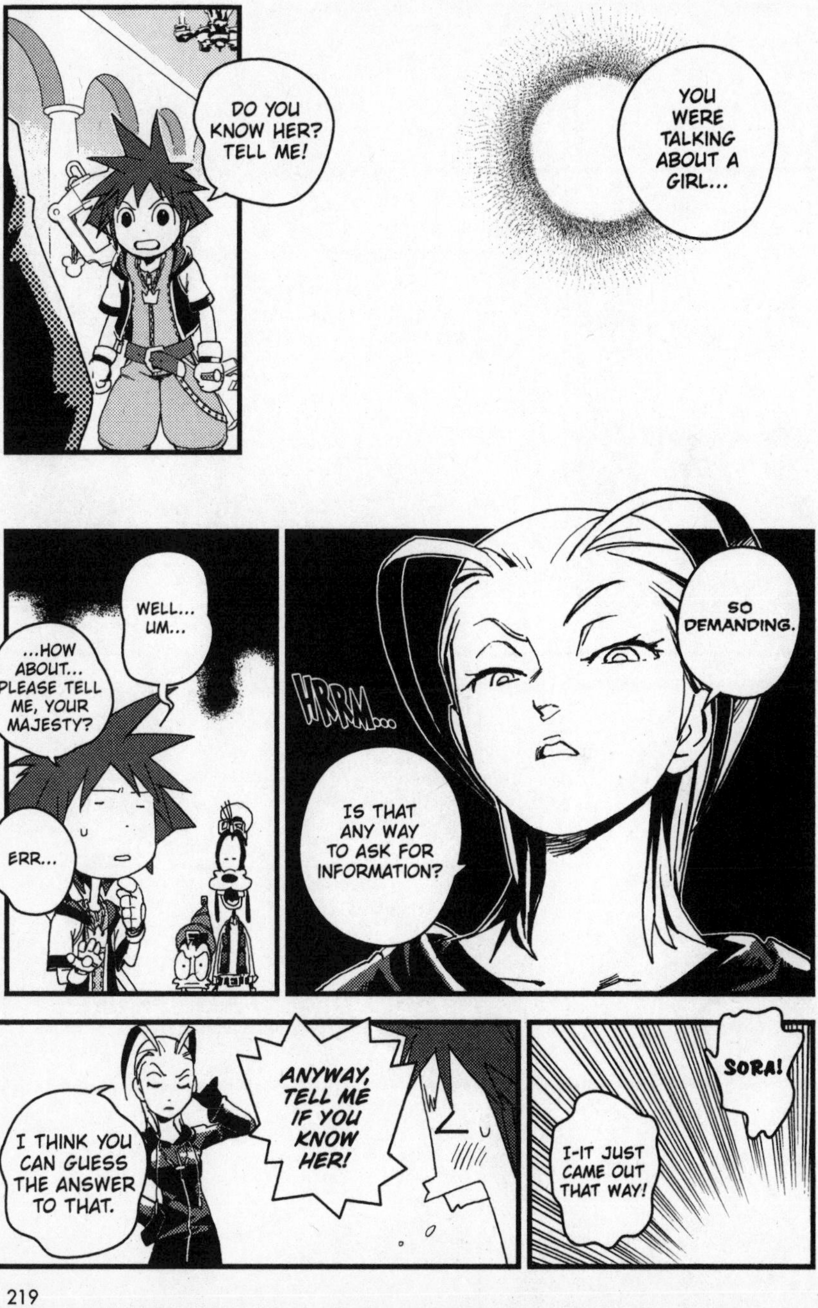
YOU WERE TALKING ABOUT A GIRL...
DO YOU KNOW HER? TELL ME!
SO DEMANDING.
HRRM...
IS THAT ANY WAY TO ASK FOR INFORMATION?
WELL... UM...
...HOW ABOUT... PLEASE TELL ME, YOUR MAJESTY?
ERR...
SORA!
I-IT JUST CAME OUT THAT WAY!
ANYWAY, TELL ME IF YOU KNOW HER!
I THINK YOU CAN GUESS THE ANSWER TO THAT.

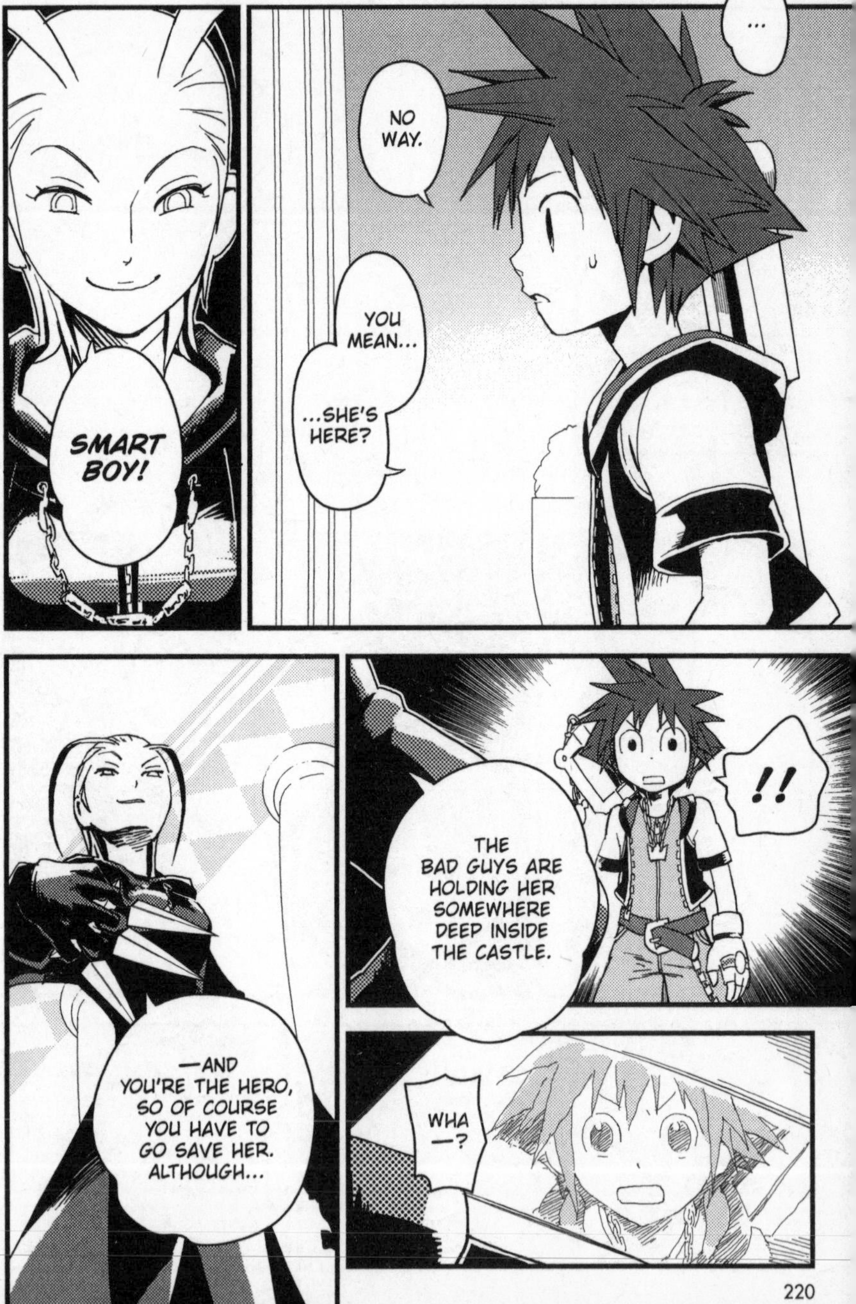
...
NO WAY.
YOU MEAN... ...SHE'S HERE?
SMART BOY!
!!
THE BAD GUYS ARE HOLDING HER SOMEWHERE DEEP INSIDE THE CASTLE.
WHA—?
—AND YOU'RE THE HERO, SO OF COURSE YOU HAVE TO GO SAVE HER. ALTHOUGH...

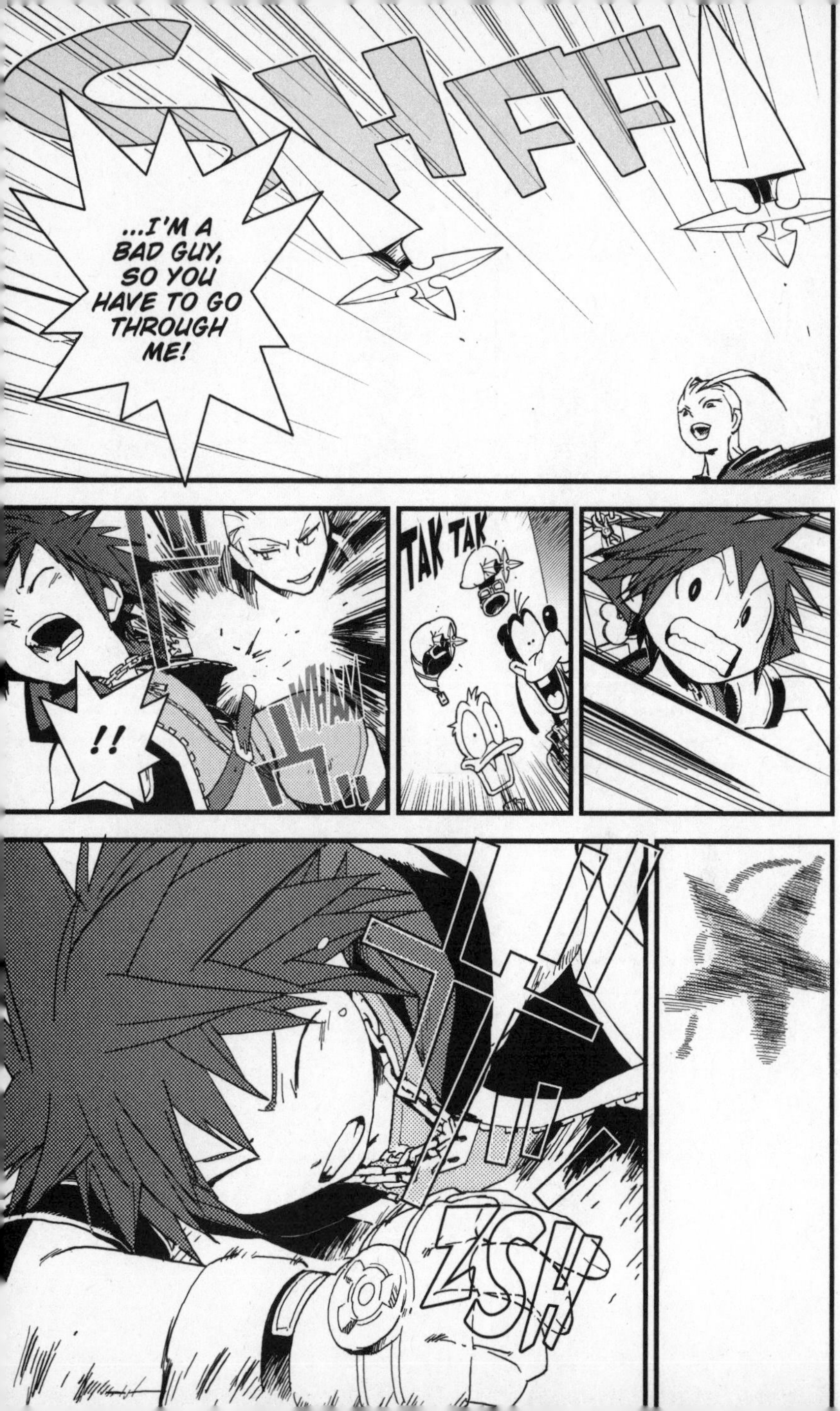
CHFF
...I'M A BAD GUY, SO YOU HAVE TO GO THROUGH ME!
TAK TAK
WHAM
!!
ZSH

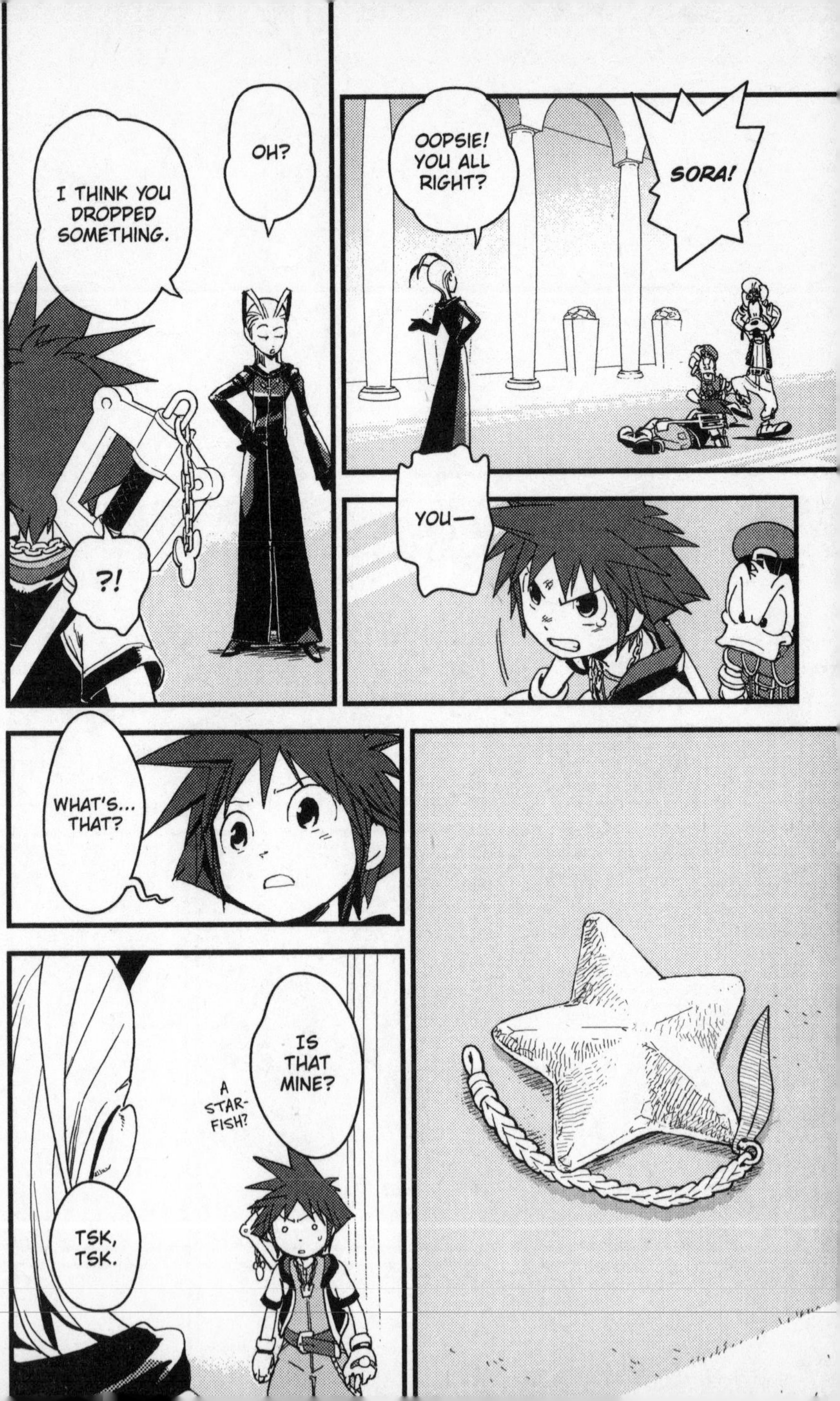
SORA!
OOPSIE! YOU ALL RIGHT?
YOU—
OH?
I THINK YOU DROPPED SOMETHING.
?!
WHAT'S... THAT?
IS THAT MINE?
A STAR-FISH?
TSK, TSK.

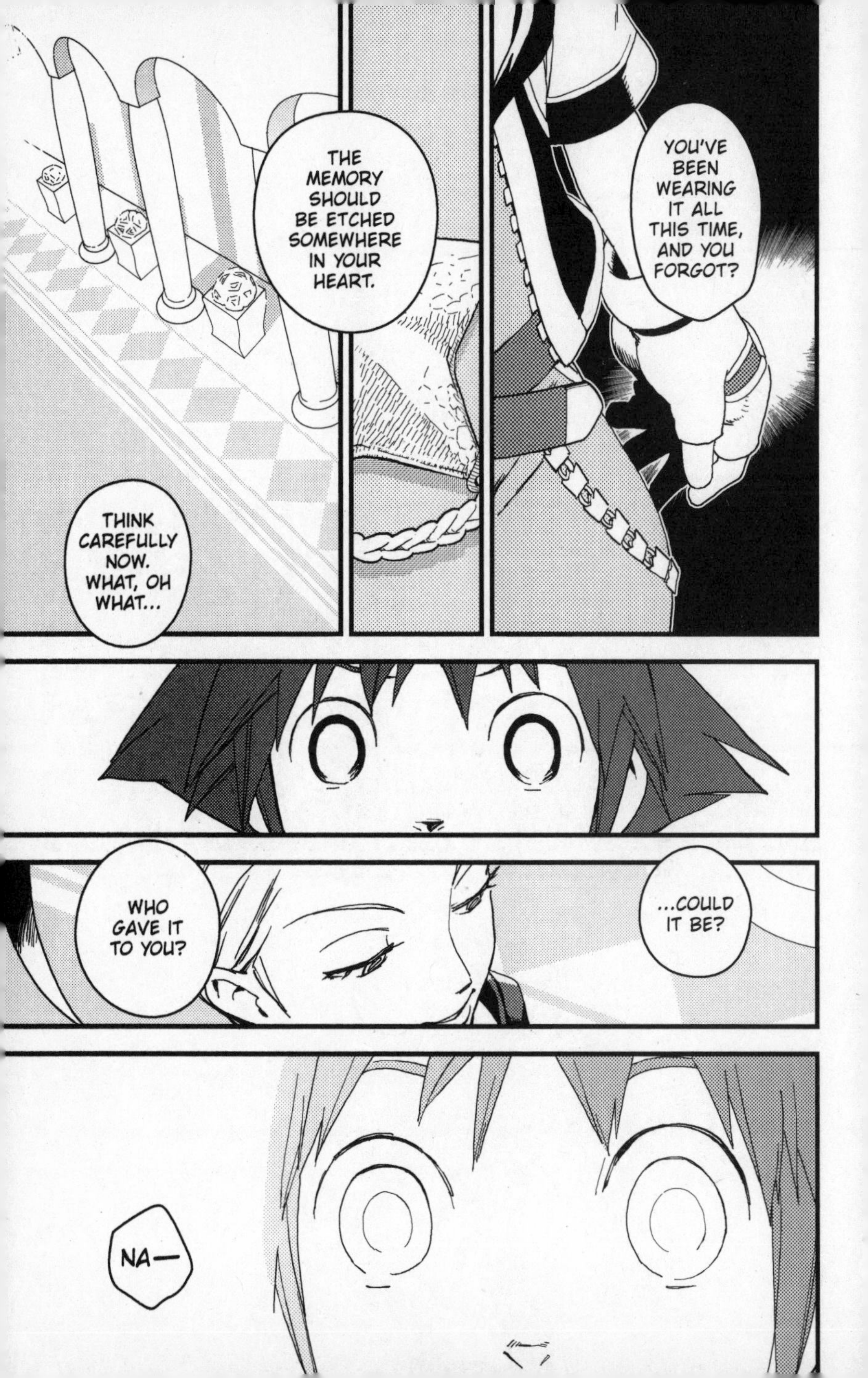
YOU'VE BEEN WEARING IT ALL THIS TIME, AND YOU FORGOT?
THE MEMORY SHOULD BE ETCHED SOMEWHERE IN YOUR HEART.
THINK CAREFULLY NOW. WHAT, OH WHAT...
...COULD IT BE?
WHO GAVE IT TO YOU?
NA—

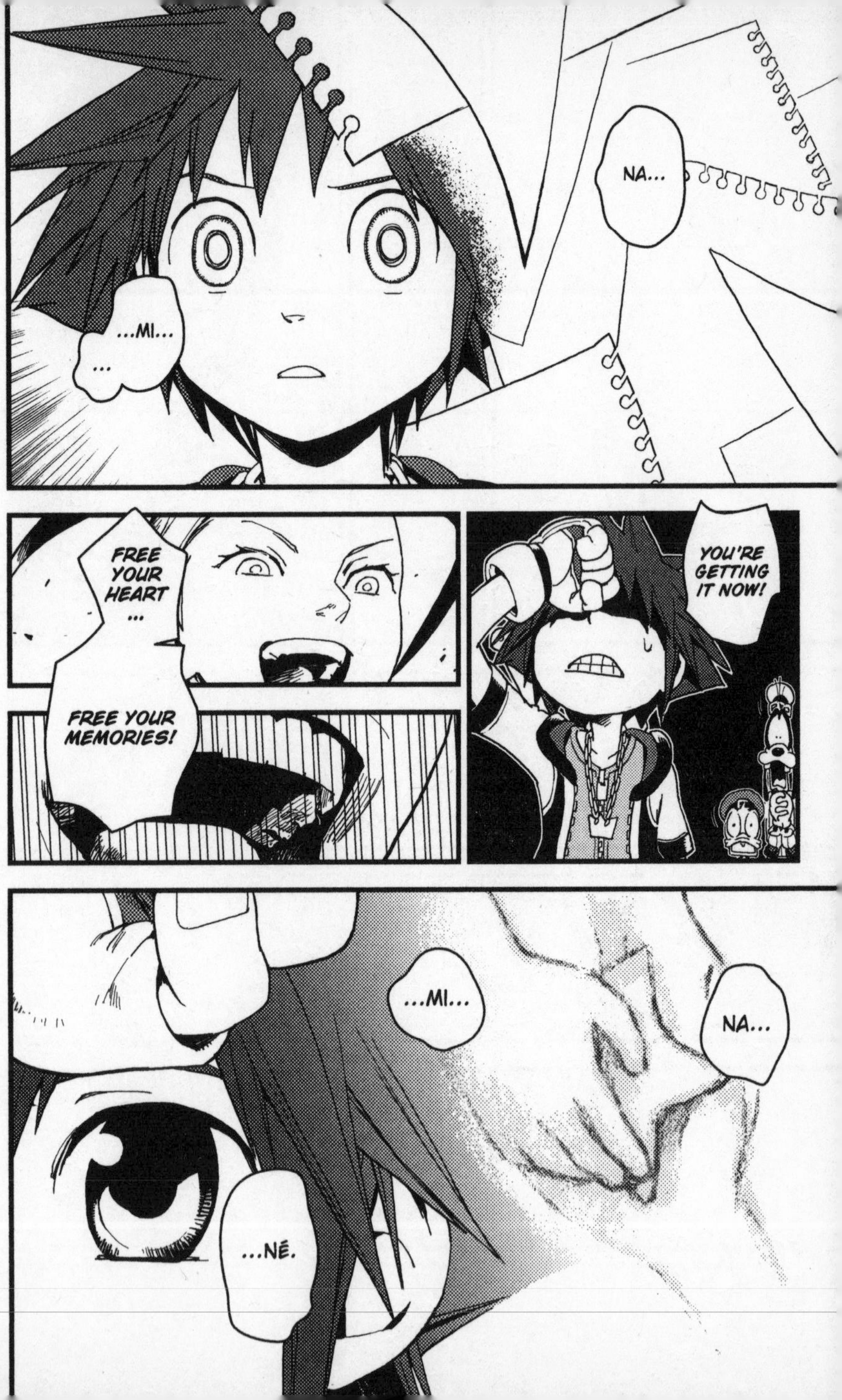
NA...
...MI...
...
YOU'RE GETTING IT NOW!
FREE YOUR HEART ...
FREE YOUR MEMORIES!
NA...
...MI...
...NÉ.

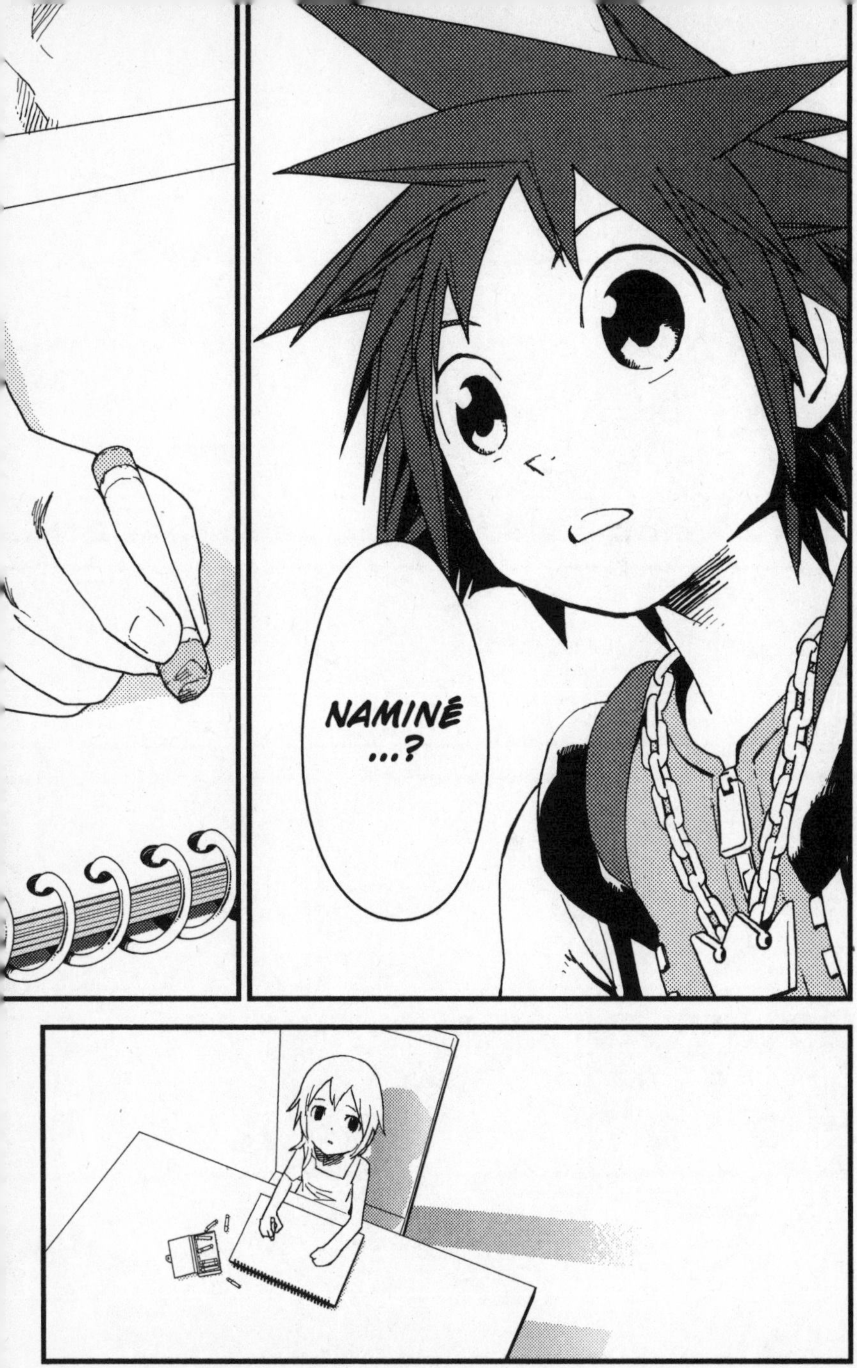
NAMINÉ ...?

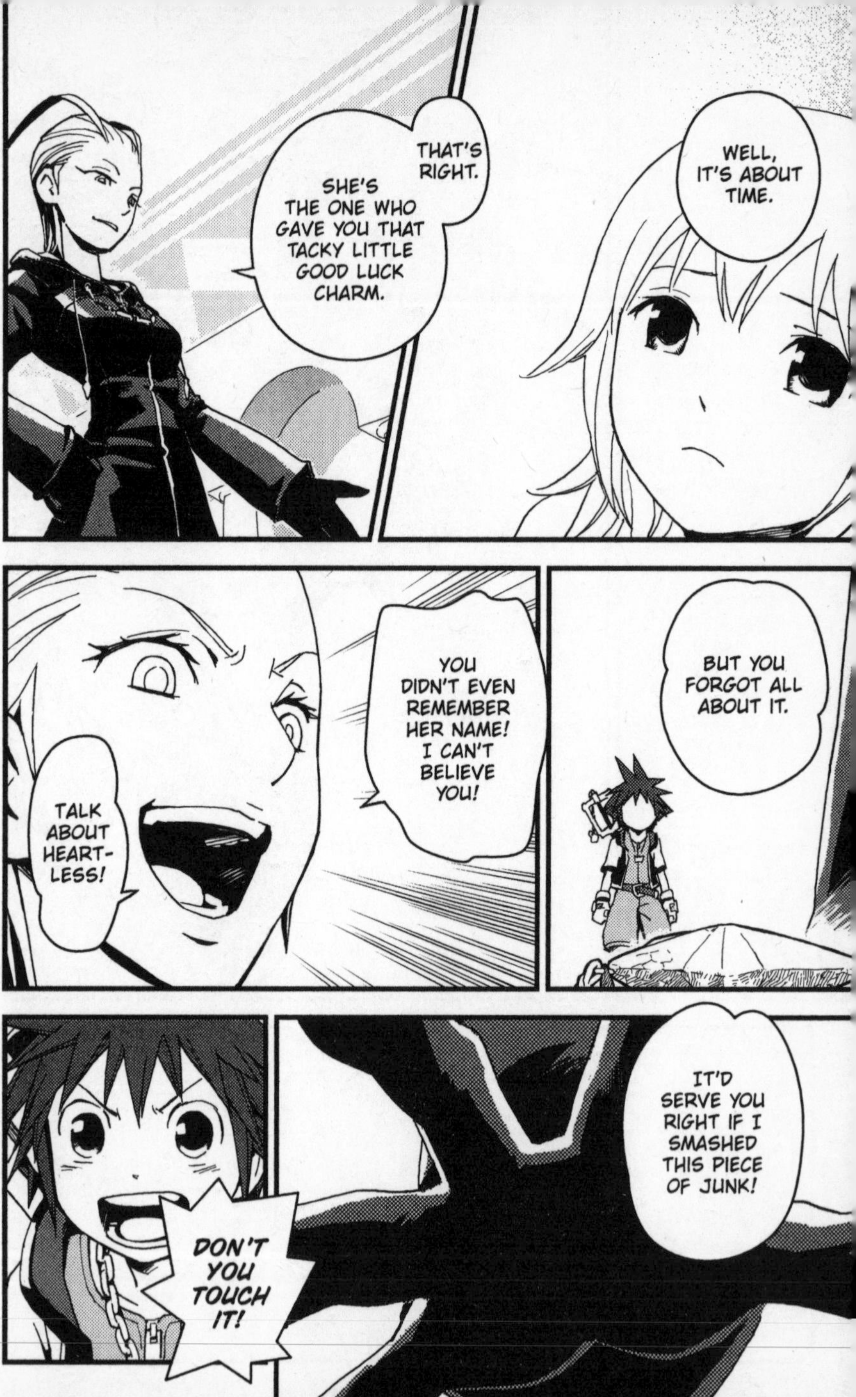
WELL, IT'S ABOUT TIME.
THAT'S RIGHT.
SHE'S THE ONE WHO GAVE YOU THAT TACKY LITTLE GOOD LUCK CHARM.
BUT YOU FORGOT ALL ABOUT IT.
YOU DIDN'T EVEN REMEMBER HER NAME! I CAN'T BELIEVE YOU!
TALK ABOUT HEART-LESS!
IT'D SERVE YOU RIGHT IF I SMASHED THIS PIECE OF JUNK!
DON'T YOU TOUCH IT!

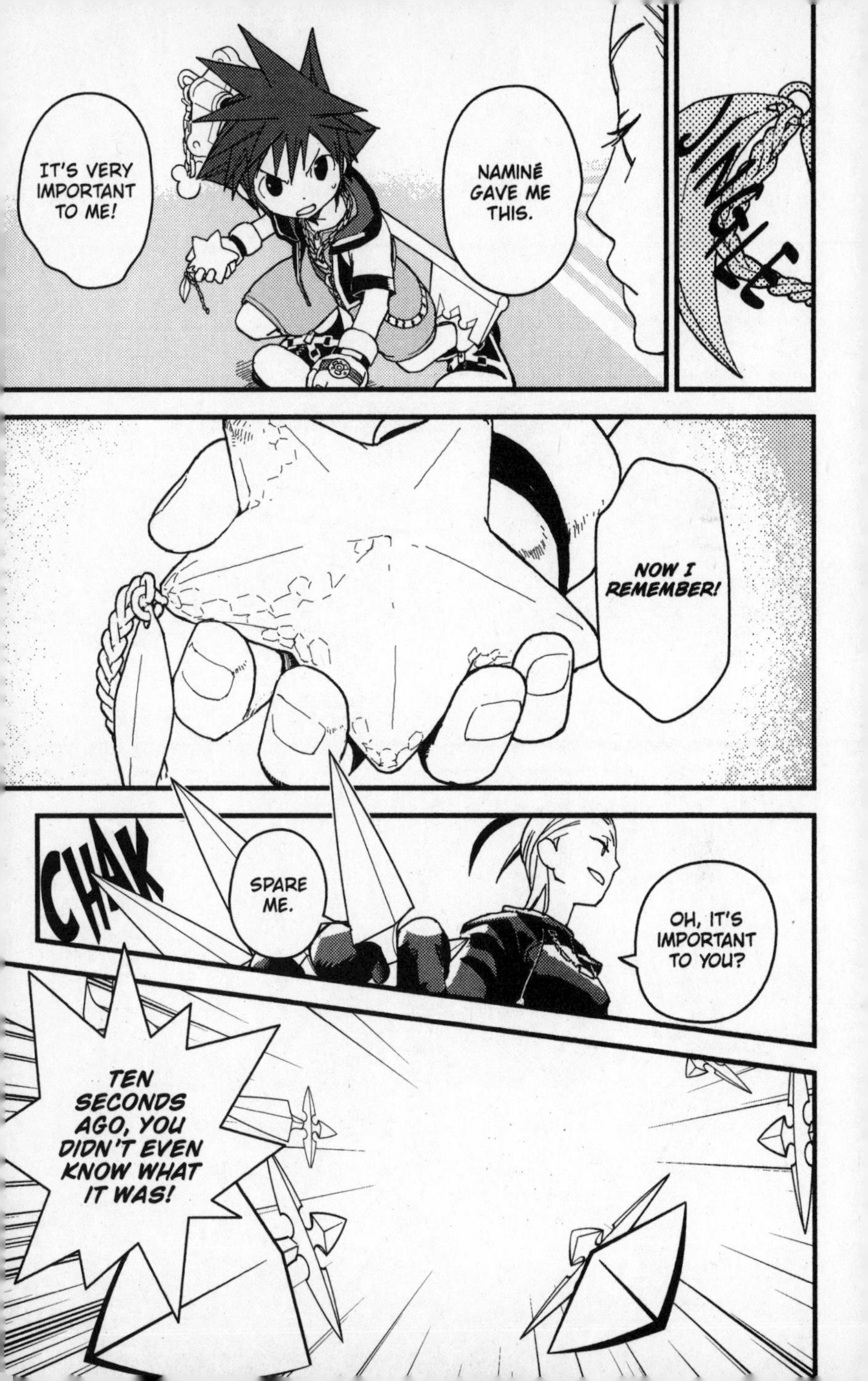
JINGLE
NAMINÉ GAVE ME THIS.
IT'S VERY IMPORTANT TO ME!
NOW I REMEMBER!
OH, IT'S IMPORTANT TO YOU?
SPARE ME.
CHAK
TEN SECONDS AGO, YOU DIDN'T EVEN KNOW WHAT IT WAS!

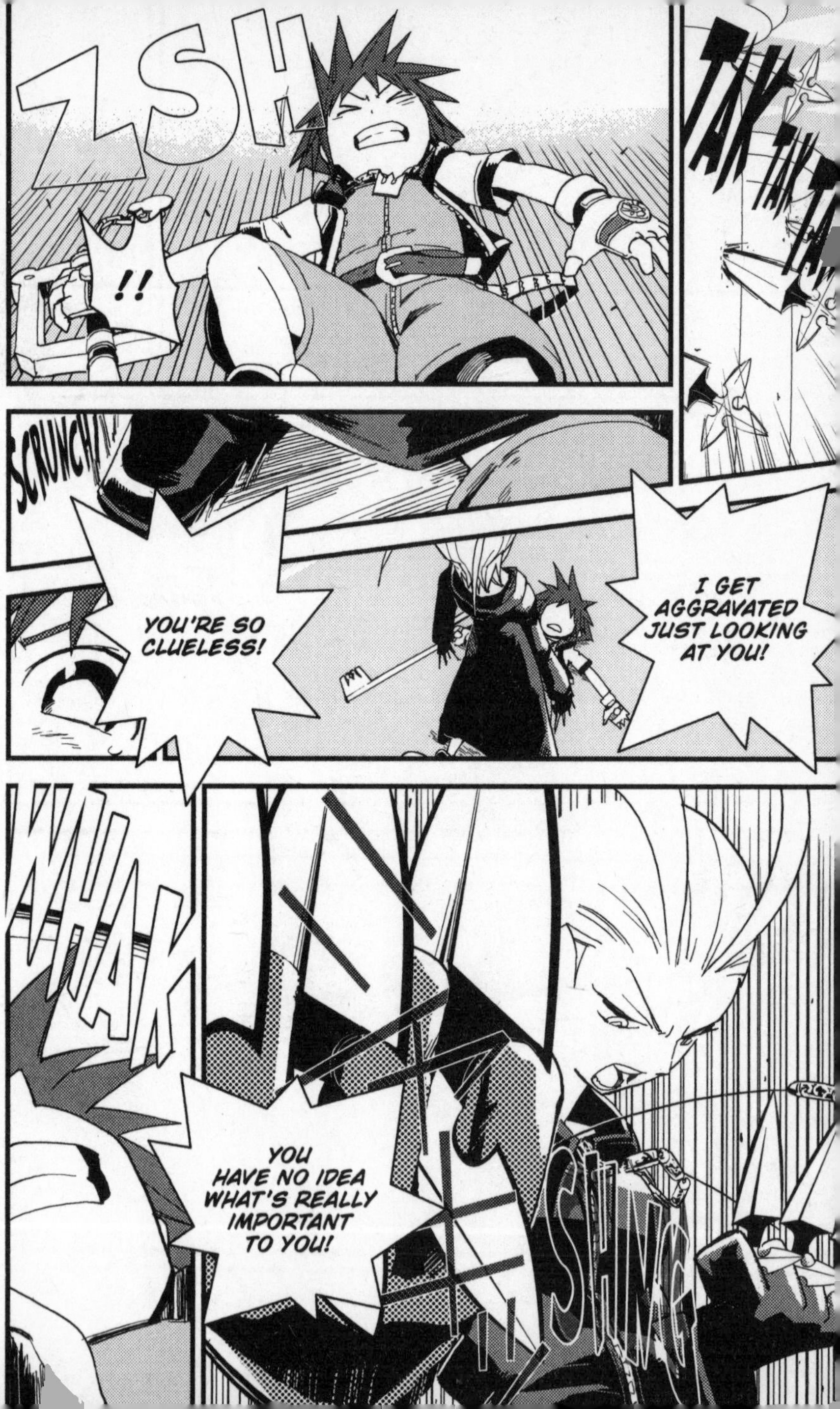
TAK TAK TA...
ZSH
!!
SCRUNCH
I GET AGGRAVATED JUST LOOKING AT YOU!
YOU'RE SO CLUELESS!
SHING
YOU HAVE NO IDEA WHAT'S REALLY IMPORTANT TO YOU!
WHAK

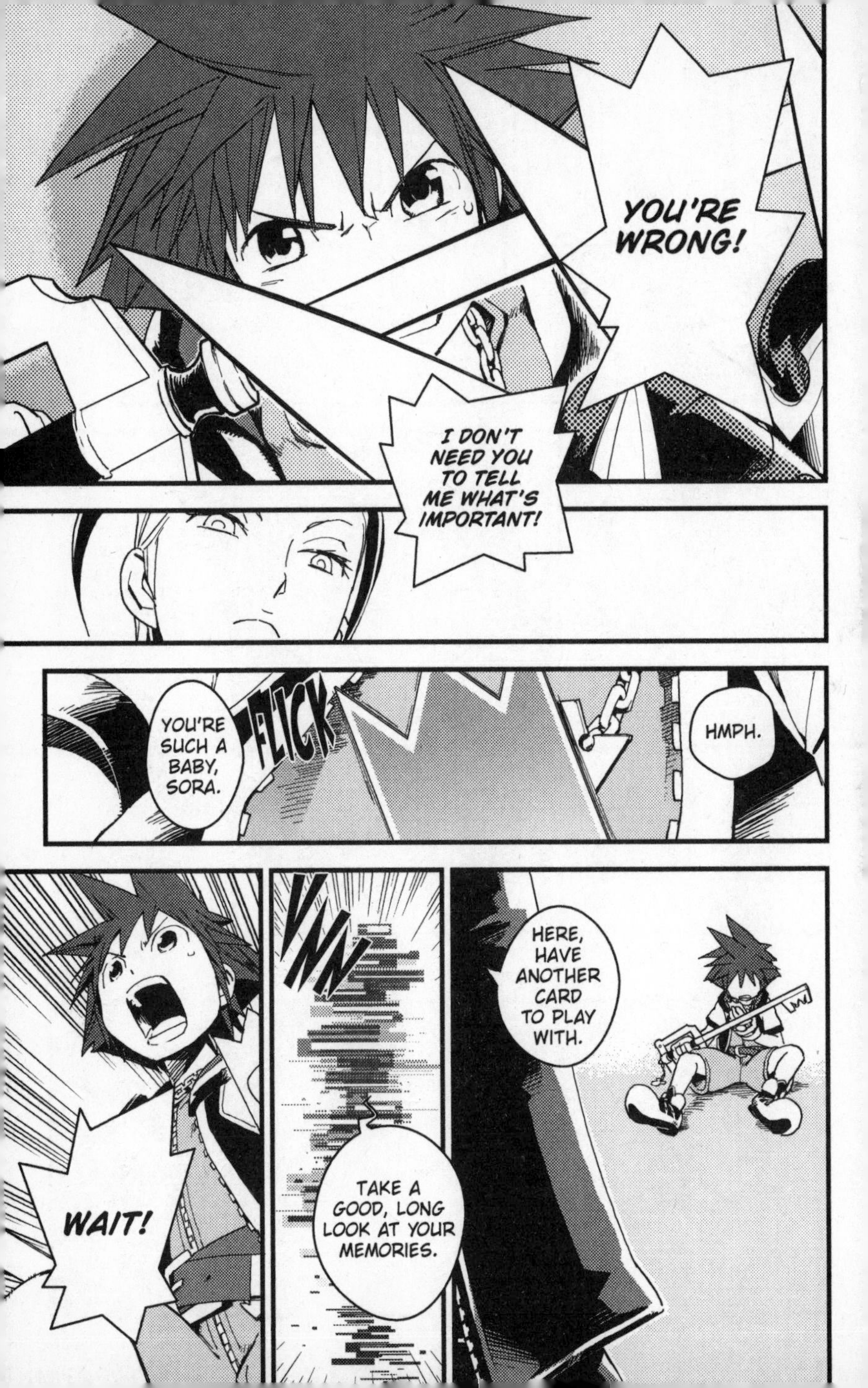
YOU'RE WRONG!
I DON'T NEED YOU TO TELL ME WHAT'S IMPORTANT!
HMPH.
FLICK
YOU'RE SUCH A BABY, SORA.
HERE, HAVE ANOTHER CARD TO PLAY WITH.
VNN
TAKE A GOOD, LONG LOOK AT YOUR MEMORIES.
WAIT!

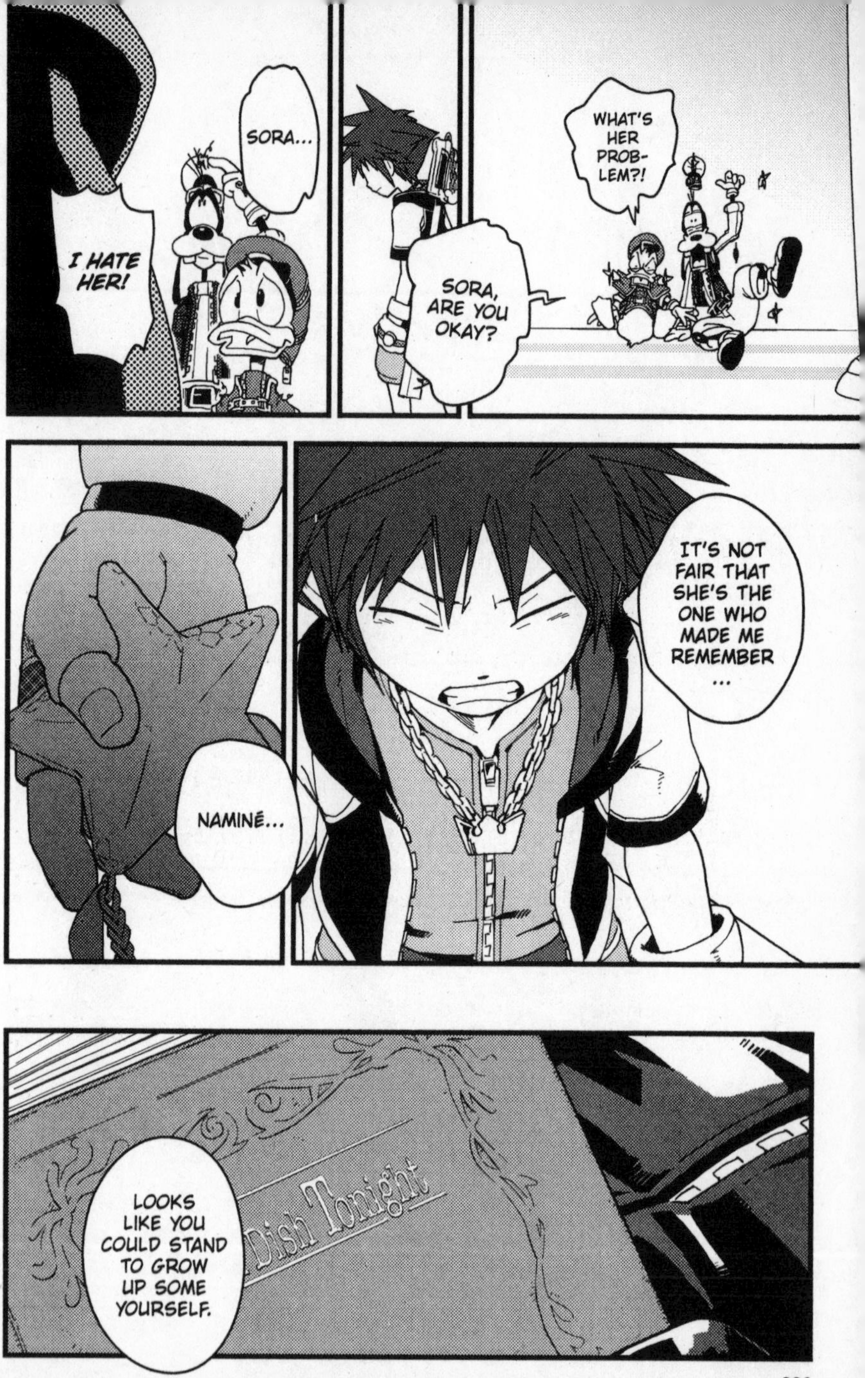
WHAT'S HER PROB-LEM?!
SORA, ARE YOU OKAY?
SORA...
I HATE HER!
IT'S NOT FAIR THAT SHE'S THE ONE WHO MADE ME REMEMBER ...
NAMINÉ...
Dish Tonight
LOOKS LIKE YOU COULD STAND TO GROW UP SOME YOURSELF.

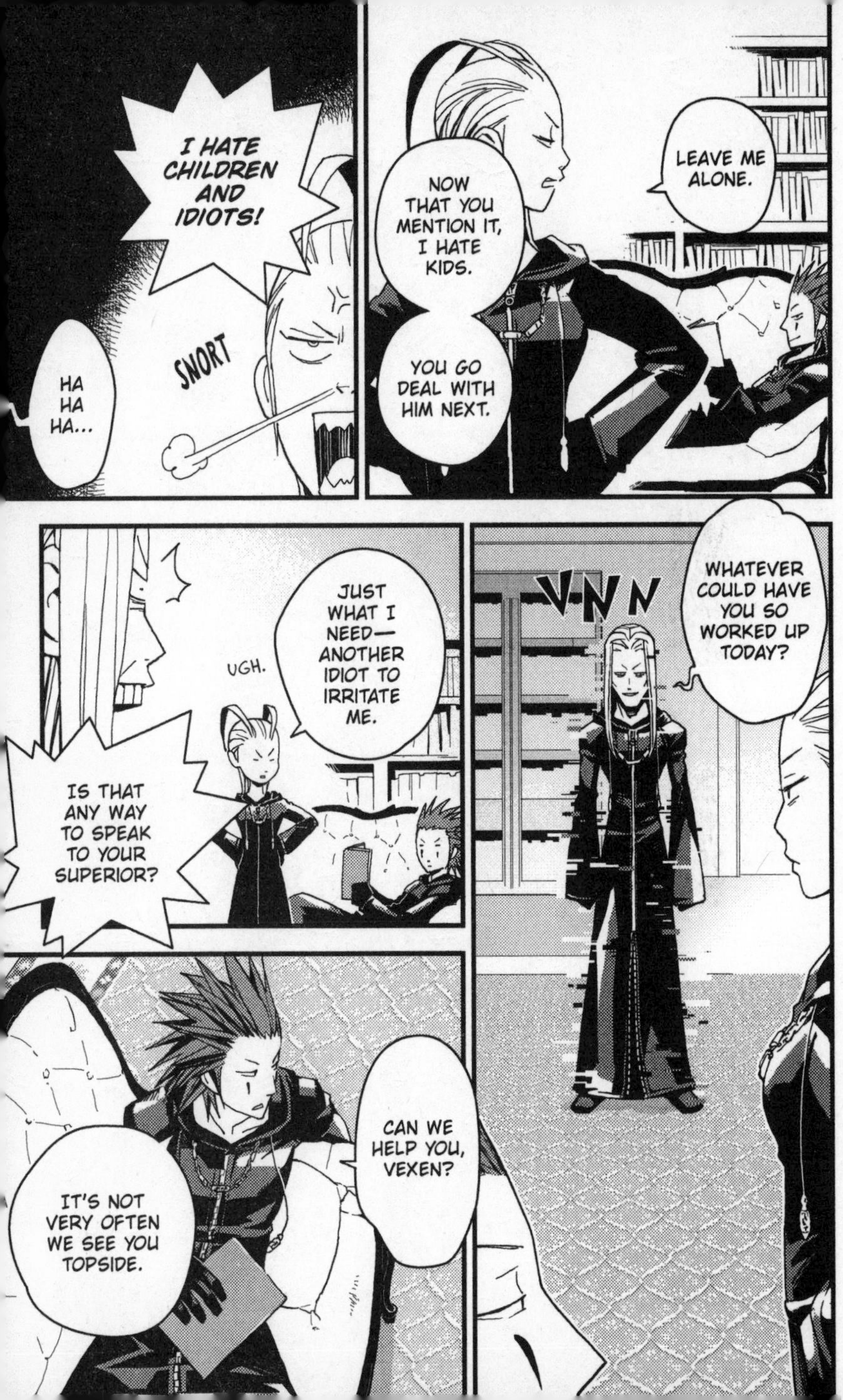
LEAVE ME ALONE.
NOW THAT YOU MENTION IT, I HATE KIDS.
YOU GO DEAL WITH HIM NEXT.
I HATE CHILDREN AND IDIOTS!
SNORT
HA HA HA...
WHATEVER COULD HAVE YOU SO WORKED UP TODAY?
VNN
JUST WHAT I NEED—ANOTHER IDIOT TO IRRITATE ME.
UGH.
IS THAT ANY WAY TO SPEAK TO YOUR SUPERIOR?
CAN WE HELP YOU, VEXEN?
IT'S NOT VERY OFTEN WE SEE YOU TOPSIDE.

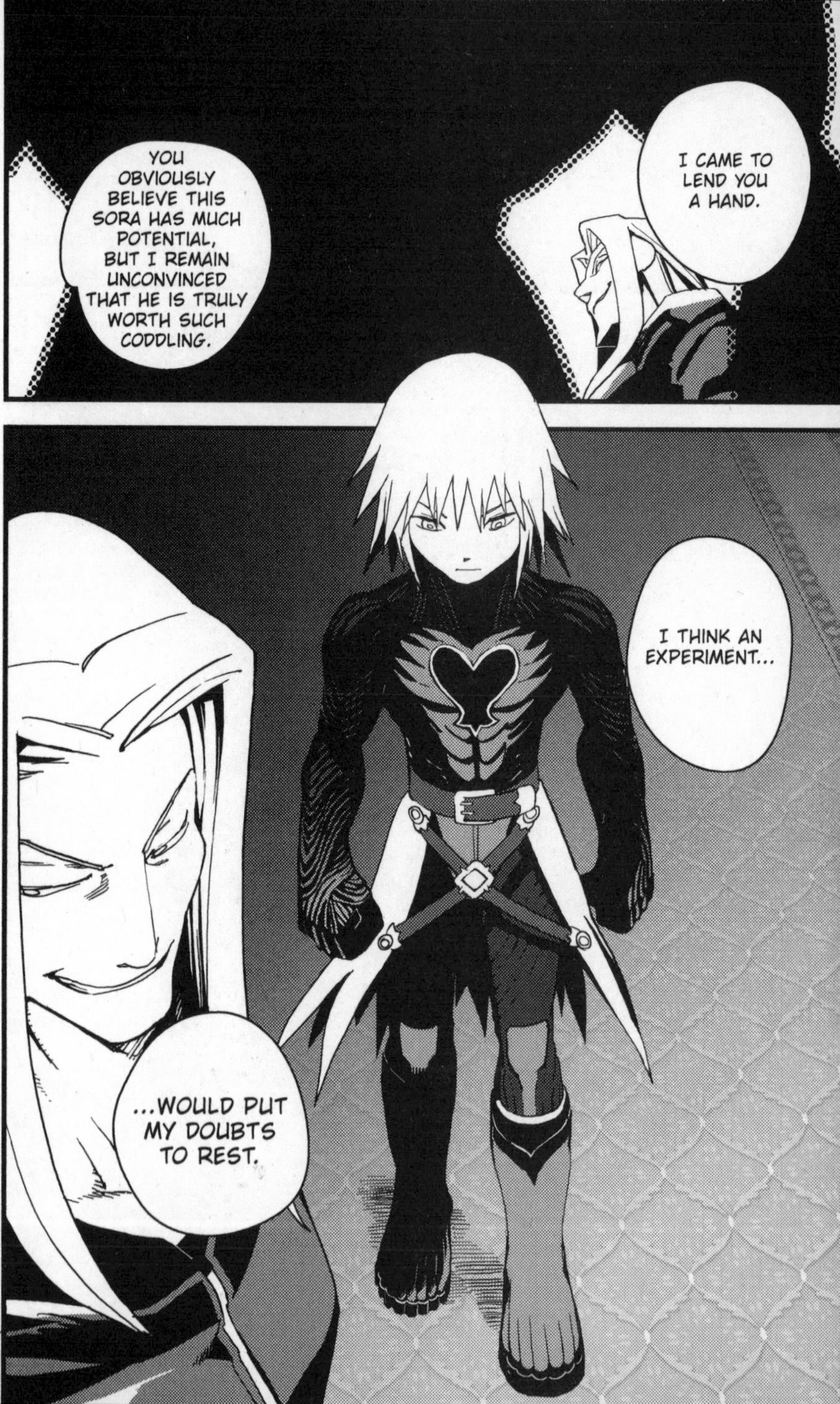
I CAME TO LEND YOU A HAND.
YOU OBVIOUSLY BELIEVE THIS SORA HAS MUCH POTENTIAL, BUT I REMAIN UNCONVINCED THAT HE IS TRULY WORTH SUCH CODDLING.
I THINK AN EXPERIMENT...
...WOULD PUT MY DOUBTS TO REST.

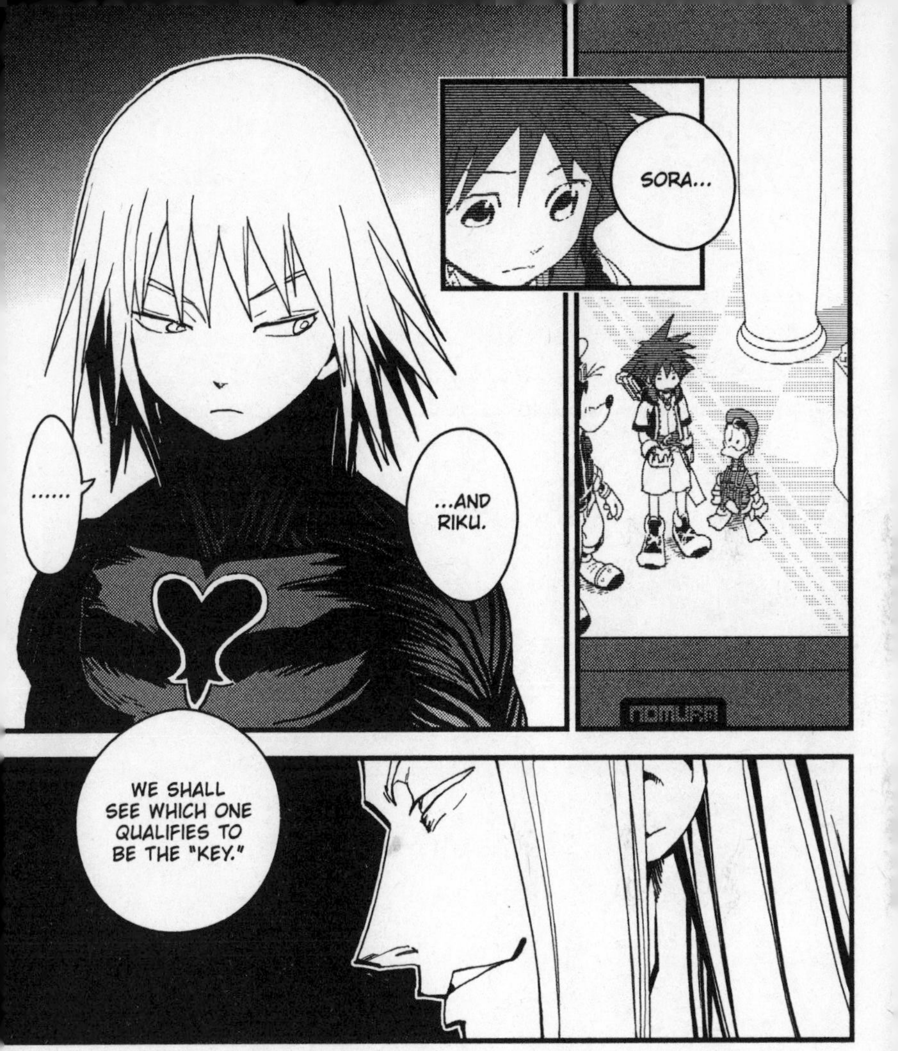
SORA...
NOMURA
...AND RIKU.
......
WE SHALL SEE WHICH ONE QUALIFIES TO BE THE "KEY."

## *Card:08* Promise

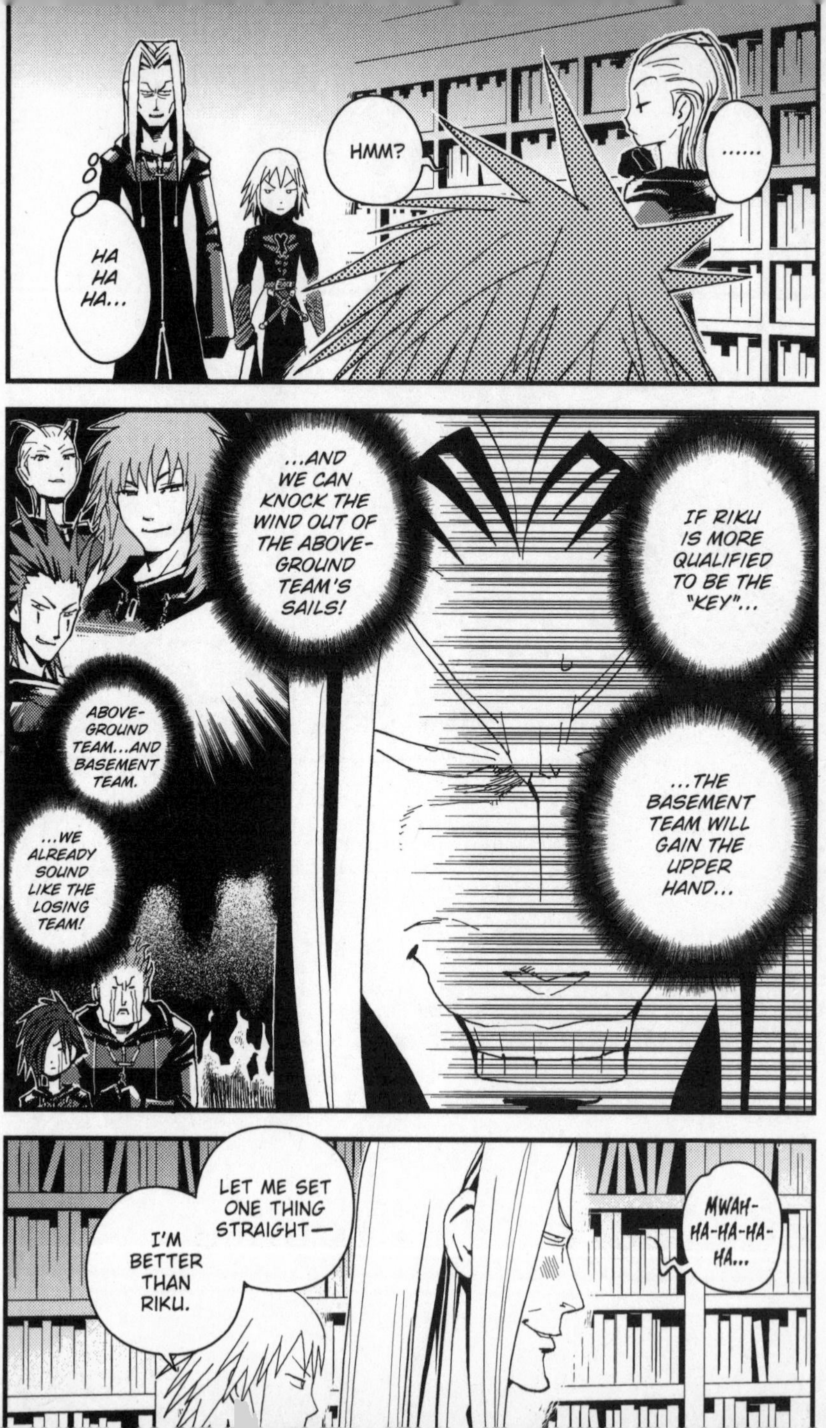
......
HMM?
HA HA HA...
IF RIKU IS MORE QUALIFIED TO BE THE "KEY"...
...THE BASEMENT TEAM WILL GAIN THE UPPER HAND...
...AND WE CAN KNOCK THE WIND OUT OF THE ABOVE-GROUND TEAM'S SAILS!
ABOVE-GROUND TEAM...AND BASEMENT TEAM.
...WE ALREADY SOUND LIKE THE LOSING TEAM!
MWAH-HA-HA-HA-HA...
LET ME SET ONE THING STRAIGHT—
I'M BETTER THAN RIKU.

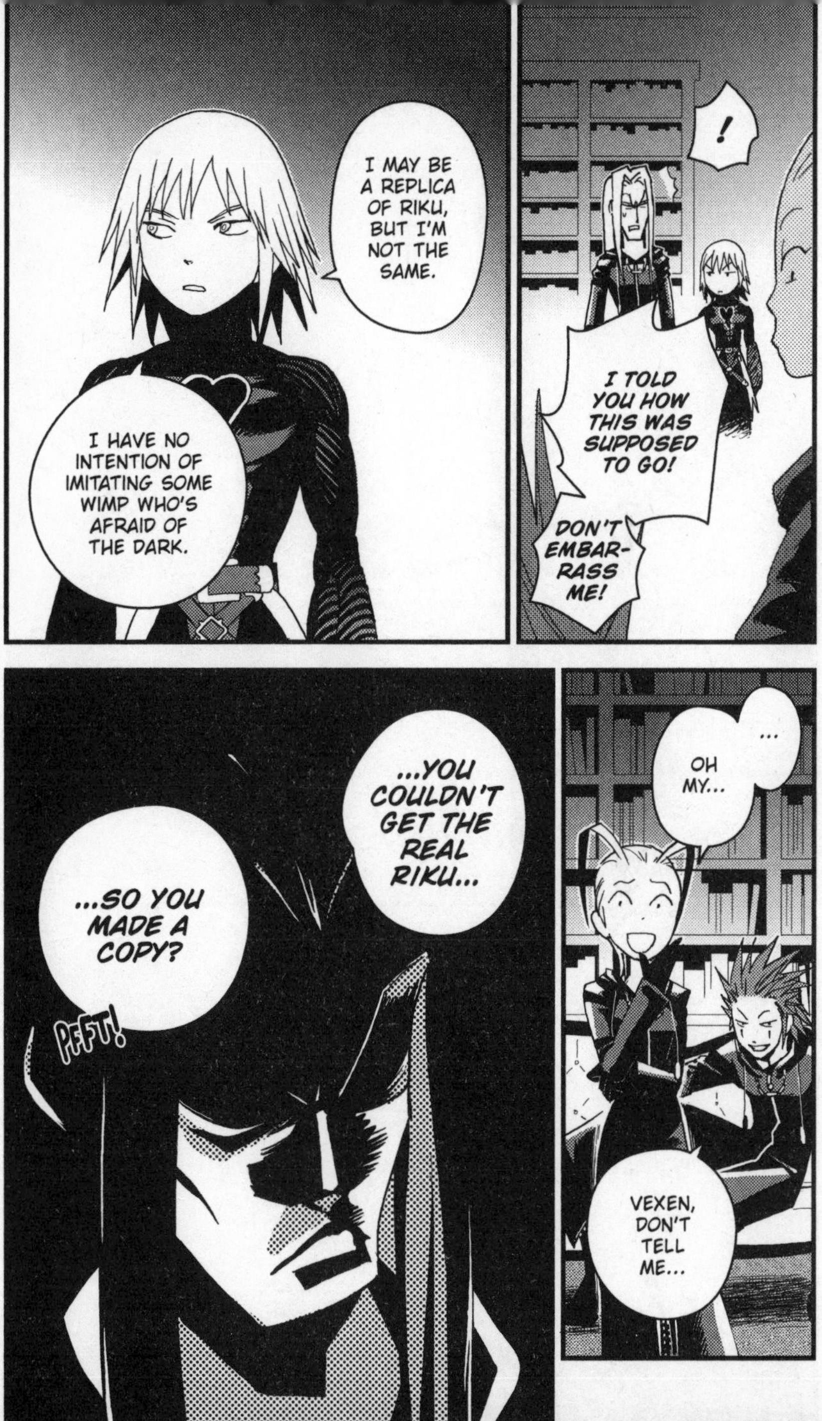
!
I TOLD YOU HOW THIS WAS SUPPOSED TO GO!
DON'T EMBAR-RASS ME!
I MAY BE A REPLICA OF RIKU, BUT I'M NOT THE SAME.
I HAVE NO INTENTION OF IMITATING SOME WIMP WHO'S AFRAID OF THE DARK.
...
OH MY...
VEXEN, DON'T TELL ME...
...YOU COULDN'T GET THE REAL RIKU...
...SO YOU MADE A COPY?
PFFT!

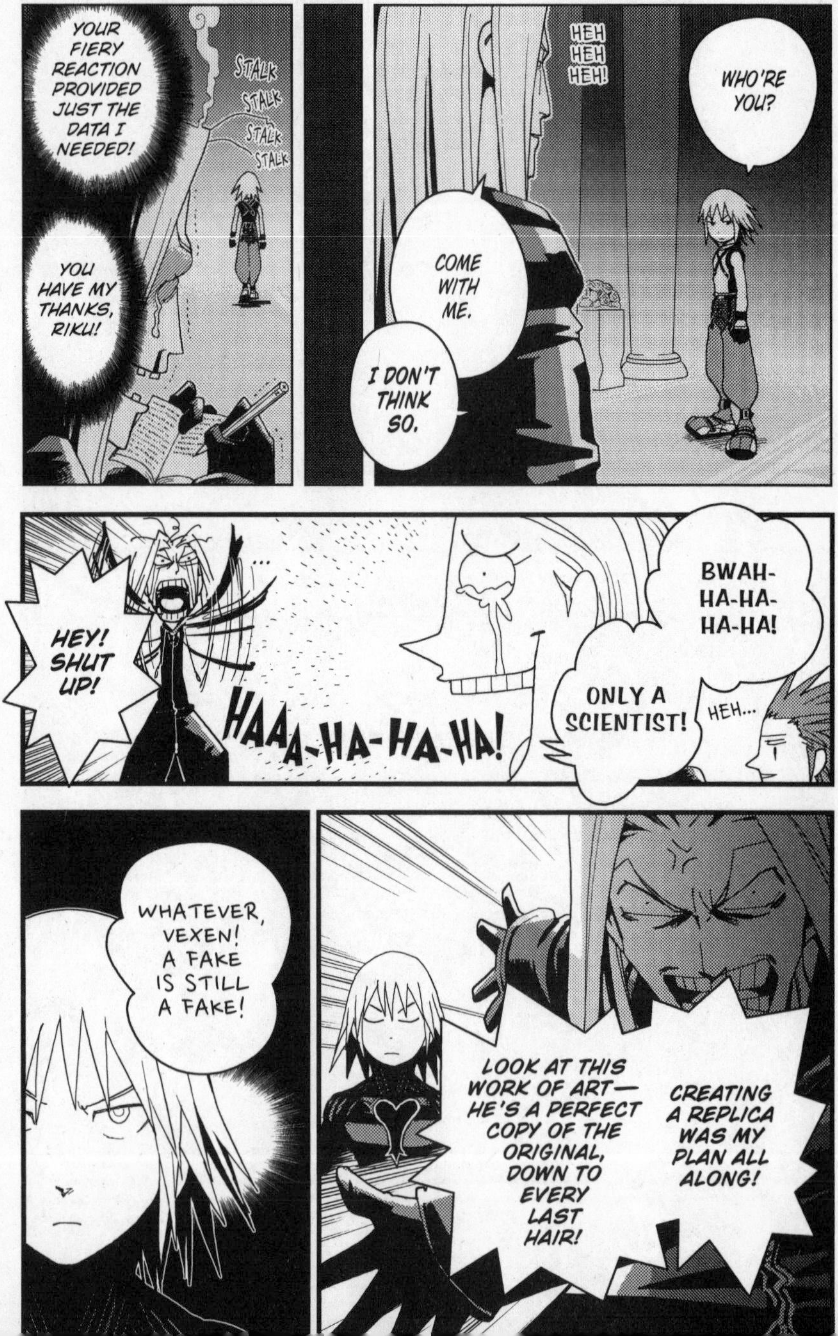
WHO'RE YOU?
HEH HEH HEH!
COME WITH ME.
I DON'T THINK SO.
YOUR FIERY REACTION PROVIDED JUST THE DATA I NEEDED!
STALK STALK STALK STALK
YOU HAVE MY THANKS, RIKU!
BWAH-HA-HA-HA-HA!
HEH...
ONLY A SCIENTIST!
HAAA-HA-HA-HA!
...
HEY! SHUT UP!
CREATING A REPLICA WAS MY PLAN ALL ALONG!
LOOK AT THIS WORK OF ART—HE'S A PERFECT COPY OF THE ORIGINAL, DOWN TO EVERY LAST HAIR!
WHATEVER, VEXEN! A FAKE IS STILL A FAKE!

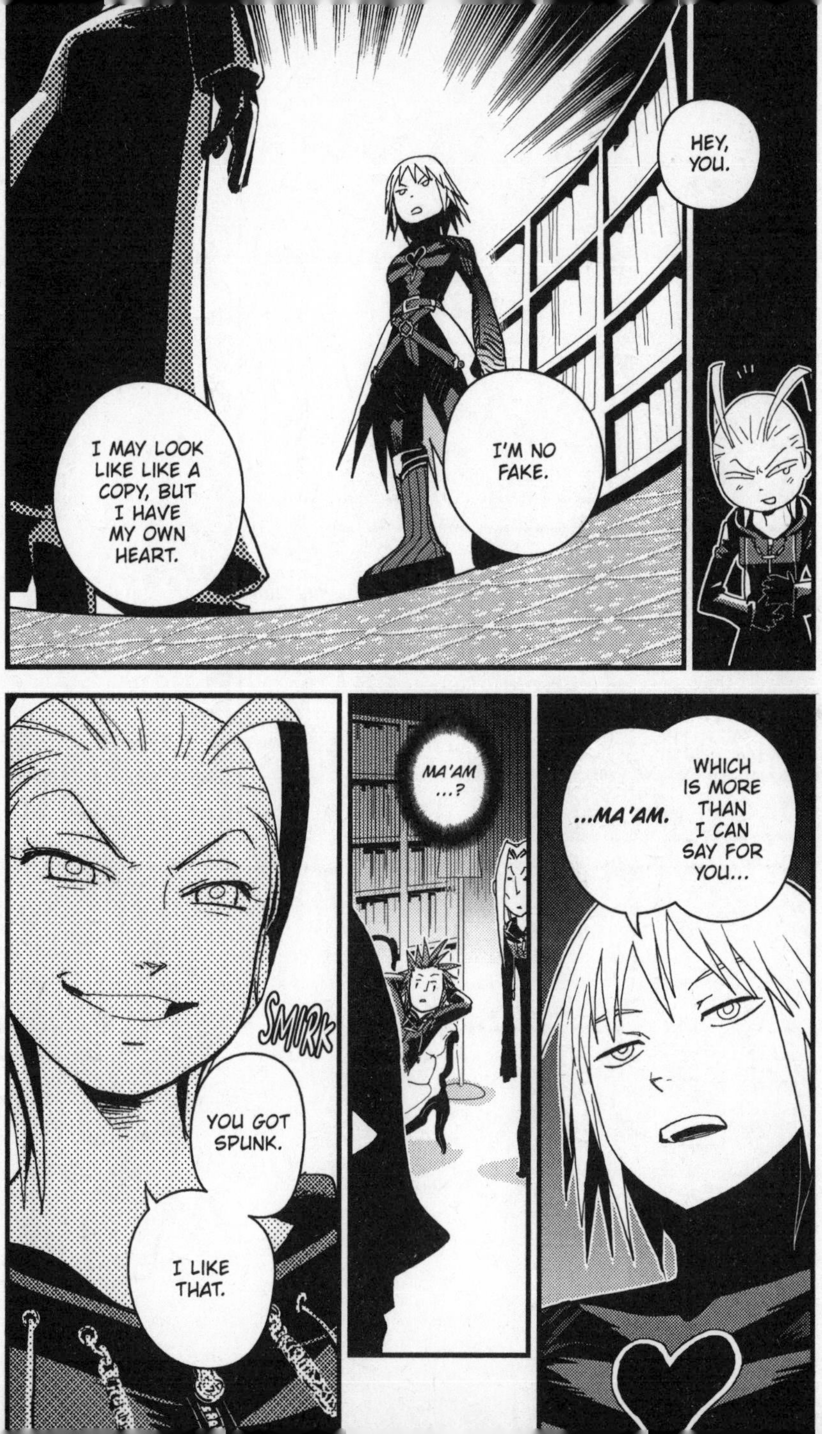
HEY, YOU.
I'M NO FAKE.
I MAY LOOK LIKE LIKE A COPY, BUT I HAVE MY OWN HEART.
WHICH IS MORE THAN I CAN SAY FOR YOU...
...MA'AM.
MA'AM ...?
SMIRK
YOU GOT SPUNK.
I LIKE THAT.

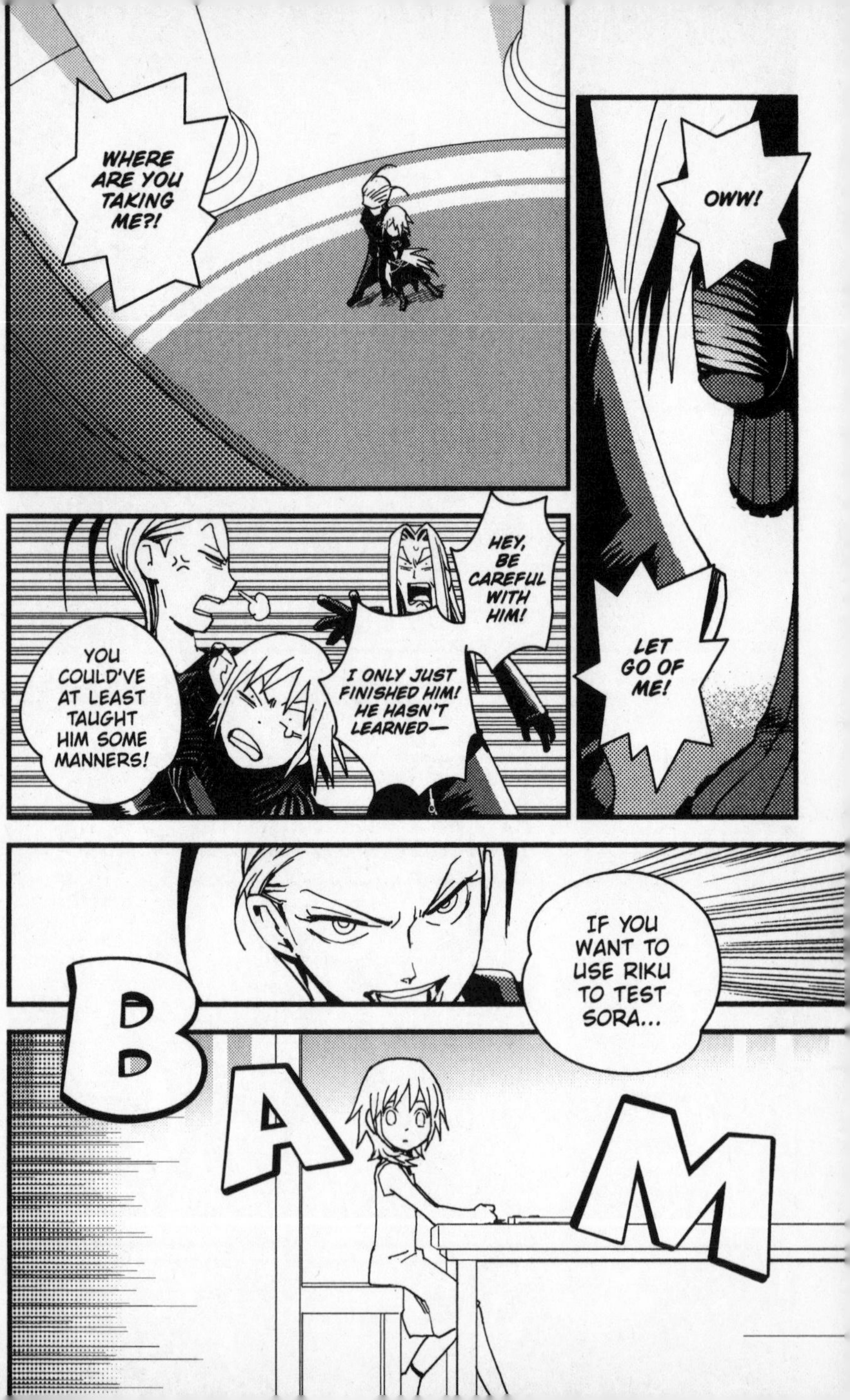
OWW!
LET GO OF ME!
WHERE ARE YOU TAKING ME?!
HEY, BE CAREFUL WITH HIM!
I ONLY JUST FINISHED HIM! HE HASN'T LEARNED—
YOU COULD'VE AT LEAST TAUGHT HIM SOME MANNERS!
IF YOU WANT TO USE RIKU TO TEST SORA...
BAM

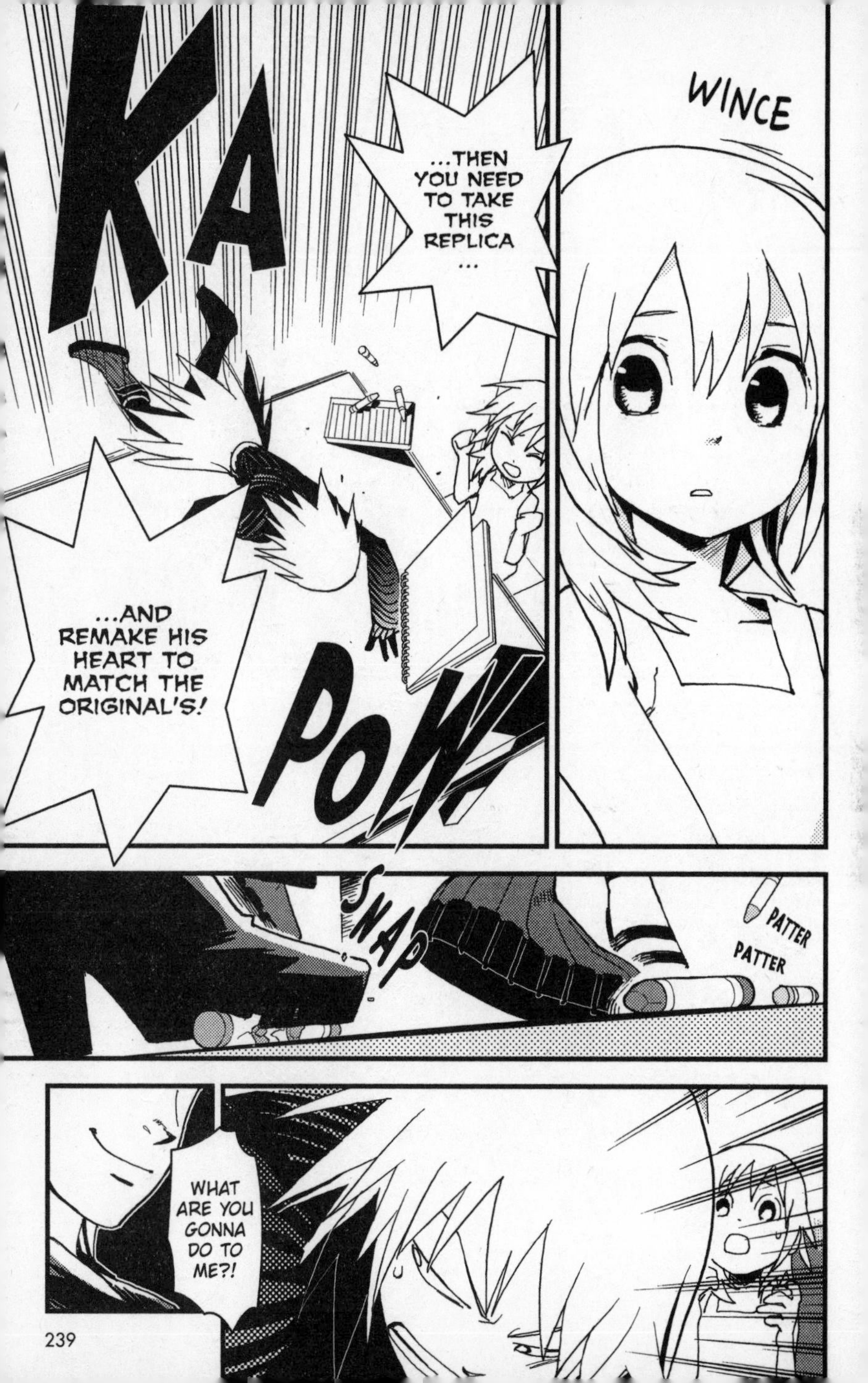
WINCE
KA
...THEN YOU NEED TO TAKE THIS REPLICA ...
...AND REMAKE HIS HEART TO MATCH THE ORIGINAL'S!
POW
PATTER PATTER
SNAP
WHAT ARE YOU GONNA DO TO ME?!

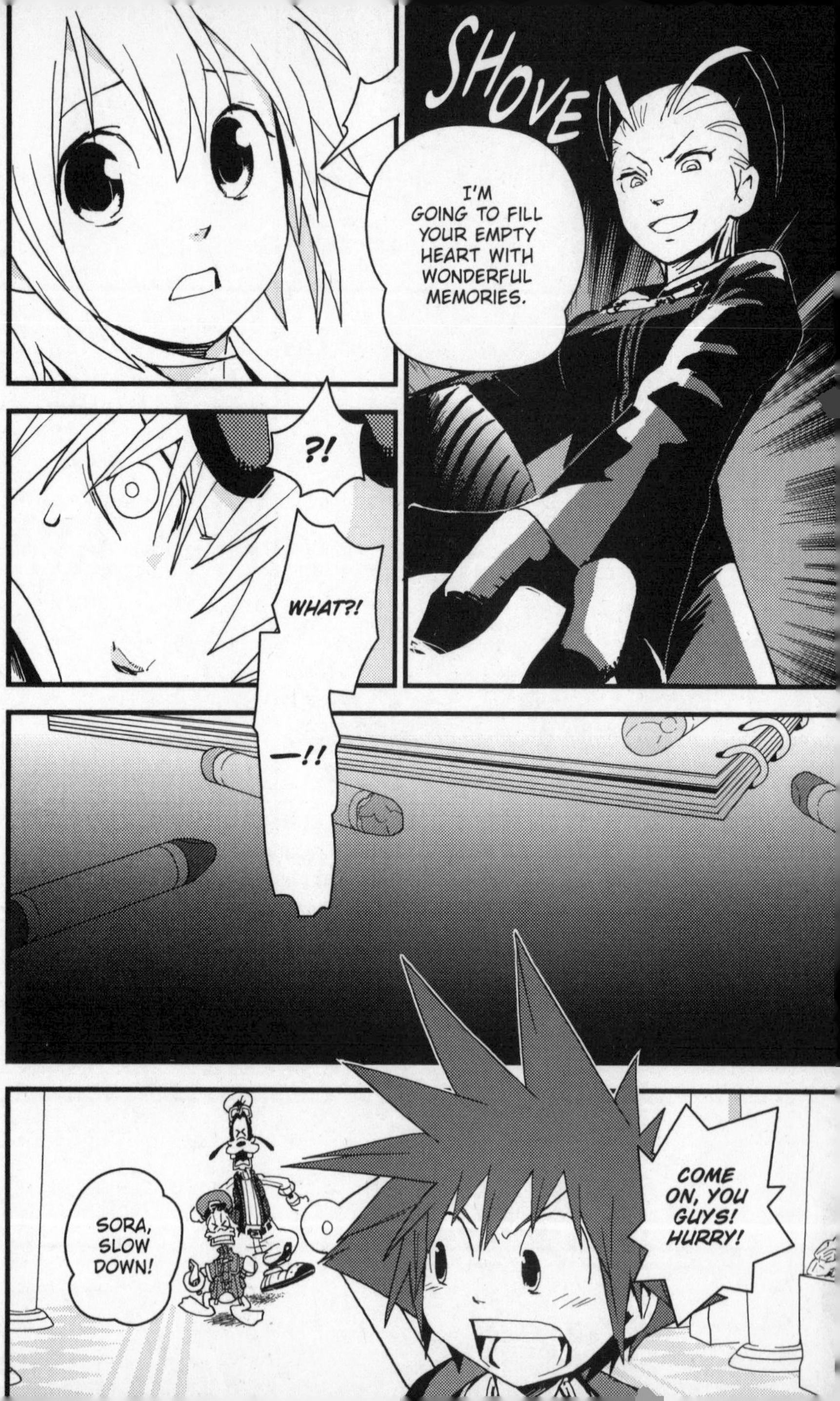
SHOVE
I'M GOING TO FILL YOUR EMPTY HEART WITH WONDERFUL MEMORIES.
?!
WHAT?!
—!!
COME ON, YOU GUYS! HURRY!
SORA, SLOW DOWN!

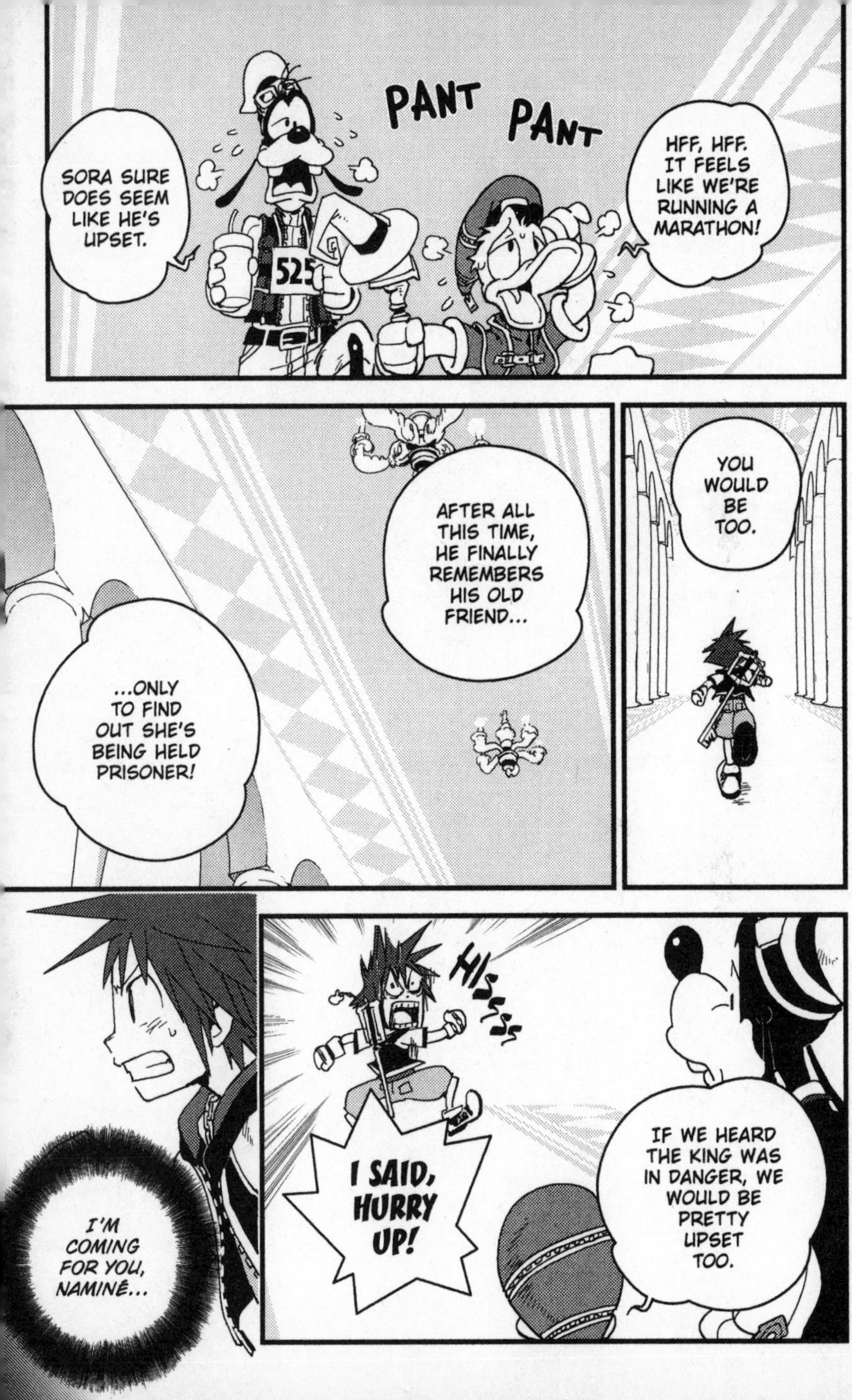
PANT PANT
HFF, HFF. IT FEELS LIKE WE'RE RUNNING A MARATHON!
SORA SURE DOES SEEM LIKE HE'S UPSET.
525
YOU WOULD BE TOO.
AFTER ALL THIS TIME, HE FINALLY REMEMBERS HIS OLD FRIEND...
...ONLY TO FIND OUT SHE'S BEING HELD PRISONER!
HISSSS
IF WE HEARD THE KING WAS IN DANGER, WE WOULD BE PRETTY UPSET TOO.
I SAID, HURRY UP!
I'M COMING FOR YOU, NAMINÉ...

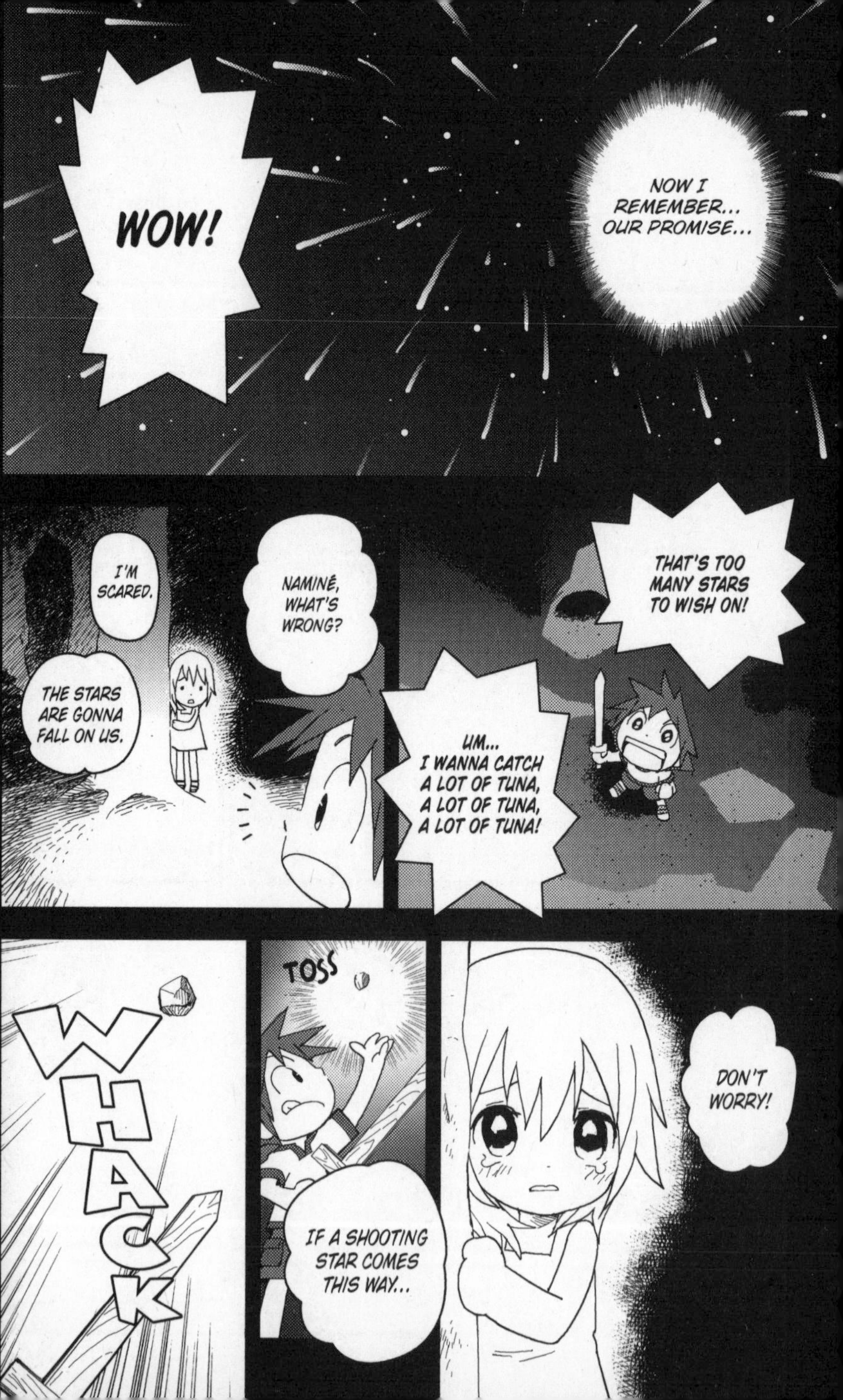
NOW I REMEMBER... OUR PROMISE...
WOW!
THAT'S TOO MANY STARS TO WISH ON!
UM... I WANNA CATCH A LOT OF TUNA, A LOT OF TUNA, A LOT OF TUNA!
NAMINÉ, WHAT'S WRONG?
I'M SCARED.
THE STARS ARE GONNA FALL ON US.
DON'T WORRY!
TOSS
IF A SHOOTING STAR COMES THIS WAY...
WHACK

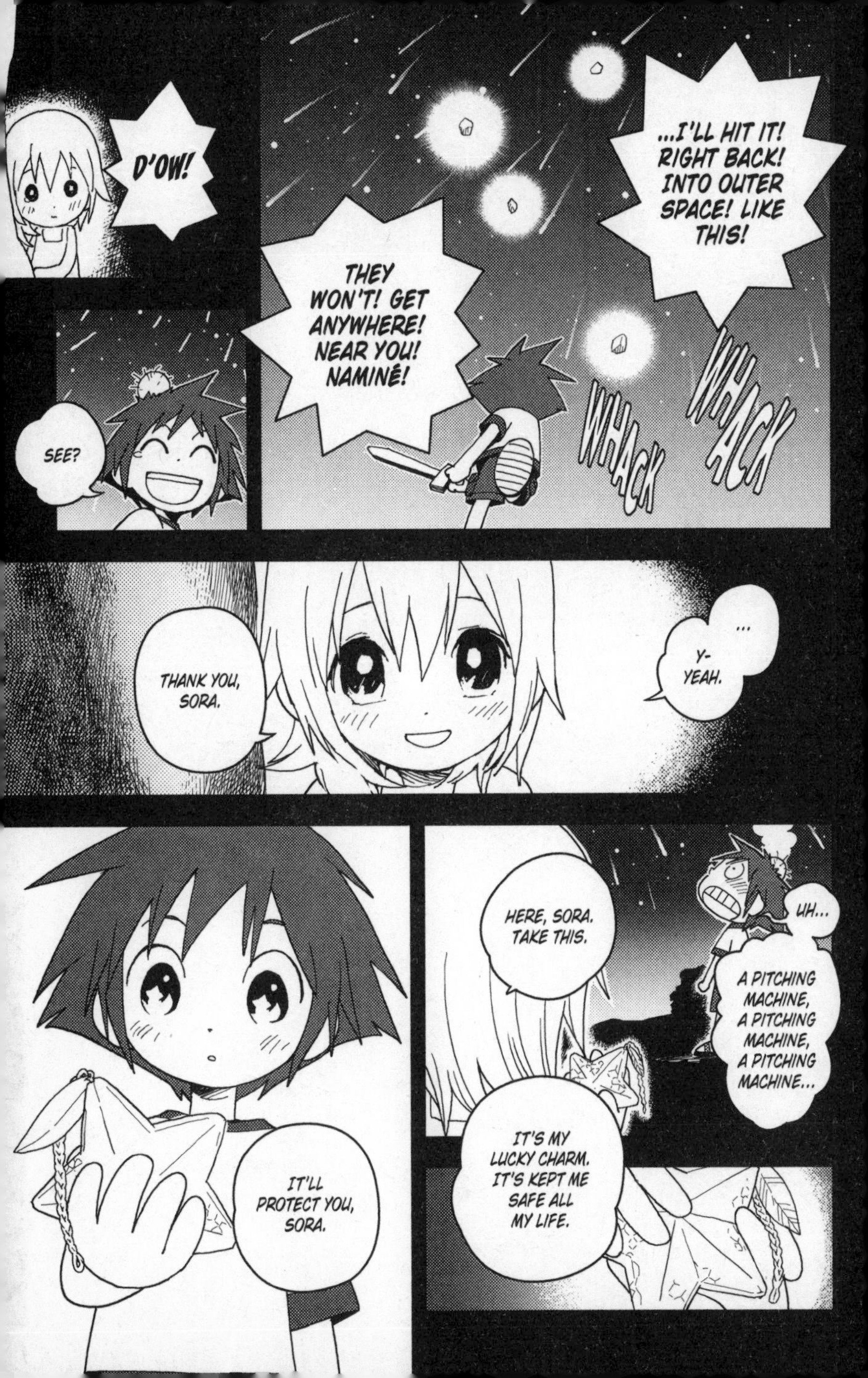
...I'LL HIT IT! RIGHT BACK! INTO OUTER SPACE! LIKE THIS!
THEY WON'T! GET ANYWHERE! NEAR YOU! NAMINÉ!
WHACK
WHACK
D'OW!
SEE?
... Y-YEAH.
THANK YOU, SORA.
UH...
A PITCHING MACHINE, A PITCHING MACHINE, A PITCHING MACHINE...
HERE, SORA. TAKE THIS.
IT'S MY LUCKY CHARM. IT'S KEPT ME SAFE ALL MY LIFE.
IT'LL PROTECT YOU, SORA.

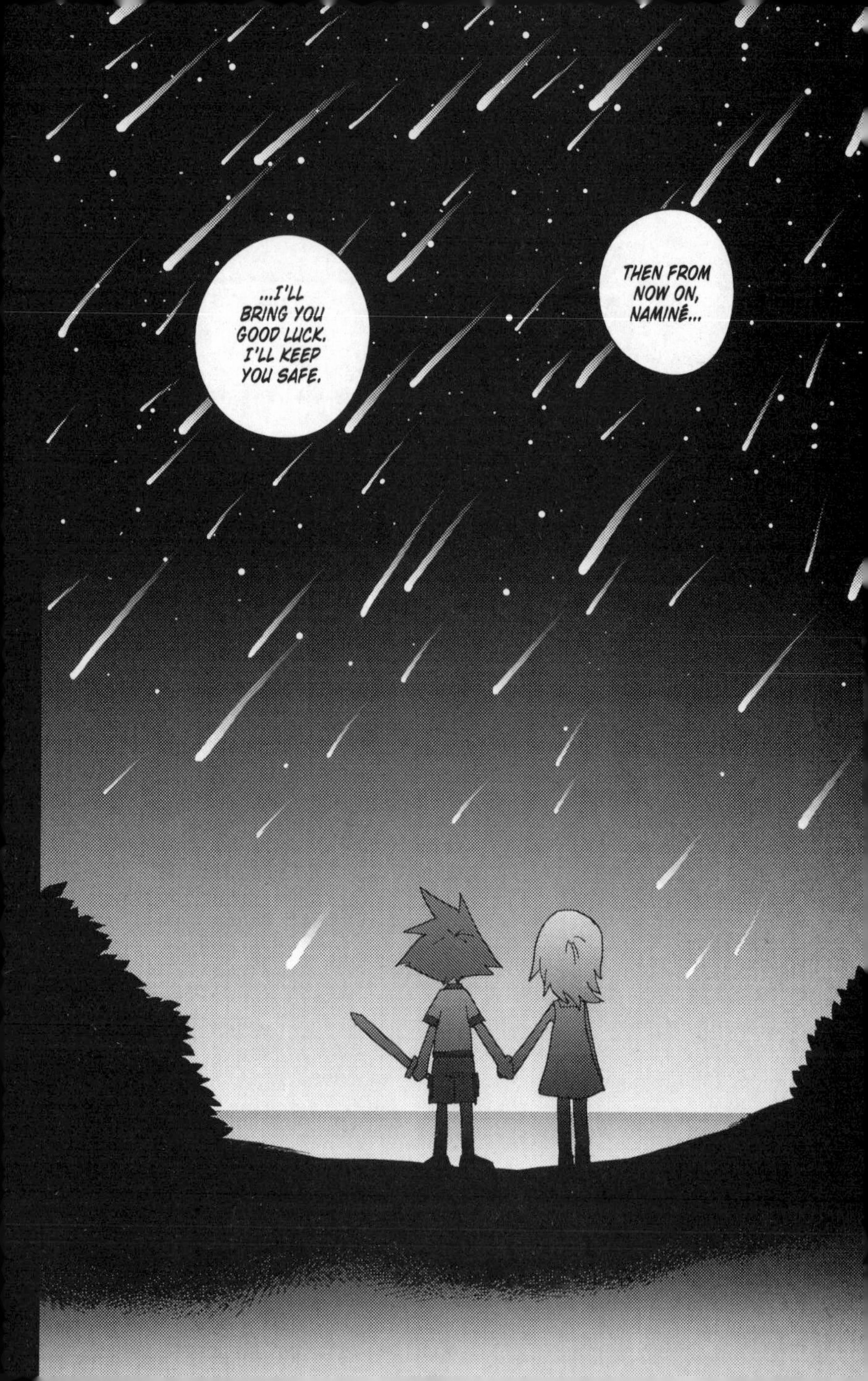
THEN FROM NOW ON, NAMINÉ...
...I'LL BRING YOU GOOD LUCK. I'LL KEEP YOU SAFE.

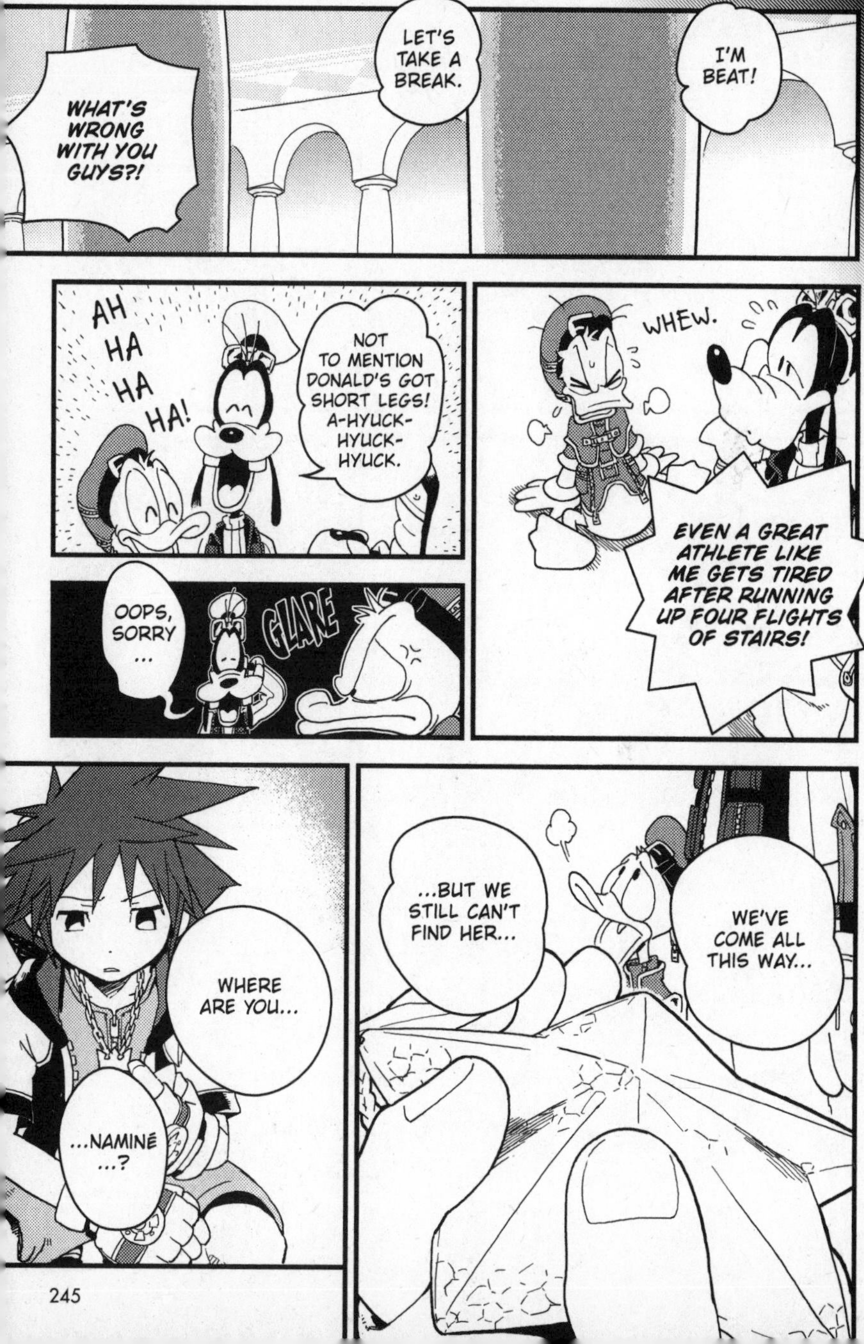
I'M BEAT!
LET'S TAKE A BREAK.
WHAT'S WRONG WITH YOU GUYS?!
WHEW.
EVEN A GREAT ATHLETE LIKE ME GETS TIRED AFTER RUNNING UP FOUR FLIGHTS OF STAIRS!
NOT TO MENTION DONALD'S GOT SHORT LEGS! A-HYUCK-HYUCK-HYUCK.
AH HA HA HA!
GLARE
OOPS, SORRY ...
WE'VE COME ALL THIS WAY...
...BUT WE STILL CAN'T FIND HER...
WHERE ARE YOU...
...NAMINÉ ...?

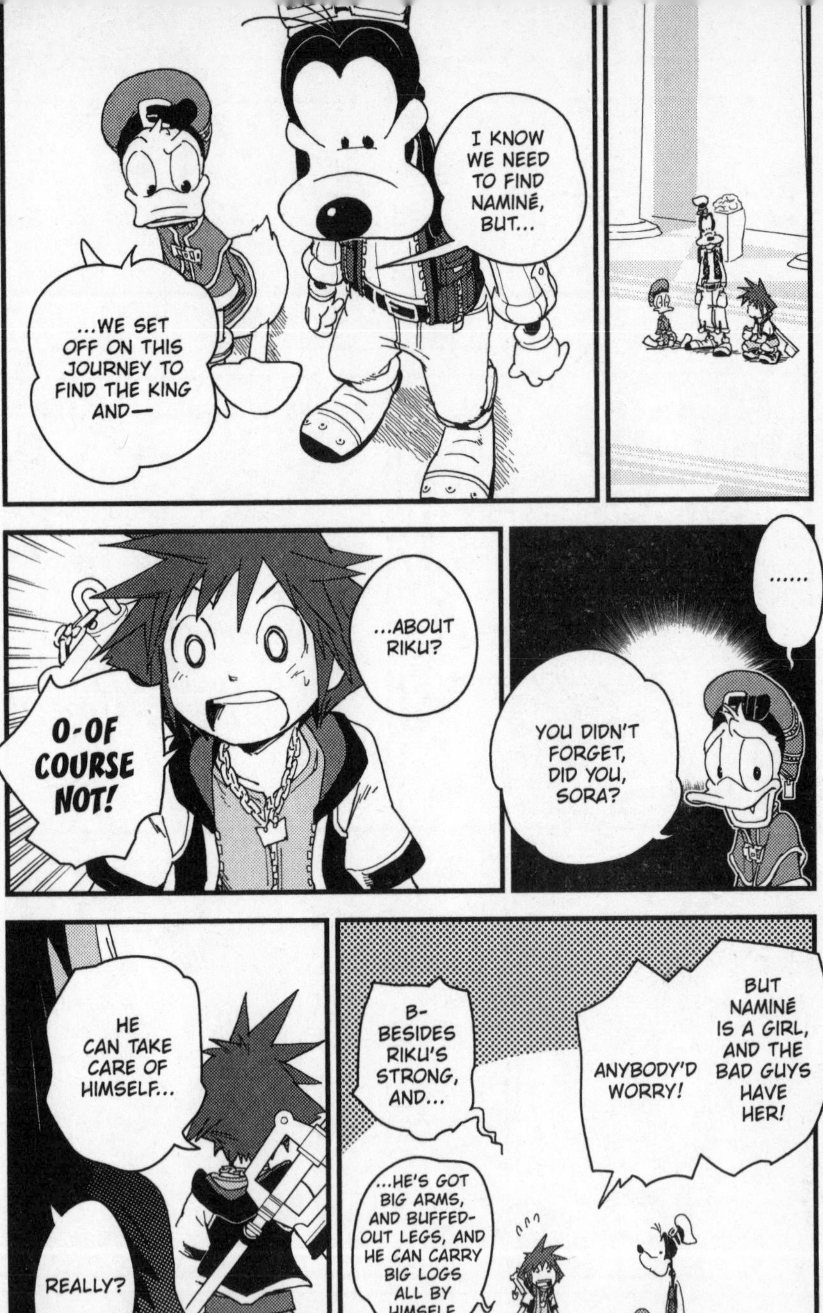
I KNOW WE NEED TO FIND NAMINÉ, BUT...
...WE SET OFF ON THIS JOURNEY TO FIND THE KING AND—
......
YOU DIDN'T FORGET, DID YOU, SORA?
...ABOUT RIKU?
O-OF COURSE NOT!
BUT NAMINÉ IS A GIRL, AND THE BAD GUYS HAVE HER!
ANYBODY'D WORRY!
B-BESIDES RIKU'S STRONG, AND...
...HE'S GOT BIG ARMS, AND BUFFED-OUT LEGS, AND HE CAN CARRY BIG LOGS ALL BY HIMSELF.
HE CAN TAKE CARE OF HIMSELF...
REALLY?

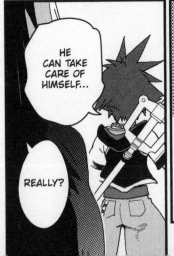

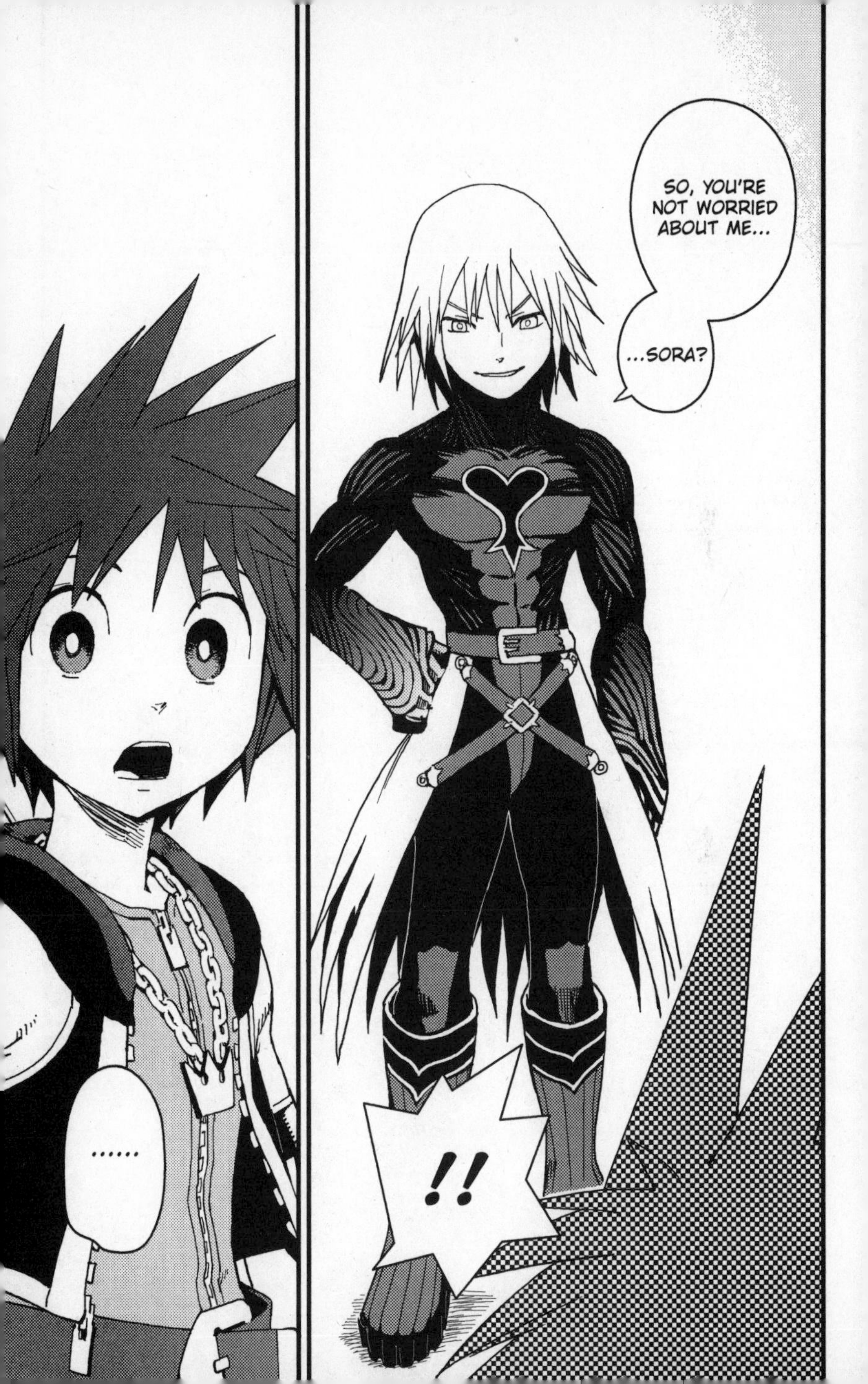
SO, YOU'RE NOT WORRIED ABOUT ME...
...SORA?
!!
......

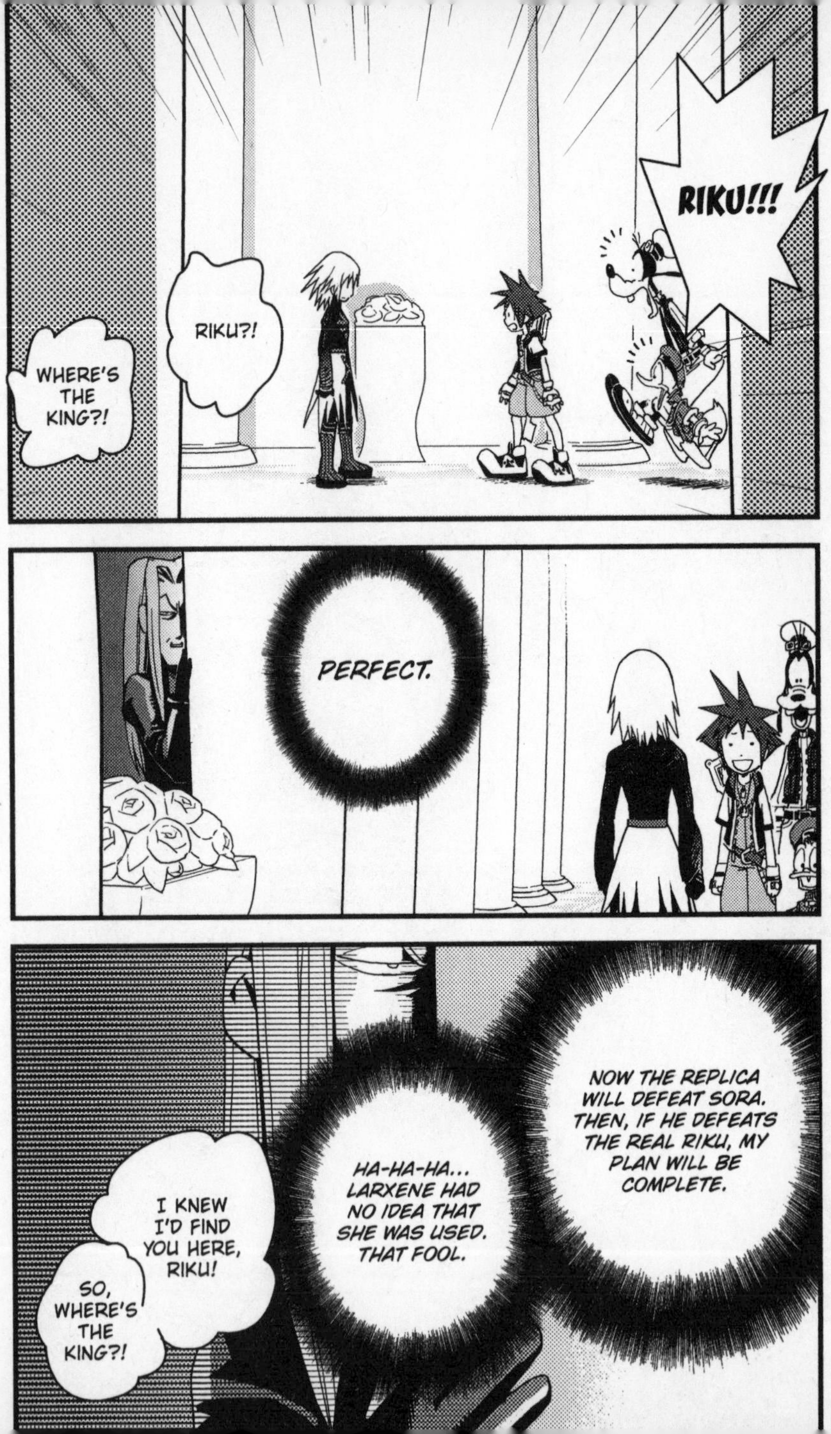
RIKU!!!
RIKU?!
WHERE'S THE KING?!
PERFECT.
NOW THE REPLICA WILL DEFEAT SORA. THEN, IF HE DEFEATS THE REAL RIKU, MY PLAN WILL BE COMPLETE.
HA-HA-HA... LARXENE HAD NO IDEA THAT SHE WAS USED. THAT FOOL.
I KNEW I'D FIND YOU HERE, RIKU!
SO, WHERE'S THE KING?!

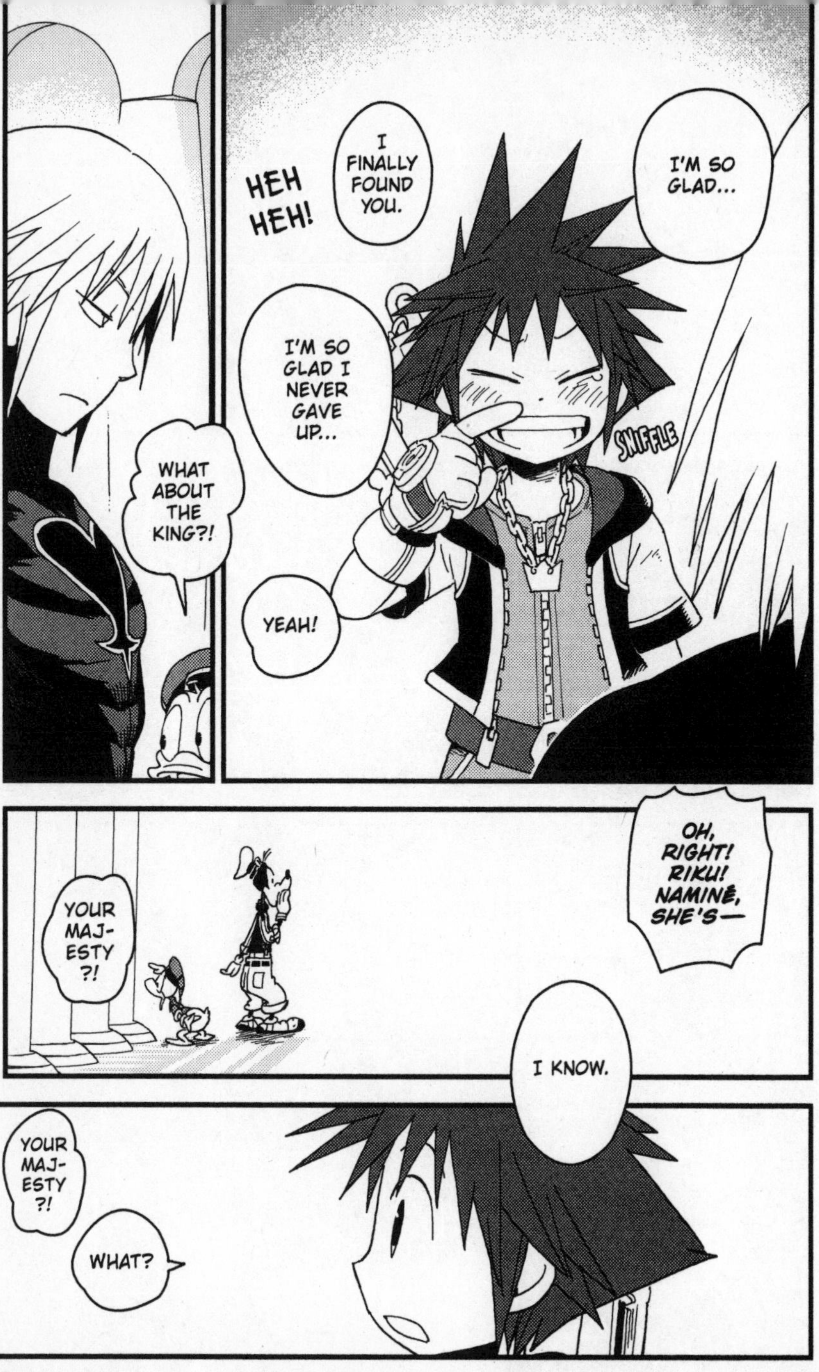
I'M SO GLAD...
I FINALLY FOUND YOU.
HEH HEH!
SNIFFLE
I'M SO GLAD I NEVER GAVE UP...
YEAH!
WHAT ABOUT THE KING?!
OH, RIGHT! RIKU! NAMINÉ, SHE'S—
YOUR MAJESTY?!
I KNOW.
YOUR MAJESTY?!
WHAT?

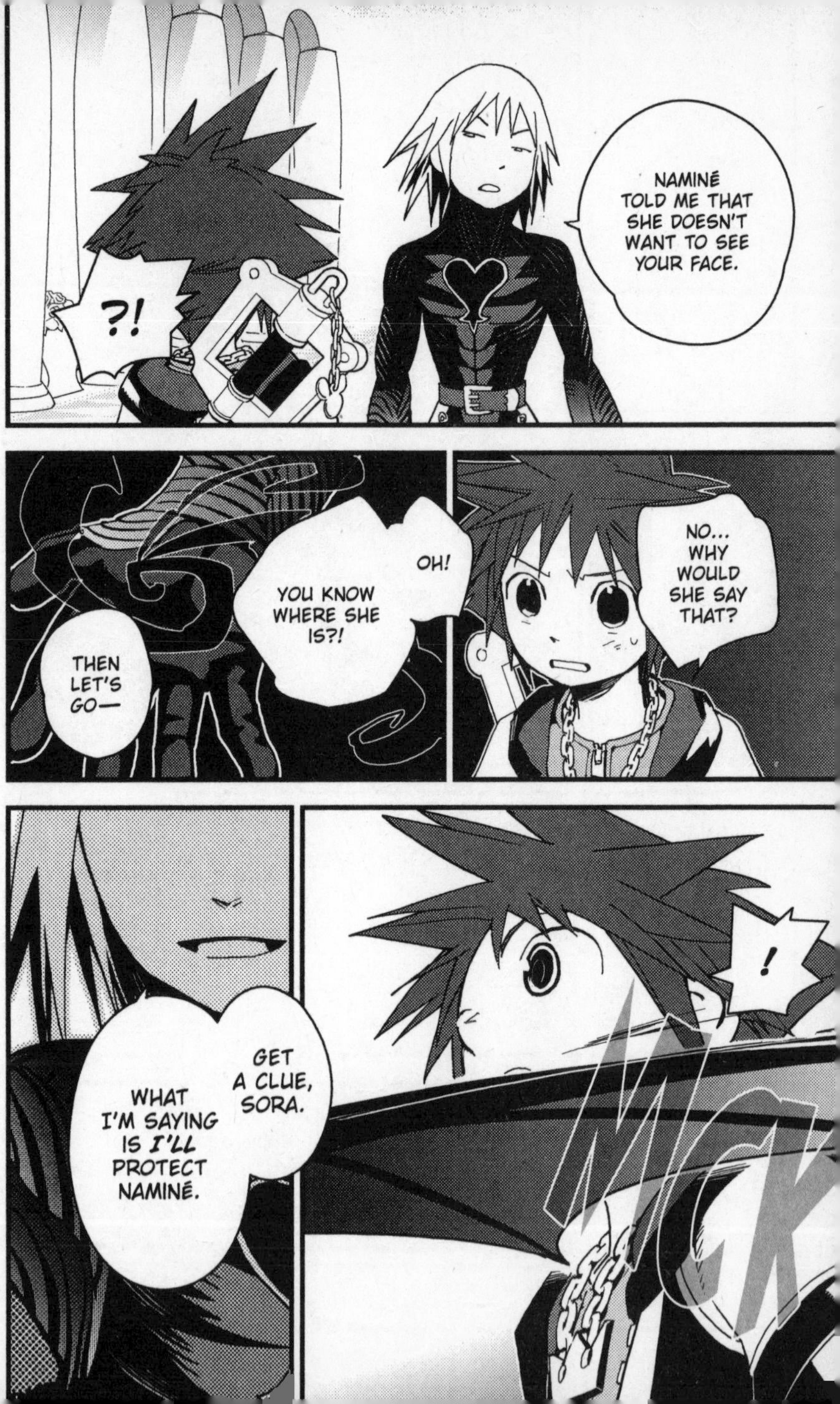
NAMINÉ TOLD ME THAT SHE DOESN'T WANT TO SEE YOUR FACE.
?!
NO... WHY WOULD SHE SAY THAT?
OH!
YOU KNOW WHERE SHE IS?!
THEN LET'S GO—
!
GET A CLUE, SORA.
WHAT I'M SAYING IS *I'LL* PROTECT NAMINÉ.

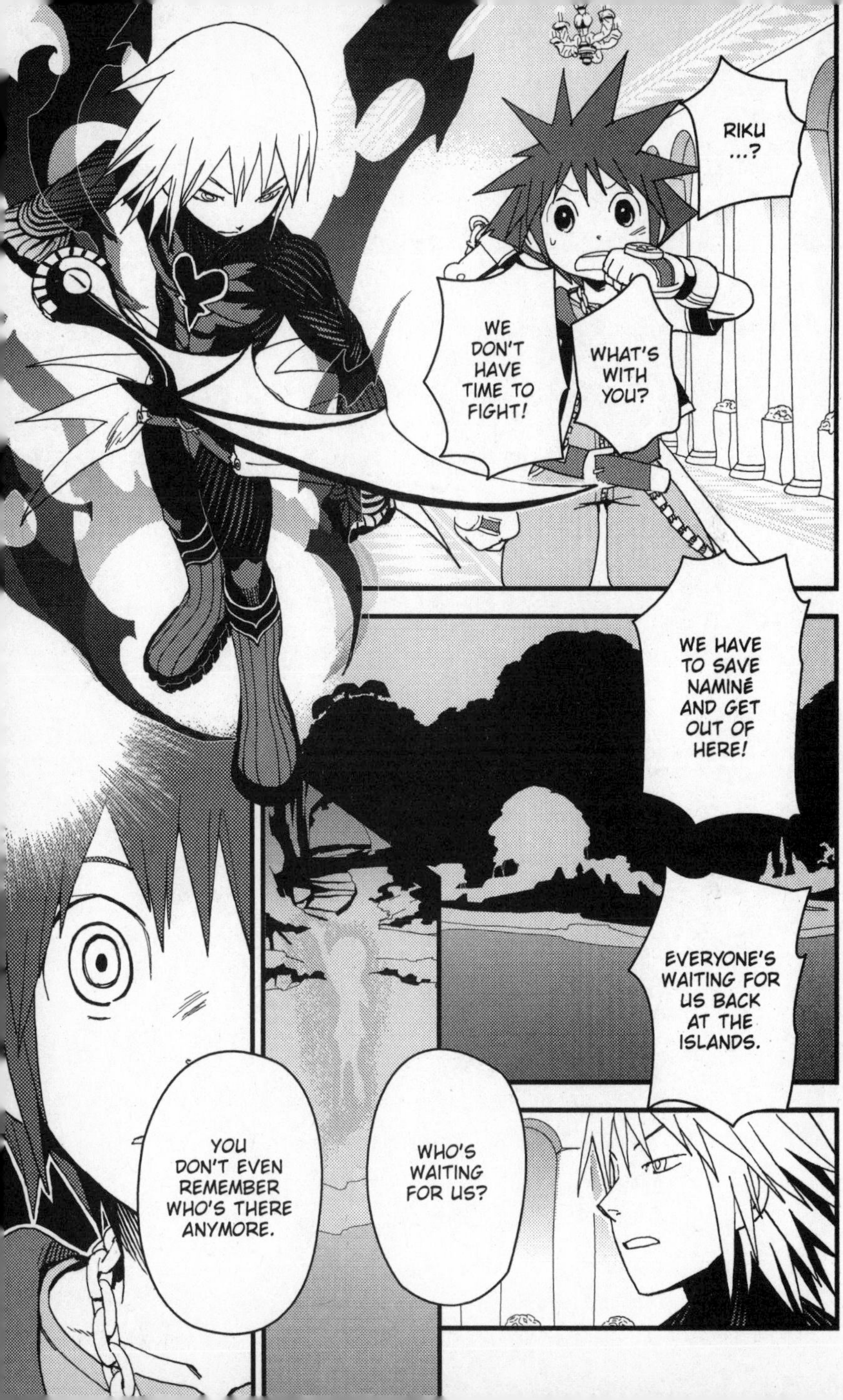
RIKU ...?
WHAT'S WITH YOU?
WE DON'T HAVE TIME TO FIGHT!
WE HAVE TO SAVE NAMINÉ AND GET OUT OF HERE!
EVERYONE'S WAITING FOR US BACK AT THE ISLANDS.
WHO'S WAITING FOR US?
YOU DON'T EVEN REMEMBER WHO'S THERE ANYMORE.

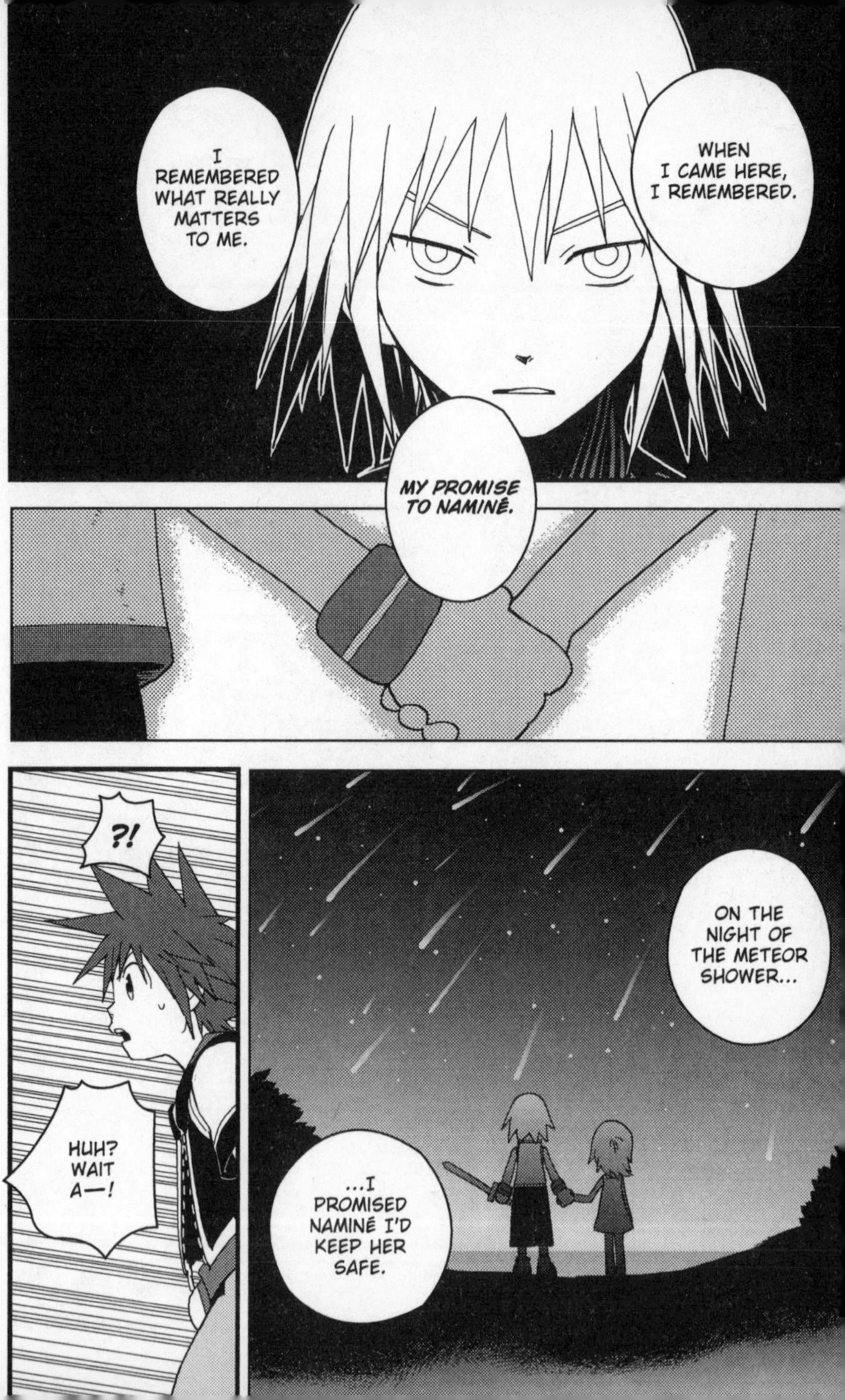
WHEN I CAME HERE, I REMEMBERED.
I REMEMBERED WHAT REALLY MATTERS TO ME.
MY PROMISE TO NAMINÉ.
ON THE NIGHT OF THE METEOR SHOWER...
...I PROMISED NAMINÉ I'D KEEP HER SAFE.
?!
HUH? WAIT A—!

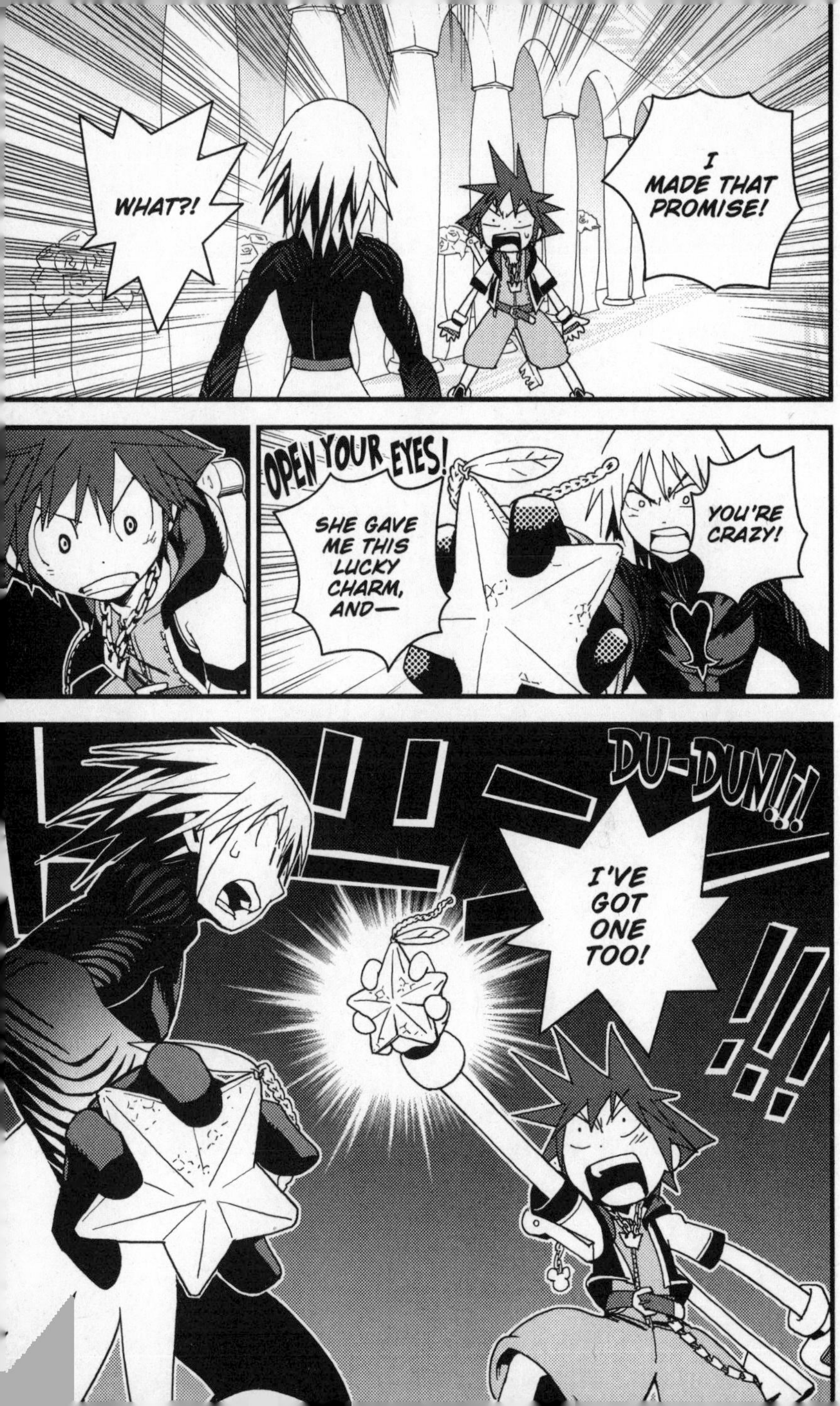
I MADE THAT PROMISE!
WHAT?!
YOU'RE CRAZY!
OPEN YOUR EYES!
SHE GAVE ME THIS LUCKY CHARM, AND—
DU-DUN!!!
I'VE GOT ONE TOO!
!!!

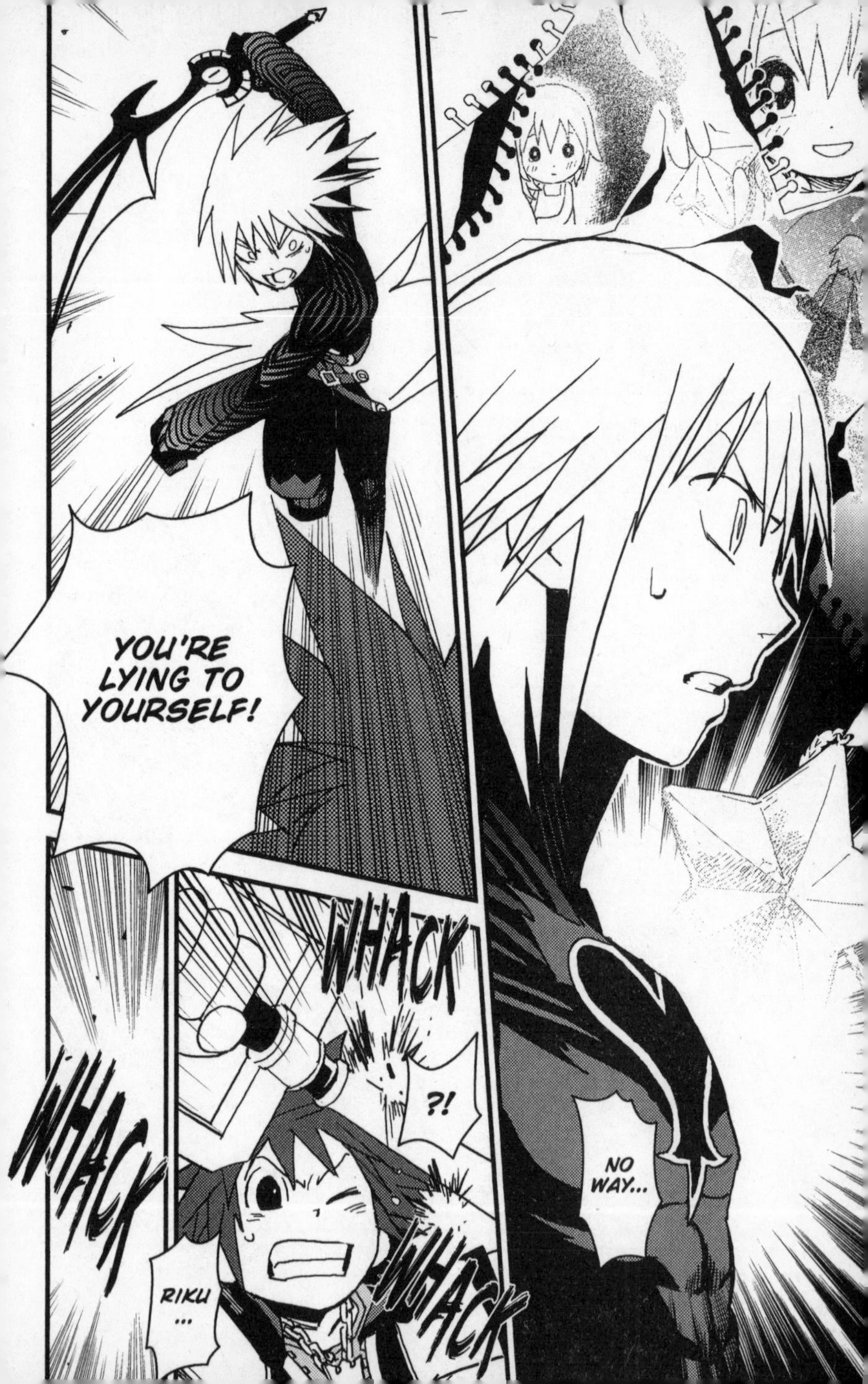
NO WAY...
YOU'RE LYING TO YOURSELF!
WHACK
?!
WHACK
WHACK
RIKU ...

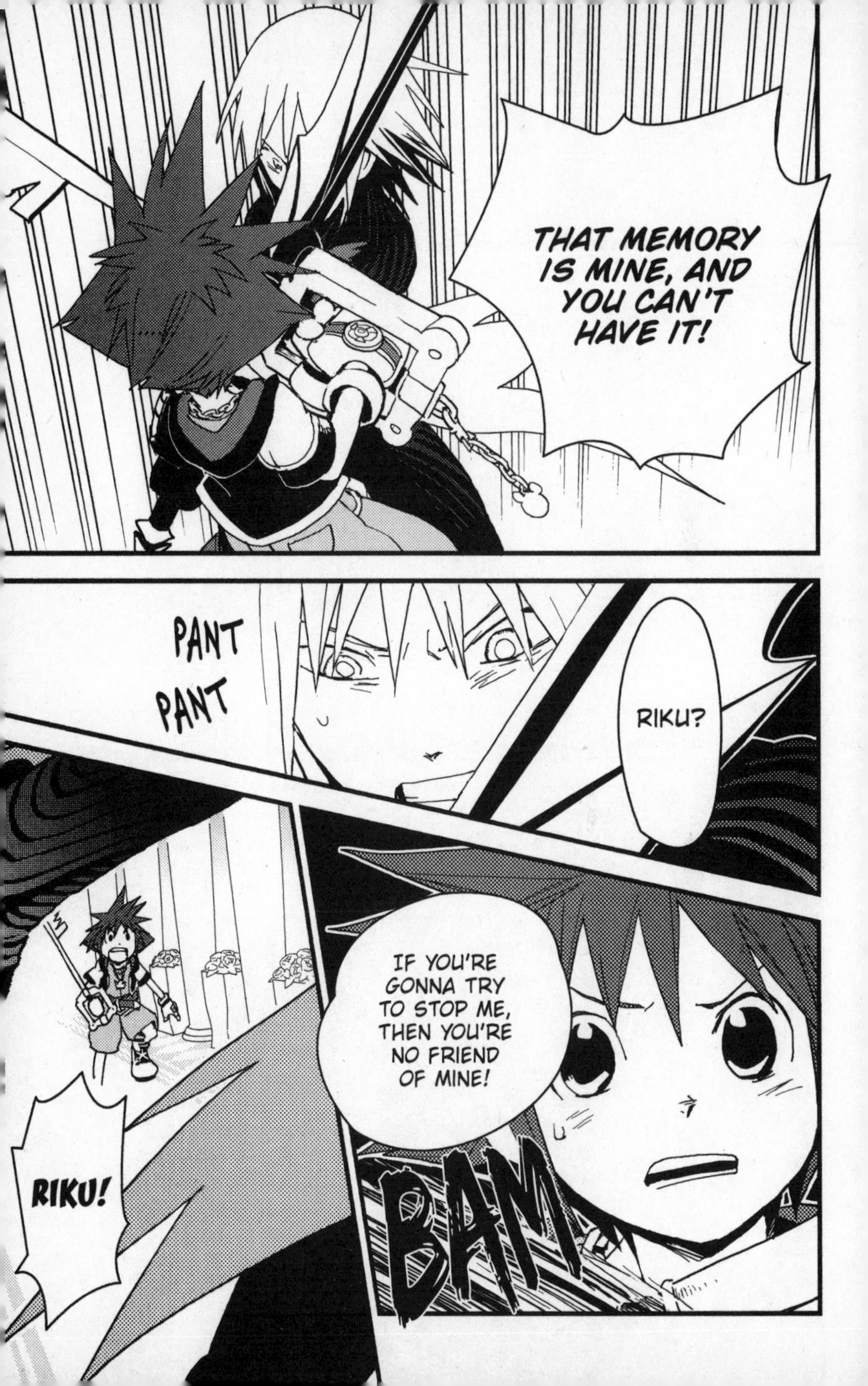
THAT MEMORY IS MINE, AND YOU CAN'T HAVE IT!
RIKU?
PANT PANT
IF YOU'RE GONNA TRY TO STOP ME, THEN YOU'RE NO FRIEND OF MINE!
BAM
RIKU!

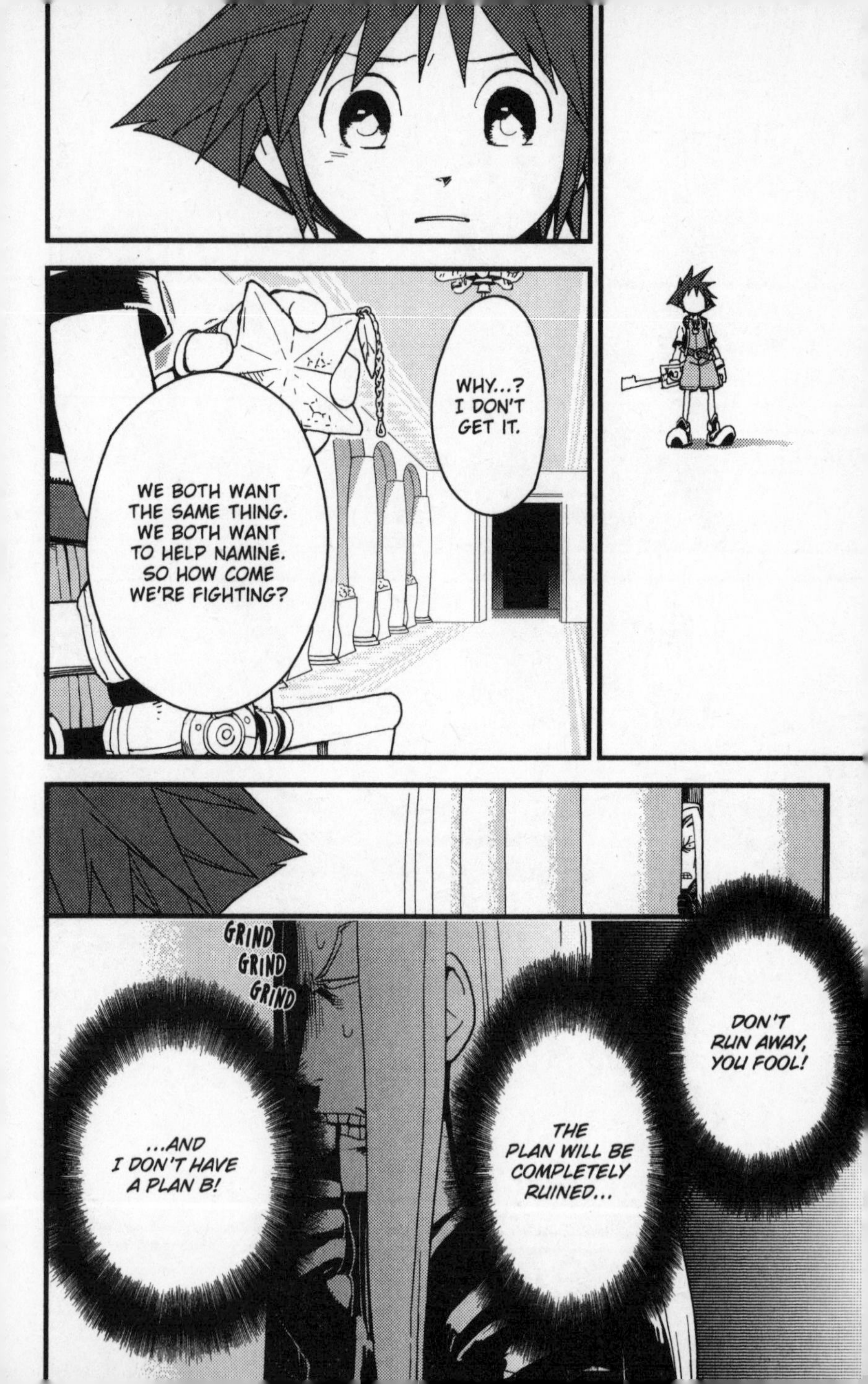
WHY...? I DON'T GET IT.
WE BOTH WANT THE SAME THING. WE BOTH WANT TO HELP NAMINÉ. SO HOW COME WE'RE FIGHTING?
GRIND GRIND GRIND
DON'T RUN AWAY, YOU FOOL!
THE PLAN WILL BE COMPLETELY RUINED...
...AND I DON'T HAVE A PLAN B!

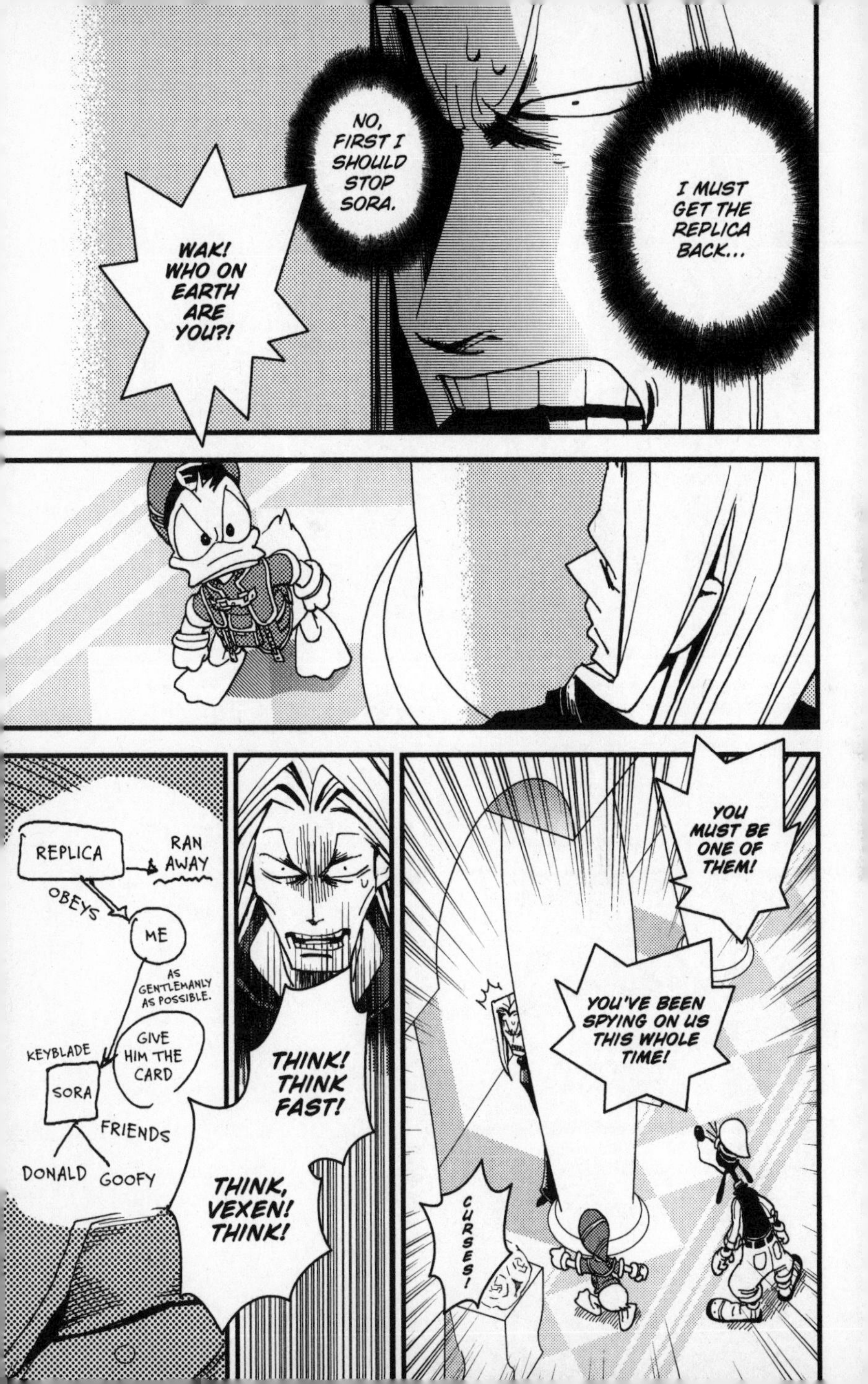
I MUST GET THE REPLICA BACK...
NO, FIRST I SHOULD STOP SORA.
WAK! WHO ON EARTH ARE YOU?!
YOU MUST BE ONE OF THEM!
YOU'VE BEEN SPYING ON US THIS WHOLE TIME!
CURSES!
THINK! THINK FAST!
THINK, VEXEN! THINK!
REPLICA
RAN AWAY
OBEYS
ME
AS GENTLEMANLY AS POSSIBLE.
GIVE HIM THE CARD
KEYBLADE
SORA
FRIENDS
DONALD
GOOFY

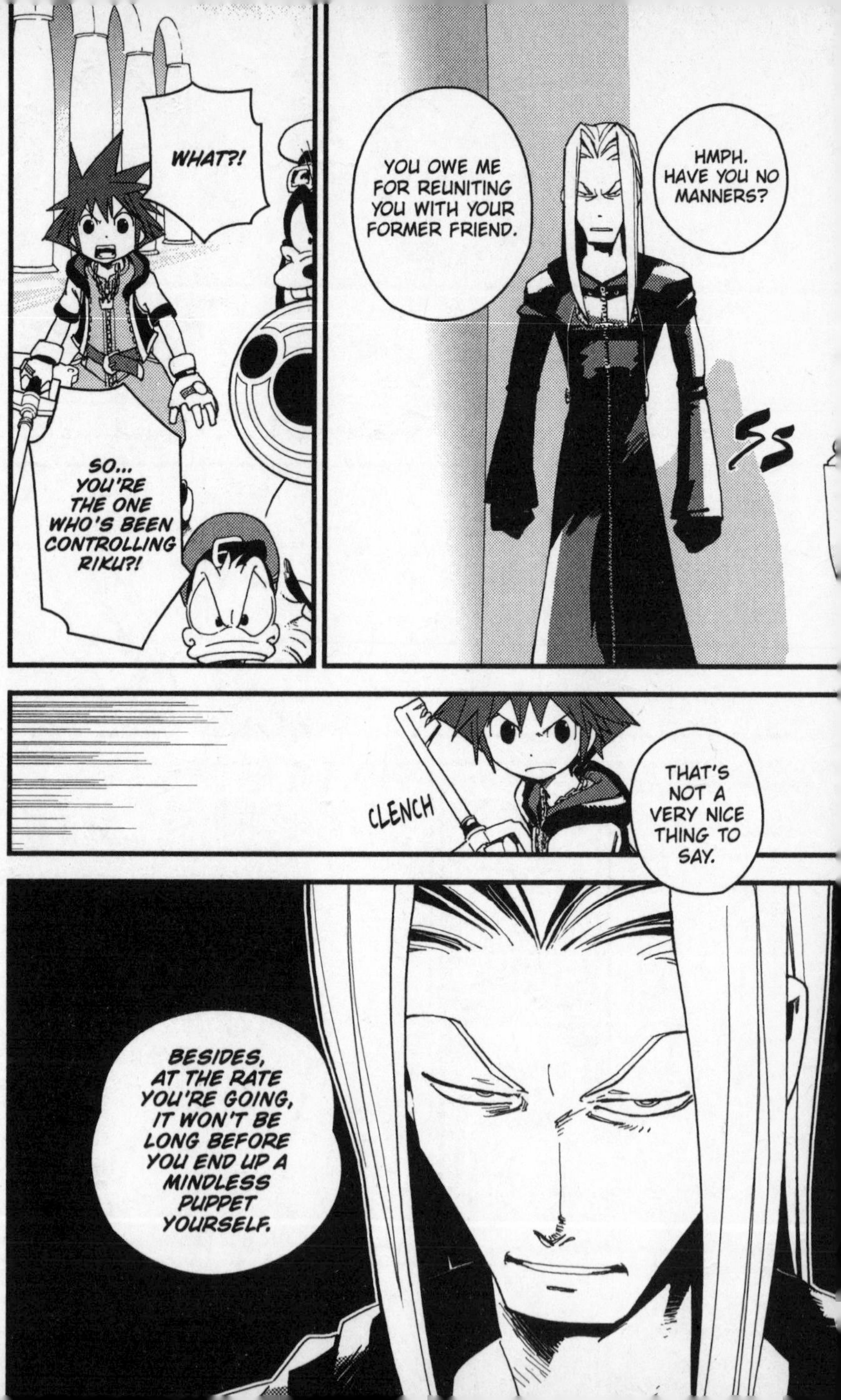
HMPH. HAVE YOU NO MANNERS?
YOU OWE ME FOR REUNITING YOU WITH YOUR FORMER FRIEND.
WHAT?!
SO... YOU'RE THE ONE WHO'S BEEN CONTROLLING RIKU?!
THAT'S NOT A VERY NICE THING TO SAY.
CLENCH
BESIDES, AT THE RATE YOU'RE GOING, IT WON'T BE LONG BEFORE YOU END UP A MINDLESS PUPPET YOURSELF.

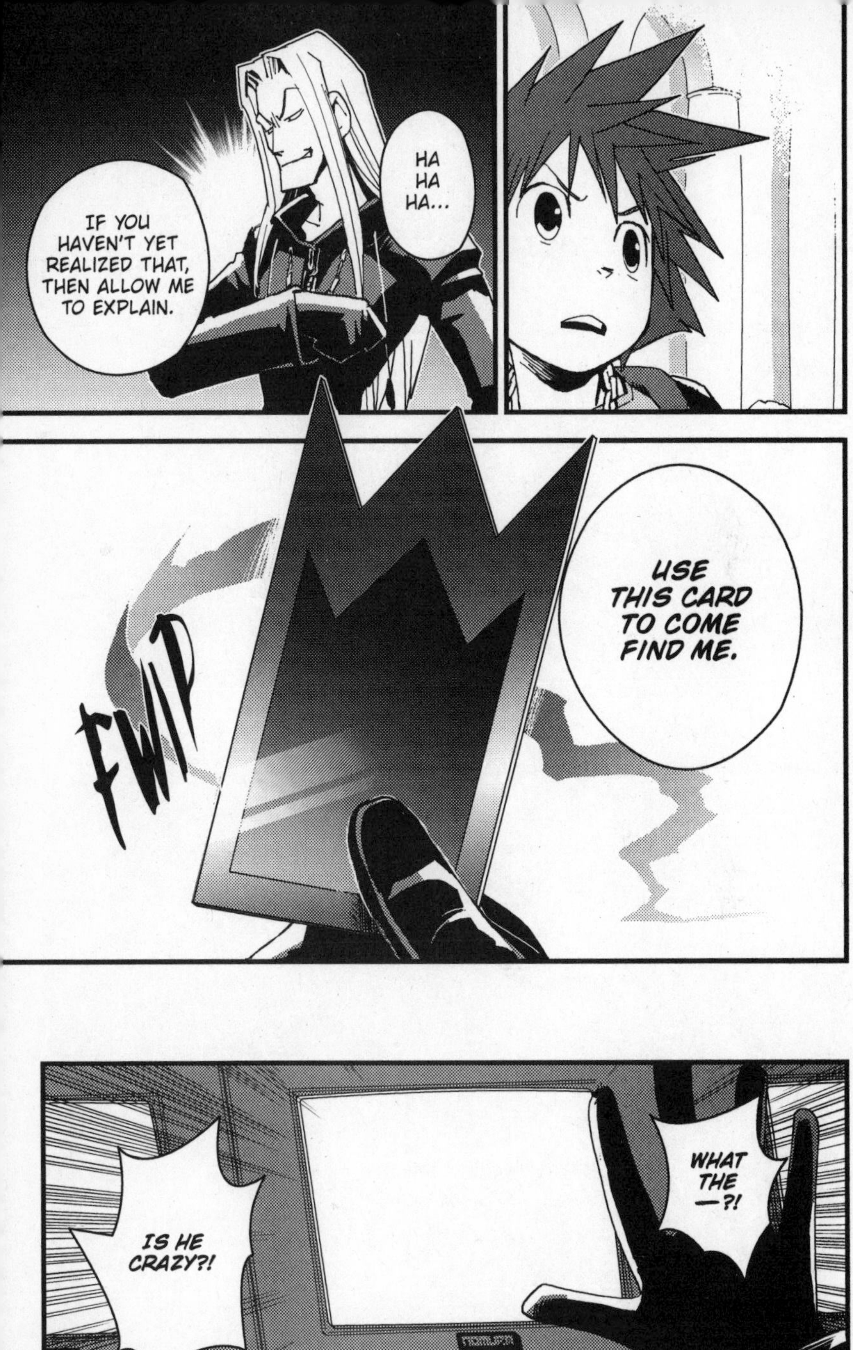
HA HA HA...
IF YOU HAVEN'T YET REALIZED THAT, THEN ALLOW ME TO EXPLAIN.
USE THIS CARD TO COME FIND ME.
FWIP
WHAT THE—?!
IS HE CRAZY?!

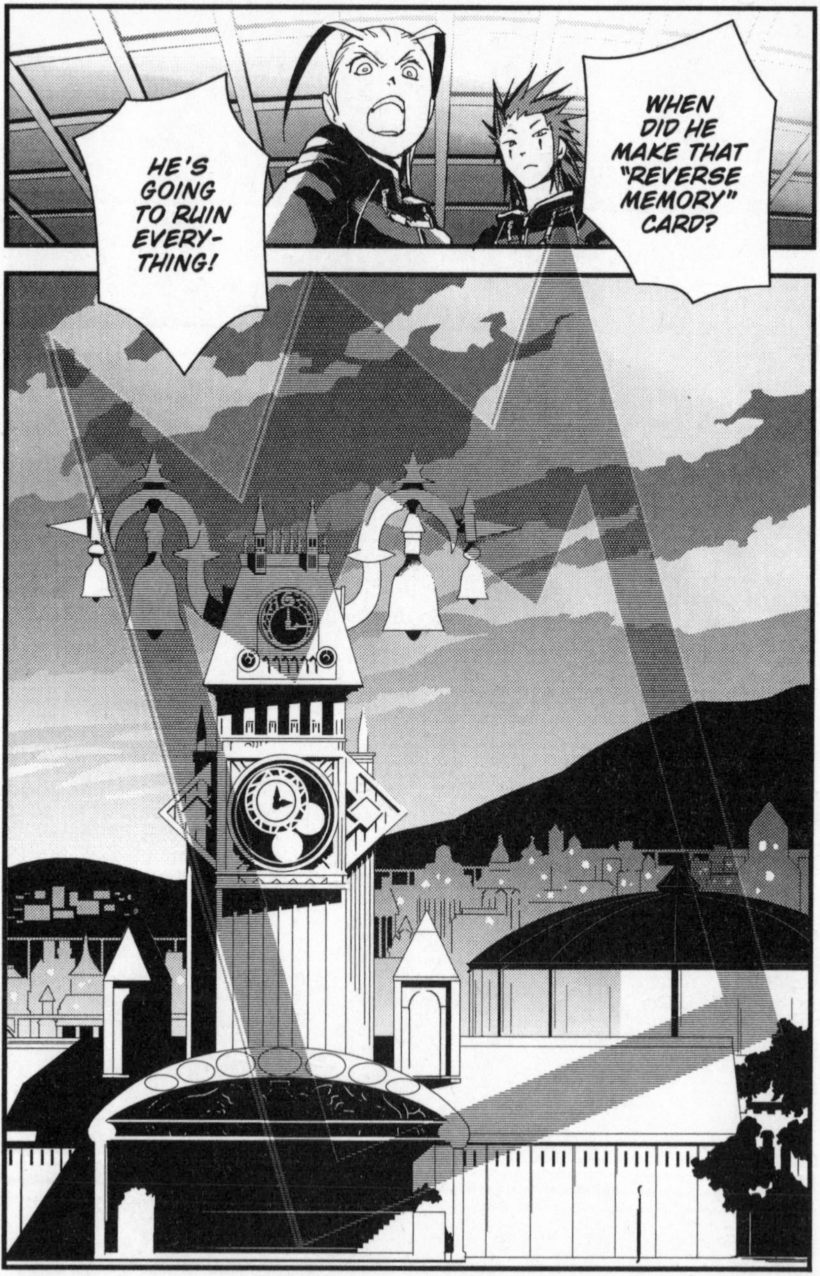
WHEN DID HE MAKE THAT "REVERSE MEMORY" CARD?
HE'S GOING TO RUIN EVERY-THING!

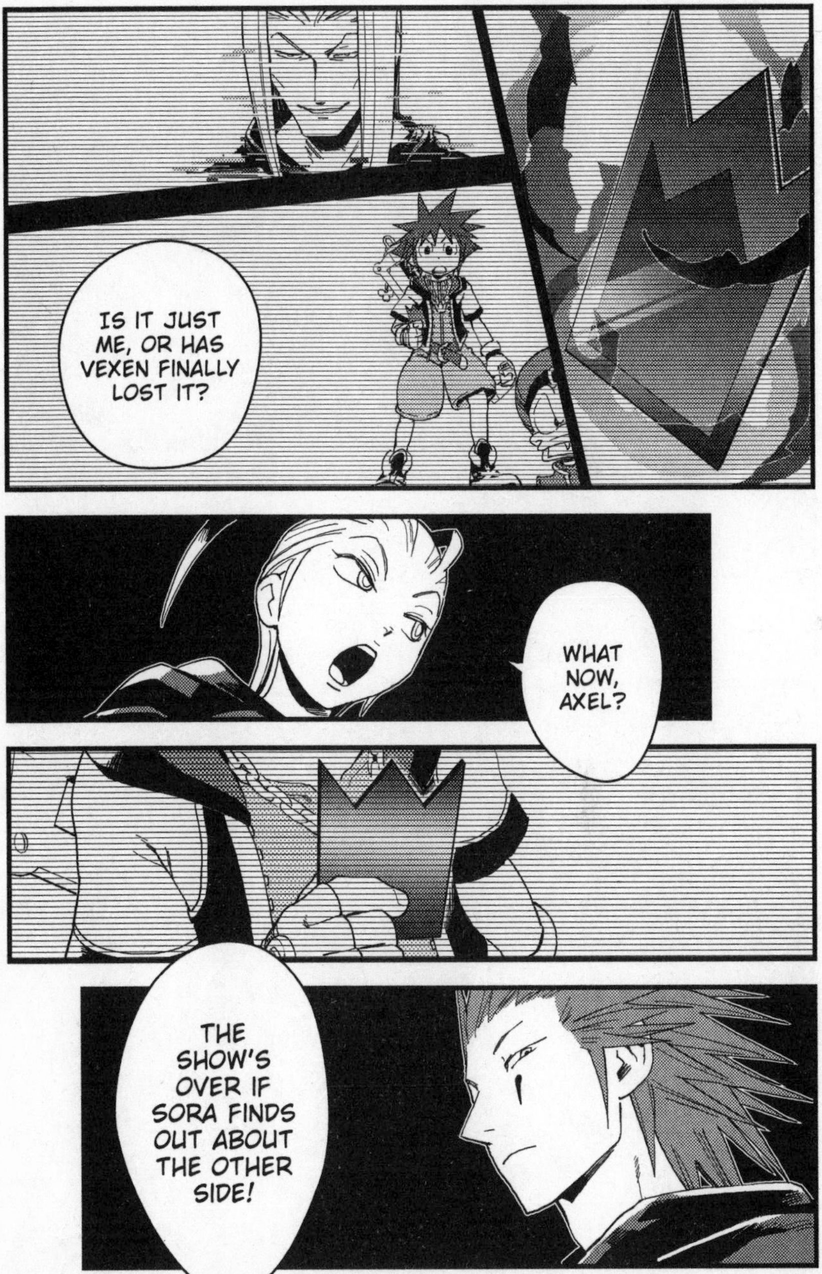
IS IT JUST ME, OR HAS VEXEN FINALLY LOST IT?
WHAT NOW, AXEL?
THE SHOW'S OVER IF SORA FINDS OUT ABOUT THE OTHER SIDE!

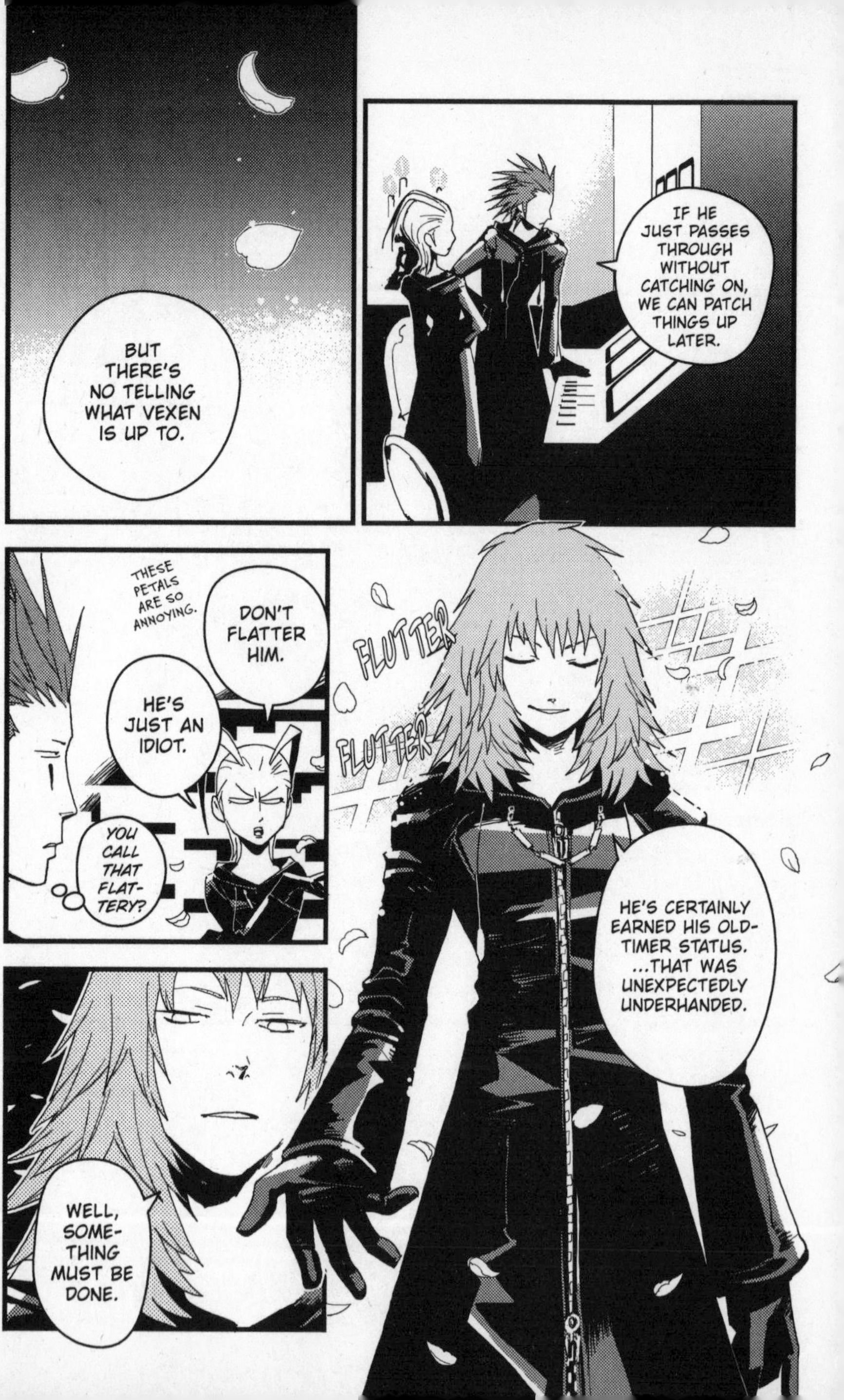
IF HE JUST PASSES THROUGH WITHOUT CATCHING ON, WE CAN PATCH THINGS UP LATER.
BUT THERE'S NO TELLING WHAT VEXEN IS UP TO.
FLUTTER
FLUTTER
HE'S CERTAINLY EARNED HIS OLD-TIMER STATUS. ...THAT WAS UNEXPECTEDLY UNDERHANDED.
THESE PETALS ARE SO ANNOYING.
DON'T FLATTER HIM.
HE'S JUST AN IDIOT.
YOU CALL THAT FLAT-TERY?
WELL, SOME-THING MUST BE DONE.

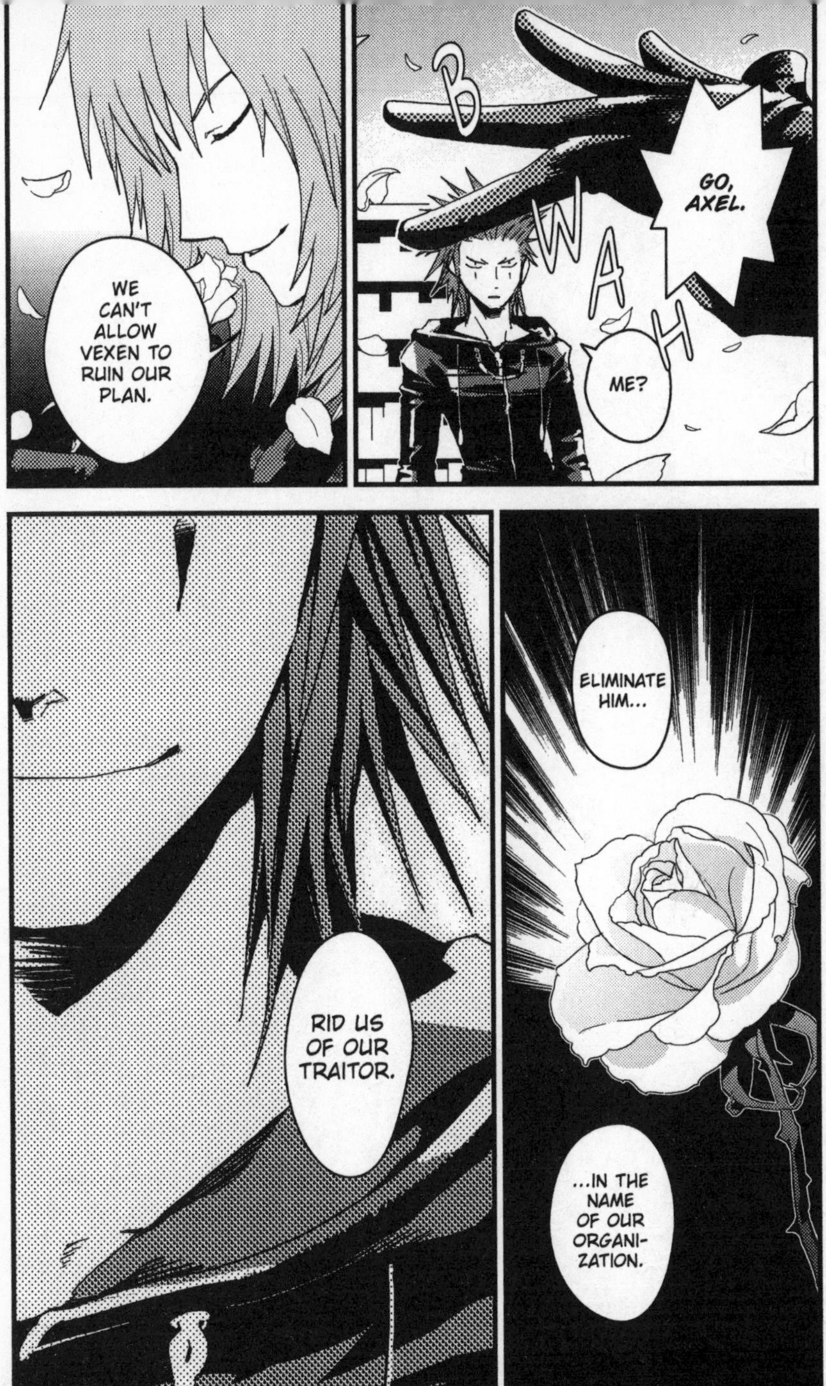
GO, AXEL.
BWAH
ME?
WE CAN'T ALLOW VEXEN TO RUIN OUR PLAN.
ELIMINATE HIM...
...IN THE NAME OF OUR ORGANI-ZATION.
RID US OF OUR TRAITOR.

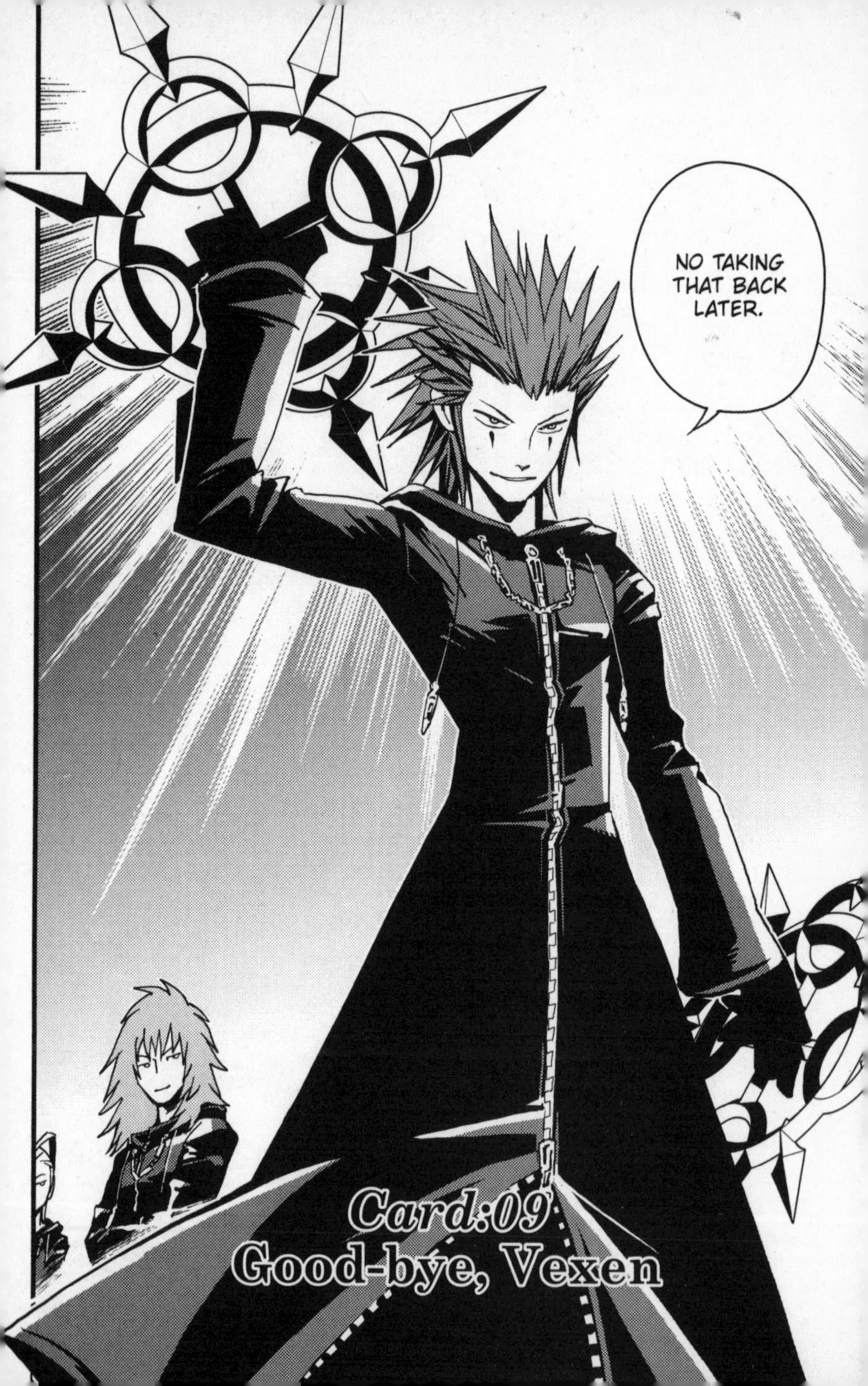
NO TAKING THAT BACK LATER.
Card:09
Good-bye, Vexen

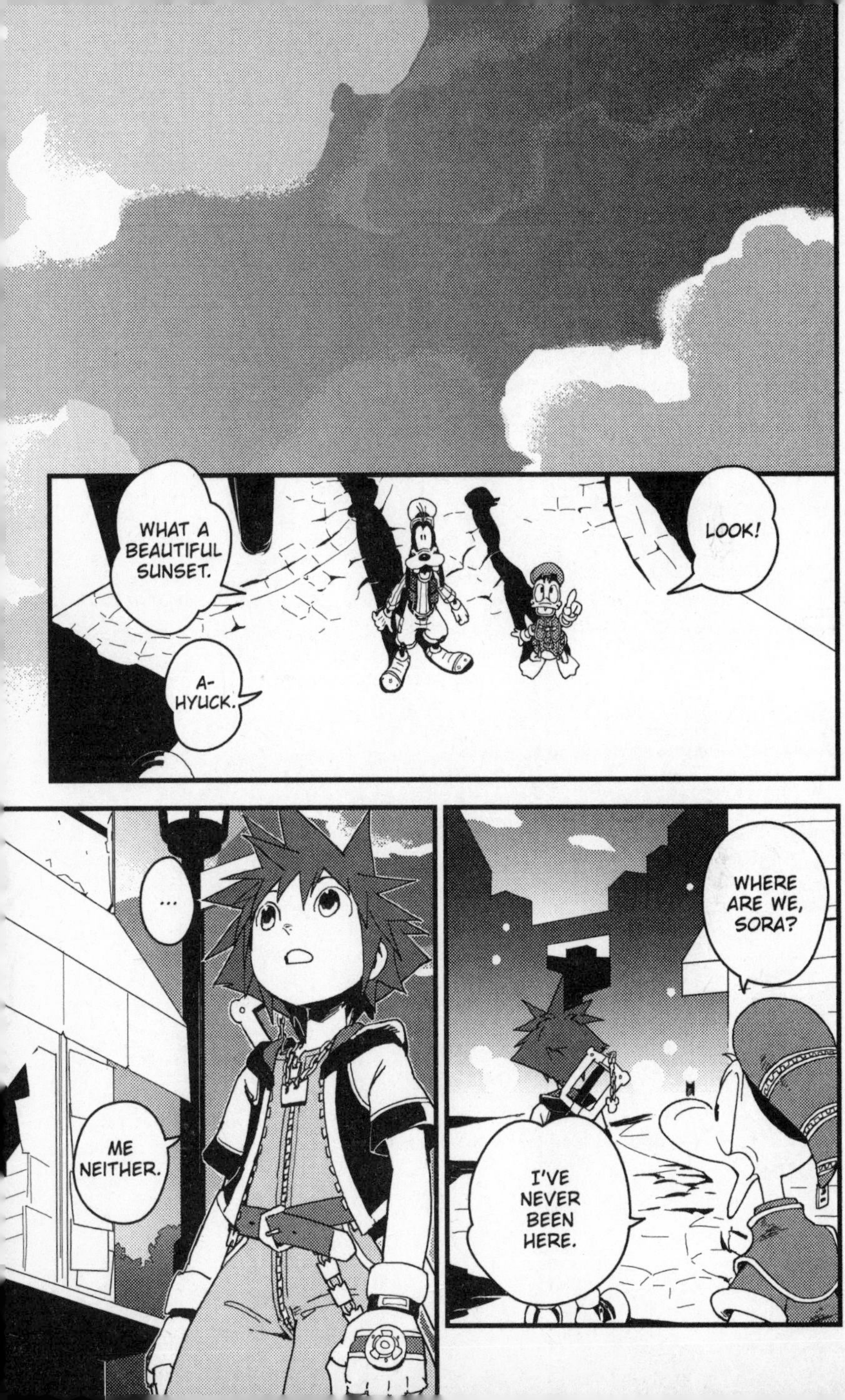
LOOK!
WHAT A BEAUTIFUL SUNSET.
A-HYUCK.
WHERE ARE WE, SORA?
I'VE NEVER BEEN HERE.
...
ME NEITHER.

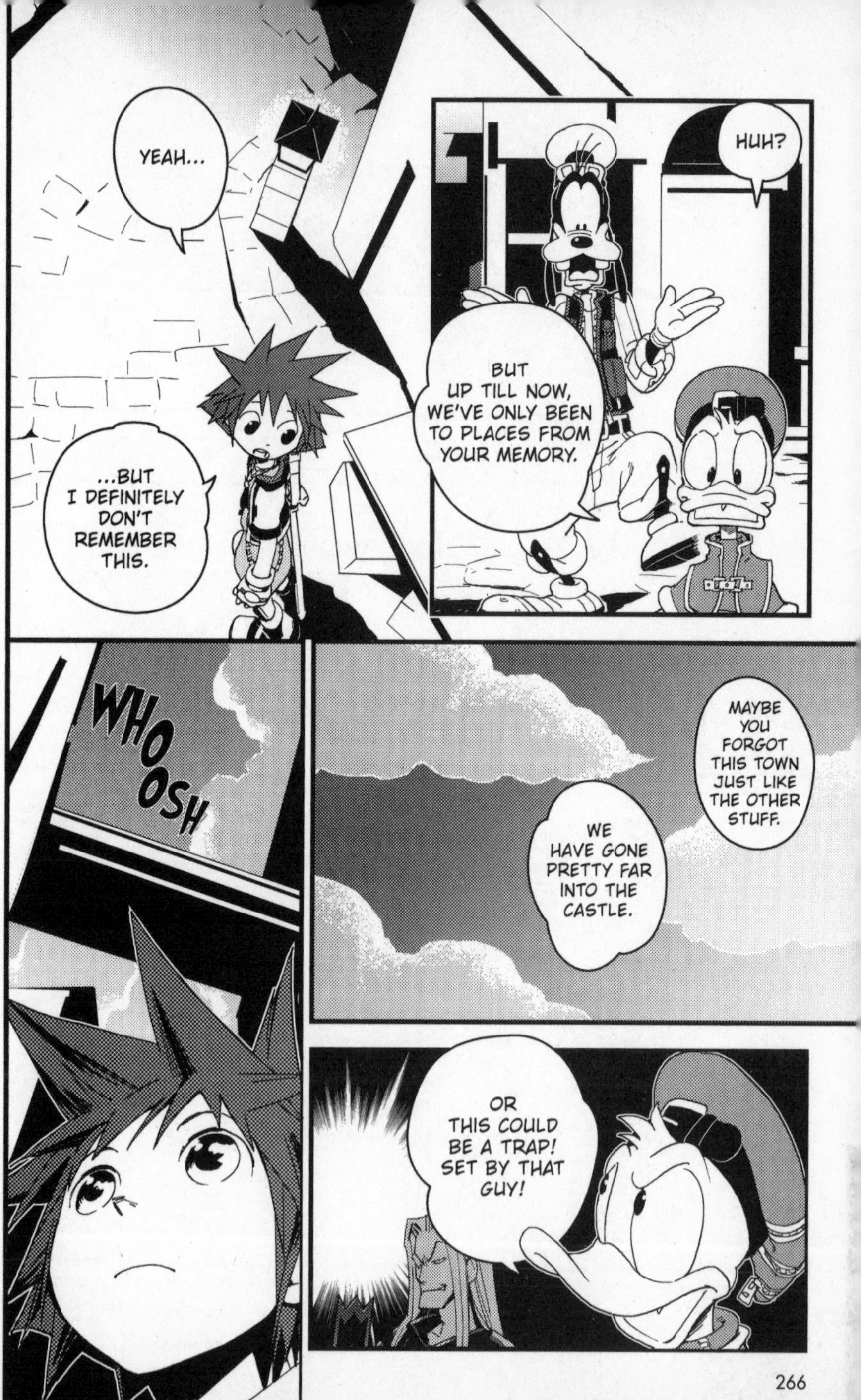
HUH?
YEAH...
BUT UP TILL NOW, WE'VE ONLY BEEN TO PLACES FROM YOUR MEMORY.
...BUT I DEFINITELY DON'T REMEMBER THIS.
MAYBE YOU FORGOT THIS TOWN JUST LIKE THE OTHER STUFF.
WE HAVE GONE PRETTY FAR INTO THE CASTLE.
OR THIS COULD BE A TRAP! SET BY THAT GUY!
WHOOSH

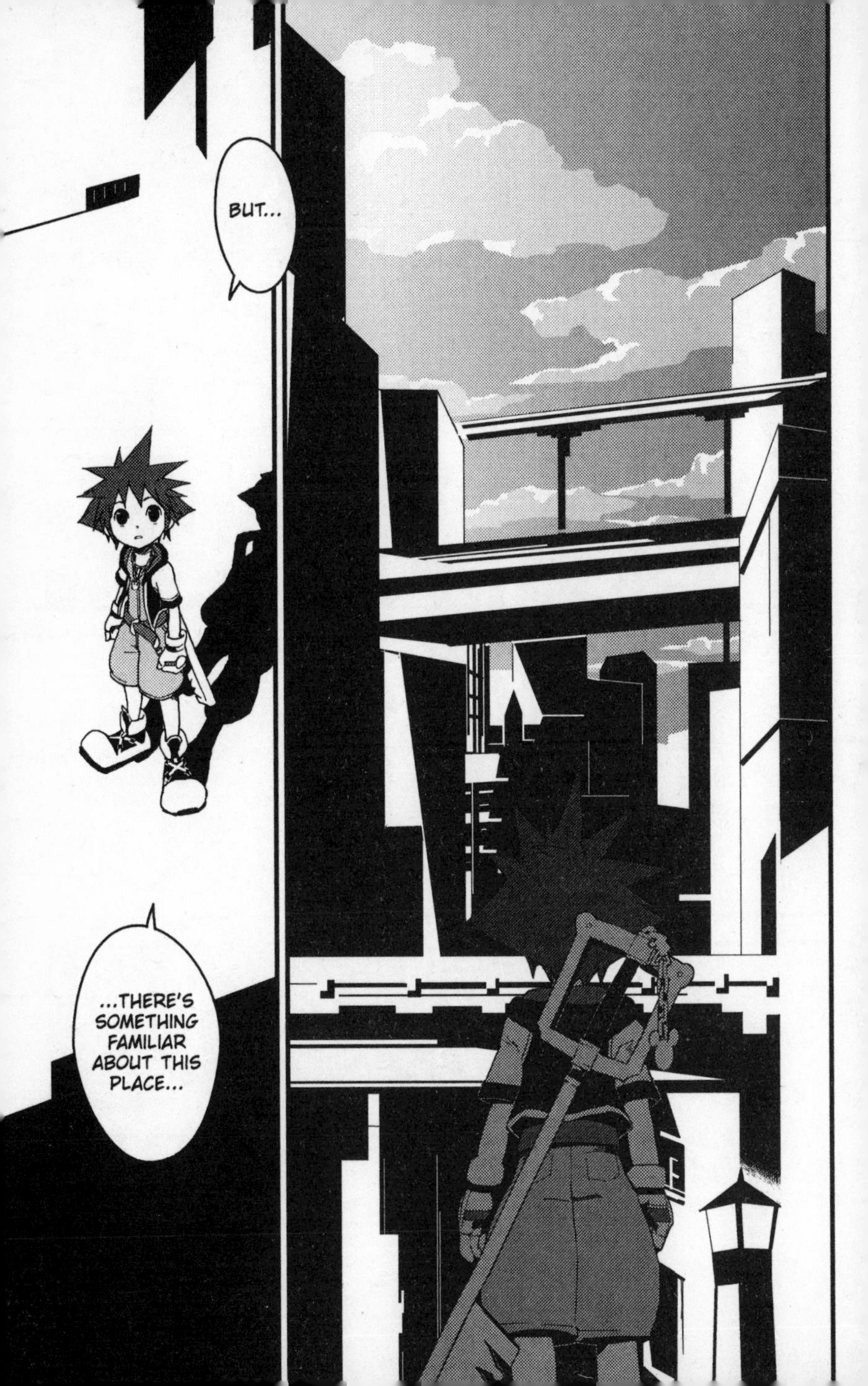
BUT...
...THERE'S SOMETHING FAMILIAR ABOUT THIS PLACE...

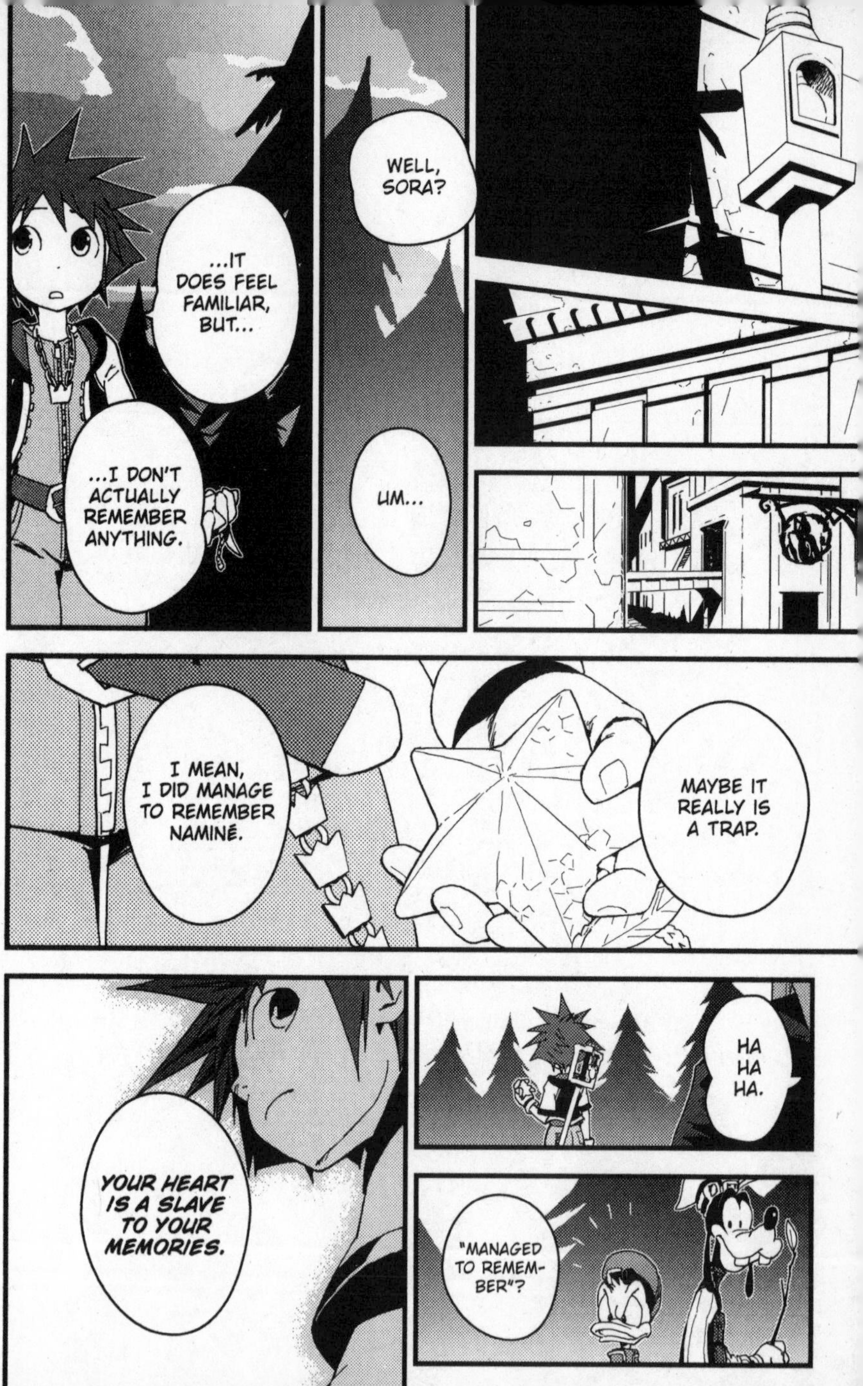
WELL, SORA?
UM...
...IT DOES FEEL FAMILIAR, BUT...
...I DON'T ACTUALLY REMEMBER ANYTHING.
MAYBE IT REALLY IS A TRAP.
I MEAN, I DID MANAGE TO REMEMBER NAMINÉ.
HA HA HA.
"MANAGED TO REMEM-BER"?
YOUR HEART IS A SLAVE TO YOUR MEMORIES.

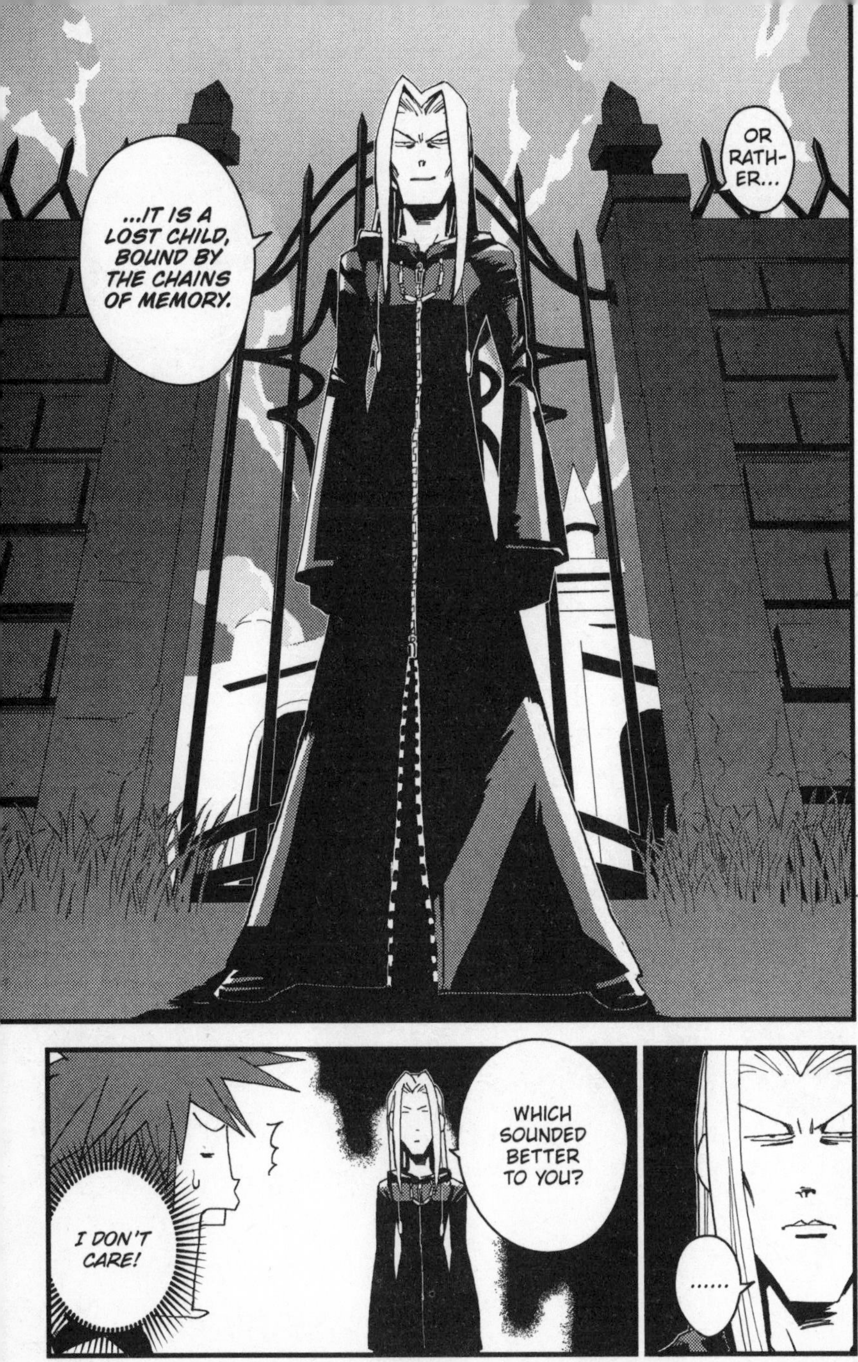
OR RATH-ER...
...IT IS A LOST CHILD, BOUND BY THE CHAINS OF MEMORY.
......
WHICH SOUNDED BETTER TO YOU?
I DON'T CARE!

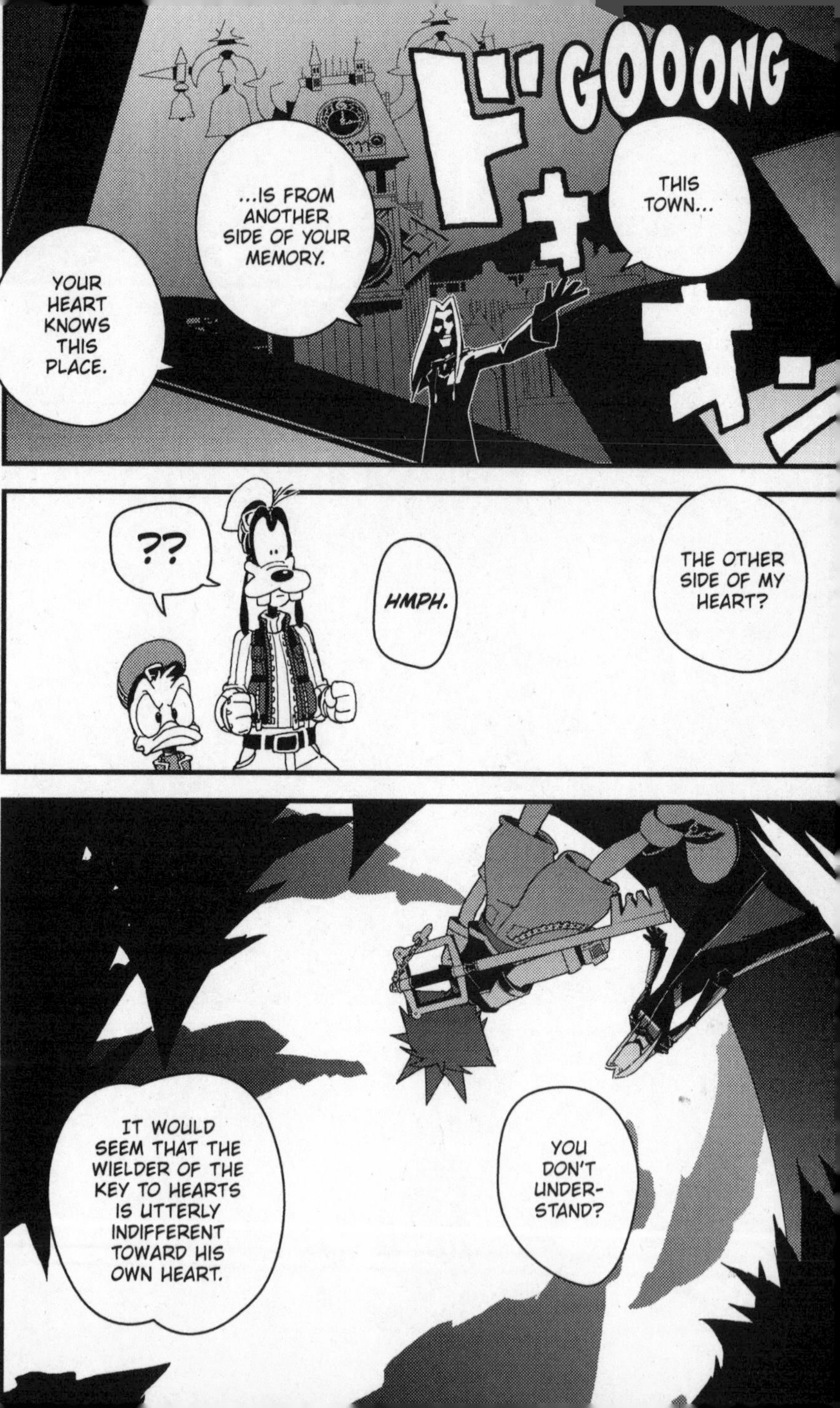
GOOONG
THIS TOWN...
...IS FROM ANOTHER SIDE OF YOUR MEMORY.
YOUR HEART KNOWS THIS PLACE.
THE OTHER SIDE OF MY HEART?
HMPH.
??
YOU DON'T UNDER-STAND?
IT WOULD SEEM THAT THE WIELDER OF THE KEY TO HEARTS IS UTTERLY INDIFFERENT TOWARD HIS OWN HEART.

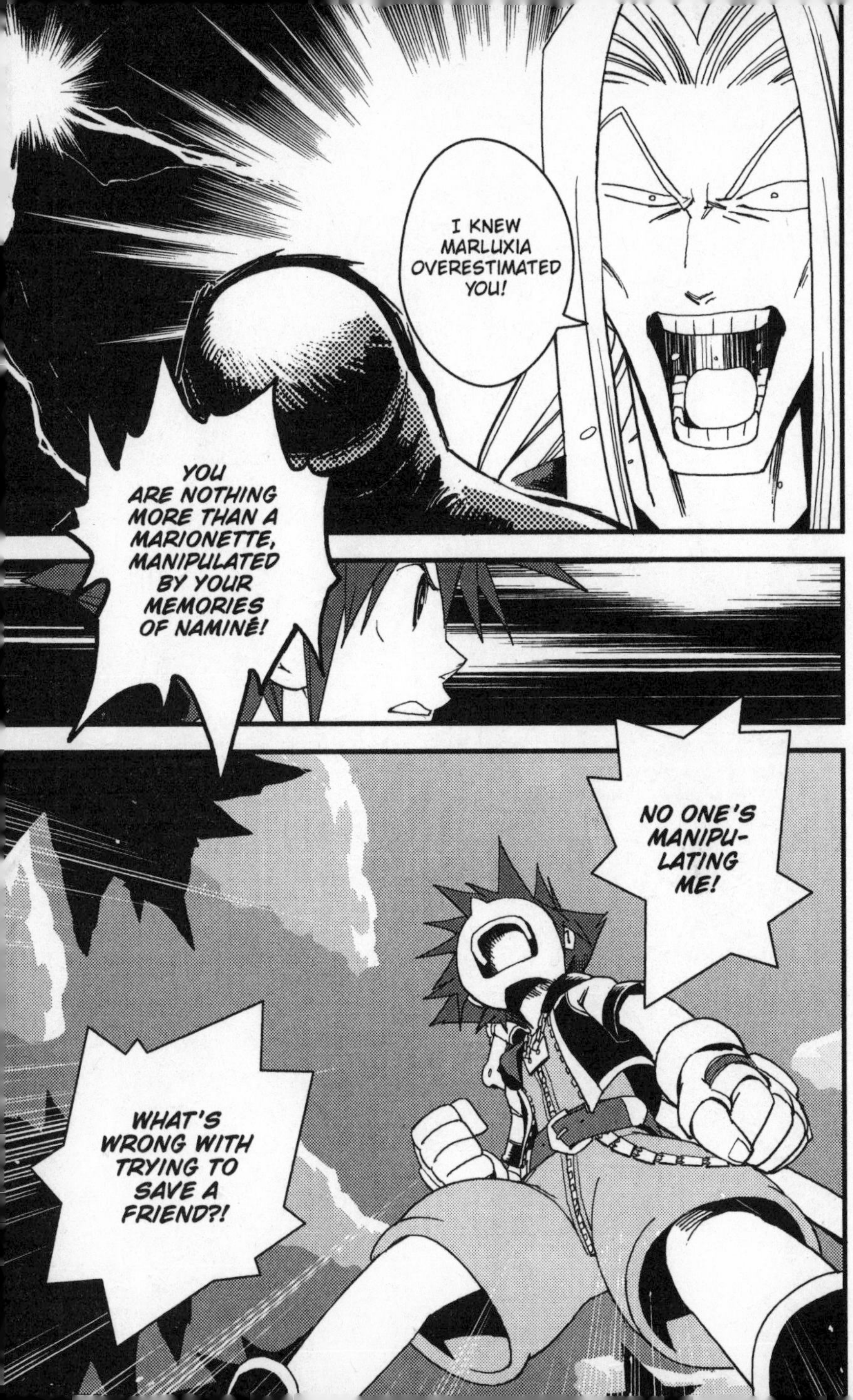
I KNEW MARLUXIA OVERESTIMATED YOU!
YOU ARE NOTHING MORE THAN A MARIONETTE, MANIPULATED BY YOUR MEMORIES OF NAMINÉ!
NO ONE'S MANIPU-LATING ME!
WHAT'S WRONG WITH TRYING TO SAVE A FRIEND?!

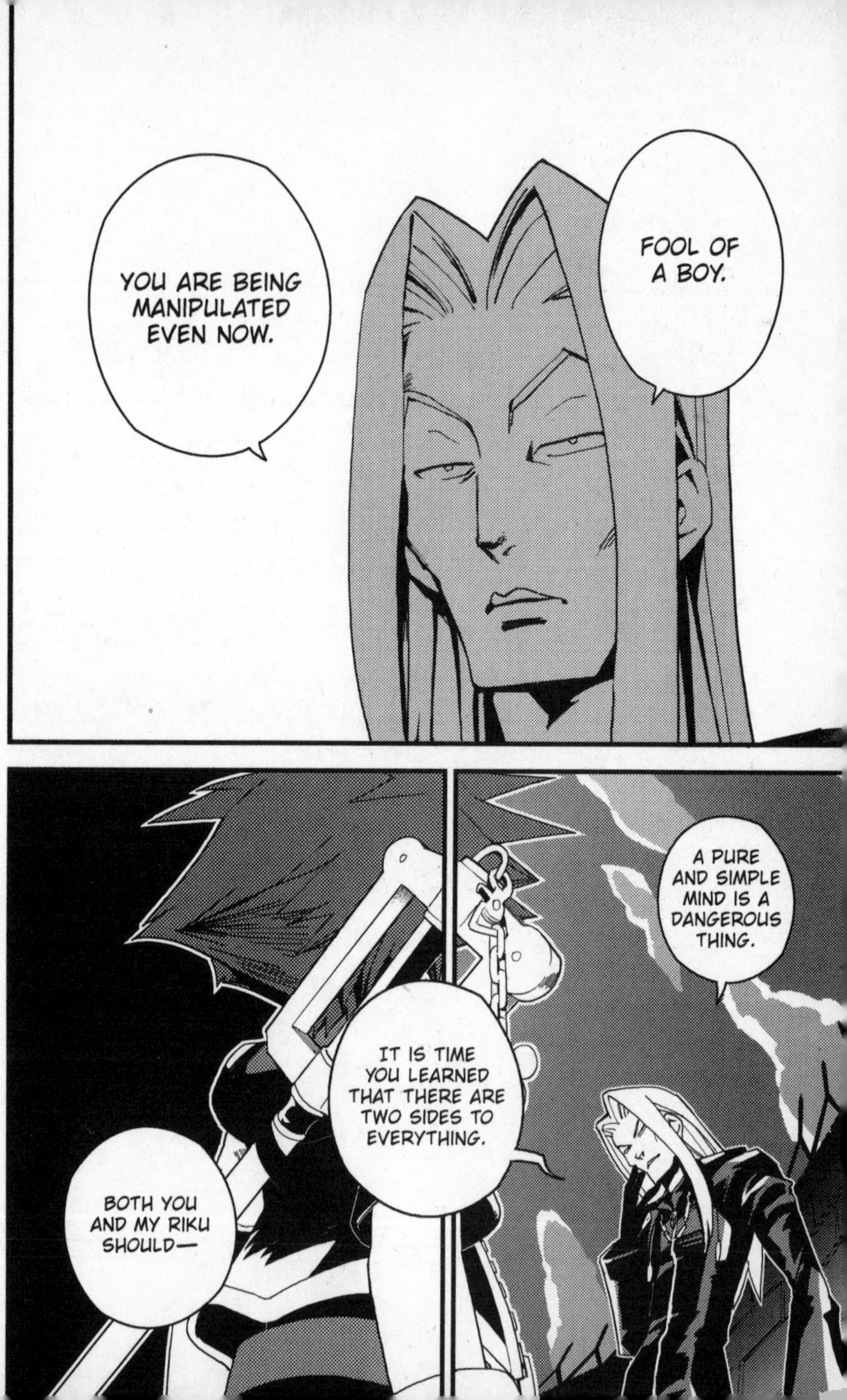
FOOL OF A BOY.
YOU ARE BEING MANIPULATED EVEN NOW.
A PURE AND SIMPLE MIND IS A DANGEROUS THING.
IT IS TIME YOU LEARNED THAT THERE ARE TWO SIDES TO EVERYTHING.
BOTH YOU AND MY RIKU SHOULD—

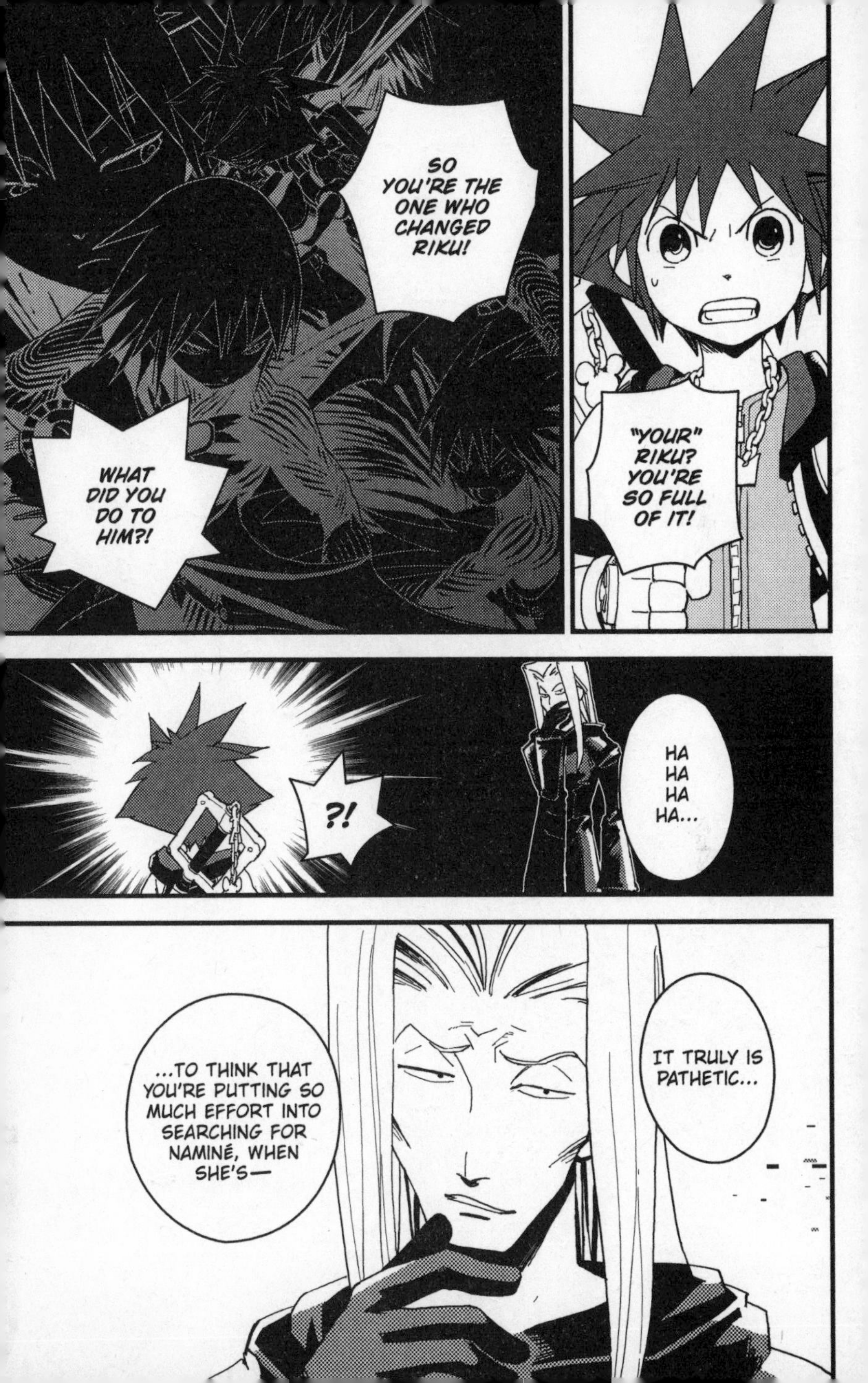
"YOUR" RIKU? YOU'RE SO FULL OF IT!
SO YOU'RE THE ONE WHO CHANGED RIKU!
WHAT DID YOU DO TO HIM?!
HA HA HA HA...
?!
IT TRULY IS PATHETIC...
...TO THINK THAT YOU'RE PUTTING SO MUCH EFFORT INTO SEARCHING FOR NAMINÉ, WHEN SHE'S—

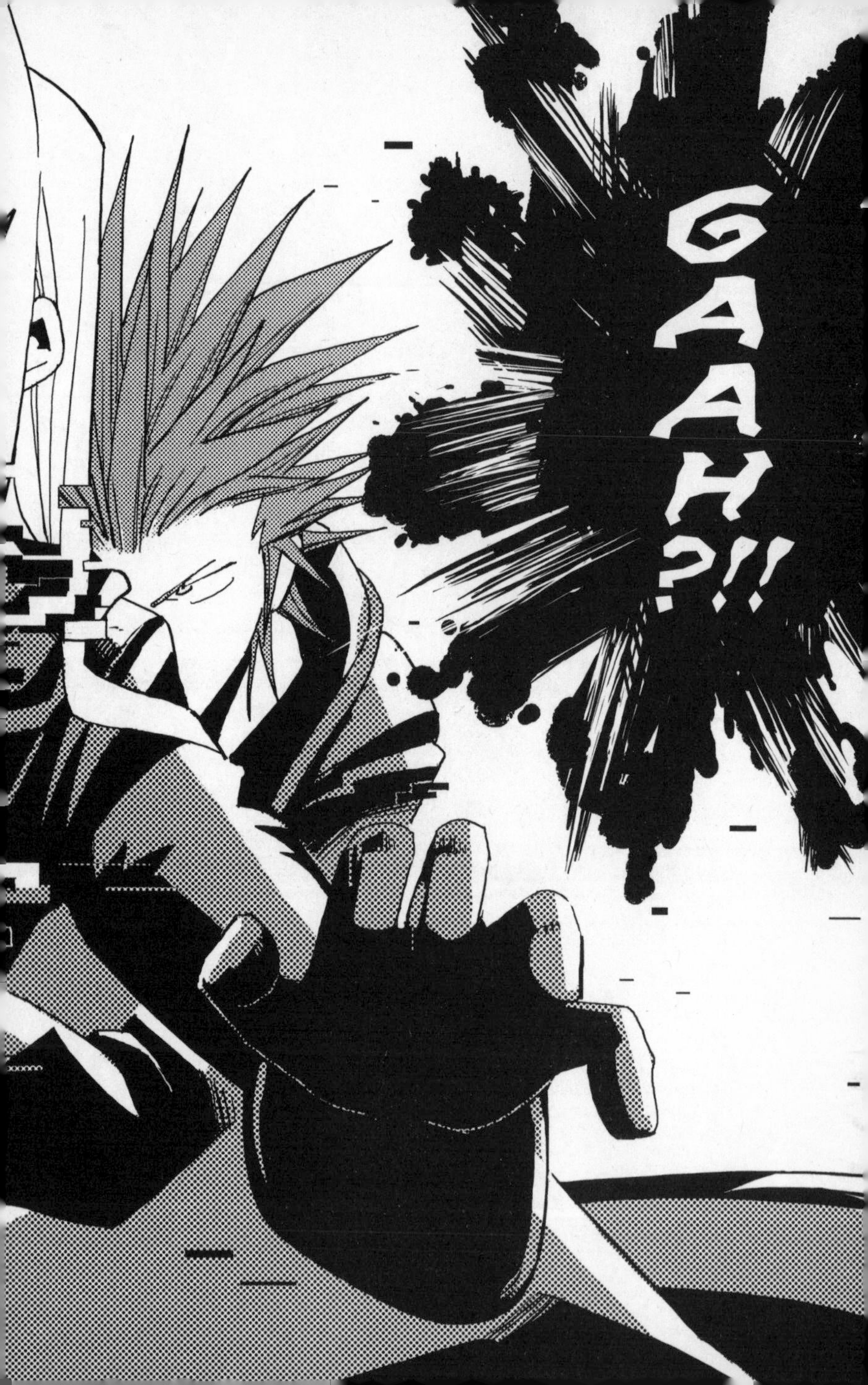
GAAH?!!

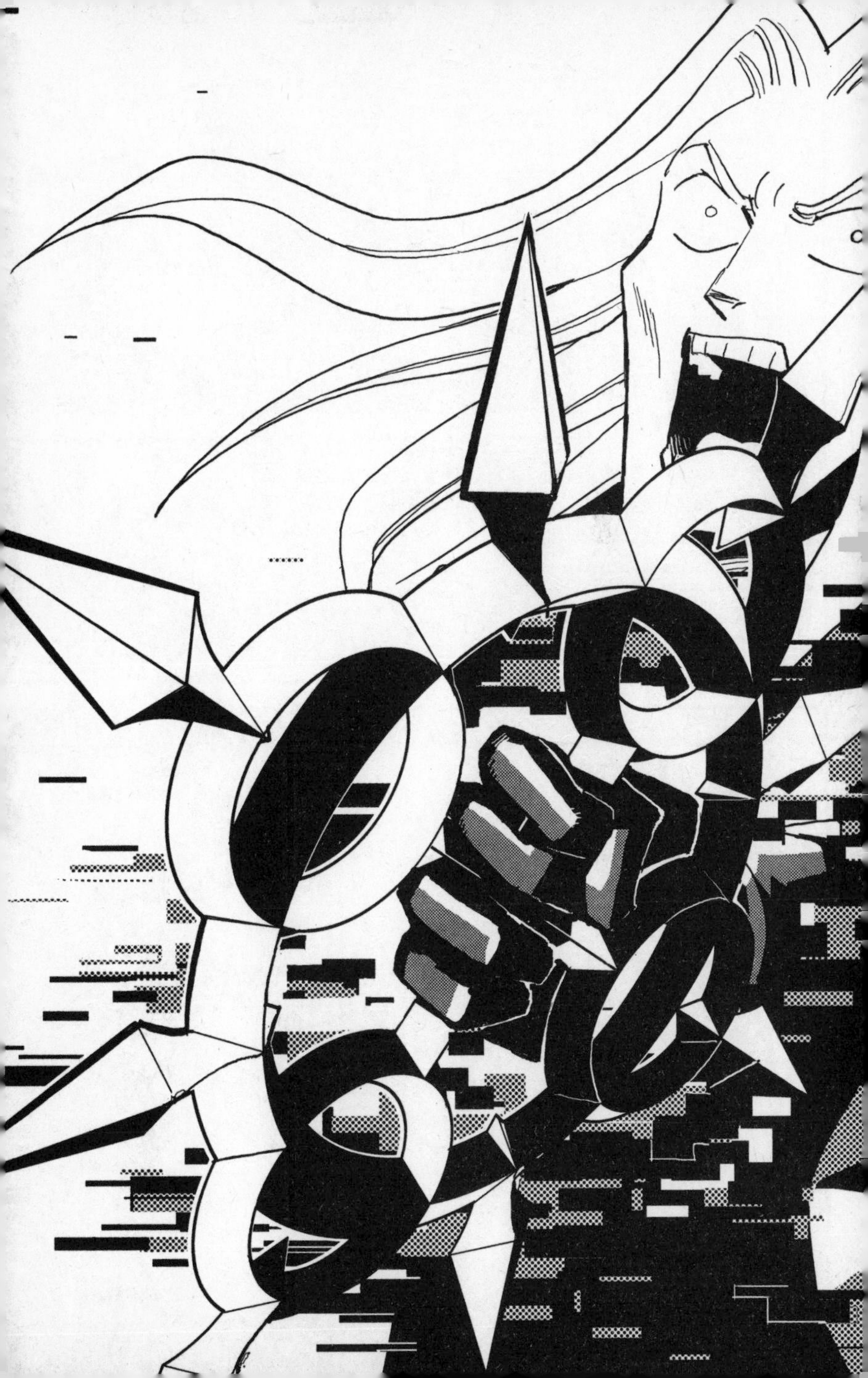

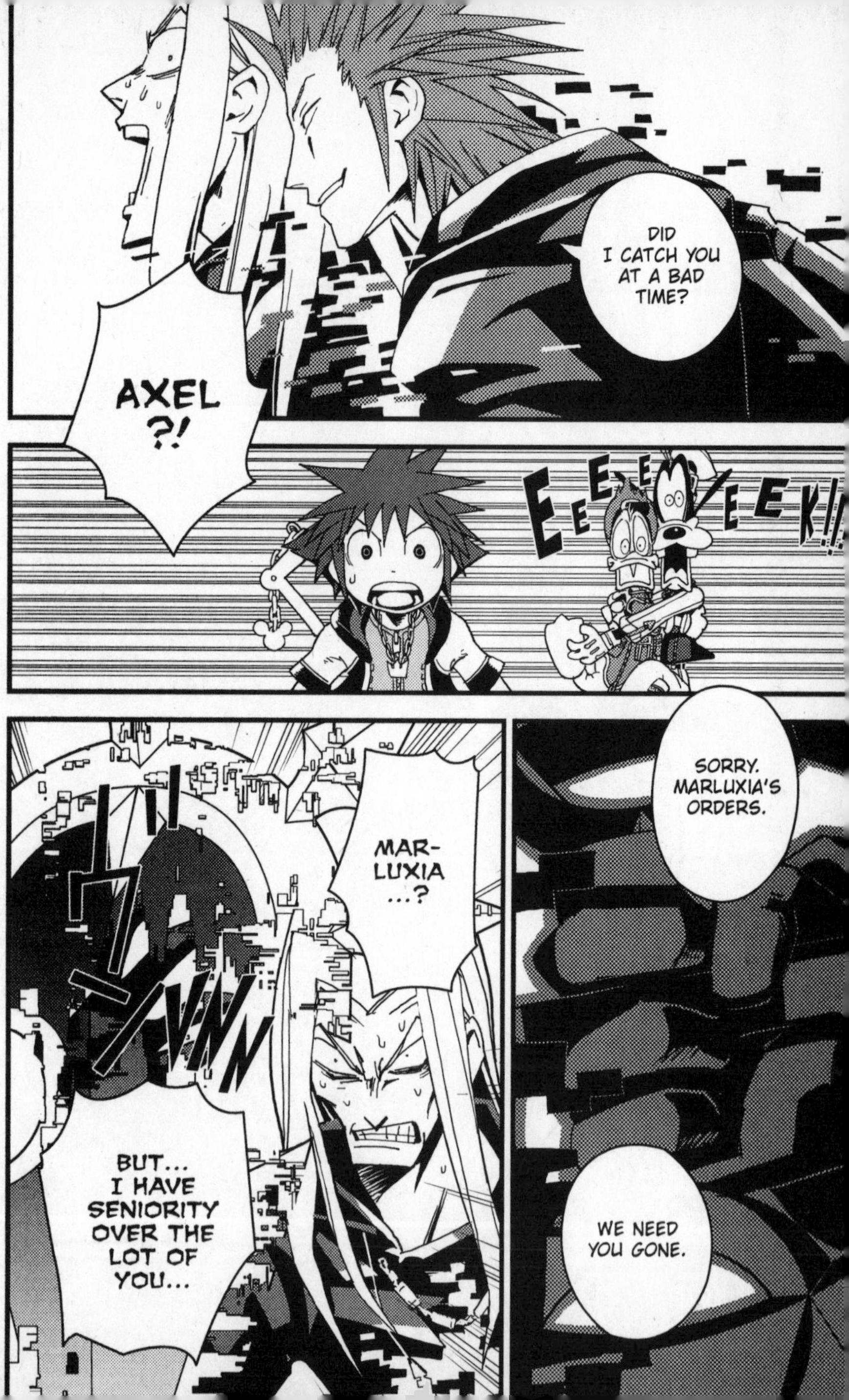
DID I CATCH YOU AT A BAD TIME?
AXEL ?!
EEEEEEEK!!!
SORRY. MARLUXIA'S ORDERS.
WE NEED YOU GONE.
MAR-LUXIA ...?
VNNN
BUT... I HAVE SENIORITY OVER THE LOT OF YOU...

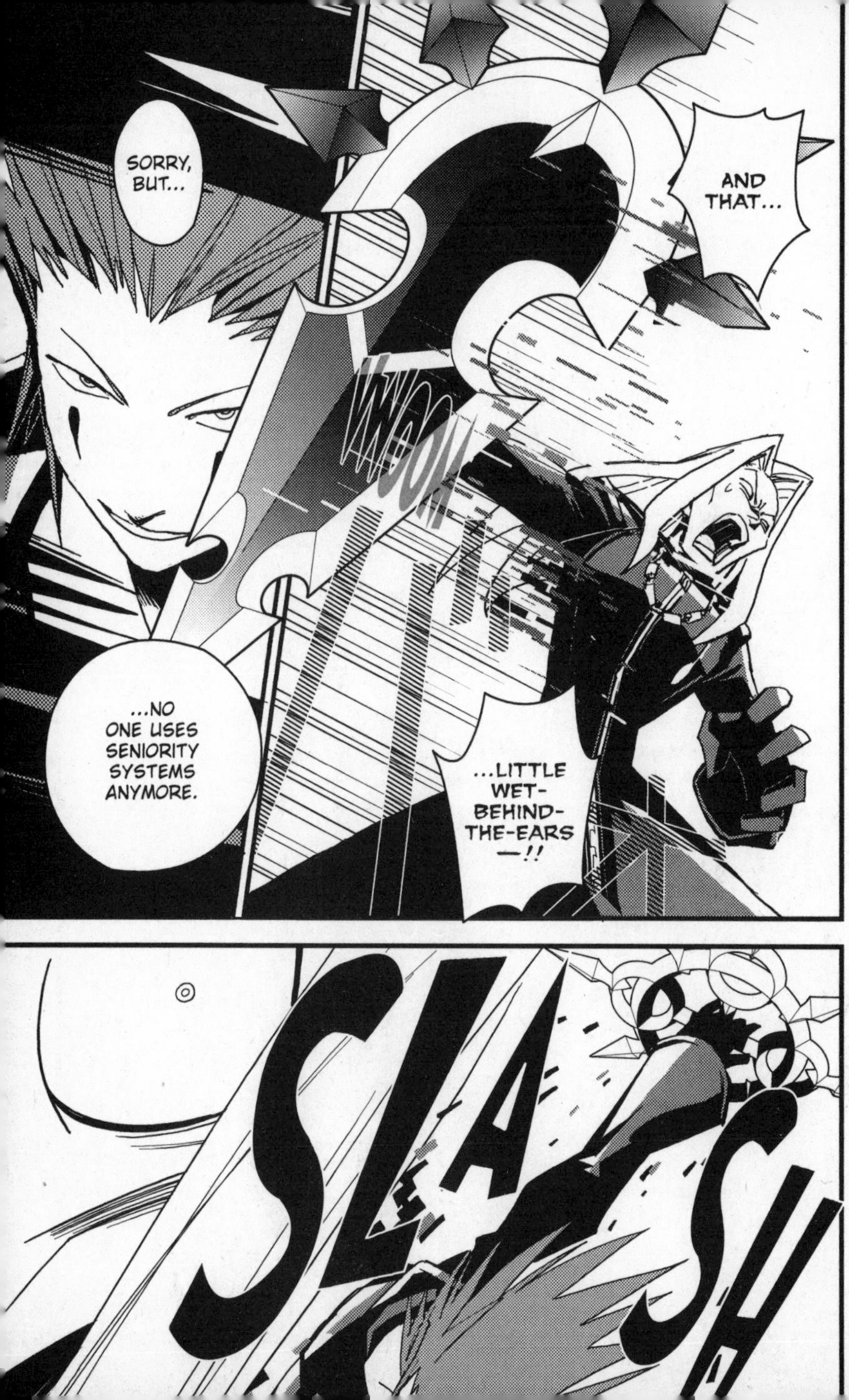
AND THAT...
SORRY, BUT...
VWOOM
...LITTLE WET-BEHIND-THE-EARS—!!
...NO ONE USES SENIORITY SYSTEMS ANYMORE.
SLASH

NO
...

N-
NO
...

I DON'T
WANT
TO...GO
YET...

THUD

YOU K-
KILLED
HIM...?!

BUT HE'S
ONE OF YOU!
HOW COULD
YOU?!

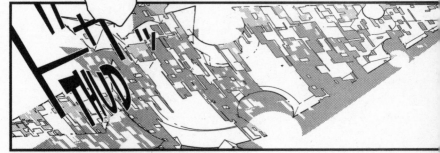

FSHH

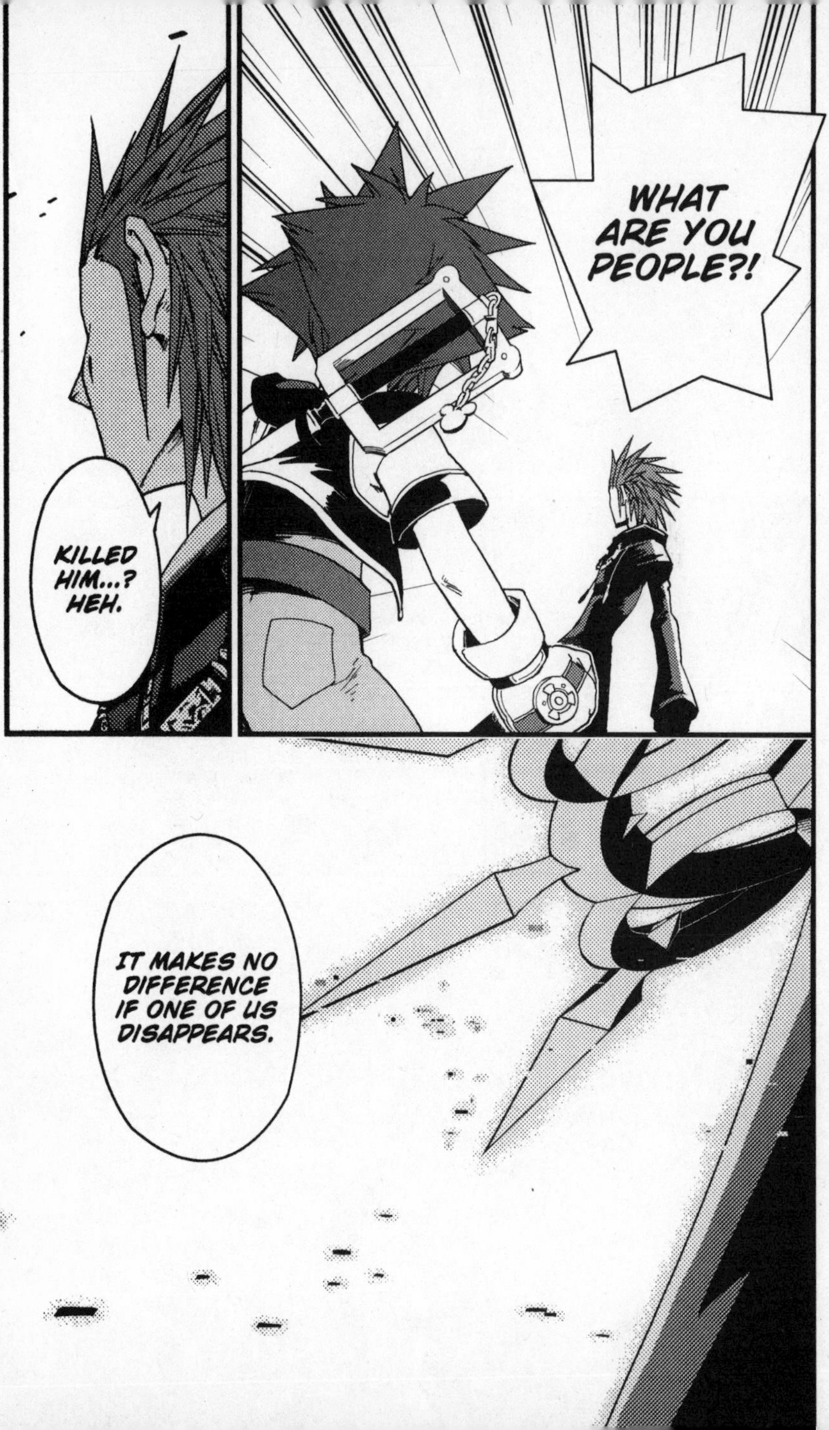
WHAT ARE YOU PEOPLE?!
KILLED HIM...? HEH.
IT MAKES NO DIFFERENCE IF ONE OF US DISAPPEARS.

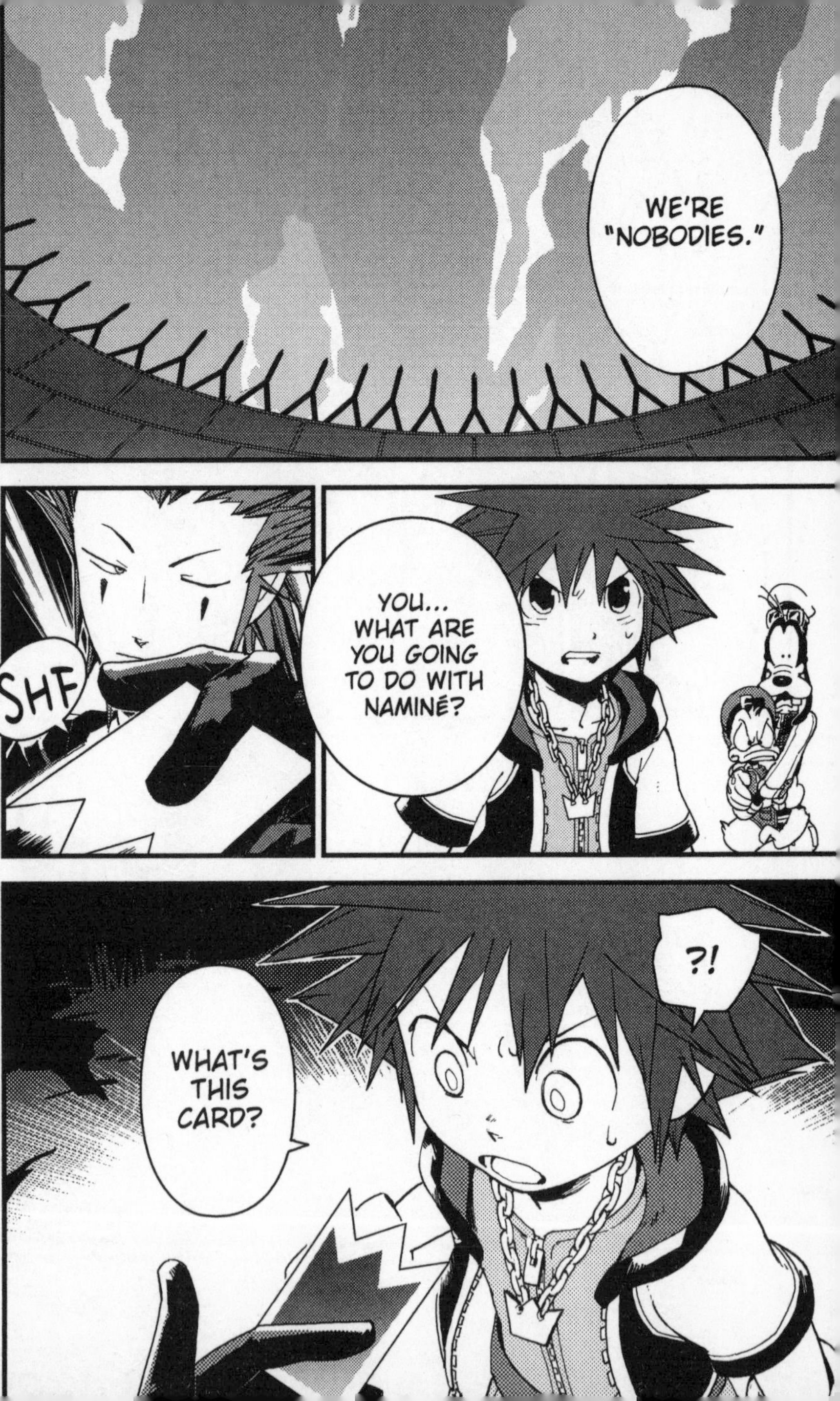
WE'RE "NOBODIES."
YOU... WHAT ARE YOU GOING TO DO WITH NAMINÉ?
SHF
?!
WHAT'S THIS CARD?

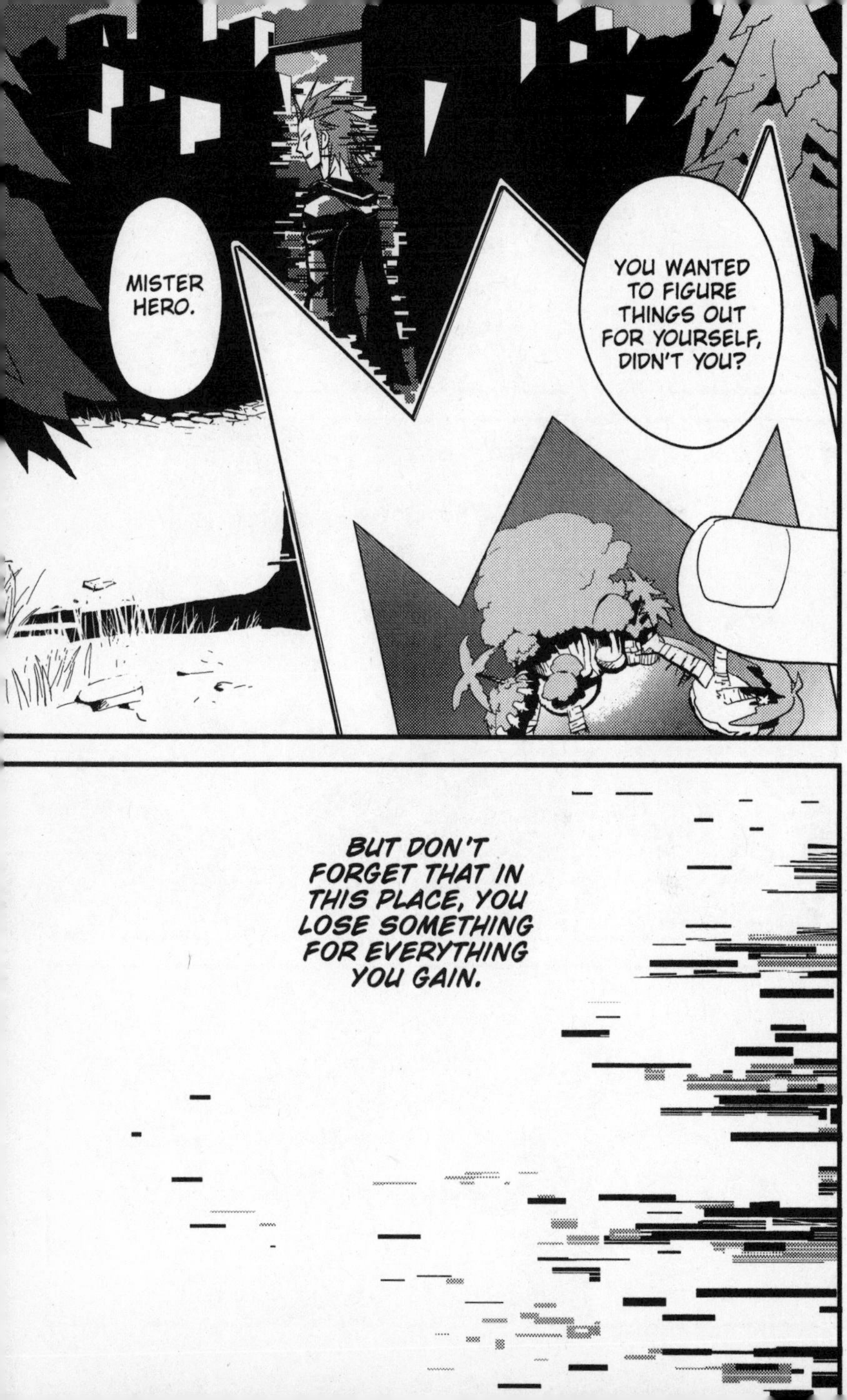
YOU WANTED TO FIGURE THINGS OUT FOR YOURSELF, DIDN'T YOU?
MISTER HERO.
BUT DON'T FORGET THAT IN THIS PLACE, YOU LOSE SOMETHING FOR EVERYTHING YOU GAIN.

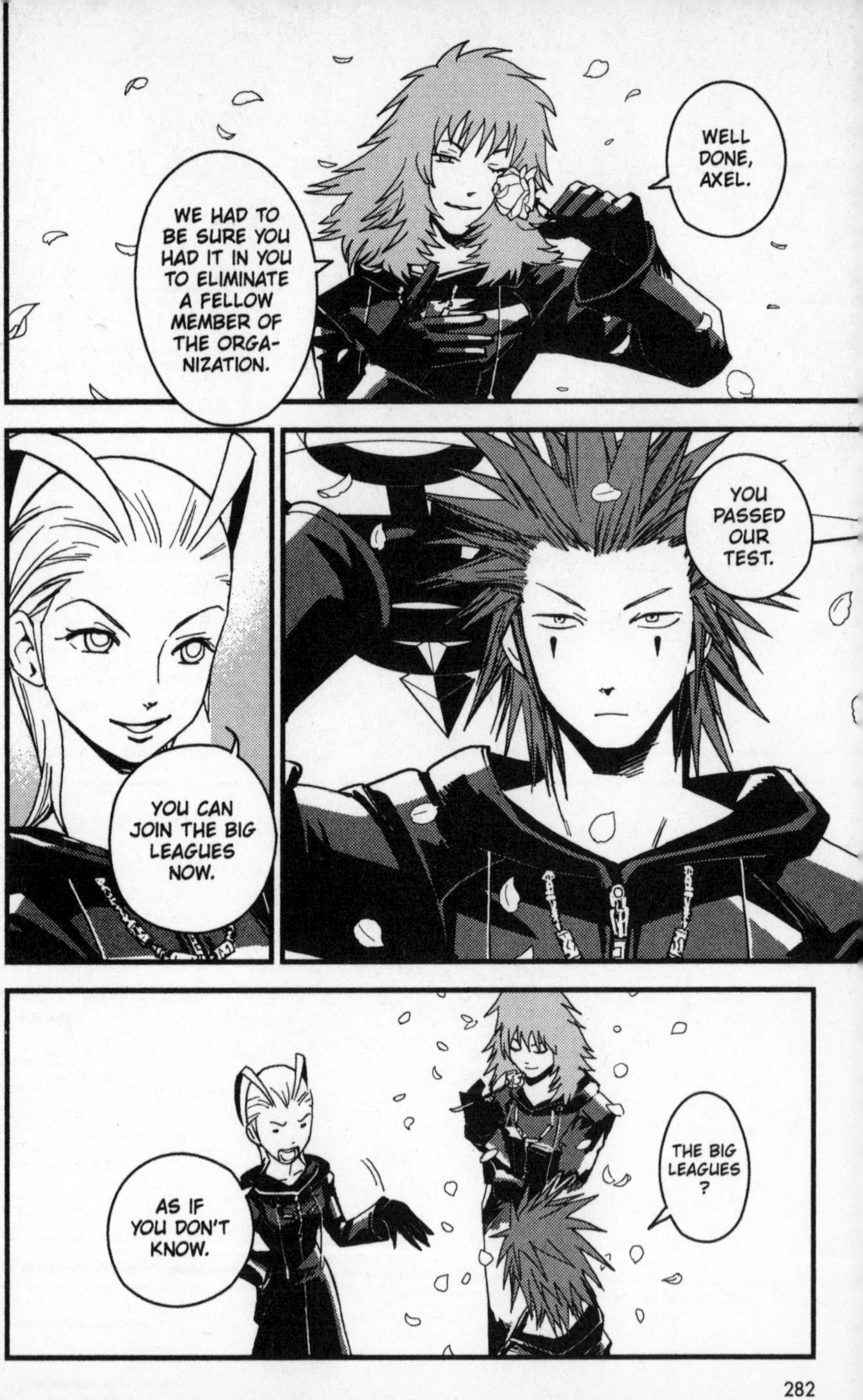
WELL DONE, AXEL.
WE HAD TO BE SURE YOU HAD IT IN YOU TO ELIMINATE A FELLOW MEMBER OF THE ORGA-NIZATION.
YOU PASSED OUR TEST.
YOU CAN JOIN THE BIG LEAGUES NOW.
THE BIG LEAGUES?
AS IF YOU DON'T KNOW.

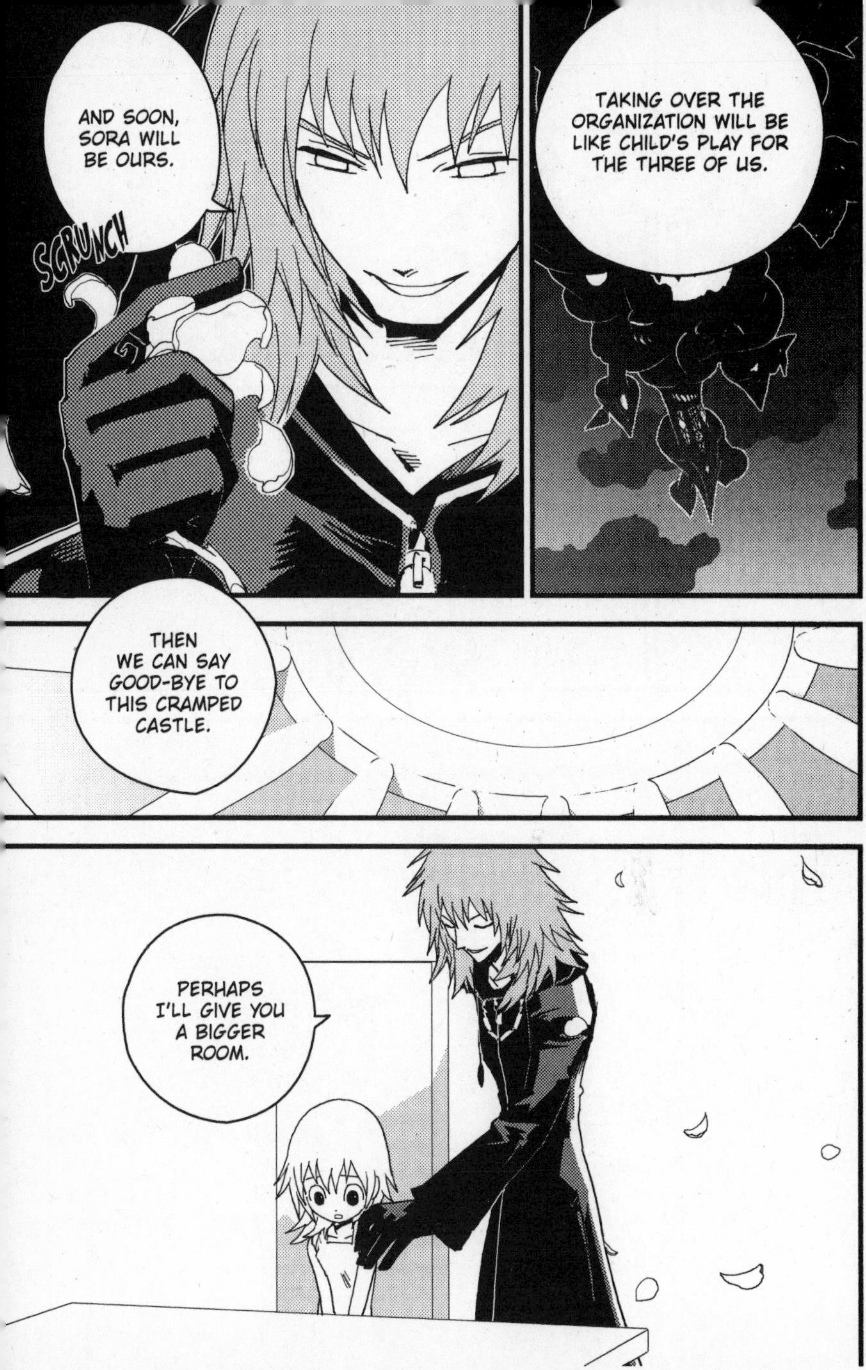
TAKING OVER THE ORGANIZATION WILL BE LIKE CHILD'S PLAY FOR THE THREE OF US.
AND SOON, SORA WILL BE OURS.
SCRUNCH
THEN WE CAN SAY GOOD-BYE TO THIS CRAMPED CASTLE.
PERHAPS I'LL GIVE YOU A BIGGER ROOM.

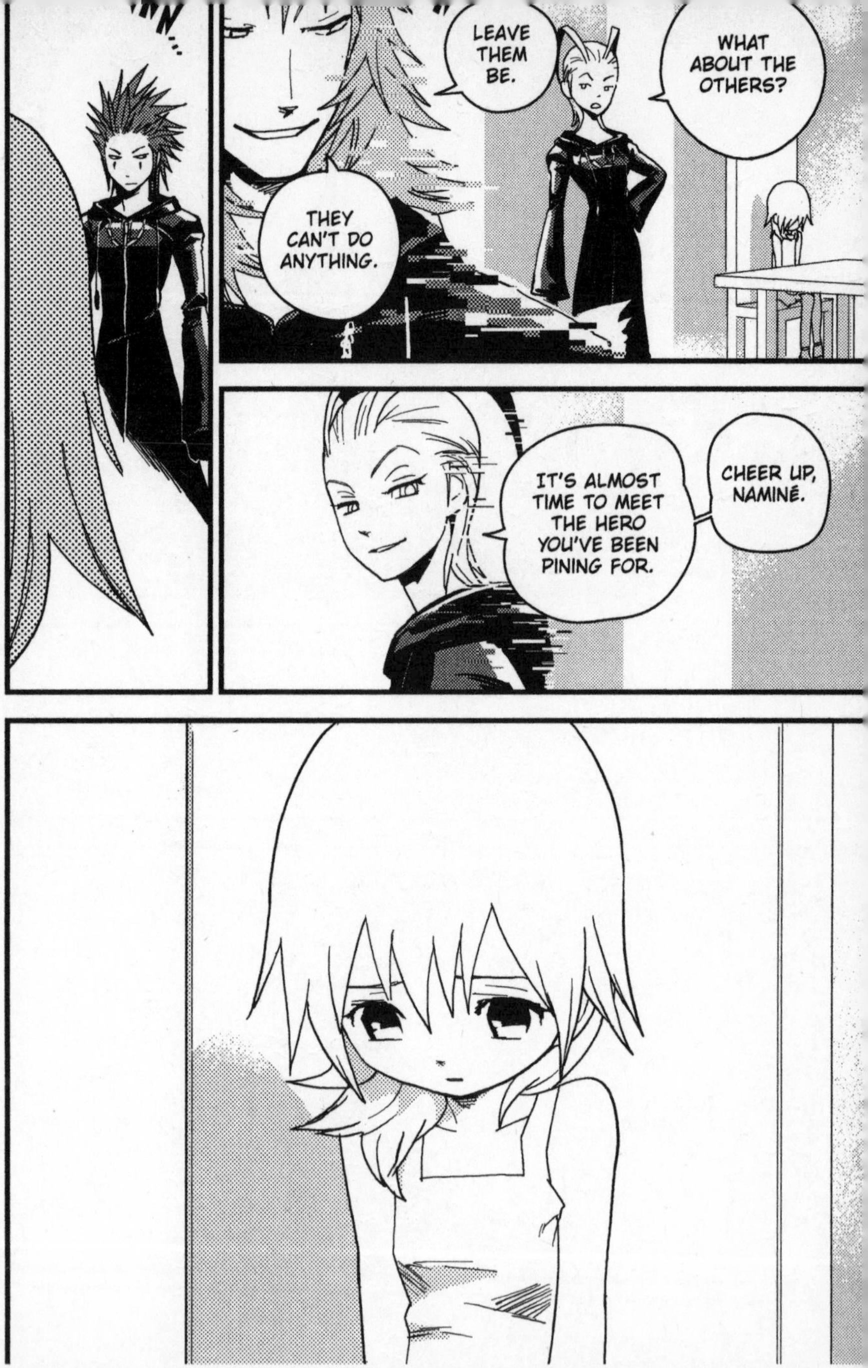
WHAT ABOUT THE OTHERS?
LEAVE THEM BE.
THEY CAN'T DO ANYTHING.
CHEER UP, NAMINÉ.
IT'S ALMOST TIME TO MEET THE HERO YOU'VE BEEN PINING FOR.

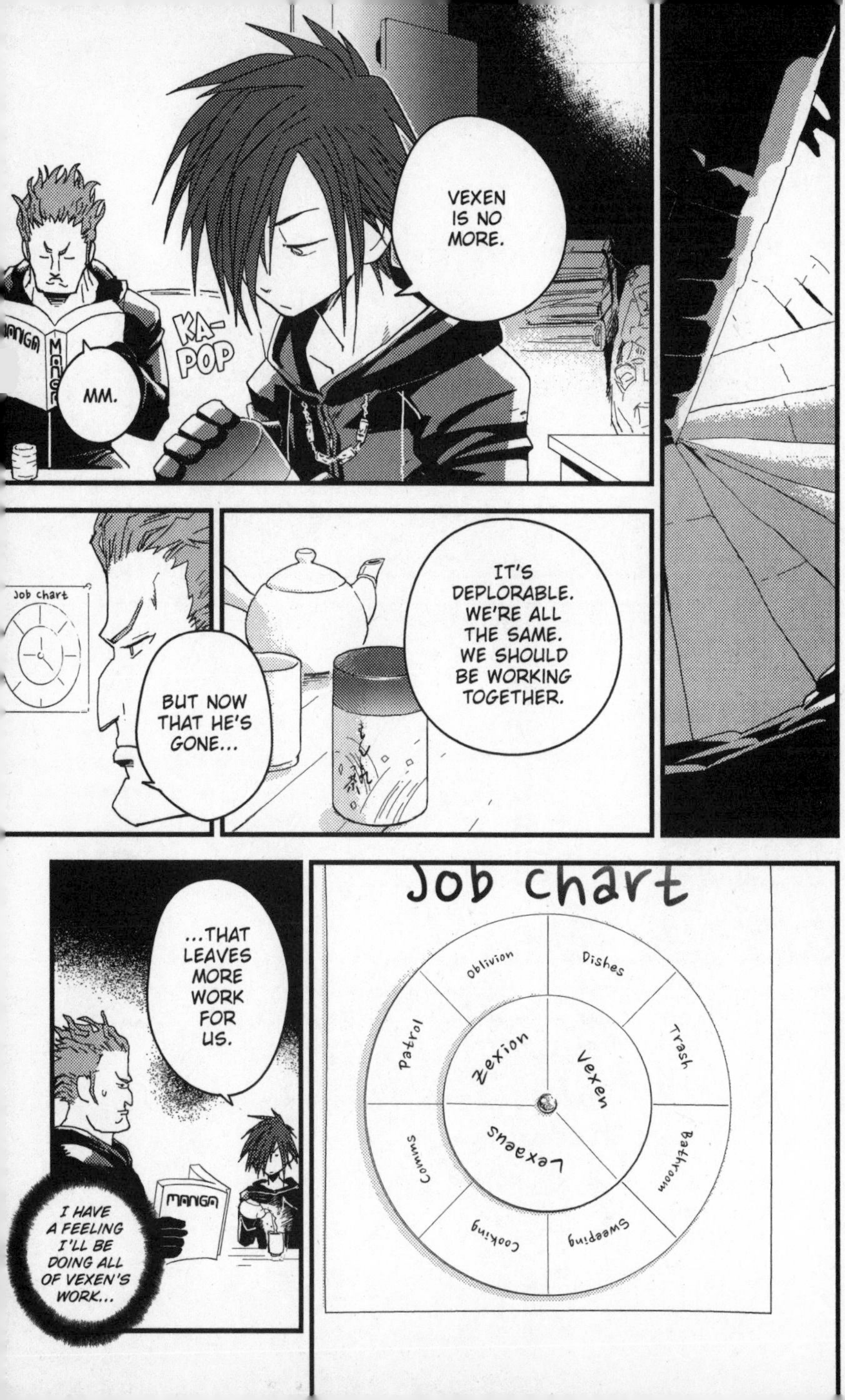
VEXEN IS NO MORE.
KA-POP
MANGA
MM.
IT'S DEPLORABLE. WE'RE ALL THE SAME. WE SHOULD BE WORKING TOGETHER.
BUT NOW THAT HE'S GONE...
Job chart
Job chart
Dishes
Trash
Bathroom
Sweeping
Cooking
Comms
Patrol
Oblivion
Vexen
Lexaeus
Zexion
...THAT LEAVES MORE WORK FOR US.
MANGA
I HAVE A FEELING I'LL BE DOING ALL OF VEXEN'S WORK...

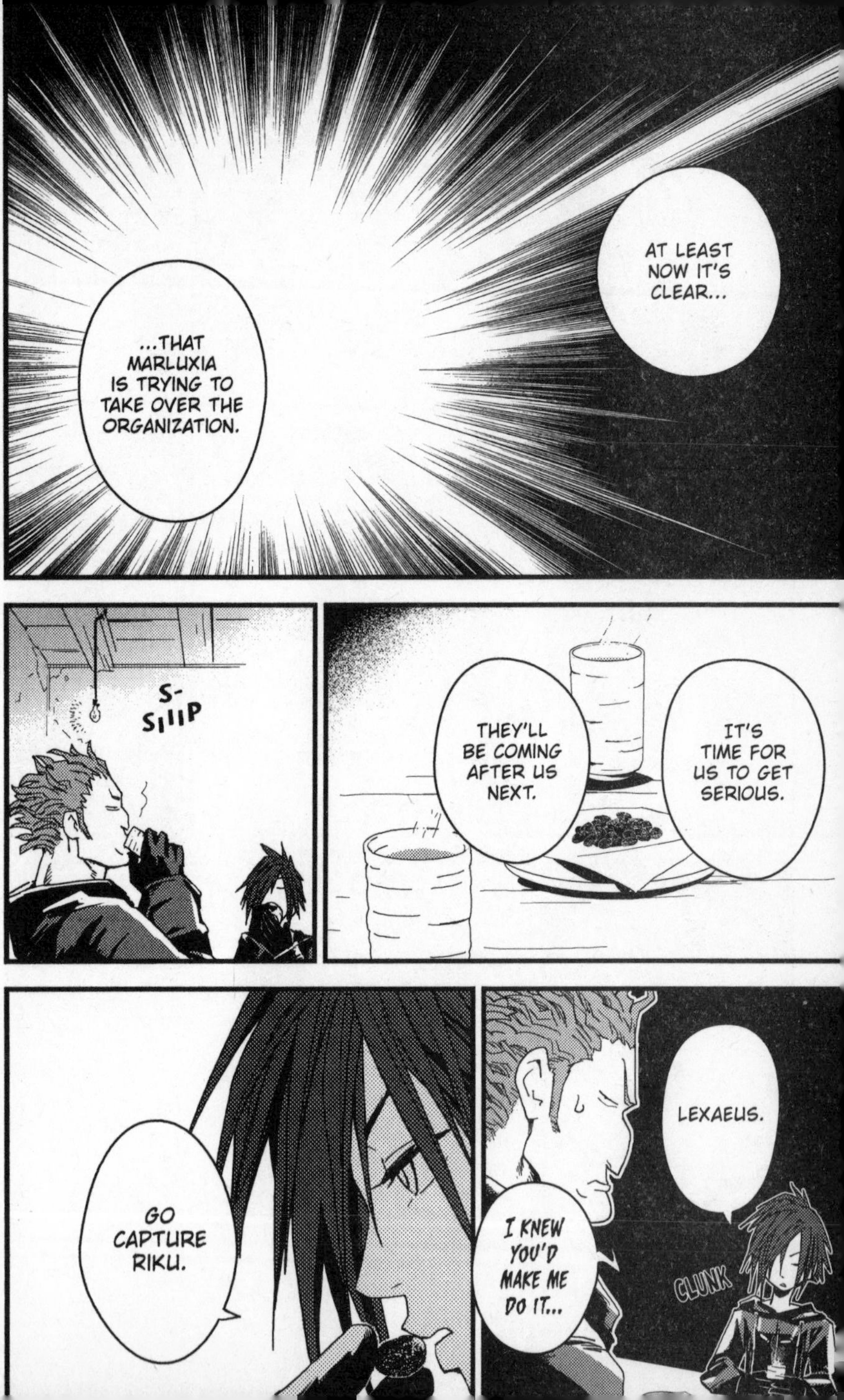
AT LEAST NOW IT'S CLEAR...
...THAT MARLUXIA IS TRYING TO TAKE OVER THE ORGANIZATION.
IT'S TIME FOR US TO GET SERIOUS.
THEY'LL BE COMING AFTER US NEXT.
S-SIIIP
LEXAEUS.
I KNEW YOU'D MAKE ME DO IT...
CLUNK
GO CAPTURE RIKU.

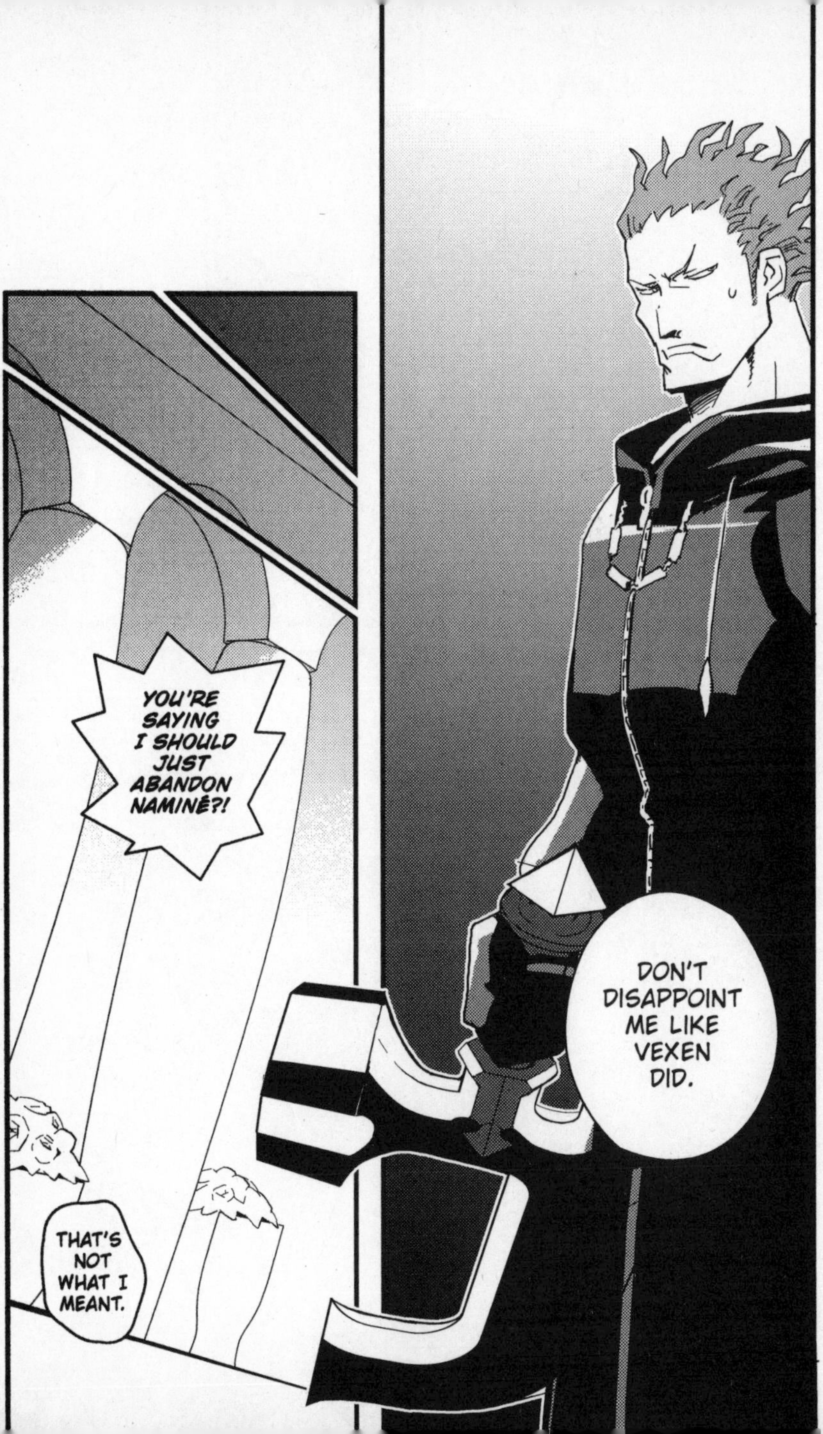
DON'T DISAPPOINT ME LIKE VEXEN DID.
YOU'RE SAYING I SHOULD JUST ABANDON NAMINÉ?!
THAT'S NOT WHAT I MEANT.

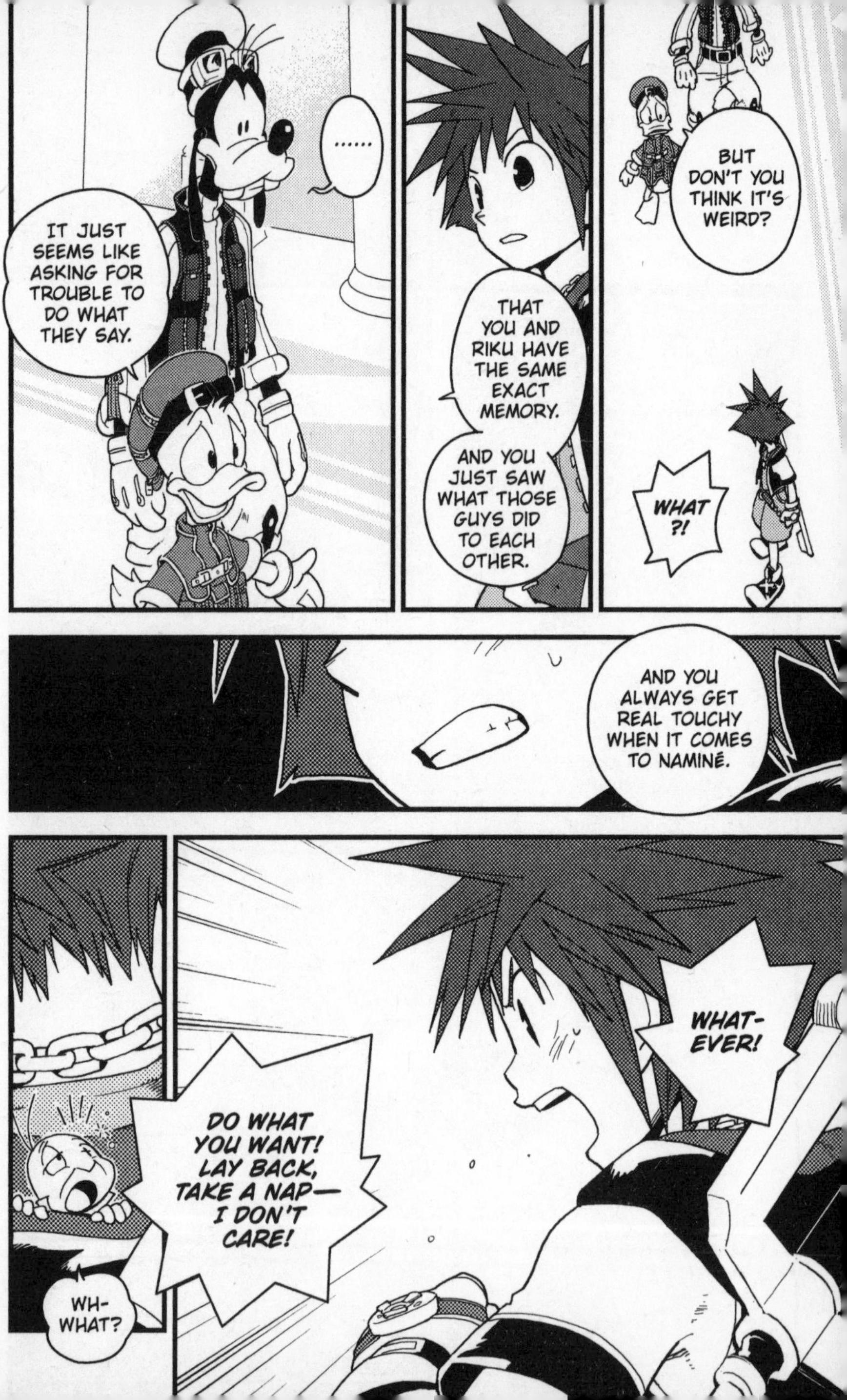
BUT DON'T YOU THINK IT'S WEIRD?
WHAT?!
THAT YOU AND RIKU HAVE THE SAME EXACT MEMORY.
AND YOU JUST SAW WHAT THOSE GUYS DID TO EACH OTHER.
......
IT JUST SEEMS LIKE ASKING FOR TROUBLE TO DO WHAT THEY SAY.
AND YOU ALWAYS GET REAL TOUCHY WHEN IT COMES TO NAMINÉ.
WHAT-EVER!
DO WHAT YOU WANT! LAY BACK, TAKE A NAP— I DON'T CARE!
WH- WHAT?

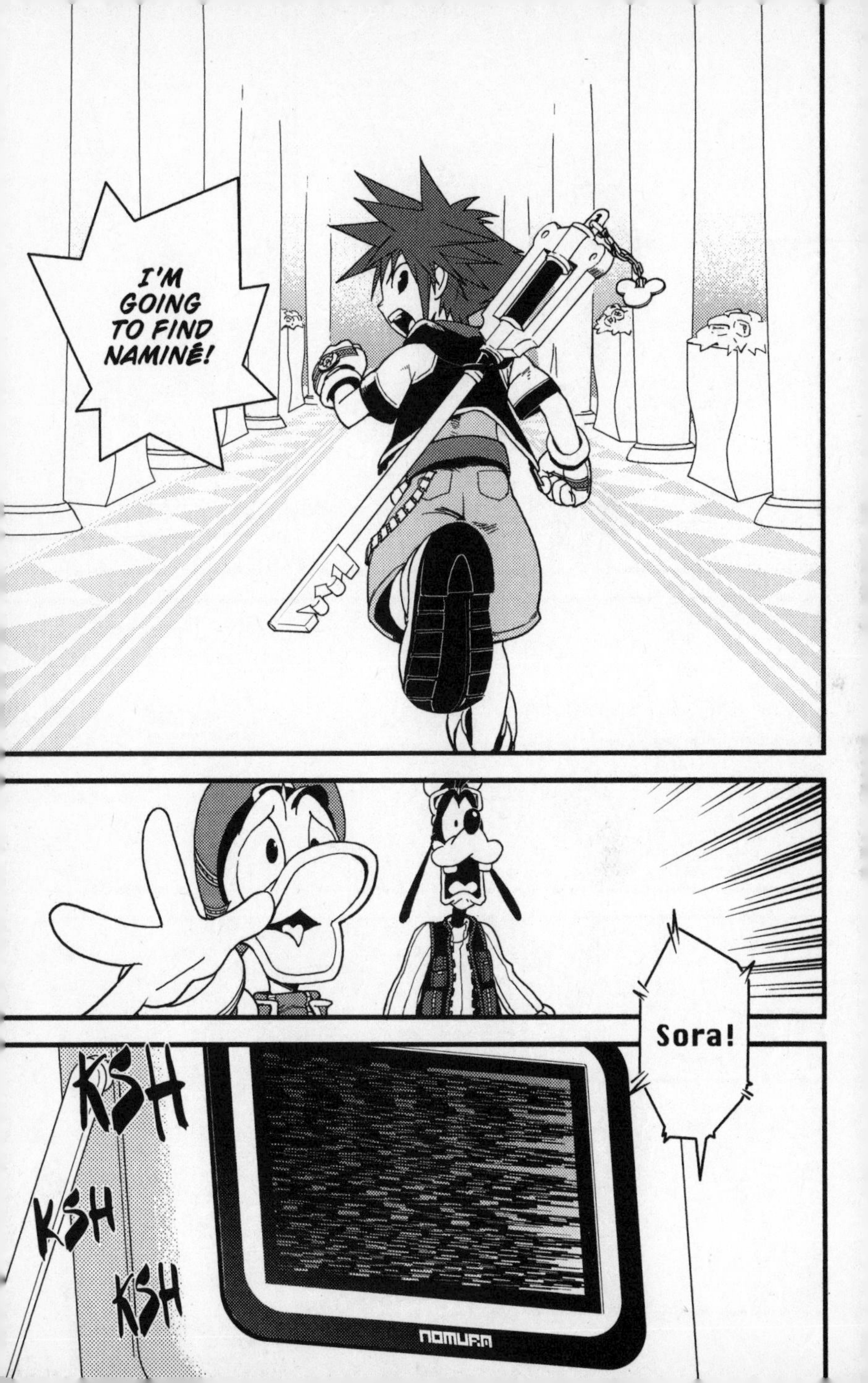
I'M GOING TO FIND NAMINÉ!
Sora!
KSH
KSH
KSH
NOMURA

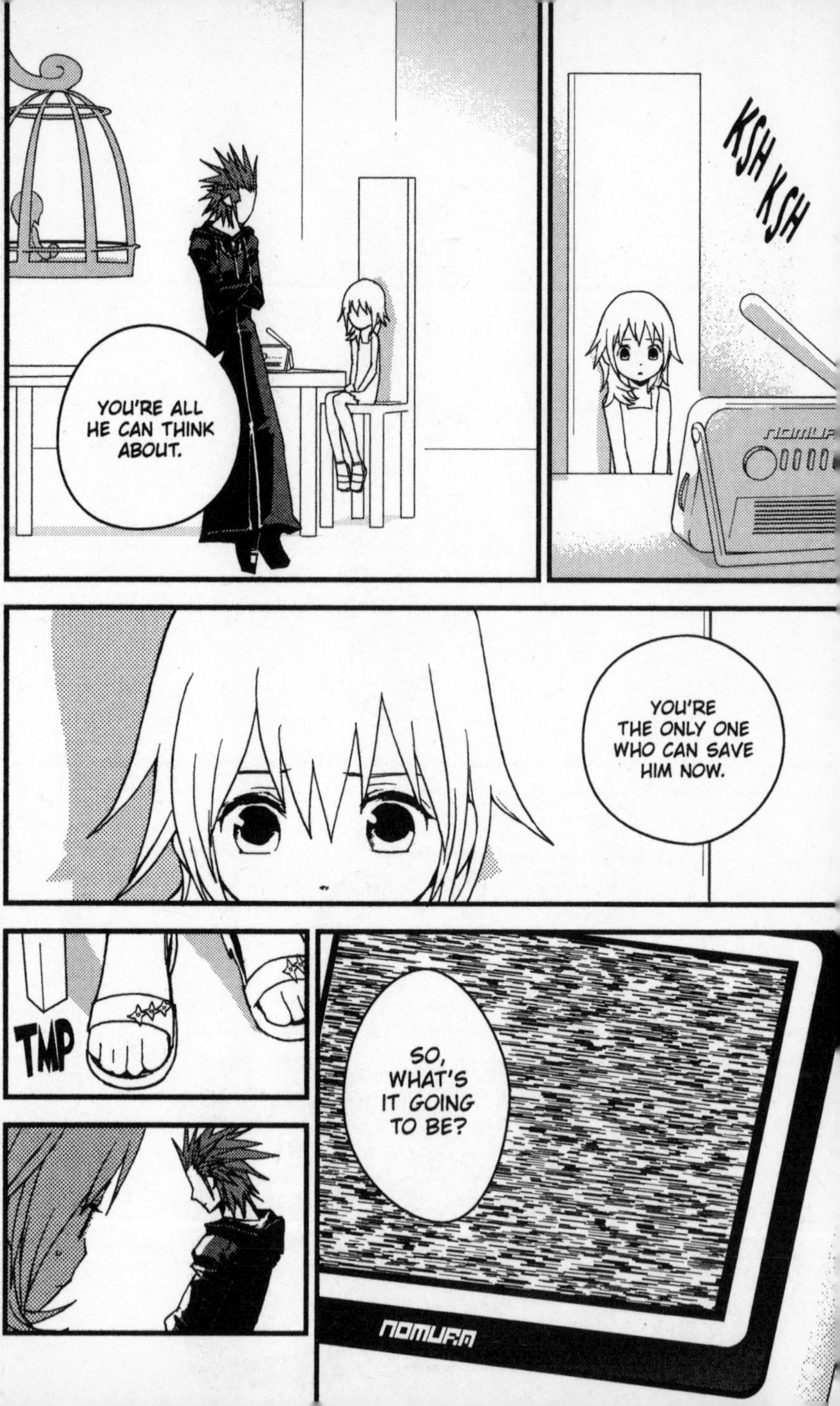
KSH KSH
YOU'RE ALL HE CAN THINK ABOUT.
YOU'RE THE ONLY ONE WHO CAN SAVE HIM NOW.
SO, WHAT'S IT GOING TO BE?
NOMURA
TMP

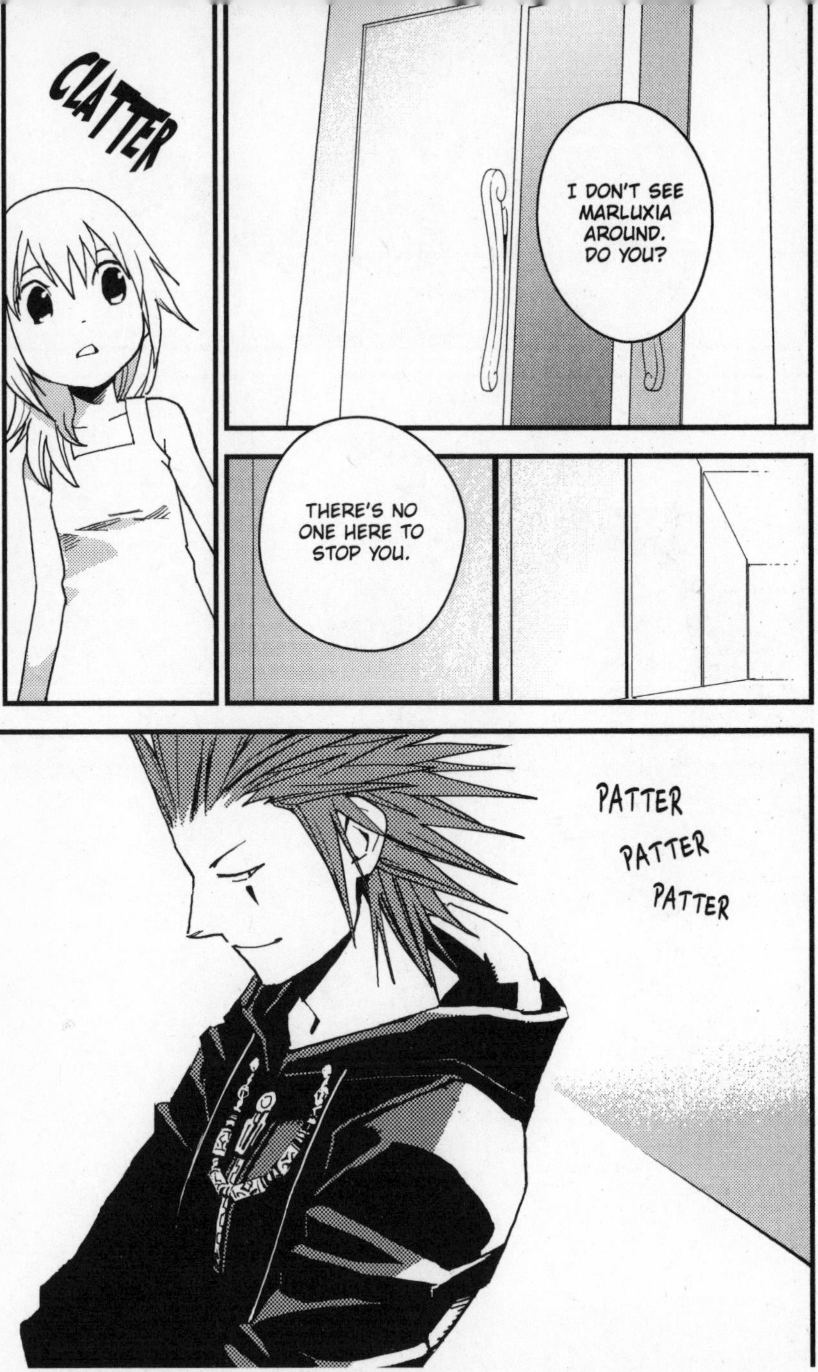
I DON'T SEE MARLUXIA AROUND. DO YOU?
THERE'S NO ONE HERE TO STOP YOU.
CLATTER
PATTER
PATTER
PATTER

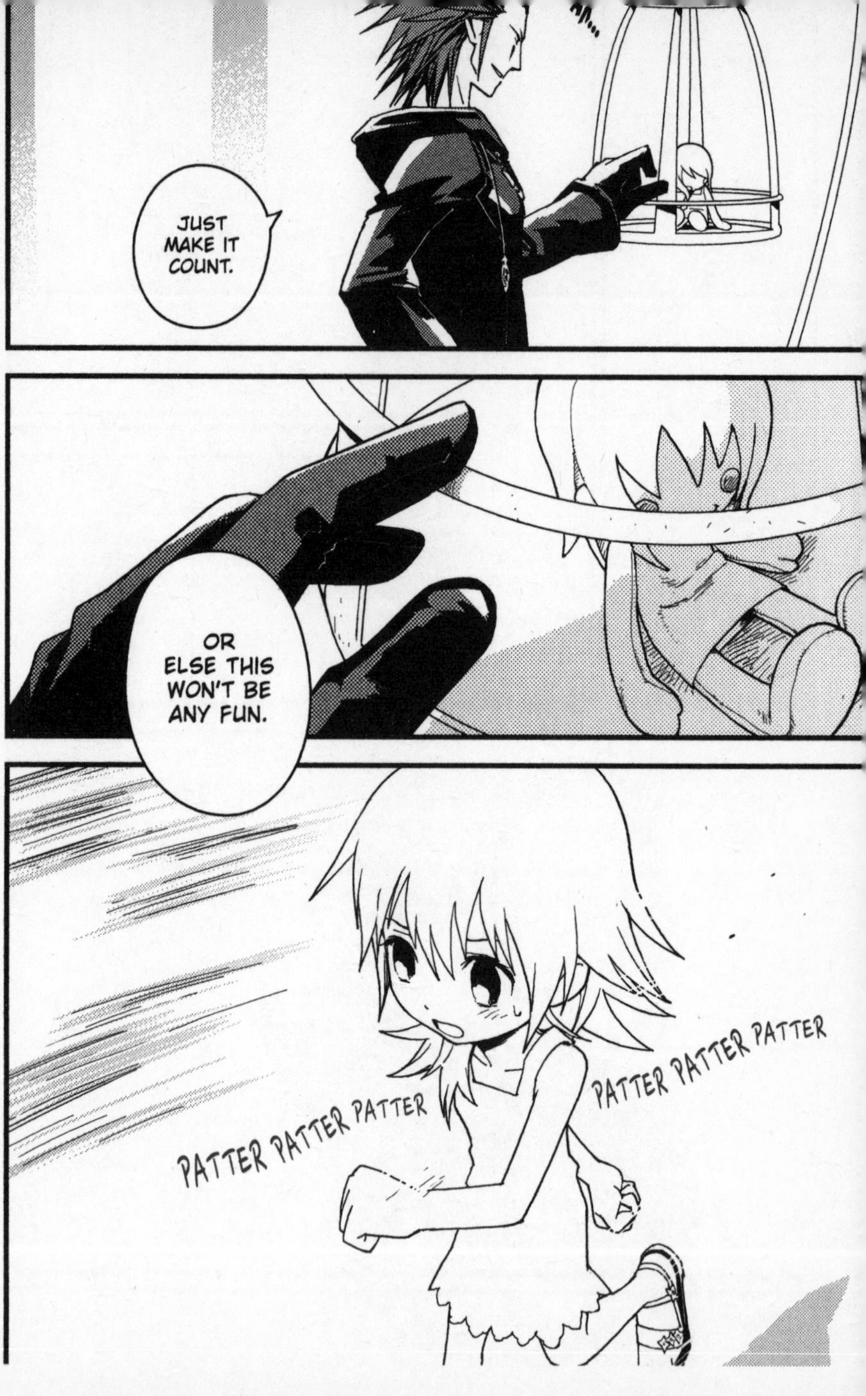
JUST MAKE IT COUNT.
OR ELSE THIS WON'T BE ANY FUN.
PATTER PATTER PATTER
PATTER PATTER PATTER

I WAS ALONE FOR SO LONG...

...I JUST COULDN'T BEAR IT ANYMORE.

THAT'S WHY I...

I'M SO SORRY, SORA.

# Card:10
# Scattered Hearts

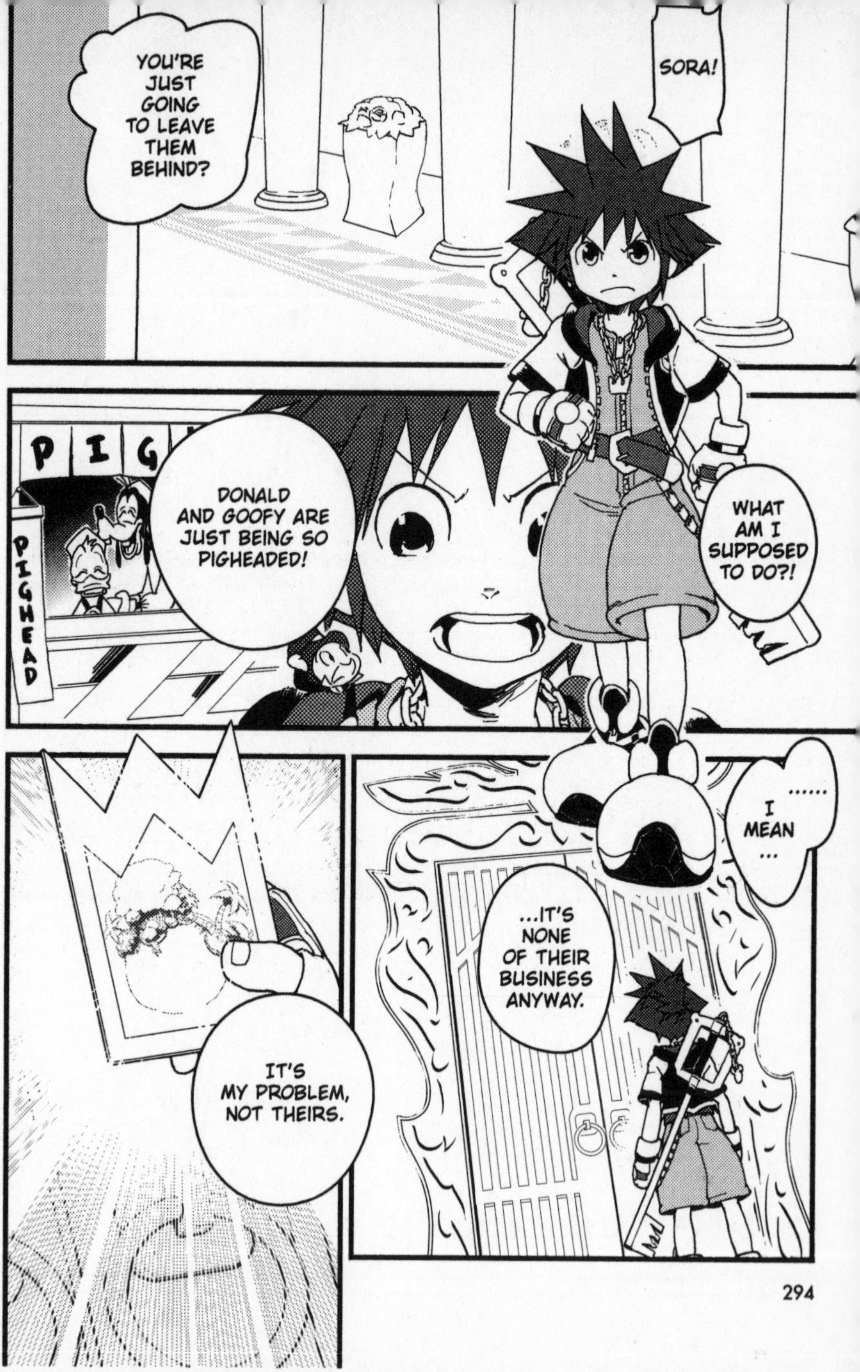
SORA!
YOU'RE JUST GOING TO LEAVE THEM BEHIND?
WHAT AM I SUPPOSED TO DO?!
DONALD AND GOOFY ARE JUST BEING SO PIGHEADED!
PIG
PIGHEAD
...... I MEAN ...
...IT'S NONE OF THEIR BUSINESS ANYWAY.
IT'S MY PROBLEM, NOT THEIRS.

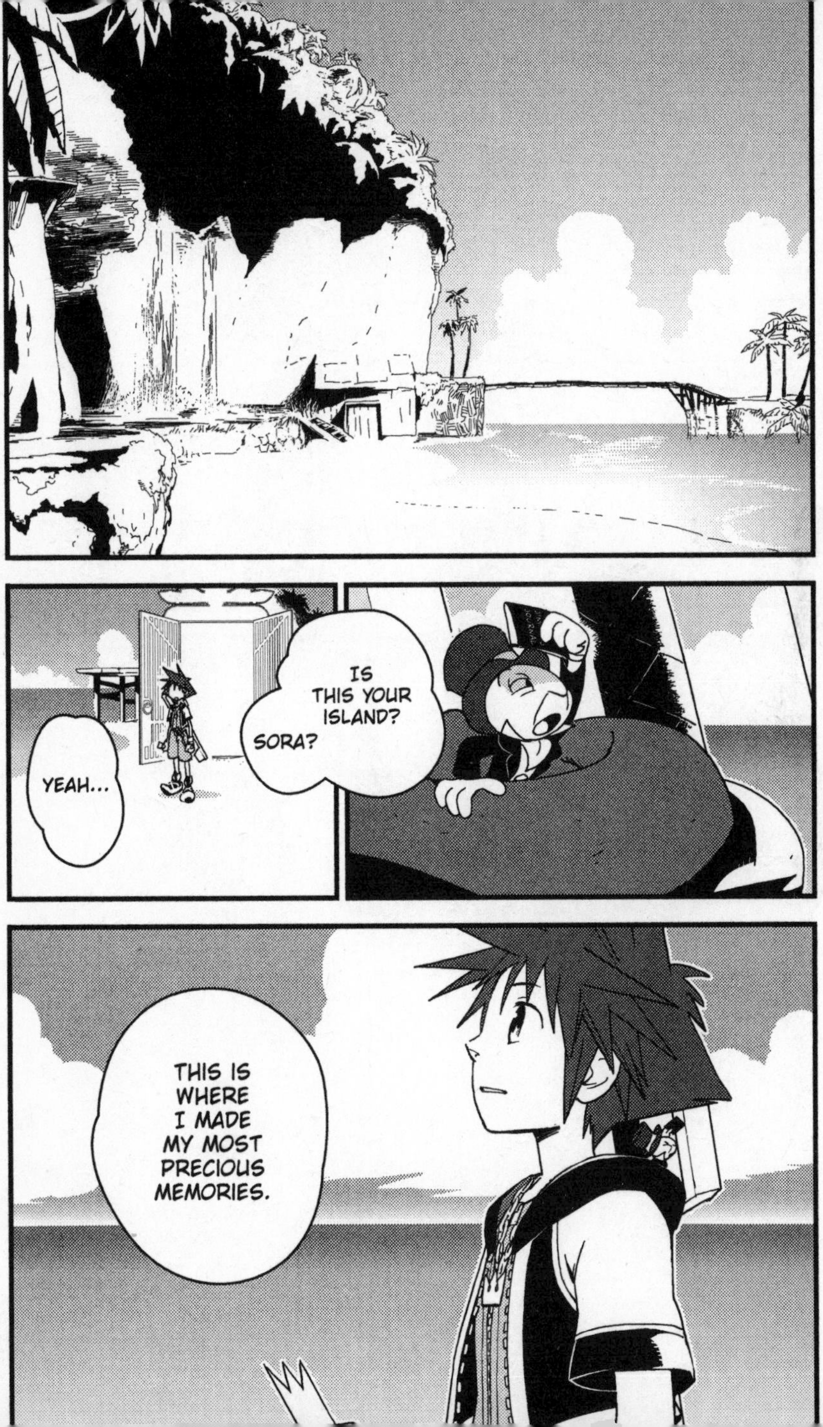
IS THIS YOUR ISLAND? SORA?
YEAH...
THIS IS WHERE I MADE MY MOST PRECIOUS MEMORIES.

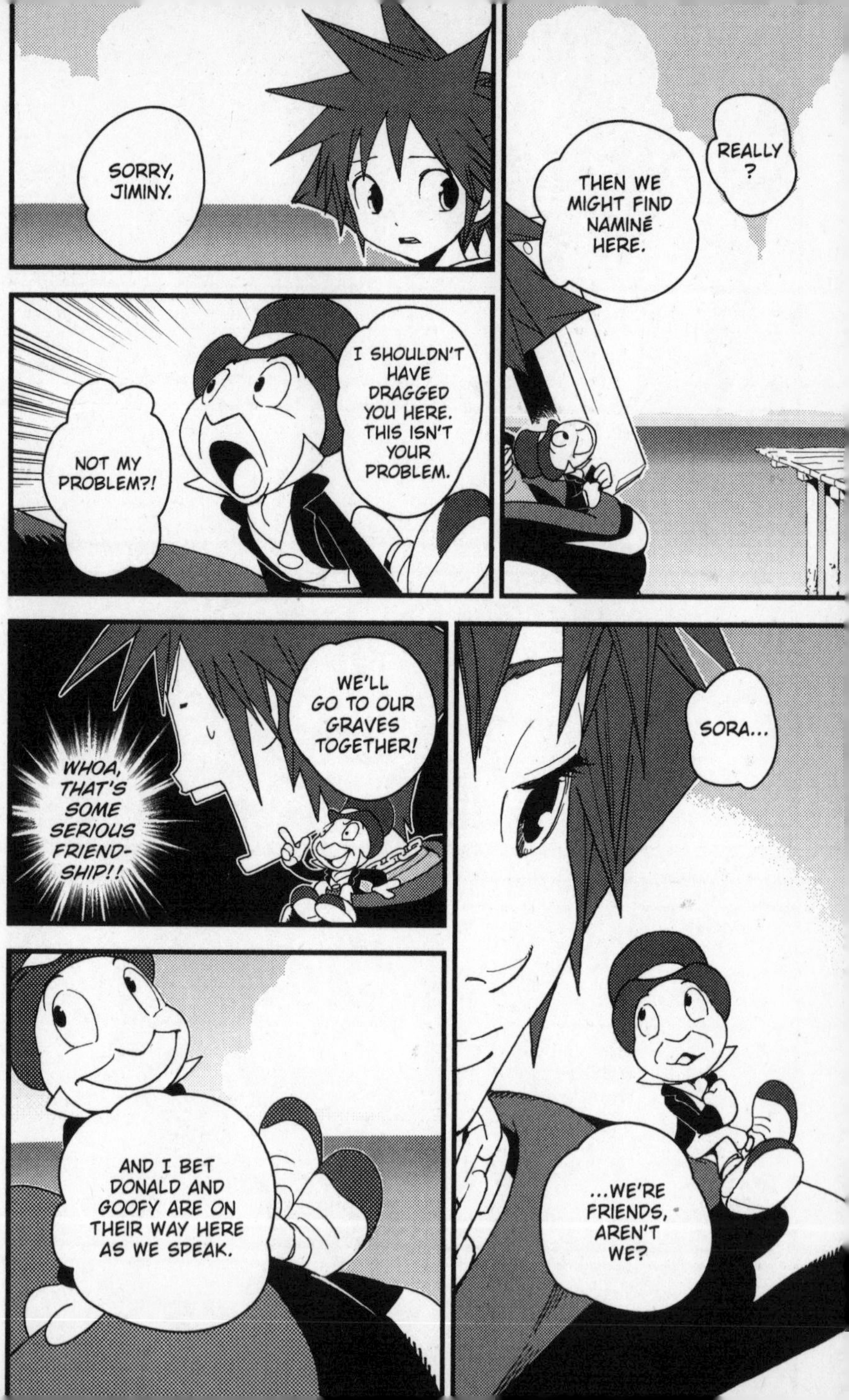
REALLY?
THEN WE MIGHT FIND NAMINÉ HERE.
SORRY, JIMINY.
I SHOULDN'T HAVE DRAGGED YOU HERE. THIS ISN'T YOUR PROBLEM.
NOT MY PROBLEM?!
SORA...
...WE'RE FRIENDS, AREN'T WE?
WE'LL GO TO OUR GRAVES TOGETHER!
WHOA, THAT'S SOME SERIOUS FRIEND-SHIP!!
AND I BET DONALD AND GOOFY ARE ON THEIR WAY HERE AS WE SPEAK.

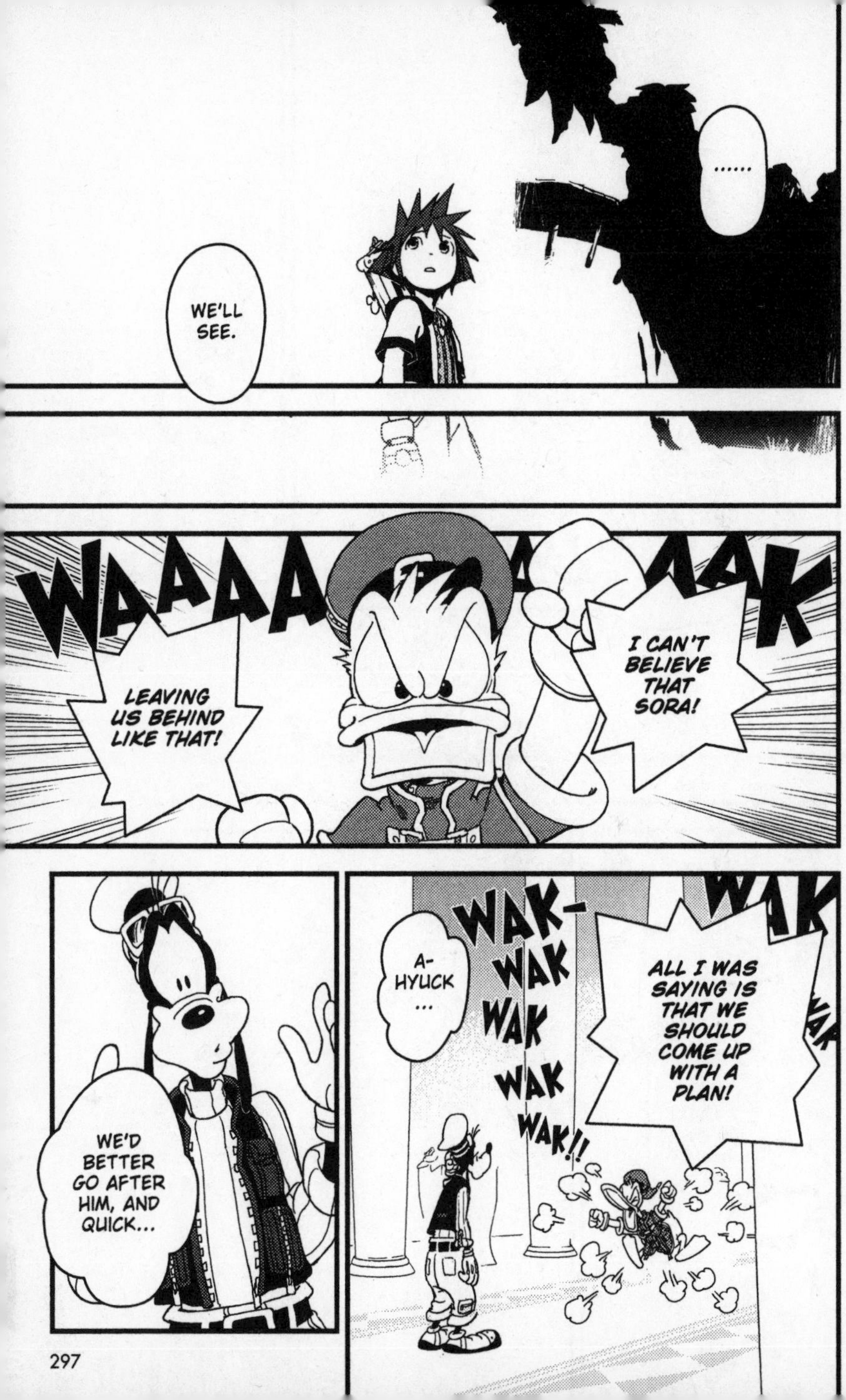
......
WE'LL SEE.
WAAAA AAAK
I CAN'T BELIEVE THAT SORA!
LEAVING US BEHIND LIKE THAT!
WAK
ALL I WAS SAYING IS THAT WE SHOULD COME UP WITH A PLAN!
WAK
WAK-WAK WAK WAK WAK!!
A-HYUCK ...
WE'D BETTER GO AFTER HIM, AND QUICK...

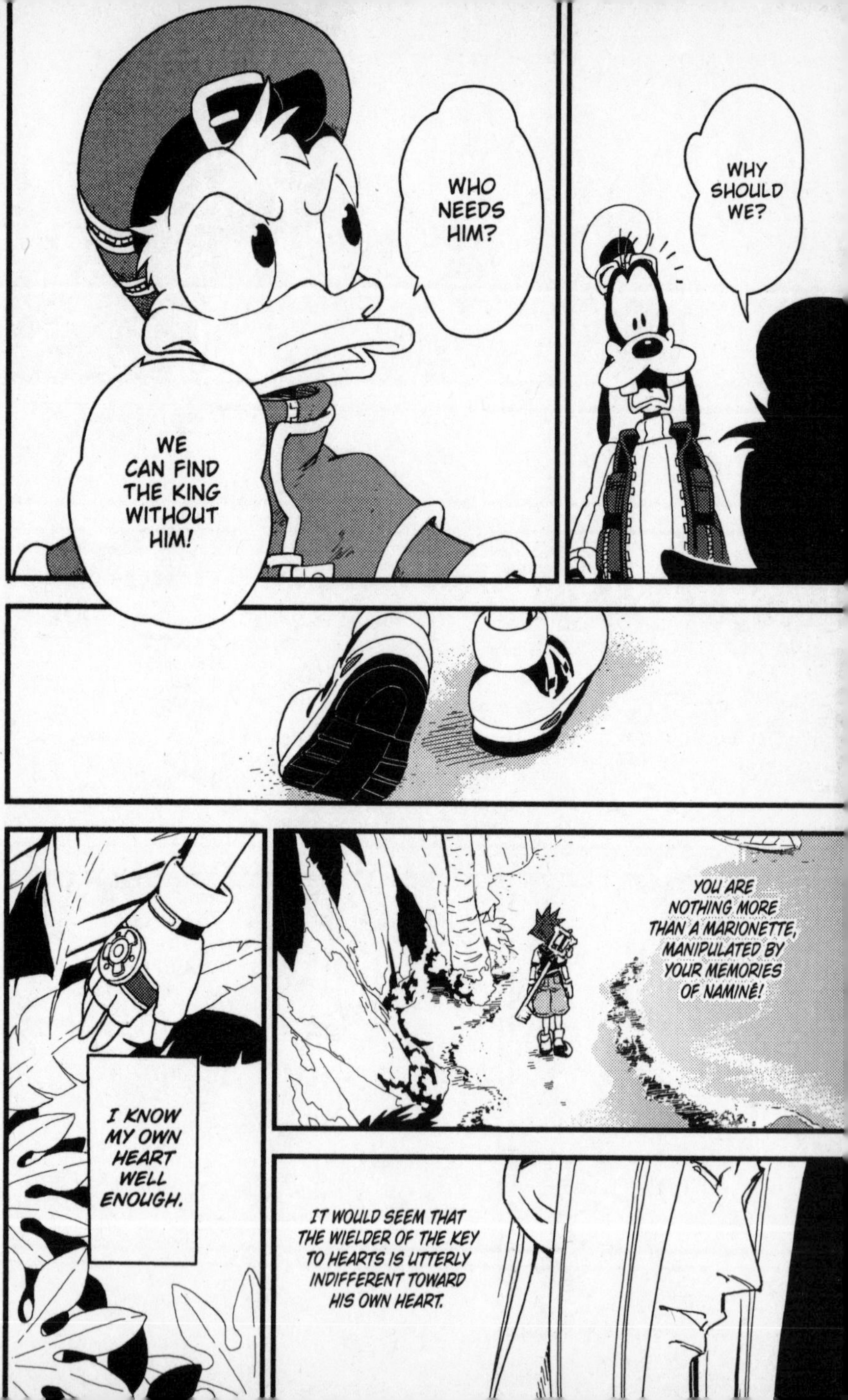
WHY SHOULD WE?
WHO NEEDS HIM?
WE CAN FIND THE KING WITHOUT HIM!
YOU ARE NOTHING MORE THAN A MARIONETTE, MANIPULATED BY YOUR MEMORIES OF NAMINÉ!
IT WOULD SEEM THAT THE WIELDER OF THE KEY TO HEARTS IS UTTERLY INDIFFERENT TOWARD HIS OWN HEART.
I KNOW MY OWN HEART WELL ENOUGH.

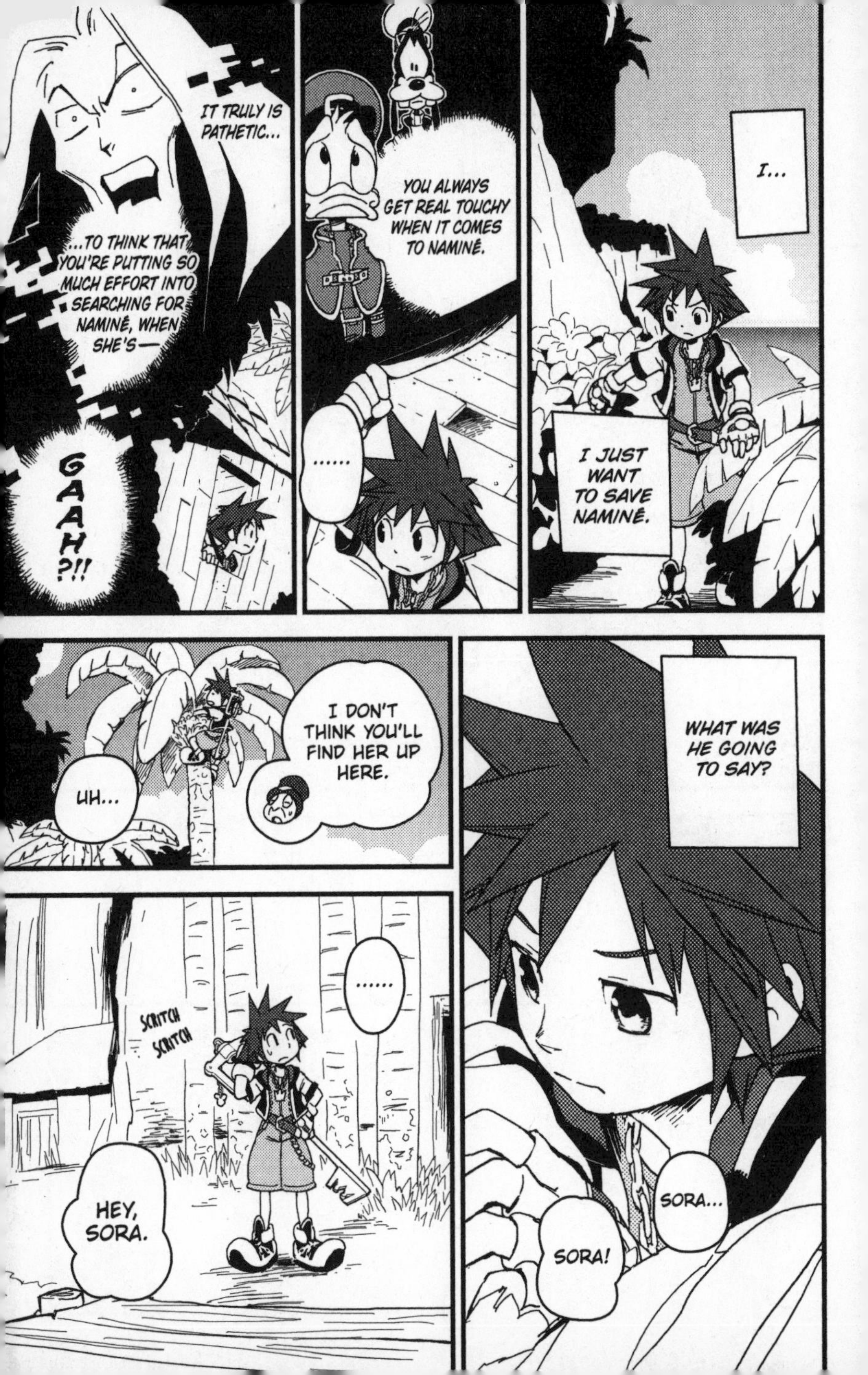
I...
I JUST WANT TO SAVE NAMINÉ.
YOU ALWAYS GET REAL TOUCHY WHEN IT COMES TO NAMINÉ.
......
IT TRULY IS PATHETIC...
...TO THINK THAT YOU'RE PUTTING SO MUCH EFFORT INTO SEARCHING FOR NAMINÉ, WHEN SHE'S—
GAAH?!!
WHAT WAS HE GOING TO SAY?
SORA...
SORA!
I DON'T THINK YOU'LL FIND HER UP HERE.
UH...
......
SCRITCH
SCRITCH
HEY, SORA.

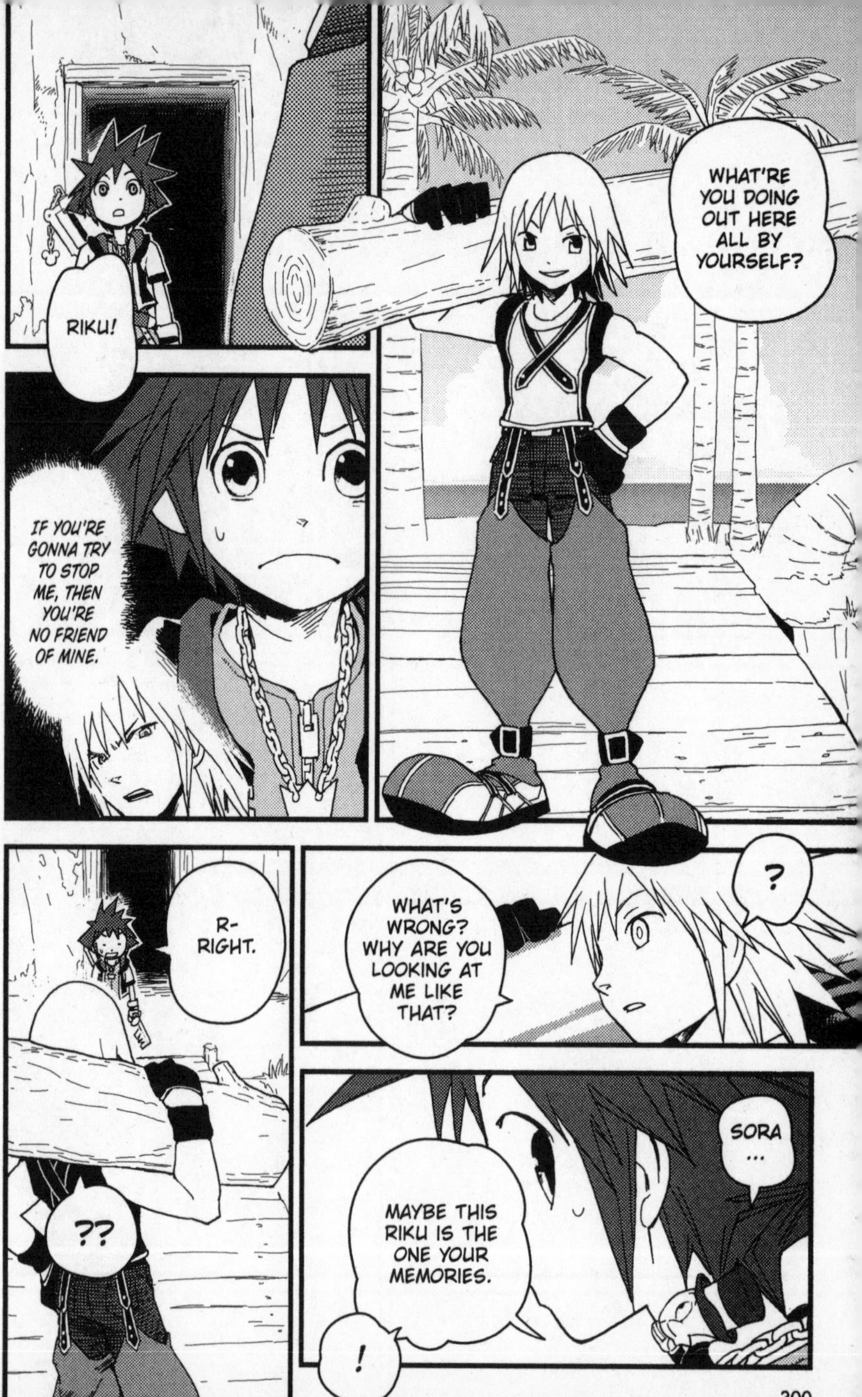
WHAT'RE YOU DOING OUT HERE ALL BY YOURSELF?
RIKU!
IF YOU'RE GONNA TRY TO STOP ME, THEN YOU'RE NO FRIEND OF MINE.
?
WHAT'S WRONG? WHY ARE YOU LOOKING AT ME LIKE THAT?
SORA ...
MAYBE THIS RIKU IS THE ONE YOUR MEMORIES.
!
R- RIGHT.
??

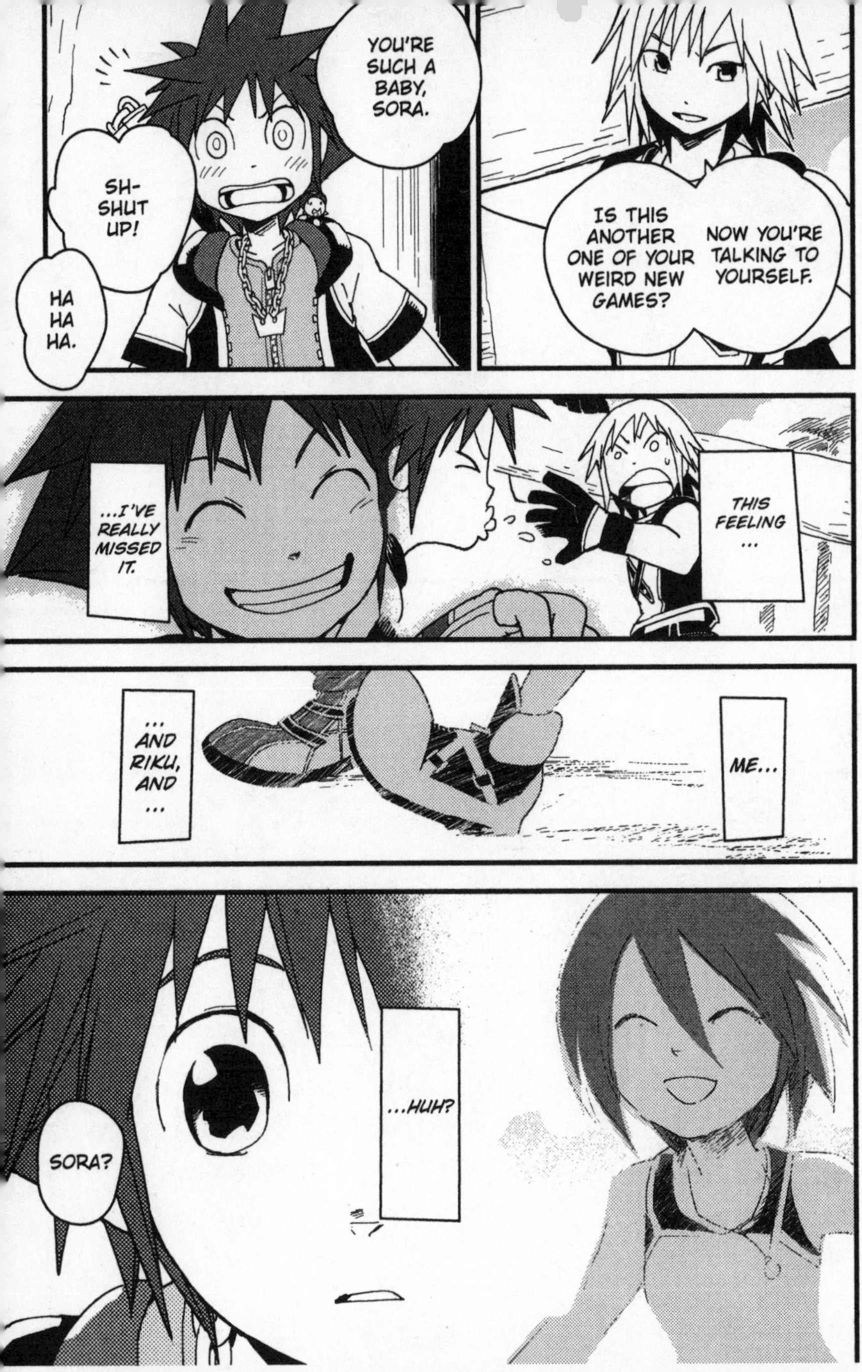
NOW YOU'RE TALKING TO YOURSELF.
IS THIS ANOTHER ONE OF YOUR WEIRD NEW GAMES?
YOU'RE SUCH A BABY, SORA.
SH-SHUT UP!
HA HA HA.
THIS FEELING ...
...I'VE REALLY MISSED IT.
ME...
... AND RIKU, AND ...
...HUH?
SORA?

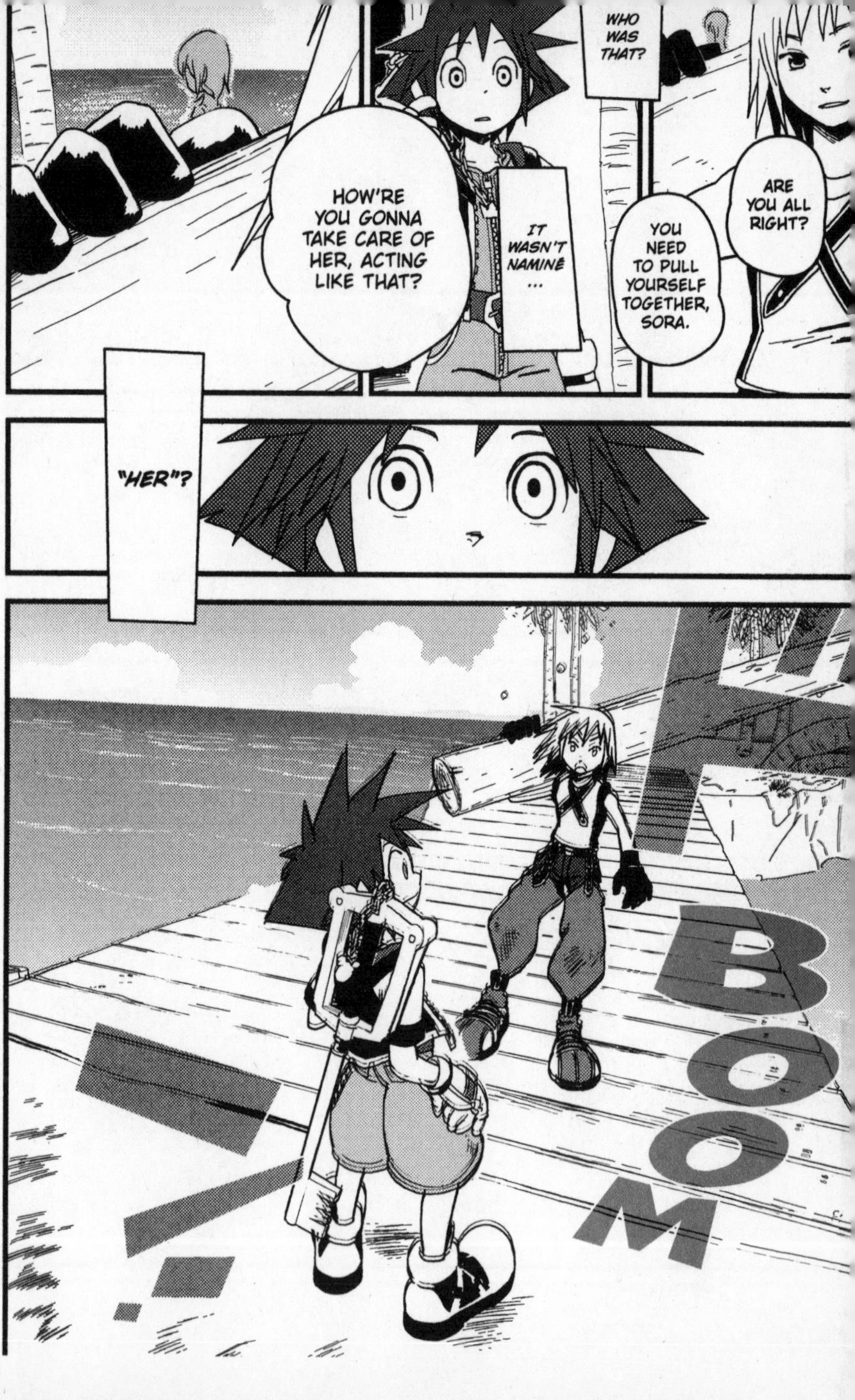
ARE YOU ALL RIGHT?
YOU NEED TO PULL YOURSELF TOGETHER, SORA.
WHO WAS THAT?
IT WASN'T NAMINÉ ...
HOW'RE YOU GONNA TAKE CARE OF HER, ACTING LIKE THAT?
"HER"?
BOOM

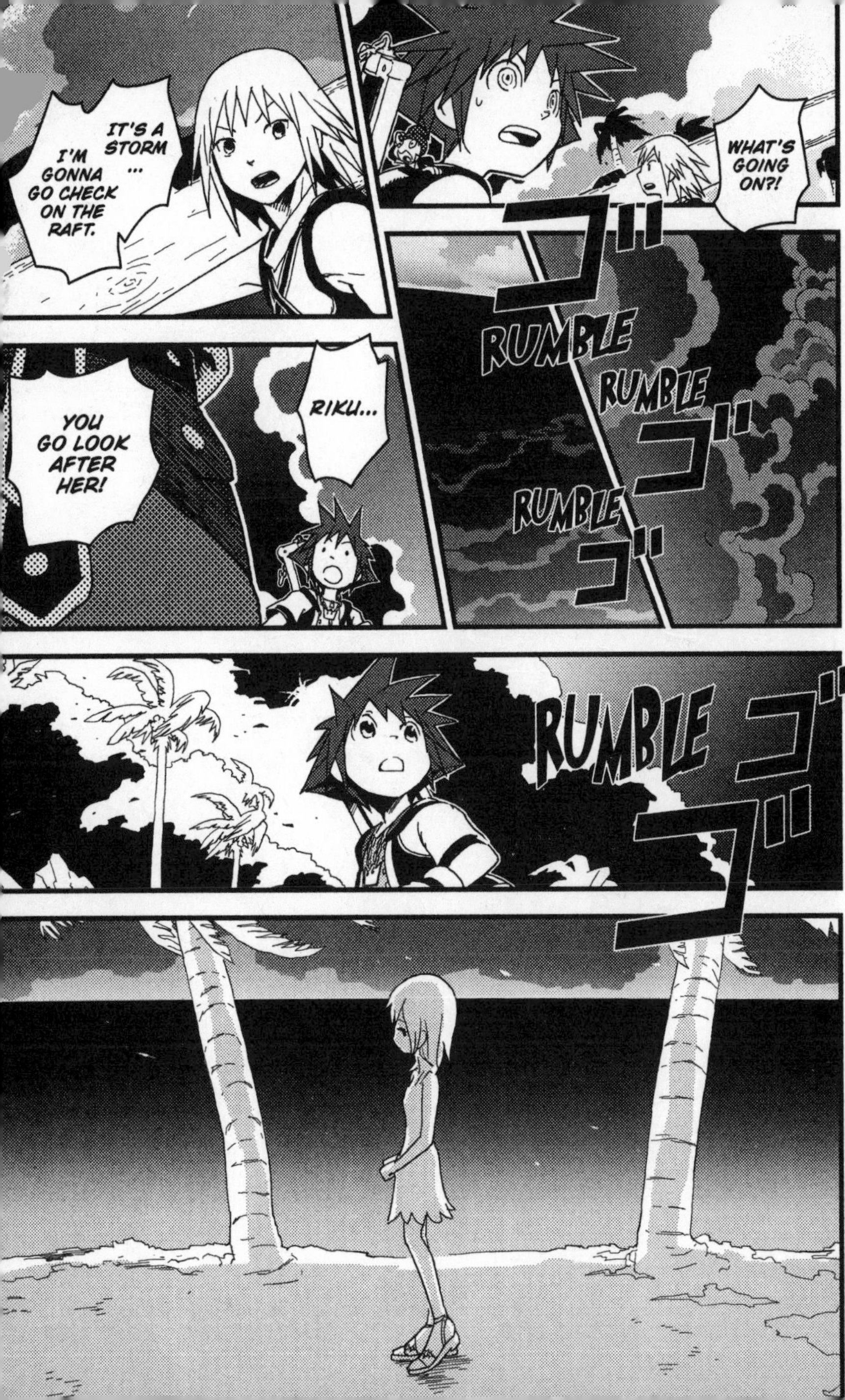
WHAT'S GOING ON?!
IT'S A STORM ...
I'M GONNA GO CHECK ON THE RAFT.
ゴ
RUMBLE
RUMBLE
ゴ
RUMBLE
ゴ
RIKU...
YOU GO LOOK AFTER HER!
ゴ
RUMBLE
ゴ
ゴ

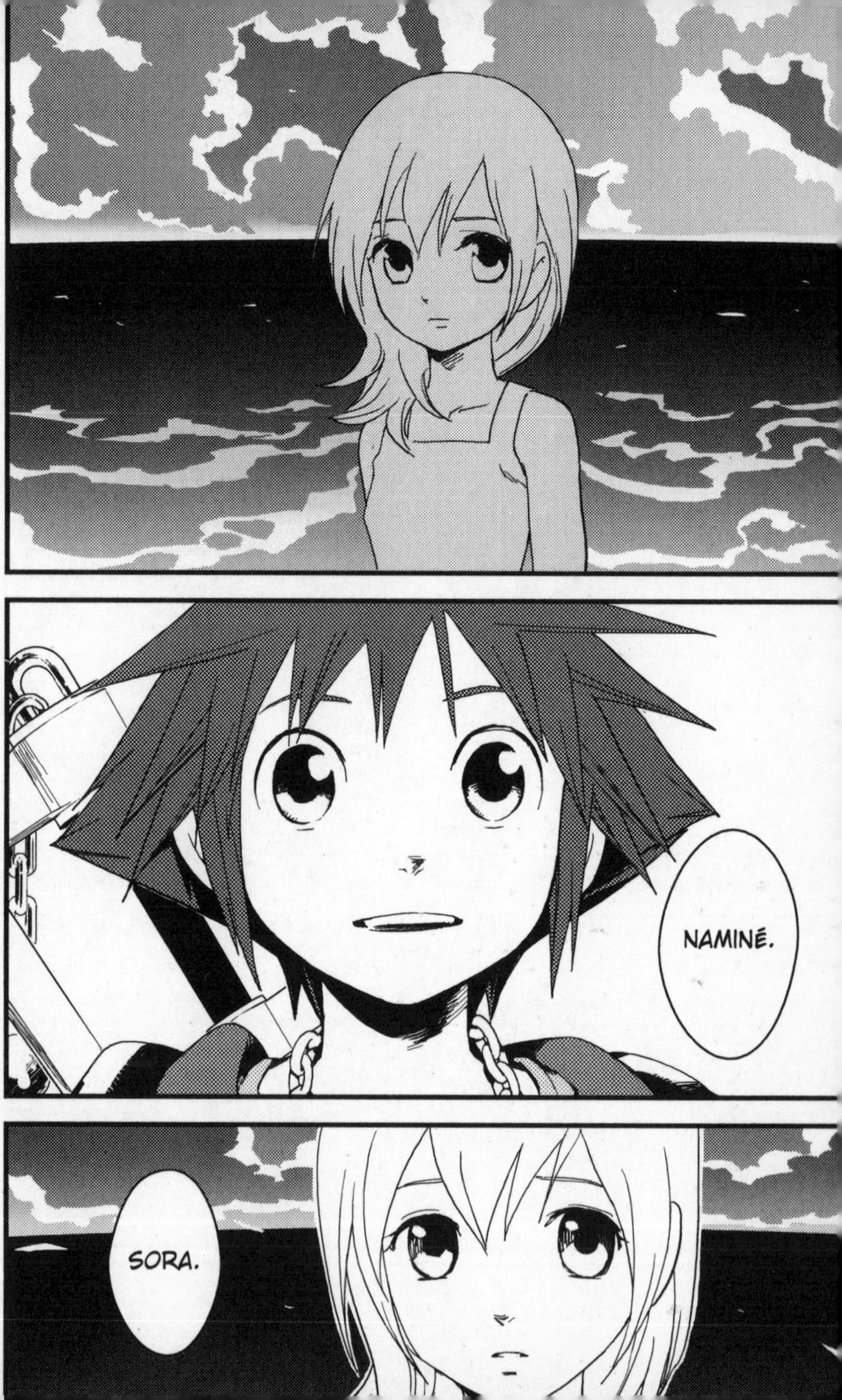
NAMINÉ.
SORA.

THANK YOU.

YOU CAME FOR ME.

Quash

% ALCOHOL / LESS THAN 1% JUICE

LESS THAN 1% JUICE

CHEERS!!

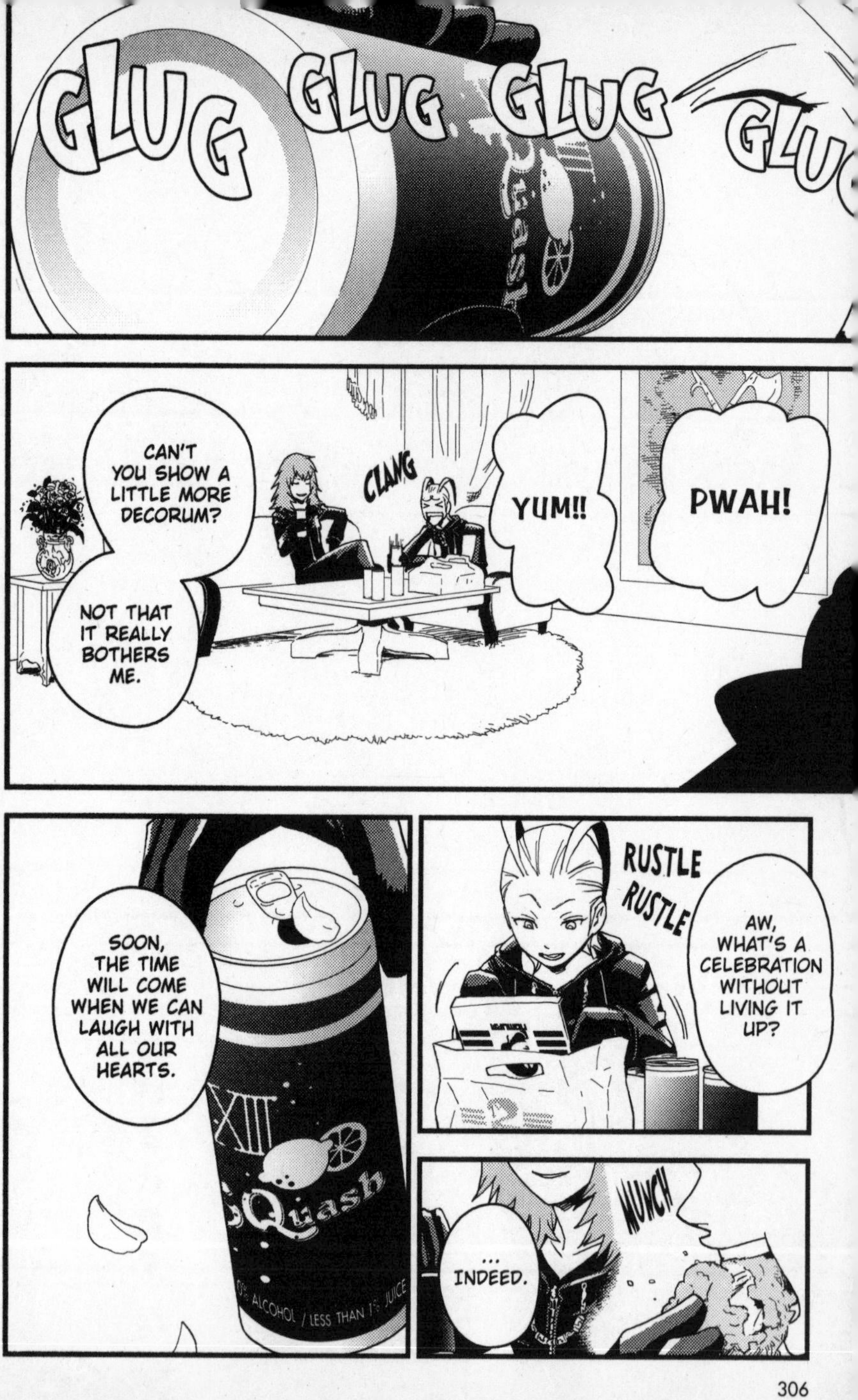
GLUG GLUG GLUG GLUG
PWAH!
YUM!!
CLANG
CAN'T YOU SHOW A LITTLE MORE DECORUM?
NOT THAT IT REALLY BOTHERS ME.
RUSTLE RUSTLE
AW, WHAT'S A CELEBRATION WITHOUT LIVING IT UP?
MUNCH
... INDEED.
SOON, THE TIME WILL COME WHEN WE CAN LAUGH WITH ALL OUR HEARTS.
XIII
SQuash
0% ALCOHOL / LESS THAN 1% JUICE

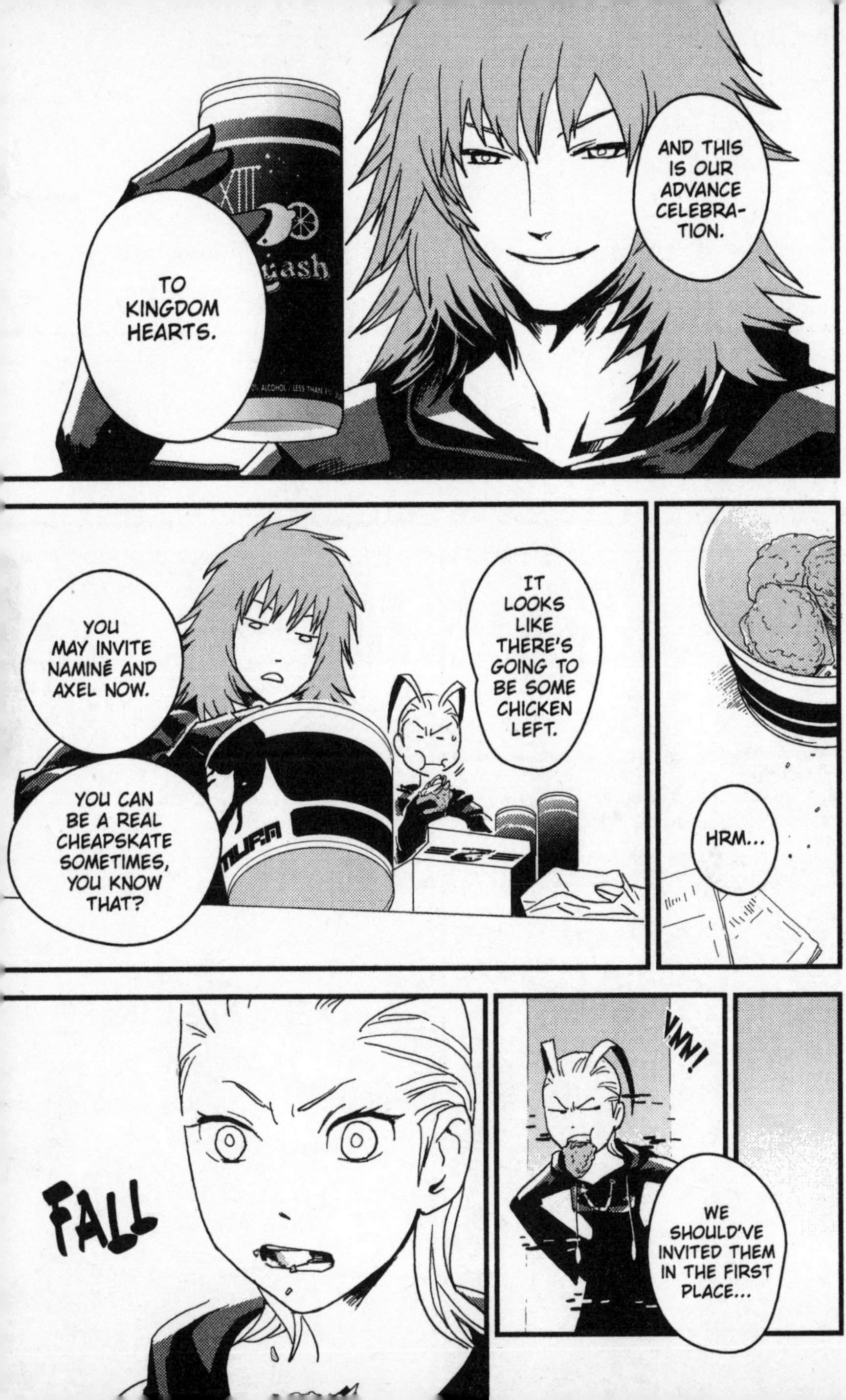

AND THIS IS OUR ADVANCE CELEBRATION.
TO KINGDOM HEARTS.
HRM...
IT LOOKS LIKE THERE'S GOING TO BE SOME CHICKEN LEFT.
YOU MAY INVITE NAMINÉ AND AXEL NOW.
YOU CAN BE A REAL CHEAPSKATE SOMETIMES, YOU KNOW THAT?
VNN!
WE SHOULD'VE INVITED THEM IN THE FIRST PLACE...
FALL

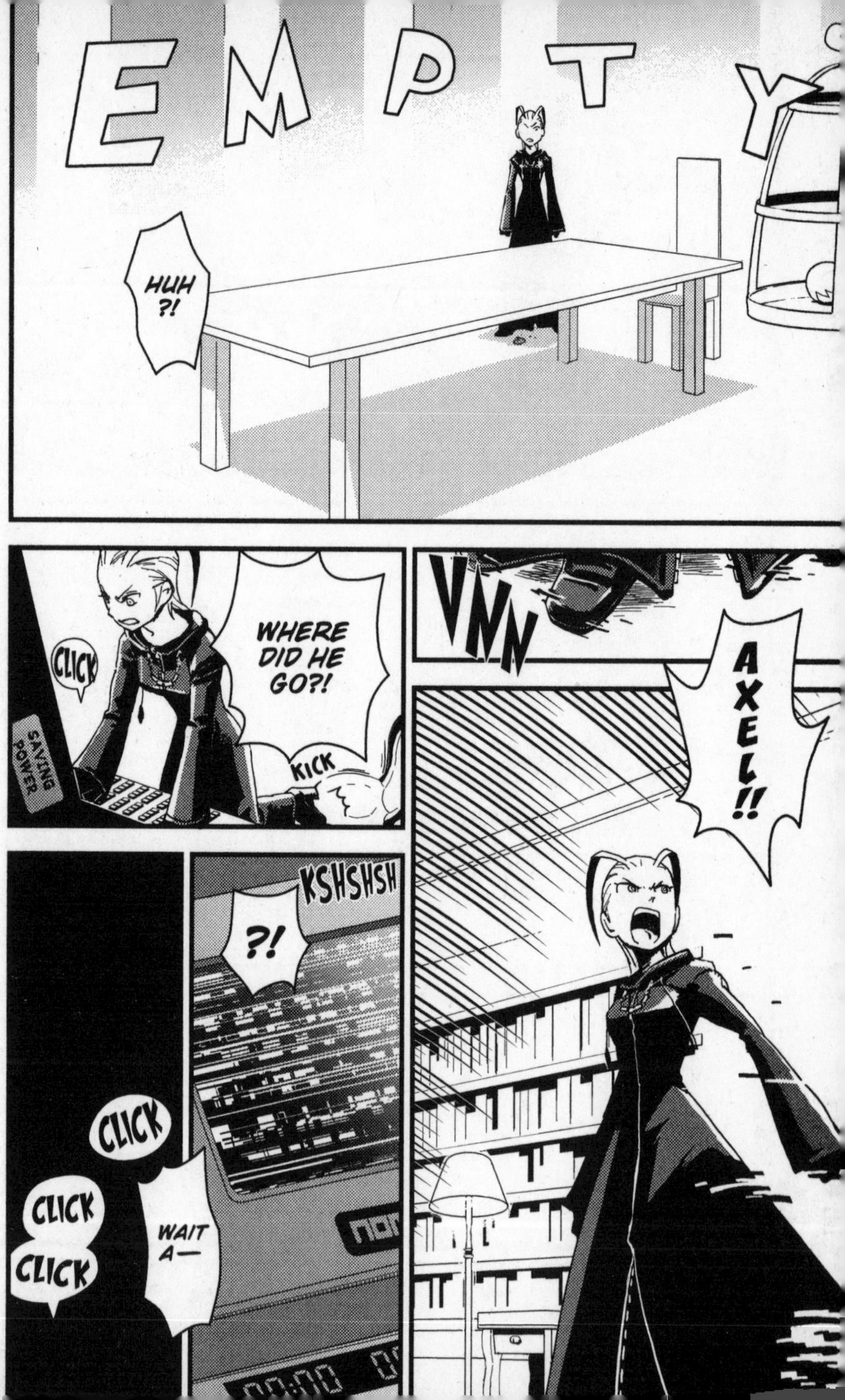
EMPTY
HUH?!
VNN
WHERE DID HE GO?!
CLICK
SAVING POWER
KICK
AXEL!!
KSHSHSH
?!
WAIT A—
CLICK
CLICK
CLICK

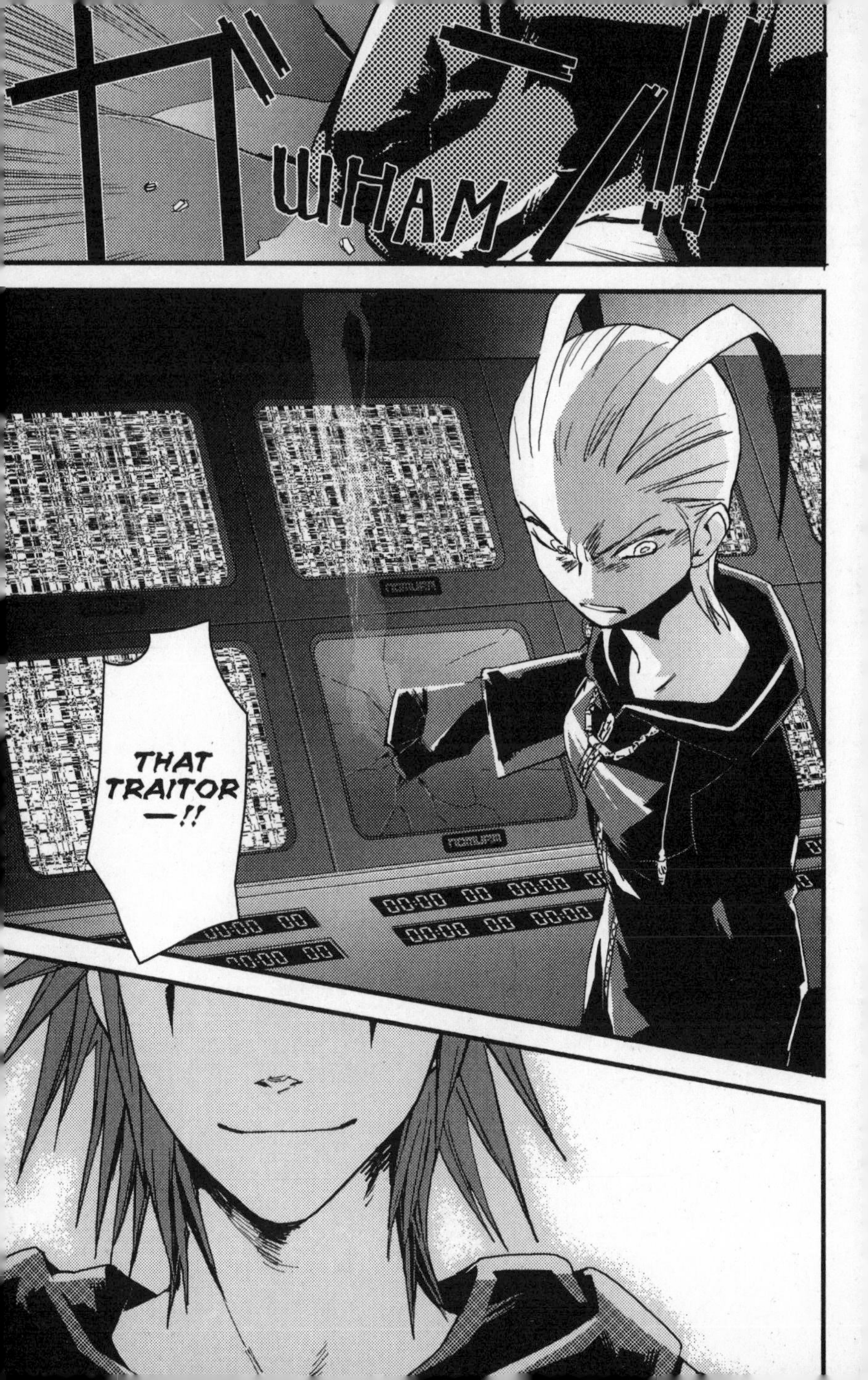
WHAM
THAT TRAITOR —!!

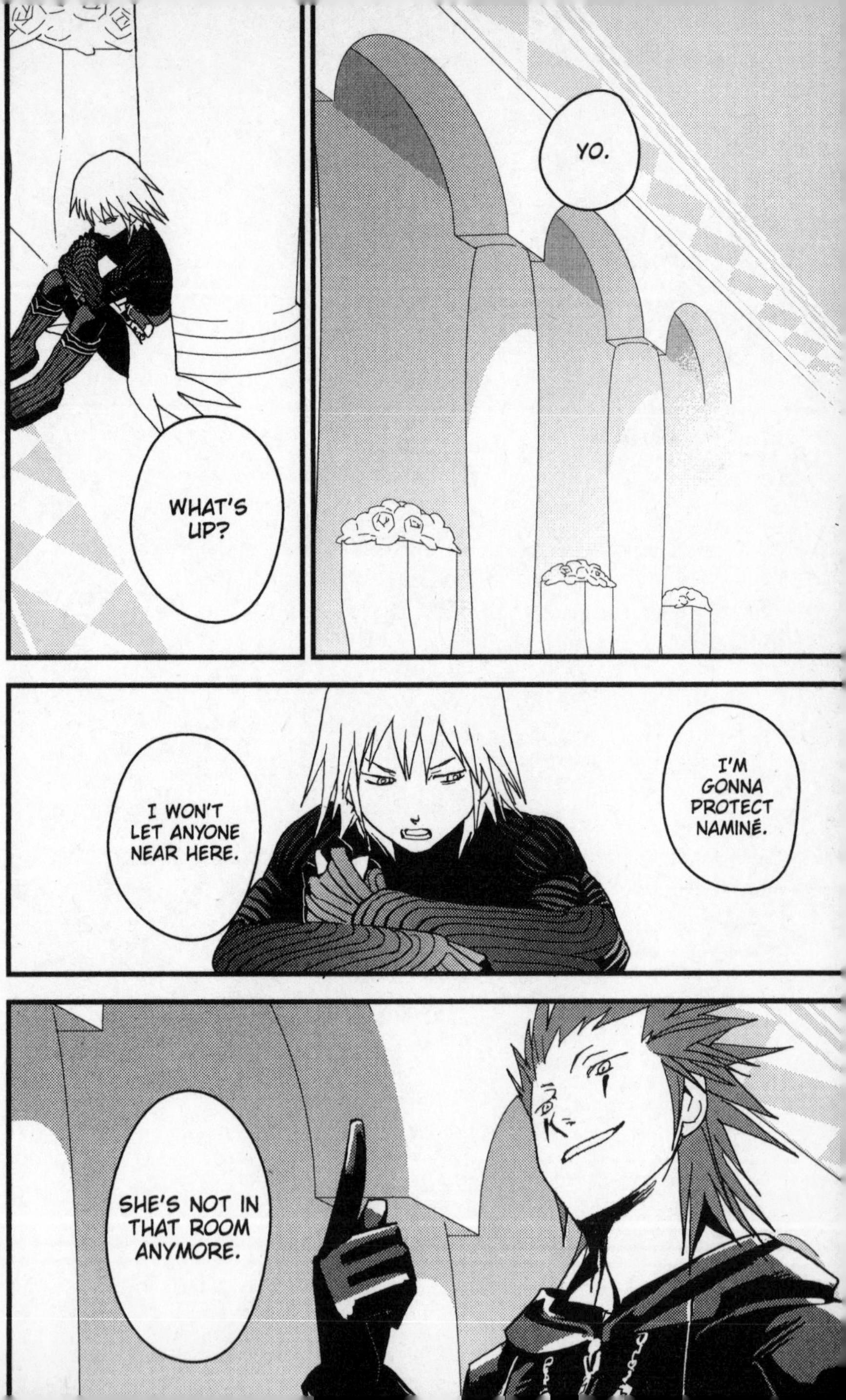
YO.
WHAT'S UP?
I'M GONNA PROTECT NAMINÉ.
I WON'T LET ANYONE NEAR HERE.
SHE'S NOT IN THAT ROOM ANYMORE.

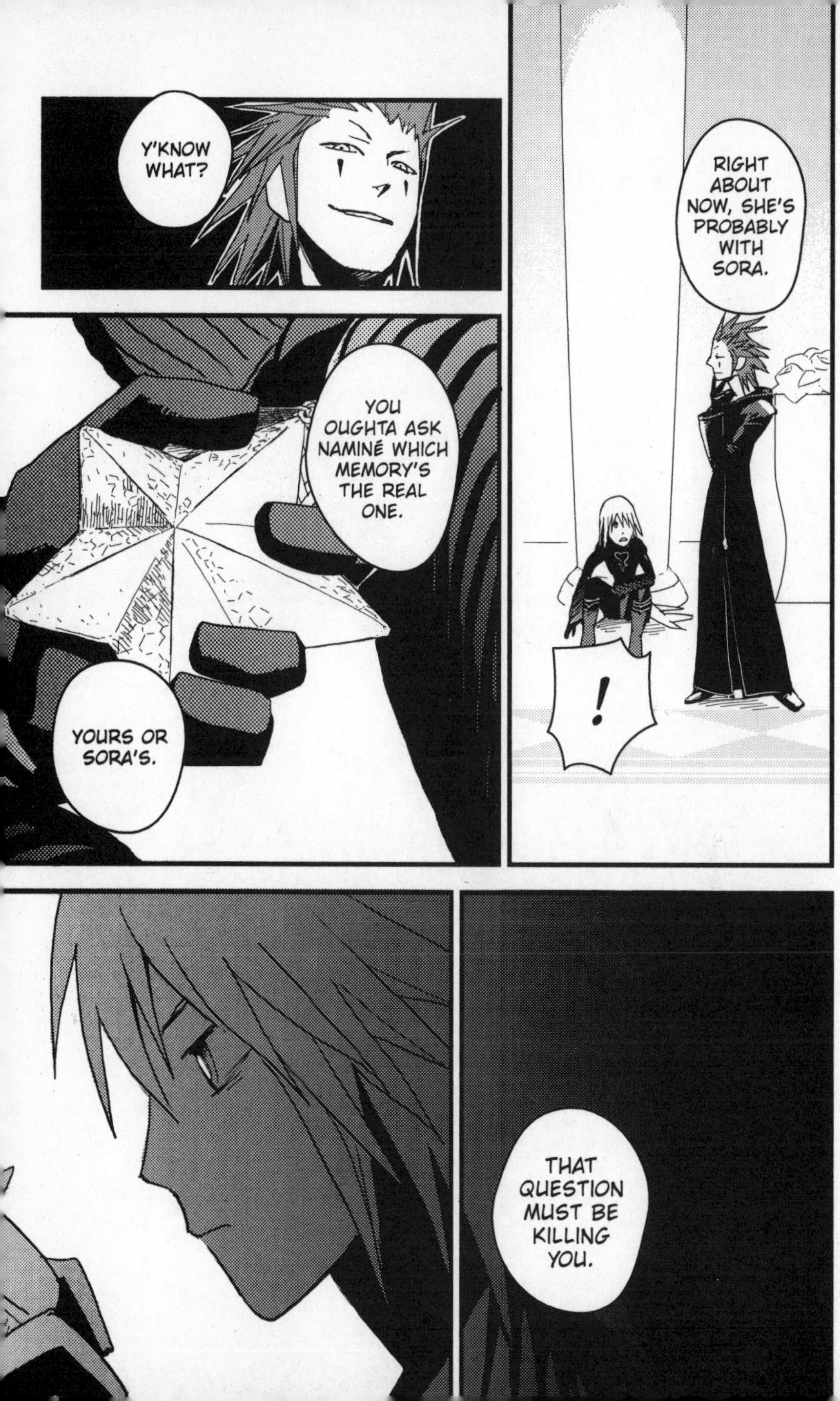
RIGHT ABOUT NOW, SHE'S PROBABLY WITH SORA.
!
Y'KNOW WHAT?
YOU OUGHTA ASK NAMINÉ WHICH MEMORY'S THE REAL ONE.
YOURS OR SORA'S.
THAT QUESTION MUST BE KILLING YOU.

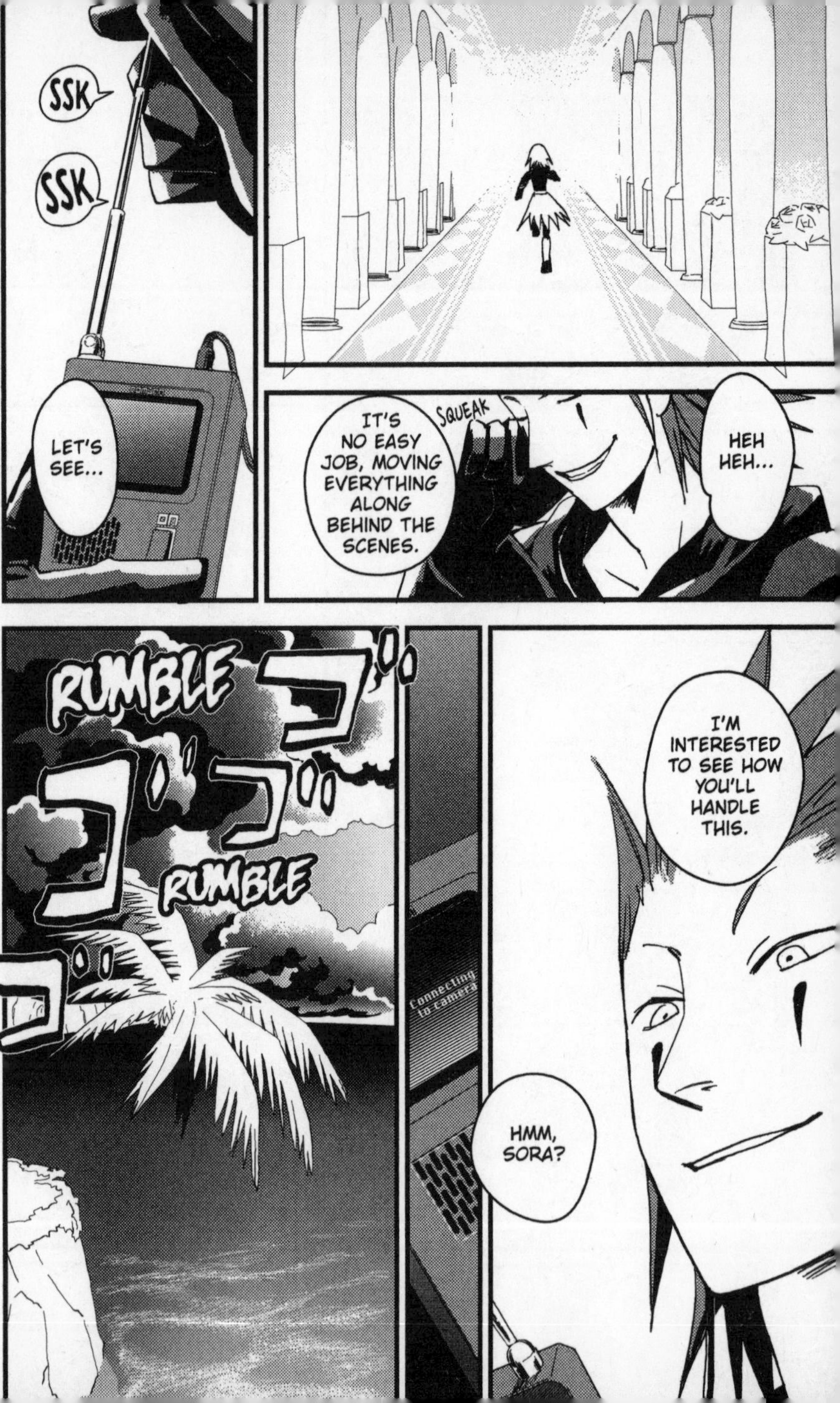
HEH HEH...
SQUEAK
IT'S NO EASY JOB, MOVING EVERYTHING ALONG BEHIND THE SCENES.
SSK
SSK
LET'S SEE...
I'M INTERESTED TO SEE HOW YOU'LL HANDLE THIS.
HMM, SORA?
Connecting to camera
RUMBLE
RUMBLE

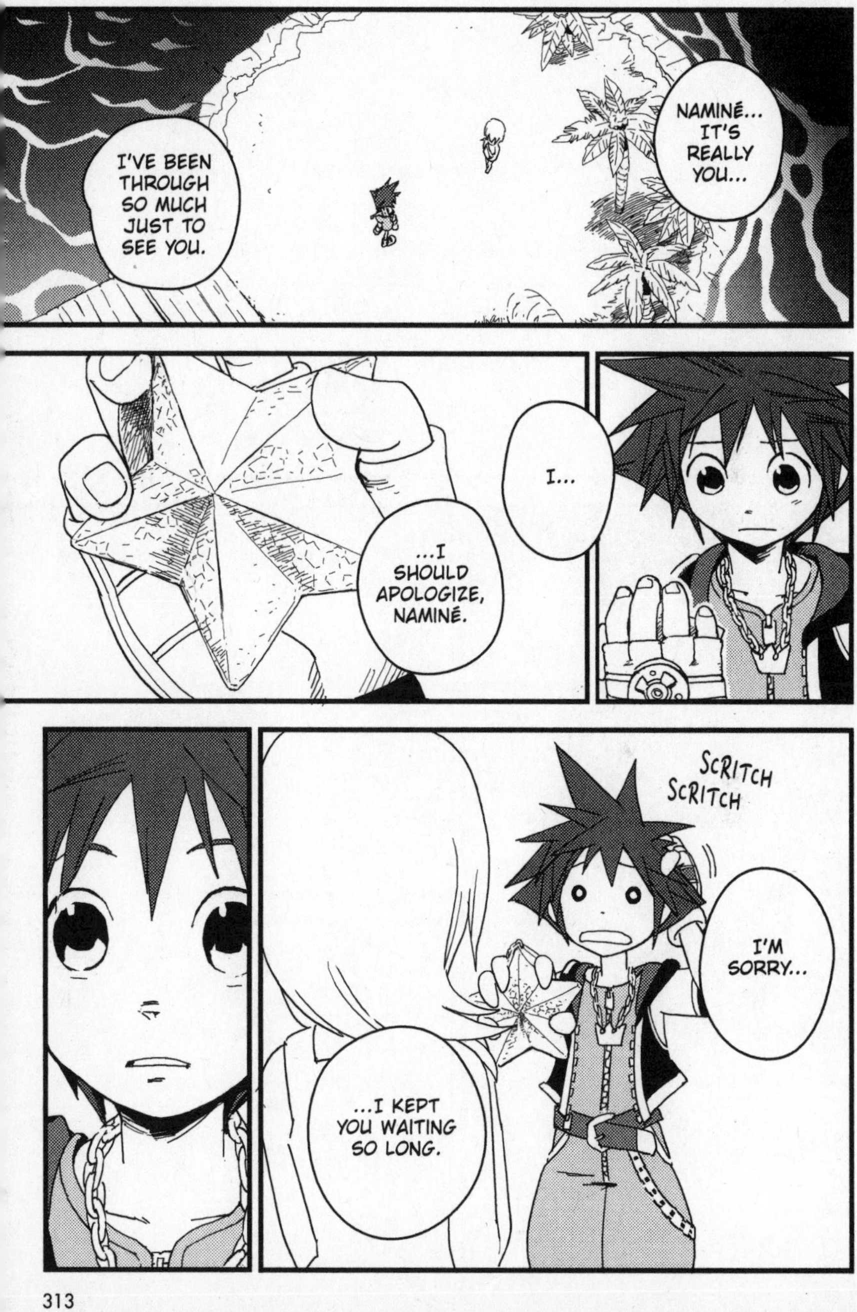
NAMINÉ... IT'S REALLY YOU...
I'VE BEEN THROUGH SO MUCH JUST TO SEE YOU.
I...
...I SHOULD APOLOGIZE, NAMINÉ.
SCRITCH SCRITCH
I'M SORRY...
...I KEPT YOU WAITING SO LONG.

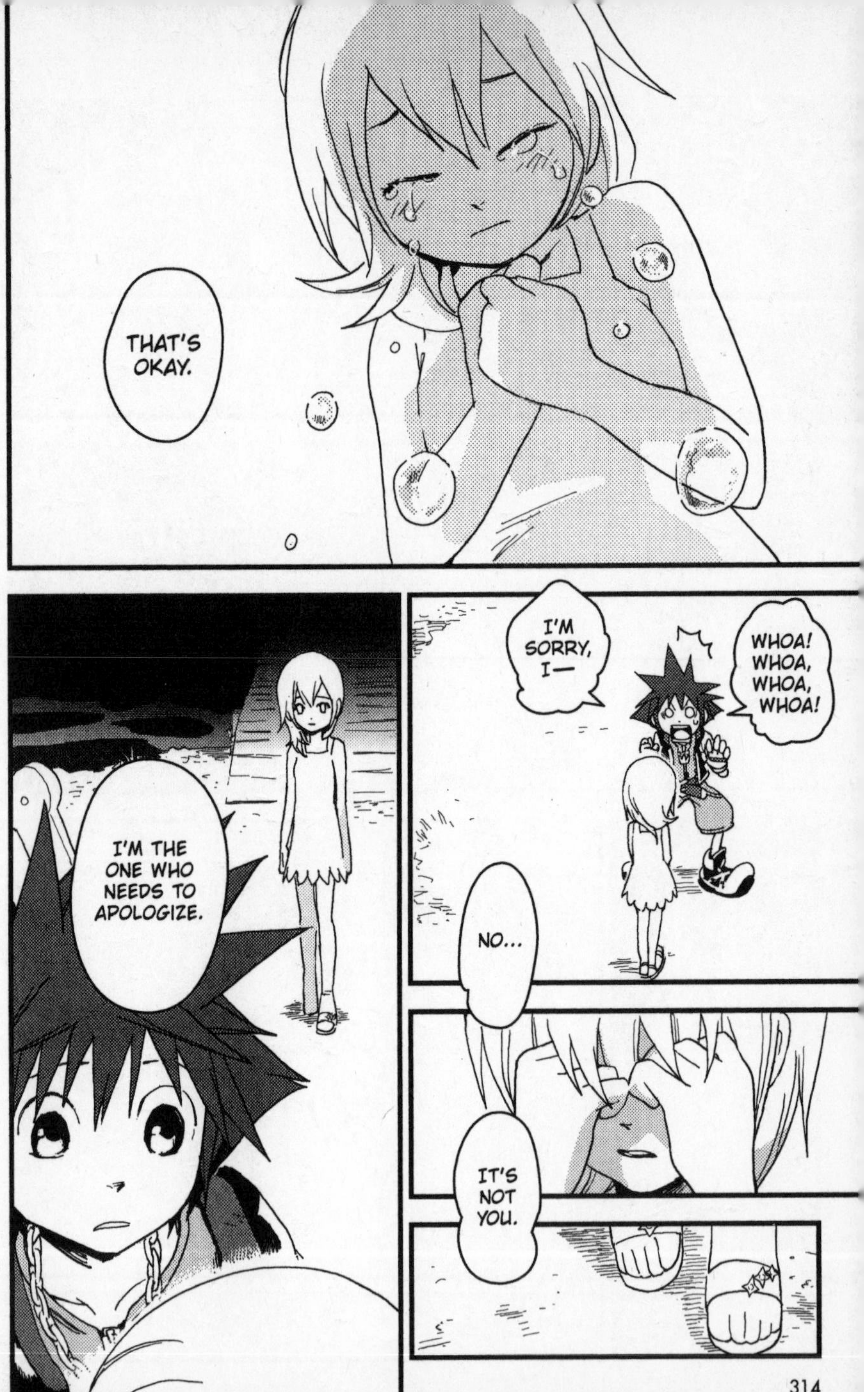
THAT'S OKAY.
WHOA! WHOA, WHOA, WHOA!
I'M SORRY, I—
NO...
IT'S NOT YOU.
I'M THE ONE WHO NEEDS TO APOLOGIZE.

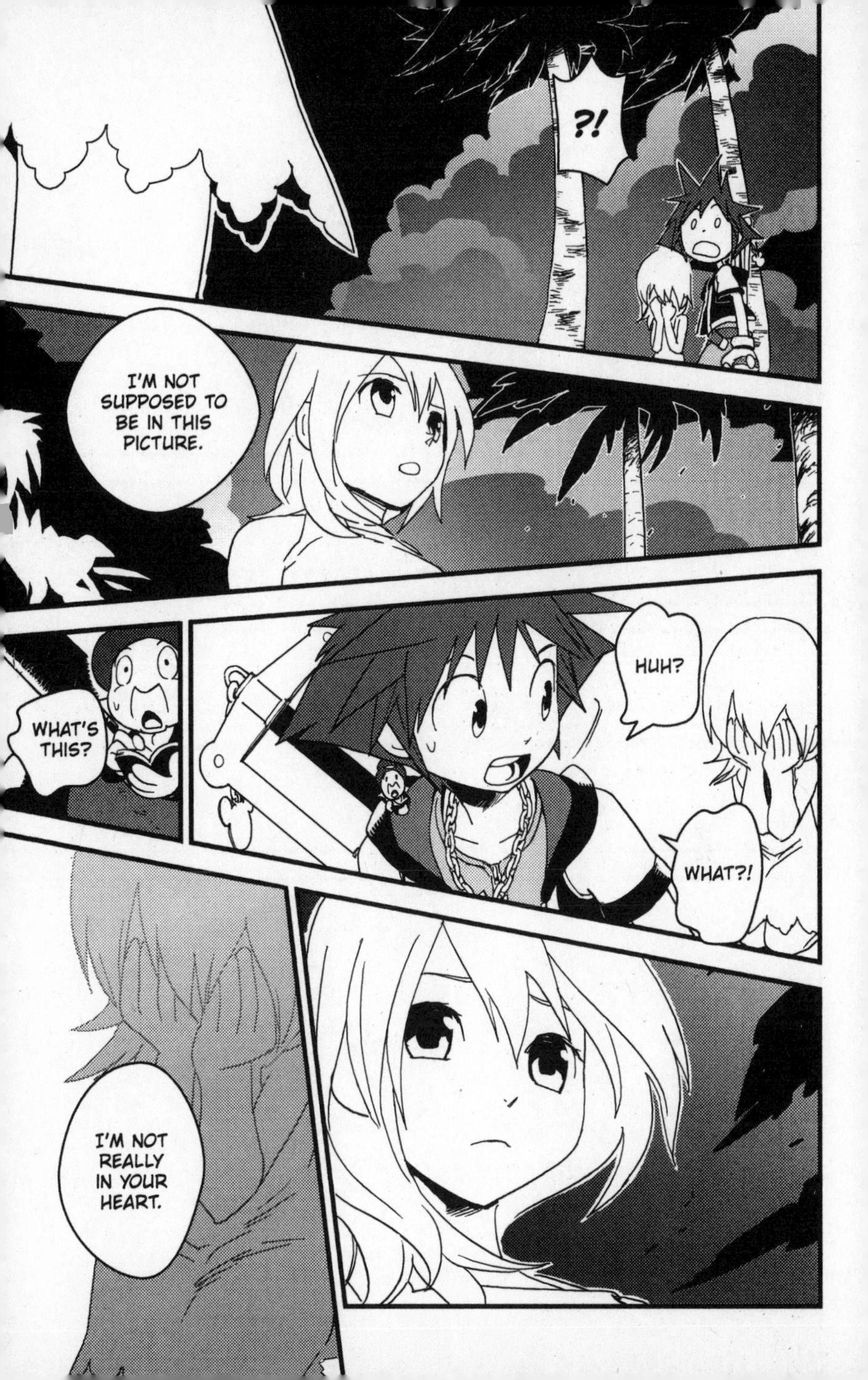
?!
I'M NOT SUPPOSED TO BE IN THIS PICTURE.
HUH?
WHAT?!
WHAT'S THIS?
I'M NOT REALLY IN YOUR HEART.

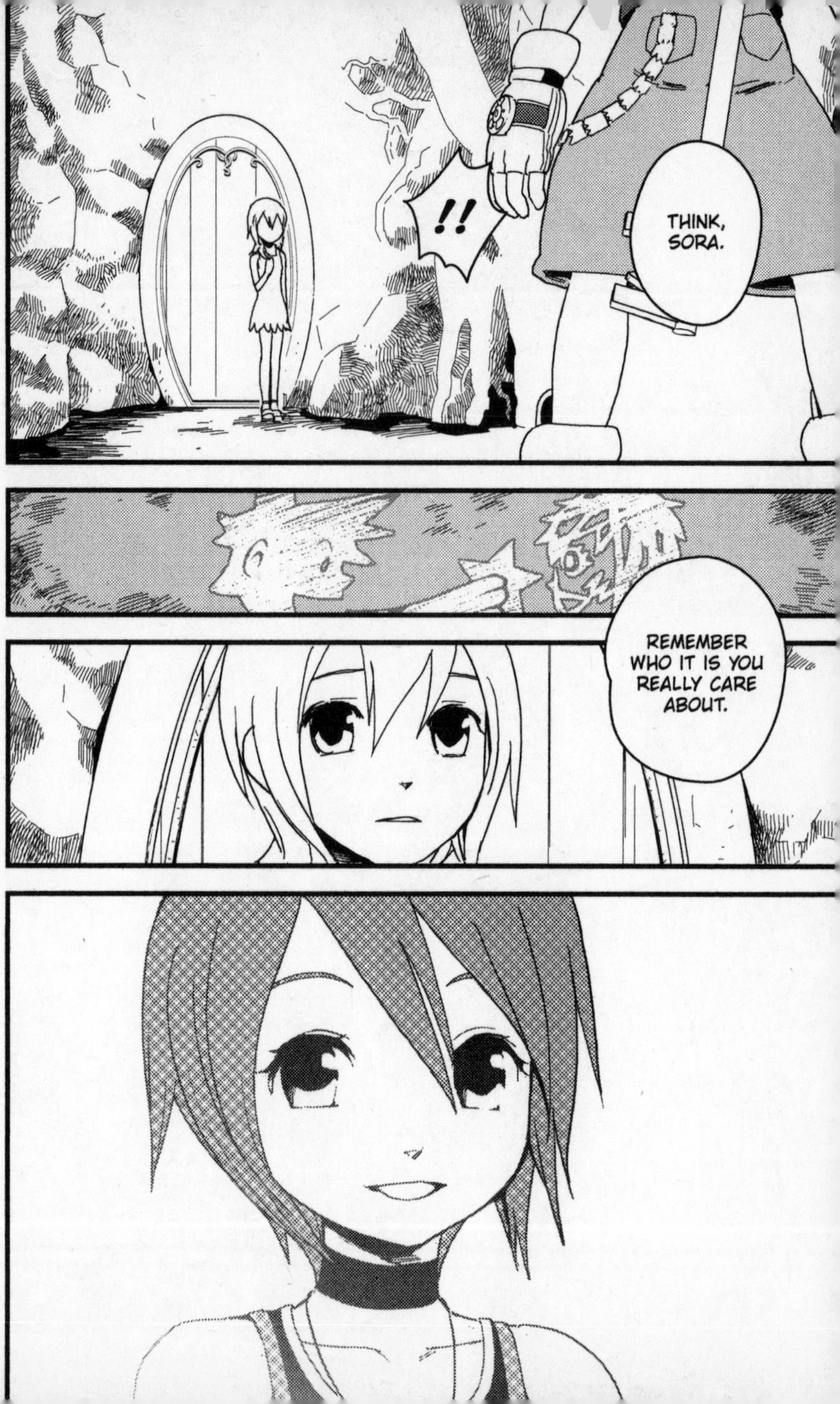
THINK, SORA.
!!
REMEMBER WHO IT IS YOU REALLY CARE ABOUT.

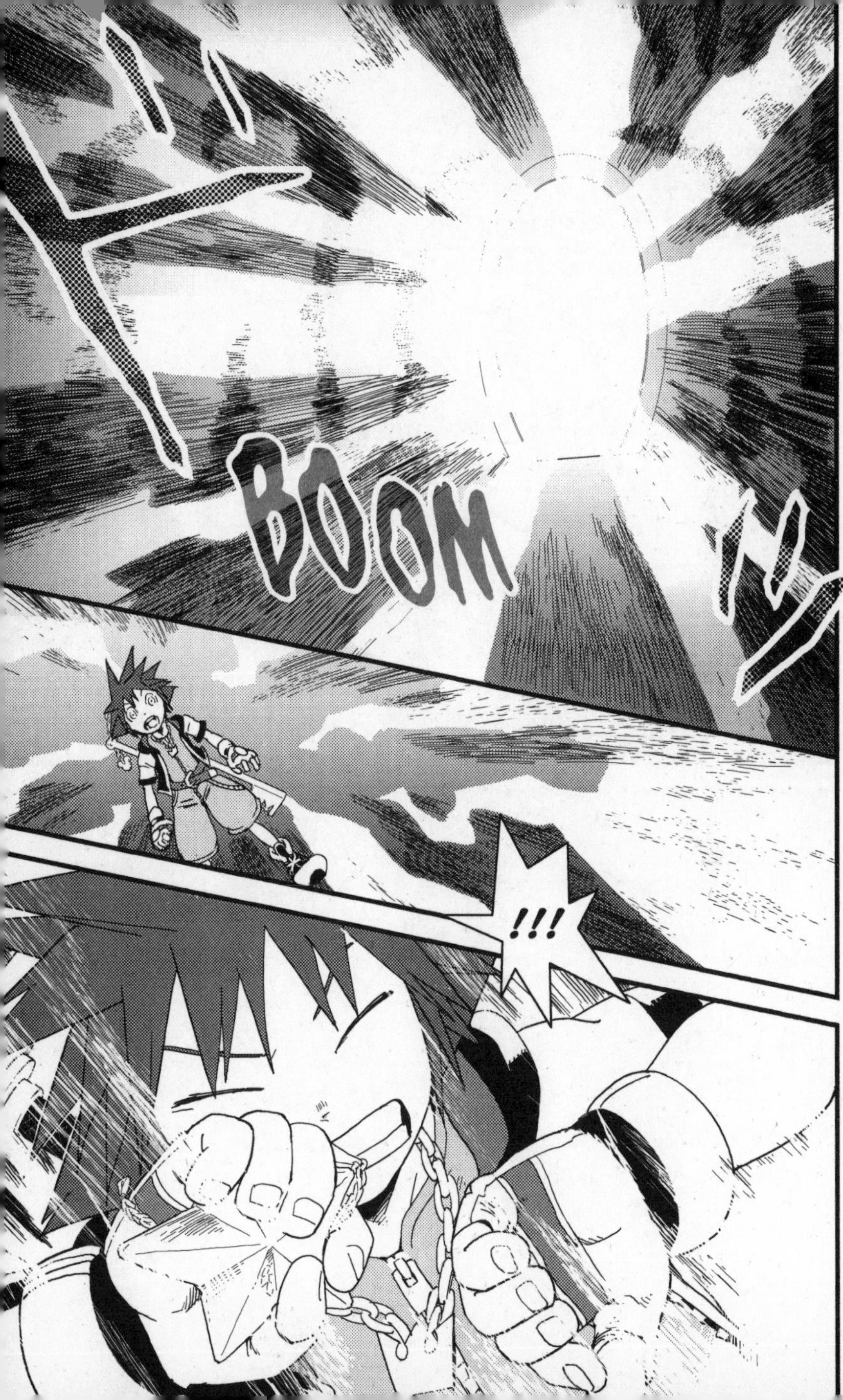
BOOM
!!!

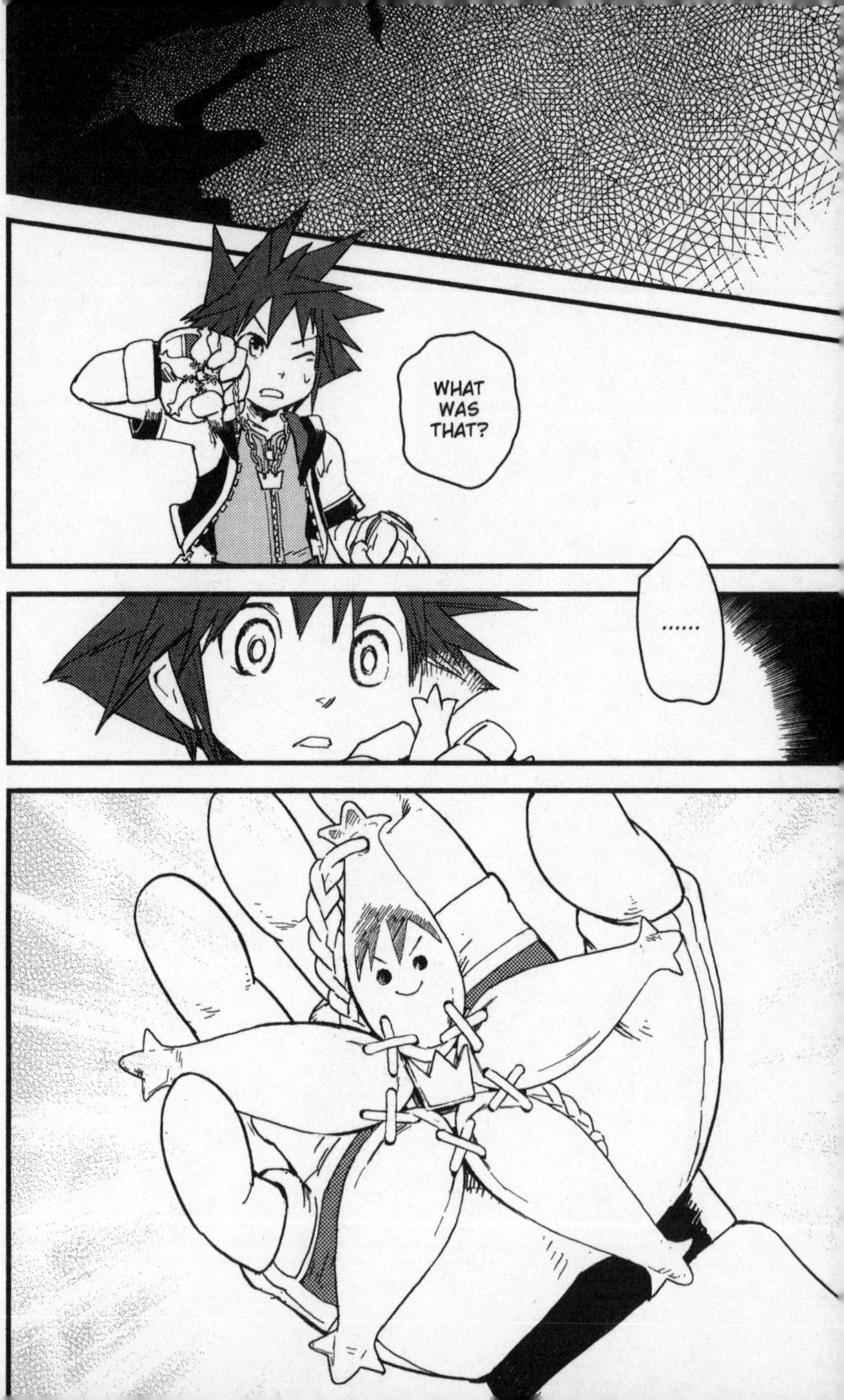
WHAT WAS THAT?
......

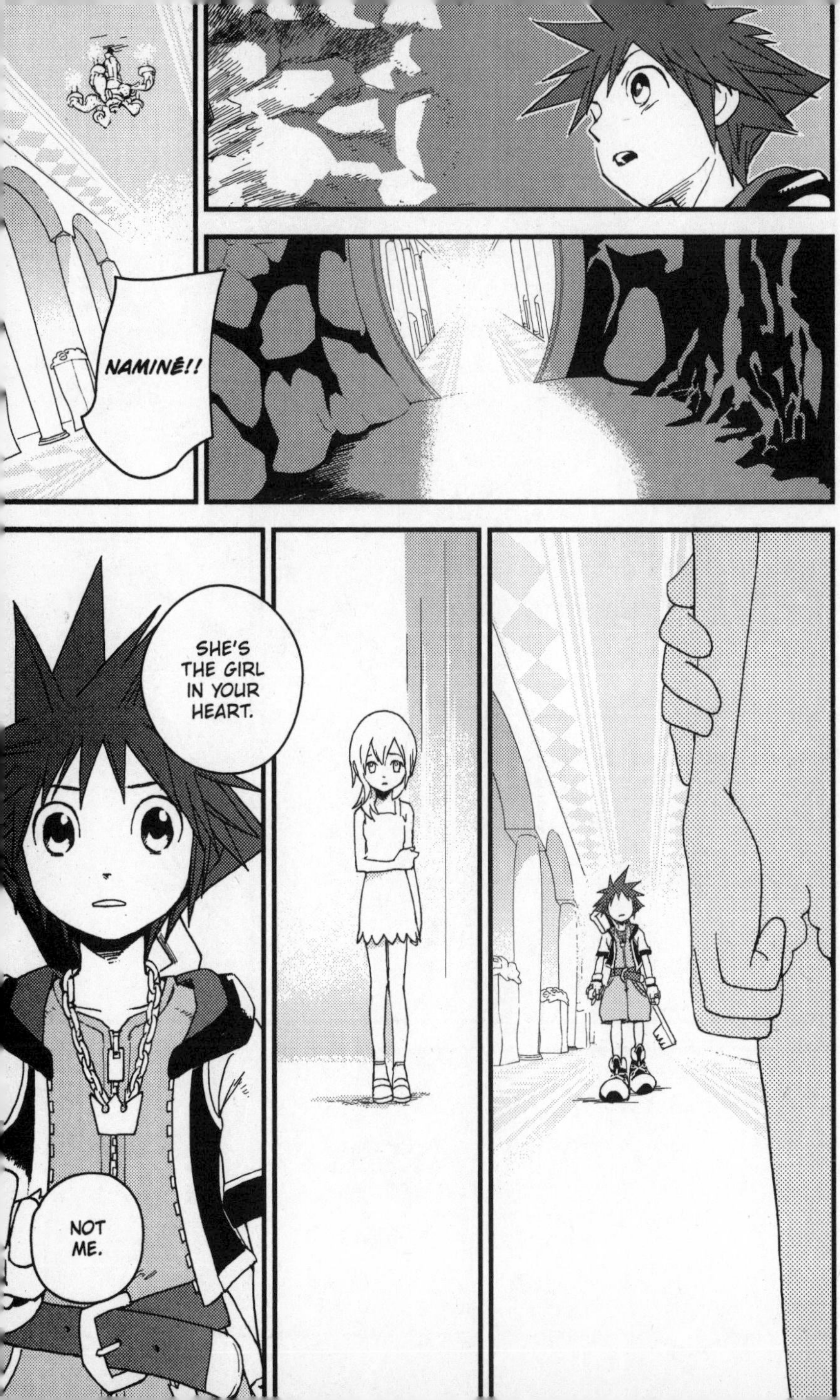
NAMINÉ!!
SHE'S THE GIRL IN YOUR HEART.
NOT ME.

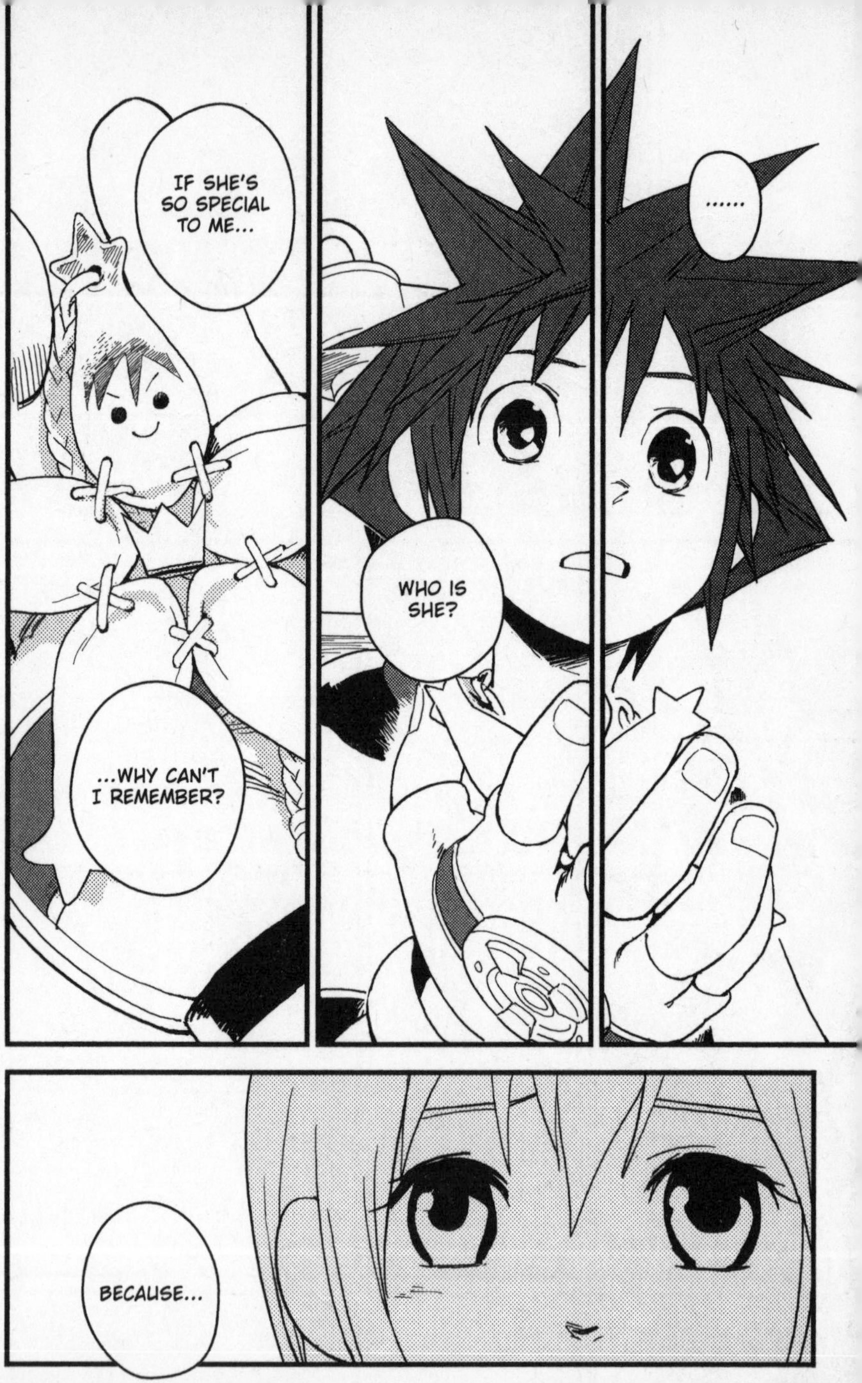
......
WHO IS SHE?
IF SHE'S SO SPECIAL TO ME...
...WHY CAN'T I REMEMBER?
BECAUSE...

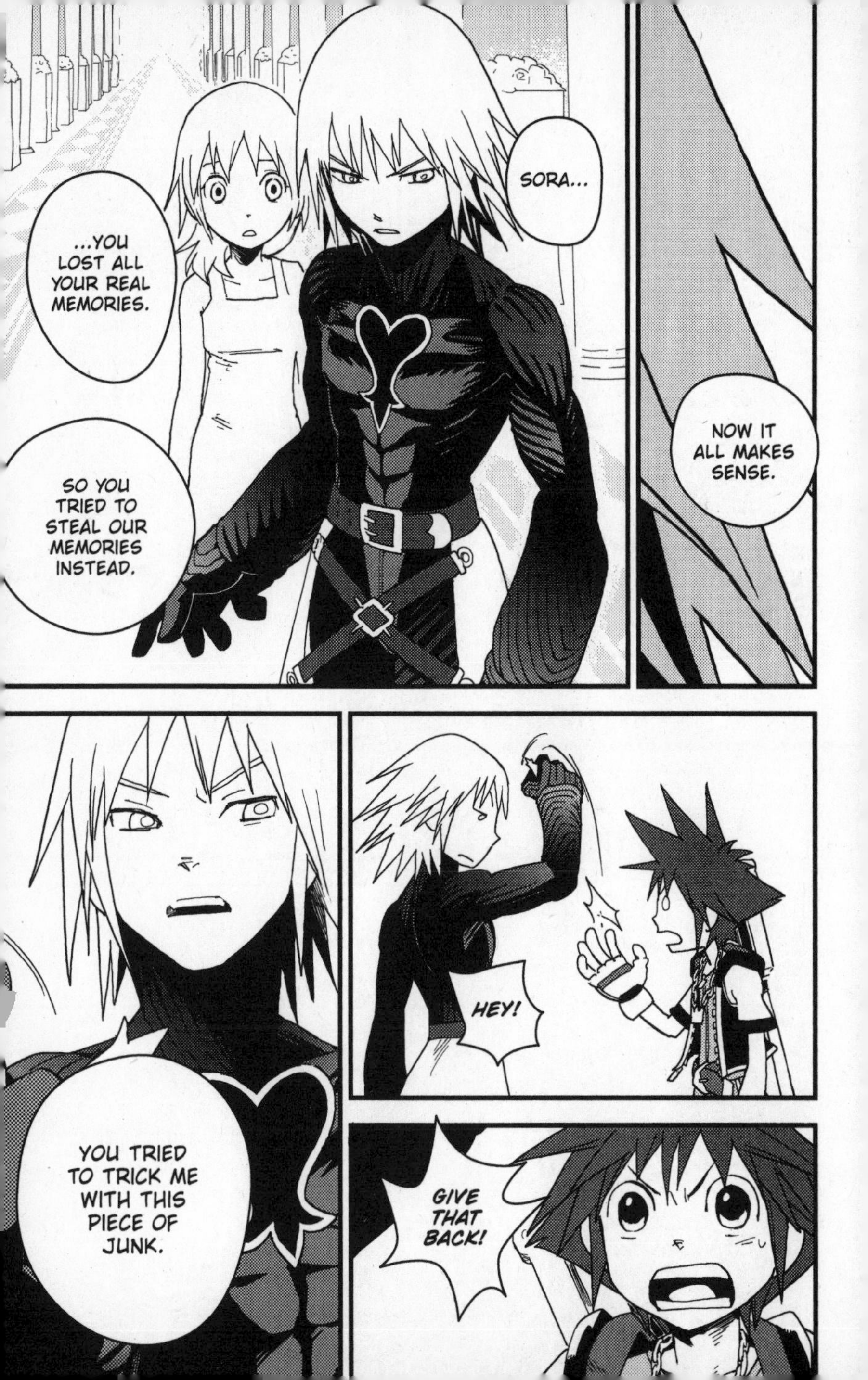
NOW IT ALL MAKES SENSE.
SORA...
...YOU LOST ALL YOUR REAL MEMORIES.
SO YOU TRIED TO STEAL OUR MEMORIES INSTEAD.
HEY!
GIVE THAT BACK!
YOU TRIED TO TRICK ME WITH THIS PIECE OF JUNK.

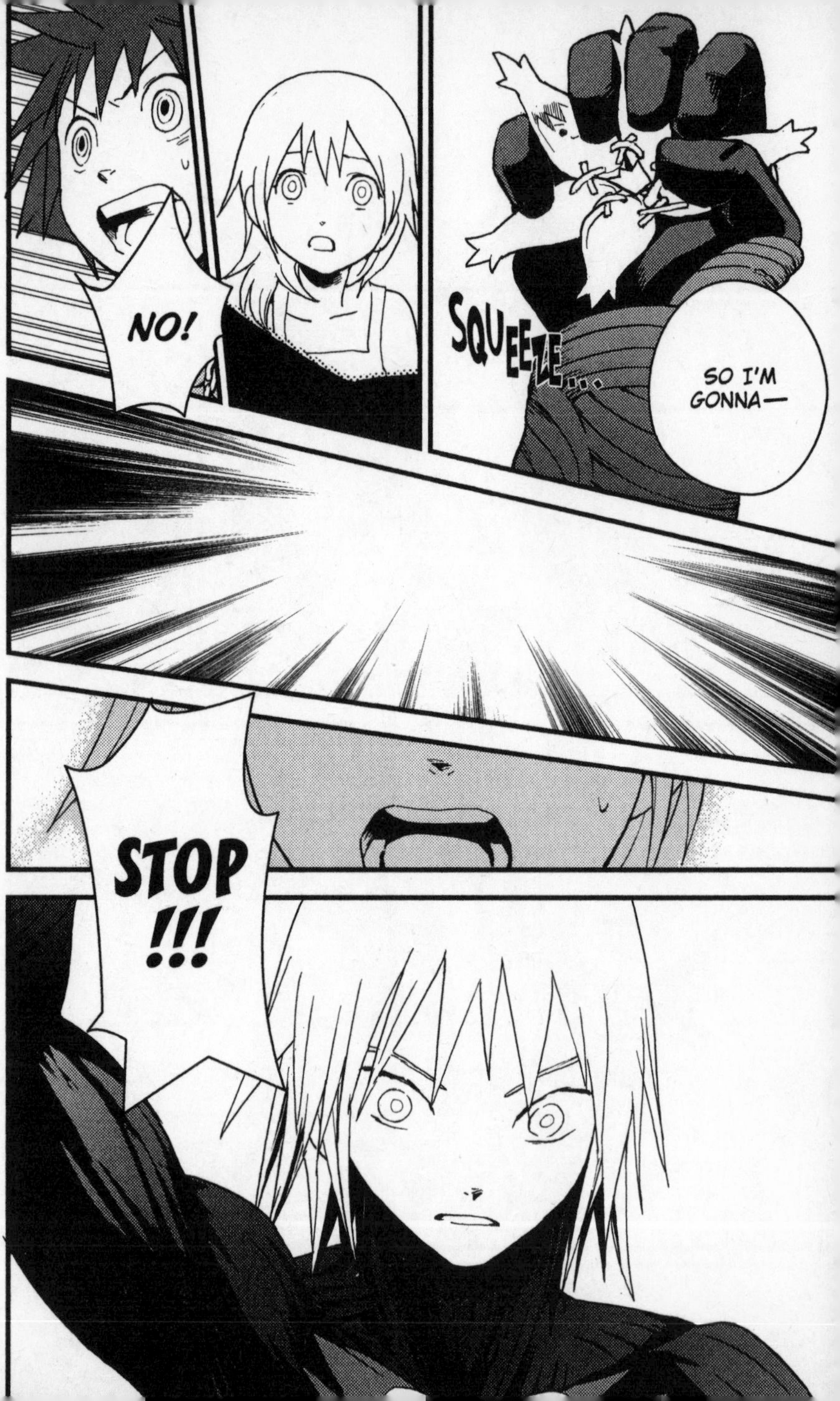
SO I'M GONNA—
SQUEEZE...
NO!
STOP !!!

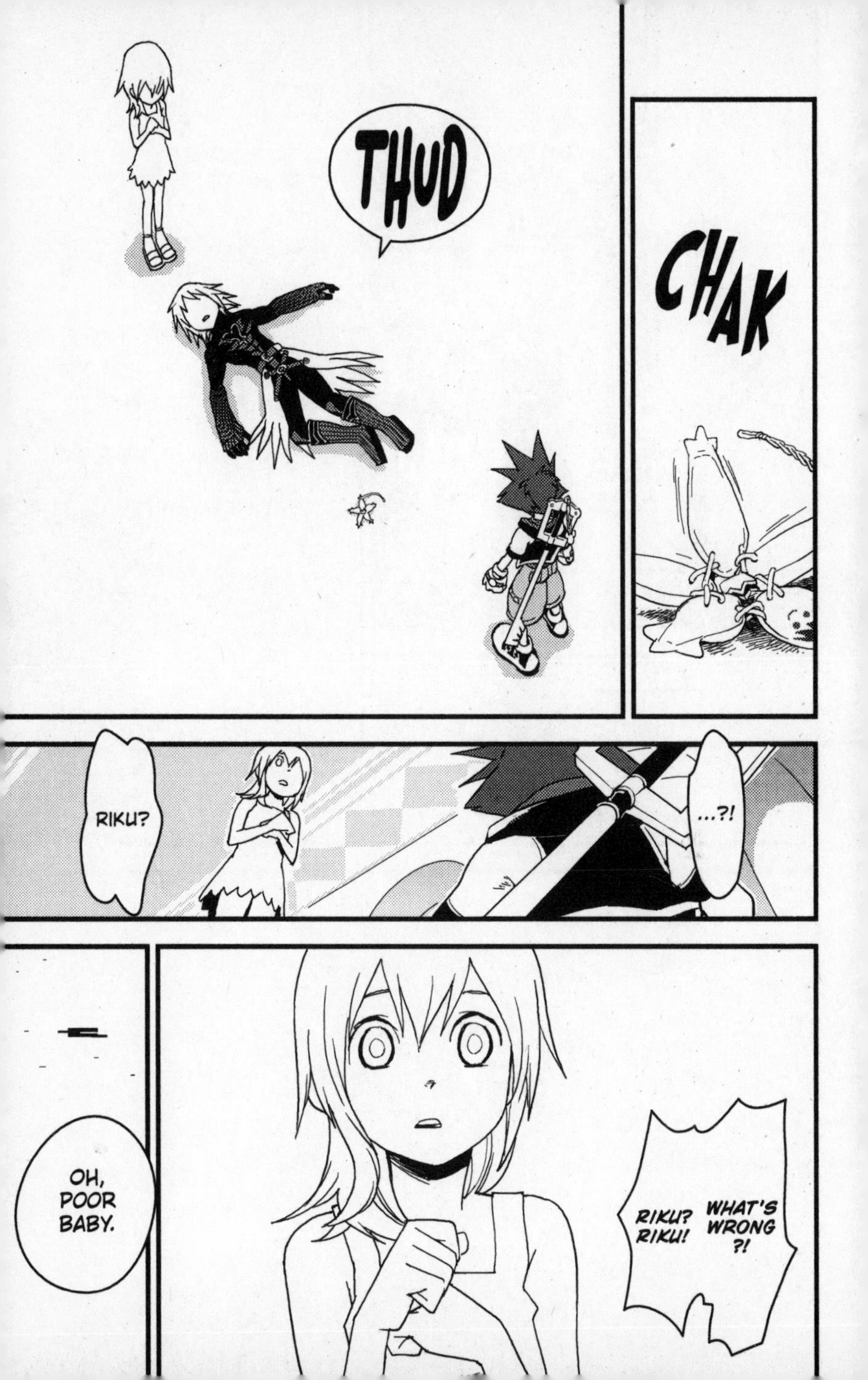
CHAK
THUD
...?!
RIKU?
RIKU? RIKU! WHAT'S WRONG ?!
OH, POOR BABY.

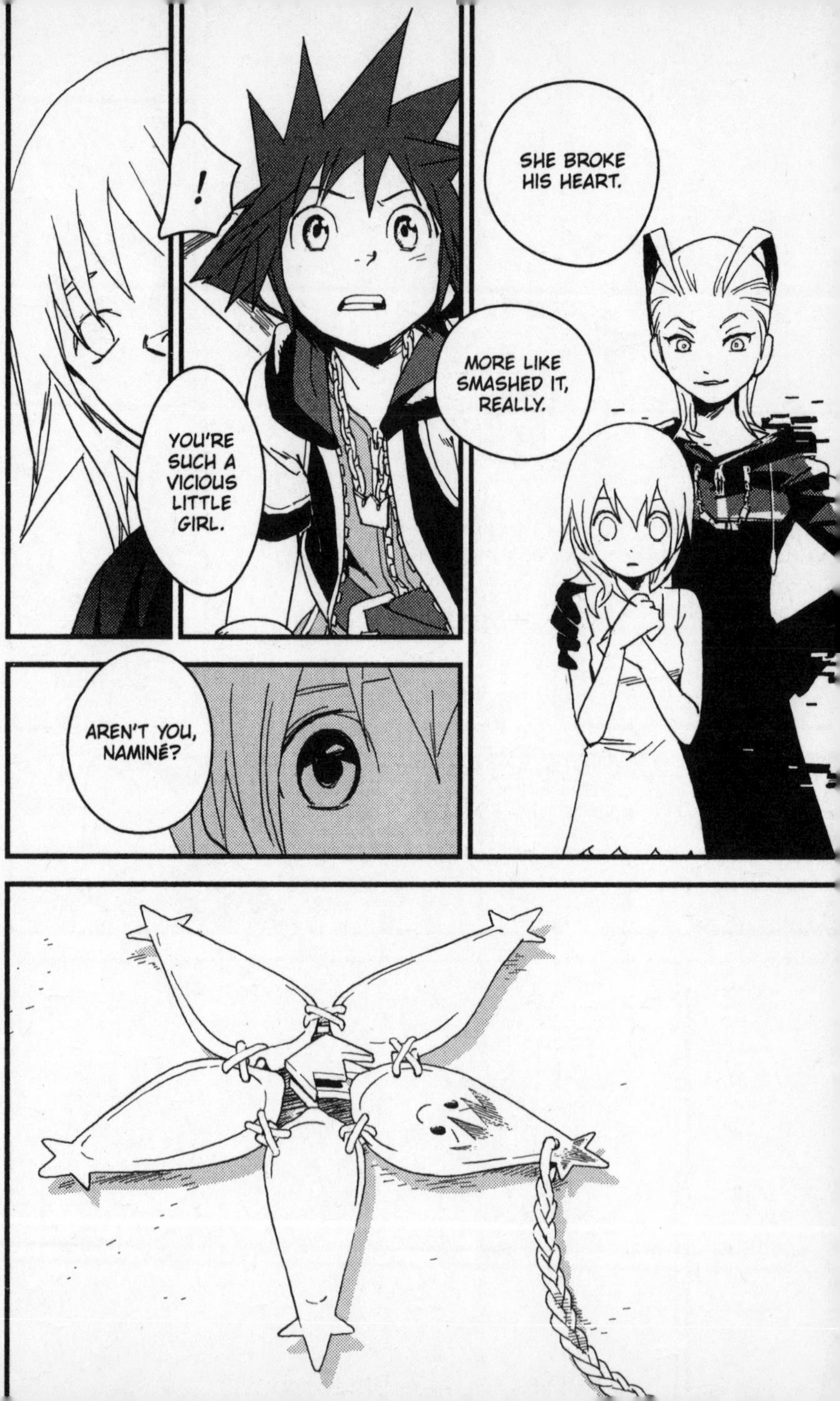
SHE BROKE HIS HEART.
MORE LIKE SMASHED IT, REALLY.
!
YOU'RE SUCH A VICIOUS LITTLE GIRL.
AREN'T YOU, NAMINÉ?

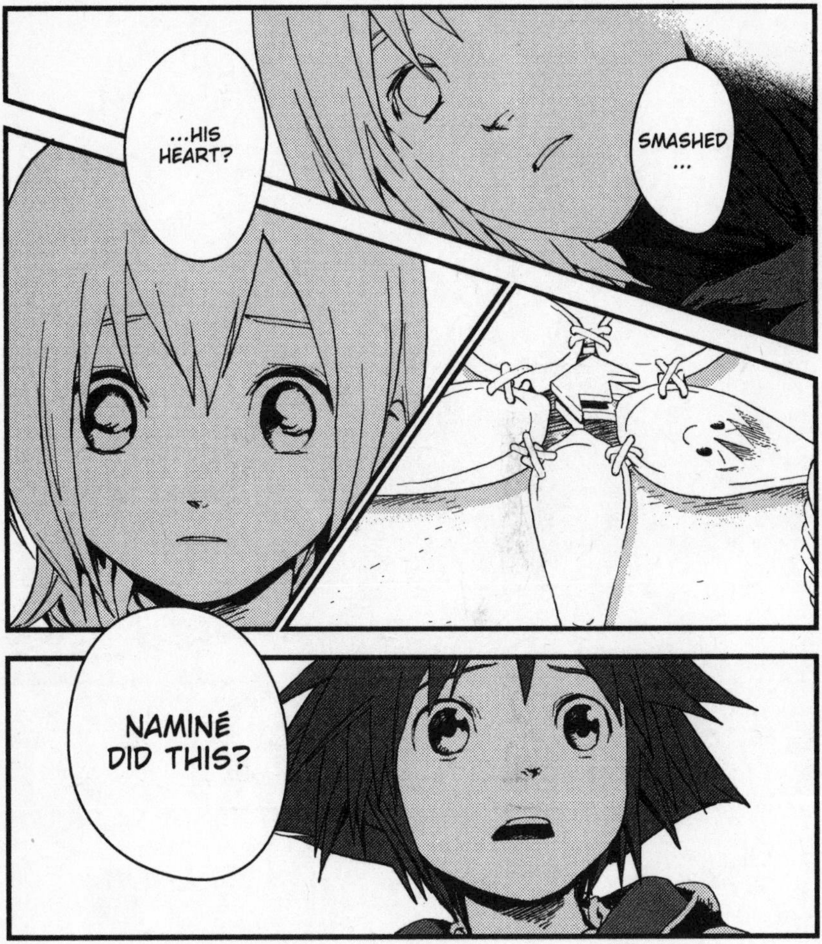
SMASHED ...
...HIS HEART?
NAMINÉ DID THIS?

## *Card:11* SHOCK!!!

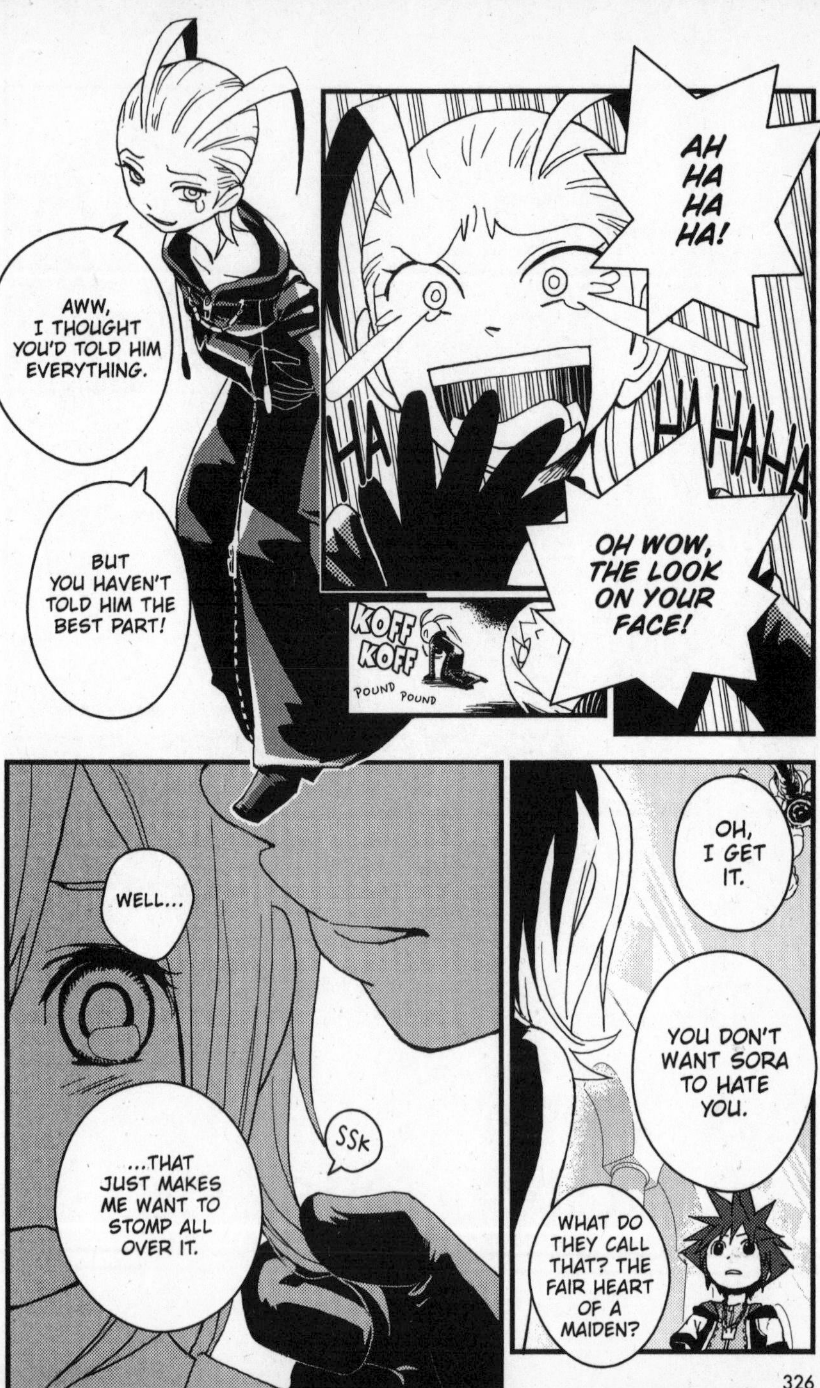
AH HA HA HA!
HA HAHAHA
HA
OH WOW, THE LOOK ON YOUR FACE!
KOFF KOFF
POUND POUND
AWW, I THOUGHT YOU'D TOLD HIM EVERYTHING.
BUT YOU HAVEN'T TOLD HIM THE BEST PART!
OH, I GET IT.
YOU DON'T WANT SORA TO HATE YOU.
WHAT DO THEY CALL THAT? THE FAIR HEART OF A MAIDEN?
WELL...
SSk
...THAT JUST MAKES ME WANT TO STOMP ALL OVER IT.

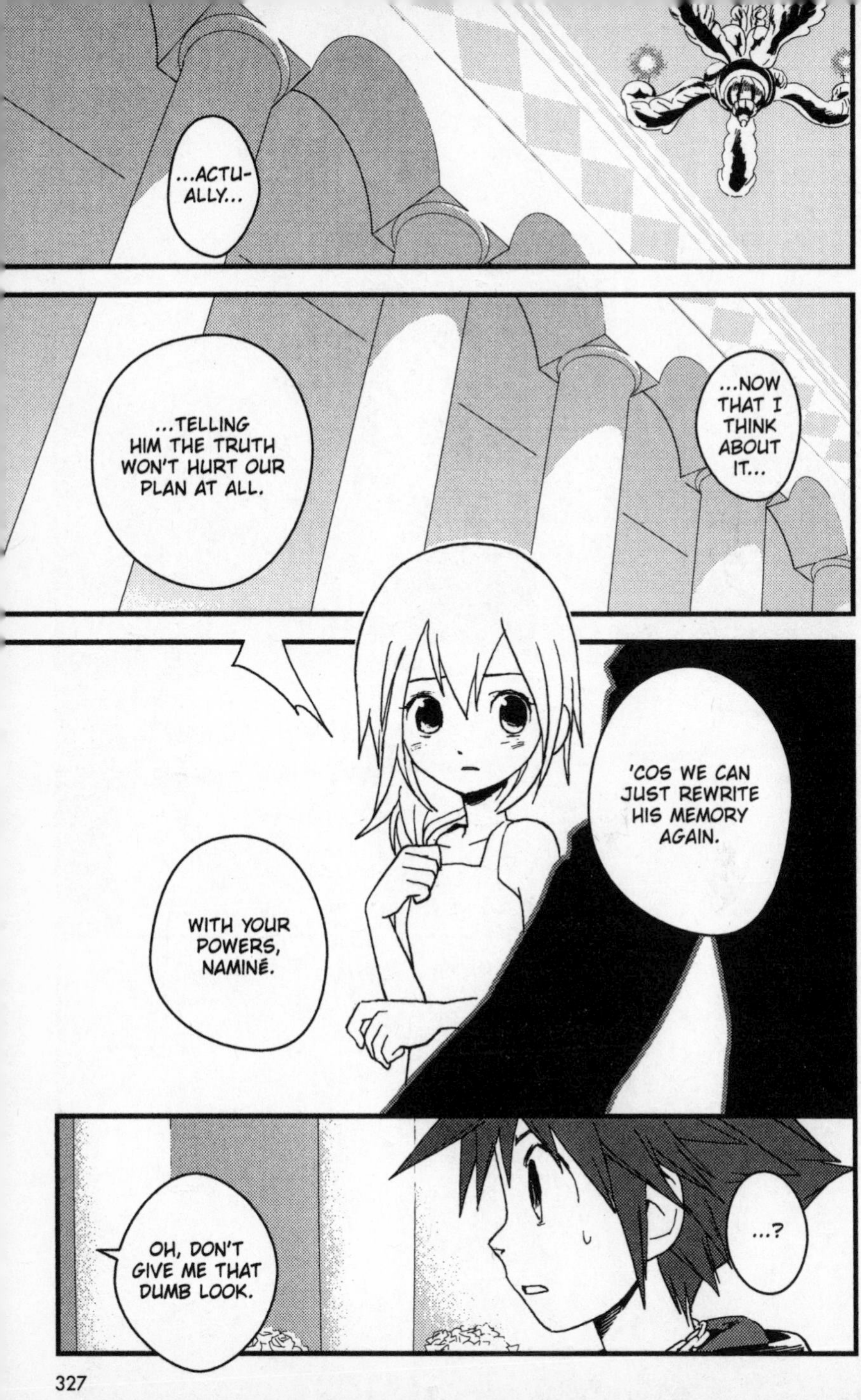
...ACTUALLY...
...NOW THAT I THINK ABOUT IT...
...TELLING HIM THE TRUTH WON'T HURT OUR PLAN AT ALL.
'COS WE CAN JUST REWRITE HIS MEMORY AGAIN.
WITH YOUR POWERS, NAMINÉ.
...?
OH, DON'T GIVE ME THAT DUMB LOOK.

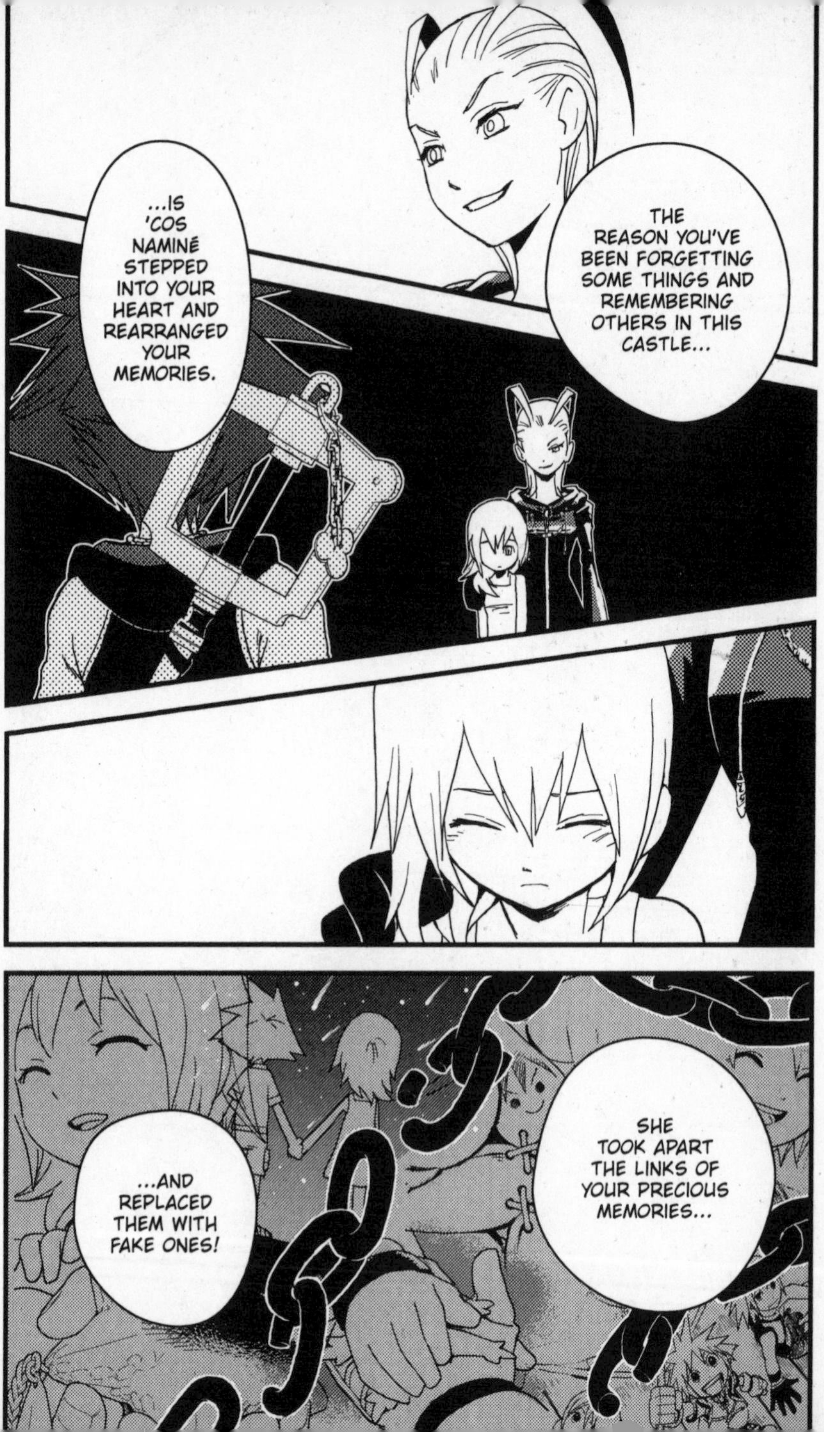
THE REASON YOU'VE BEEN FORGETTING SOME THINGS AND REMEMBERING OTHERS IN THIS CASTLE...
...IS 'COS NAMINÉ STEPPED INTO YOUR HEART AND REARRANGED YOUR MEMORIES.
SHE TOOK APART THE LINKS OF YOUR PRECIOUS MEMORIES...
...AND REPLACED THEM WITH FAKE ONES!

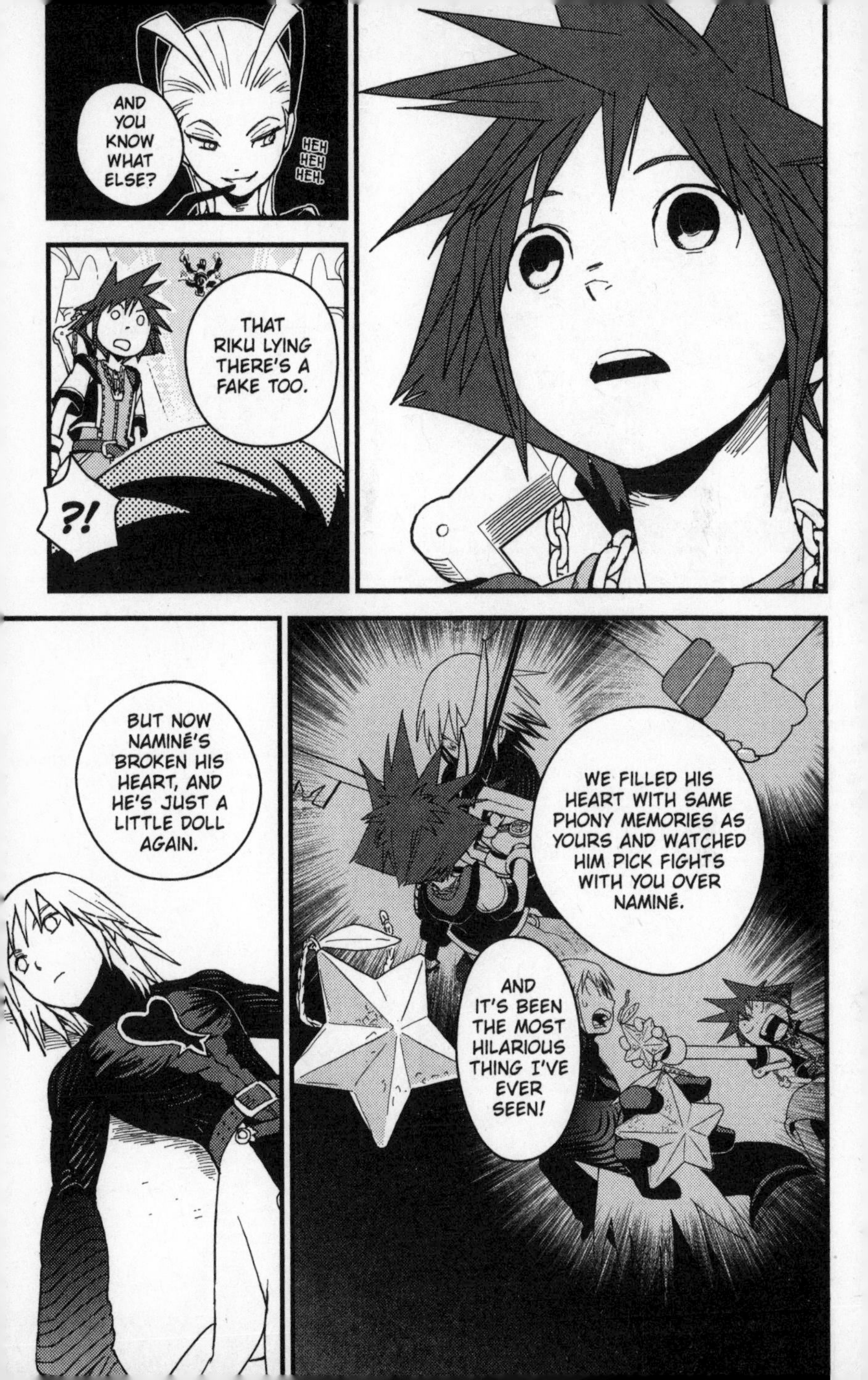
AND YOU KNOW WHAT ELSE?
HEH HEH HEH.
THAT RIKU LYING THERE'S A FAKE TOO.
?!
WE FILLED HIS HEART WITH SAME PHONY MEMORIES AS YOURS AND WATCHED HIM PICK FIGHTS WITH YOU OVER NAMINÉ.
AND IT'S BEEN THE MOST HILARIOUS THING I'VE EVER SEEN!
BUT NOW NAMINÉ'S BROKEN HIS HEART, AND HE'S JUST A LITTLE DOLL AGAIN.

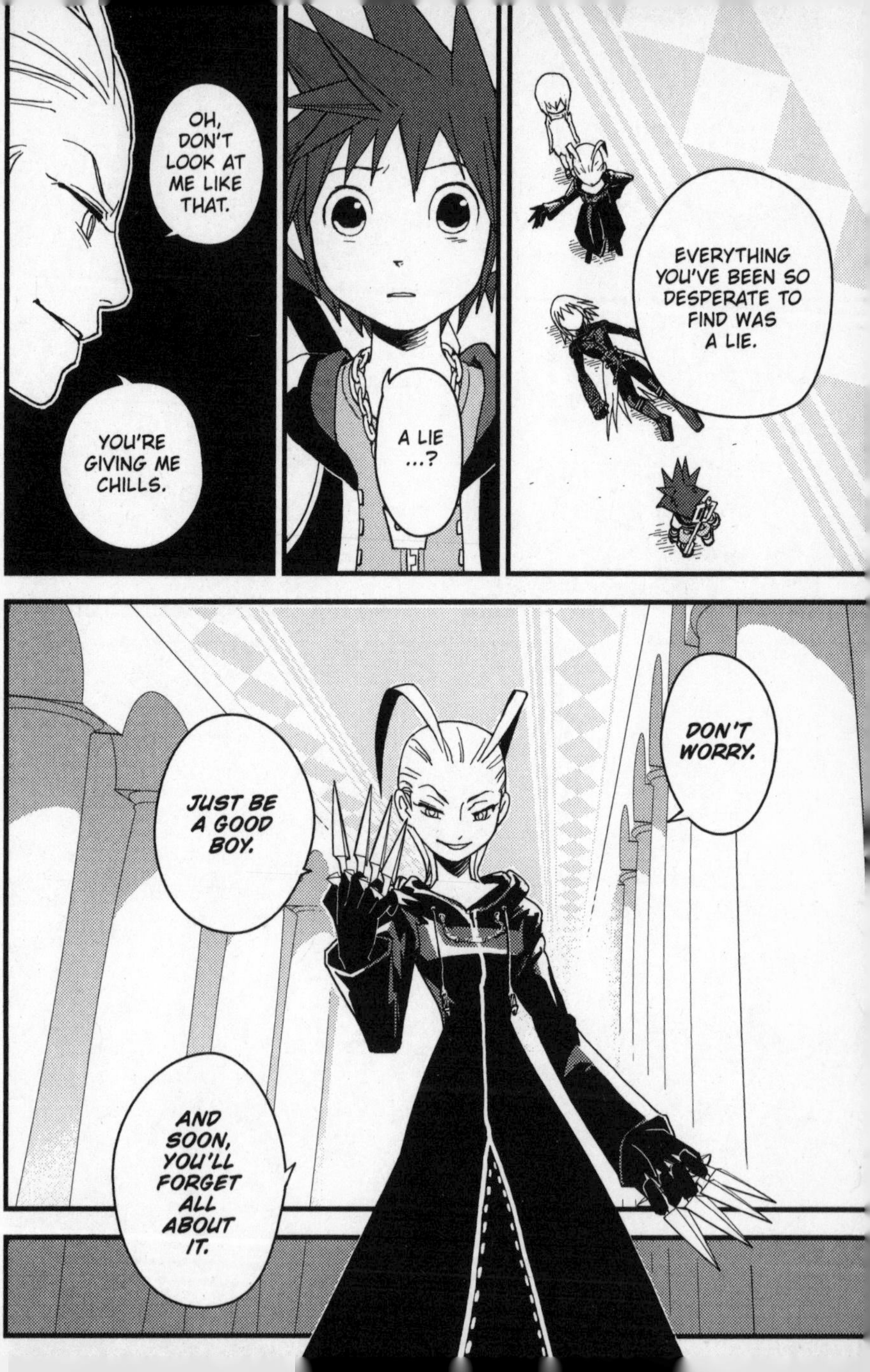
EVERYTHING YOU'VE BEEN SO DESPERATE TO FIND WAS A LIE.
A LIE ...?
OH, DON'T LOOK AT ME LIKE THAT.
YOU'RE GIVING ME CHILLS.
DON'T WORRY.
JUST BE A GOOD BOY.
AND SOON, YOU'LL FORGET ALL ABOUT IT.

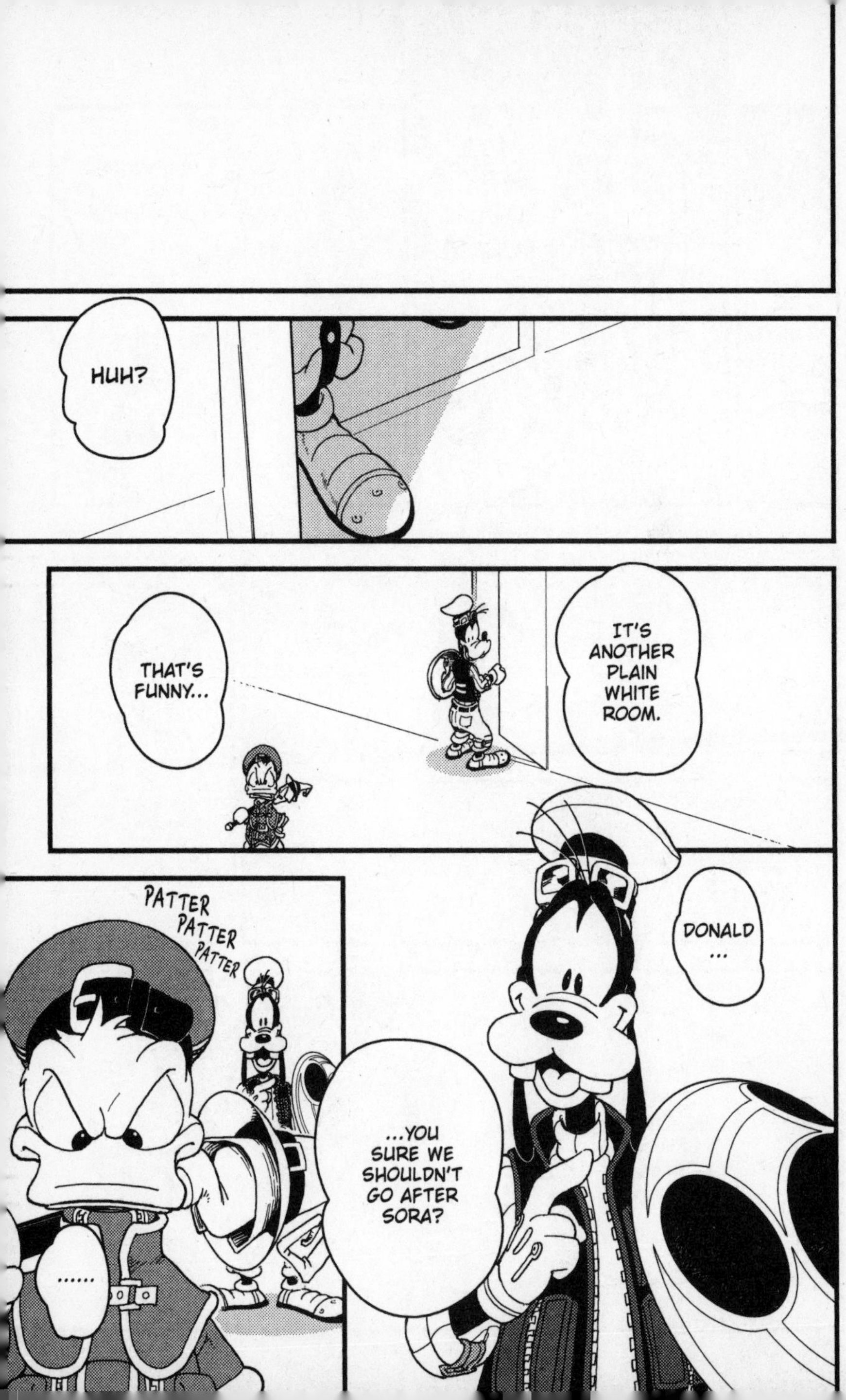
HUH?
IT'S ANOTHER PLAIN WHITE ROOM.
THAT'S FUNNY...
DONALD ...
...YOU SURE WE SHOULDN'T GO AFTER SORA?
PATTER PATTER PATTER
......

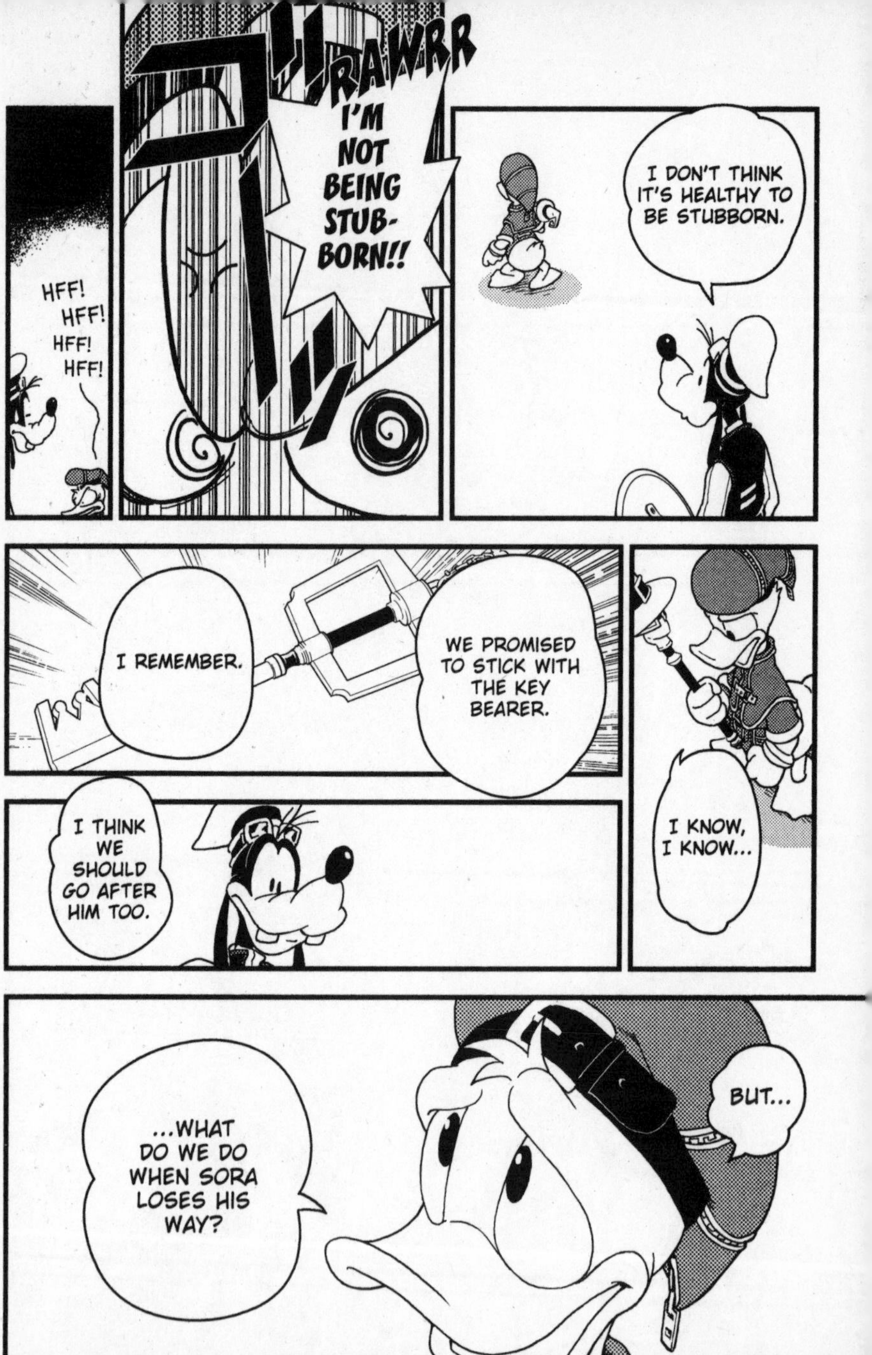
I DON'T THINK IT'S HEALTHY TO BE STUBBORN.
RAWRR
I'M NOT BEING STUB-BORN!!
HFF! HFF! HFF! HFF!
I KNOW, I KNOW...
WE PROMISED TO STICK WITH THE KEY BEARER.
I REMEMBER.
I THINK WE SHOULD GO AFTER HIM TOO.
BUT...
...WHAT DO WE DO WHEN SORA LOSES HIS WAY?

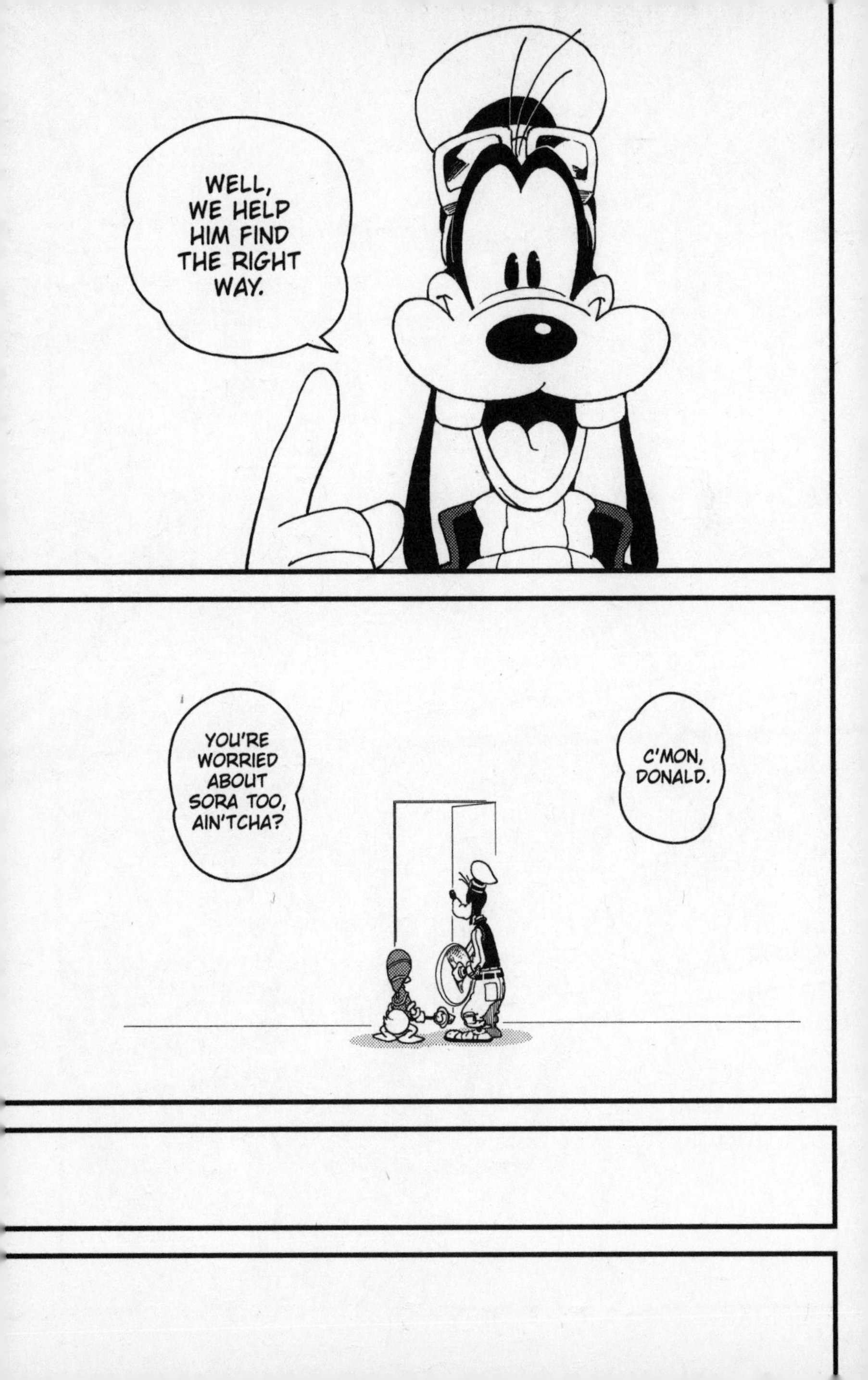
WELL, WE HELP HIM FIND THE RIGHT WAY.
C'MON, DONALD.
YOU'RE WORRIED ABOUT SORA TOO, AIN'TCHA?

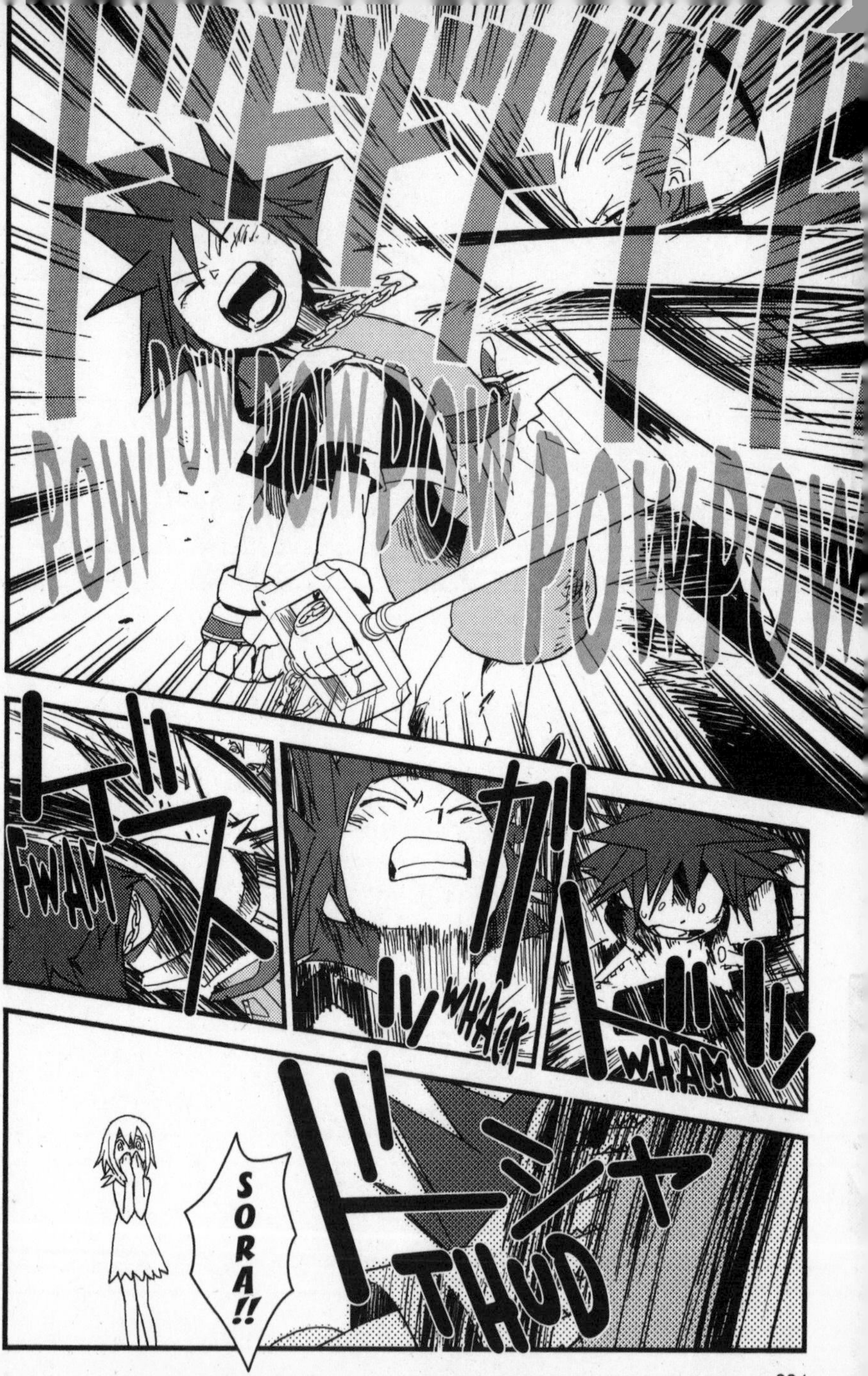
POW POW POW POW POW POW POW POW
WHAM
WHACK
FWAM
THUD
SORA!!

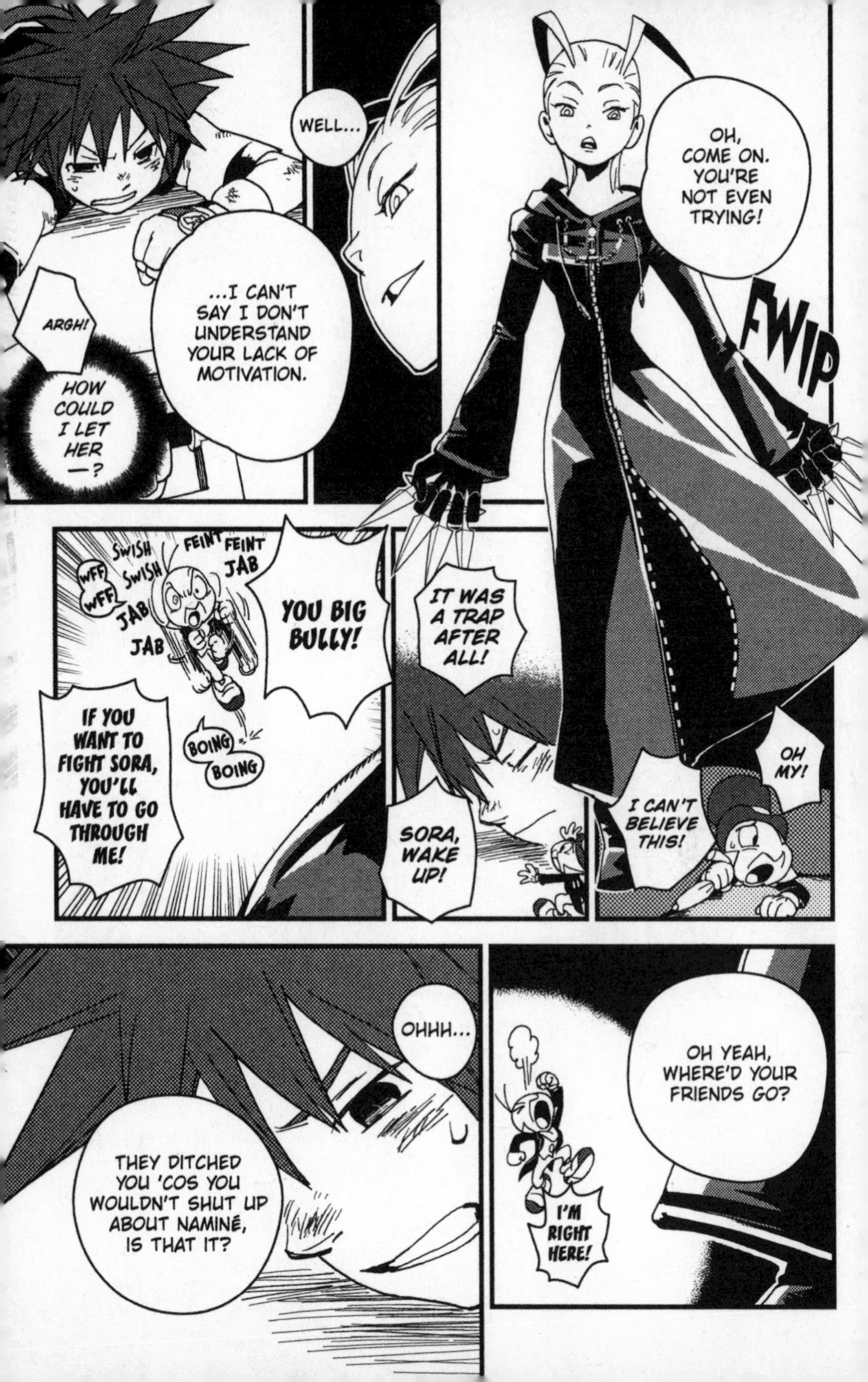
OH, COME ON. YOU'RE NOT EVEN TRYING!
FWIP
WELL...
...I CAN'T SAY I DON'T UNDERSTAND YOUR LACK OF MOTIVATION.
ARGH!
HOW COULD I LET HER—?
OH MY!
I CAN'T BELIEVE THIS!
IT WAS A TRAP AFTER ALL!
SORA, WAKE UP!
YOU BIG BULLY!
FEINT FEINT
JAB
SWISH SWISH
WFF WFF
JAB JAB
IF YOU WANT TO FIGHT SORA, YOU'LL HAVE TO GO THROUGH ME!
BOING BOING
OH YEAH, WHERE'D YOUR FRIENDS GO?
I'M RIGHT HERE!
OHHH...
THEY DITCHED YOU 'COS YOU WOULDN'T SHUT UP ABOUT NAMINÉ, IS THAT IT?

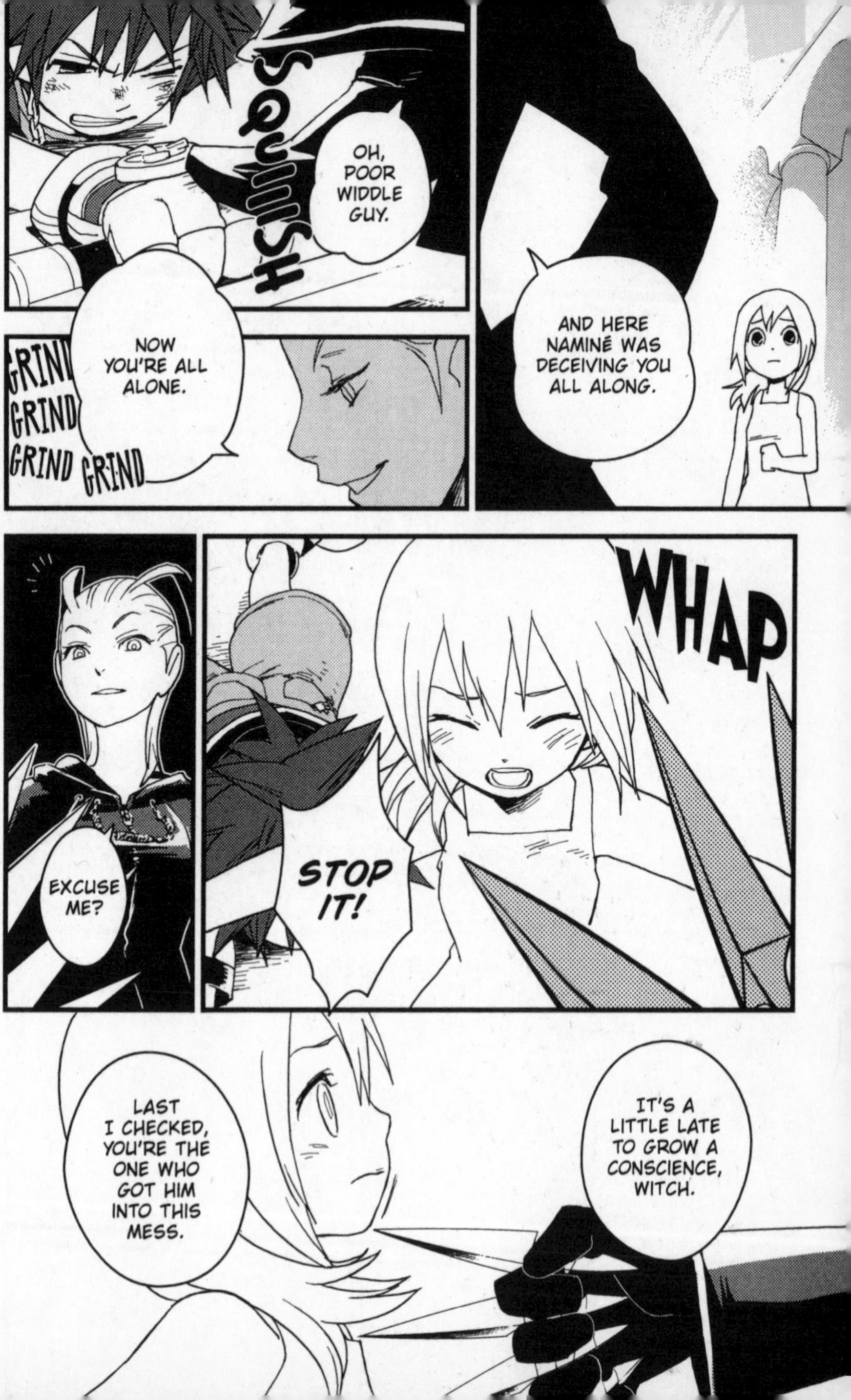
AND HERE NAMINÉ WAS DECEIVING YOU ALL ALONG.
SQUIISH
OH, POOR WIDDLE GUY.
NOW YOU'RE ALL ALONE.
GRIND GRIND GRIND GRIND GRIND
WHAP
STOP IT!
EXCUSE ME?
IT'S A LITTLE LATE TO GROW A CONSCIENCE, WITCH.
LAST I CHECKED, YOU'RE THE ONE WHO GOT HIM INTO THIS MESS.

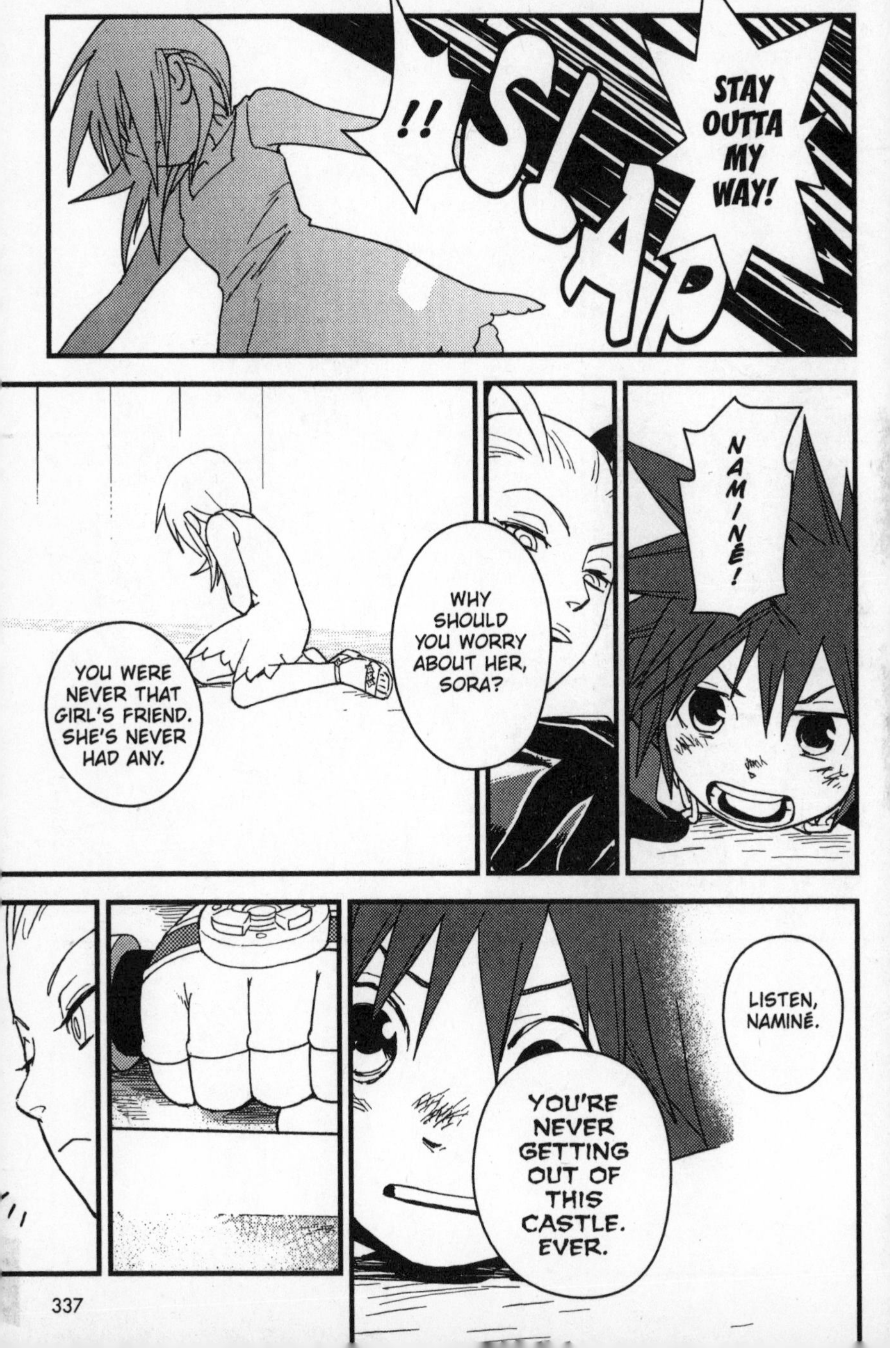
STAY OUTTA MY WAY!
SLAP
!!
NAMINÉ!
WHY SHOULD YOU WORRY ABOUT HER, SORA?
YOU WERE NEVER THAT GIRL'S FRIEND. SHE'S NEVER HAD ANY.
LISTEN, NAMINÉ.
YOU'RE NEVER GETTING OUT OF THIS CASTLE. EVER.

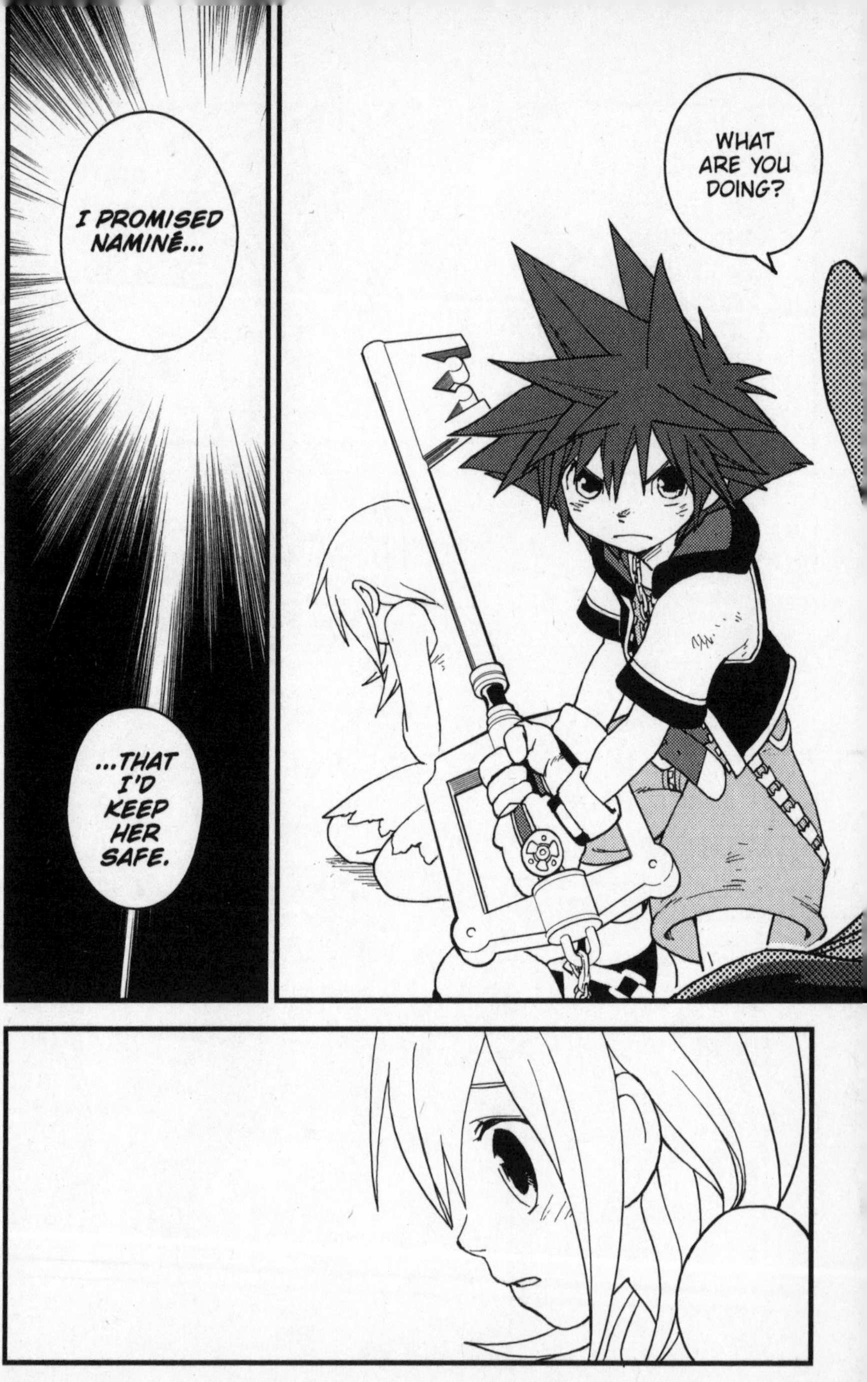
WHAT ARE YOU DOING?
I PROMISED NAMINÉ...
...THAT I'D KEEP HER SAFE.

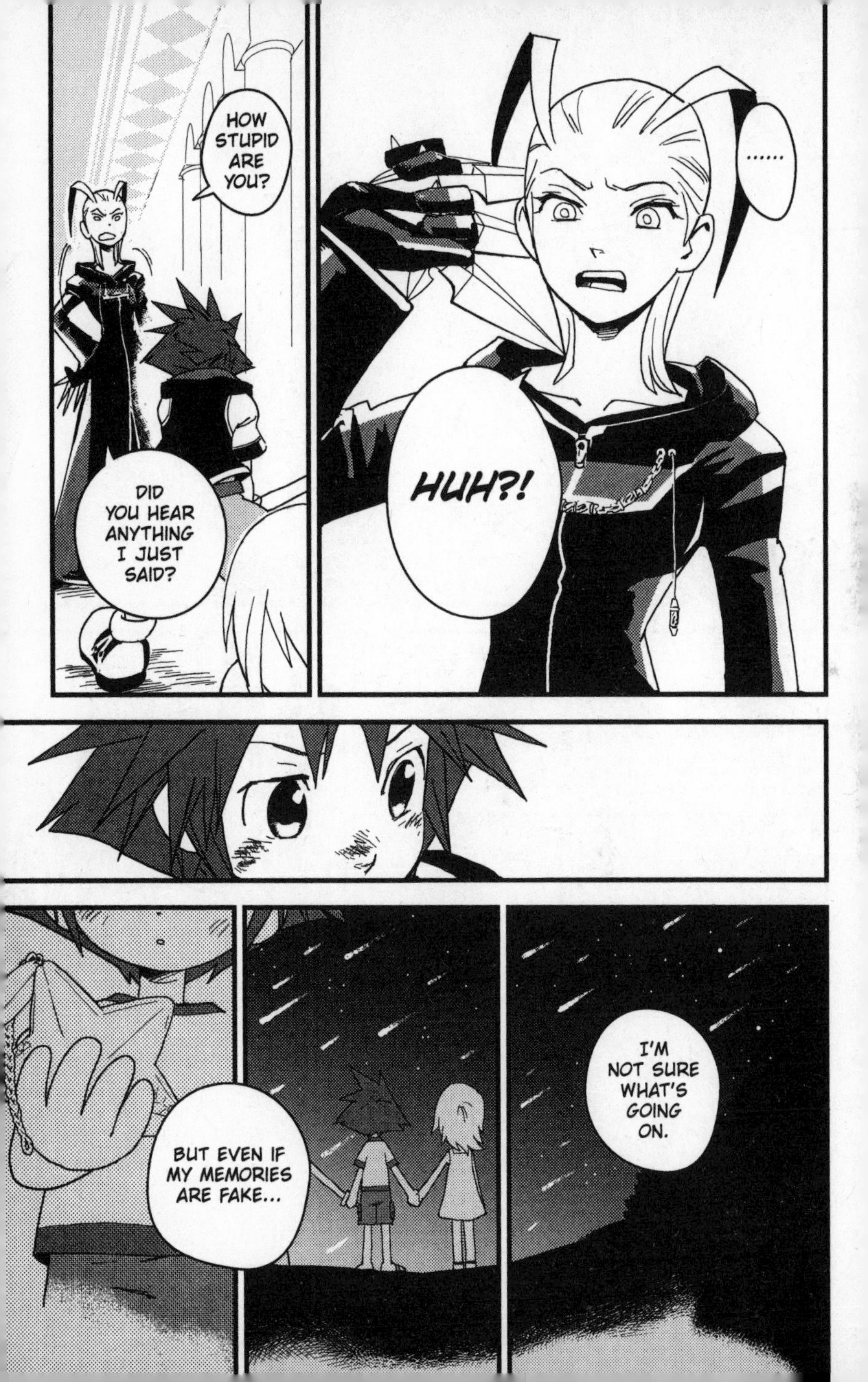
......
HUH?!
HOW STUPID ARE YOU?
DID YOU HEAR ANYTHING I JUST SAID?
I'M NOT SURE WHAT'S GOING ON.
BUT EVEN IF MY MEMORIES ARE FAKE...

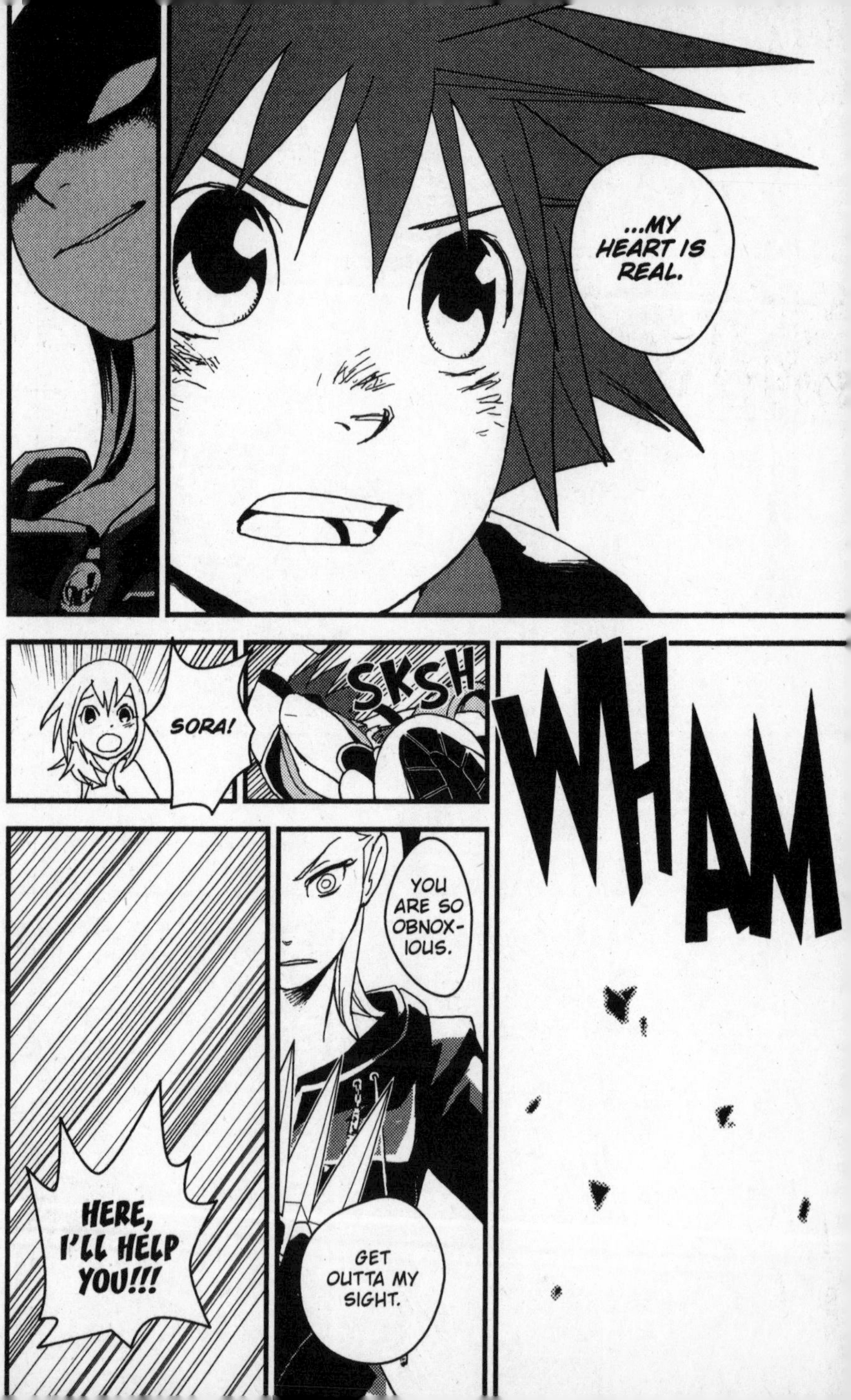
...MY HEART IS REAL.
WHAM
SKSH
SORA!
YOU ARE SO OBNOX-IOUS.
GET OUTTA MY SIGHT.
HERE, I'LL HELP YOU!!!

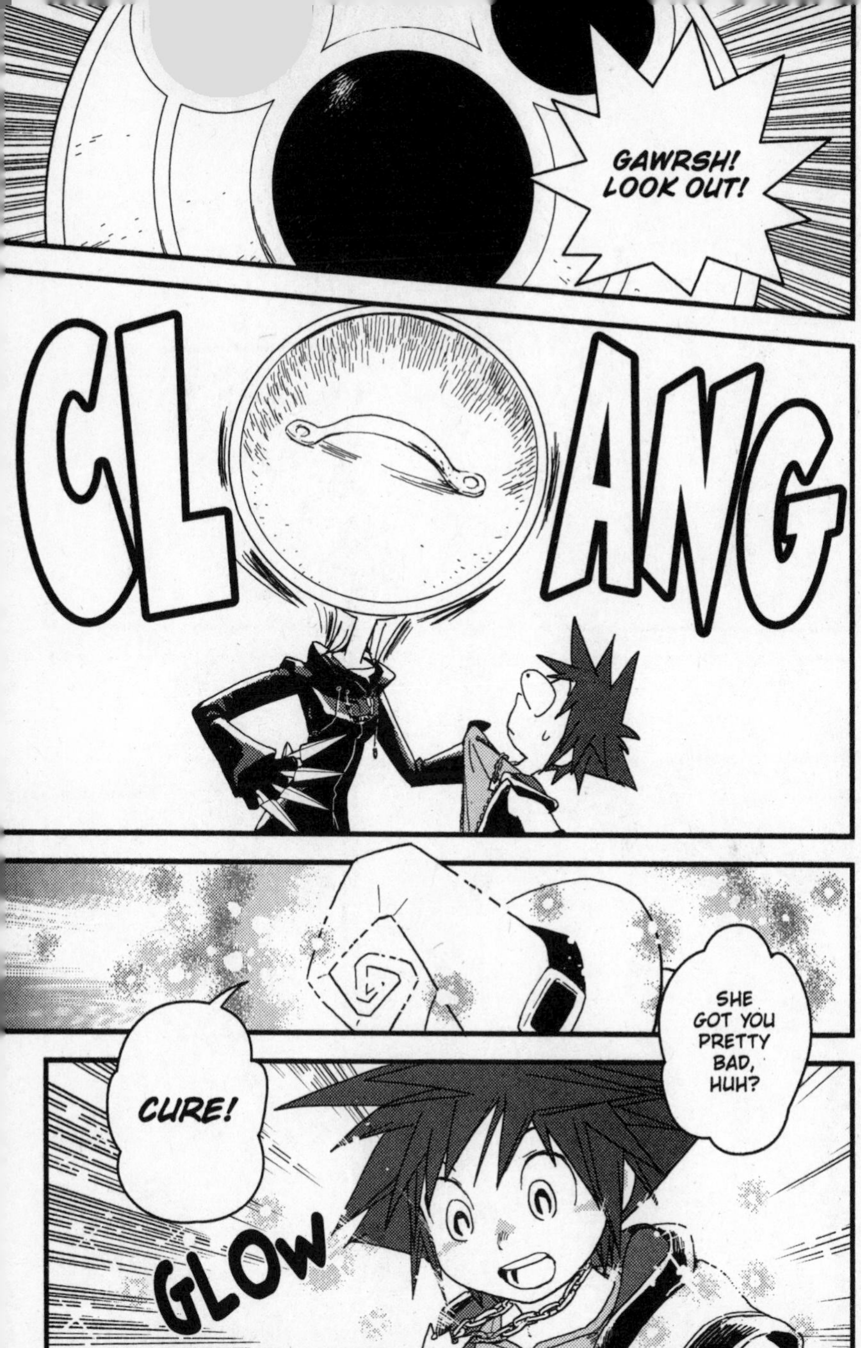
GAWRSH! LOOK OUT!
CLANG
SHE GOT YOU PRETTY BAD, HUH?
CURE!
GLOW

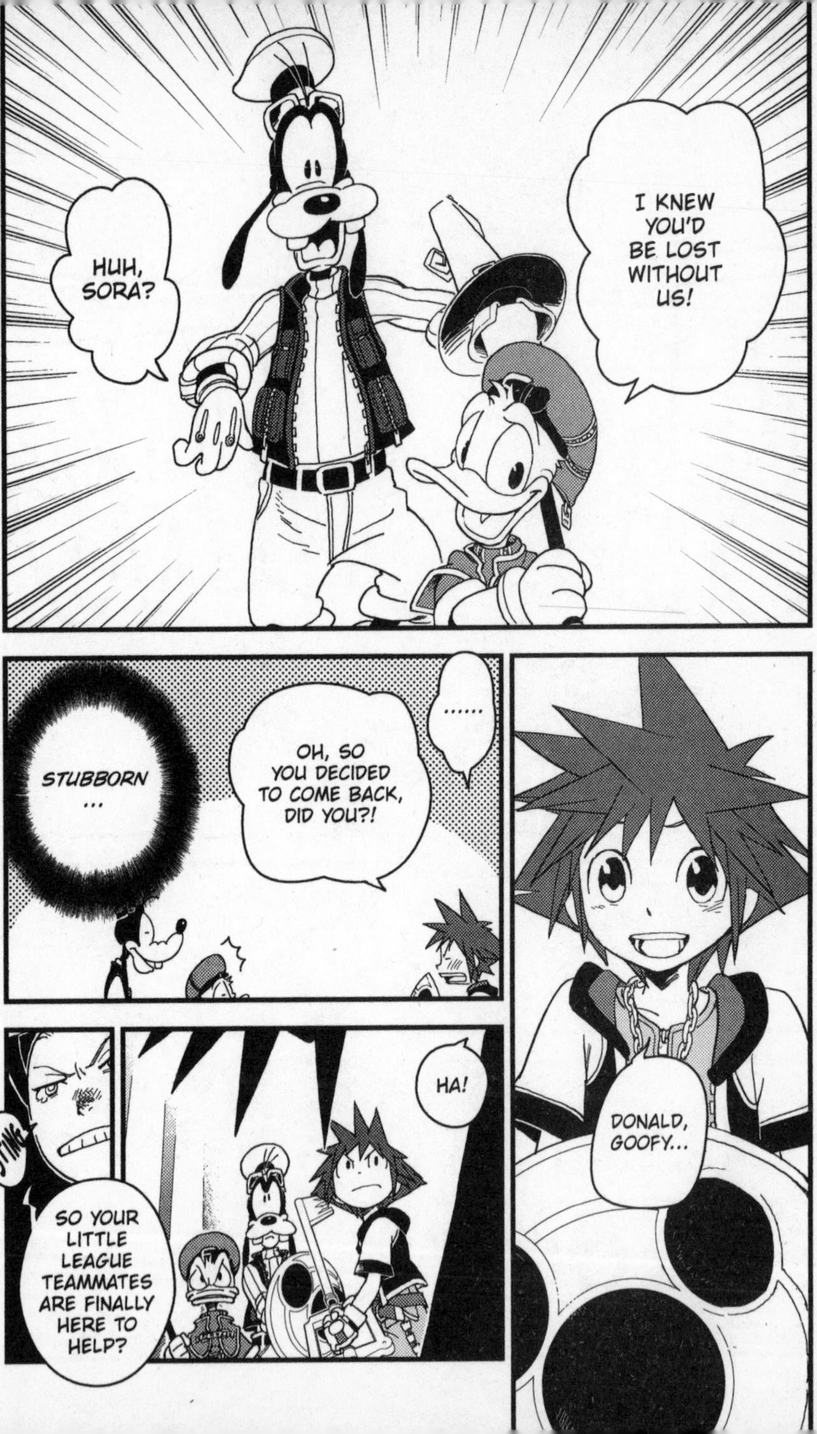
I KNEW YOU'D BE LOST WITHOUT US!
HUH, SORA?
DONALD, GOOFY...
......
OH, SO YOU DECIDED TO COME BACK, DID YOU?!
STUBBORN ...
HA!
STING
SO YOUR LITTLE LEAGUE TEAMMATES ARE FINALLY HERE TO HELP?

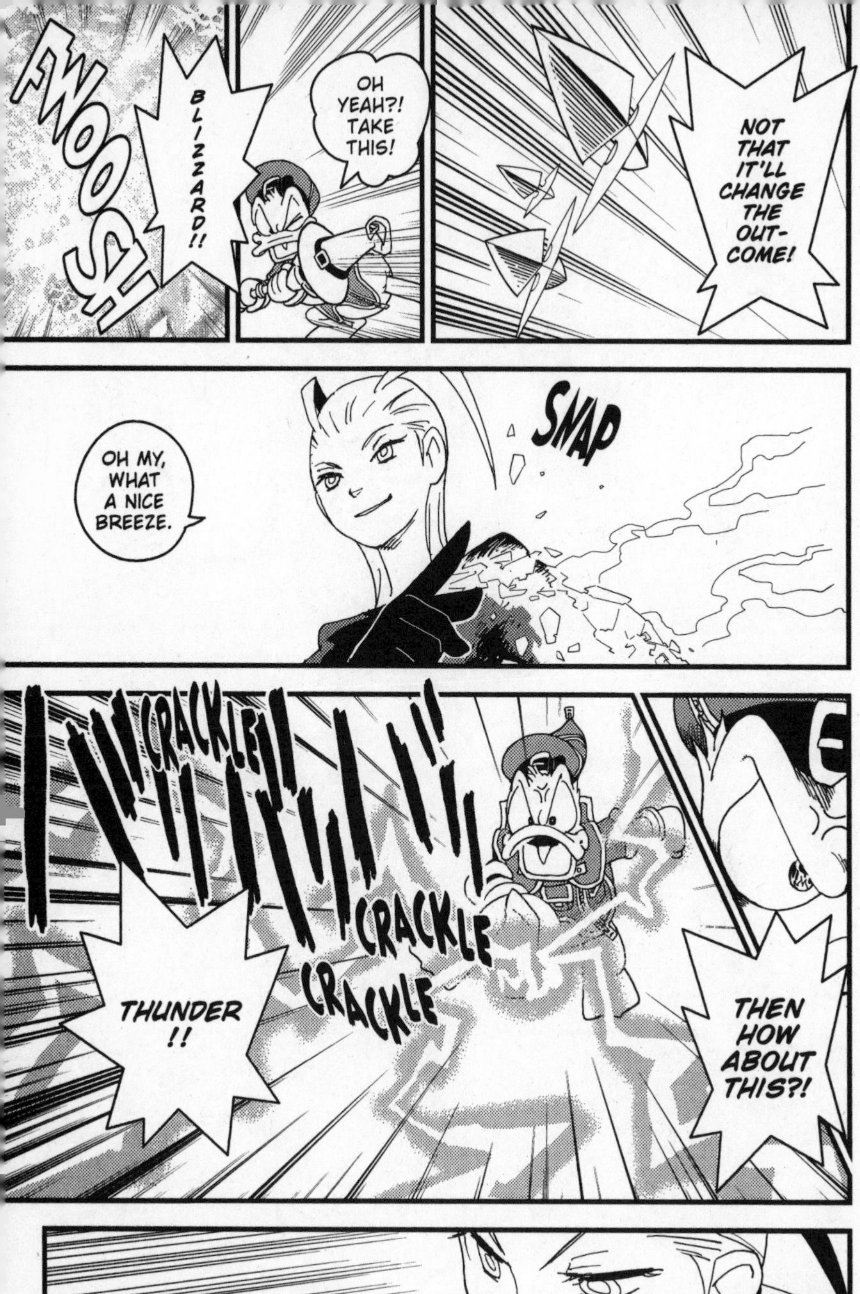
NOT THAT IT'LL CHANGE THE OUT-COME!
OH YEAH?! TAKE THIS!
BLIZZARD!!
FWOOSH
SNAP
OH MY, WHAT A NICE BREEZE.
THEN HOW ABOUT THIS?!
CRACKLE
CRACKLE
CRACKLE
THUNDER!!

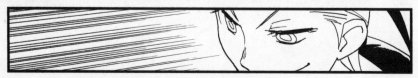

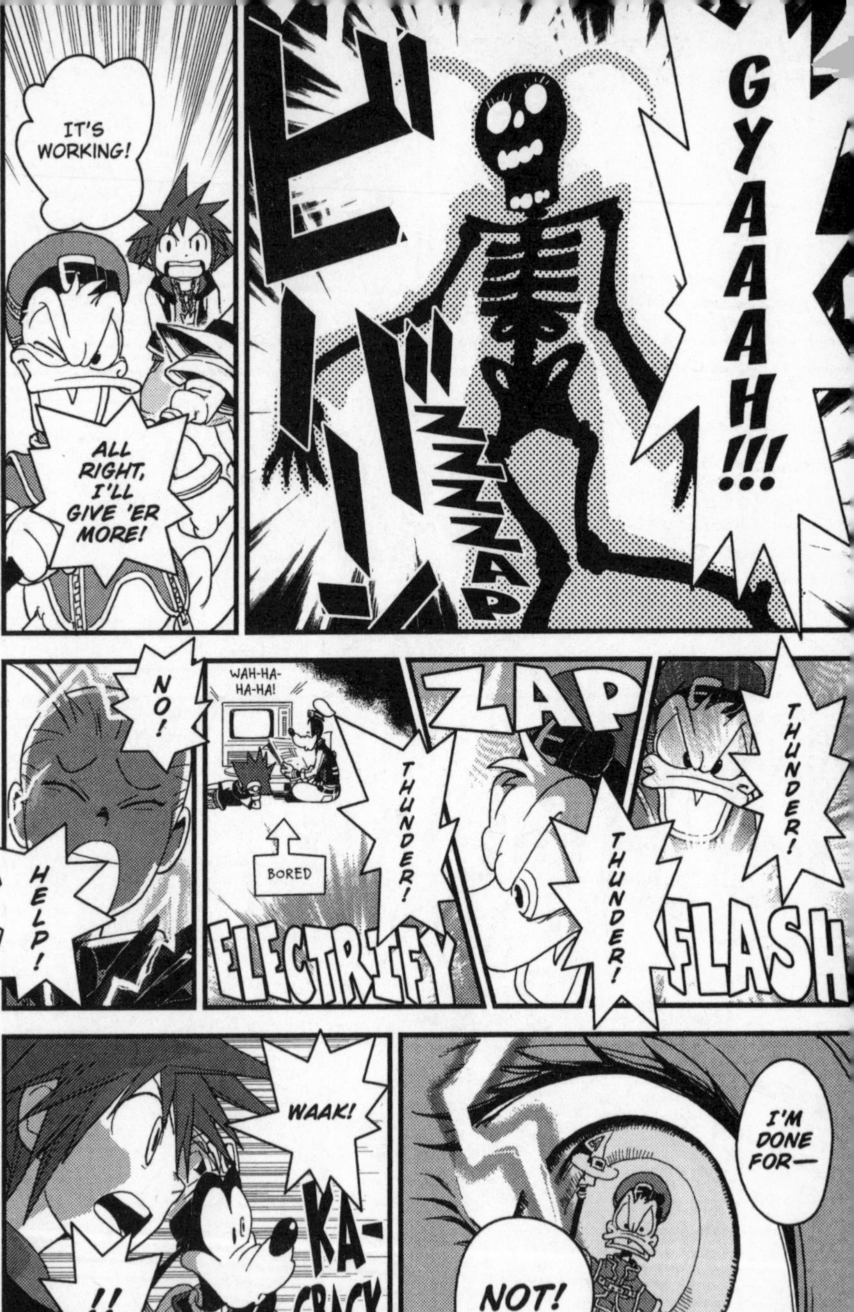
GYAAAH!!!
ZZZZZAP
IT'S WORKING!
ALL RIGHT, I'LL GIVE 'ER MORE!
THUNDER!
FLASH
ZAP
THUNDER!
WAH-HA-HA-HA!
THUNDER!
BORED
ELECTRIFY
NO!
HELP!
I'M DONE FOR—
NOT!
WAAK!
KA-CRACK
!!

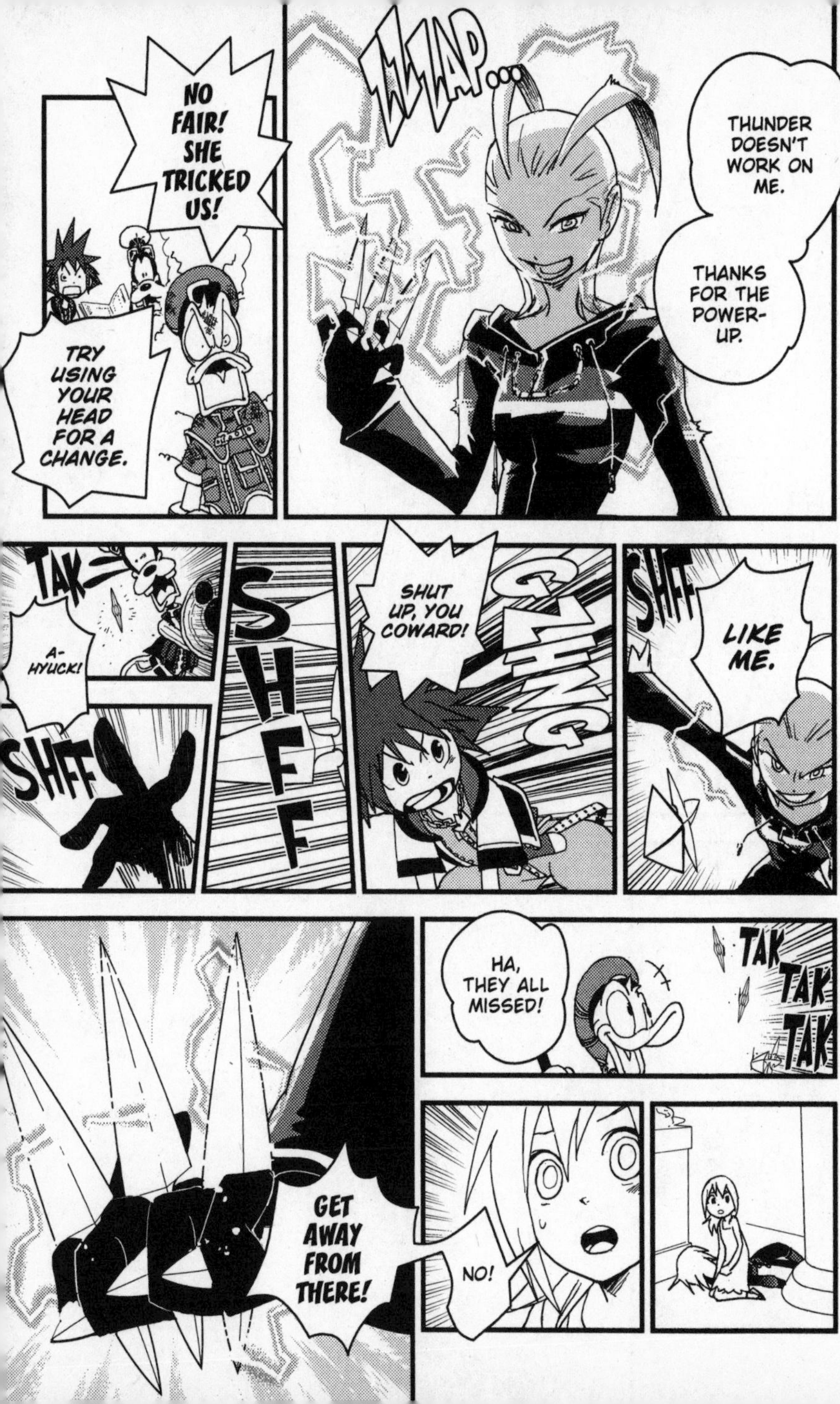
ZZZAP...
THUNDER DOESN'T WORK ON ME.
THANKS FOR THE POWER-UP.
NO FAIR! SHE TRICKED US!
TRY USING YOUR HEAD FOR A CHANGE.
SHFF
LIKE ME.
SHUT UP, YOU COWARD!
SHFF
TAK
A-HYUCK!
SHFF
HA, THEY ALL MISSED!
TAK TAK TAK
NO!
GET AWAY FROM THERE!

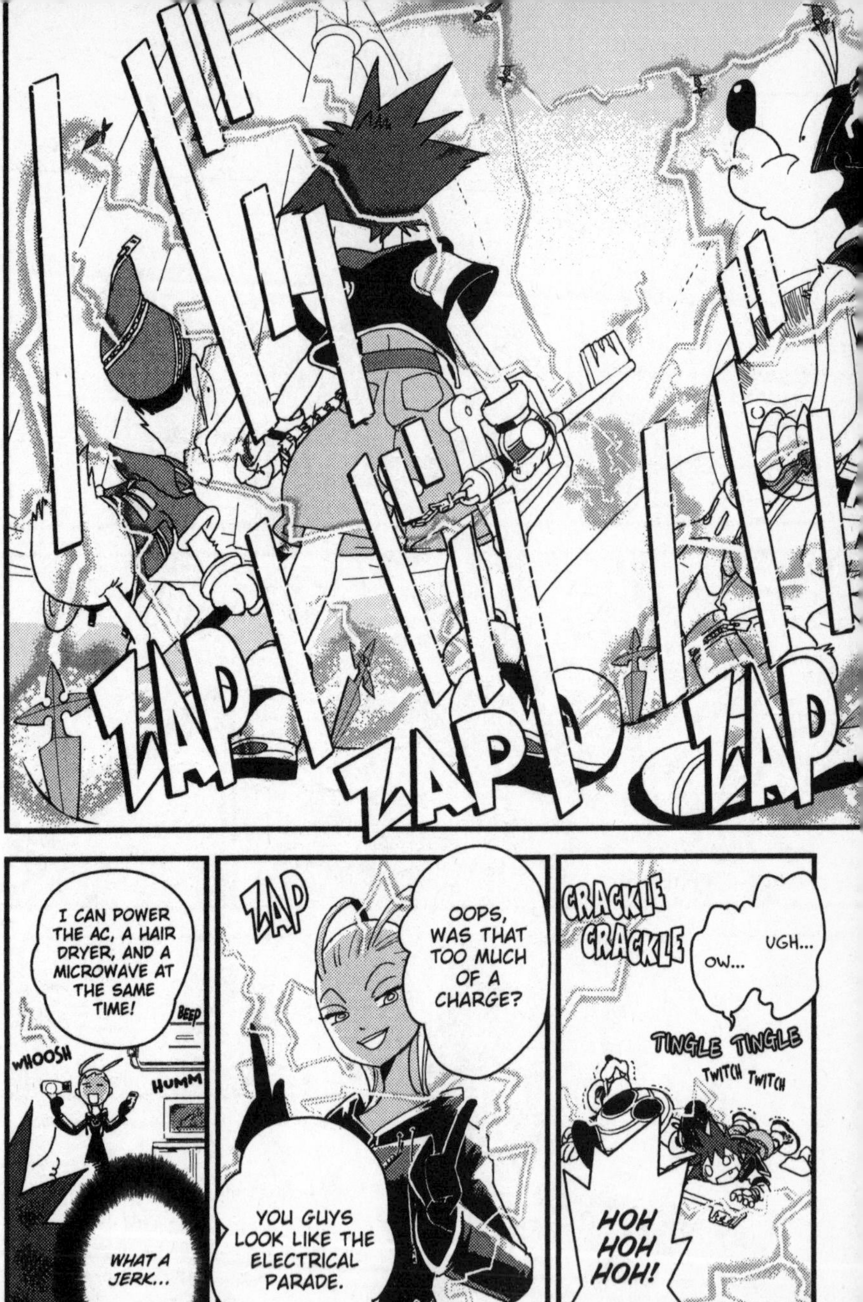
ZAP
ZAP
ZAP
CRACKLE
CRACKLE
UGH...
OW...
TINGLE TINGLE
TWITCH TWITCH
HOH HOH HOH!
ZAP
OOPS, WAS THAT TOO MUCH OF A CHARGE?
YOU GUYS LOOK LIKE THE ELECTRICAL PARADE.
I CAN POWER THE AC, A HAIR DRYER, AND A MICROWAVE AT THE SAME TIME!
BEEP
WHOOSH
HUMM
WHAT A JERK...

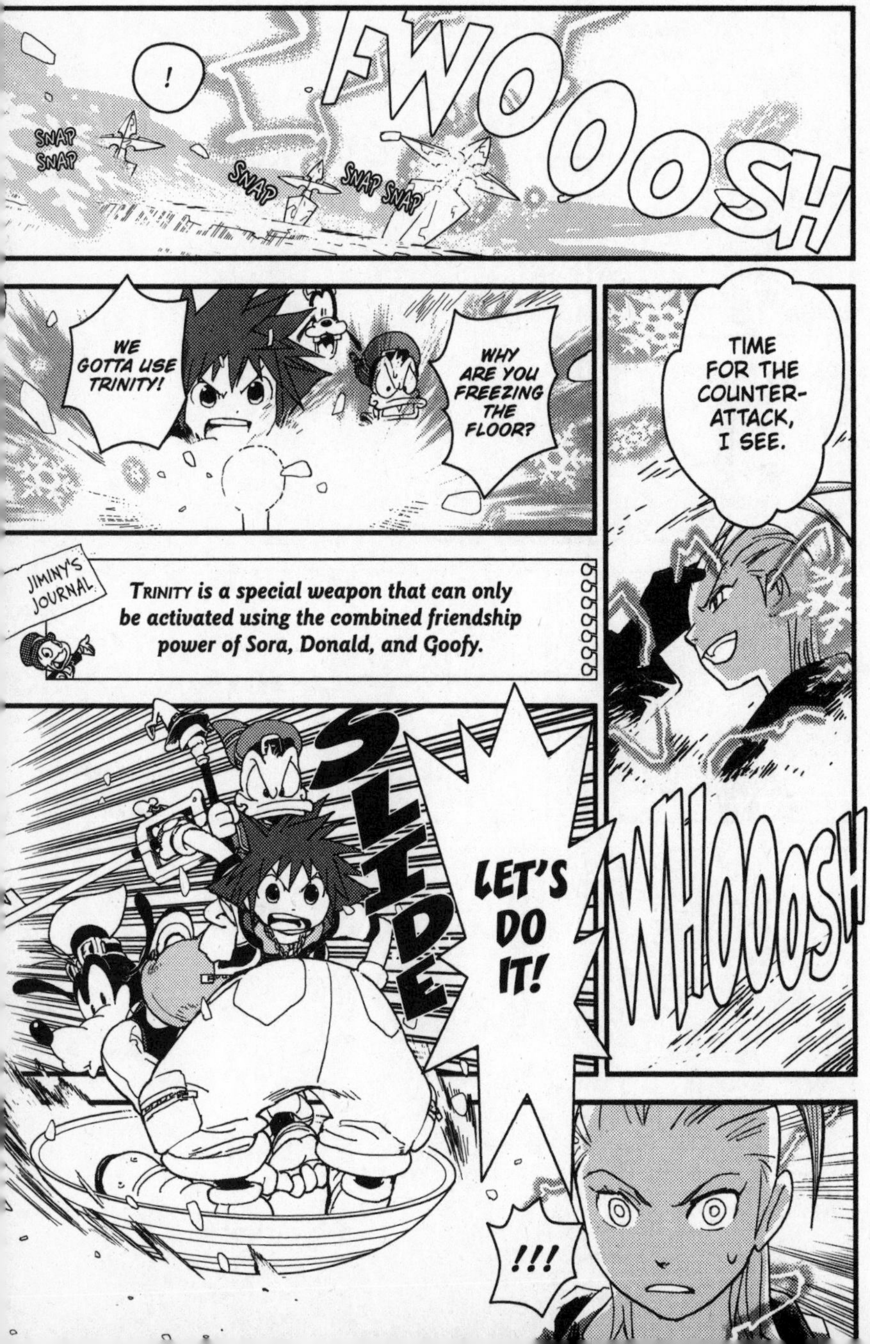
FWOOOSH
!
SNAP SNAP
SNAP
SNAP SNAP
TIME FOR THE COUNTER-ATTACK, I SEE.
WHOOOSH
WHY ARE YOU FREEZING THE FLOOR?
WE GOTTA USE TRINITY!
JIMINY'S JOURNAL
TRINITY is a special weapon that can only be activated using the combined friendship power of Sora, Donald, and Goofy.
SLIDE
LET'S DO IT!
!!!

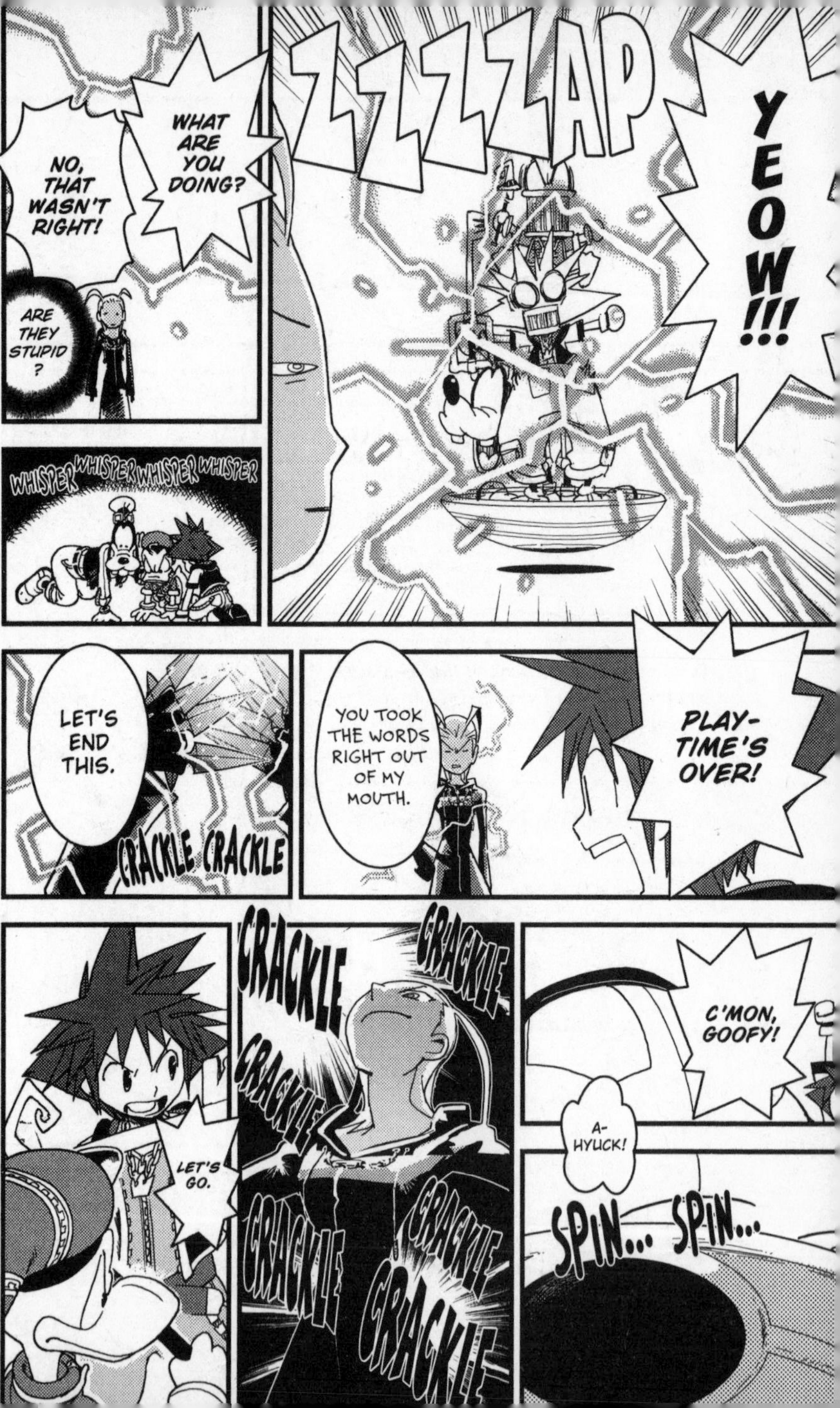
ZZZZZAP
YEOW!!!
WHAT ARE YOU DOING?
NO, THAT WASN'T RIGHT!
ARE THEY STUPID?
WHISPER WHISPER WHISPER WHISPER
PLAY-TIME'S OVER!
YOU TOOK THE WORDS RIGHT OUT OF MY MOUTH.
LET'S END THIS.
CRACKLE CRACKLE
C'MON, GOOFY!
A-HYUCK!
SPIN... SPIN...
CRACKLE CRACKLE CRACKLE CRACKLE CRACKLE CRACKLE
LET'S GO.

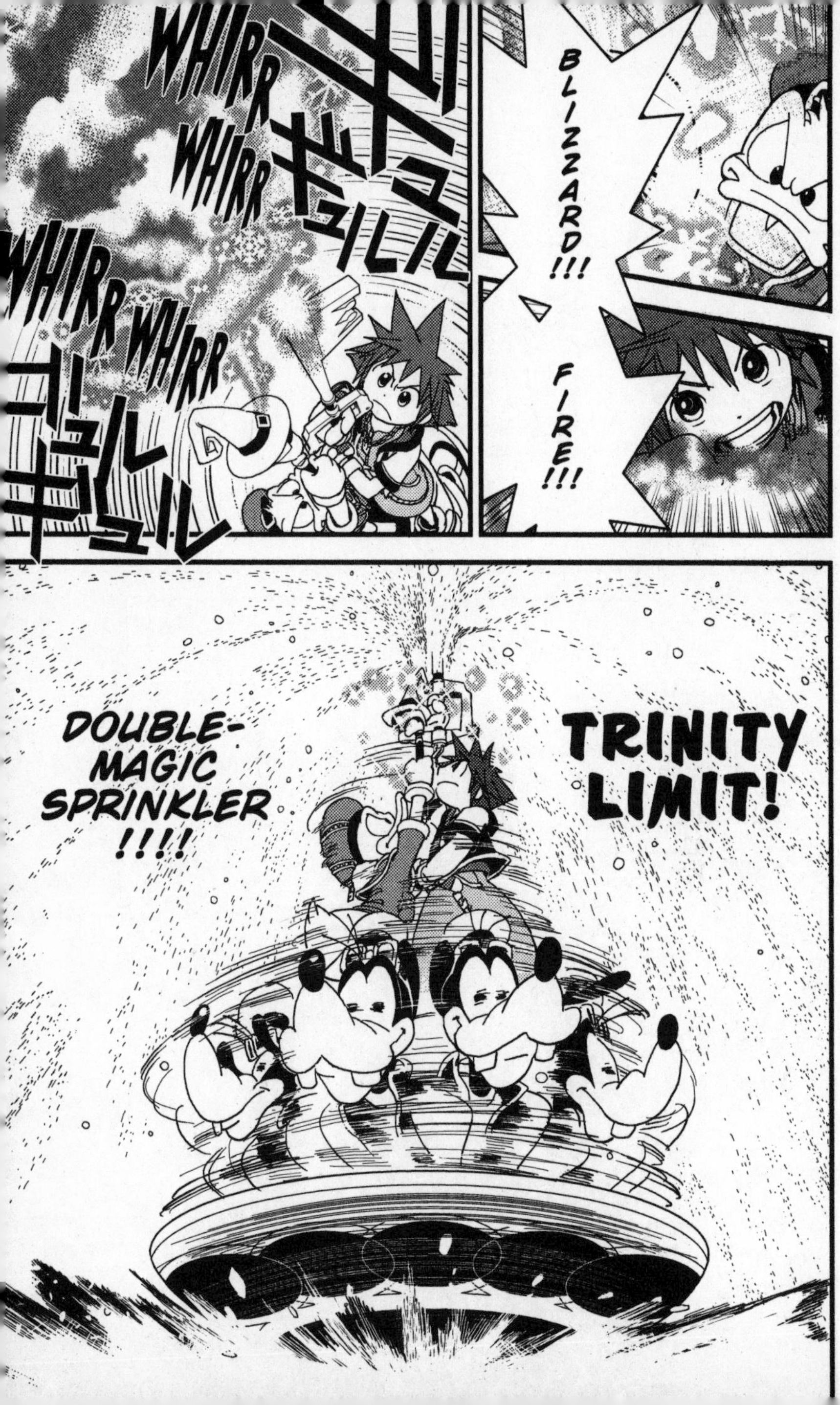
BLIZZARD!!!
FIRE!!!
WHIRR WHIRR
WHIRR WHIRR
TRINITY LIMIT!
DOUBLE-MAGIC SPRINKLER!!!!

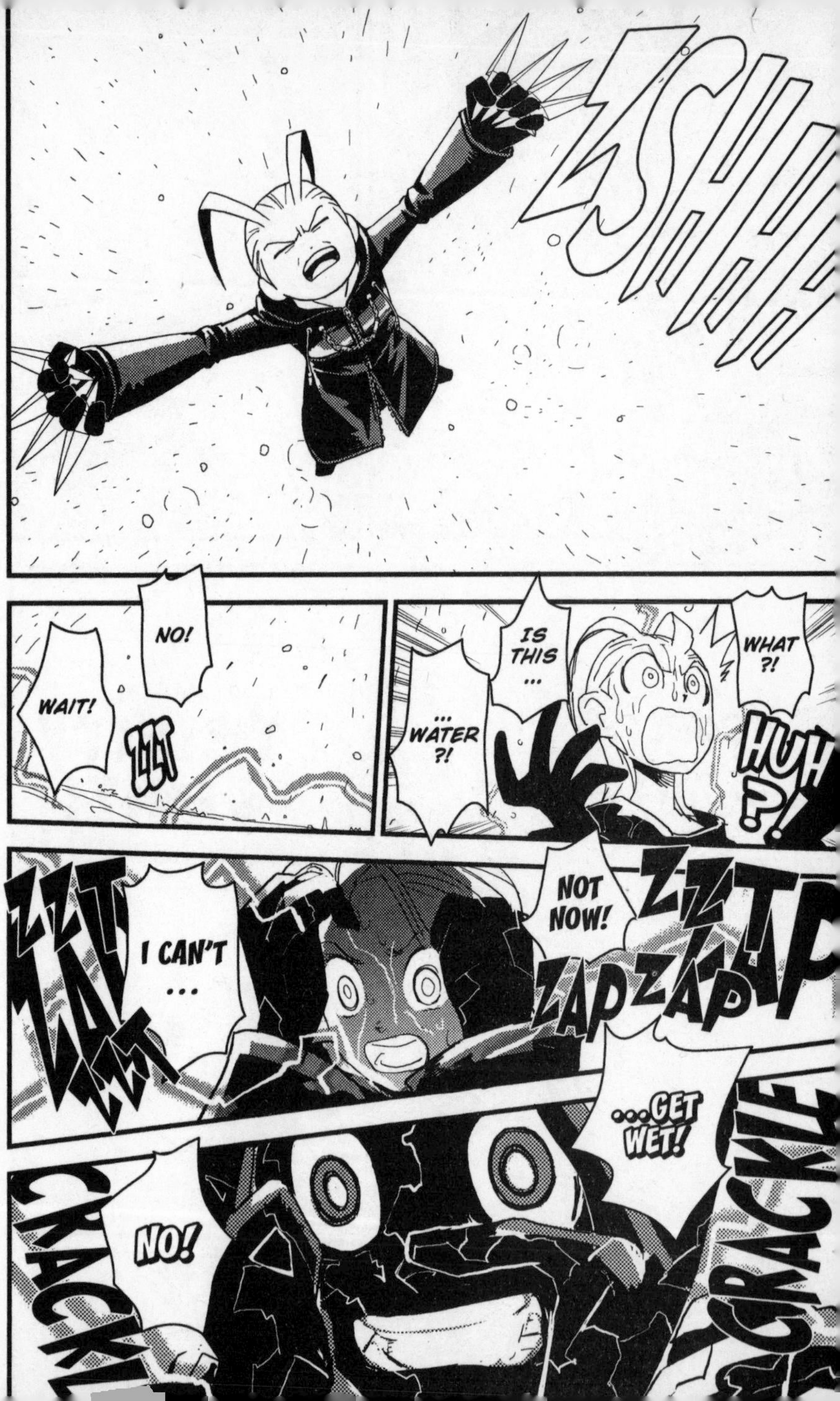
ZSHH
WHAT ?!
IS THIS ...
... WATER ?!
HUH ?!
NO!
WAIT!
ZZT
NOT NOW!
ZZZT
ZAP ZAP
I CAN'T ...
...GET WET!
CRACKLE
NO!
CRACKL

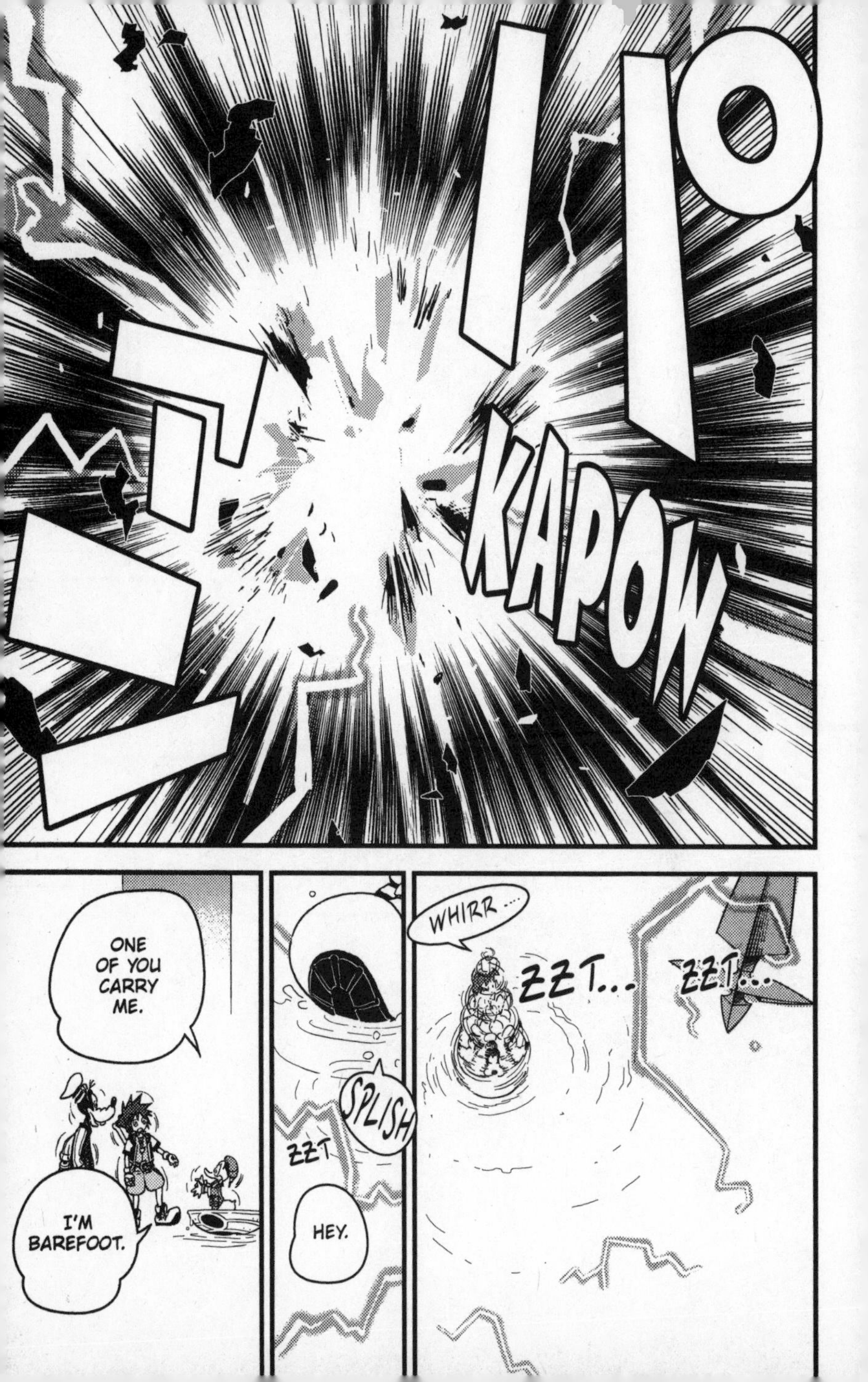
KAPOW
WHIRR ....
ZZT...
ZZT...
SPLISH
ZZT
HEY.
ONE OF YOU CARRY ME.
I'M BAREFOOT.

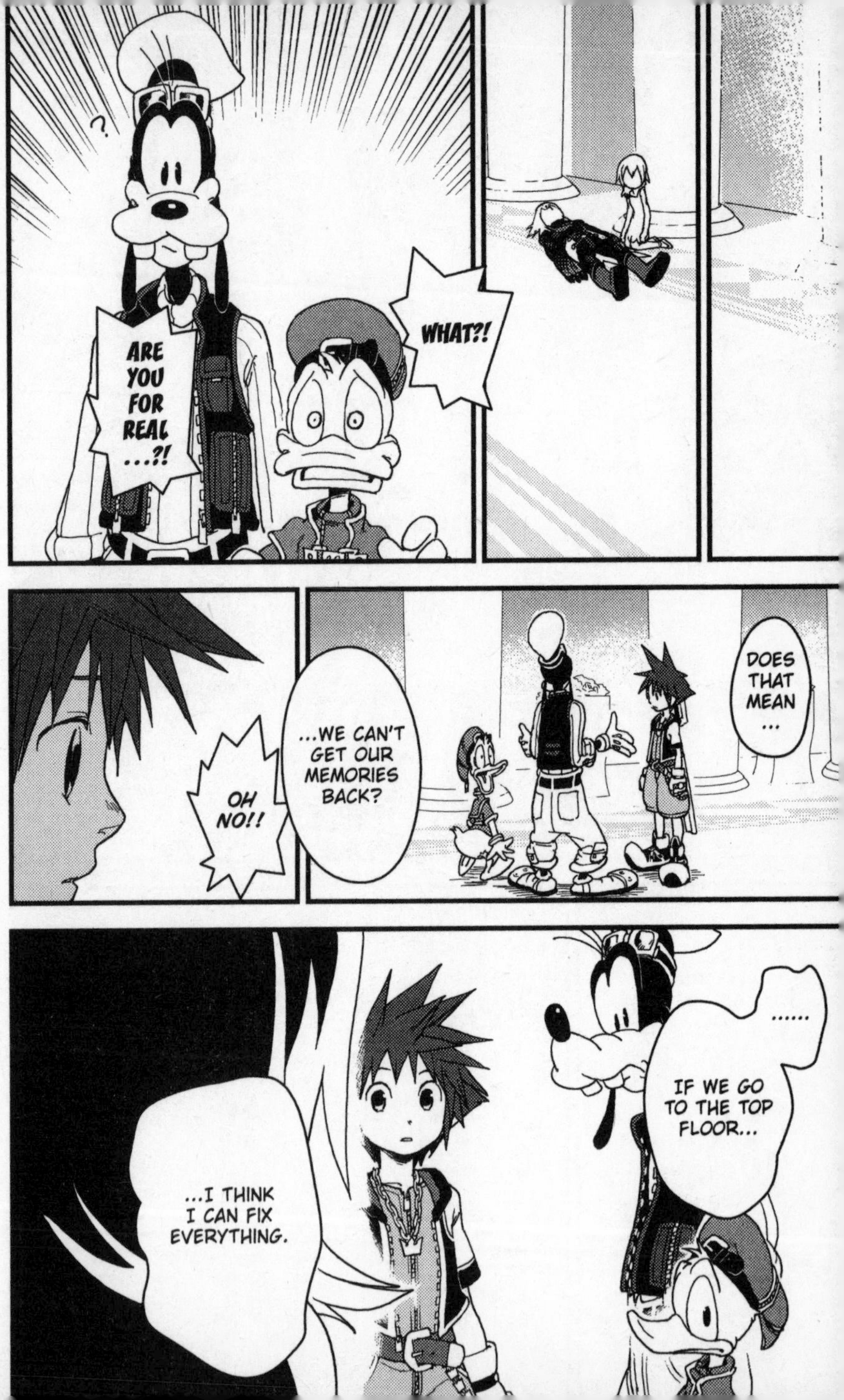
WHAT?!
ARE YOU FOR REAL...?!
DOES THAT MEAN...
...WE CAN'T GET OUR MEMORIES BACK?
OH NO!!
......
IF WE GO TO THE TOP FLOOR...
...I THINK I CAN FIX EVERYTHING.

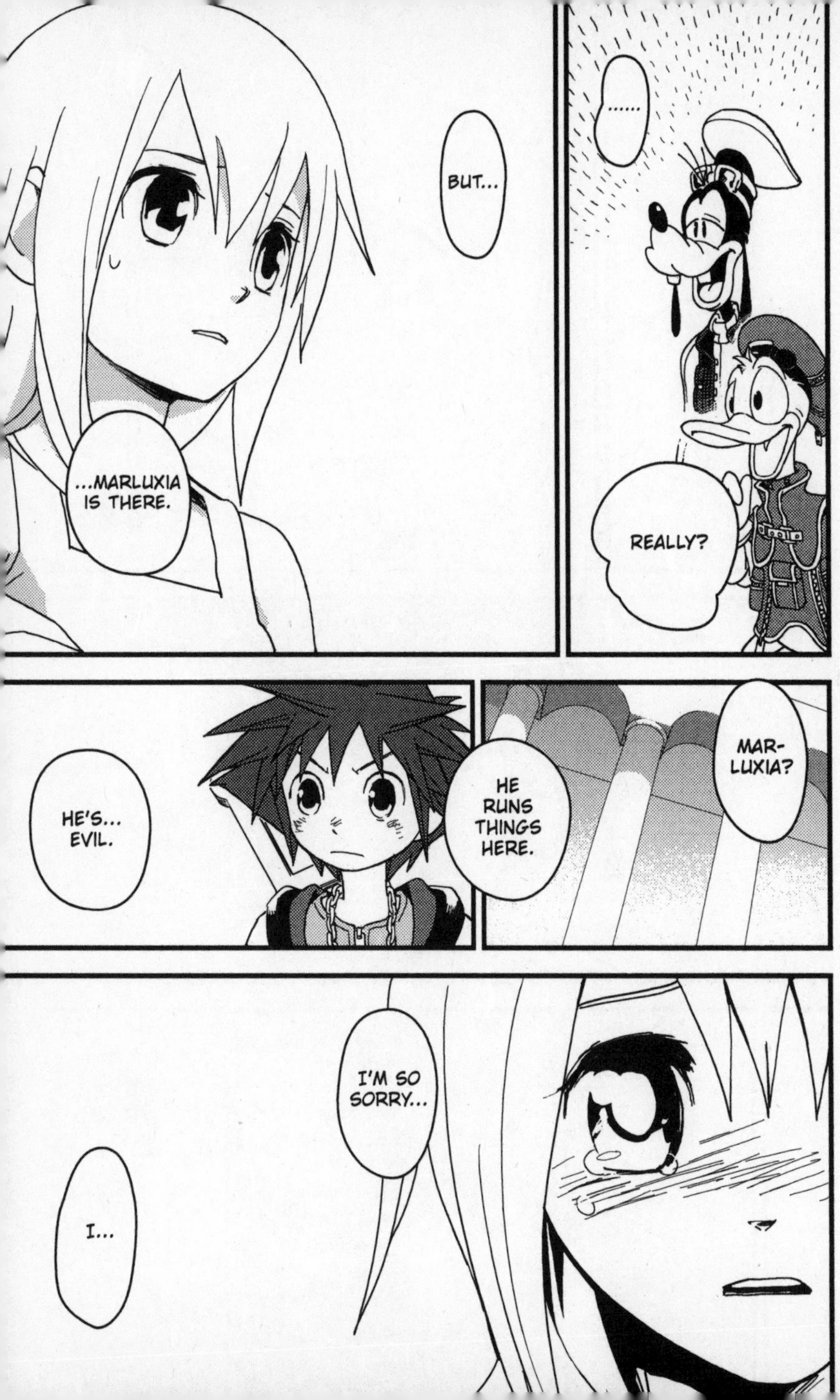
......
REALLY?
BUT...
...MARLUXIA IS THERE.
MAR-LUXIA?
HE RUNS THINGS HERE.
HE'S... EVIL.
I'M SO SORRY...
I...

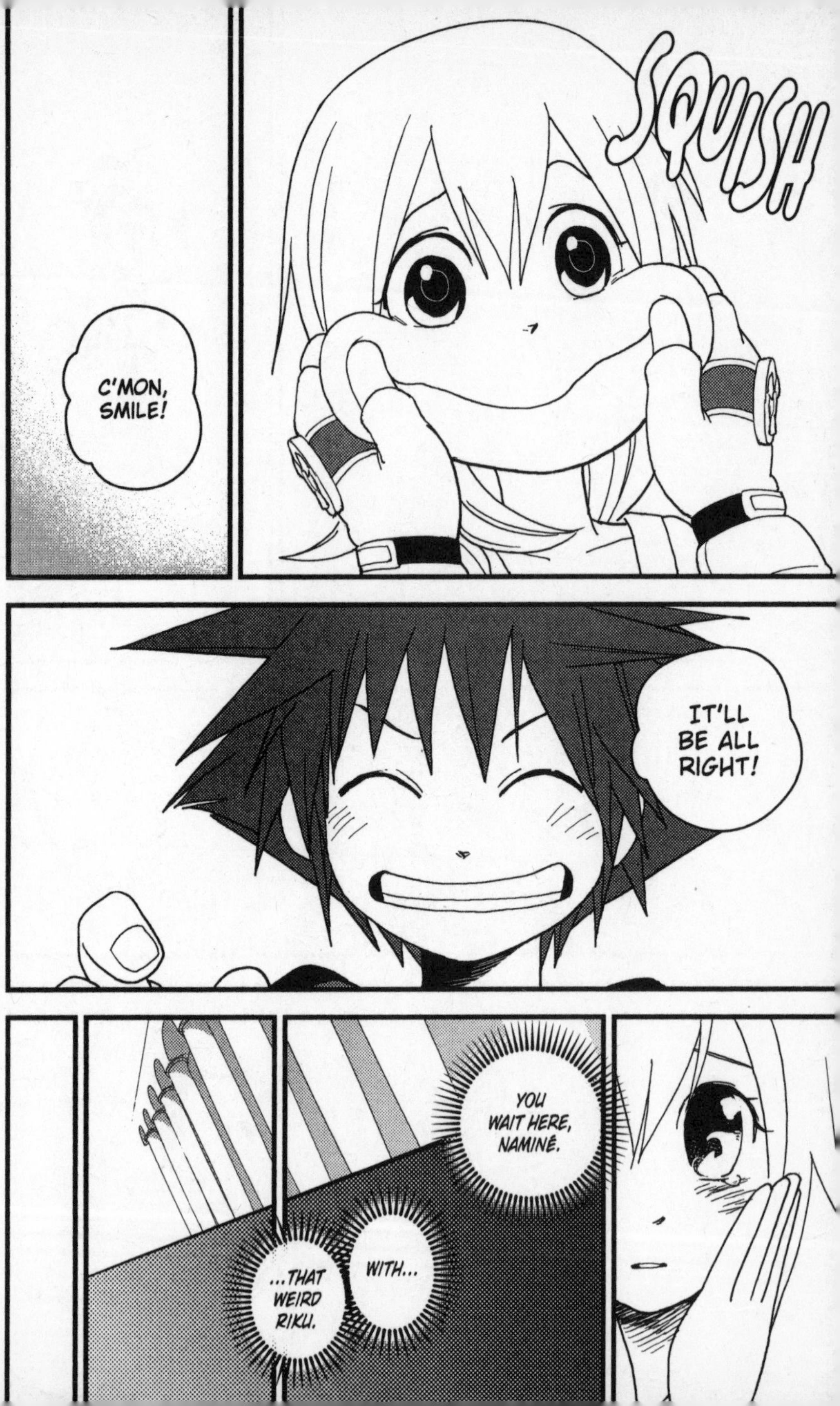
SQUISH
C'MON, SMILE!
IT'LL BE ALL RIGHT!
YOU WAIT HERE, NAMINÉ.
WITH...
...THAT WEIRD RIKU.

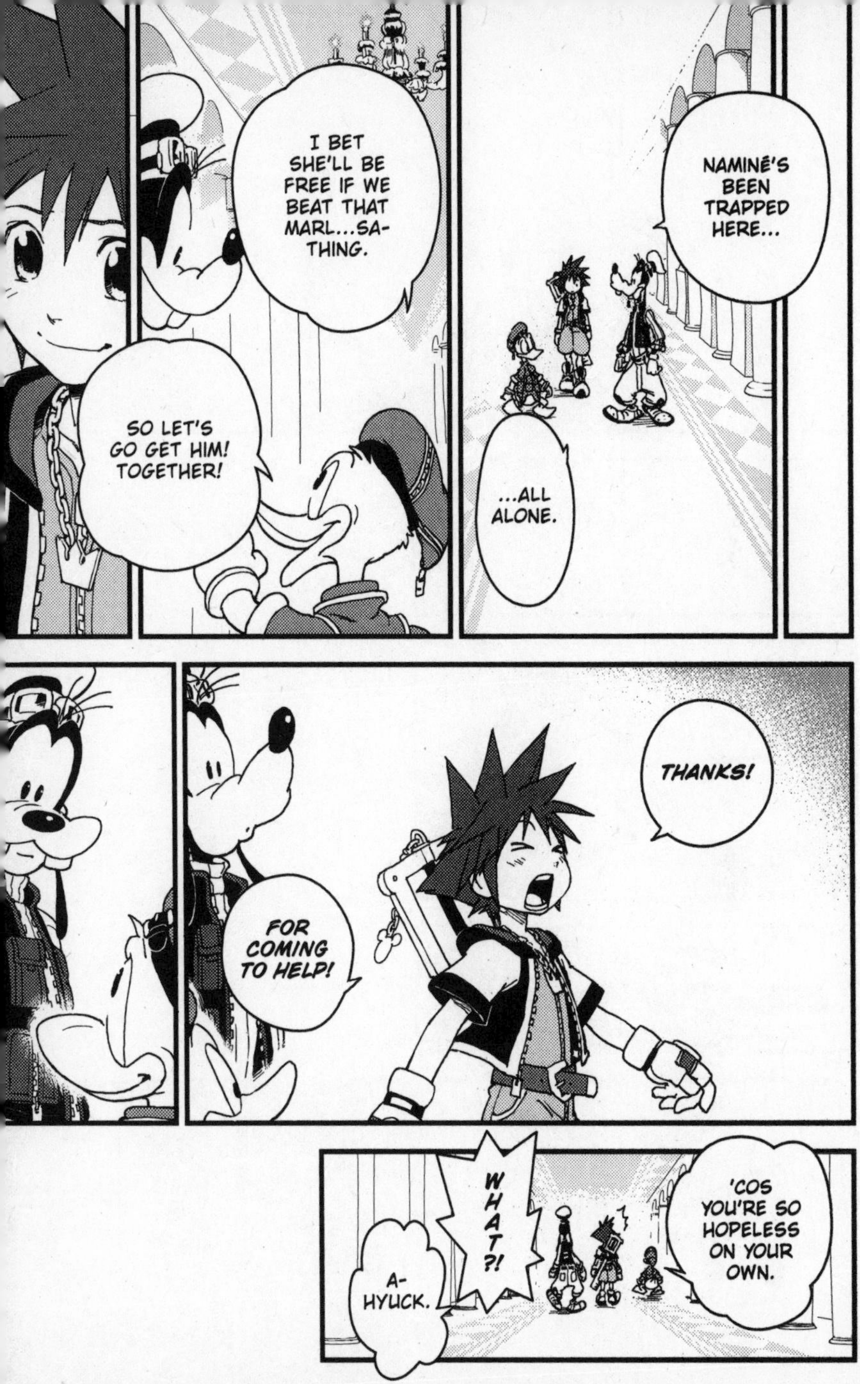
NAMINÉ'S BEEN TRAPPED HERE...
...ALL ALONE.
I BET SHE'LL BE FREE IF WE BEAT THAT MARL...SA-THING.
SO LET'S GO GET HIM! TOGETHER!
THANKS!
FOR COMING TO HELP!
'COS YOU'RE SO HOPELESS ON YOUR OWN.
WHAT?!
A-HYUCK.

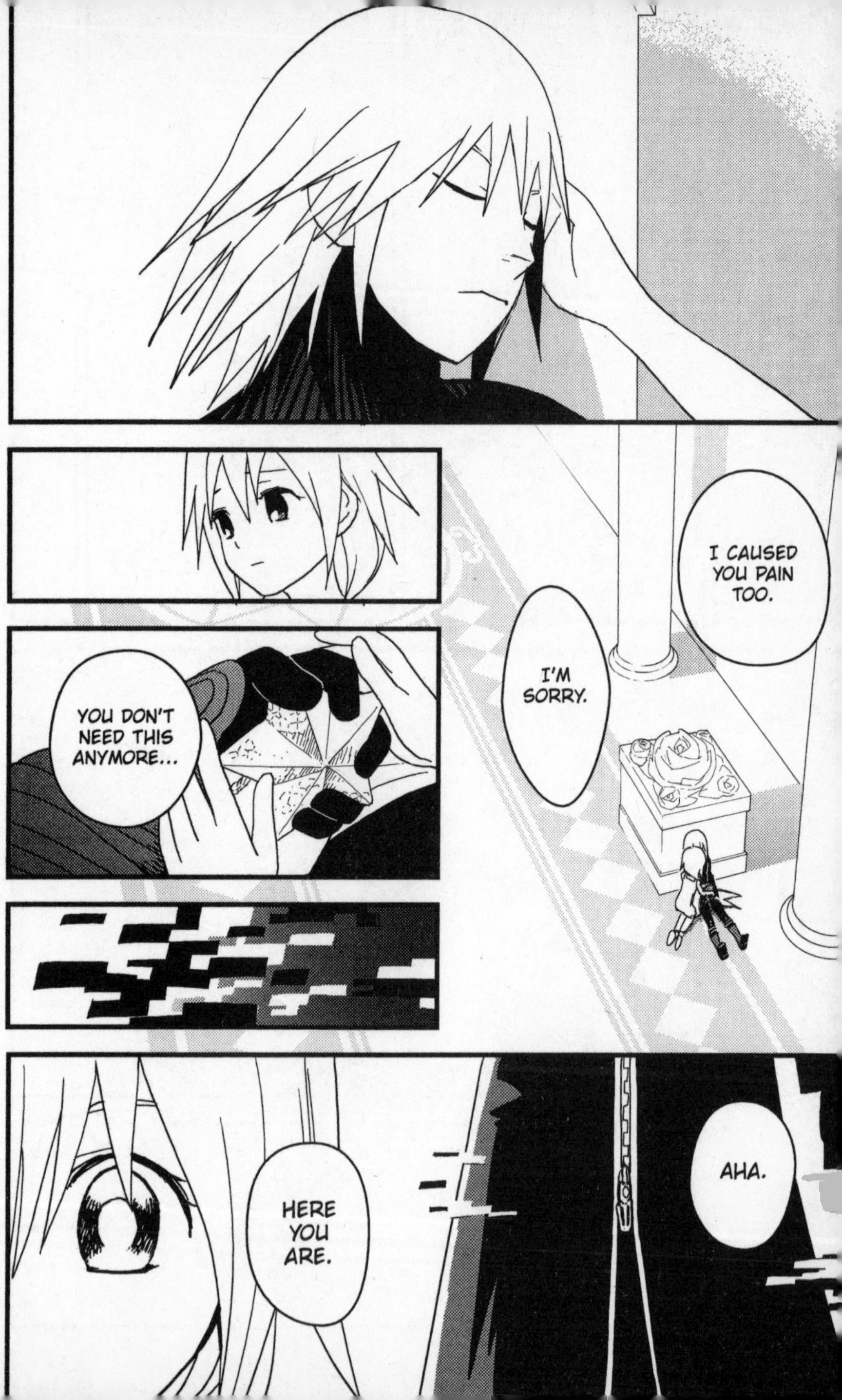
I CAUSED YOU PAIN TOO.
I'M SORRY.
YOU DON'T NEED THIS ANYMORE...
AHA.
HERE YOU ARE.

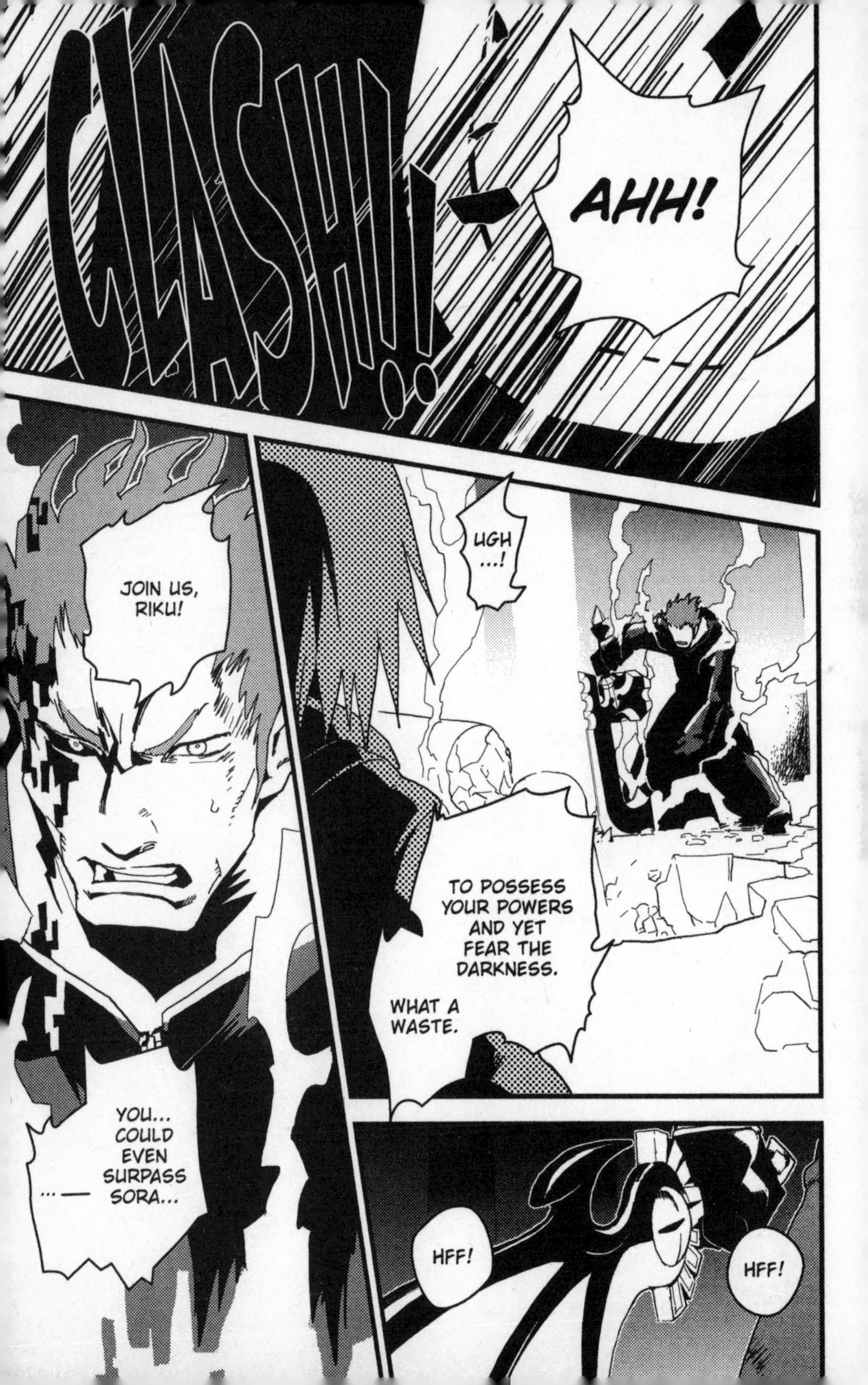
AHH!
CLASH!!
UGH ...!
TO POSSESS YOUR POWERS AND YET FEAR THE DARKNESS.
WHAT A WASTE.
HFF!
HFF!
JOIN US, RIKU!
YOU... COULD EVEN SURPASS SORA...
... —

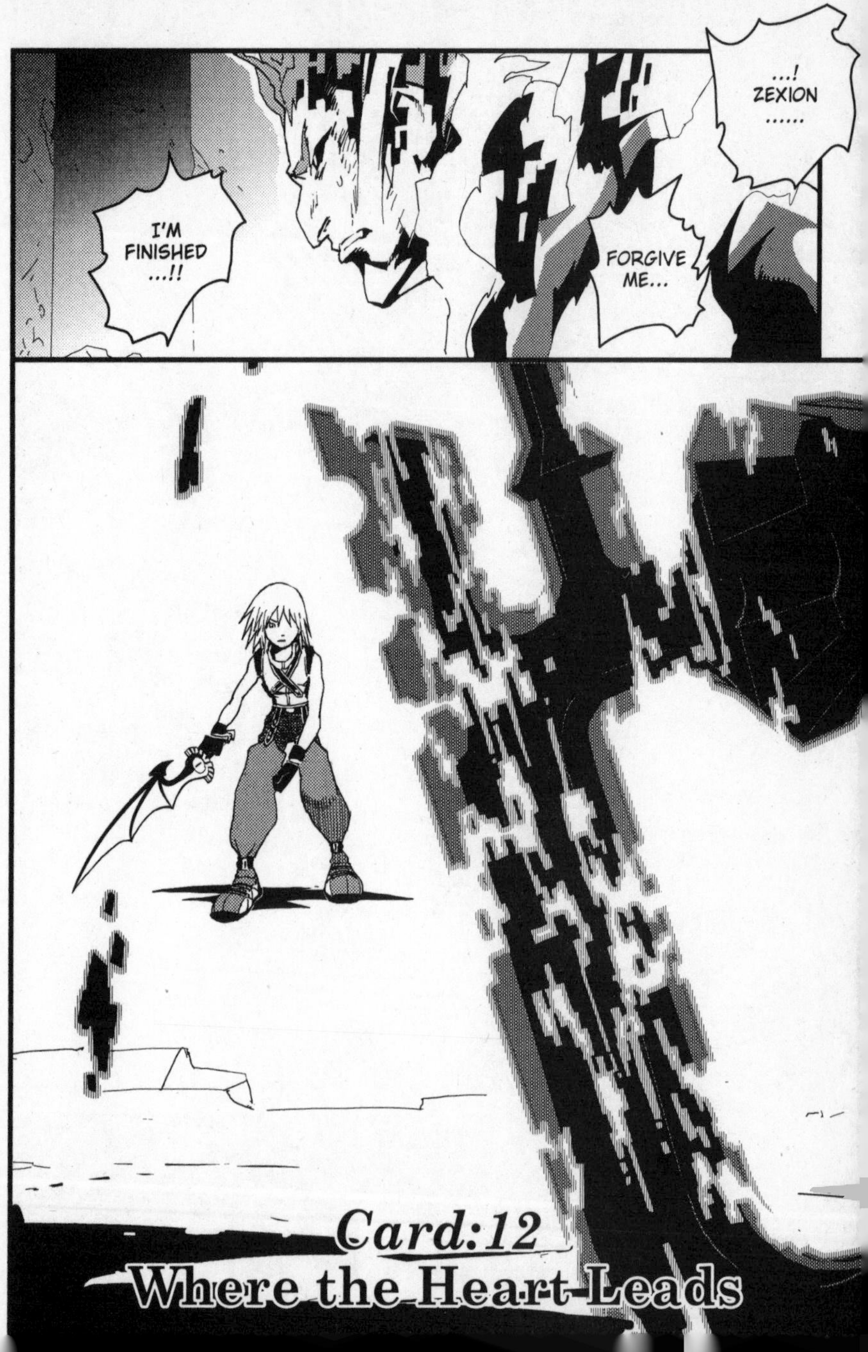
...! ZEXION ......
FORGIVE ME...
I'M FINISHED ...!!
Card:12
Where the Heart Leads

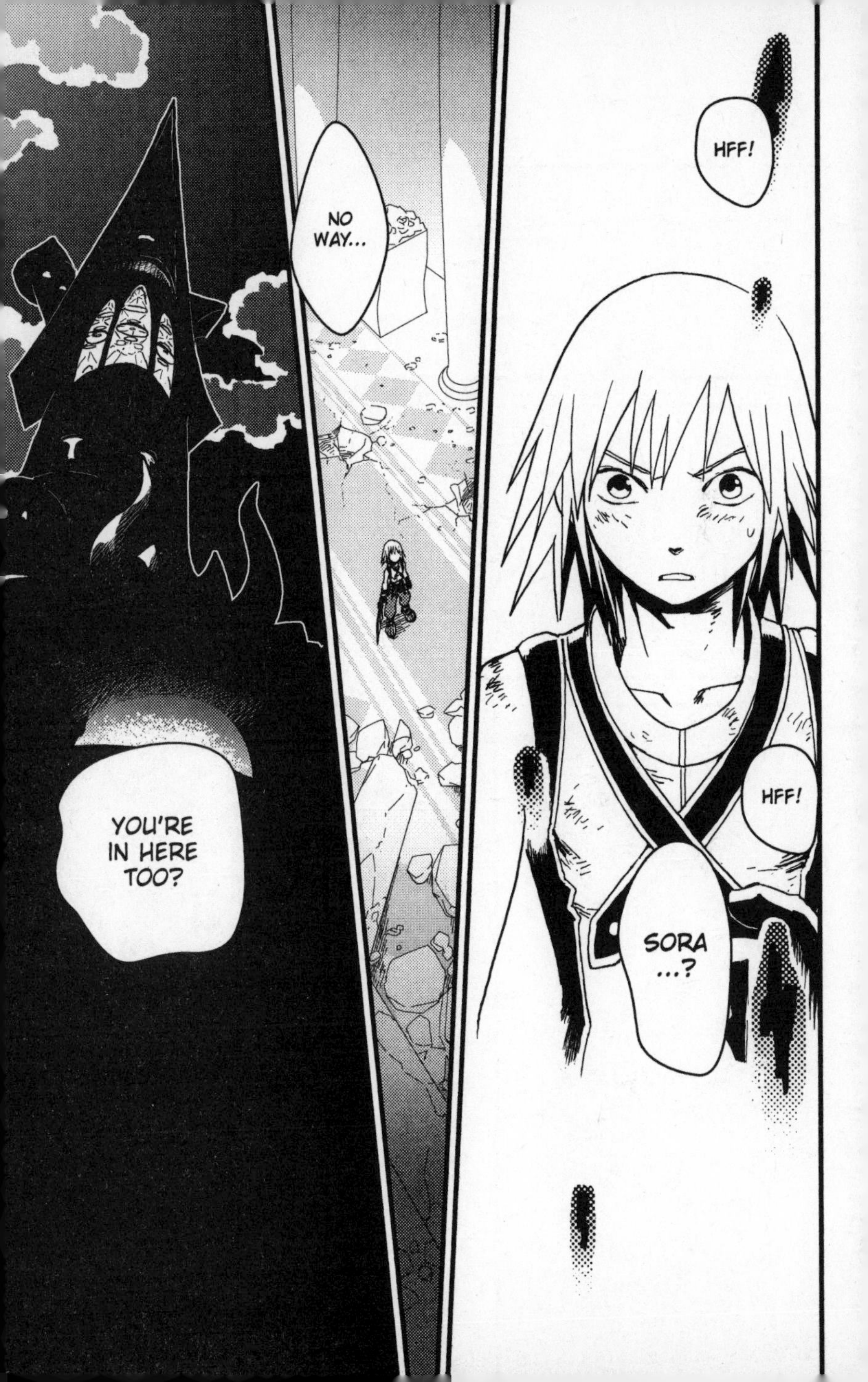
HFF!
HFF!
SORA ...?
NO WAY...
YOU'RE IN HERE TOO?

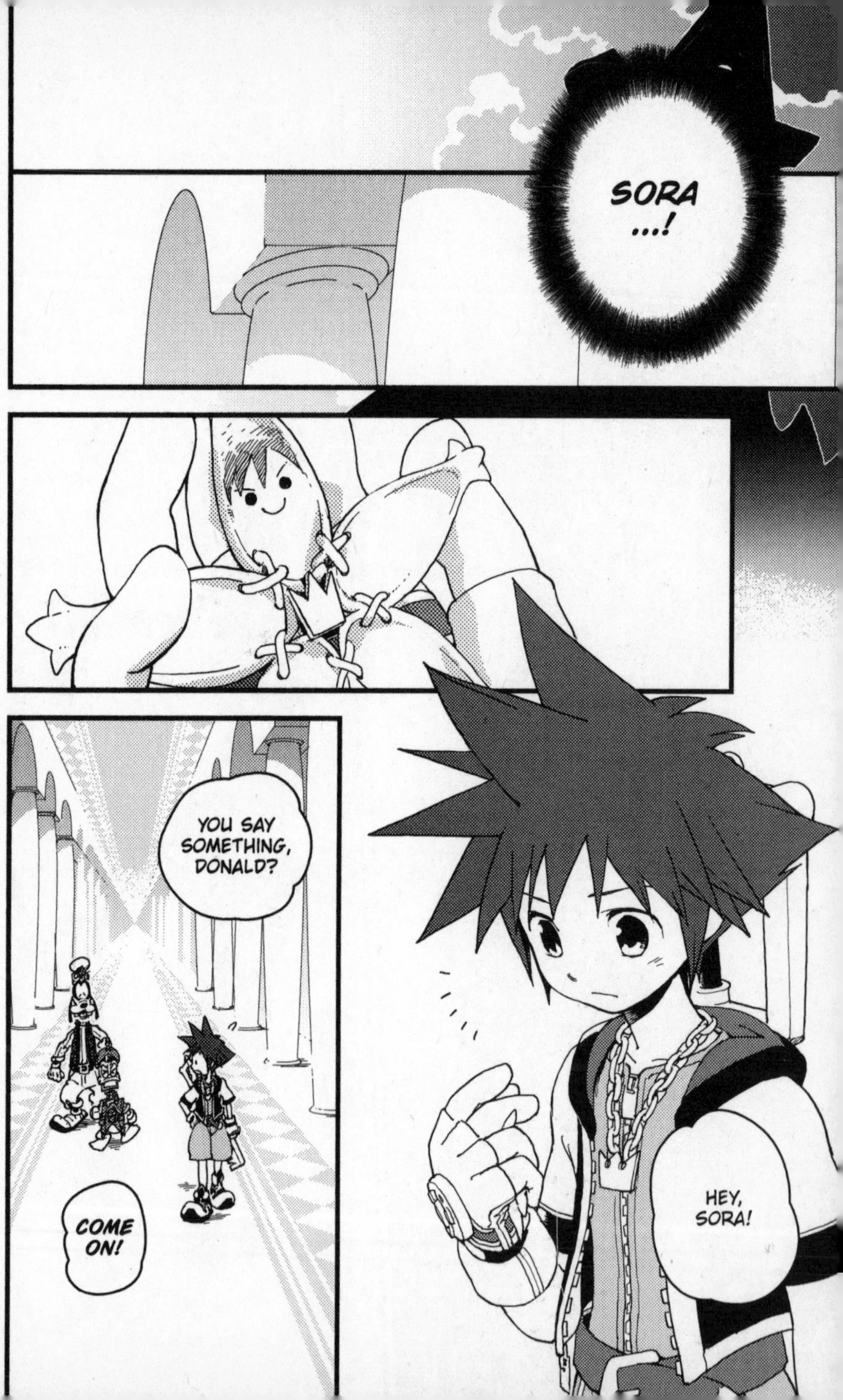
SORA ...!
HEY, SORA!
YOU SAY SOMETHING, DONALD?
COME ON!

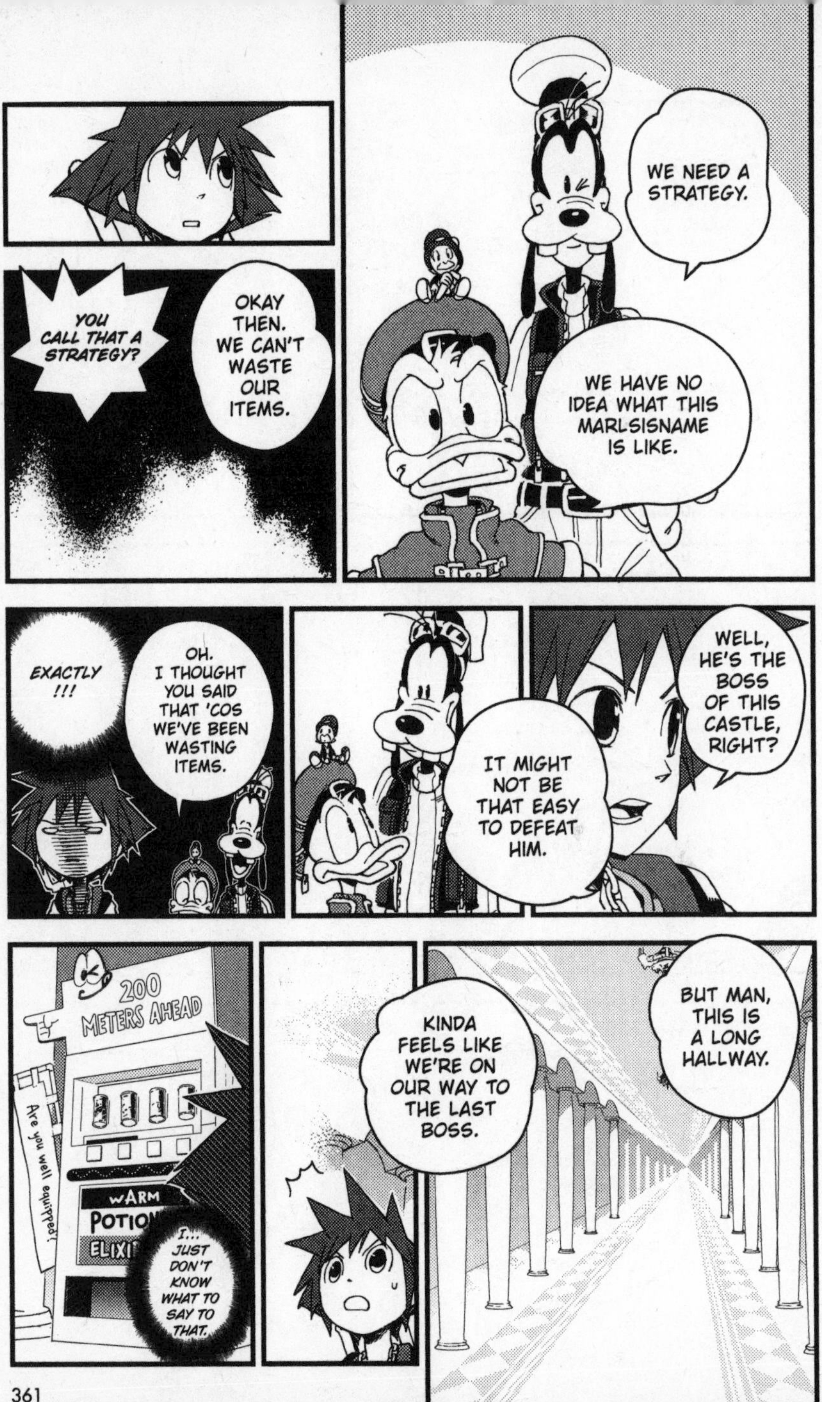
WE NEED A STRATEGY.
WE HAVE NO IDEA WHAT THIS MARLSISNAME IS LIKE.
OKAY THEN. WE CAN'T WASTE OUR ITEMS.
YOU CALL THAT A STRATEGY?
WELL, HE'S THE BOSS OF THIS CASTLE, RIGHT?
IT MIGHT NOT BE THAT EASY TO DEFEAT HIM.
OH. I THOUGHT YOU SAID THAT 'COS WE'VE BEEN WASTING ITEMS.
EXACTLY!!!
BUT MAN, THIS IS A LONG HALLWAY.
KINDA FEELS LIKE WE'RE ON OUR WAY TO THE LAST BOSS.
200 METERS AHEAD
Are you well equipped?
WARM
I... JUST DON'T KNOW WHAT TO SAY TO THAT.

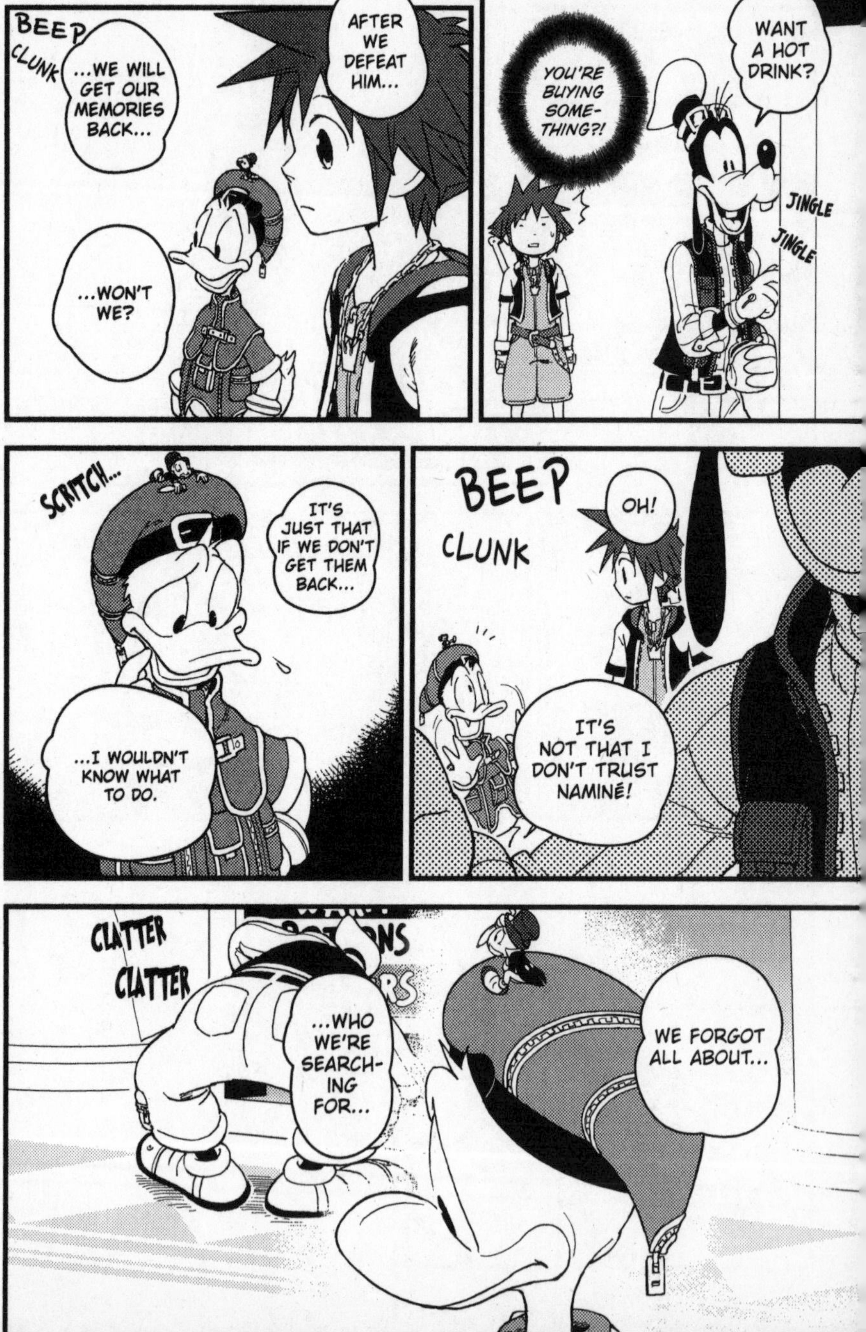
WANT A HOT DRINK?
YOU'RE BUYING SOME-THING?!
JINGLE
JINGLE
AFTER WE DEFEAT HIM...
BEEP
CLUNK
...WE WILL GET OUR MEMORIES BACK...
...WON'T WE?
OH!
BEEP
CLUNK
IT'S NOT THAT I DON'T TRUST NAMINÉ!
IT'S JUST THAT IF WE DON'T GET THEM BACK...
SCRITCH...
...I WOULDN'T KNOW WHAT TO DO.
WE FORGOT ALL ABOUT...
...WHO WE'RE SEARCH-ING FOR...
CLATTER
CLATTER

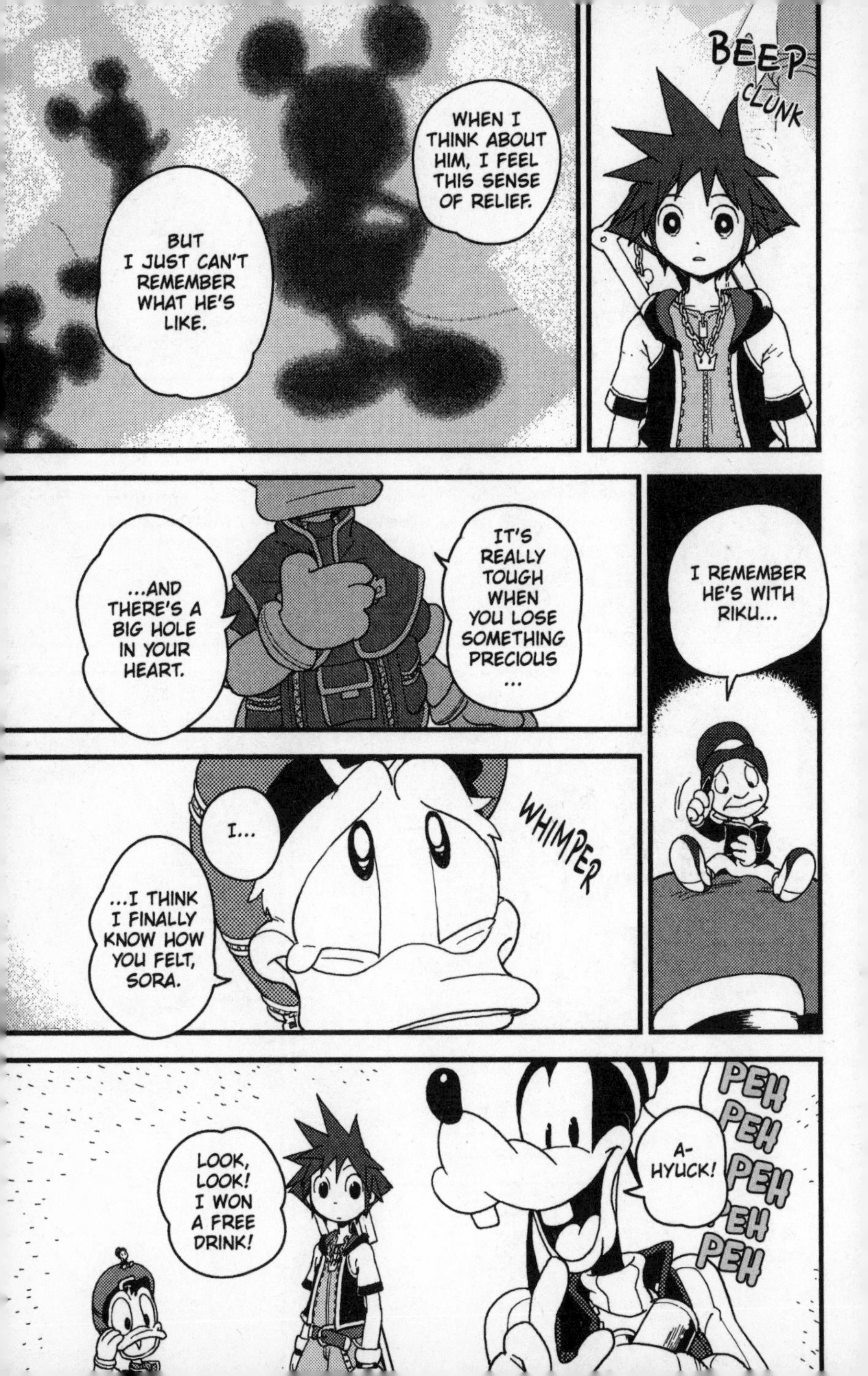
BEEP
CLUNK
WHEN I THINK ABOUT HIM, I FEEL THIS SENSE OF RELIEF.
BUT I JUST CAN'T REMEMBER WHAT HE'S LIKE.
I REMEMBER HE'S WITH RIKU...
IT'S REALLY TOUGH WHEN YOU LOSE SOMETHING PRECIOUS...
...AND THERE'S A BIG HOLE IN YOUR HEART.
WHIMPER
I...
...I THINK I FINALLY KNOW HOW YOU FELT, SORA.
PEH PEH PEH EH PEH
A-HYUCK!
LOOK, LOOK! I WON A FREE DRINK!

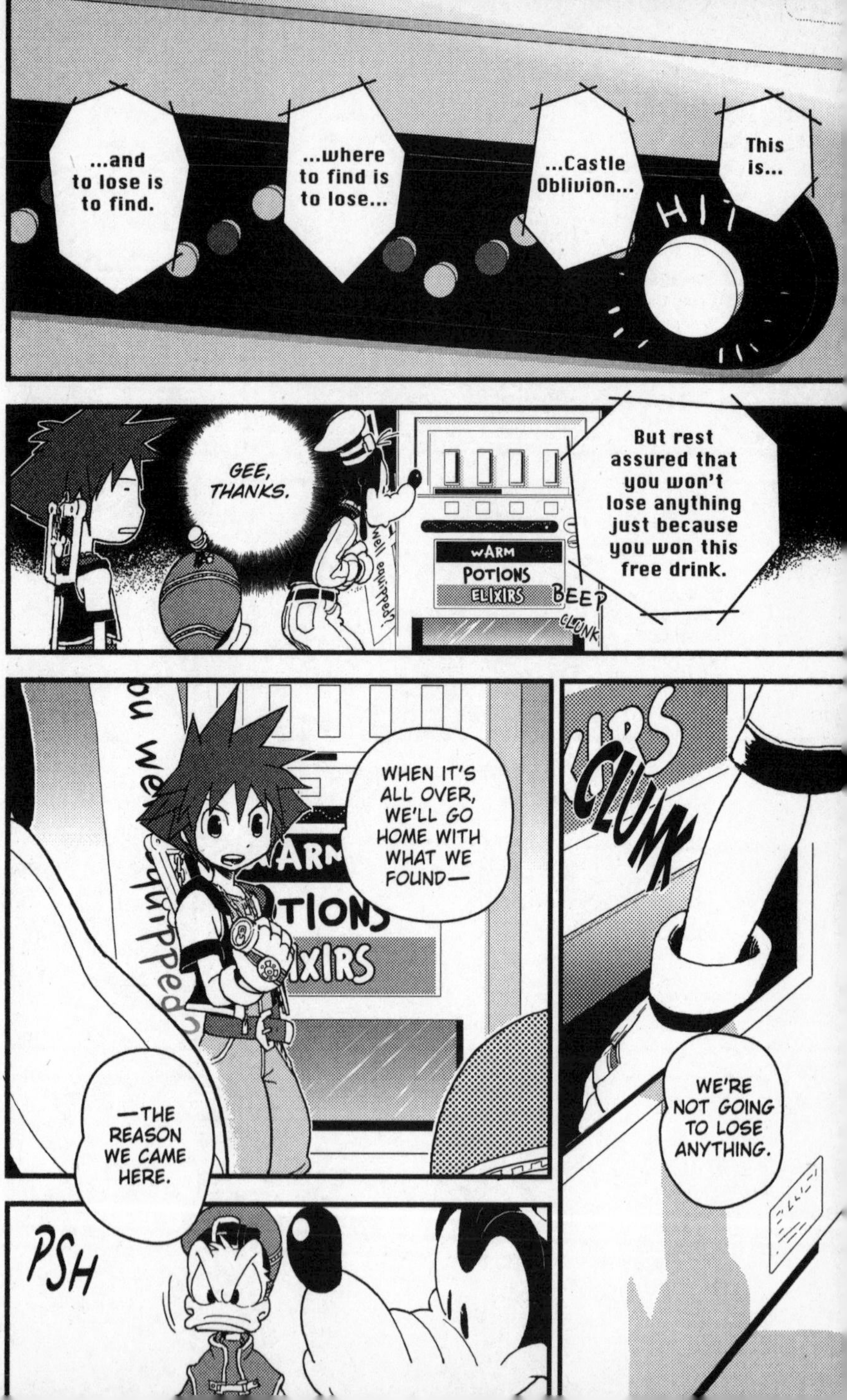
This is...
HIT
...Castle Oblivion...
...where to find is to lose...
...and to lose is to find.
But rest assured that you won't lose anything just because you won this free drink.
BEEP
CLUNK
WARM
POTIONS
ELIXIRS
well equipped?
GEE, THANKS.
CLUNK
WE'RE NOT GOING TO LOSE ANYTHING.
WHEN IT'S ALL OVER, WE'LL GO HOME WITH WHAT WE FOUND—
—THE REASON WE CAME HERE.
PSH

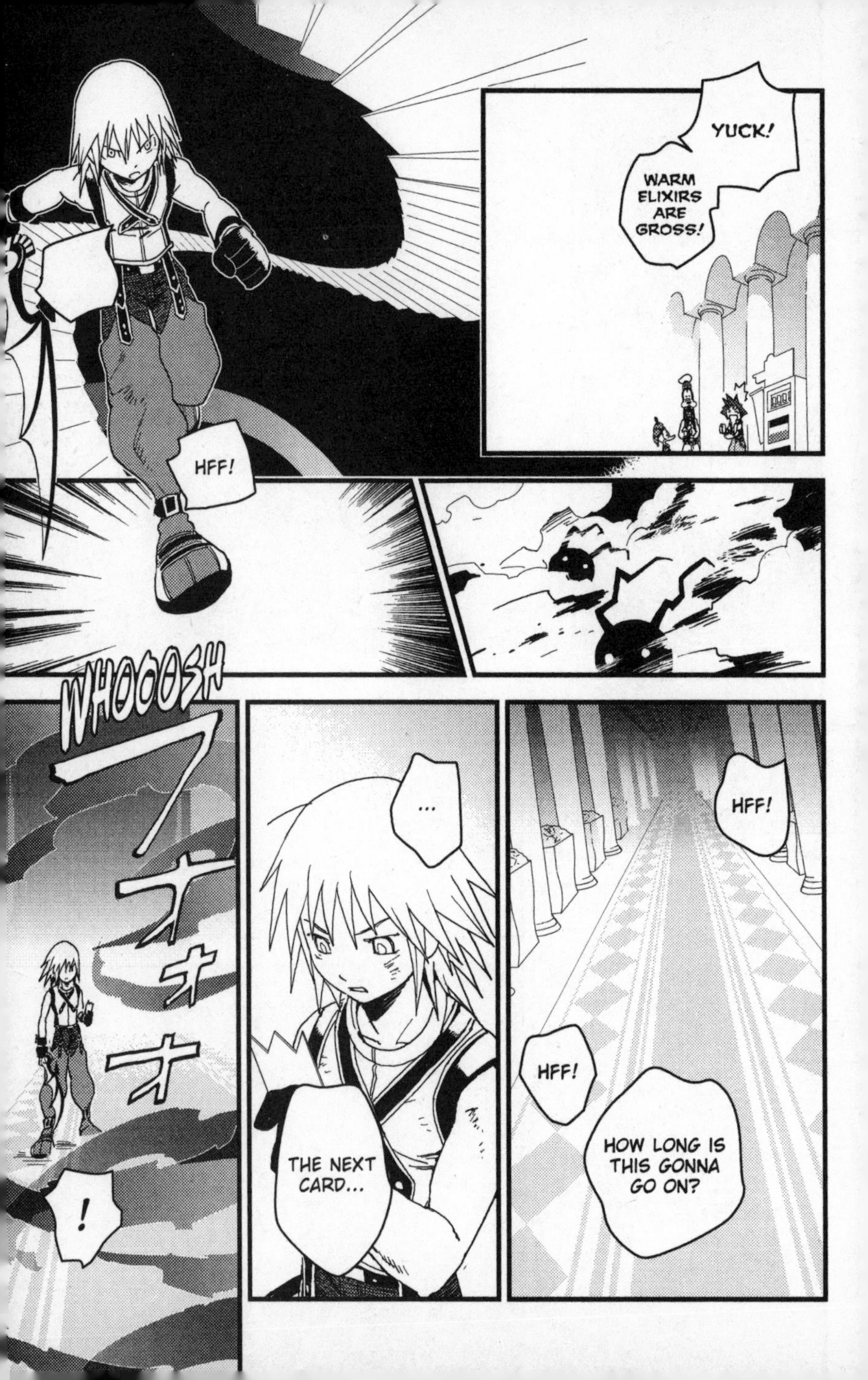
YUCK!
WARM ELIXIRS ARE GROSS!
HFF!
WHOOOSH
フォォォ
HFF!
HFF!
HOW LONG IS THIS GONNA GO ON?
...
THE NEXT CARD...
!

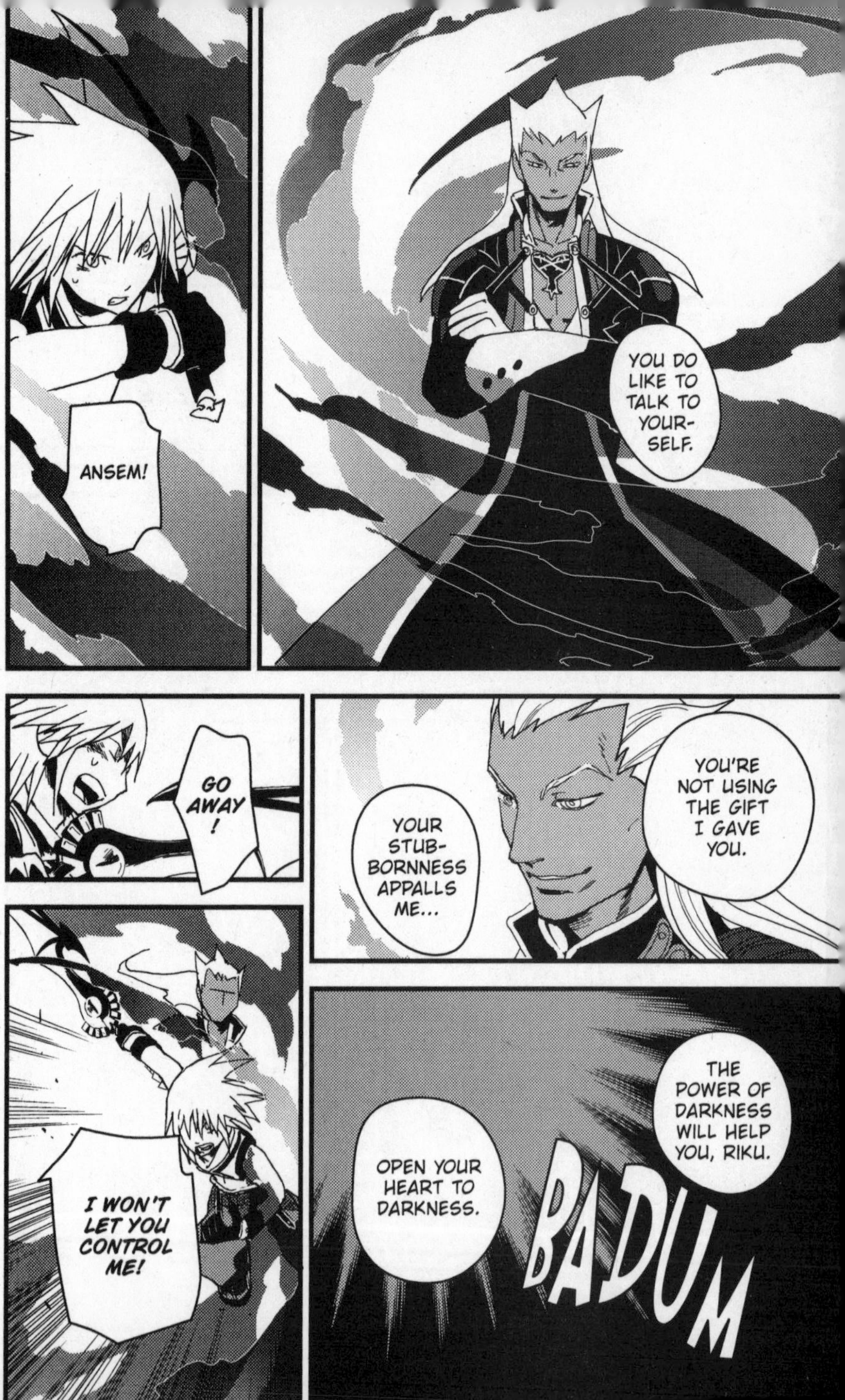
YOU DO LIKE TO TALK TO YOUR-SELF.
ANSEM!
YOU'RE NOT USING THE GIFT I GAVE YOU.
YOUR STUB-BORNNESS APPALLS ME...
GO AWAY!
THE POWER OF DARKNESS WILL HELP YOU, RIKU.
OPEN YOUR HEART TO DARKNESS.
BADUM
I WON'T LET YOU CONTROL ME!

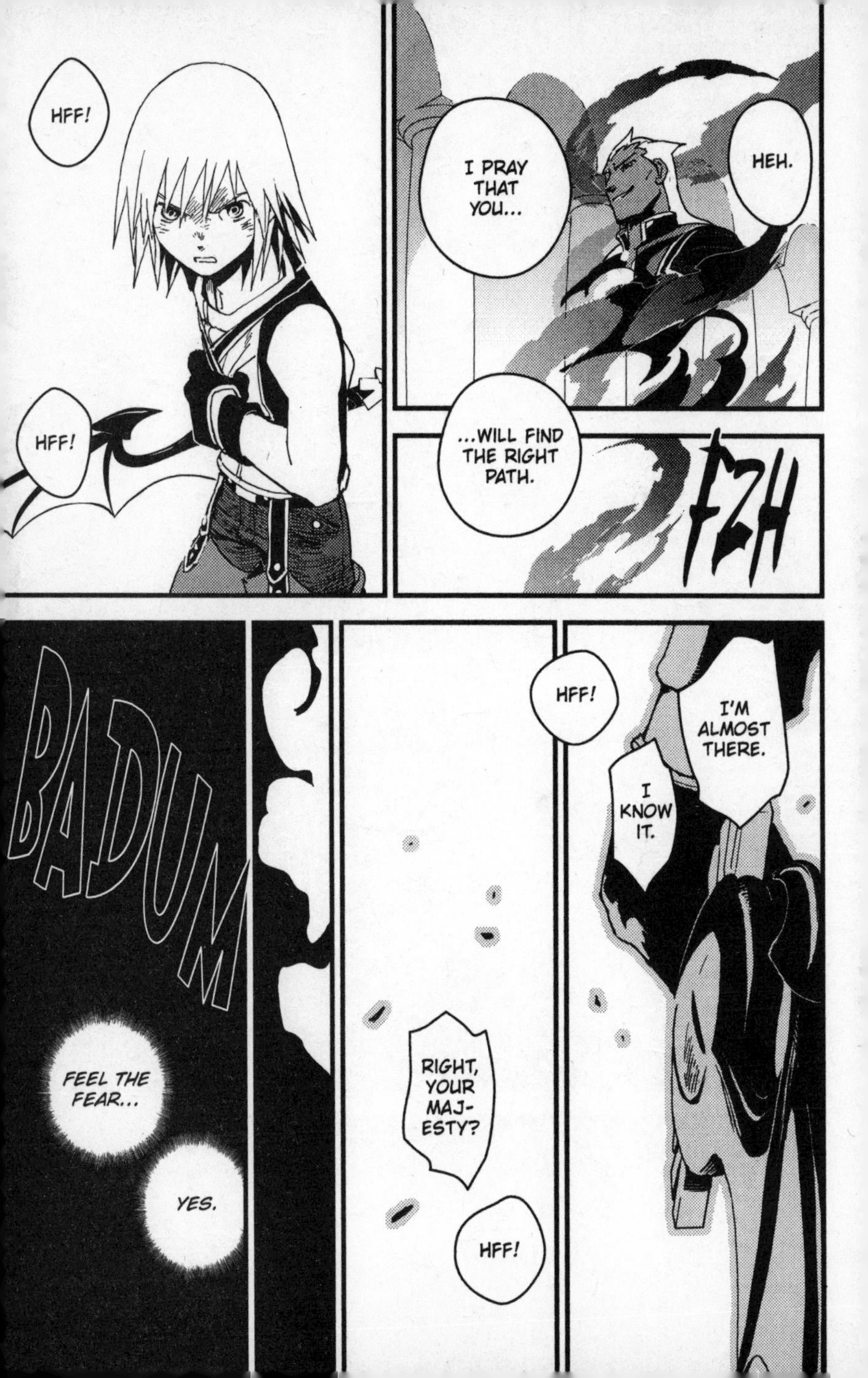
HEH.
I PRAY THAT YOU...
...WILL FIND THE RIGHT PATH.
FZH
HFF!
HFF!
HFF!
I'M ALMOST THERE.
I KNOW IT.
RIGHT, YOUR MAJ-ESTY?
HFF!
BADUM
FEEL THE FEAR...
YES.

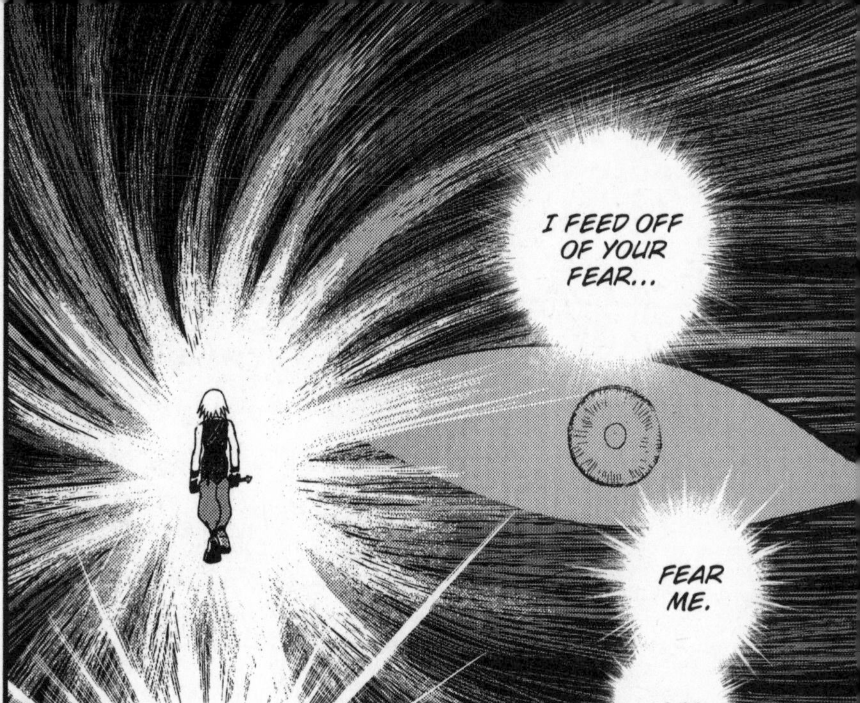
I FEED OFF OF YOUR FEAR...
FEAR ME.
HATE ME.
FIGHT ME.
WITH MORE INTENSITY!

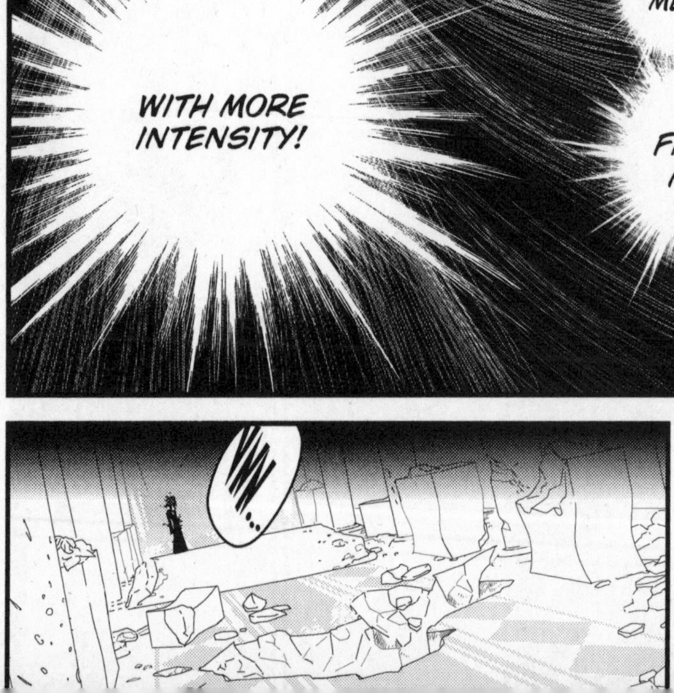
NNN...

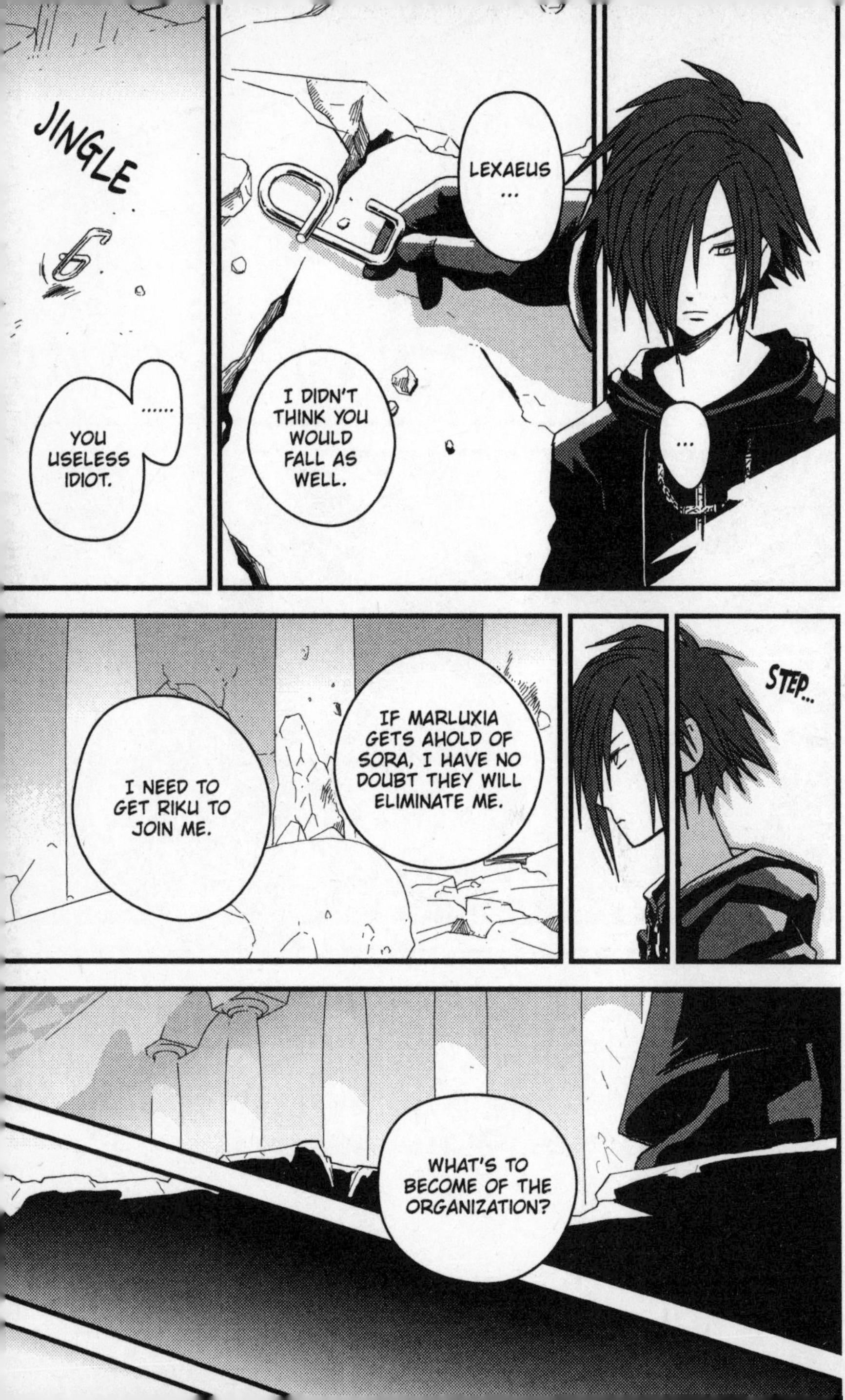
LEXAEUS ...
...
I DIDN'T THINK YOU WOULD FALL AS WELL.
JINGLE
......
YOU USELESS IDIOT.
STEP...
IF MARLUXIA GETS AHOLD OF SORA, I HAVE NO DOUBT THEY WILL ELIMINATE ME.
I NEED TO GET RIKU TO JOIN ME.
WHAT'S TO BECOME OF THE ORGANIZATION?

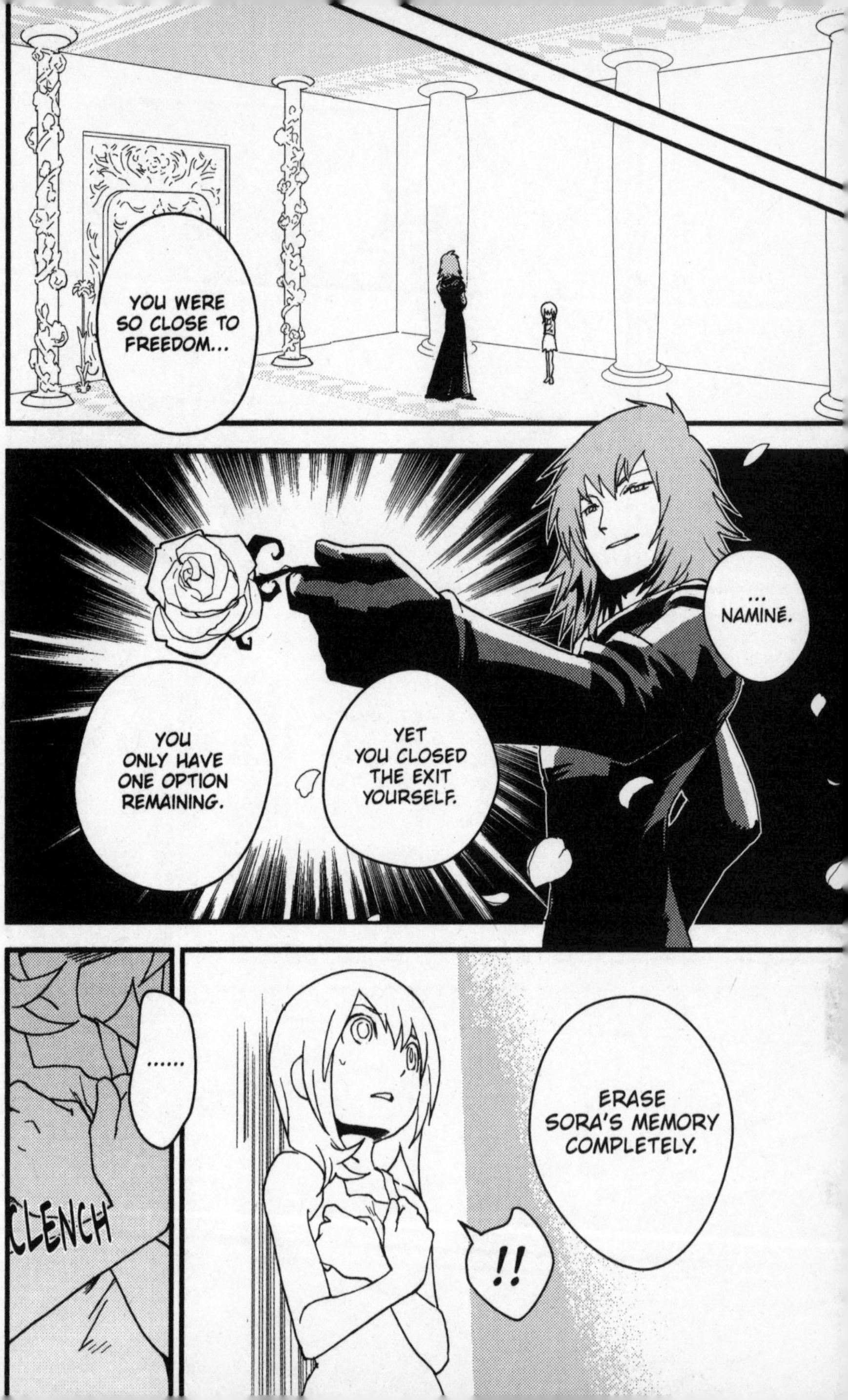
YOU WERE SO CLOSE TO FREEDOM...
... NAMINÉ.
YET YOU CLOSED THE EXIT YOURSELF.
YOU ONLY HAVE ONE OPTION REMAINING.
ERASE SORA'S MEMORY COMPLETELY.
!!
......
CLENCH

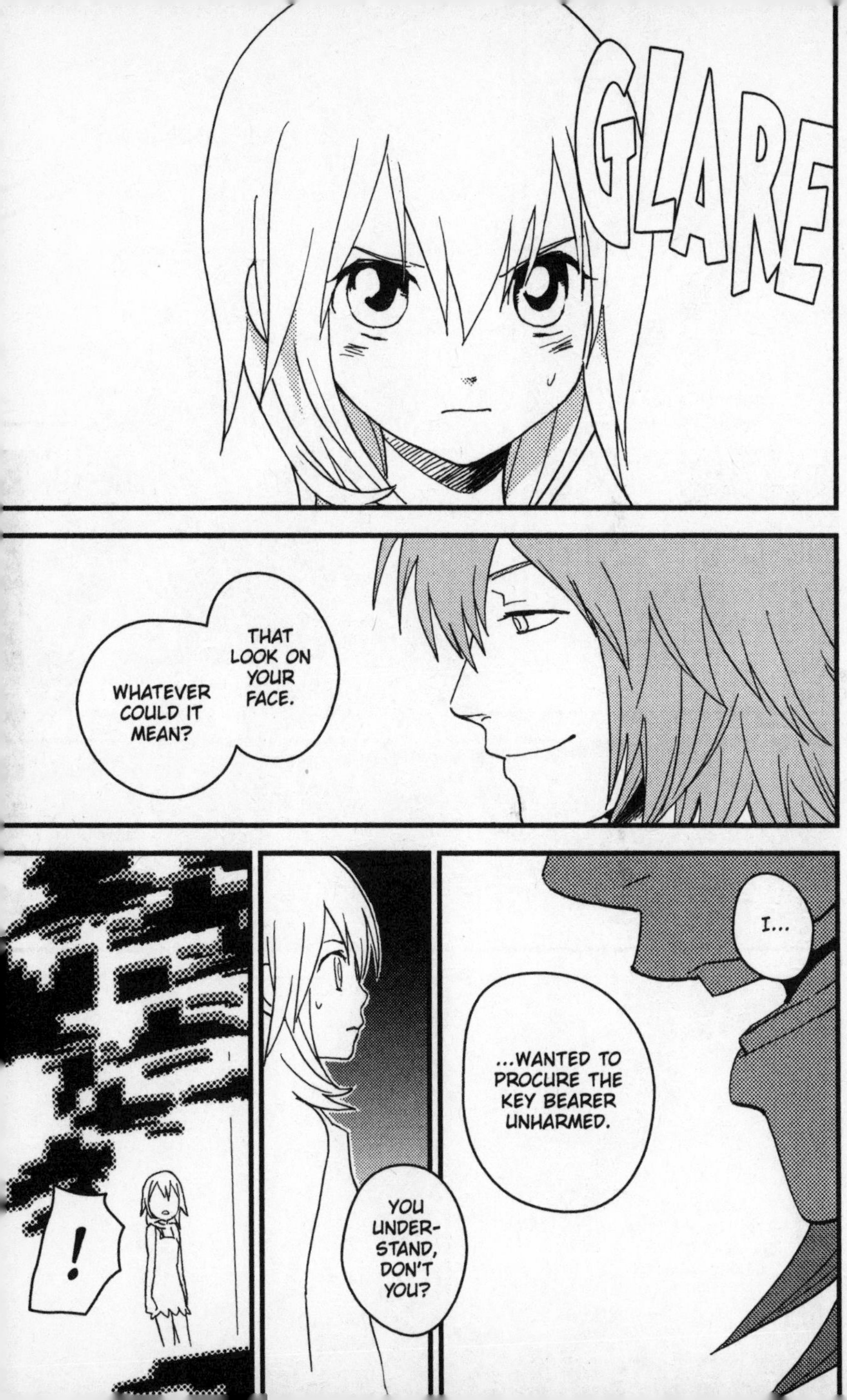
GLARE
THAT LOOK ON YOUR FACE.
WHATEVER COULD IT MEAN?
I...
...WANTED TO PROCURE THE KEY BEARER UNHARMED.
YOU UNDER-STAND, DON'T YOU?
!

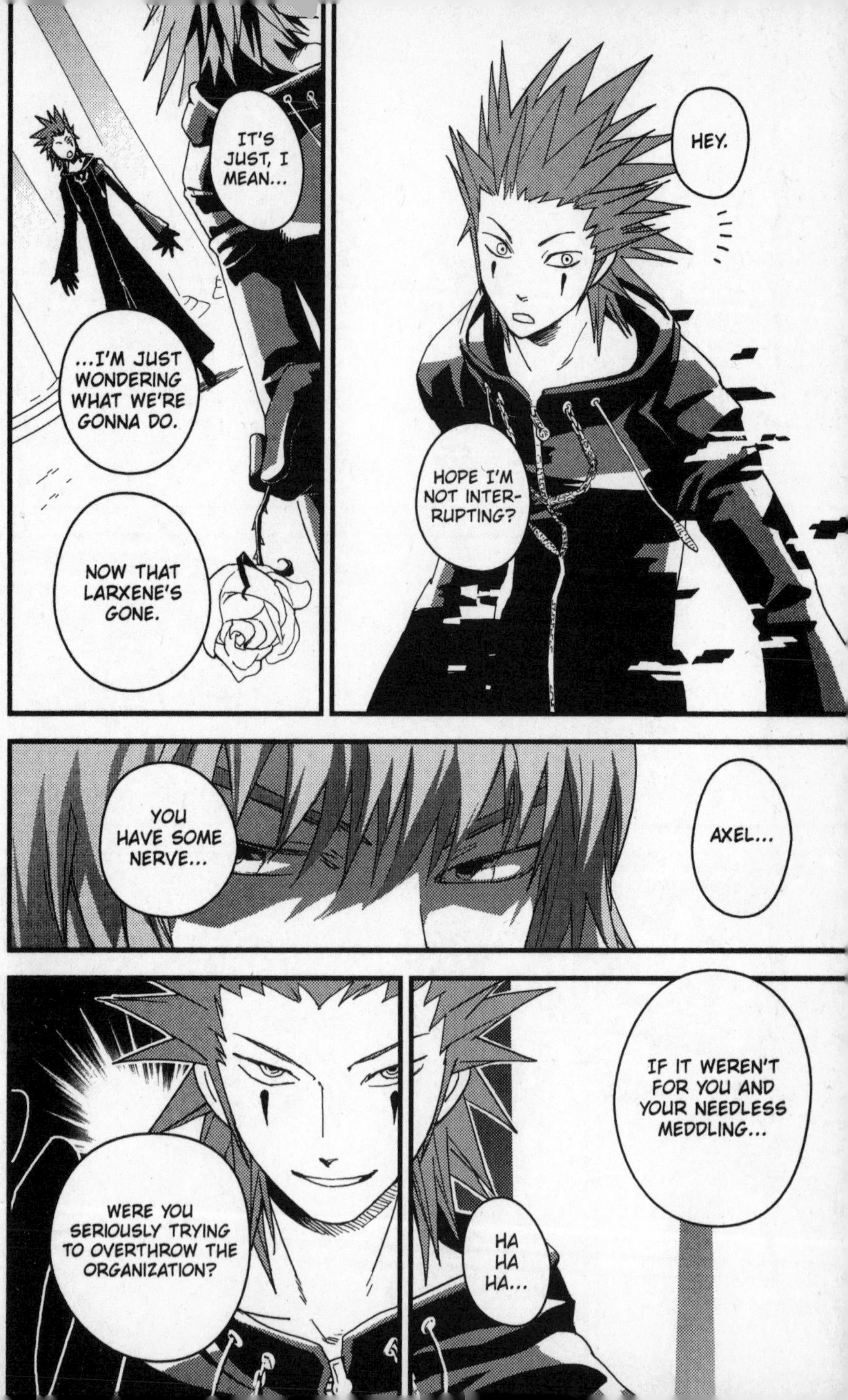
HEY.
HOPE I'M NOT INTER-RUPTING?
IT'S JUST, I MEAN...
...I'M JUST WONDERING WHAT WE'RE GONNA DO.
NOW THAT LARXENE'S GONE.
AXEL...
YOU HAVE SOME NERVE...
IF IT WEREN'T FOR YOU AND YOUR NEEDLESS MEDDLING...
HA HA HA...
WERE YOU SERIOUSLY TRYING TO OVERTHROW THE ORGANIZATION?

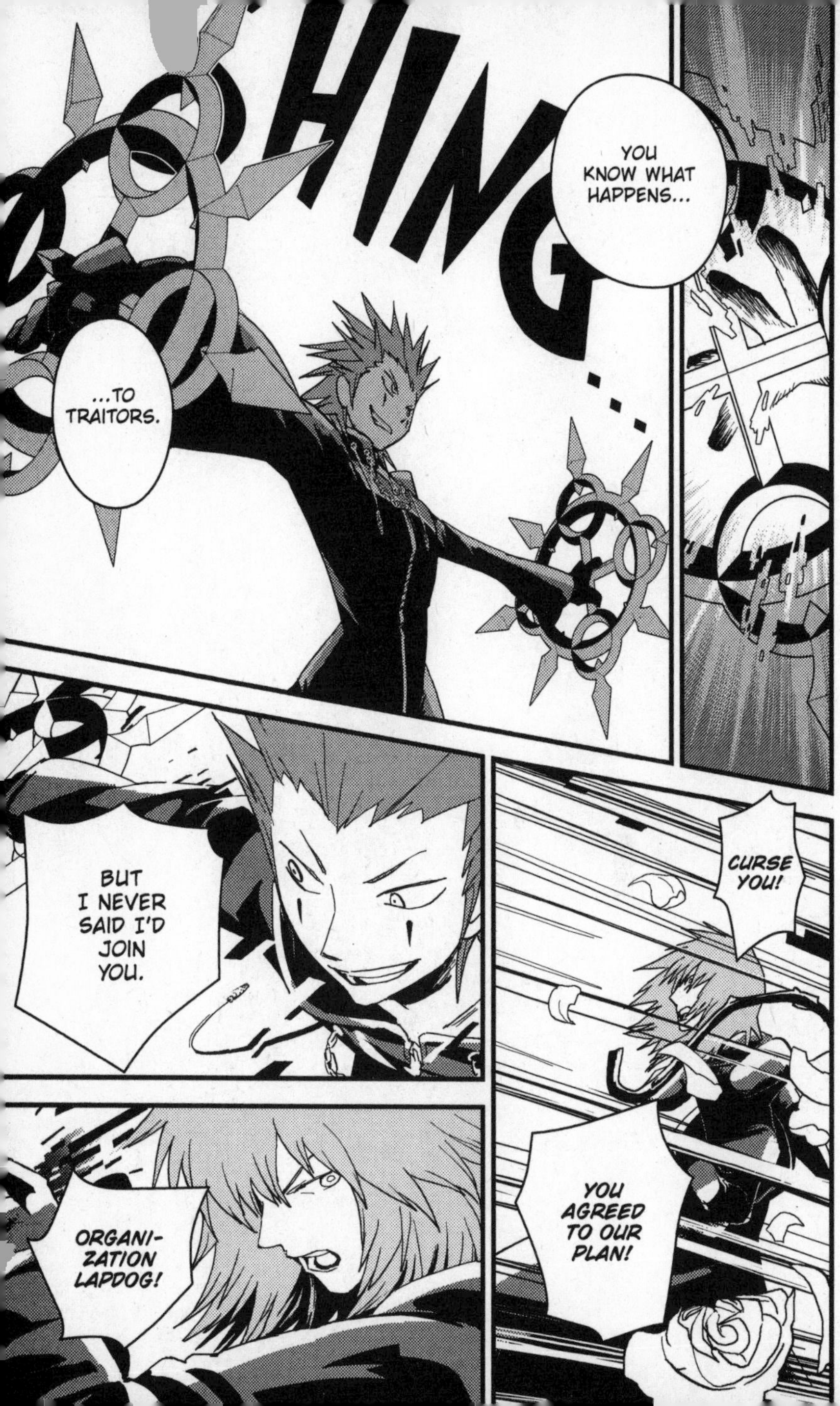
HING
YOU KNOW WHAT HAPPENS...
...TO TRAITORS.
CURSE YOU!
YOU AGREED TO OUR PLAN!
BUT I NEVER SAID I'D JOIN YOU.
ORGANI-ZATION LAPDOG!

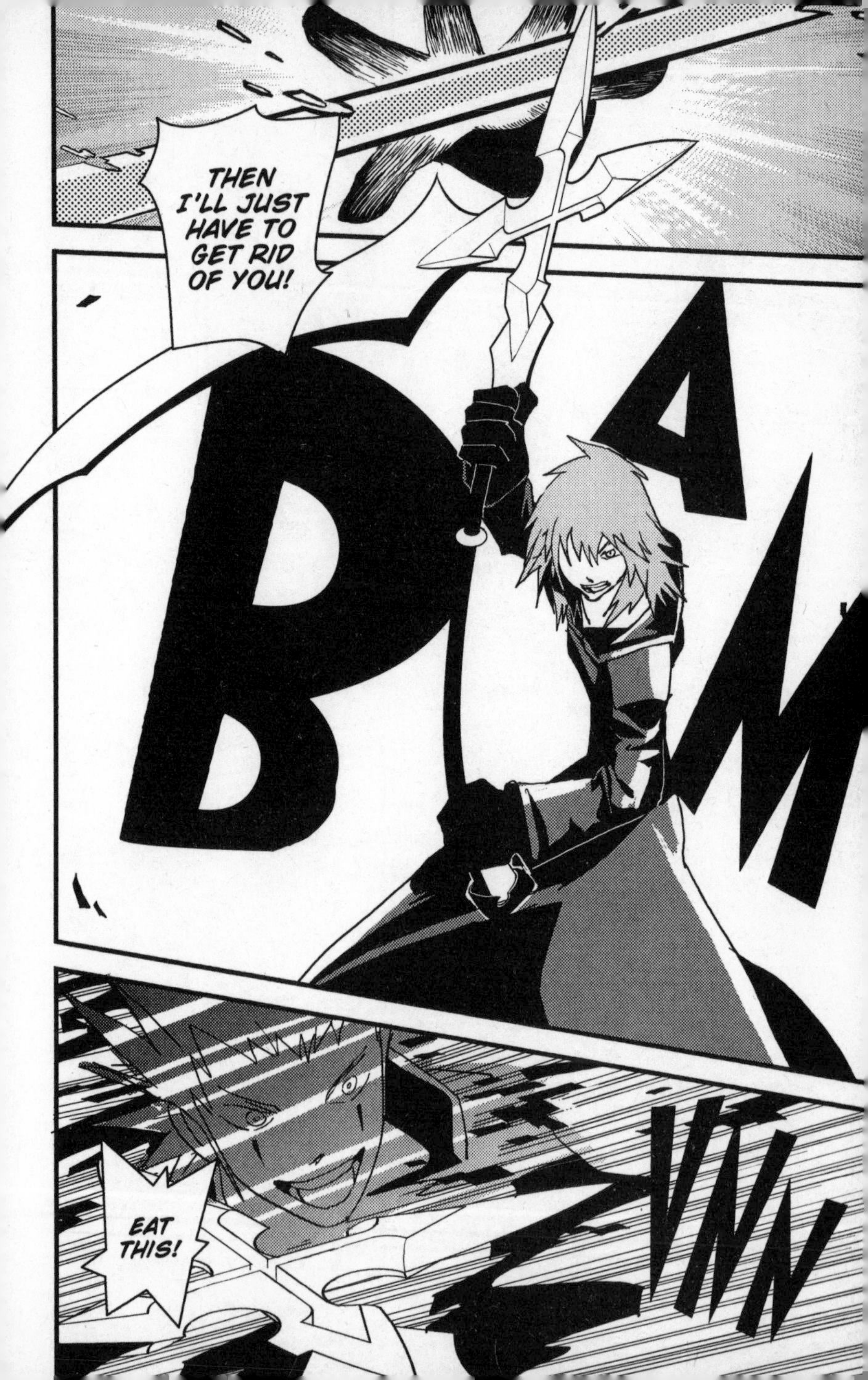
THEN I'LL JUST HAVE TO GET RID OF YOU!
BAM
EAT THIS!

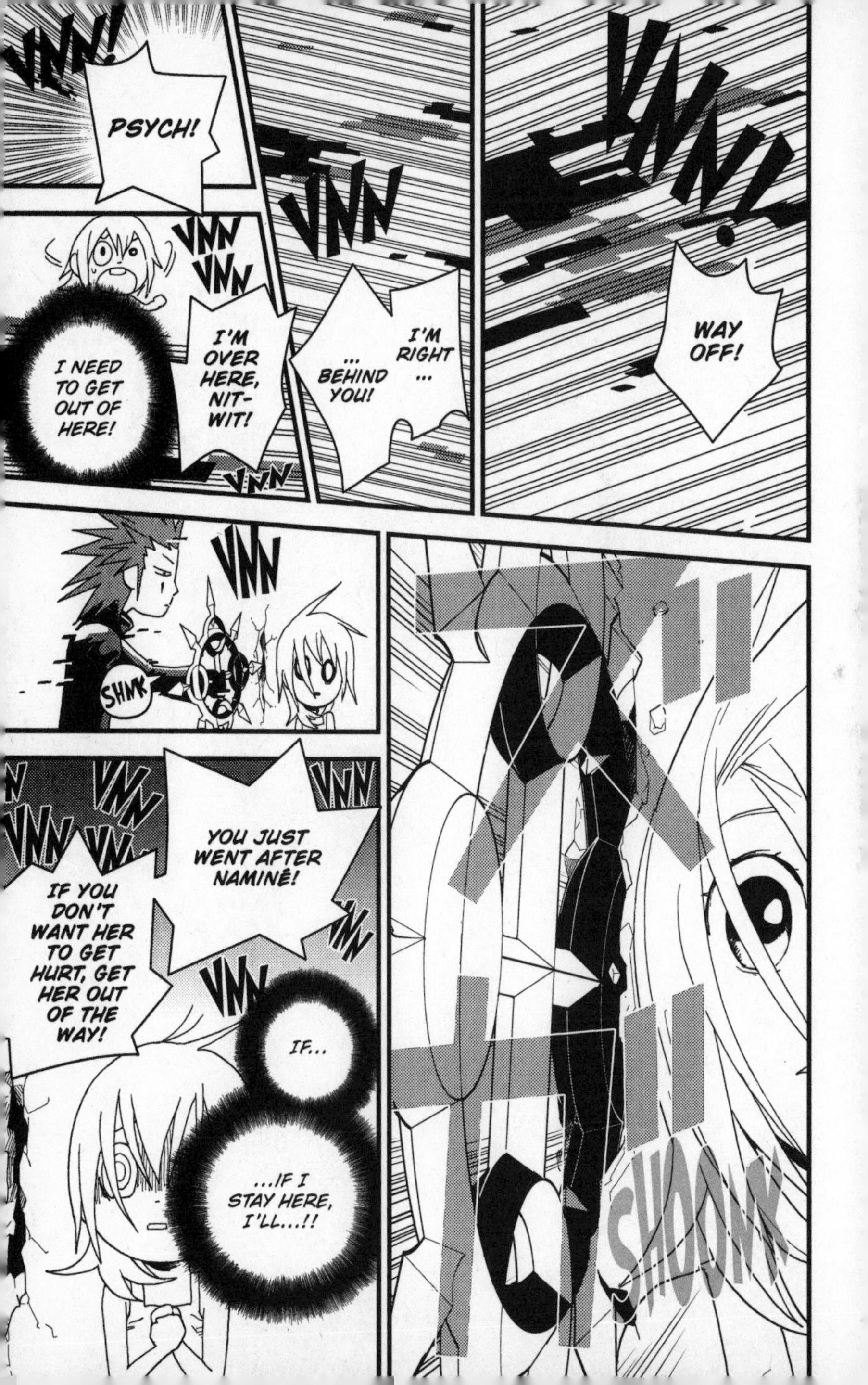

VNN!
WAY OFF!
VNN
I'M RIGHT ...
... BEHIND YOU!
VNN!
PSYCH!
VNN VNN
I'M OVER HERE, NIT-WIT!
I NEED TO GET OUT OF HERE!
VNN
SHOOM
VNN
SHNK
VNN VNN VNN VNN
YOU JUST WENT AFTER NAMINÉ!
IF YOU DON'T WANT HER TO GET HURT, GET HER OUT OF THE WAY!
VNN
IF...
...IF I STAY HERE, I'LL...!!

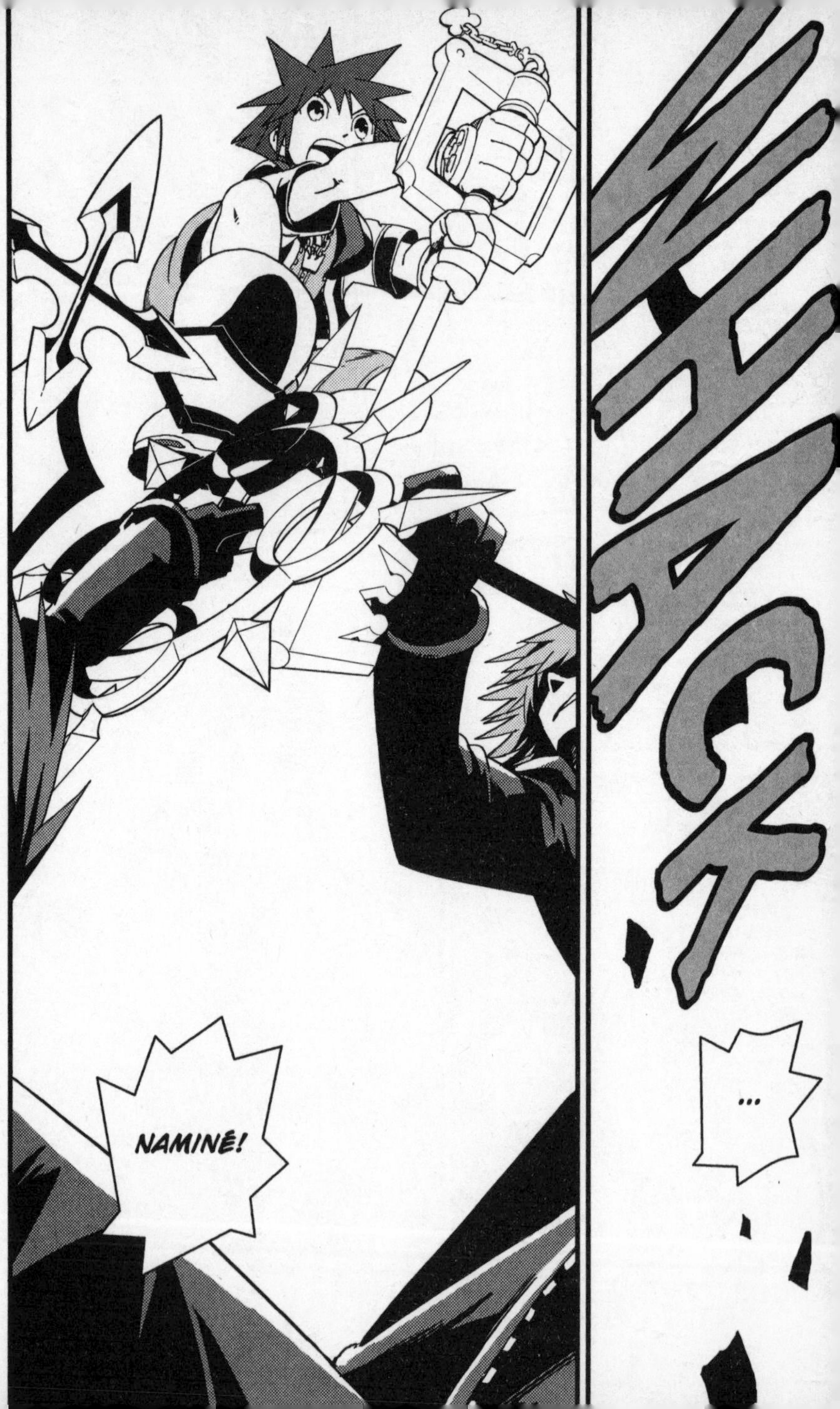
WHACK
...
NAMINÉ!

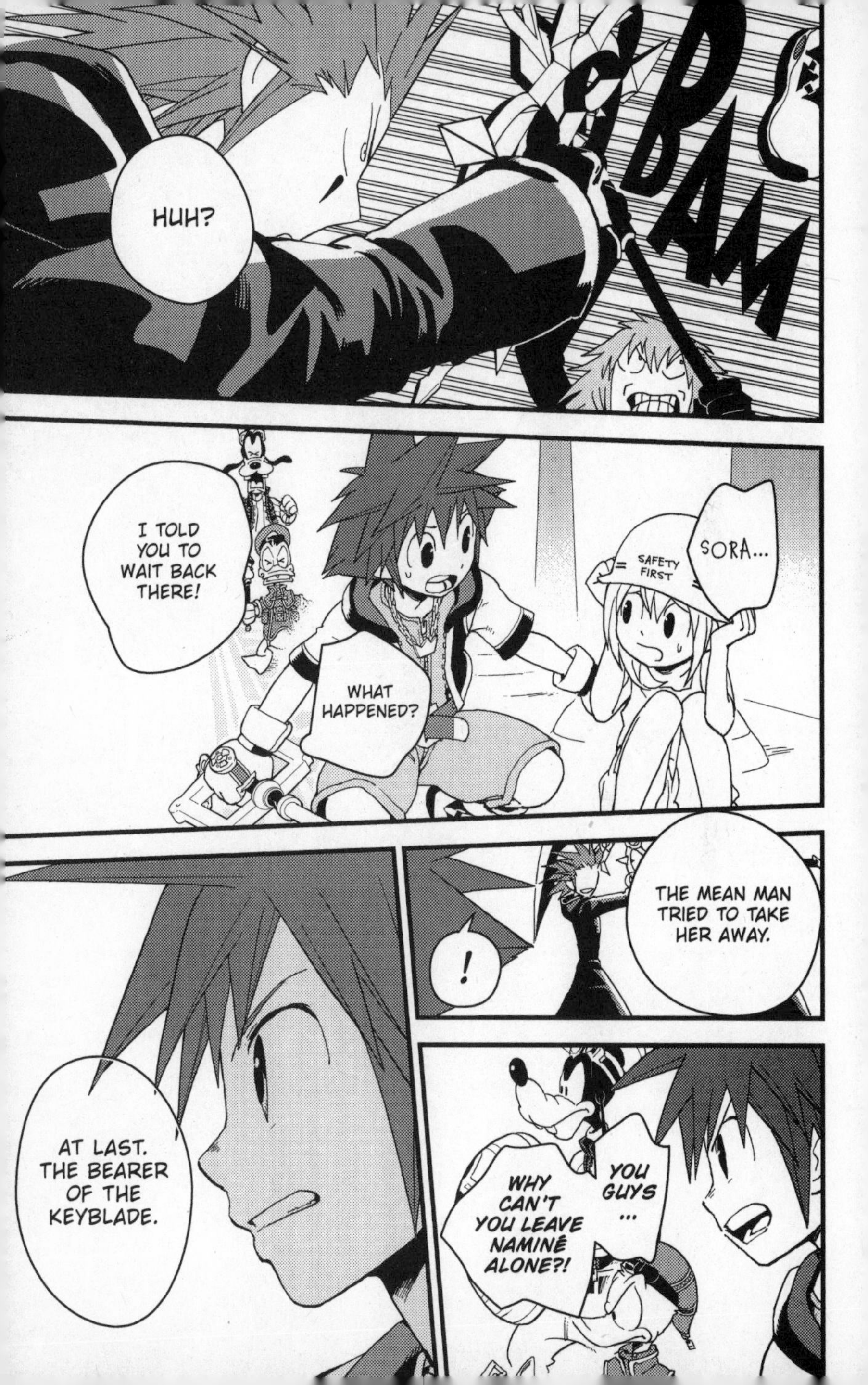
BADAM
HUH?
SORA...
SAFETY FIRST
I TOLD YOU TO WAIT BACK THERE!
WHAT HAPPENED?
THE MEAN MAN TRIED TO TAKE HER AWAY.
!
YOU GUYS ...
WHY CAN'T YOU LEAVE NAMINÉ ALONE?!
AT LAST. THE BEARER OF THE KEYBLADE.

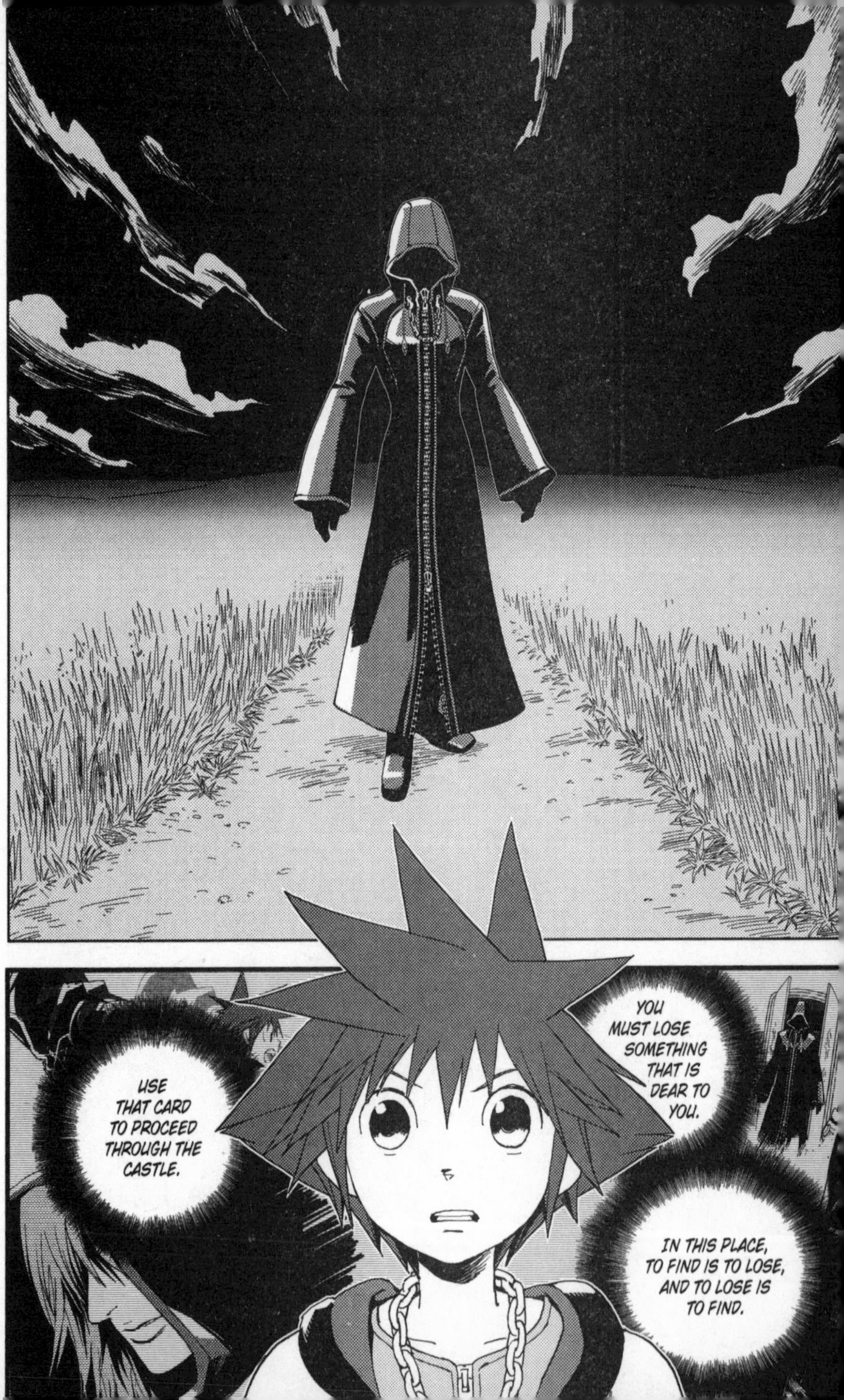
YOU MUST LOSE SOMETHING THAT IS DEAR TO YOU.
USE THAT CARD TO PROCEED THROUGH THE CASTLE.
IN THIS PLACE, TO FIND IS TO LOSE, AND TO LOSE IS TO FIND.

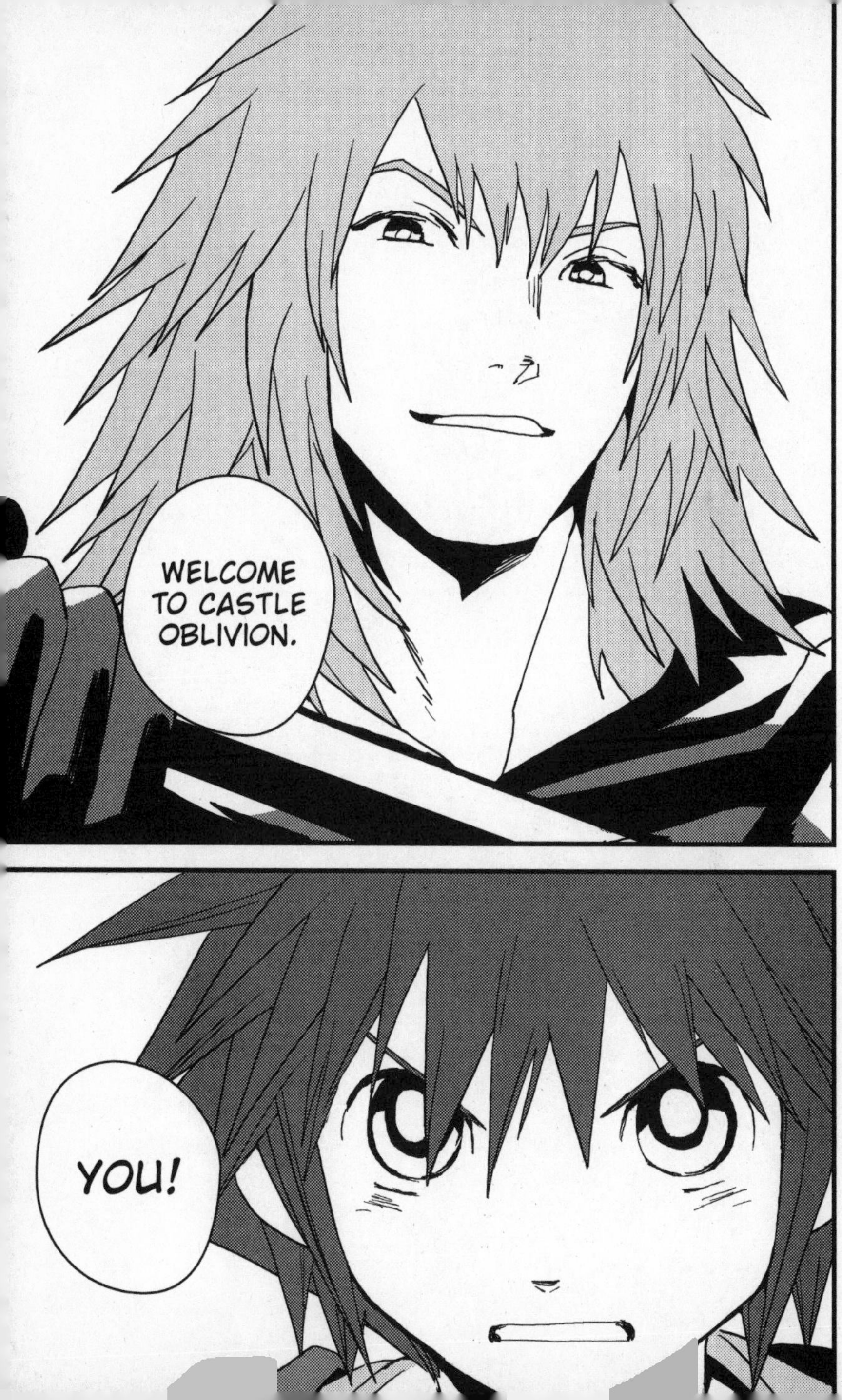
WELCOME TO CASTLE OBLIVION.
YOU!

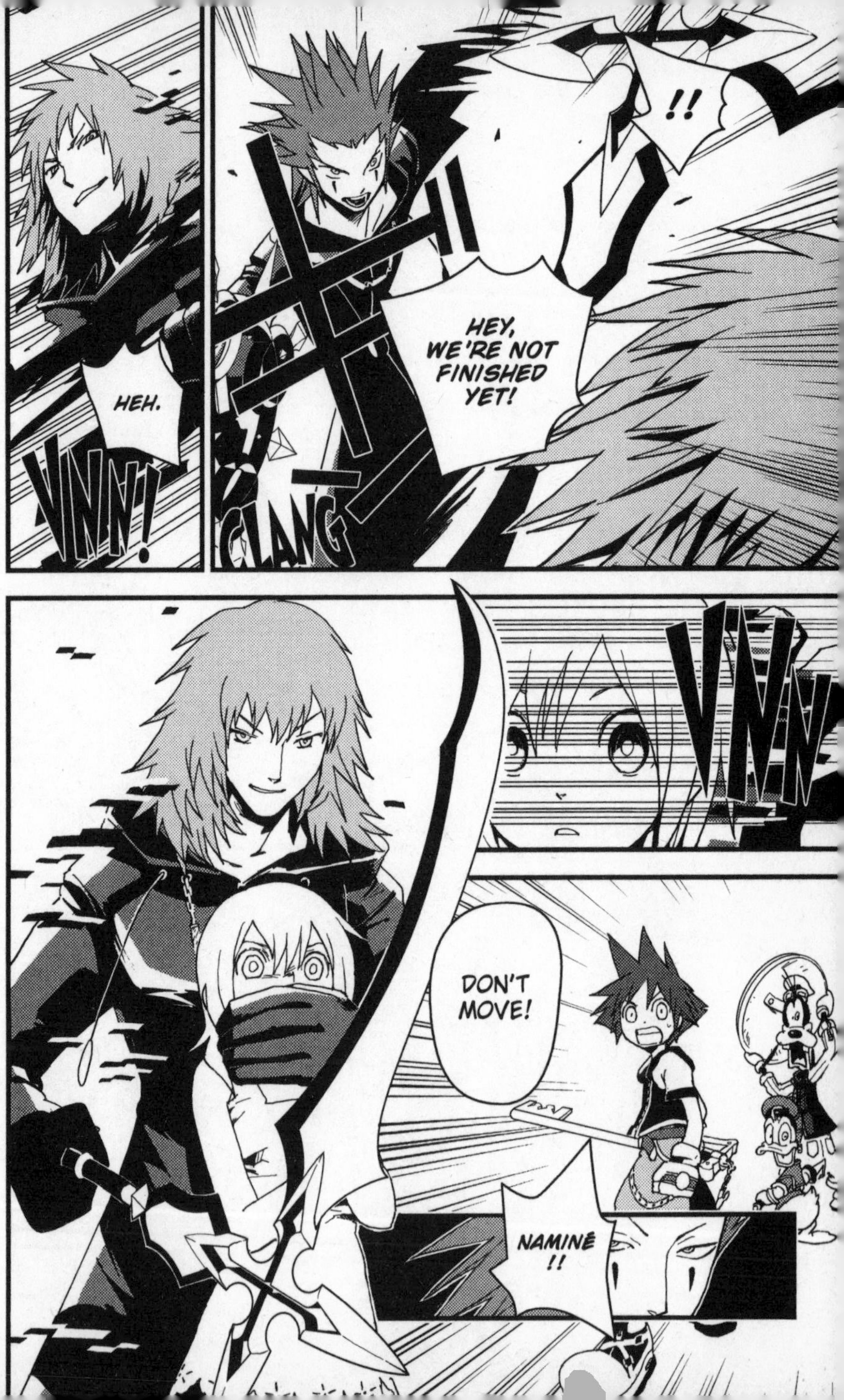
!!
HEY, WE'RE NOT FINISHED YET!
CLANG
HEH.
VNNN!
VNN
DON'T MOVE!
NAMINÉ !!

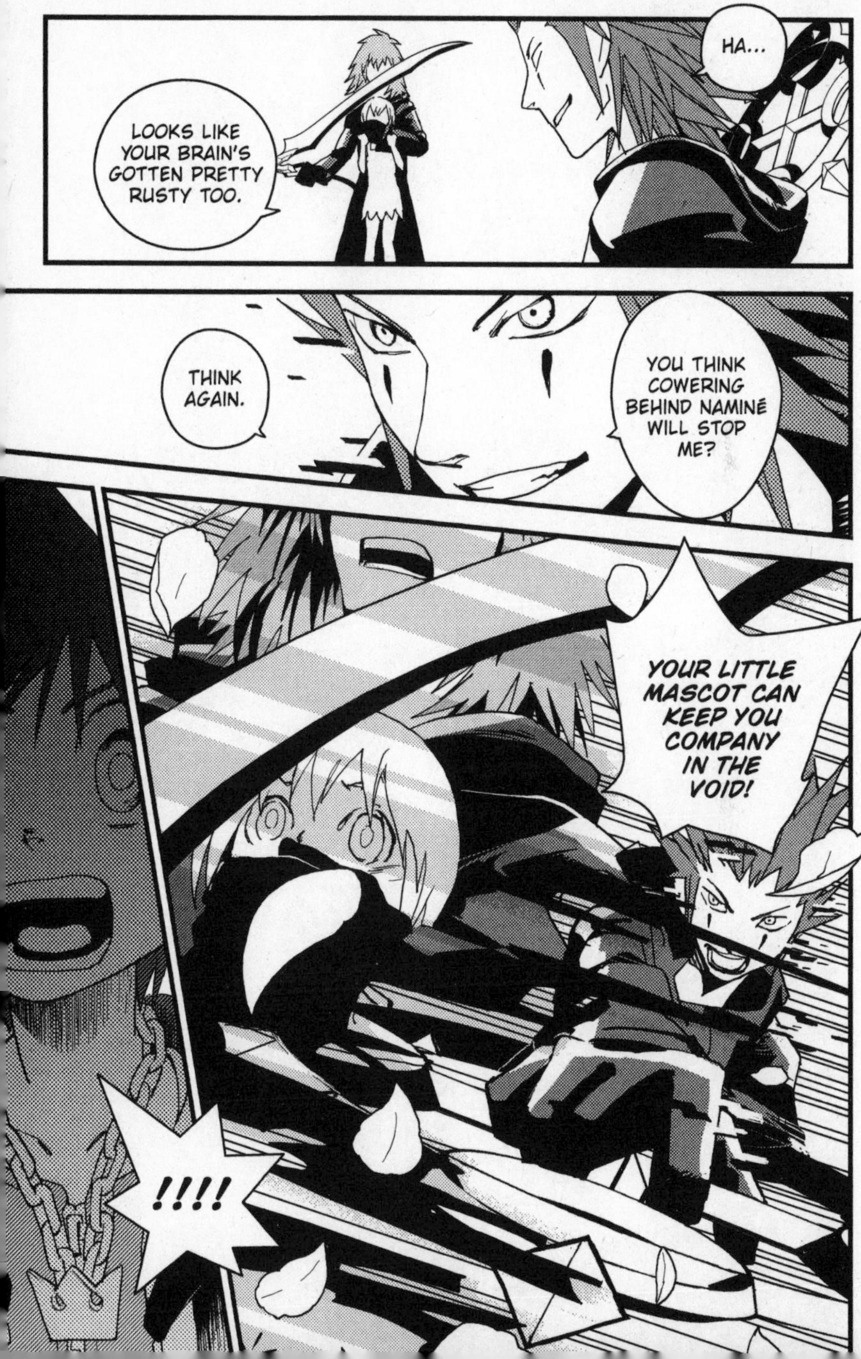
HA...
LOOKS LIKE YOUR BRAIN'S GOTTEN PRETTY RUSTY TOO.
YOU THINK COWERING BEHIND NAMINÉ WILL STOP ME?
THINK AGAIN.
YOUR LITTLE MASCOT CAN KEEP YOU COMPANY IN THE VOID!
!!!!

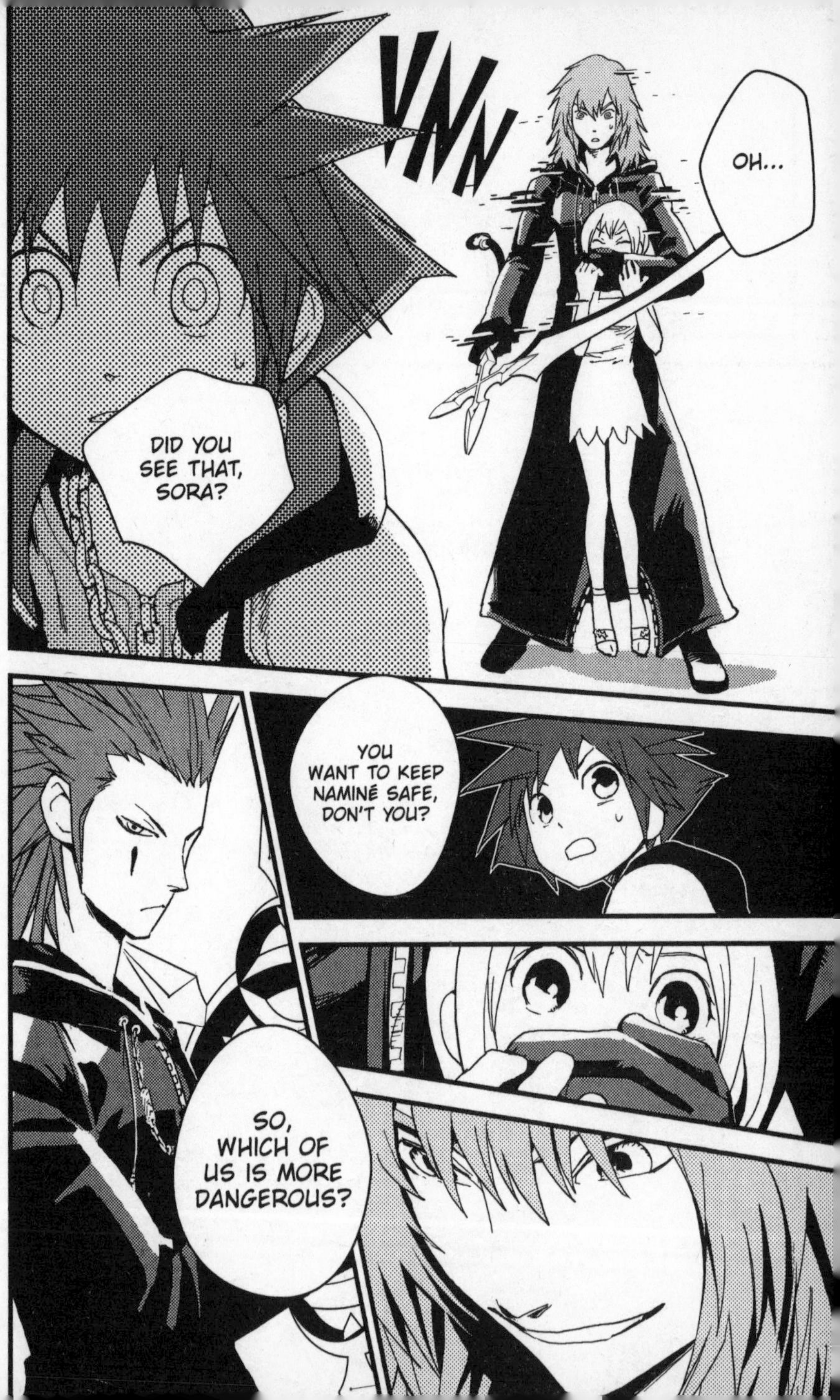
VNN
OH...
DID YOU SEE THAT, SORA?
YOU WANT TO KEEP NAMINÉ SAFE, DON'T YOU?
SO, WHICH OF US IS MORE DANGEROUS?

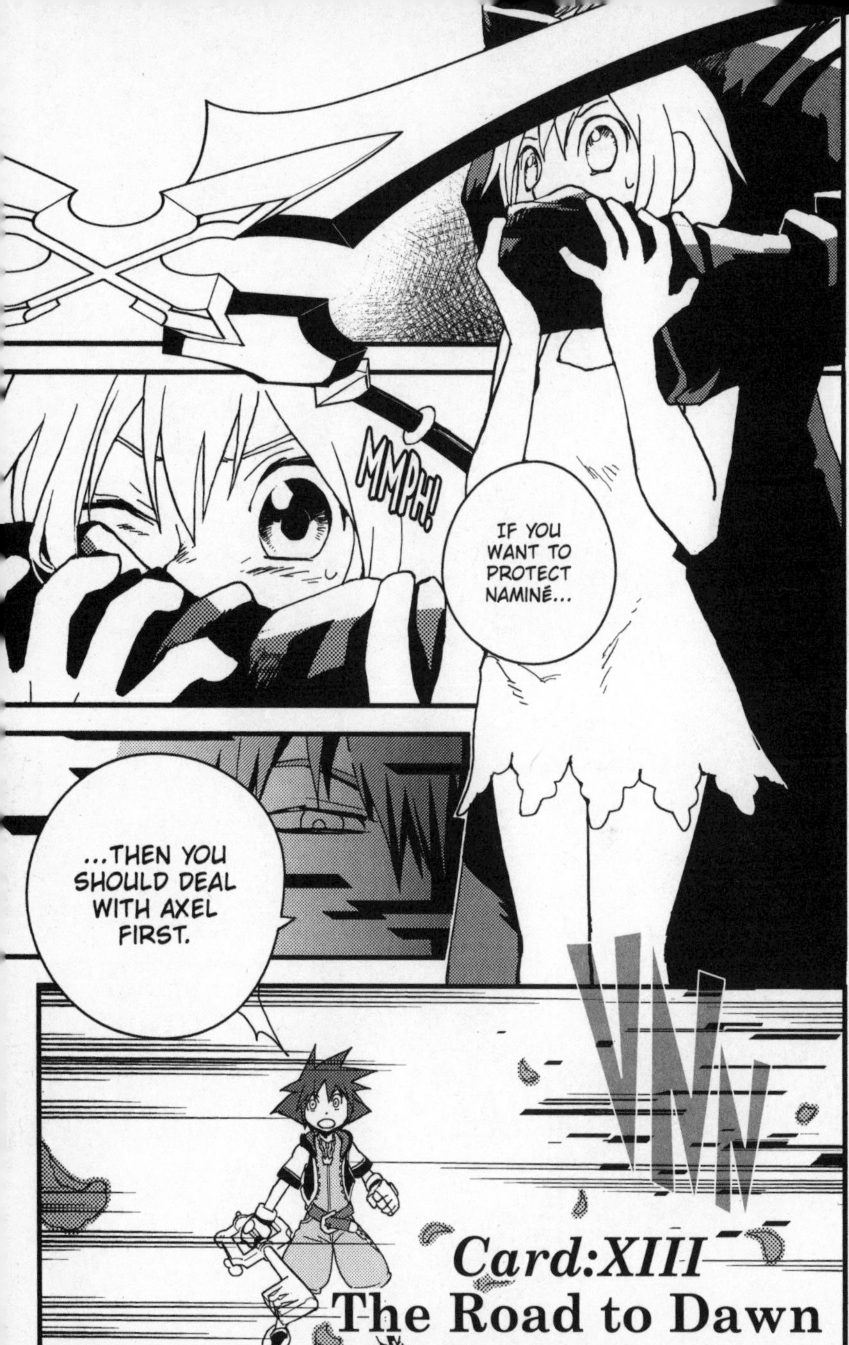
IF YOU WANT TO PROTECT NAMINÉ...
MMPH!
...THEN YOU SHOULD DEAL WITH AXEL FIRST.
VNN
Card:XIII
The Road to Dawn

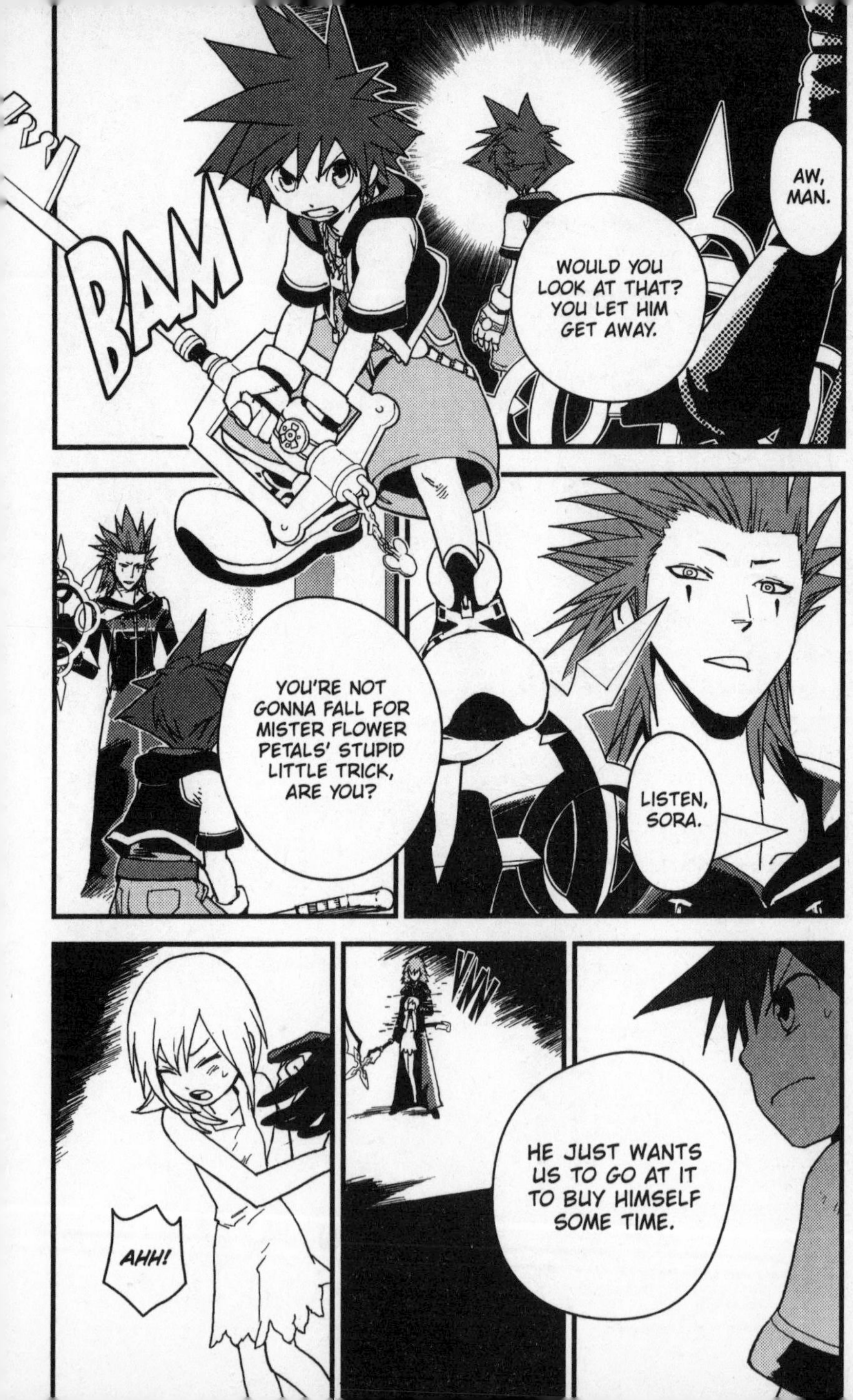
AW, MAN.
WOULD YOU LOOK AT THAT? YOU LET HIM GET AWAY.
BAM
LISTEN, SORA.
YOU'RE NOT GONNA FALL FOR MISTER FLOWER PETALS' STUPID LITTLE TRICK, ARE YOU?
HE JUST WANTS US TO GO AT IT TO BUY HIMSELF SOME TIME.
VNN
AHH!

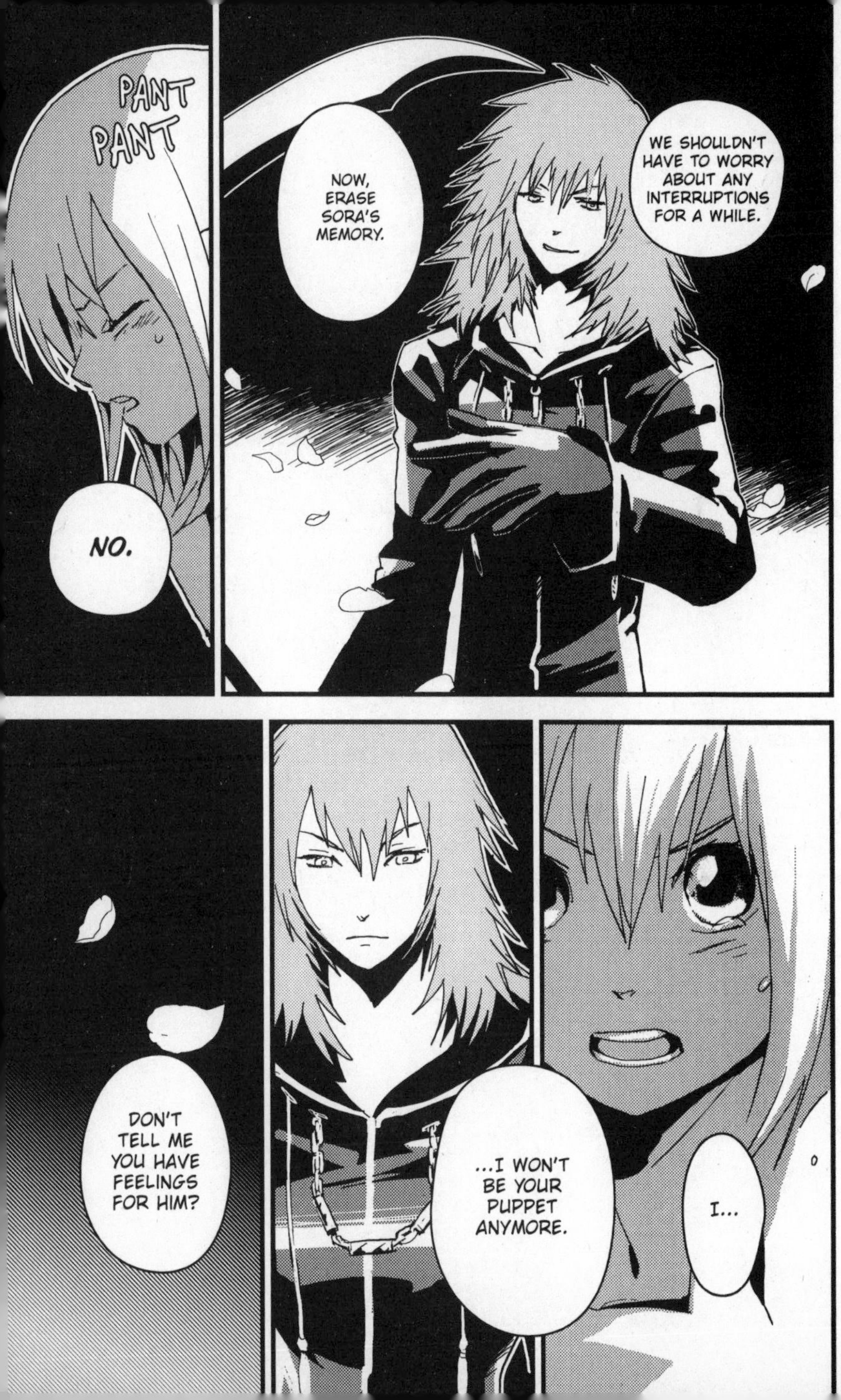
WE SHOULDN'T HAVE TO WORRY ABOUT ANY INTERRUPTIONS FOR A WHILE.
NOW, ERASE SORA'S MEMORY.
PANT PANT
NO.
I...
...I WON'T BE YOUR PUPPET ANYMORE.
DON'T TELL ME YOU HAVE FEELINGS FOR HIM?

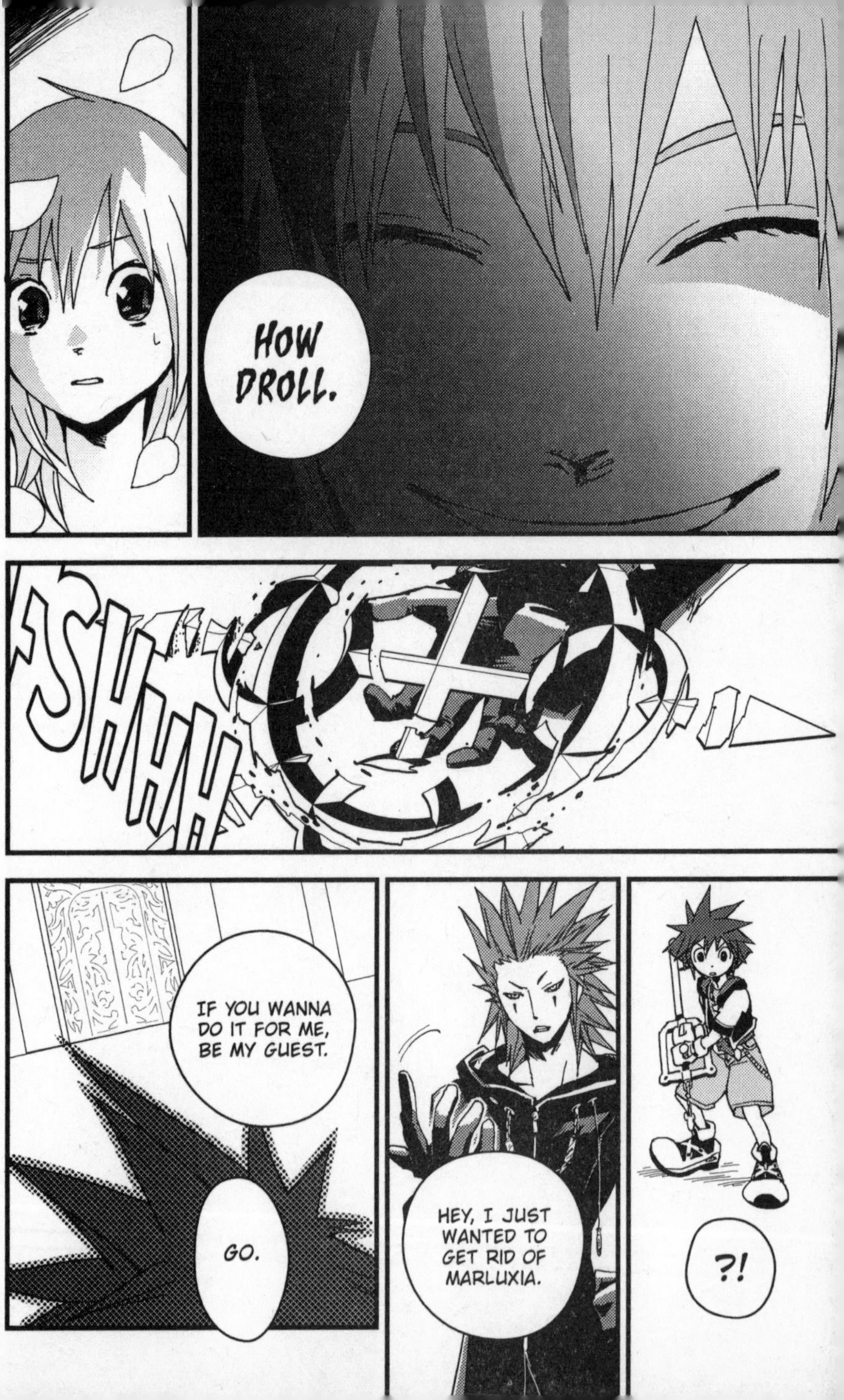
HOW DROLL.
SHHH
?!
HEY, I JUST WANTED TO GET RID OF MARLUXIA.
IF YOU WANNA DO IT FOR ME, BE MY GUEST.
GO.

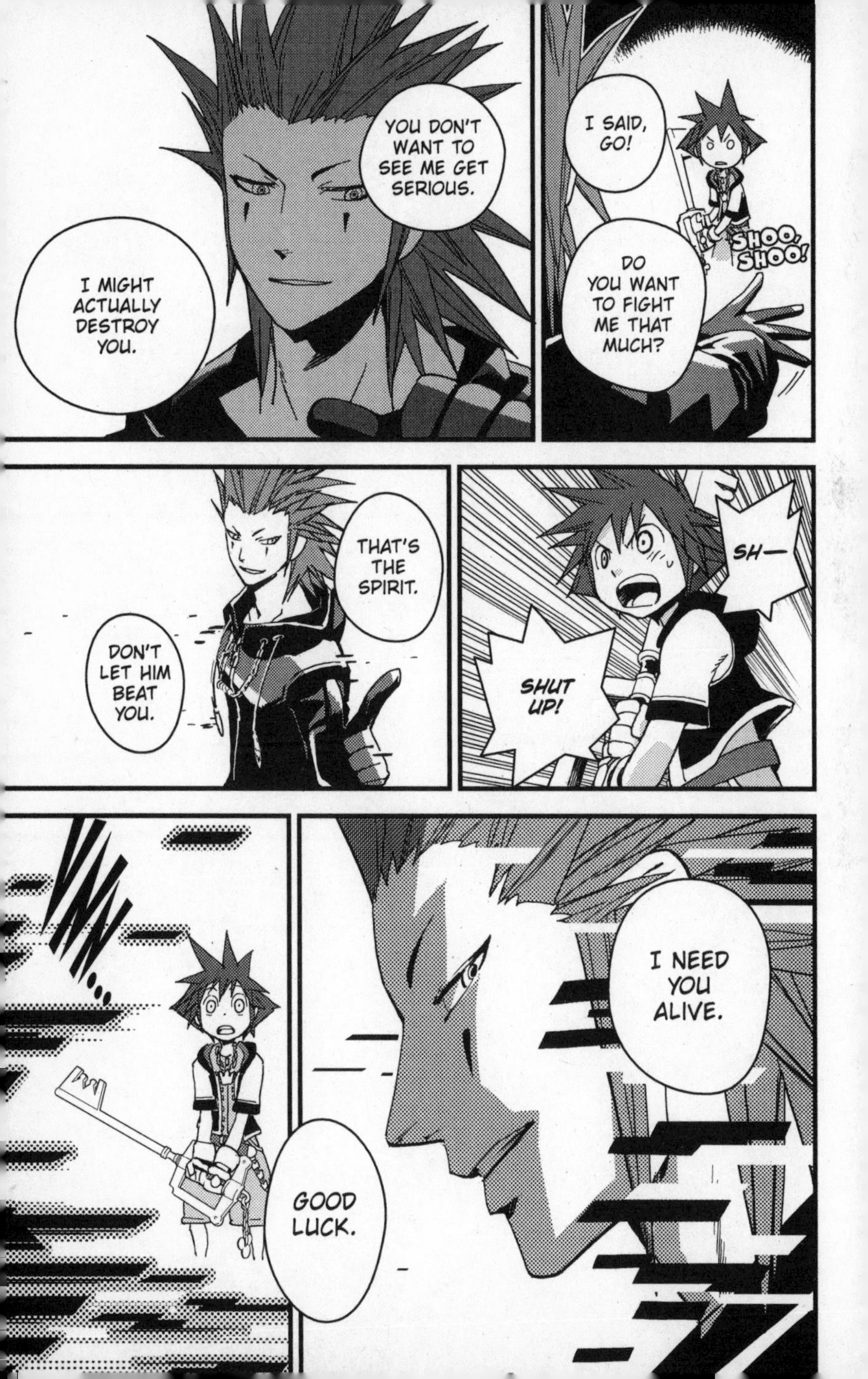
I SAID, GO!
SHOO, SHOO!
DO YOU WANT TO FIGHT ME THAT MUCH?
YOU DON'T WANT TO SEE ME GET SERIOUS.
I MIGHT ACTUALLY DESTROY YOU.
SH—
SHUT UP!
THAT'S THE SPIRIT.
DON'T LET HIM BEAT YOU.
I NEED YOU ALIVE.
GOOD LUCK.

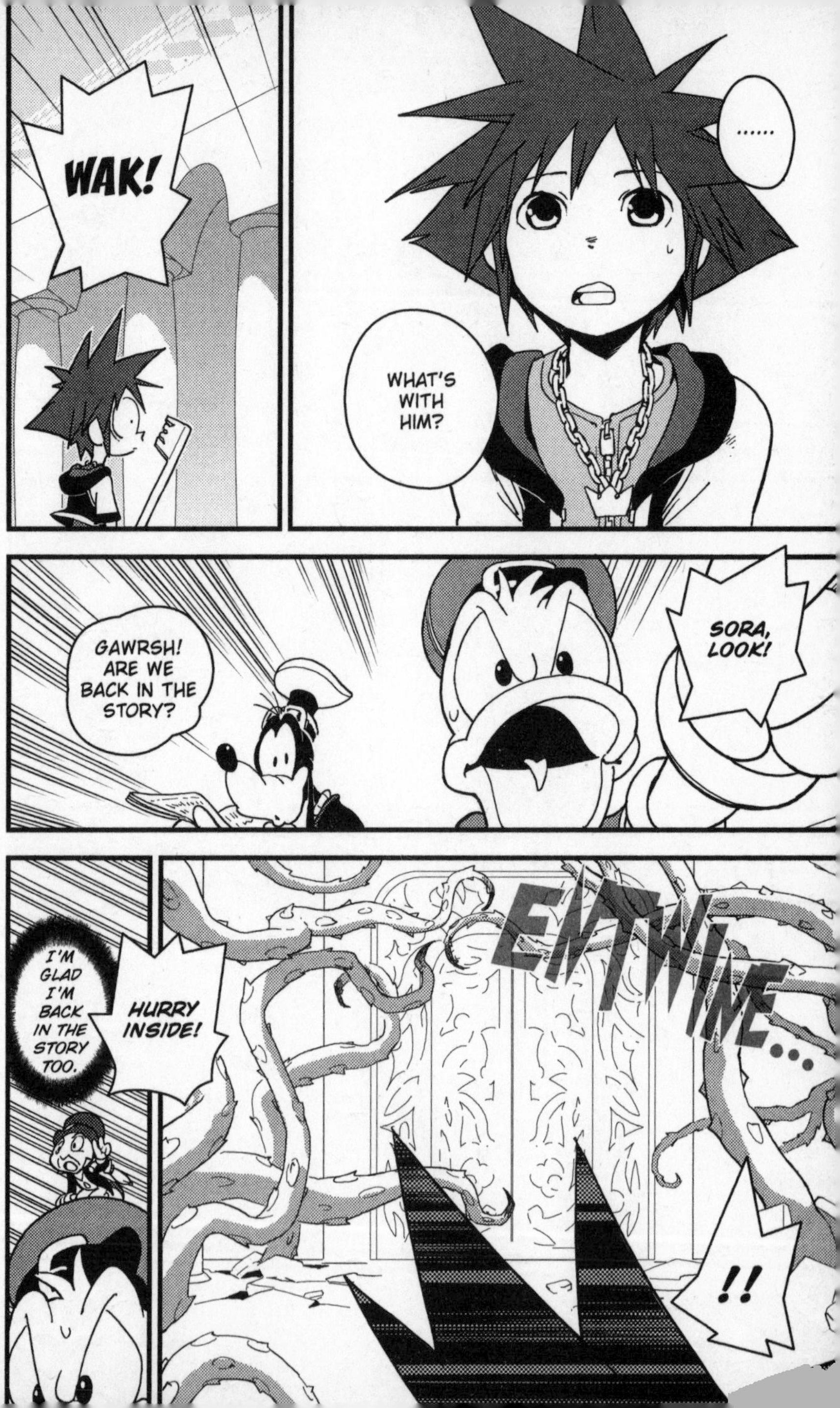
......
WHAT'S WITH HIM?
WAK!
SORA, LOOK!
GAWRSH! ARE WE BACK IN THE STORY?
ENTWINE...
!!
HURRY INSIDE!
I'M GLAD I'M BACK IN THE STORY TOO.

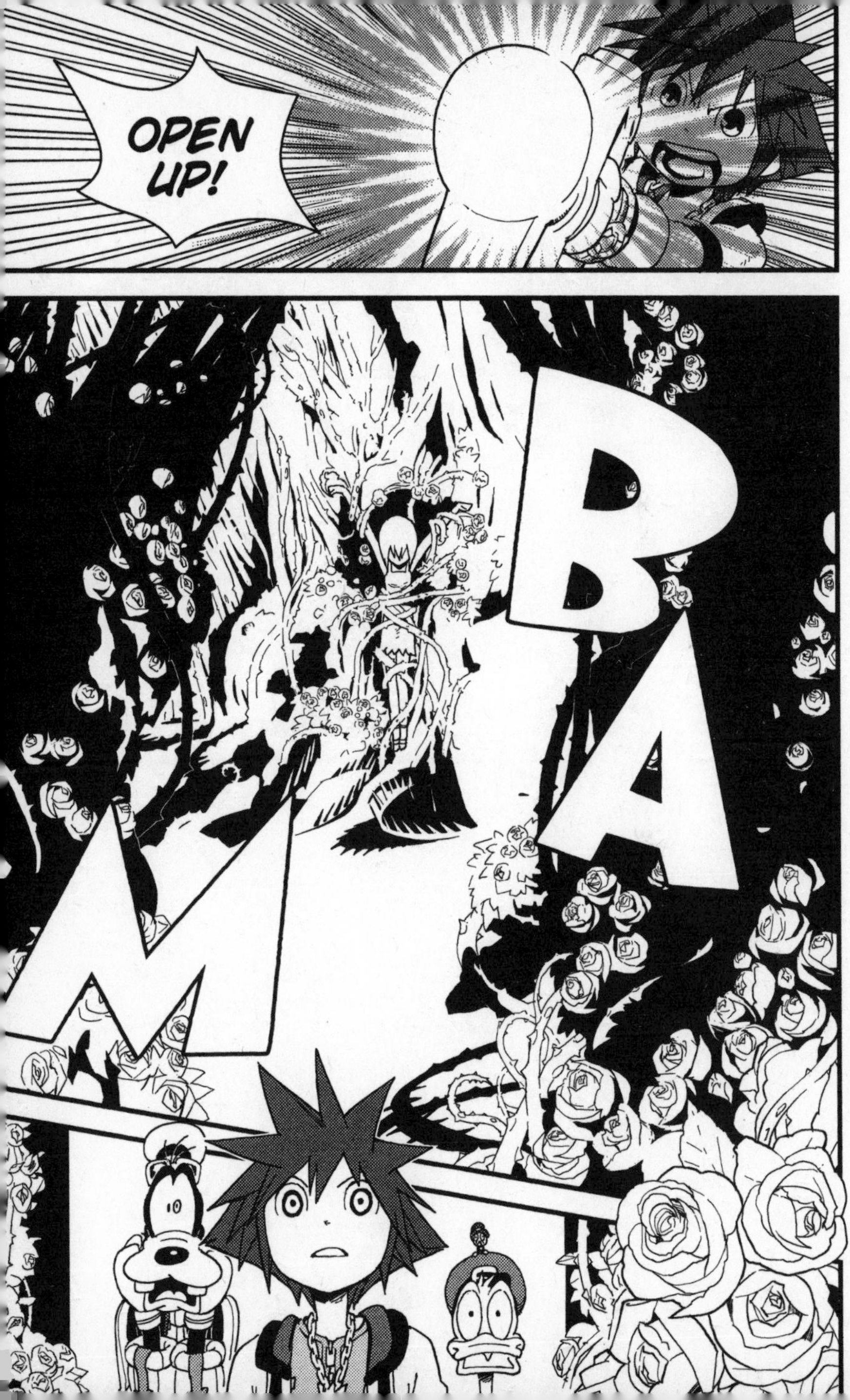
OPEN UP!
BAM

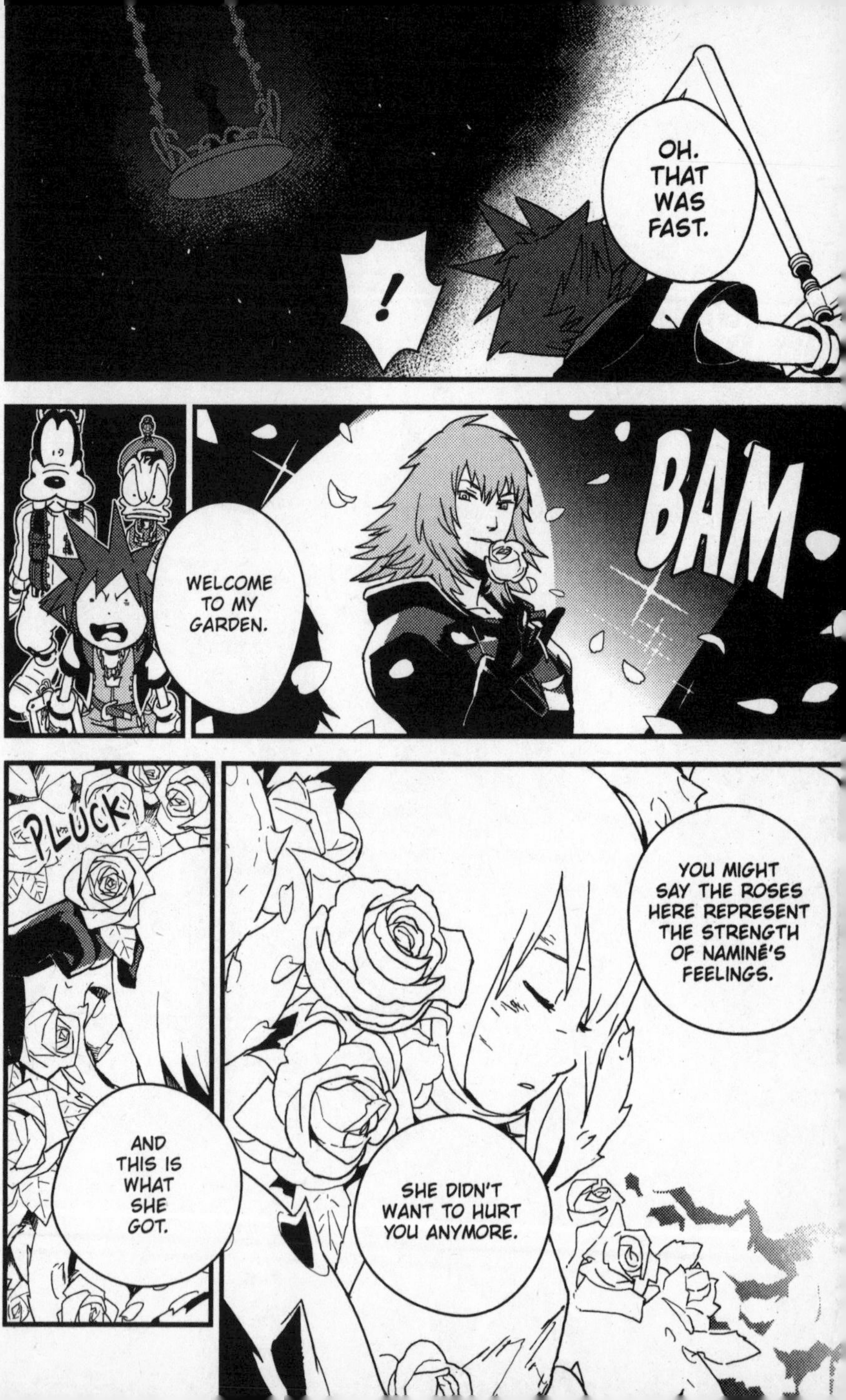
OH. THAT WAS FAST.
!
BAM
WELCOME TO MY GARDEN.
YOU MIGHT SAY THE ROSES HERE REPRESENT THE STRENGTH OF NAMINÉ'S FEELINGS.
SHE DIDN'T WANT TO HURT YOU ANYMORE.
PLUCK
AND THIS IS WHAT SHE GOT.

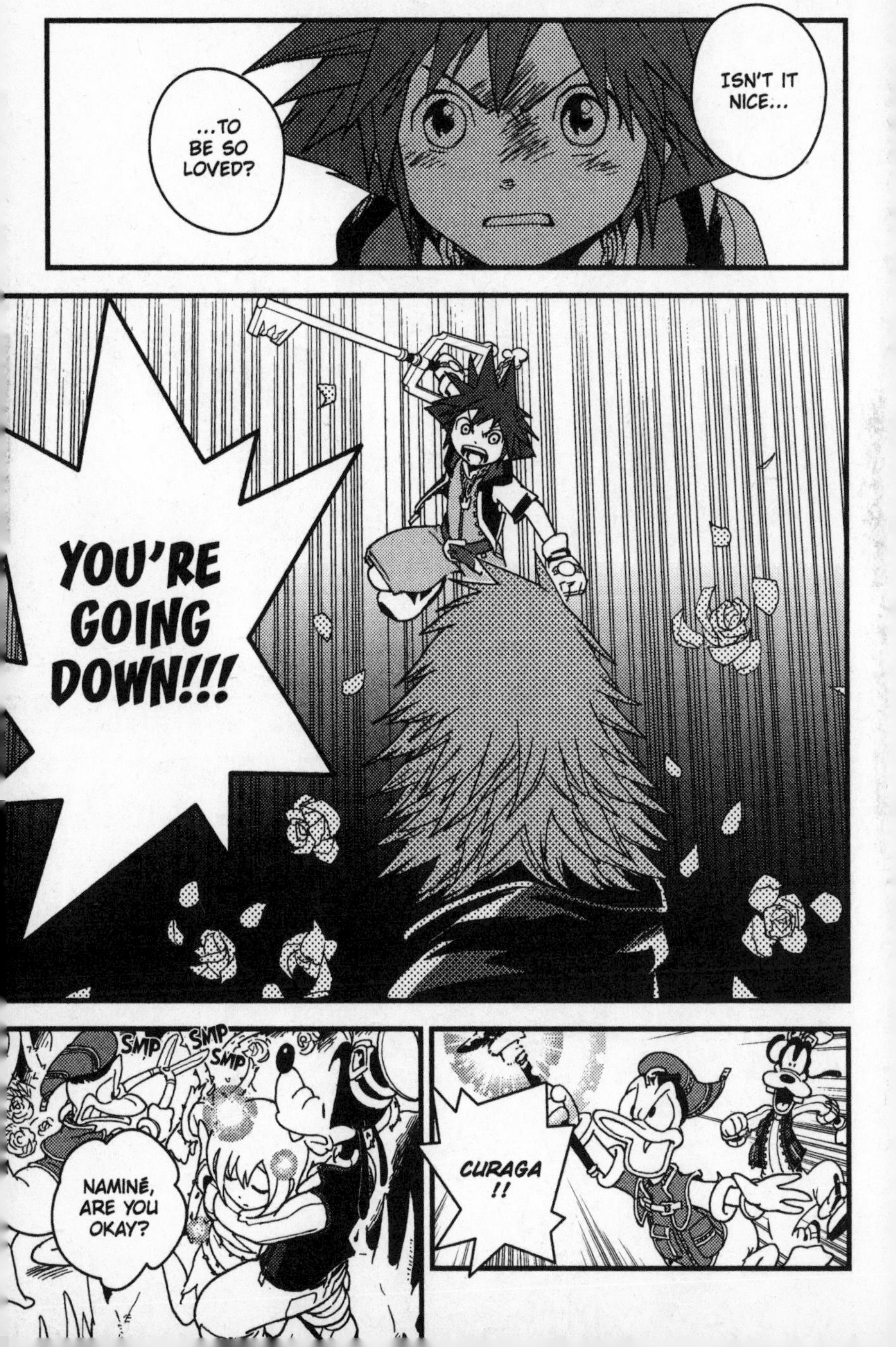
ISN'T IT NICE...
...TO BE SO LOVED?
YOU'RE GOING DOWN!!!
CURAGA!!
SMP SMP SMP
NAMINÉ, ARE YOU OKAY?

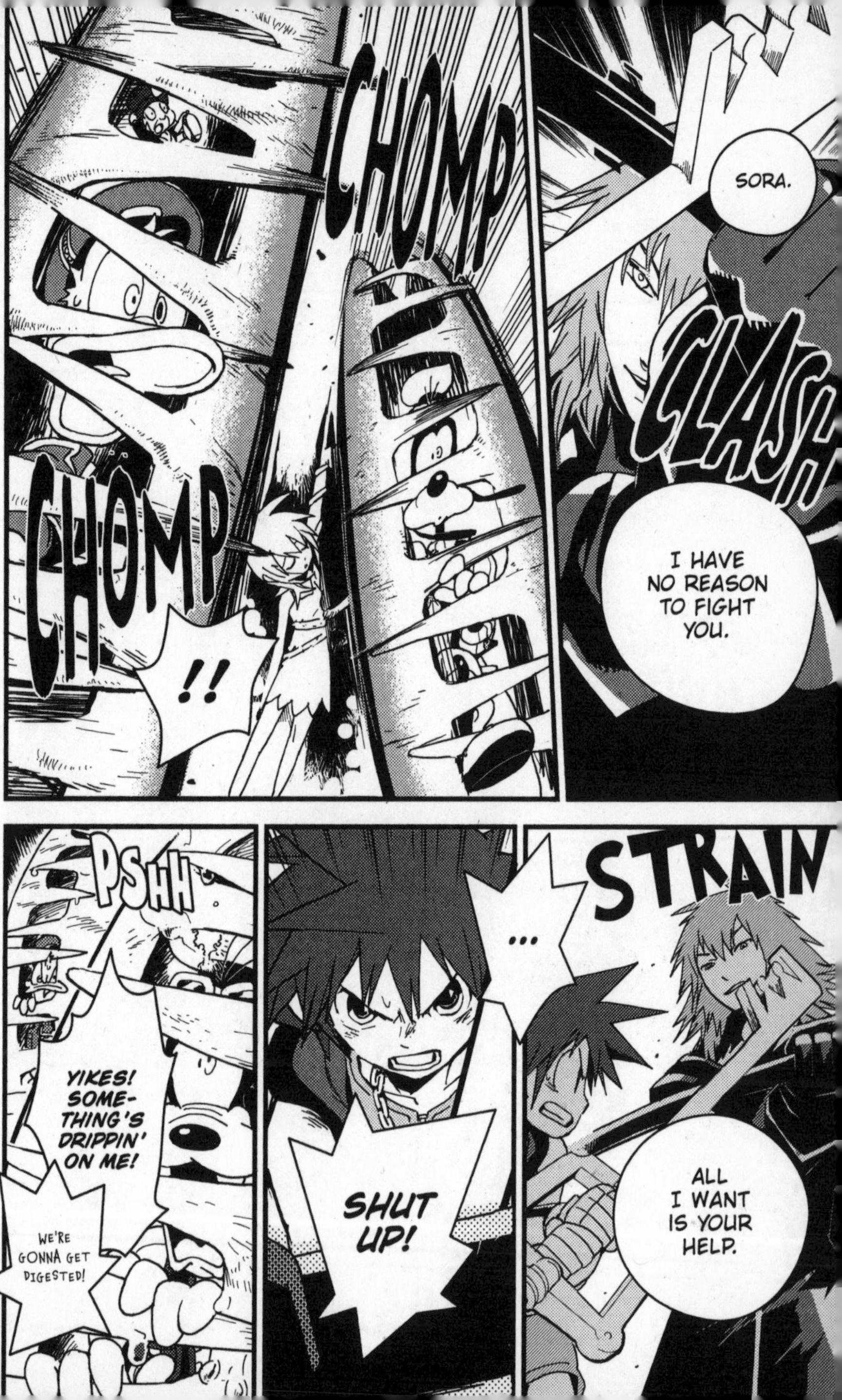
SORA.
CLASH
I HAVE NO REASON TO FIGHT YOU.
CHOMP
CHOMP
!!
STRAIN
ALL I WANT IS YOUR HELP.
...
SHUT UP!
PSHH
YIKES! SOME-THING'S DRIPPIN' ON ME!
WE'RE GONNA GET DIGESTED!

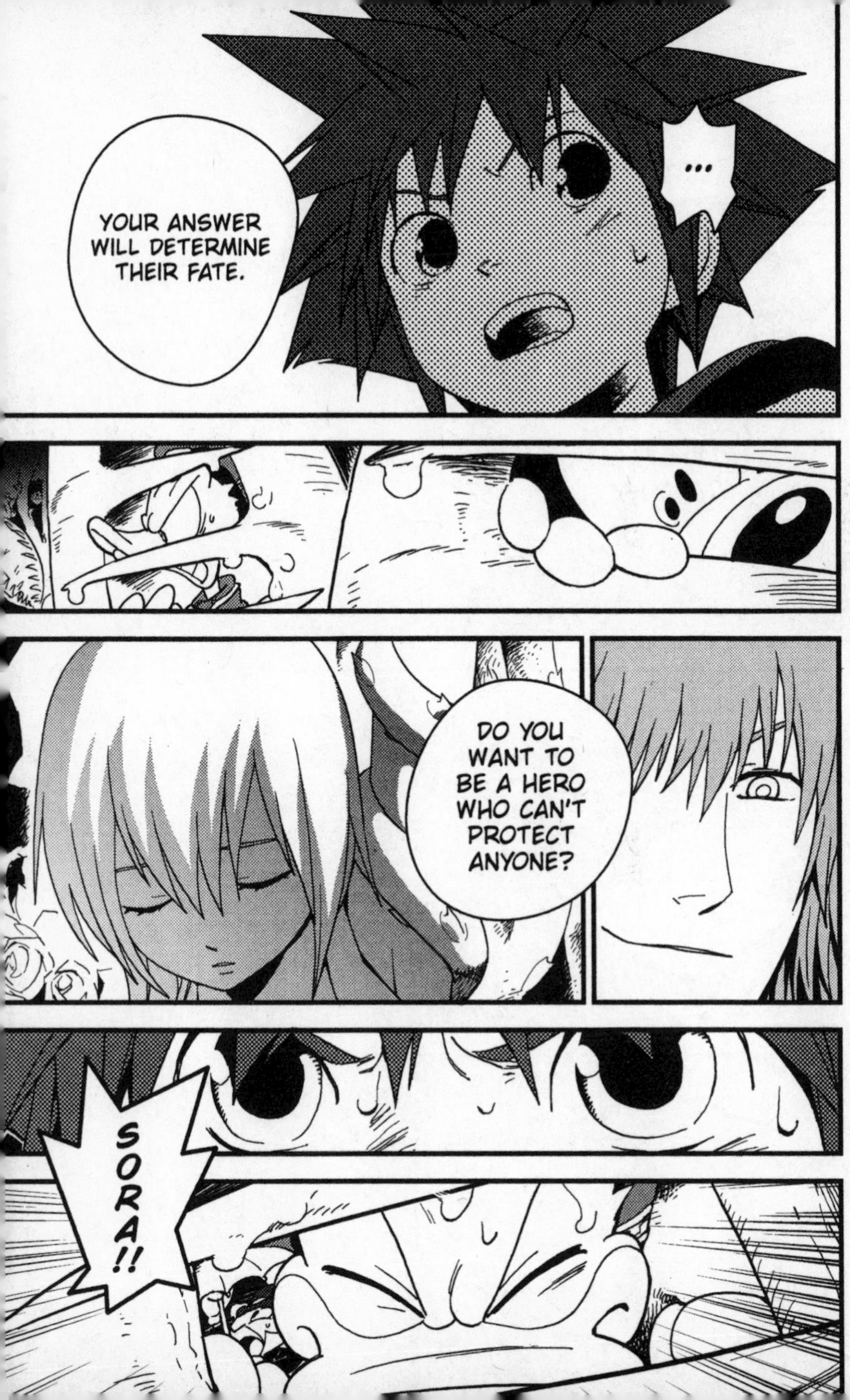
...
YOUR ANSWER WILL DETERMINE THEIR FATE.
DO YOU WANT TO BE A HERO WHO CAN'T PROTECT ANYONE?
SORA!!

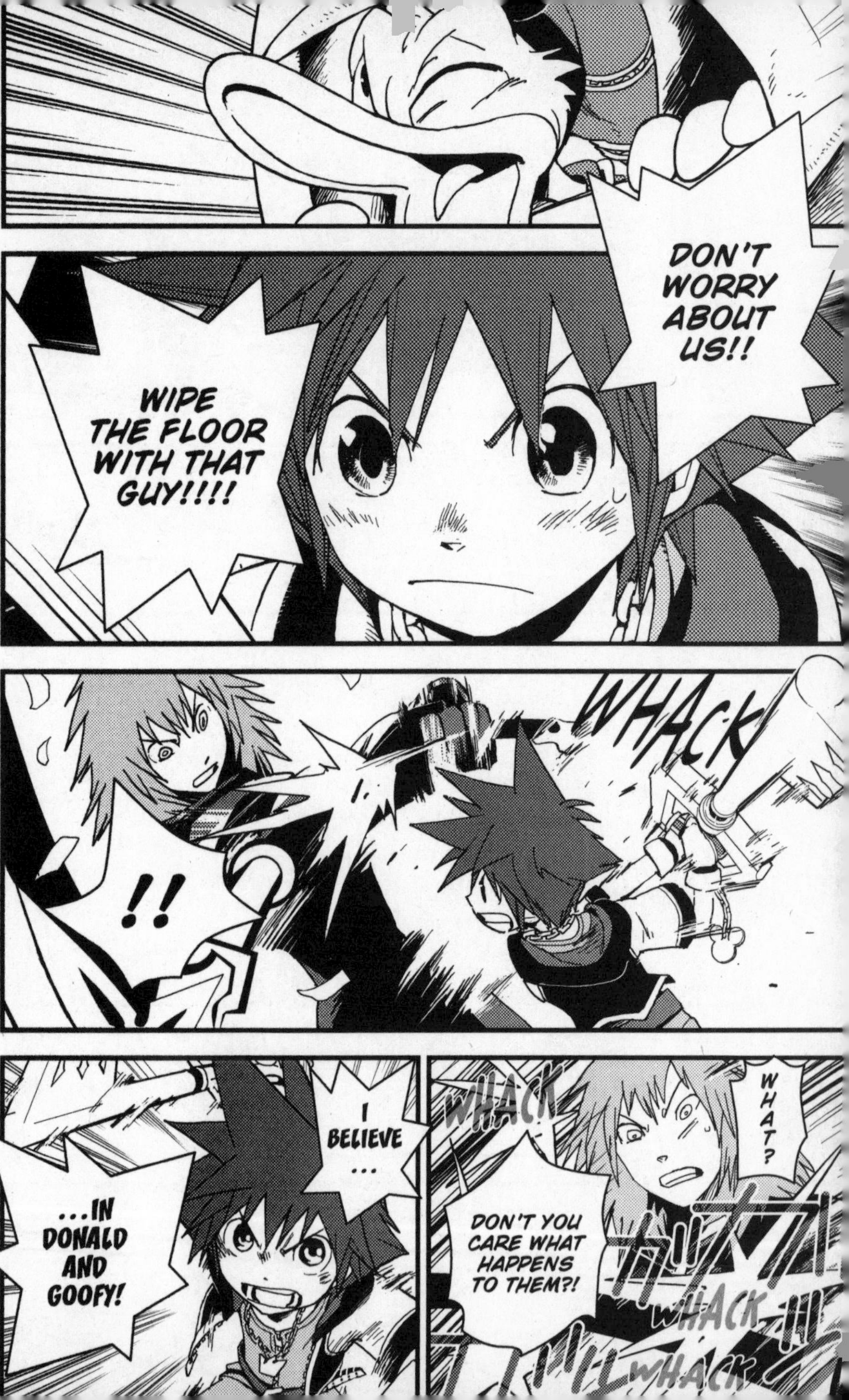
DON'T WORRY ABOUT US!!
WIPE THE FLOOR WITH THAT GUY!!!!
WHACK
!!
WHACK
WHAT?
DON'T YOU CARE WHAT HAPPENS TO THEM?!
WHACK
WHACK
I BELIEVE...
...IN DONALD AND GOOFY!

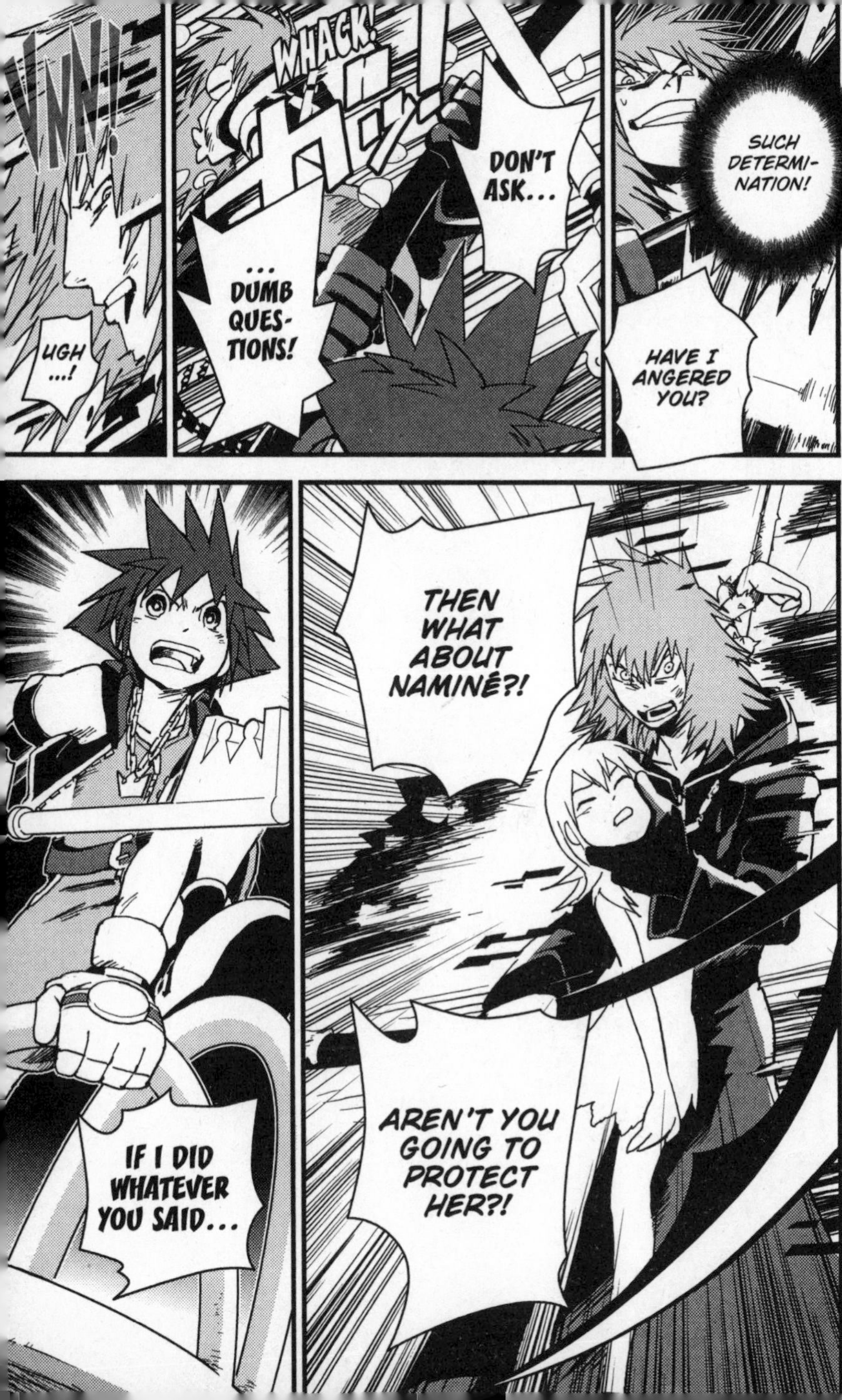
SUCH DETERMINATION!
HAVE I ANGERED YOU?
WHACK!
DON'T ASK...
... DUMB QUESTIONS!
VNN!
UGH ...!
THEN WHAT ABOUT NAMINÉ?!
AREN'T YOU GOING TO PROTECT HER?!
IF I DID WHATEVER YOU SAID...

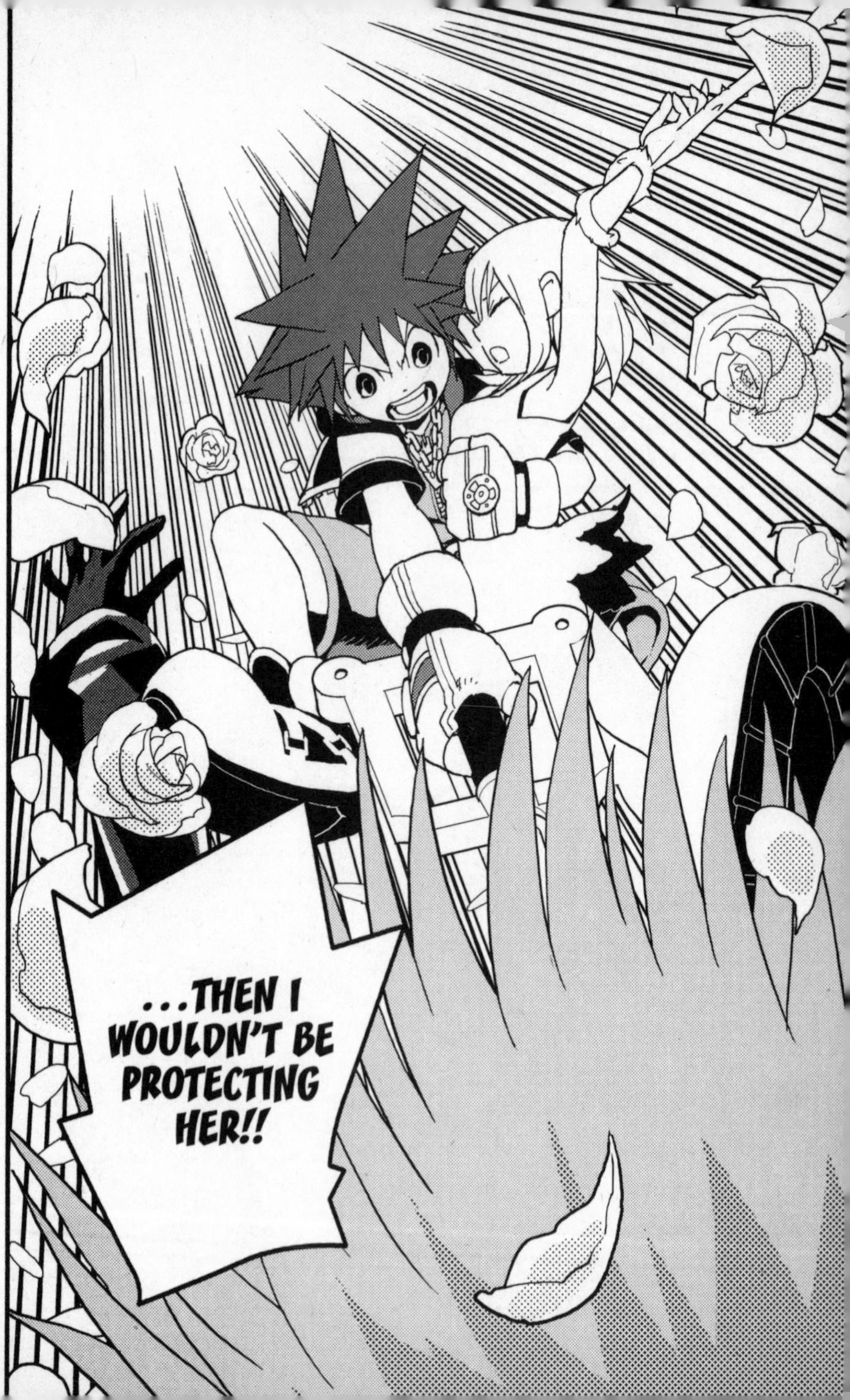
...THEN I WOULDN'T BE PROTECTING HER!!

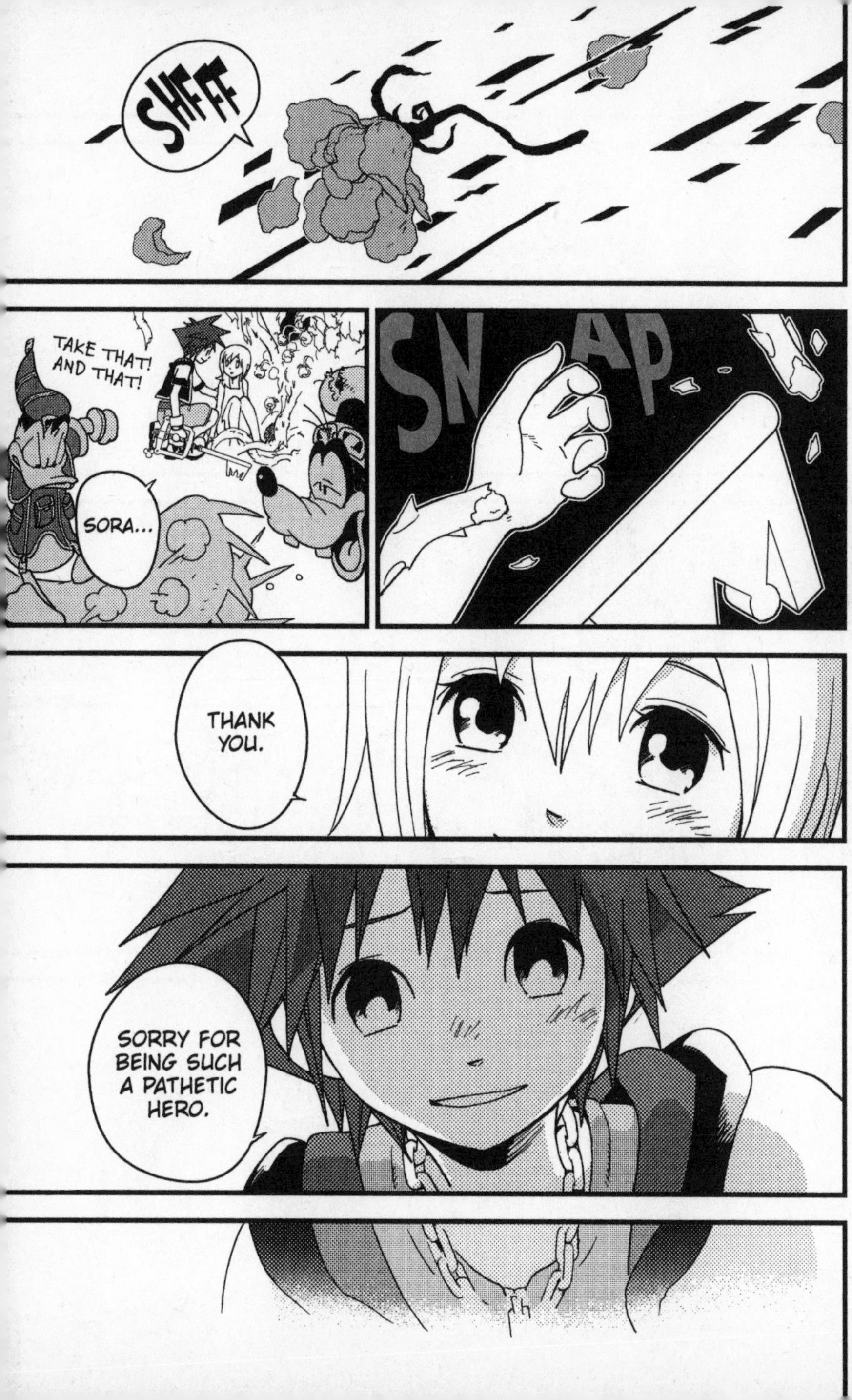
SHFFF
SNAP
TAKE THAT! AND THAT!
SORA...
THANK YOU.
SORRY FOR BEING SUCH A PATHETIC HERO.

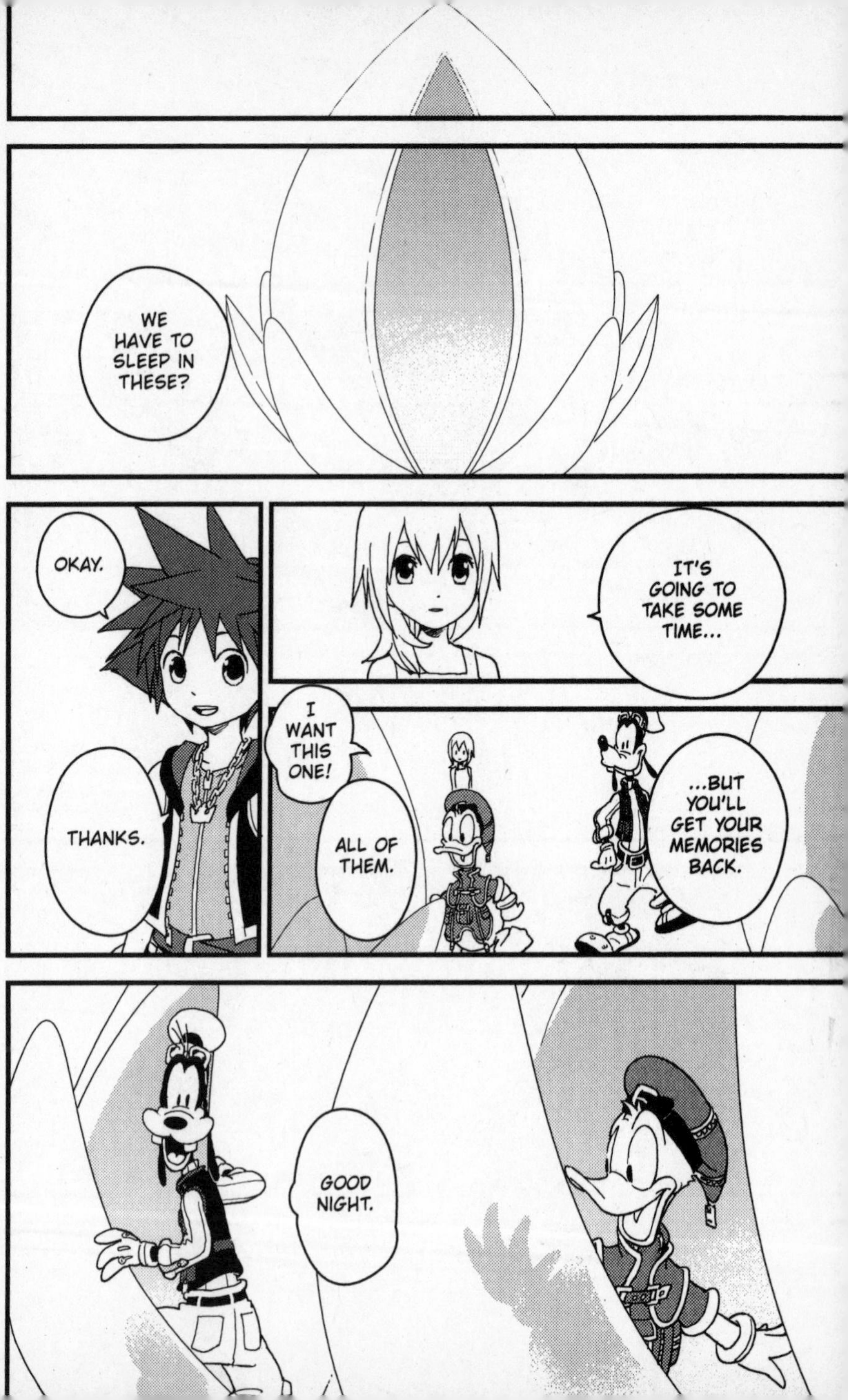
WE HAVE TO SLEEP IN THESE?
IT'S GOING TO TAKE SOME TIME...
...BUT YOU'LL GET YOUR MEMORIES BACK.
I WANT THIS ONE!
ALL OF THEM.
OKAY.
THANKS.
GOOD NIGHT.

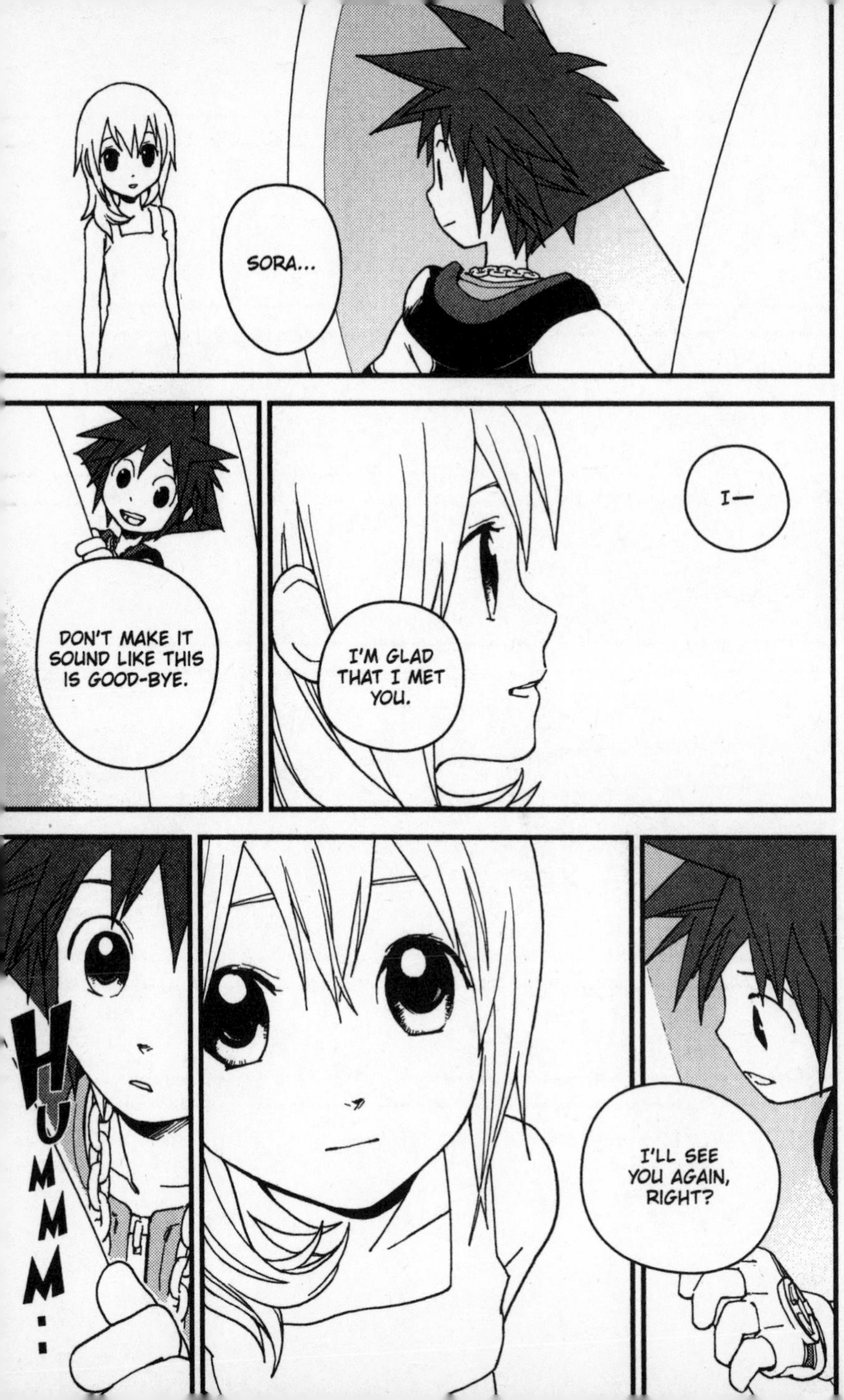
SORA...
I—
I'M GLAD THAT I MET YOU.
DON'T MAKE IT SOUND LIKE THIS IS GOOD-BYE.
I'LL SEE YOU AGAIN, RIGHT?
HUMMM..

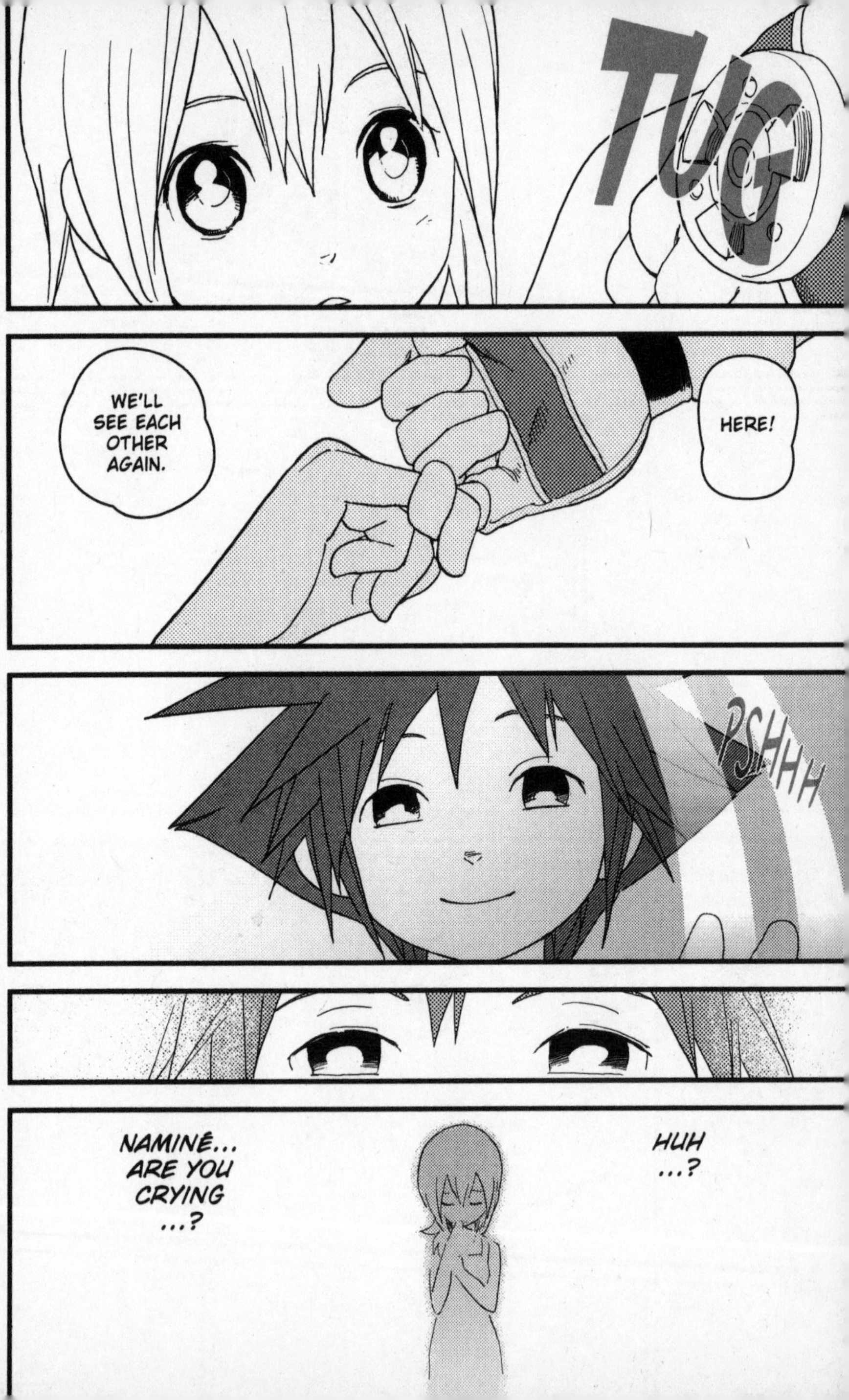
TUG
HERE!
WE'LL SEE EACH OTHER AGAIN.
PSHHH
HUH ...?
NAMINÉ... ARE YOU CRYING ...?

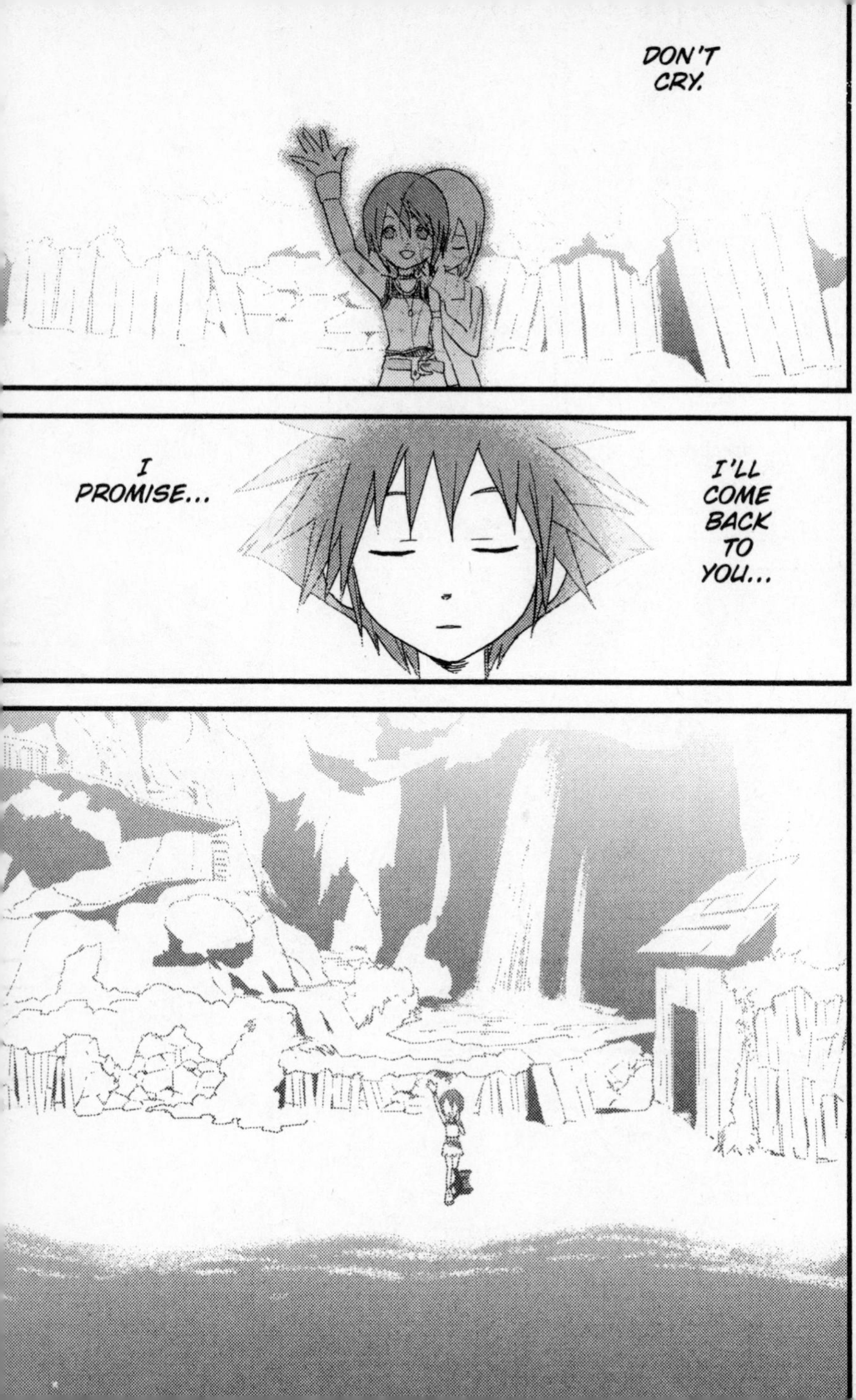
DON'T CRY.
I'LL COME BACK TO YOU...
I PROMISE...

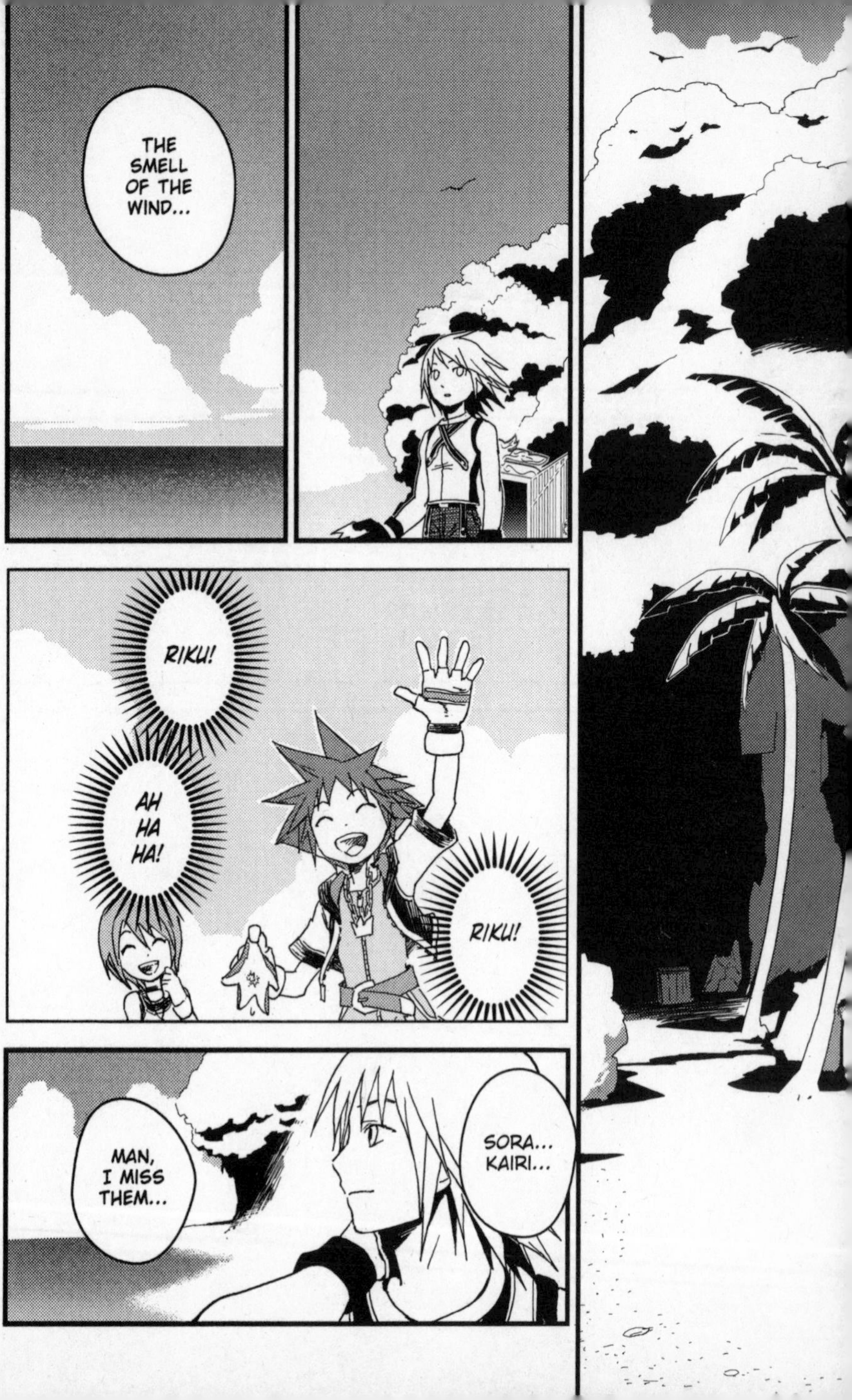
THE SMELL OF THE WIND...
RIKU!
AH HA HA!
RIKU!
SORA... KAIRI...
MAN, I MISS THEM...

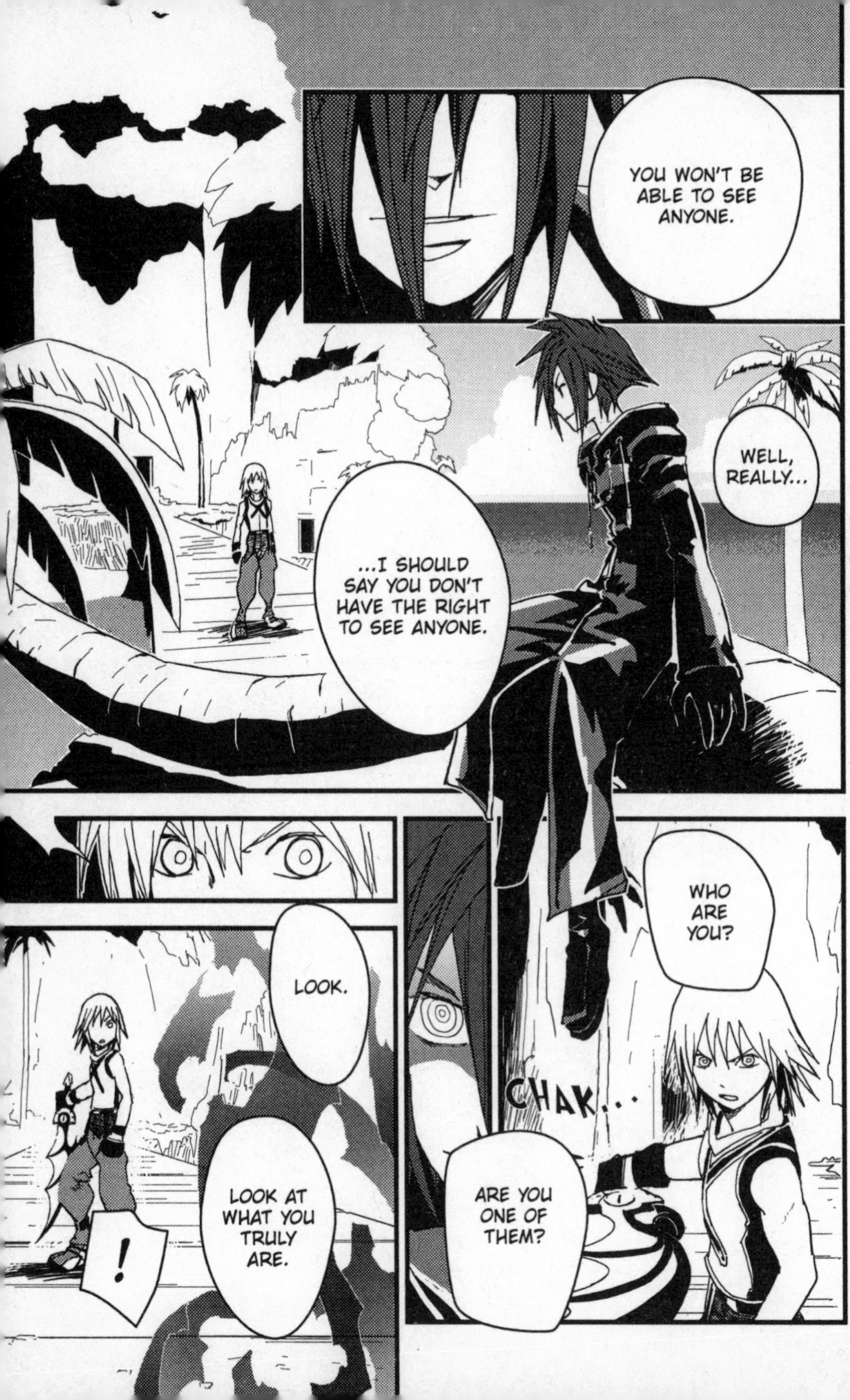
YOU WON'T BE ABLE TO SEE ANYONE.
WELL, REALLY...
...I SHOULD SAY YOU DON'T HAVE THE RIGHT TO SEE ANYONE.
WHO ARE YOU?
CHAK...
ARE YOU ONE OF THEM?
LOOK.
LOOK AT WHAT YOU TRULY ARE.
!

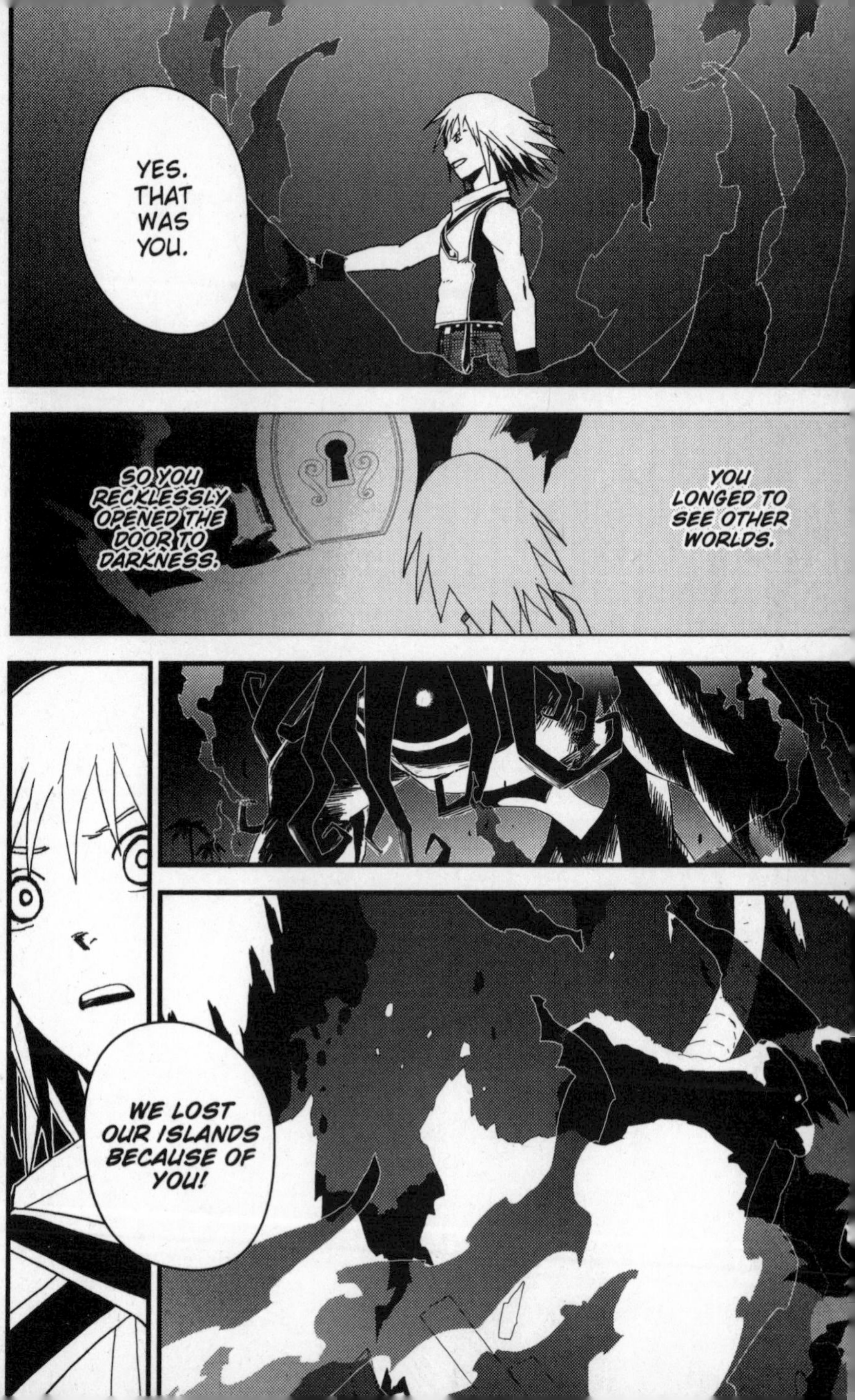
YES. THAT WAS YOU.
YOU LONGED TO SEE OTHER WORLDS.
SO YOU RECKLESSLY OPENED THE DOOR TO DARKNESS.
WE LOST OUR ISLANDS BECAUSE OF YOU!

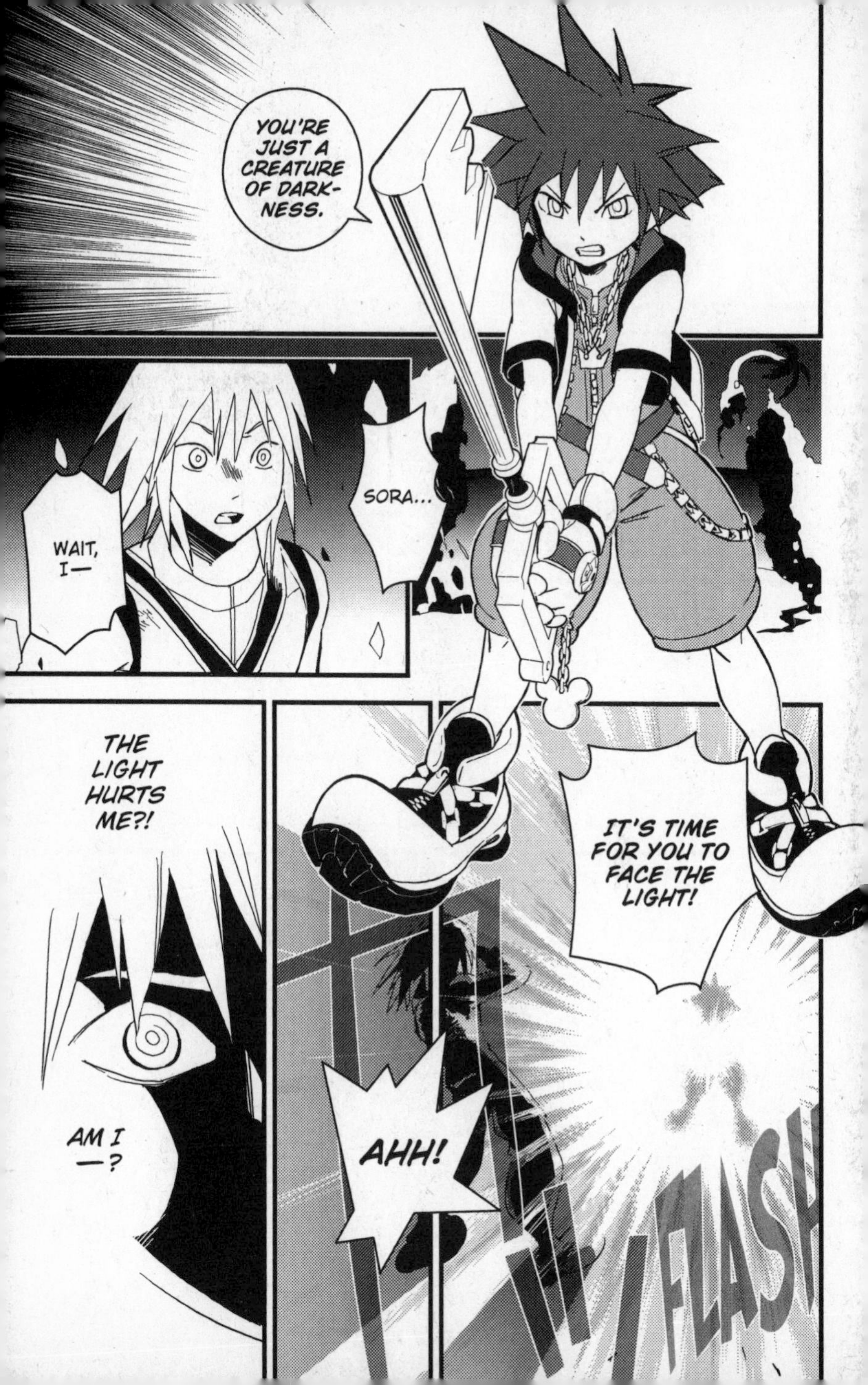
YOU'RE JUST A CREATURE OF DARK-NESS.
SORA...
WAIT, I—
IT'S TIME FOR YOU TO FACE THE LIGHT!
AHH!
FLASH
THE LIGHT HURTS ME?!
AM I —?

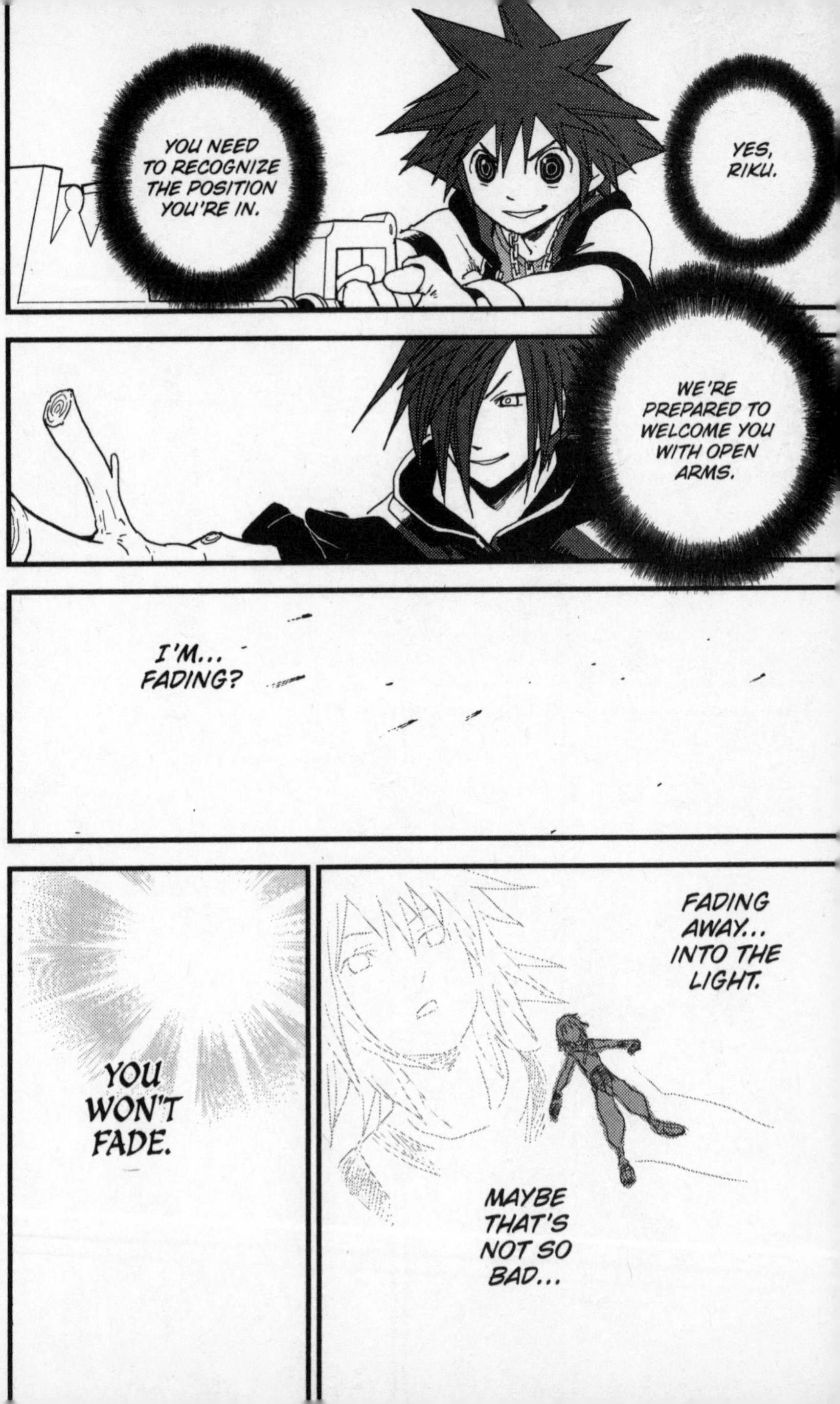
YES, RIKU.
YOU NEED TO RECOGNIZE THE POSITION YOU'RE IN.
WE'RE PREPARED TO WELCOME YOU WITH OPEN ARMS.
I'M... FADING?
FADING AWAY... INTO THE LIGHT.
MAYBE THAT'S NOT SO BAD...
YOU WON'T FADE.

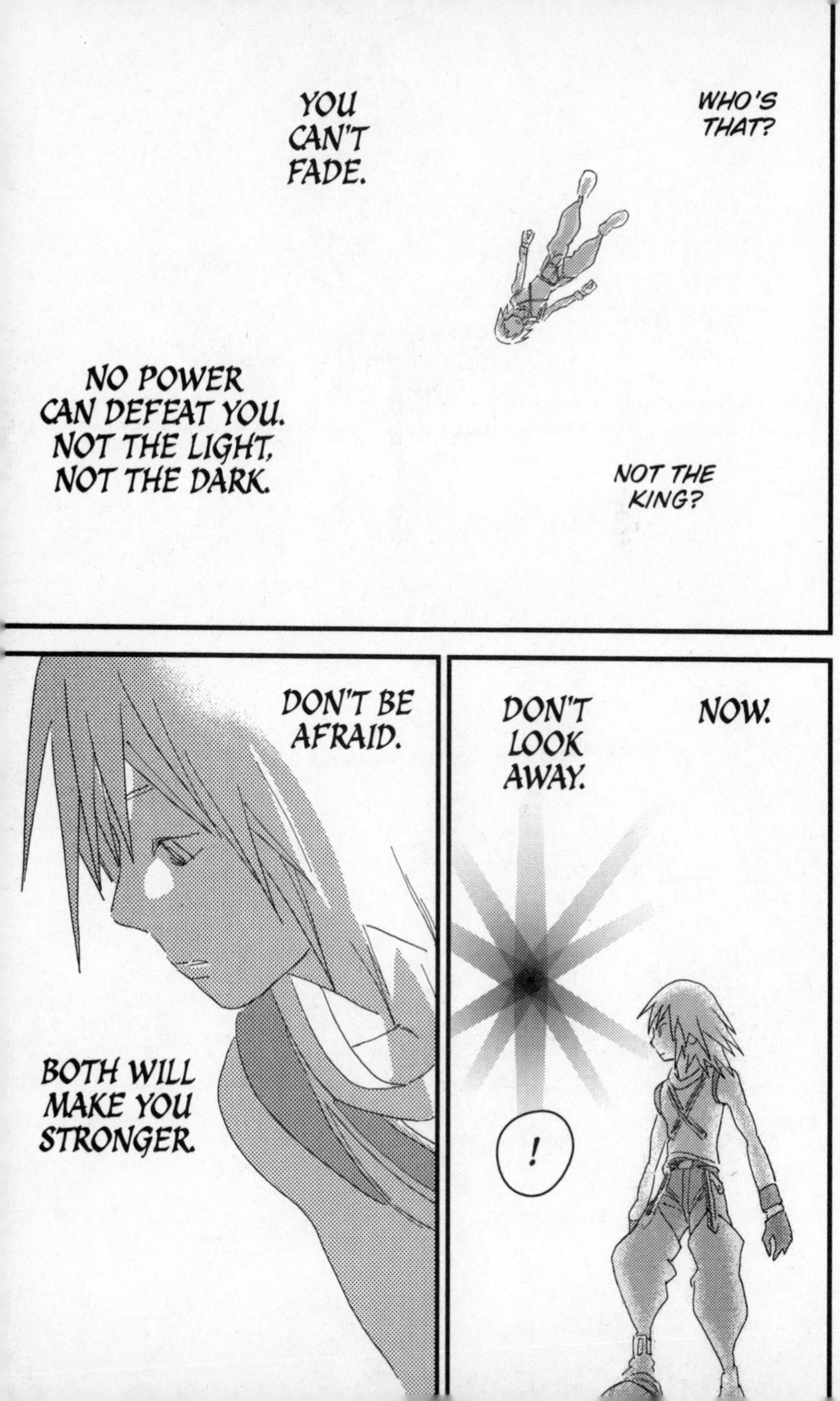
WHO'S THAT?
YOU CAN'T FADE.
NO POWER CAN DEFEAT YOU. NOT THE LIGHT, NOT THE DARK.
NOT THE KING?
NOW.
DON'T LOOK AWAY.
!
DON'T BE AFRAID.
BOTH WILL MAKE YOU STRONGER.

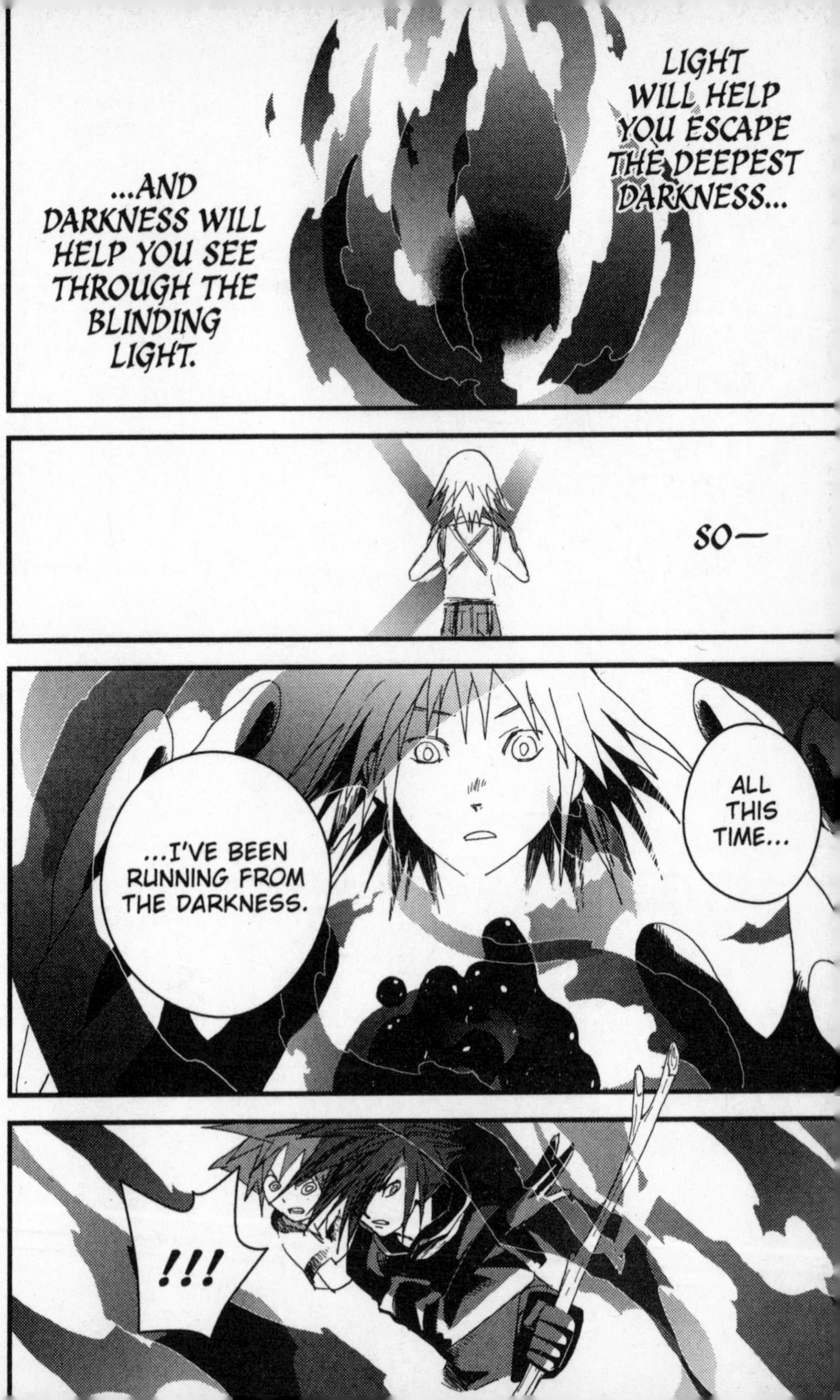
LIGHT WILL HELP YOU ESCAPE THE DEEPEST DARKNESS...
...AND DARKNESS WILL HELP YOU SEE THROUGH THE BLINDING LIGHT.
SO—
ALL THIS TIME...
...I'VE BEEN RUNNING FROM THE DARKNESS.
!!!

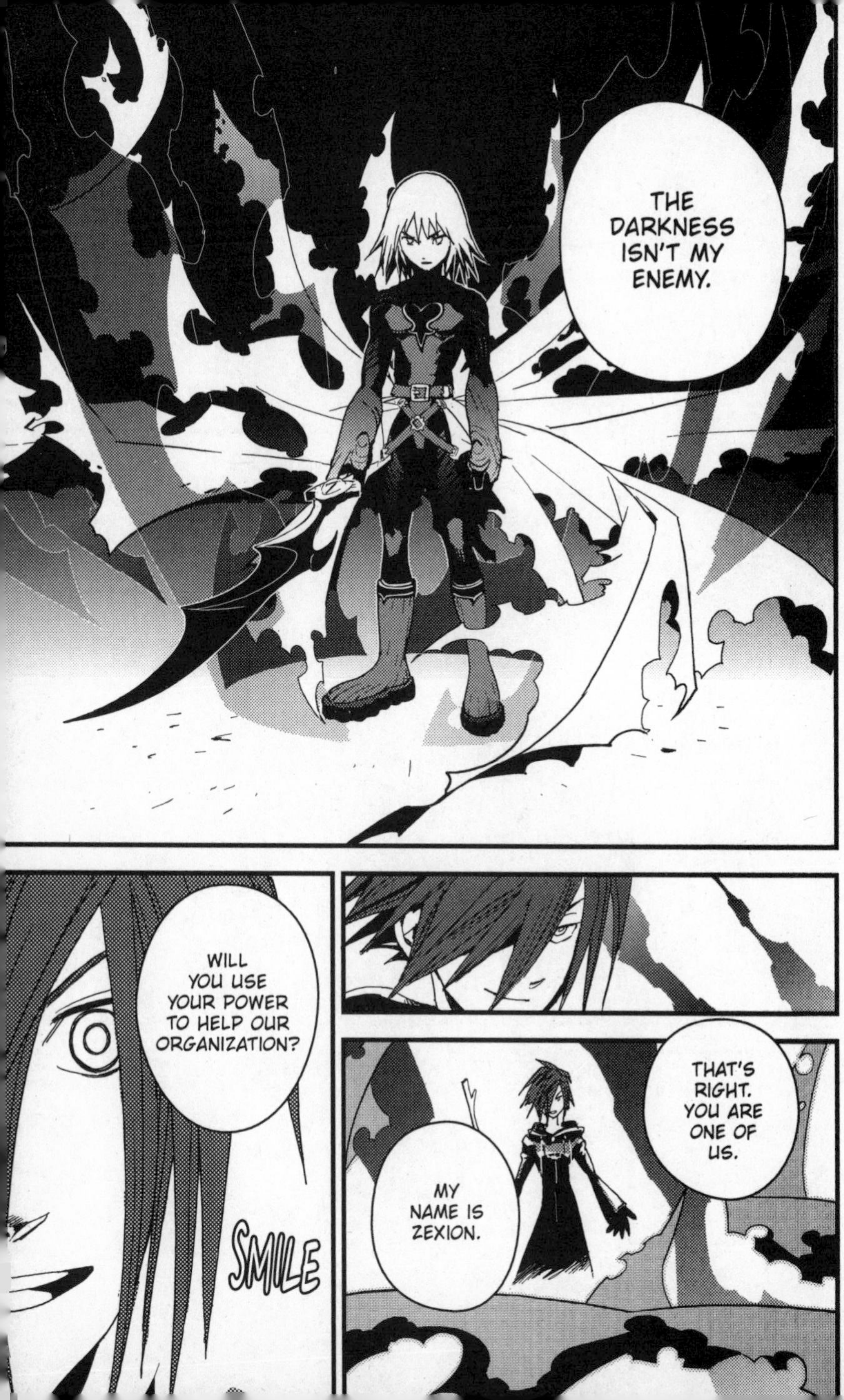
THE DARKNESS ISN'T MY ENEMY.
THAT'S RIGHT. YOU ARE ONE OF US.
MY NAME IS ZEXION.
WILL YOU USE YOUR POWER TO HELP OUR ORGANIZATION?
SMILE

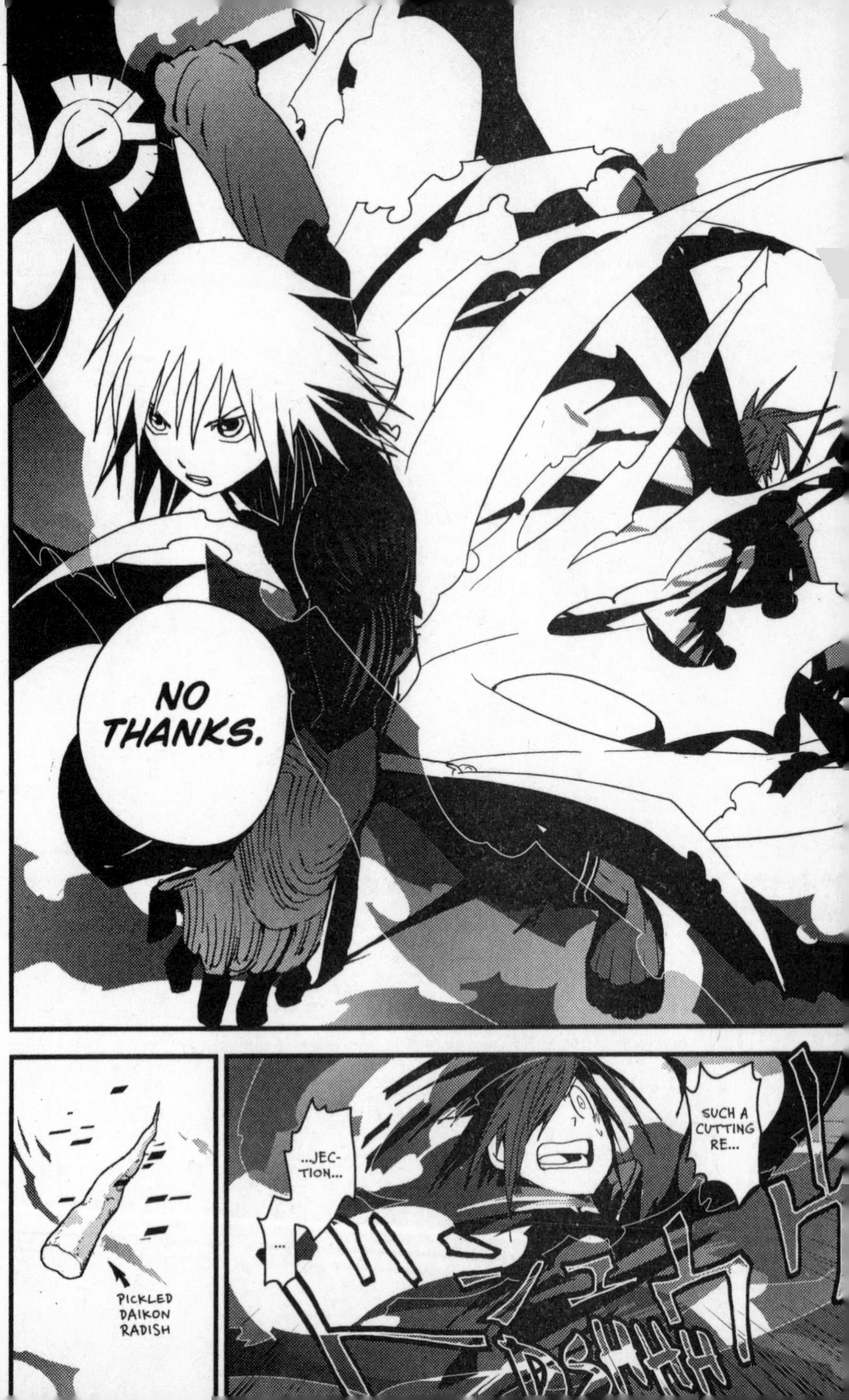
NO THANKS.
SUCH A CUTTING RE...
...JEC-TION...
...
DSHHH
PICKLED DAIKON RADISH

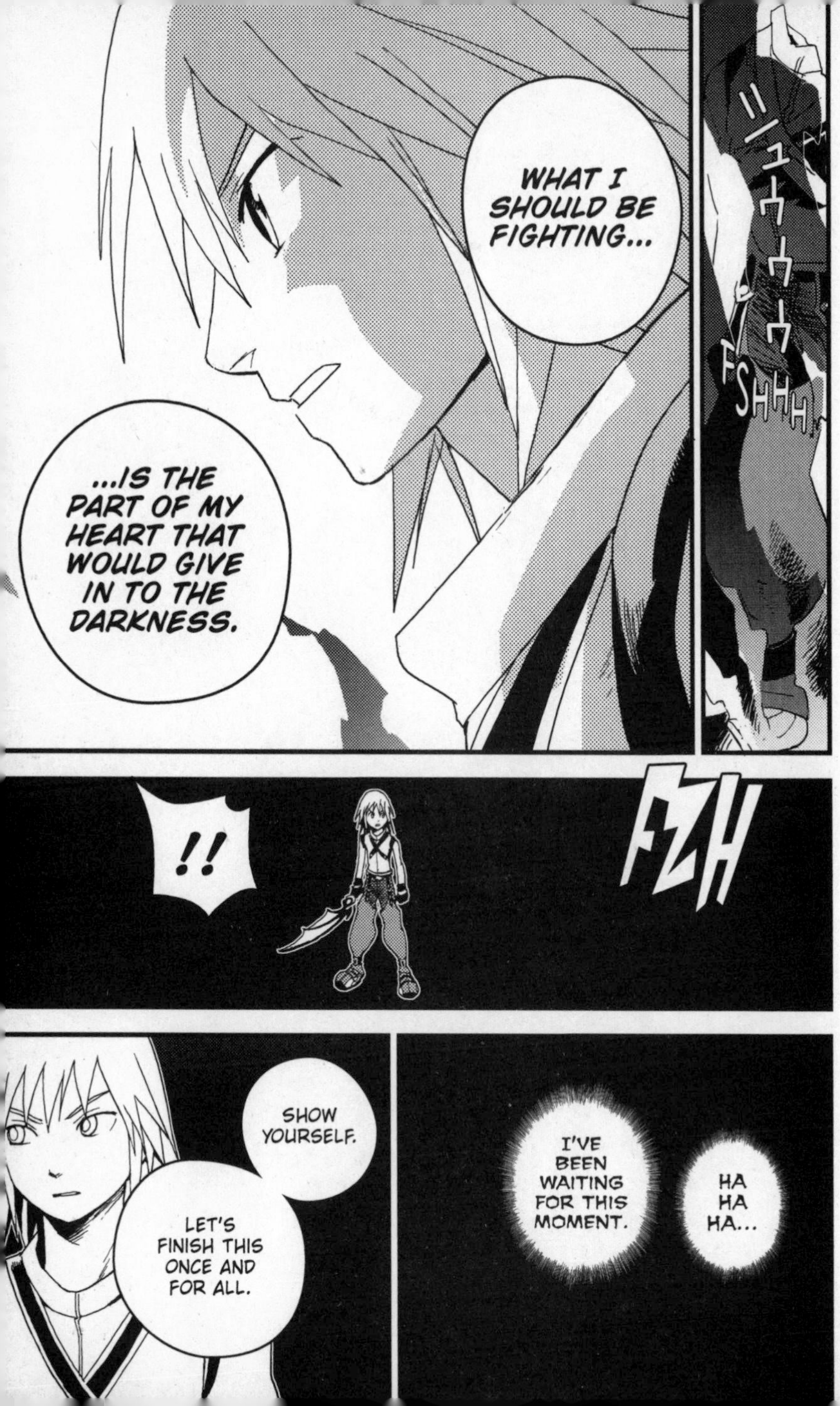
FSHHH
WHAT I SHOULD BE FIGHTING...
...IS THE PART OF MY HEART THAT WOULD GIVE IN TO THE DARKNESS.
FZH
!!
HA HA HA...
I'VE BEEN WAITING FOR THIS MOMENT.
SHOW YOURSELF.
LET'S FINISH THIS ONCE AND FOR ALL.

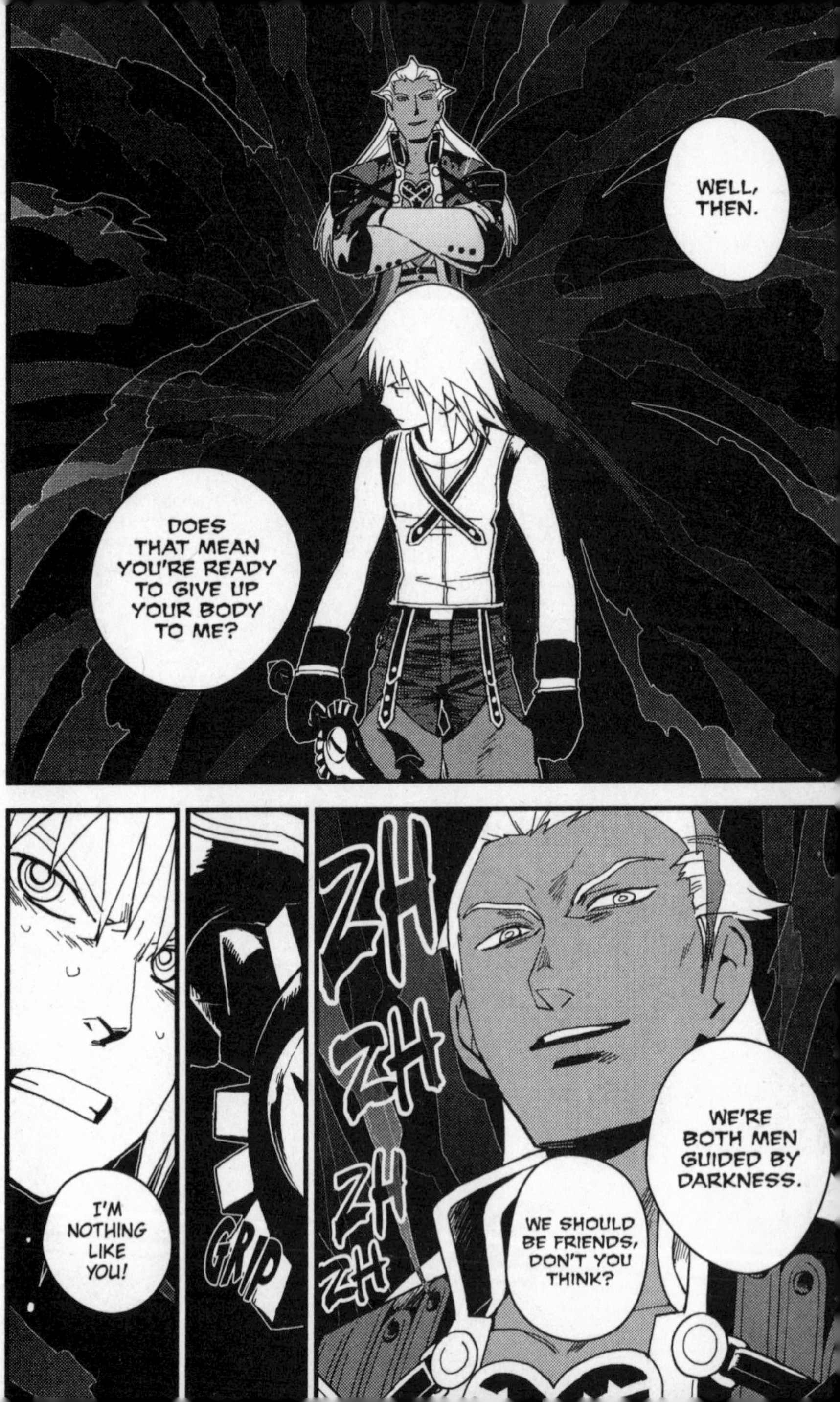
WELL, THEN.
DOES THAT MEAN YOU'RE READY TO GIVE UP YOUR BODY TO ME?
WE'RE BOTH MEN GUIDED BY DARKNESS.
WE SHOULD BE FRIENDS, DON'T YOU THINK?
ZH ZH ZH ZH
GRIP
I'M NOTHING LIKE YOU!

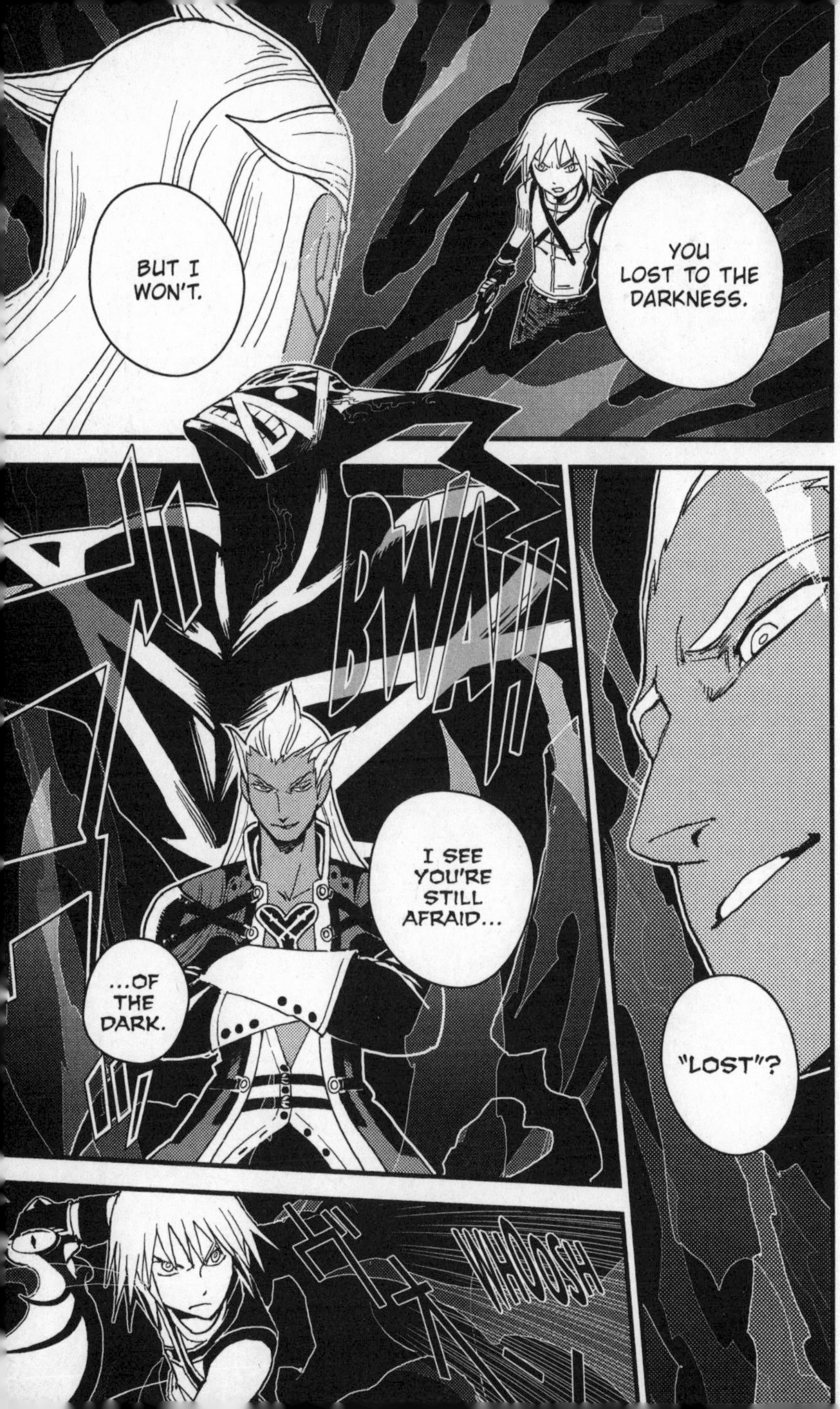
YOU LOST TO THE DARKNESS.
BUT I WON'T.
"LOST"?
BWAH
I SEE YOU'RE STILL AFRAID...
...OF THE DARK.
WHOOSH

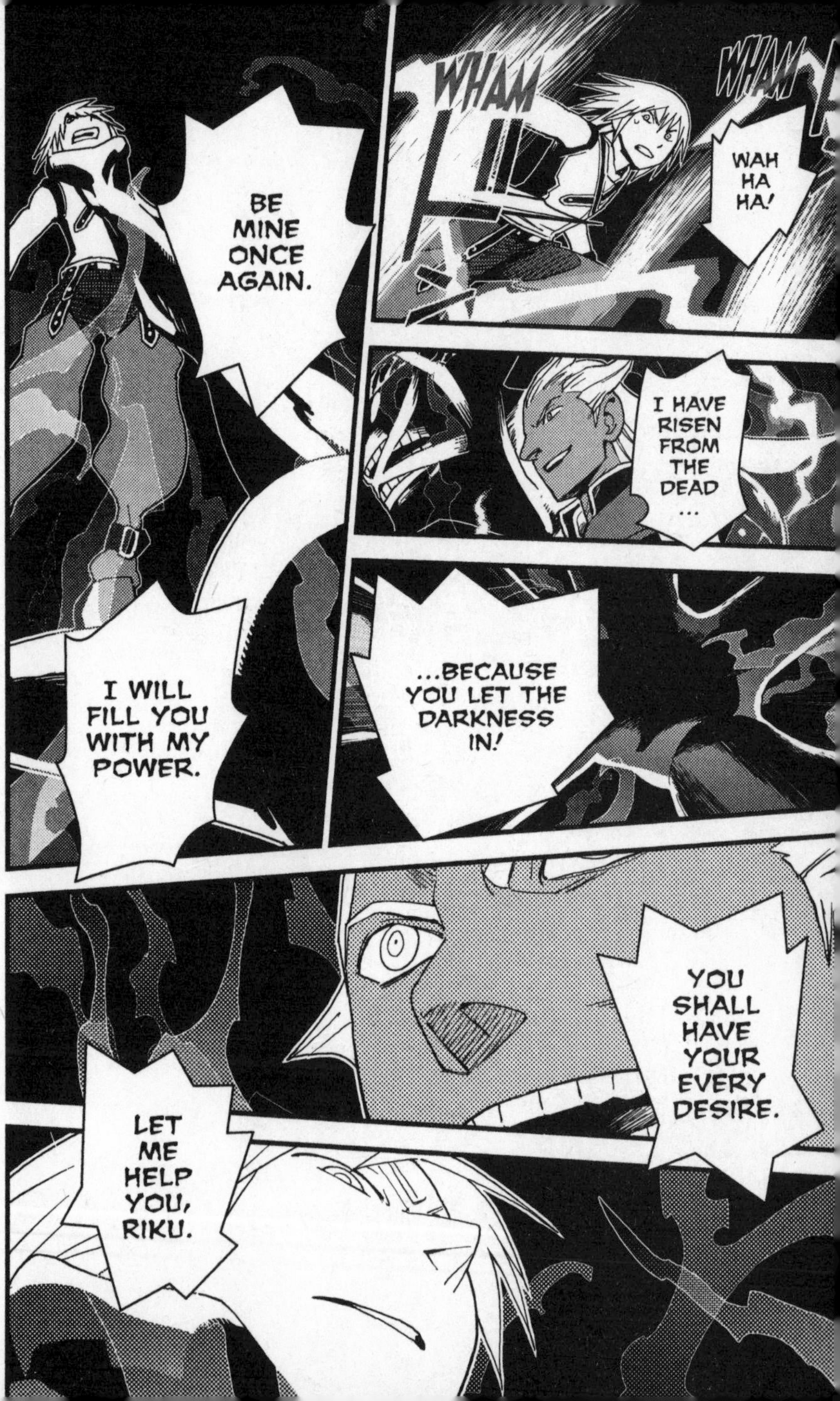
WHAM
WAH HA HA!
WHAM
I HAVE RISEN FROM THE DEAD ...
...BECAUSE YOU LET THE DARKNESS IN!
BE MINE ONCE AGAIN.
I WILL FILL YOU WITH MY POWER.
YOU SHALL HAVE YOUR EVERY DESIRE.
LET ME HELP YOU, RIKU.

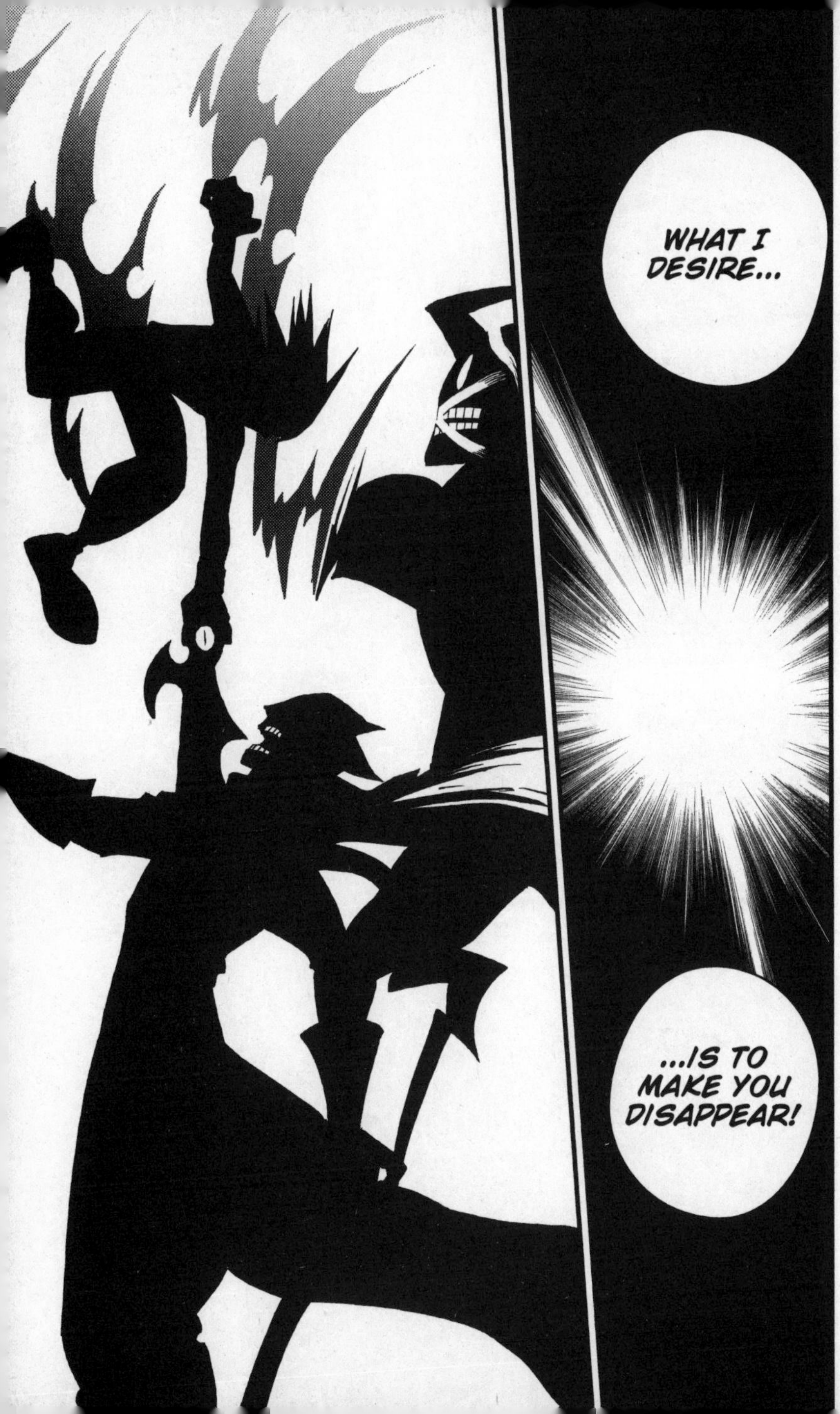
WHAT I DESIRE...
...IS TO MAKE YOU DISAPPEAR!

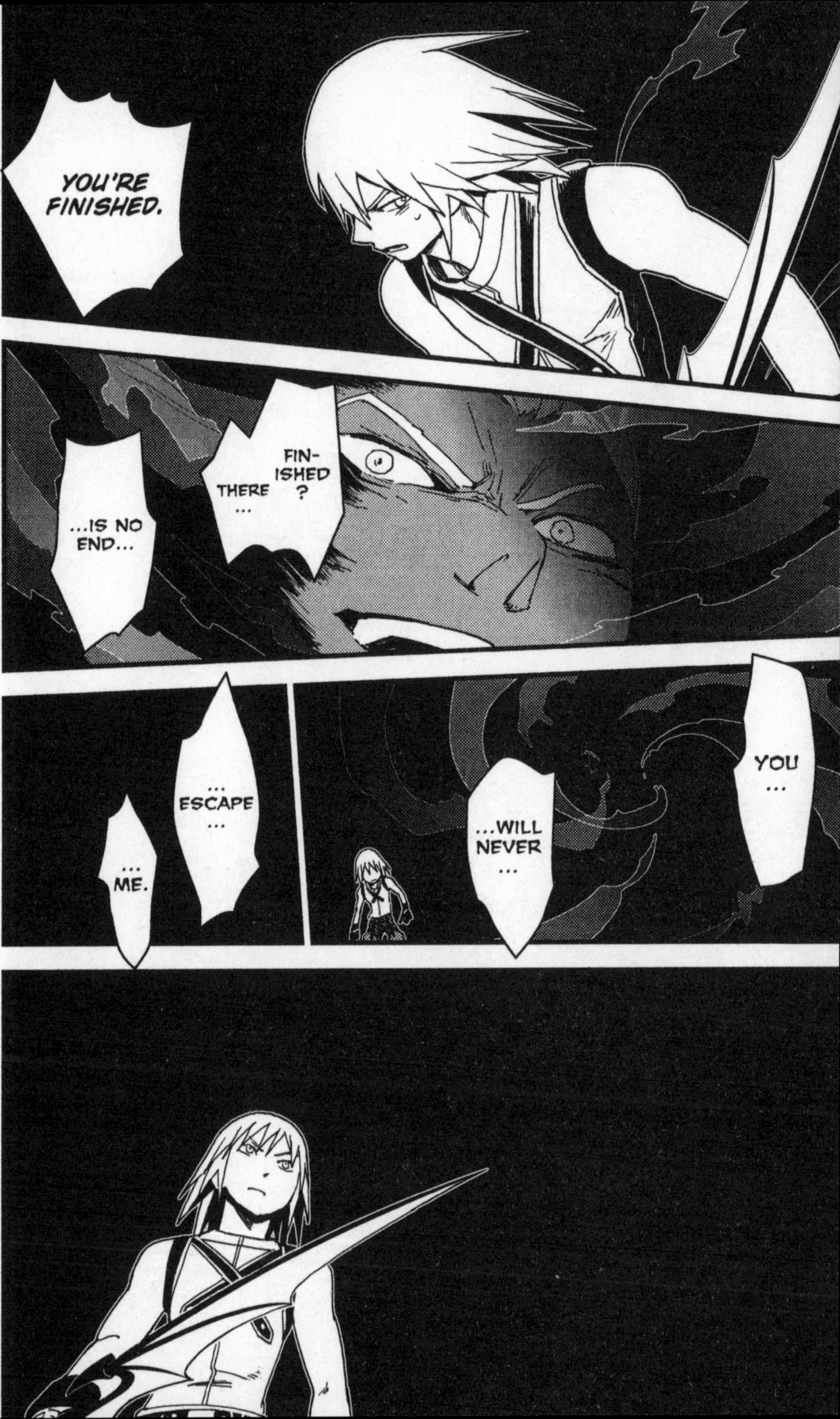
YOU'RE FINISHED.
FIN-ISHED?
THERE...
...IS NO END...
YOU...
...WILL NEVER...
...ESCAPE...
...ME.

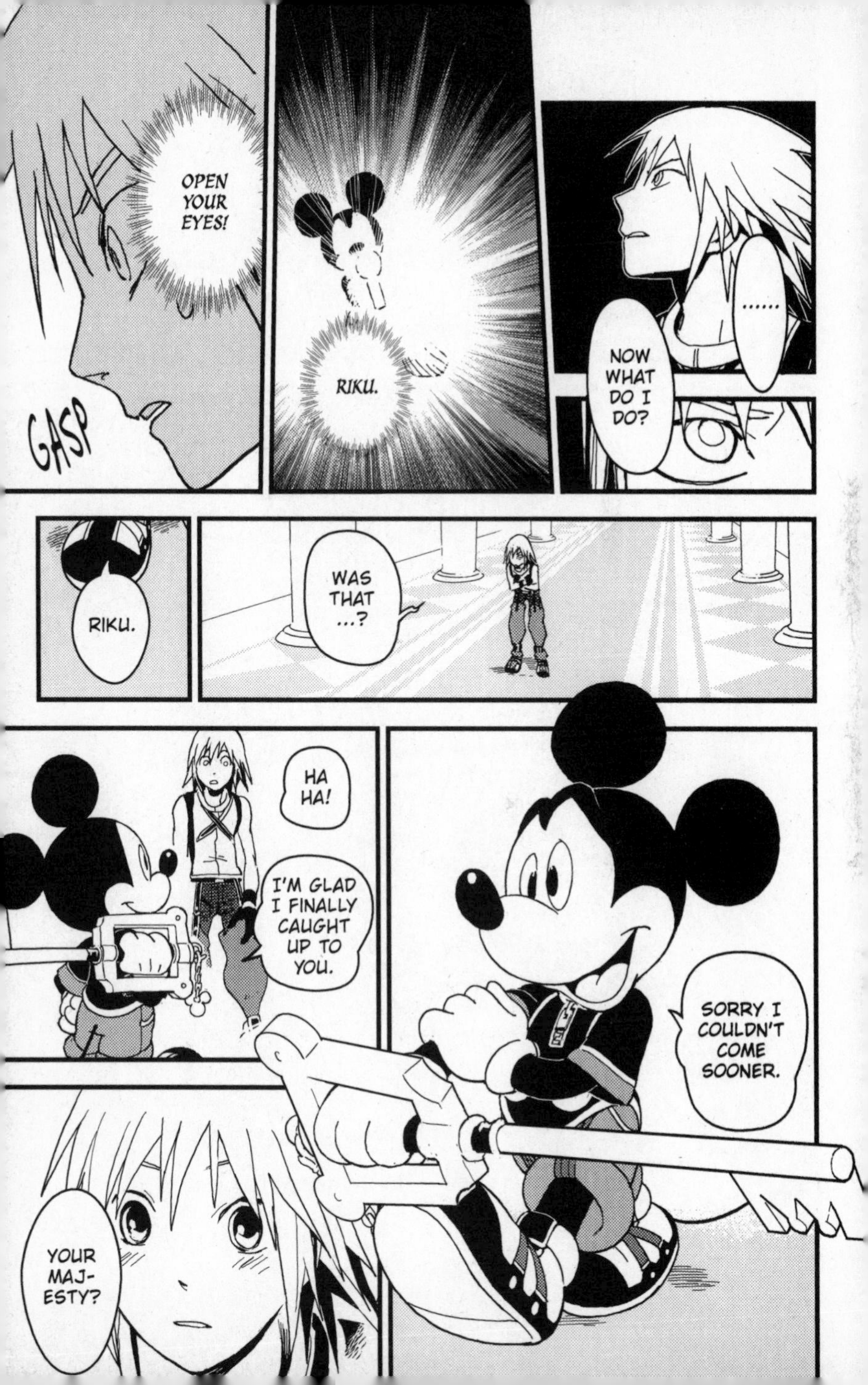
......
NOW WHAT DO I DO?
RIKU.
OPEN YOUR EYES!
GASP
WAS THAT ...?
RIKU.
SORRY I COULDN'T COME SOONER.
HA HA!
I'M GLAD I FINALLY CAUGHT UP TO YOU.
YOUR MAJ-ESTY?

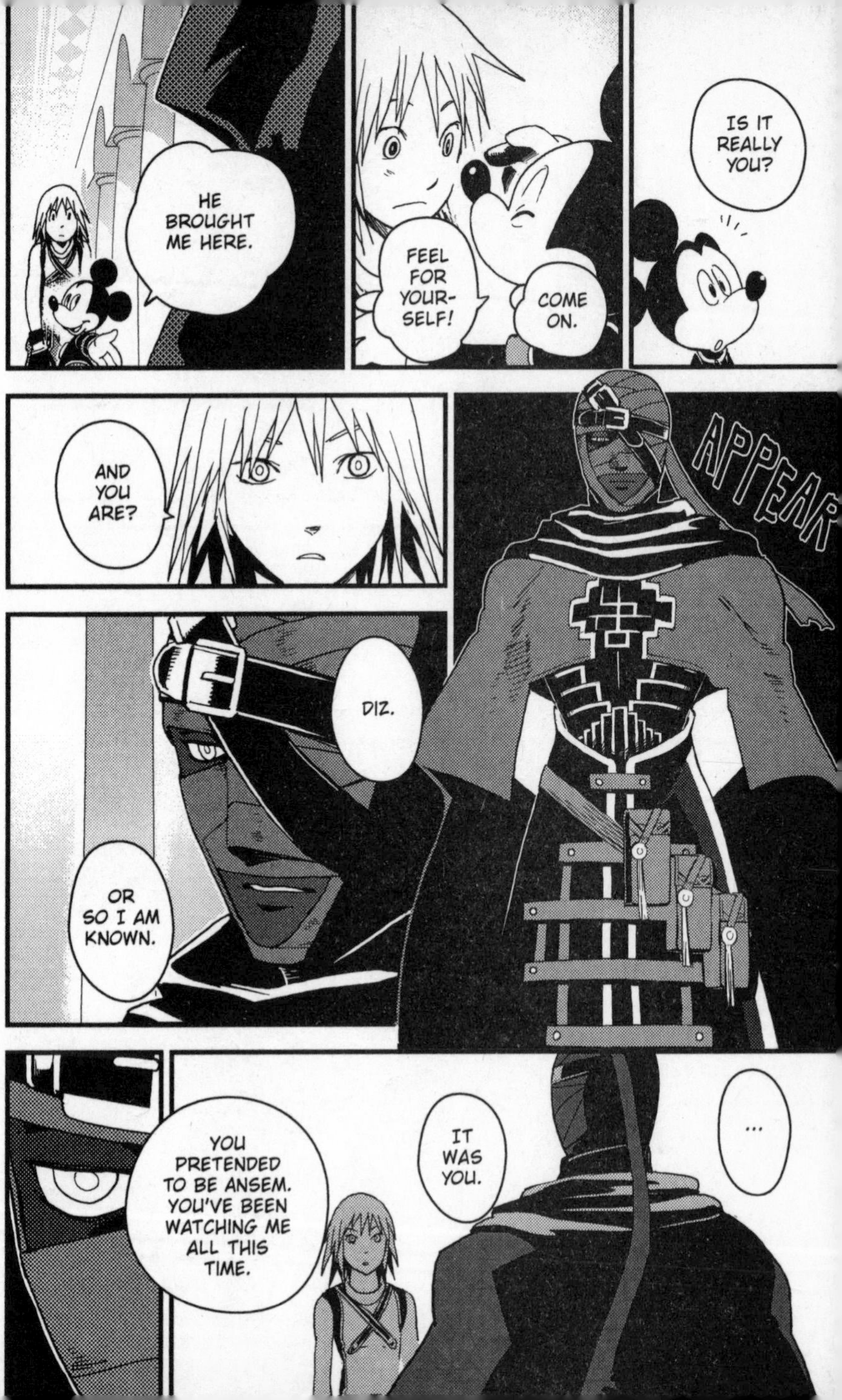
IS IT REALLY YOU?
COME ON.
FEEL FOR YOUR-SELF!
HE BROUGHT ME HERE.
APPEAR
AND YOU ARE?
DIZ.
OR SO I AM KNOWN.
...
IT WAS YOU.
YOU PRETENDED TO BE ANSEM. YOU'VE BEEN WATCHING ME ALL THIS TIME.

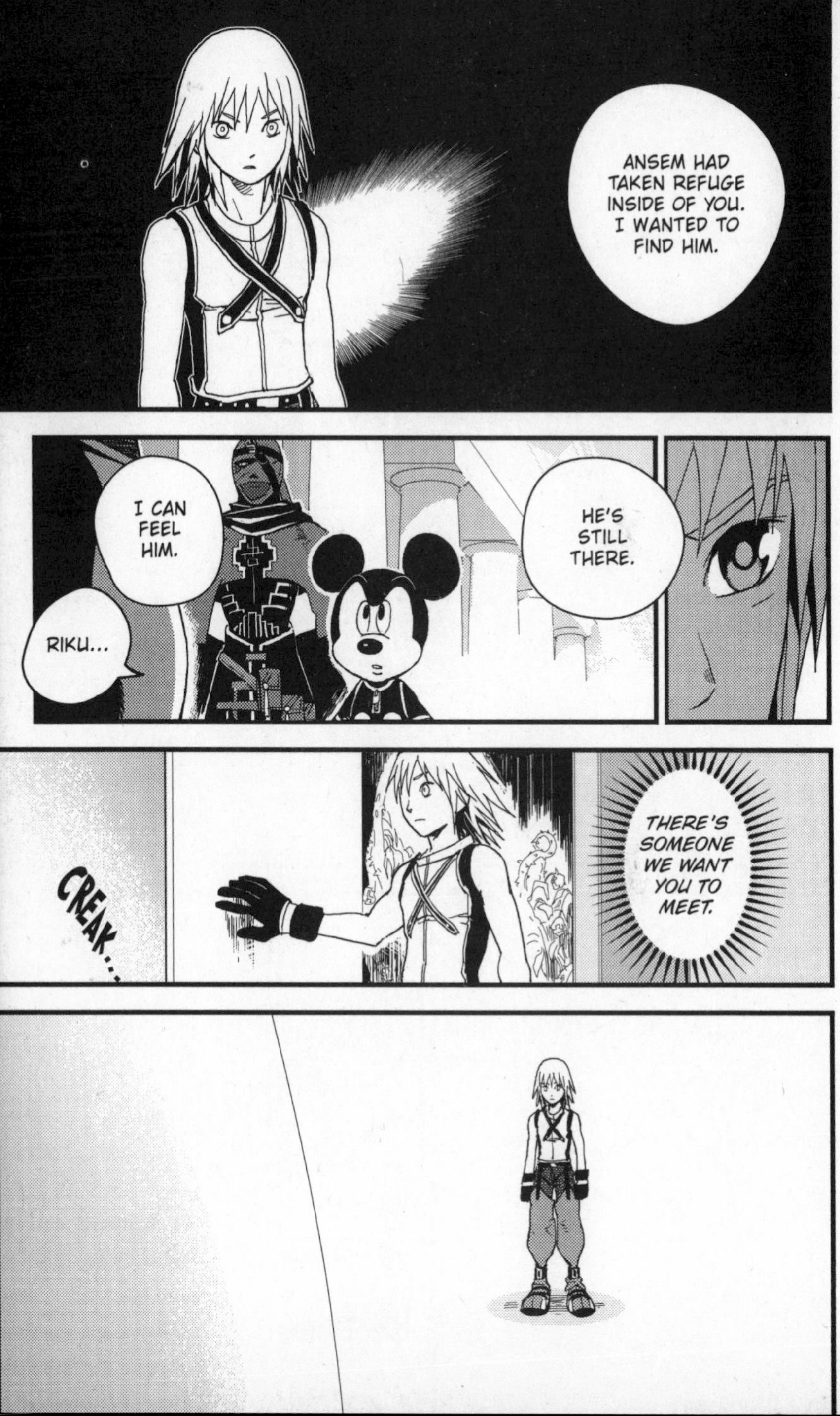
ANSEM HAD TAKEN REFUGE INSIDE OF YOU. I WANTED TO FIND HIM.
HE'S STILL THERE.
I CAN FEEL HIM.
RIKU...
THERE'S SOMEONE WE WANT YOU TO MEET.
CREAK...

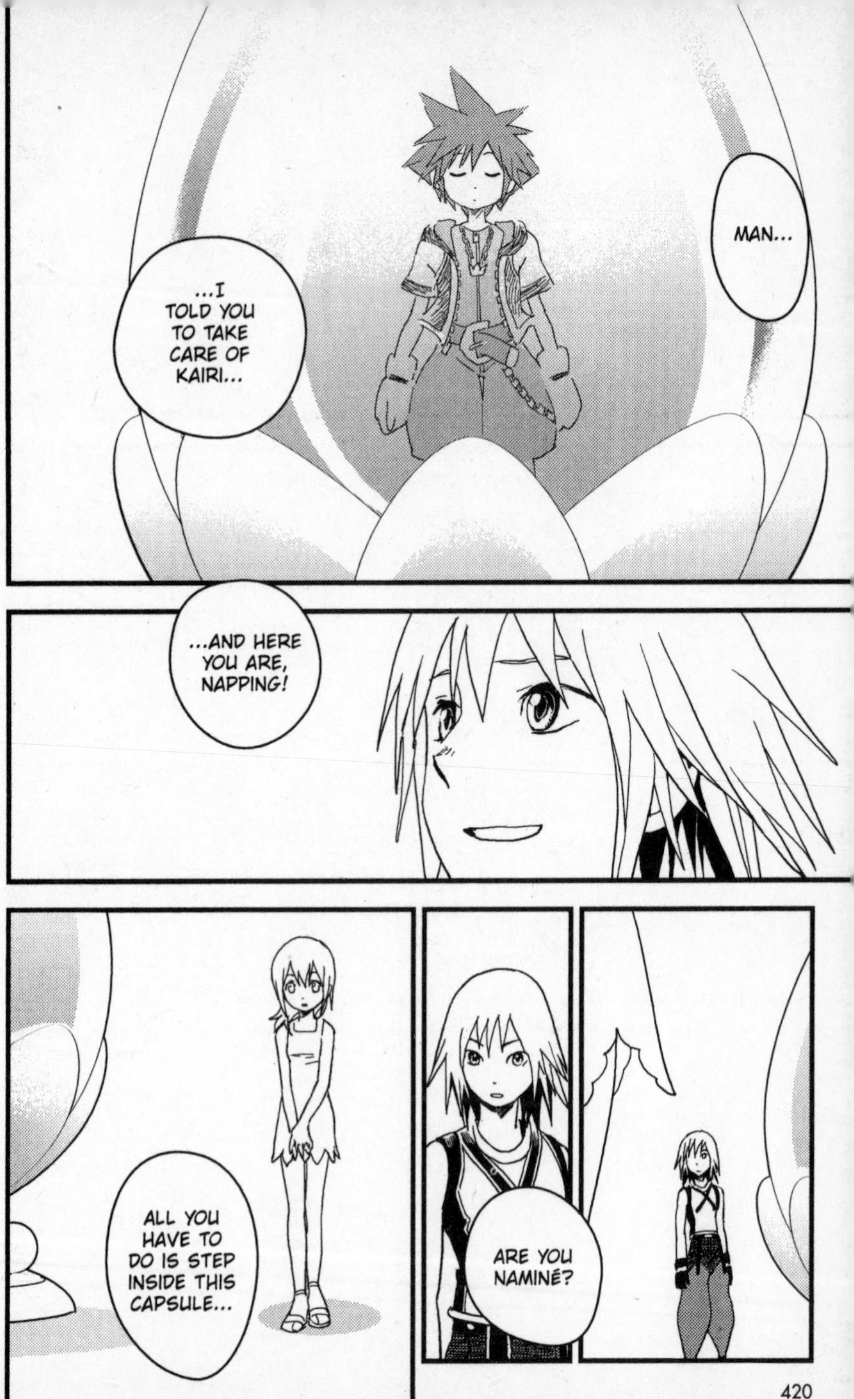
MAN...
...I TOLD YOU TO TAKE CARE OF KAIRI...
...AND HERE YOU ARE, NAPPING!
ARE YOU NAMINÉ?
ALL YOU HAVE TO DO IS STEP INSIDE THIS CAPSULE...

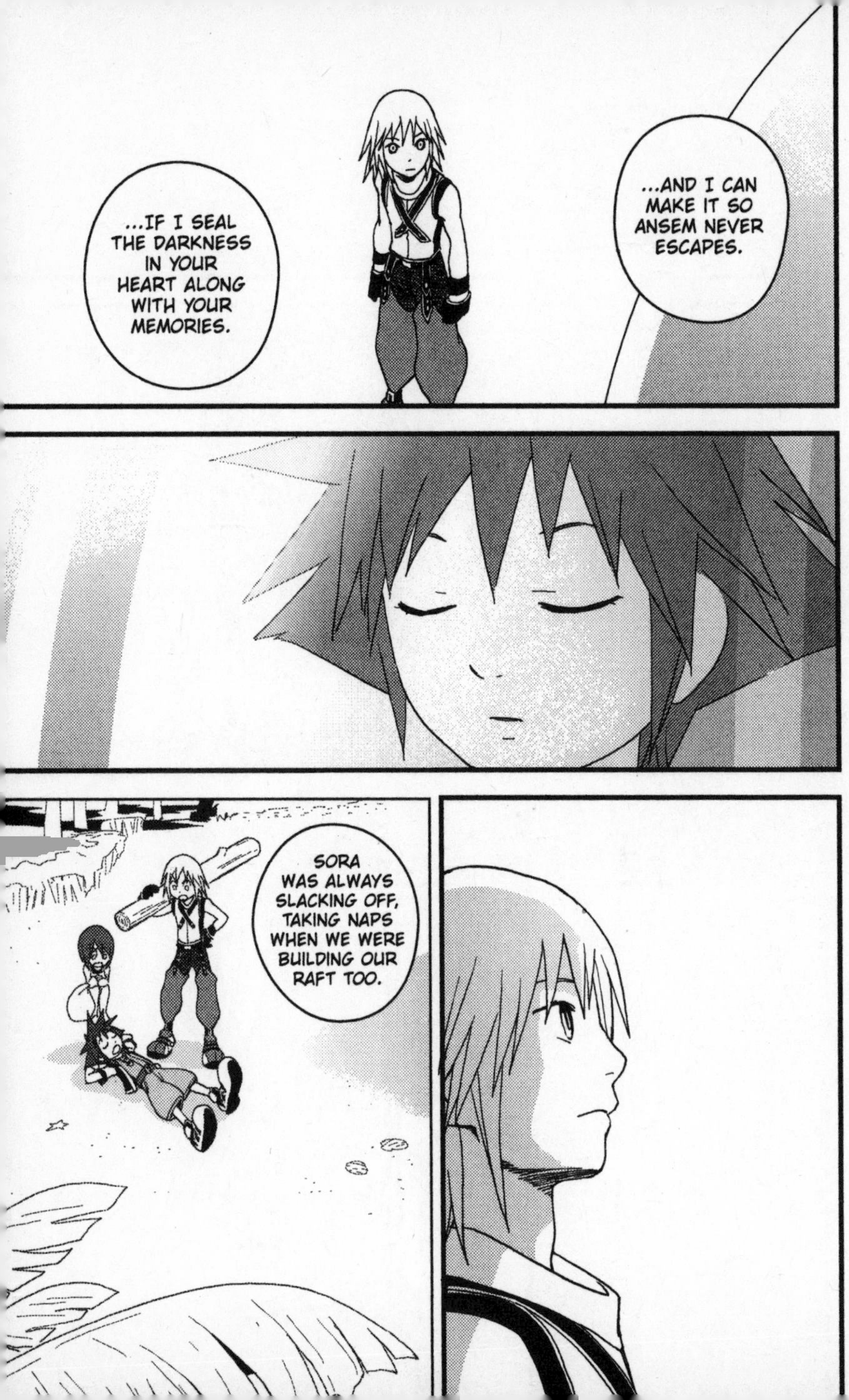
...IF I SEAL THE DARKNESS IN YOUR HEART ALONG WITH YOUR MEMORIES.
...AND I CAN MAKE IT SO ANSEM NEVER ESCAPES.
SORA WAS ALWAYS SLACKING OFF, TAKING NAPS WHEN WE WERE BUILDING OUR RAFT TOO.

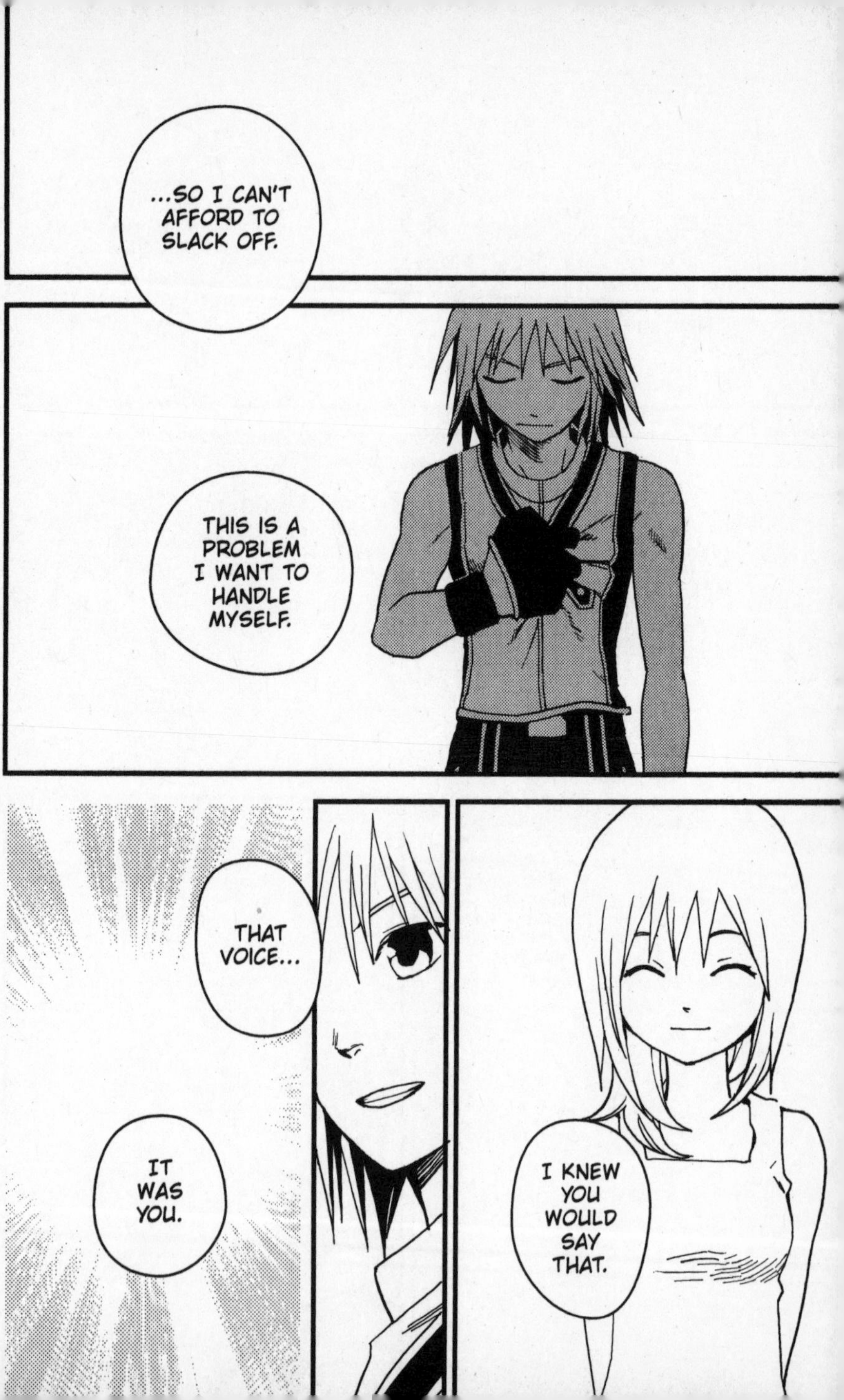
...SO I CAN'T AFFORD TO SLACK OFF.
THIS IS A PROBLEM I WANT TO HANDLE MYSELF.
I KNEW YOU WOULD SAY THAT.
THAT VOICE...
IT WAS YOU.

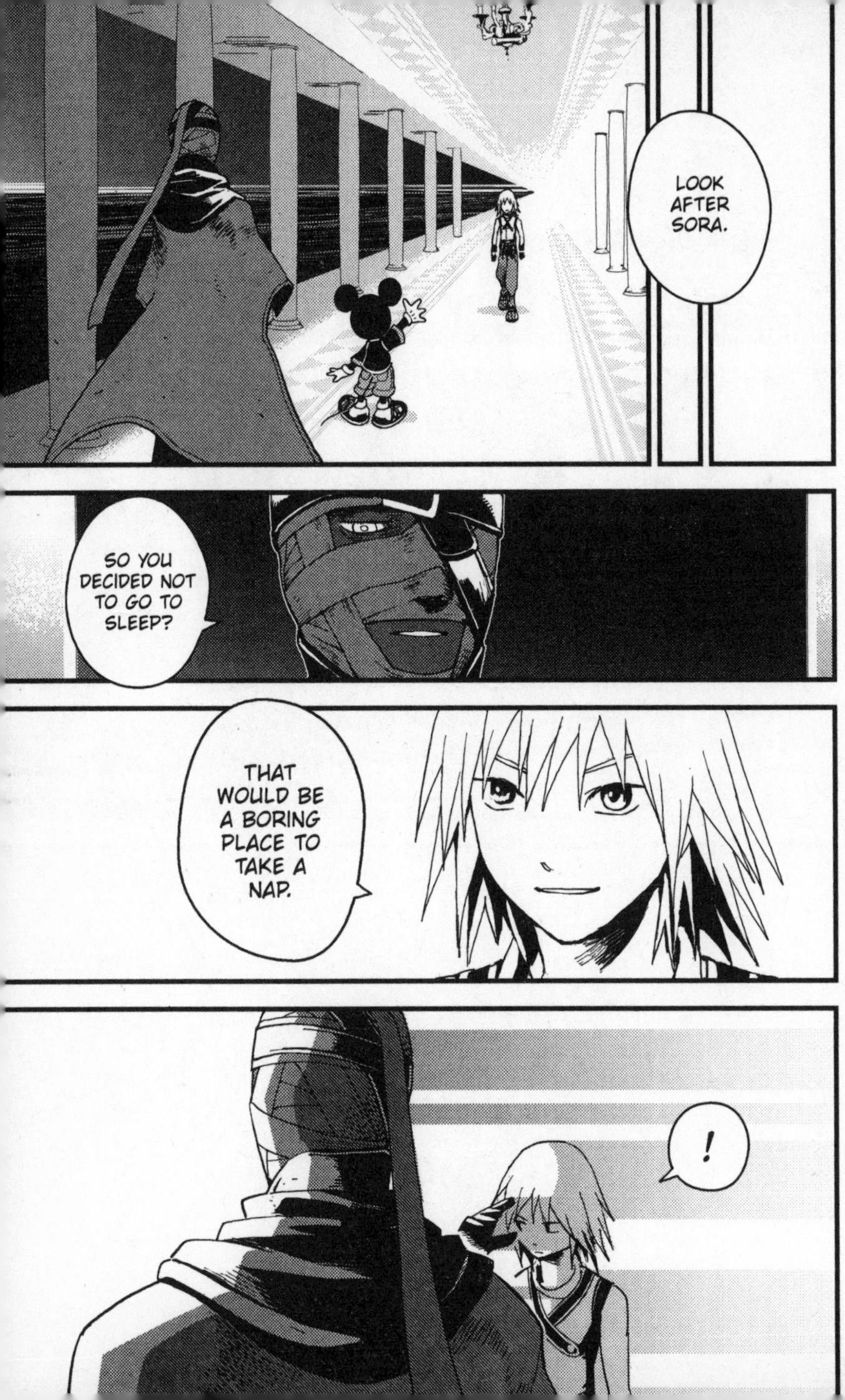
LOOK AFTER SORA.
SO YOU DECIDED NOT TO GO TO SLEEP?
THAT WOULD BE A BORING PLACE TO TAKE A NAP.
!

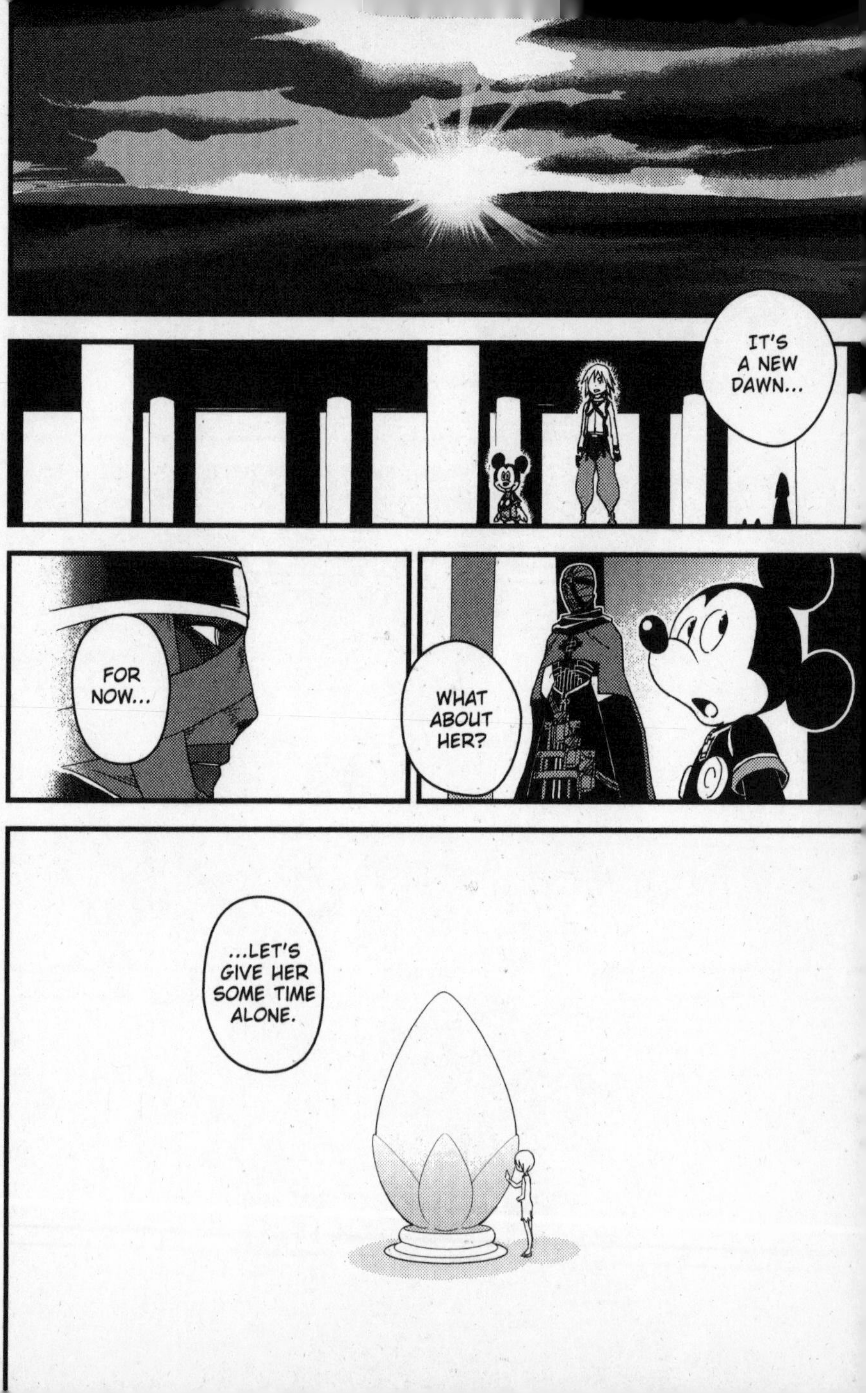
IT'S A NEW DAWN...
WHAT ABOUT HER?
FOR NOW...
...LET'S GIVE HER SOME TIME ALONE.

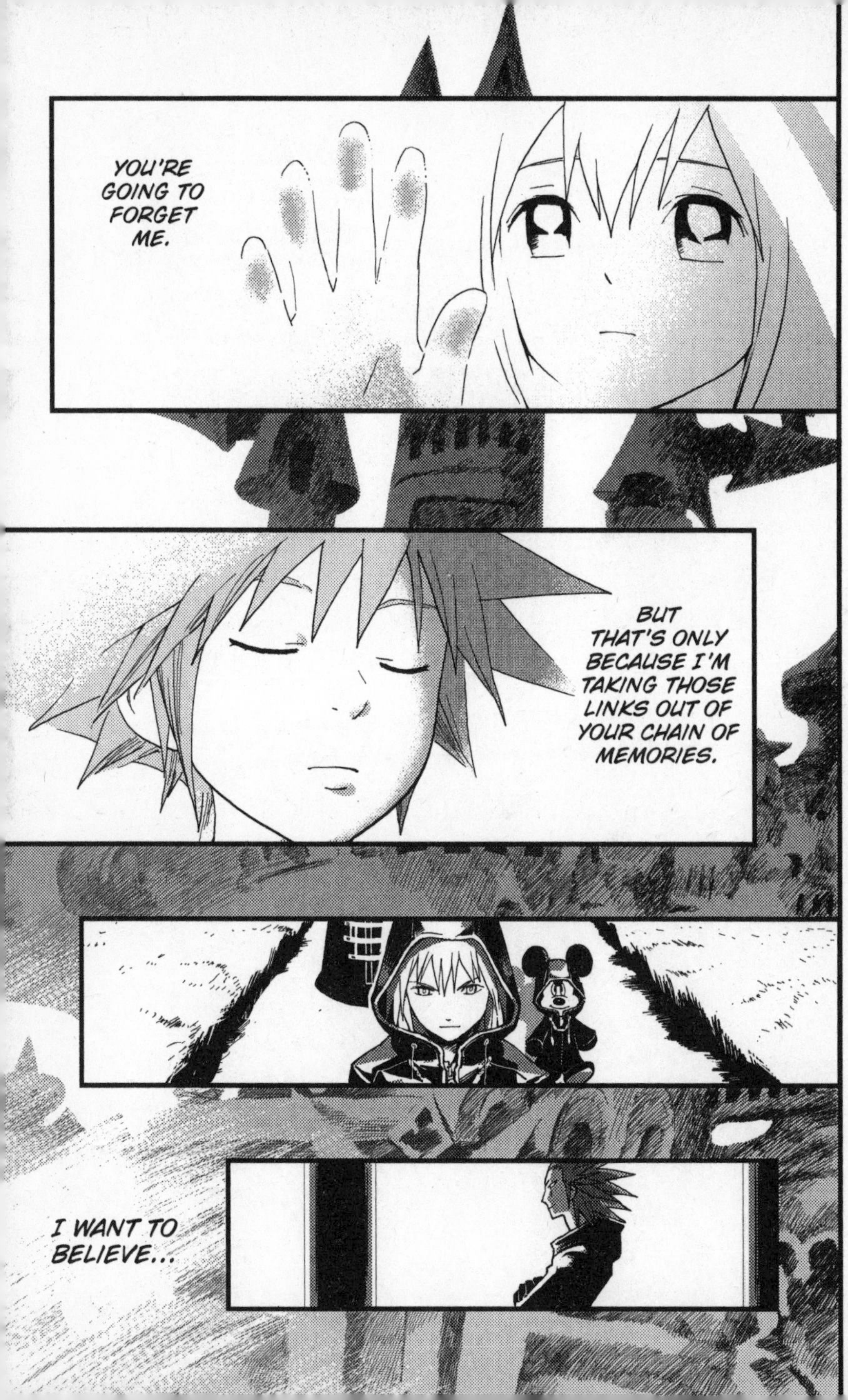
YOU'RE GOING TO FORGET ME.
BUT THAT'S ONLY BECAUSE I'M TAKING THOSE LINKS OUT OF YOUR CHAIN OF MEMORIES.
I WANT TO BELIEVE...

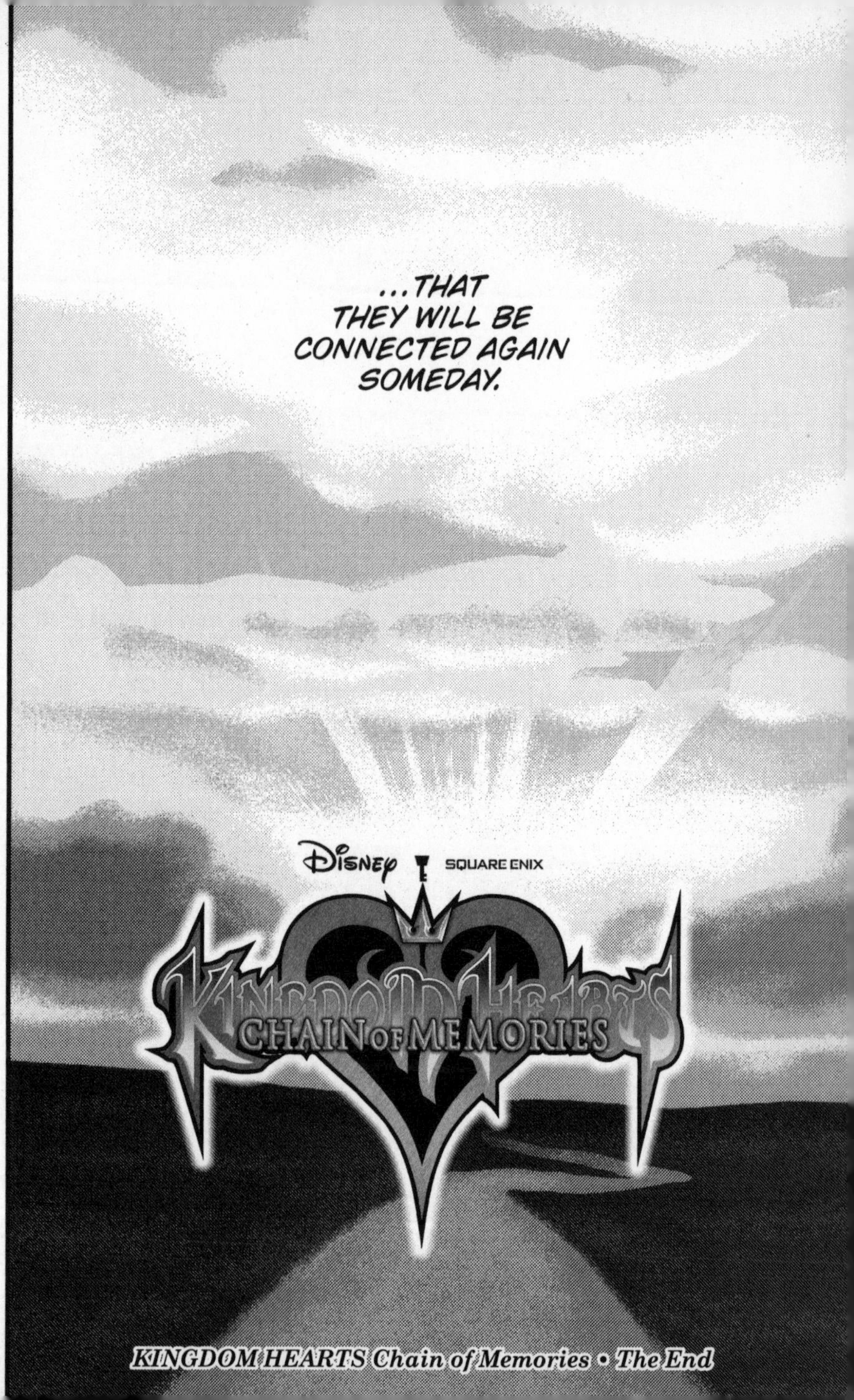
...THAT THEY WILL BE CONNECTED AGAIN SOMEDAY.
DISNEY SQUARE ENIX
KINGDOM HEARTS CHAIN OF MEMORIES
KINGDOM HEARTS Chain of Memories • The End

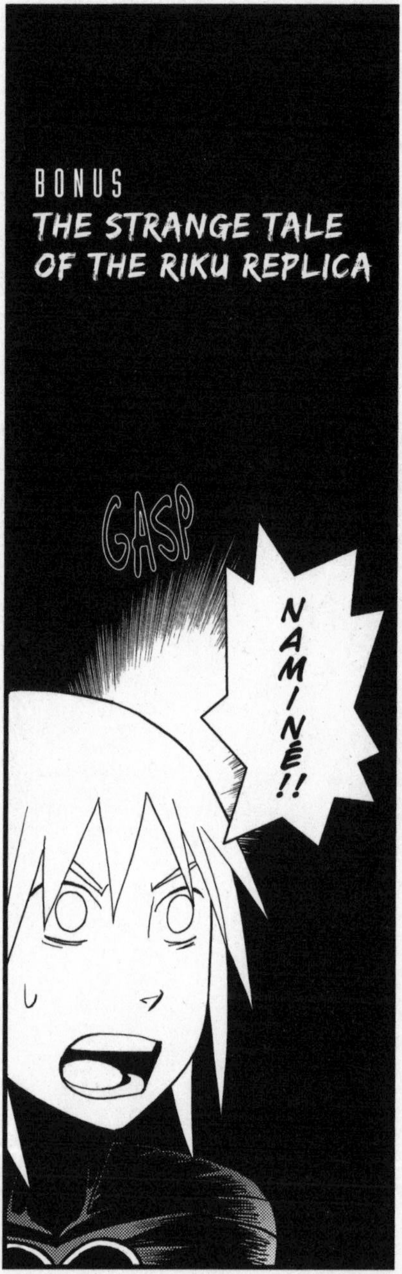
BONUS
THE STRANGE TALE OF THE RIKU REPLICA
GASP
NAMINÉ!!
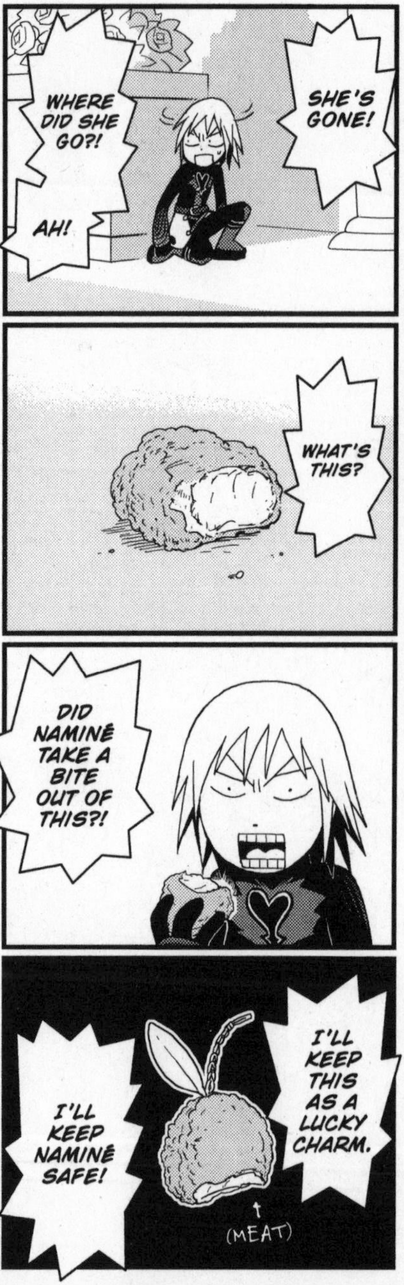
SHE'S GONE!
WHERE DID SHE GO?!
AH!
WHAT'S THIS?
DID NAMINÉ TAKE A BITE OUT OF THIS?!
I'LL KEEP THIS AS A LUCKY CHARM.
I'LL KEEP NAMINÉ SAFE!
(MEAT)

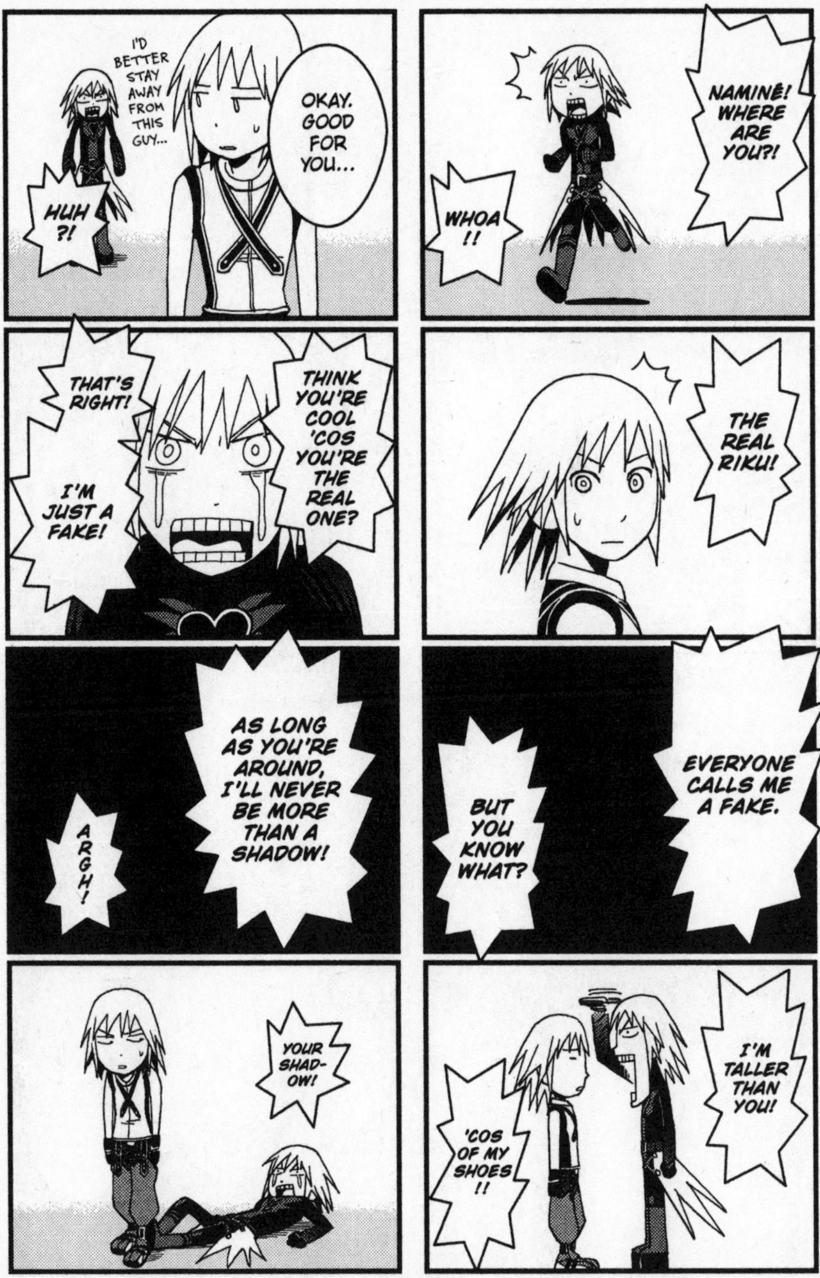
NAMINÉ! WHERE ARE YOU?!
WHOA !!
OKAY. GOOD FOR YOU...
I'D BETTER STAY AWAY FROM THIS GUY...
HUH ?!
THE REAL RIKU!
THINK YOU'RE COOL 'COS YOU'RE THE REAL ONE?
THAT'S RIGHT!
I'M JUST A FAKE!
EVERYONE CALLS ME A FAKE.
BUT YOU KNOW WHAT?
AS LONG AS YOU'RE AROUND, I'LL NEVER BE MORE THAN A SHADOW!
ARGH!
I'M TALLER THAN YOU!
'COS OF MY SHOES !!
YOUR SHAD-OW!

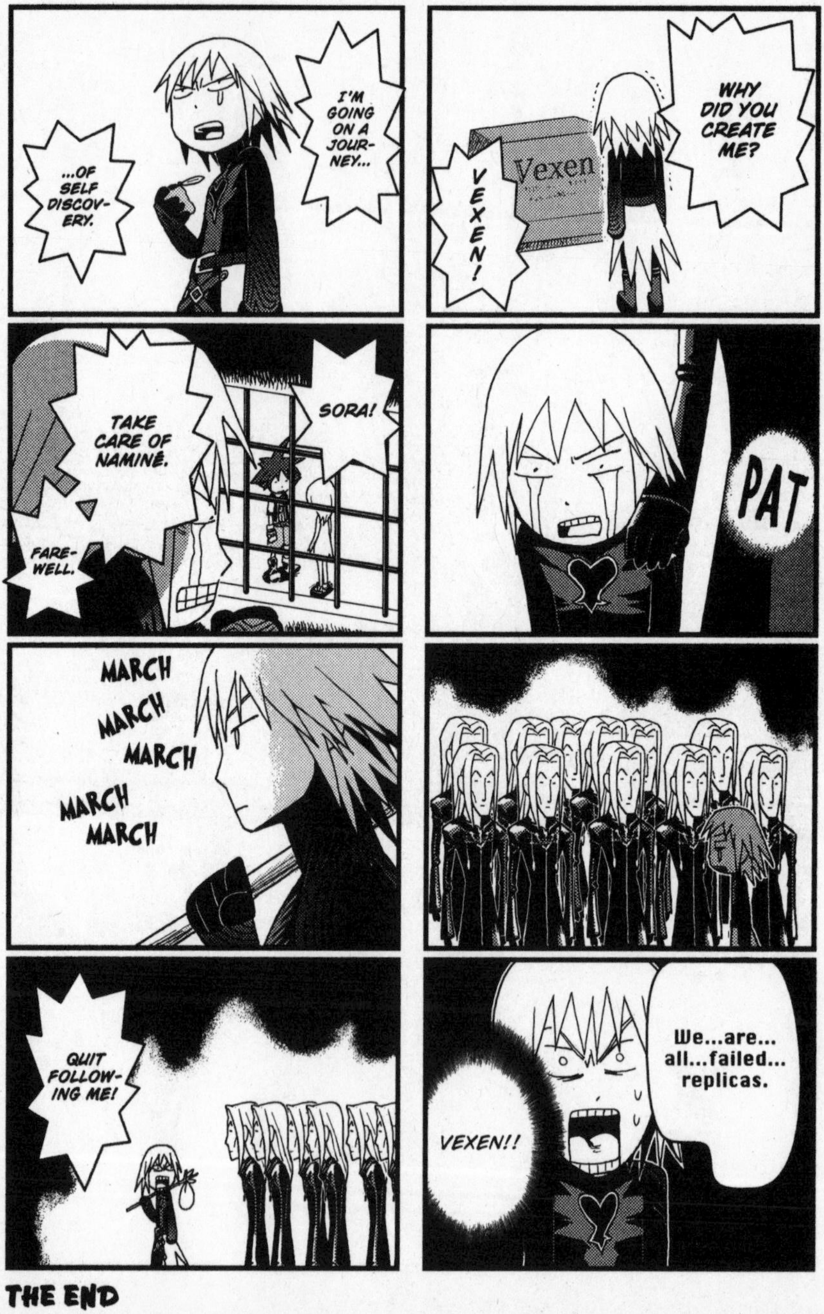
WHY DID YOU CREATE ME?
VEXEN!
PAT
We...are...all...failed...replicas.
VEXEN!!
I'M GOING ON A JOURNEY...
...OF SELF DISCOVERY.
SORA!
TAKE CARE OF NAMINÉ.
FAREWELL.
MARCH MARCH MARCH MARCH MARCH
QUIT FOLLOWING ME!
THE END

Disney SQUARE ENIX

KINGDOM HEARTS
CHAIN OF MEMORIES

# KINGDOM HEARTS
## CHAIN OF MEMORIES

### SHIRO AMANO

ORIGINAL CONCEPT:
TETSUYA NOMURA

Translation: Alethea and Athena Nibley • Lettering: Terri Delgado, Lys Blakeslee

KINGDOM HEARTS © Disney Enterprises, Inc. Characters from FINAL FANTASY video game series © 1990, 1997, 1999, 2001, 2002 Square Enix Co., Ltd. All rights reserved.

Translation © 2013 by Disney Enterprises, Inc.

Yen Press
Hachette Book Group
1290 Avenue of the Americas, New York, NY 10104

www.HachetteBookGroup.com
www.YenPress.com

Yen Press is an imprint of Hachette Book Group, Inc. The Yen Press name and logo are trademarks of Hachette Book Group, Inc.

First Yen Press Edition: June 2013

ISBN: 978-0-316-25562-2

10 9 8 7 6 5 4

BVG

Printed in the United States of America